BY WESLEY CHU

The Art of Prophecy

The Art of Destiny

The Art of Legend

THE ART OF LEGEND

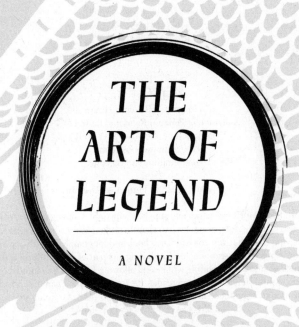

THE
ART OF
LEGEND

A NOVEL

THE WAR ARTS SAGA: BOOK THREE

WESLEY CHU

NEW YORK

Del Rey
An imprint of Random House
A division of Penguin Random House LLC
1745 Broadway, New York, NY 10019
randomhousebooks.com
penguinrandomhouse.com

Map on pages viii–ix by Sunga Park

Hardcover ISBN 978-0-593-23769-4
Ebook ISBN 978-0-593-23770-0

Printed in the United States of America on acid-free paper

1st Printing

First Edition

BOOK TEAM: Production editor: Abby Duval • Managing editor: Paul Gilbert • Production manager: Mark Maguire • Copy editor: Michael Burke • Proofreaders: Rachael Clements, Drew Goter, Lara Kennedy, Lawrence Krauser

Book design by Jo Anne Metsch

The authorized representative in the EU for product safety and compliance is Penguin Random House Ireland, Morrison Chambers, 32 Nassau Street, Dublin D02 YH68, Ireland. https://eu-contact.penguin.ie

To childhood dreams,

may they all come true

WHITE GHOST
LANDS

DIYU
MOUNTAIN

CLOUD
PILLARS

VAUZAN

YUKIAN RIVER

WUG

MANJING

SKYFALL
TEMPLE

NGYN OCEAN

TRUE FREEZE

HRUSHA

MT. SHELTY

ALLANTO

SHINGYONG
MOUNTAINS

JIAYI

DANZIYI

CELESTIAL
PALACE

EA OF
OWERS

XUSAN

SANBA

BLUE
SEA

SAND SNAKE

THE ORIGINAL TEMPLE
OF THE TIANDI

DRAMATIS PERSONAE

THE TIANDI

Ayque High lord of the Shulan Court. Leader of the stupid faction.

Bhasani, Narwani Master of the Drowned Fist.

Dongshi Duke of Lawkan. Former whisperlord of the empire. Leader of the Ten Hounds.

Fausan, Noon also God of Gamblers. Master of the Whipfinger Style Song Family Ho Lineage.

Goramh Legendary Tiandi monk. His wisdom is renowned throughout the world. Likely starved to death on a mountain.

Guanshi, Sasha also Beautiful Boy. Daughter of Guanshi Kanyu. Boss of the Worst Today Boys.

Guiman Hansoo monk. One ring. Pahm's little brother.

Hachi Heir to the Whipfinger Style Song Family Ho Lineage. Close friend to Jian.

Haiksong Gardener at Skyfall Temple.

Huakt Captain in the Shulan Displayguards.

Hua, Shao Latest protagonist in the popular long-running Burning Hearts romance series written by a Xhu Weh Sahri. Not a real person.

Hujo, Akai also Longsleeves. High lord and a general of the Caobiu Cinderblossoms.

Huyyi Prisoner at the Happy Glow Retirement Home. Lover to Cyyk.

Jian, Wen also Lu Hiro. Champion of the Five Under Heaven. The Prophesied Hero of the Tiandi. Heir to the Windwhispering School of the Zhang Lineage. #1 Most Wanted Fugitive in the Enlightened States.

Kaiyu, Hwang Heir of the Houtou style Third Lin Lineage. Close friend to Jian.

Kasa, Hwang also the Sky Monkey. Master of the Houtou style Third Lin Lineage. Father to Kaiyu. Killed while saving Wen Jian from the Lotus Lotus monks.

Koranajah Battleabbess of the Black Orchid sect in Vauzan. Friend to Taishi.

Kuolong Master war artist of the Tea Bears of Xing. Slain by the Eternal Khan of Katuia during the siege of Xusan.

Liuman Hansoo monk. Twelve rings. Pahm's former master. Killed by Qisami.

Meehae Apprentice acupuncturist. Close friend to Jian in Sanba.

Mori, Lee Templeabbot of the Temple of the Tiandi in Vauzan. Former lover to Taishi.

Munnam, Ling Former Master windwhisper. Father to Ling Taishi. Deceased.

Neehong Resident of Vauzan. Mother to Neeshan.

Neeshan Former box girl in Vauzan. Lover to Hachi.

Oban, Ori High lord of the Shulan Court. Close friend to former Duke Saan and interim leader of Shulan Duchy. Leader of the idiotic faction.

Obeen, Ori Lord of the Shulan Court. Brother and personal mind trust to Highlord Oban.

Pahm Hansoo war monk. Ten rings. Close friend to Xinde and Jian.

Pei Child Oracle of the Tiandi. Friend to Taishi.

Pengzo Initiate at the Skyfall Temple.

Qinhhwanan Former battleabbess of the Black Orchids, friend of Taishi, slain by a Katuia champion.

Saan also the Painted Tiger. Duke of Shulan. Former Emperor Xuanshing's second son. Former student to Taishi. Killed by Sunri.

Saku Saku High lady of the Shulan Court. Leader of the capitulation caucus.

Sanso, Ling Son of Ling Taishi. Deceased.

Sohi, Soa Former Eternal Bright Light master. Younger brother to Sohn.

Sohn, Soa Master of the Eternal Bright Light Fist Pan Family Pan Lineage. Lost heir to the family's schools. Formerly nicknamed Pan's Pillaging Playboy. Wanted Fugitive.

Sohnsho, Soa Eternal Bright Light master. Head of the Pan family Pan Lineage. Nephew to Sohn.

Sonaya, Ras Daughter of the Drowned Fist. Bhasani's heir. Love interest to Jian.

Sunri also the Desert Lioness. Duchess of Caobiu. Former concubine to Emperor Xuanshing.

Taishi, Ling also Nai Roha. Grandmaster of the Windwhispering School of the Zhang Lineage; Windwhispering School of the Zhang Lineage of the Ling Family Branch. Distant #2 Most Wanted Fugitive in the Enlightened States.

Waylin Duke of Xing. Cousin to the Emperor Xuanshing.

Xinde Magistrate in Vauzan. Former captain of the Caobiu Stone Watchers long eyes unit. Former First Senior of the Longxian War Art Academy. Close friend to Jian from back in Jiayi.

Xuamio Worst Boy Thug of the Worst Today Boys.

Yanso Duke of Gyian. Former purselord to Emperor Xuanshing. Killed by Sunri.

Yinshi, Hui Former songmistress of the Xing Court. Mother to Ling Taishi. Deceased.

Zofi, Wu Taishi's close confidante and assistant. Adopted daughter to Ling Taishi. Best friend and tutor to Jian.

THE SHADOW

Akiana, Aki Lady of Aki household. Twin to Akiya. Youngest daughter of Lord Aki Niam. Under the care of Qisami as Child Companion Kiki. Deceased.

Akiya, Aki Lady of Aki household. Twin to Akiana. Youngest daughter of Lord Aki Niam. Under the care of Qisami as Child Companion Kiki. Deceased.

Badgasgirl Member of Cyyk's Grunt Gang. Prisoner of the Happy Glow Retirement Home.

Big Lettuce Member of Cyyk's Grunt Gang. Prisoner of the Happy Glow Retirement Home.

Bingwing Shadowkill in Koteuni's copper-tier cell.

Burandin Shadowkill in Qisami's cell. Husband to Koteuni.

Chalkface Member of Cyyk's Grunt Gang. Prisoner of the Happy Glow Retirement Home.

Chiafana also Firstwife. The Minister of Critical Purpose. Adviser to Duchess Sunri of Caobiu.

Cyyk, Quan also Cyknan. Lord in the Quan family of Caobiu. Son of Highlord General Quan Sah. Former student of the Longxian School. Grunt in Qisami's cell. Prisoner at the Happy Glow Retirement Home.

Fungusfeet Member of Cyyk's Grunt Gang. Prisoner of the Happy Glow Retirement Home.

Haaren Shadowkill in Qisami's cell. Opera. Killed by Taishi.

Hair Bear Boss of Barrack Twelve, also known as the Goons, of the Happy Glow Retirement Home.

Issa, Tawara Mother of the River, former Lawkan lord. Prisoner at the Happy Glow Retirement Home.

Ito, Tawara One of the leaders of the Lawkan faction at the Happy Glow Retirement Home.

Jahko Shadowkill in Koteuni's copper-tier cell.

Koteuni Leader of a copper-tier shadowkill cell. Former second-in-command in Maza Qisami's cell. Wife to Burandin. No longer friends with Qisami.

Qisami, Maza also Kiki. Former copper-tier shadowkill from the Bo Po Mo Fo training pool. Former diamond-tier operative under demotion and garnishment from the Consortium. Resident at the Happy Glow Retirement Home.

Snoutnose Member of Cyyk's Grunt Gang. Prisoner of the Happy Glow Retirement Home.

Soy, Mubaan Former minor Gyian taxlord. Prisoner at the Happy Glow Retirement Home. Castrated by Qisami.

Sunxia Warden of Happy Glow Retirement Home. Possibly cousin to Sunri.

Surratoo Sister of the Black Orchids. Nanny to Pei, Oracle of the Tiandi. Excommunicated.

Svent Barrack Three boss of the Happy Glow Retirement Home.

Three Chins Elevator king of the Hope You Get Rich Mine at the Happy Glow Retirement Home.

Tsang Former grunt of Maza Qisami's cell. Now promoted to the Consortium training pool.

Ushmu Shulan lord defending Vauzan's Prime Ward.

Ziyak, Maza Emeritus Senior Mnemonic of the Gyian Court. Father to Maza Qisami.

Zwei also Zweilang. Shadowkill in Koteuni's cell. Opera. A Yiyang.

THE KATUIA

Alyna Viperstrike of the Nezra clan. Former mentor to Salminde. Deceased.

Bhusui Will of the Khan to Visan.

Daewon Master tinker. Council member of the Nezra clan. Husband to Malinde. Father to young Hampa.

Dai Ninth Yazgur of Sunjawa Outpost.

Faalsa Viperstrike and a clan chief of the Nezra clan. Father to Salminde. Deceased.

Hampa Viperstrike. Neophyte to Salminde. Killed by Raydan.

Hanus Yar of the *Honest Run*. Member of the Great Deals Galore Guild.

Hoquo Nezra warrior. Slain during the Nezra attack on the *Honest Run* trade barge.

Horsaw Will of the Khan to Visan.

Huong First Yazgur of Sunjawa Outpost.

Hwashi Will of the Khan to Visan.

Jawapa Hrusha cobbler of the Sun Under Lagoon. His crap is garbage.

Jhamsa Elder Spirit Shaman of Katuia. Council member of Chaqra, the Black City. Former heart-father to Sali.

Jiamin also the Eternal Khan of Katuia. The Lord of the Grass Sea. Childhood friend of Sali. Deceased.

Joum Will of the Khan to Visan.

Lehuangxi Thiraput Cungle Captain of the *Hana Iceberg*. Friend to Sali.

Mali also Malinde the Master Tinker. Sectchief to Nezra tinker sect. Council member of the Nezra clan. Sister to Salminde. Wife to Daewon. Mother to young Hampa.

Marhi also Hoisannisi Jayngnaga Marhi. Neophyte viperstrike to Salminde. Former rumblerlead of Hightop cluster. Friend to Hampa.

Mileene Viperstrike of the Nezra clan. Mother to Salminde. Deceased.

Nanka Crew member of the *Not Loud Not Fat*. Former howler monkey of Nezra clan.

Raydan also Raydan the Stormchaser. The Stormchaser. Former raidbrother to Sali. Killed by Sali.

Sali also Salminde the Viperstrike. The Viperstrike. Former Will of the Khan. Council member of the Nezra clan. Leader of the Exiles Rebellion against Katuia.

Shobansa Nezra Supplychief. Trader and wealthiest person in Nezra.

Suriptika also Conchitsha Abu Suriptika. Happan ritualist. Cobbler in Hrusha. Healer to Sali. Keeper of the Xoangiagu.

Surumptipa Clan chief of Liqusa.

Thuaia Will of the Khan to Visan.

Visan also the new Eternal Khan of Katuia. The Lord of the Grass Sea.

Wani Viperstrike of Nezra clan. Neophyte to Salminde. Former howler monkey.

Weigo Nezra tinker under Daewon.

Yuraki also Rich Man Yuraki. Elder of Hightop cluster. Important politician in Hrusha.

Zowna First of the Coldshatters of Clan Liqusa.

*For a summary of the events of the War Arts Saga so far,
please turn to "The Story So Far" in the appendix.*

ACT I

CHAPTER ONE

AT THE GATES

The Siege of Vauzan began during a sunny Tenth Day Prayer. Ling Taishi was gnawing on a thousand-layer flaky bun at the Tall Wall Dim Sum restaurant set up at the parapet of the Dauntless Wall, which ran along the eastern perimeter of Vauzan city, the ducal capital of Shulan Duchy. The wall didn't serve as much of a deterrent. It was wider and squatter than it was tall, and no opposing army had ever been intimidated by a fat wall. The court often rented the grounds of the outer battlement to various businesses and special events. Wedding processions circling the city were especially popular.

Today was Breakfast Club, which happened at every Tenth Day Prayer. Taishi would never admit it, but she savored these meals with the other women of the club. These events were some of her most enjoyable moments in a world increasingly devoid of such small pleasures. The Vauzan Temple of the Tiandi during Tenth Day Prayer was insufferable, so this gave her an excuse to leave the temple grounds and stay as far away from the ghastly, pious rabble yearning to tithe their way into heaven. With the troubles brewing across the Enlightened States, the business of religion was doing well.

She continued to nibble the edges of her bun. Like the wall, her breakfast was also falsely advertised. The so-called thousand-layer flaky bun had many layers, yes, but not close to a thousand. Probably not even twenty. Even worse, it was dry and bland. Every bite sucked the moisture out of her mouth. It was a good thing that Taishi was prepared. She reached for one of the six cups arrayed before her. The one on the left was hot soy milk for dipping. Next to it was the black poison tea—not actually poisonous. Beside that was the plum wine, the ginseng drink, and then the monk fruit drink. The last cup was water, for washing of course.

Taishi drained the hot soy milk in one burning gulp, and then scooped up another bun. It wasn't that the Tall Wall's pastries were that good; it was that there was competition here, and Zofi ate enough for three.

Sitting across from Taishi, smirking, was Narwani Bhasani, Master of the Drowned Fist, who said, "Ling Taishi, grandmaster war artist, legend of the lunar court, the most-wanted fugitive—sometimes second—in the Enlightened States, is a messy eater. We can't take you anywhere respectable, master."

Flakes dribbled onto Taishi's lap as she sucked her fingers. "I might not be alive next time we get a table here. I'll eat how I like."

It was true; reservations at the Tall Wall Dim Sum, a pop-up open only during Tenth Day Prayers, were difficult to land. That was the thing about time. When she first entered the lunar court, reputation was everything, especially for young women starting out in a man's world. Now that these masters were older legends, they were practically invisible, which suited Taishi fine. Once you're close to death, you tend to stop worrying about what other people think of you.

Taishi popped the last bit of bun into her mouth and flagged down one of the servers moving between the tables. "Hey, pretty miss, another round of soy milk, please."

The girl with the bright green apron rolled her pushcart next to the table and swapped out the empty pitcher with a piping hot one. She also brought out three stacks of wicker baskets and placed them on the table before scribbling markings on a small wooden tablet next to Bhasani.

She bowed to Taishi. "Will that be all, holy dowager?"

"That's it, pretty miss." Taishi objected to the title, but not everyone gets the chance to choose their own identity. She did her best to play the part. She now lived in Vauzan under the alias Dowager Nun Nai Roha.

The legendary grandmaster war artist and criminal Ling Taishi was, by all official accounts, deceased, although she still had the second-largest bounty in all the Enlightened States on her head. According to the carefully crafted and then leaked story that she and Templeabbot Lee Mori had concocted, Taishi had been killed two years ago by her disciple, Wen Jian, the Prophesied Hero—or Villain, depending on which clergy you asked—of the Tiandi, the Champion of the Five Under Heaven, and *still* the most wanted man in the Enlightened States. It annoyed Taishi that her bounty never surpassed his, and never would now that she was dead.

The rumors surrounding them were equally fantastic and unbelievable. The facts were decidedly murkier and needed to be kept under wraps for a while longer. Taishi was not yet ready to reveal Jian to the world, and honestly, *he* wasn't ready.

Ras Sonaya and Wu Zofi joined the two masters at the table a little while later. The drowned fist heir was Jian's tutor, and Taishi's assistant and ward rounded out the last two members of the Breakfast Club. As usual, the girls were late. Both were dragging a little, their heads bowed and shoulders slumped as they fell into their seats. It must have been another late night for the young people.

Taishi used her chopsticks to pick up a couple pieces of garlic green beans. "Have a seat. There's more soy milk coming."

"You're late, daughter," Bhasani scolded. She was always a stickler about her heir's timeliness even though *she* was the one who was often criminally tardy.

"Apologies, Mother." Sonaya looked hungover. She double-fisted a cup of water and a cup of tea and took turns sipping from each. The

drowned fist didn't have a strong tolerance, and any drinking the previous night now showed on her usually unblemished face. After Sonaya
finished her second cup, she helped herself to the blood orange wine,
gulping that until she was out of breath. She set it down and burped,
earning a disapproving glare from Bhasani. Sonaya had been spending
her free time with Jian, and the two had rubbed off on each other in
the worst and best ways.

Bhasani's puckered lips reflected her views on the two young wom-
en's late-night escapades, but Taishi didn't mind. They were young,
assertive women in one of the grandest cities in the world. Taishi had
once been just like them, except with more bar brawls. Bhasani had
been too, if the haughty drowned fist master bothered to remember.

Zofi, on the other hand, had an iron stomach and could match the
God of Gamblers gourd for gourd. She could probably go for another
binge after breakfast if she chose. The former mapmaker's daughter
immediately reached for the wooden menu tablet and took inventory
of the spread on the table, as she was wont to do, as if she were running
her father's map shop. She began to mark up the orders as if she were
grading one of Jian's tests, adding two extra plates of garlic spinach and
removing one of the small dragon buns.

"You always get too many," she chided Taishi.

After she was satisfied with the business of ordering breakfast, Zofi
began to dig into her plate as if this were her last meal. The girl ate like
a large Lawkan ring-push wrestler, swallowing a potsticker with one
bite. "This could use a little salt and sesame oil." She was a food snob
too, with an opinion on everything. She crunched a thousand-layer
flaky bun. "Gah, so dry." Zofi slurped her soy milk and made a face.
"This could use some sugar."

The drowned fist daughter had drained her cups and was flagging
down the server for a refill. "Excuse me, pretty miss. Girl, hey, excuse
me . . . hey!"

The server walked past their table. It was a particularly peculiar
trait among the Shulan. If an elderly person was around, they ignored
the younger people as if they were toddlers. It was their way of showing
deference, but as with everything else, they took it to an extreme. Tai-

shi enjoyed sipping her steaming soy milk as Sonaya tried to flag someone down. The young woman was so used to attention that she got
easily riled when it was withheld. Jian might love her, even if he didn't
realize it yet, but she was a handful.

"Little stinkfish!" Sonaya hissed the fifth time the server walked
past her. Her eyes narrowed, boring into the back of the server girl's
head. Her lips parted . . . and then closed when Bhasani smacked her
across the shoulder.

"Don't abuse your powers, daughter."

"But, Mother . . ." She started to sulk, but a sharp look silenced her.

Taishi wished Jian could be so dutiful. She raised a limp hand, and
the server immediately rushed over. "Yes, dowager, how may I serve
you?"

Taishi smirked. "Refresh our cups, pretty miss, and we've added to
the order."

"Very good, dowager."

Another server arrived a few minutes later with his pushcart carrying an extravagantly glazed green soup bowl shaped like a turtle. He
removed the lid with a flourish, revealing bubbling red liquid inside.

"Dragon egg soup." Zofi rounded on Taishi. "Did you order this?
We're on a budget!"

Taishi frowned. "This must be a mistake, handsome boy. We didn't
order this. You have the wrong table."

The server bowed, his voice cracking. "Pardon, holy dowager.
Courtesy of the gentlemen at table three." He pointed to a large eight-
top with a rotating center. Four men sat around it, throwing attention
their way. It was likely at Sonaya, who had become a striking young
woman. Too much so, in fact, which wasn't necessarily a good thing
when you're a fugitive.

Zofi sneaked a peek. "Fancy any of them?"

The drowned fist daughter sniffed. "I cannot be bought with soup."

"Pardon, mistress, but the gift is for the dowager nun." The server's
cheeks turned a darker shade of red. "The generous gentleman re-
quests the pleasure of your presence."

Taishi shrouded her face. Either someone recognized her or someone had a fetish for old, dying women. Both were nonstarters. She looked over, not bothering to be subtle. All four were impeccably dressed, with pale painted faces and perfectly manicured eyebrows. All were staring directly at her. She snorted. They were either court officials or gangsters. Neither would do. "Tell my gracious patrons that I thank them for the fine offer, but if they look my way again, they'll be reincarnated as toads."

The server was taken aback. "But you accepted his gift. It's only courteous you accept—"

Taishi cut him off. "It's not a gift if I have to pay for it. Take it back if you like."

Not everyone agreed. Bhasani wrapped her arms around it and hissed. "Dragon eggs are worth their weight in gold. It's disgusting, but I doubt I'll get the chance to taste it again."

The server acted as if he were going to try to take the bowl from her anyway, but then changed his mind. He bowed. "As you wish, mistresses." He retreated back to the young men.

The four ladies settled back into their seats and helped themselves to their newfound bounty. The men, obviously courtiers, had looked puzzled and then furious when the server had relayed the message, but what were they going to do about it? The Breakfast Club had already slurped the expensive soup. They were not under any obligation to cater to these dumb hatchlings' whims simply because they were gifted an expensive appetizer. The dragon egg soup was delicious, although Taishi doubted it was liquid-gold good.

The four women forgot about those silly boys and resumed their meal. They had nearly checked off every dish on the menu tablet when several patrons rushed to the wall, looking to the east. A crowd began to gather at the edge of the outer wall. Some put their hands to their mouths. A few cried out and fled, leaving their tables with breakfast half uneaten.

Zofi looked over first. "Is a thunderstorm approaching?"

Sonaya followed her gaze and squinted. "It's too low for clouds. Perhaps an incoming fog?"

Taishi had been busy making out with the sweet potato bread but finally looked over. It was a strange sight at first, a thin plume of smoke rising up toward the heavens. Then the dark, cloudy pillar expanded, spreading out on both sides until it became a vast wall of smoke rising on the horizon where the land met sky. She had witnessed it before, and terrible things always followed shortly after. There went her pleasant morning. "We better finish our breakfast." She turned her attention back to making love with the sweet potato bread. This could be the last piece she would ever eat.

Bhasani had recognized it too. She was the first to stand. "Smoke."

"What was that?" asked Sonaya.

"It's a Smoke Curtain. Caobiu armies use them as a fog of war. It's their calling card to incite panic."

" 'The Smoke Curtain parts ways to invite death in,' " recited Taishi. "It's always been a clunky battle cry."

A few moments later, several lines of soldiers flooded onto the battlement. Fresh tension began to sour her breakfast. The table next to them abruptly got up and left. They were followed by several more, including the four men who'd tried to lure Taishi away with soup. The flow of traffic fleeing the walls became a rush. Others went histrionic, falling to their knees and praying, ruining the mood. It wasn't long before the four women were the only ones left at the tables.

Zofi, as always, was the first to become alarmed. "Shouldn't we get going somewhere as well?"

Taishi continued to chew her food. "After breakfast. Do you know how hard it is to get these reservations?"

"There's an army approaching!"

Taishi glanced at the growing Smoke Curtain and shrugged. It was still half a day away. By the size of it, the army was big, probably filled with siege towers and massive war wagons and legions upon legions of soldiers. Sunri never warred small.

She reached over for her cup of plum wine and found it empty, as were all her other cups. She raised her arm and looked around. "Pretty miss? Handsome boy?" All the servers had fled. She scowled. "Fine. Let's go."

She stood and made her way toward the stairs. The crowds of worried people parted before her as she led the other three women down the stairs toward the city level. It was one of the perks of being a dowager nun. Zofi hurried up next to her. "What should we do, Taishi? Should we leave the city? We should get out of here, right?"

Taishi didn't love the idea of dying on the run, but it appeared they had no choice. "The sooner the better, child."

A groan came from both of the drowned fists. Bhasani made a disgusted face as if she had just passed gas. "Or . . ." The drowned fist master held up a fingernail-painted, manicured hand. "We could lay low and mind our own business until things blow over. We're set up well within the city. We have shelter, food, and most importantly, anonymity. We go on the run, we risk being exposed or encountering bounty hunters or—"

"Drifting helplessly right into a naval battle," said Sonaya.

"Being taken prisoner by an enemy army and stuffed into a corpse wagon," added Zofi unhelpfully. "That was fun."

"Even if Caobiu takes the city, they would certainly leave the Ti-andi temple alone. Why rile the local populace?" Bhasani raised her cup and sipped. "Besides, you said the other day that Jian wasn't ready to reveal himself to the world yet."

Both Zofi and Sonaya bobbed their heads. No one relished being on the run again, either as fugitives or refugees. Taishi didn't blame them. She did not care to be out in the open either, especially in her condition, partially sickness but also just old age, which weakened her with each passing day.

She stayed firm, however. "I'd rather risk the dangers outside these walls than the ones inside once the Caobiu are here. Sunri is a monster. She'll find Jian eventually and turn him into a puppet, assuming he lives that long."

"Fair," Bhasani conceded. She sounded almost grudgingly admiring of the duchess.

All of them did. Taishi didn't blame them for that either. She must be getting soft with her old age, but the truth was the truth. As terrible as she was, Sunri certainly deserved to be empress. A woman needed to be ruthless to triumph in a world ruled by men. Duchess Sunri was, at the same time, the best and worst role model for little murderous girls everywhere.

They reached the bottom of the stairs and started into the city proper. The main square near the Gate of Meaning was a panicked mob of citizens trying to flee deeper into the city while soldiers pushed upstream to get to the city's defenses.

Taishi turned to Zofi. "Start gathering necessary supplies. We'll head west, circle south around the Cloud Pillars, and then head south along the Tyk Coast. We'll need garb that can withstand rain. Maybe an amphibious wagon if you can obtain one."

"And then what?" asked the mapmaker's daughter.

Taishi shrugged. "We'll decide once we get there."

"I'll head to the market to pick up travel supplies."

"Good girl." Taishi turned to the others.

Sonaya wrinkled her nose. "I don't like touching food unless it's being served to me. I'll be in the fashion ward. I need a new travel wardrobe."

"And I," added Bhasani, "am not missing my spa appointment. I won't let Sunri have that power over me. If Sunri is going to run me out of Vauzan, I intend to have a memory of a grand spa day to relive for the rest of my life."

Everyone remembered their fond memories, but the drowned fists had the ability to relive them fully with their jing. Taishi was jealous of that power, although she would probably abuse it to relive her most tragic moments in life.

The Breakfast Club broke up, each woman going her separate way, leaving Taishi standing alone at the base of the Gate of Stillness leading outside the city. Something about this moment gave her pause as she watched her friends disappear into the crowded streets. Sadness swept over her, and she wondered if today's Breakfast Club would be the last good morning she would have for the rest of her life.

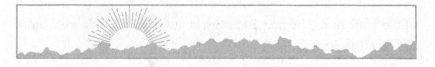

CHAPTER TWO

THE PENAL LIFE

The gong rang once, reverberating across the prison barrack.

Maza Qisami woke up to the sound of rain drumming against the roof and walls of the large but cramped room. Her eyes opened to the misshapen beams of rotting wood and dirty ice haphazardly cobbled together like a building about to collapse into itself. She wiggled her toes and fingers, making sure they still worked, and then continued the motion up her limbs to her neck. Satisfied she was still in one piece, she yawned and let a long breath escape. She sat up, the crown of her head narrowly missing the curved ceiling that met at a point in the center of the large sloping roof, and looked around the long rectangular room of her barrack. She was still here, still breathing, still in one piece.

Everything was fine.

The second gong rang. Qisami reached under her sand-filled pillow and retrieved her clothing—five cut-up burlap sacks and four more she wore as cloaks—to add to the five she slept in. Lastly, she donned the last bit of her uniform: a rotting wooden plaque secured by a string of hemp hanging around her neck. Burned onto the discolored wood were large ashen characters: 1439 ROOM 3. Scribbled below were roughly carved Zhingzhi letters: NO UTENSILS. NO TOOLS. NO ROPE.

Qisami swung her leg over the side of her bed and began her descent down the five levels of bunk beds toward the ground floor.

The loud snorer directly below was still asleep, his ragged breathing sucking air through his nostrils like a clogged sewer line. The woman in the bunk below him rolled away from Qisami as she passed on her way down. The man on the second level had just awoken and was massaging his right arm. The poor sap had the ill luck of it getting frostbite and turning blue the other day. He might not realize it yet, but that hand was as good as gone. He stopped getting dressed and stared at her as she continued down to the ground level.

The last person in her stack at the bottom bunk, a middle-aged man who had arrived during the last supply shipment, lay on his side in a fetal position with his arms wrapped around his already rigid body. His eyes stared at Qisami as her foot touched the floor.

She stared back. Someone must have stolen his burlap sack last night. It was a common occurrence for fresh fish, as newcomers were called. Those residing on the bottom bunks had to learn to guard their sacks, lest they suffer this same fate. A few unfortunate predators had tried to steal Qisami's sack during her first few days here, when she had been assigned a bottom bunk. She still wore their four sacks five years later. Layering was important for survival in this frigid land of eternal cold. No one bothered her anymore.

Poor guy. That left only one thing to do.

Qisami patted the body and rummaged through his pockets, coming away with a small vial of burnroot and a short string of liang tucked in his underpants. She also found a small pouch with a small painted wooden regiment insignia. The corpse had been an artillery officer in the Caobiu army. He must have done something terrible to get sent up here. He probably accidentally fired upon his own troops, deserted, or had been caught raping. Sunri did not tolerate incompetence or poor behavior, especially the latter. Either way, he was dead and Qisami was nine coppers wealthier. Coins were of particular value around

these parts. They carried a better exchange rate than the other curren-
cies, they didn't deteriorate like paper bills or wooden chips, and in a
pinch you could toss your coins in a sock and use it like a flail in a
fight.

The water basin line was fifteen deep by the time she reached the
end of the barrack. The piss line was even longer considering there
were only three squats for over fifty souls, which was the typical barrack size. Fortunately, Qisami was known, so the crowds parted before
her as she walked past them. No one objected when she cut in line.
Seniority, or rather notoriety, had its privileges at the Happy Glow Retirement Home.

"Chopstick," came the smattering of greetings and nods. Most
were begrudging. That was the nickname she had earned shortly after
she arrived. Just one stick.

No one used her real name. None here knew it, save for one person and he didn't count. Most were terrified of her, for good reason,
and looked away when she passed. Qisami had made her reputation
shortly after she had arrived, and she had enjoyed this authority over
the years. Now it was tiresome. At least it allowed her to cut in line for
the piss hole, so that was something.

The gong banged louder and a bit more urgently a third time.

Qisami emptied her bowels and finished cleaning up before joining the rest of the crowd as they filed out. Barrack Three lined up ten
rows, five people deep in front of their building in the main yard,
which was a large, circular open space surrounded by the barracks,
which were divided into four unequal quadrants with the Caobiu corner by far the largest.

It was a warmer day than usual in the Grass Tundra, meaning it
wasn't snowing and they could actually see the dull King floating
across the clear blue sky. Late spring in the first cycle of the year was
as good as it got around here: the wind didn't bite so hard, the snow
was softer and crunchier, and the ice blocks that formed most of the
buildings at the colony were wet and weepy.

A rotund, well-fed man, equally wide as he was tall, walked out from the large building alone in the center of the circle, and approached their group. "Good morning, friends!"

"Good morning, Lord Svent," the chorus replied.

Svent was the boss of Barrack Three and technically an inmate. The difference was that he hailed from a wealthy merchant family in Danziyi, which made him management. He was a jovial man, and he forced that same cheerfulness on his customers, as he liked to call them. And like most of the affluent here, Svent made sure to remind the rest of Barrack Three that while they were all technically inmates, he was a higher class of prisoner than the rest. The nobles were still nobles, the wealthy still had status, and the commoners were there to get stepped on. Everyone lived their sentences here that reflected their social status back at home. Management consisted of the nobility, and the wealthy worked as administrators or guards, leaving the remaining inmates—the commoners—serving as laborers or miners.

The Happy Glow Retirement Home was an infamous place and widely considered the worst prison to get sent to. It was located in the ass end of the world, deep in the Grass Tundra past the borders of the Enlightened States. The prisoners were divided by where they came from, with everyone sorted into a corner based on their home duchy. In a way, the Happy Glow Retirement Home was somewhat of a microcosm of the Enlightened States. This was also the hole where Sunri tossed her political enemies.

"Listen up, customers. Who wants a full belly today?" Svent was a miserable man, thinking himself more silver-tongued than he actually was. The man aspired to climb the corporate prison ladder. He was easy to annoy, quick to temper, and had an appetite for flesh. He had tried to come on to Qisami when she had first transferred to Three from the Goons, and had been lucky to walk away with only a few broken fingers. They had a solid understanding ever since. It still made him a piggy that she wouldn't mind making squeal, but as long as the trades he made with the women in Three were voluntary, it was none of her business.

"We do," came a smattering of replies.

Svent scrunched his face. His voice was louder the second time. "It seems like everyone wants to starve today. Do you all want to freeze to death too?" Escalating his threats was always an effective way to build enthusiasm and team spirit.

"No, Lord Svent!" The chorus made more effort this time.

He nodded. "Good. You're all on ore-panning duty this week at Warehouse Two. Lucky you, always the plum assignments. You can thank your boss for that." When no one answered, rage flashed across his face. His fists clenched. "Now is a good time to thank your generous lord, you snow ticks."

"Thank you, Boss Svent," the chorus grumbled.

The smile returned as if it had never left. "Splendid! Get me three full quotas today and the furnace gets to eat tonight. You all want to keep your fingers and toes from falling off, am I right?"

"Yes, Lord Svent," they chorused.

Qisami even joined in this time. It actually was a good deal, but she berated herself for sinking that low. She was a woman who, just a few short years ago, was living on top of the world: wealthy, powerful, and could do whatever she wanted to whomever she wanted. She didn't even answer to dukes. Now she was giddy over a bowl of watered-down mushy rice.

Sure, everything was fine.

"Hit four and there may be an extra bowl of congee for you. Maybe even chicken," Svent continued. "How do you like that? Everyone thank Boss Svent now, yeah?"

"Thanks, Boss Svent."

The inmates dispersed, moving quicker than usual. Bonus food was a treat. Everyone was usually a step ahead of starvation. Barrack Three was known as the good fortune house. They always seemed to get assigned better jobs and higher bonuses. There was a logical reason for that, and it wasn't due to the strength of Svent's charm and influence.

Svent threw his arm across Qisami's chest as she passed, touching her chest and opposite shoulder. "Not you, Chopstick. Warden wants to see you."

She looked at his arm barring her way. In another lifetime, it would have been separated from his shoulder. "You got it, boss."

Qisami broke away from the rest of the pack and backtracked, moving against traffic. By now, just as the predawn rays of the King appeared in the distance, a weak piss-colored glow blanketed by gray clouds and white flurries was beginning to crawl across the darkened landscape. It never really got dark in the Grass Tundra, just like it never really got any brighter. There was always a constant blanket of stark grayness as far as the eyes could see.

The Happy Glow Retirement Home was an open-air prison. It had no walls or fortifications. Archers were not manning guard towers. Management did not send hunting parties to chase escaping inmates. That was the first thing every inmate was told the first day they arrived. *If you want to go, then go.* They'd usually just wish you luck and wave as you walked the Grass Tundra to your likely demise. There was no escape or shelter for over a hundred miles. No civilization, no refuge, no hope. All there was in the Grass Tundra was frigid death or slow starvation.

Qisami continued toward the heart of the colony, passing by Barrack Two and Barrack Five, and then past the kitchen and holding area storing ore, awaiting the shipment of inbound supplies and outbound ore scheduled at the beginning of first cycle spring and near the end of the second cycle fall. Having fallen behind due to a particularly harsh third cycle winter near the end of last year, management was trying to catch up with their quota, which explained why they were offering extra bowls of congee for extra work.

The management office was a large two-story manor at the center of the main field. It was one of the few buildings built from stone and wood. Most others were constructed from packed snow and ice. The lone guard leaning against the wall next to the door let her pass with a lazy wave of his hand and continued his staring contest with the floor. The Happy Glow was manned by a small militia that had just enough bodies to put down a riot, guard the mine, and chase off the occasional polar bear or woolly rhinoceros or mammoth. They consisted mostly of low-standing nobles from court or wealthier business types, who were able to bribe their way into management during their sentencing.

She crossed the main hall with several dozen wristwaggers working at tables huddled around small fireplaces. Most had been sentenced for fraud, bribery, or tax evasion, or they were considered threats to the duchess's regime. Sunri had a way of maximizing the usefulness of her assets.

Qisami passed by one young noble sitting at a table playing a game of Siege with another. "Hey, One-Ball."

As always, Mubaan Soy flinched when she neared. Soy was an unpleasant minor Gyian taxlord who had tried to impose himself upon the house staff back in Allanto. Qisami had ended that hobby by separating one of his testicles from its sack with a knife after he had made an attempt on her. After Sunri seized Allanto, she sent a quarter of the Gyian Court to the Happy Glow. While most inmates were here for legitimate reasons, some were here because Sunri simply didn't like them. The entire Mubaan family was here due to the latter, and Soy was the last of them.

The duchess had no tolerance for men behaving poorly. That didn't mean Qisami wouldn't gut her at the first opportunity. That bitch was at the top of Qisami's list of death marks. By now it was a lengthy list, although Qisami had to admit she had become lax in remembering all the names these days. Reciting them didn't make her feel alive the way it used to.

She reached the warden's chamber on the second floor, where two young Caobiu nobles posing as guards flanked a pitifully narrow wooden door. Why these limpweeds needed to guard anything was beyond her. The two nobles looked almost too young to have committed any offense that would deserve being sent up here. They were more likely the victims of being born into a noble family who had crossed the duchess. Maybe the lord of the family hadn't bowed low enough to Sunri or maybe had looked at her the wrong way.

"He's expecting you, Chopstick," the one on the right said as the other opened the door. Qisami appreciated that her reputation preceded her.

The door behind her closed firmly as she entered the warden's sanctum. Unlike the rest of the penal colony, the warden's private quarters were richly decorated with many of the trappings worthy of court. The floors were lined with dark mahogany wood. Thick tapestries covered three walls from floor to ceiling, while a bank of windows—with actual glass—lined the fourth. Two golden chandeliers hung from the ceiling. The people of Caobiu had a thing for chandeliers. Every room had one, if possible, even bathrooms. It must have cost a fortune for the duchy to transport so much material so far north.

The large man sitting behind a desk facing the door at the other end of the room didn't look up when she walked in. He flicked his hand, dismissively. "Sit."

Qisami remained at the doorway for a beat, then moved toward a sofa off to the side.

"Not the cushioned seats. The bench next to the door." He still hadn't looked up from his work.

A growl sprang from her throat, but she buried it and did as ordered. There was a time when she would have stabbed a man for that insult, but that was Maza Qisami, not 1439. Not Chopstick. As the minutes ticked by, her annoyance increased. Some old habits are never broken.

One could always tell when someone was born with a stick up their ass by the way they played the waiting game. It was a power play often used in court by someone of higher standing to remind someone lower exactly how much lesser they were in the hierarchy. The greater the difference, the longer the wait. That stupid Duchess Sunri once made her wait several days *after* summoning her before they finally had an audience.

Qisami passed the minutes by staring at her surroundings. This was the only place in the entire accursed colony that didn't feel like a prison. For one thing, it was warm here. The one constant at the Happy Glow was that the chill was always nipping at you, no matter where you were or what you were doing. For another, this room didn't smell like piss or death or both. Not to mention the seats were dry and soft, even this wooden one. Sitting usually involved hard uneven stone, wet ice, muddy earth, or rotting wood full of splinters.

Qisami closed her eyes, and for a few moments she let her mind roam free. She was on a beach enjoying the sun. She was in a salon getting drunk with someone soft sitting on her lap. She was—

Qisami's daydream was interrupted when the warden coughed and snorted in the loudest and most obnoxious way. He sounded like a boar feeding. She grimaced and focused on the man before her.

Warden Sunxia was a distinct man, large and tall with the bearing of a war artist, if not for his sedentary lifestyle adding weight to his frame. With a face half-burnt on the left side and a deep scar running down his right, he was ugly. Actually, no, he wasn't. She could tell the man had once been handsome, with long black hair, his one good eye striking and large, and a chin worthy of a duke. Those days were long gone, but she still found him attractive even with his scars, or perhaps because of them.

What was more interesting about the warden, however, wasn't just his once-obvious good looks, but who he looked like. All someone had to do was hold a silver liang next to his face to see the striking resemblance to a certain Duchess of Caobiu, not to mention that the two shared the same surname. The gossip at the Happy Glow was that Sunri and Sunxia were cousins, and that Sunri had brought him to the imperial court after she was raised to fourth wife of Emperor Xuanshing, may his greatness ever last. Supposedly, Sunxia had attempted a coup in the Caobiu Duchy shortly after the empire broke apart, and he had come out on the losing end.

Another rumor that persisted was that Sunxia was simply *too* handsome for the duchess to keep around court, which earned him not only his burnt and cut-up face but banishment to this penal colony. But since he still was a noble, and more importantly, a Sun, his sentence was to rule the Happy Glow Retirement Home. Nobles were weird like that.

The water clock on the wall had just emptied a full hour when an attendant came in with a breakfast tray, which made the wait even more unbearable. At least it stirred Sunxia from his work. He finished his wristwagging and stood, his wide frame causing his chair to scrape against the floor. His time spent standing was brief, and then he was sitting at the dining table breaking a large piece of bread and stuffing it into his mouth as if he were smoking a pipe.

He beckoned to her. "Chopsticks, I have a dirty job, and I'd rather not sully management. I need my most rabid dog."

"It's one stick," she grumbled. Qisami approached the edge of the table. The spread was decent. The heady scent of sugary pastries, savory sausages, and steaming soy milk wafted into Qisami's nostrils. There were taro cubes, scallion and flat noodles, deep-fried dough and hot soy milk, scallion crepes and sweet buns. There were even moon cakes. Where was the warden hiding all this stuff? Finding it would be her next hobby. It wasn't like she had much else to do. Her stomach growled, not only from hunger but from the sharp though fading memory of what decent food tasted like. She couldn't remember the last time she had a meal other than watered-down congee. "What's the ask, Warden?"

Sunxia took his time picking assorted foods onto his plate and savoring every bite. Again, this stupid waiting game. It was another five minutes before he addressed her. "The wagons on the west end of mine five are coming back with weak loads. Same weight but with disproportionately poor ratios of valuable ore to dirt and stone."

Qisami was only half listening as she watched the warden's scanning eyes. This was a good time to practice a little shoplifting. As soon as he was distracted, her fingers got busy on the table. She gesticulated with one hand to distract from the other. "Those ungrateful dogs, the nerve! Could it be because those particular shafts have dried up?"

"Doubtful." The warden shook his head. "Sent the foreman last night. Claimed he was tripping over sparkstone, coal, and silver. I had them go over reports from several weeks back. Same issue with submine sixteen, nineteen, and twenty-three, all assigned to the same Lawkan crew from Barrack Twenty-Four. Some white rice are shaving off the top and the pruneskins are the only ones with the expertise to pull it off. Find those responsible and teach them a lesson. No one dares steal from the Caobiu, not even in prison. Especially in prison."

"Do you know how they're doing it, boss?"

"Who knows how those pruneskins are pulling it off? It's in their blood."

Lawkan Duchy was known for two things: its extensive waterways and its beaches. Those people loved to bake in the sun, thus the pruneskin slur. And because of their naval and merchant expertise, the Lawkan also happened to home-grow the best smugglers in the Enlightened States.

Qisami kept him talking for a little while longer, peppering him with pointless questions. This five-minute conversation had proved fruitful. Cookies, pastries, and other sweets were high-value black market items. Finally, after her pockets were full, she worked toward an exit plan.

"Take care of them like this?" She ran a finger across her neck. "Or take care of them like this?" She made a bonking motion with her fist.

Sunxia shook his head. "There were fourteen accidents last month. The blasted shipments are falling behind schedule."

"Kneecaps it is." Qisami brushed her hands free of crumbs and rose from the table.

"Concussions," the warden corrected. "Unfortunately, only eight of those fourteen died, so now we have six useless mouths to feed until they recover. No need to waste a good bed. As always, keep management above the fray."

"Any extra scratch for me?" Qisami decided to push her luck. "How about a room here, in this nice warm building?"

The warden snorted. "You do as you're told, dog, or you go back to the Goons in the deep mines. No more luxury with Barrack Three, yeah?" The warden's eyes lowered to Qisami's legs. "You'll get a new pair of shoes, and I won't chop off your hands for those pastries you just pocketed." The warden was more observant than he let on.

A pair of new shoes and getting to keep her hands? Good enough deal. "Fine, but I'll need some muscle and a couple extra pairs of shoes."

Sunxia considered her request. He pulled out his wooden circular marker the size of her hand and slid it across the table. "Here's a marker. You get six pairs of shoes, that's it. Be done by tomorrow. I won't tolerate more theft on my watch. Now go. Your stink is ruining my appetite."

"Sure, Warden." Qisami stuffed one of the cookies into her mouth. There was no use hiding them if she had already been caught.

"Actually," the warden called as she was about to leave the room, "I changed my mind. Kill a ringleader. I don't care who. Set an example for the rest of the thieves."

Qisami closed the door after she left the warden's sanctum, and broke into a satisfied grin. Her pockets were bulging with sweets, and she was about to get a much-needed new pair of shoes. Overall, it had been a productive morning.

Getting excited over cookies and shoes was just another reminder of how far Qisami had fallen. But sure, everything was fine.

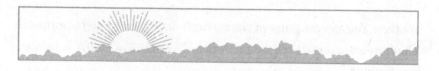

CHAPTER THREE

VAUZAN

Taishi's mind raced as she hurried back toward her cottage hidden in the back of the bamboo forest on the Vauzan Temple of the Tiandi grounds. There wasn't much to pack. Most of her worldly possessions were entombed in her family plot back on the burial mountain. She had given Jian instructions on how to retrieve them after she was gone. Everything else she could carry in her satchel.

The only things she needed to retrieve were her favorite llama sleeping robes, a few Burning Hearts romance books, and the sketch of her mother. Even her straight sword, the Swallow Dances, had been passed down to Jian. The thought of no longer being her beloved blade's owner still brought a lump to her throat.

The curving path Taishi followed broke off from the main road and ran in a descending spiral down a wooden walkway circling a tall waterfall and then broke off through a dank tunnel and into the Jewel in the Eye of the Lotus residential ward that led toward Peony Peak, where the Vauzan Temple of the Tiandi resided. A constant breeze sprayed mist over her from the water flowing over the crest of the waterfall directly overhead and plunging to the pool several stories below.

Vauzan might be beautiful, but it was dank and wet, and lacked railings. It was a wonder more older citizens didn't break their necks walking about. The importance of safety mechanisms had never occurred to Taishi until she no longer was able to soar atop the wind currents.

That was the hardest part. Taishi deeply missed flying. It had been over a year since she last tried. *Maybe* she could do it, but age made one cautious, especially now that her once-stone-grounded sense of balance had abandoned her. She had already promised herself that, Tiandi willing, she would fly one last time.

Unfortunately, traversing these hills and valleys felt like hiking uphill both ways. Her knees ached, as did her back and feet and neck and everything else. People with a lifetime of battle trauma weren't meant to live this long. She was tired of being old. People often waxed poetic about how wisdom came with age, but no one talked about the hardship of simply taking a breath. The tremors were frequent and so bad that she often couldn't hide them beneath her many layers of clothing. Another thing no one bothered to mention was how her body was literally shriveling up. The other ladies might have valid reasons for not wanting to go on the road again, but this journey would likely kill her, if Sunri didn't find her first.

A gaggle of young Tiandi monks—initiates by their plain robes— stopped in, lined up, and bowed as she passed. She nodded back, if only to maintain the pretense. The young ones were always the most fervent. Her robes were those of a hanma, an old, retired dowager battle-nun particularly revered among the devout. More importantly, local businesses always offered her discounts. It also gave her an excuse to wear a weapon, which, in her case, was a hollow sword that she primarily used as a walking cane as she stepped out from the tunnel along the slippery path.

Taishi had nearly made it to the Big Faith Ward, where the temple was located, when the street suddenly emptied of traffic, leaving her standing alone. Strange. She stopped at the middle of the walkway when two figures stepped in front of her. She felt the presence of someone approaching from behind as well. Taishi's body immediately sank down as her feet instinctively took a wider stance. She subcon-

sciously checked the direction of the breeze. There was heavy moisture in the air, which made for slow air currents. Not that it mattered,
but old habits die hard.

One man bowed, fist to open palm, formal but shallow. His irritation showed. "It did not have to be this difficult, master. You should
have accepted the soup."

"It's still easy, young lord," she replied. "You don't want difficult,
trust me."

"By the decree of the Regent Council of Shulan, you have been
ordered to present yourself to the ducal court."

Taishi considered her options. To disobey the summons was grounds
for high treason. But what the hell. The Shulan Court had bigger
things to worry about right now. Taishi put a hand on the hilt of her
blade. She held her hollow sword at chest level and let the hilt slip to
reveal the exposed blade. Hollow swords were as described: sword-
shaped blades that were hollow inside, allowing the weapon to be a
quarter of the weight with none of the effectiveness. They were for
show, props to intimidate rabble and cutpurses. Unfortunately for Taishi, all court officials were war artists to some degree. A year ago, she
would have cracked these four eggs and not even gotten warmed up.

Time changed things. Taishi was a shell of her former self. Her
mind was still sharp, but her jing had long wasted alongside her body.
So now she had to defend herself in other ways.

She stared the four men down. Her glare was still fierce. Three of
the young men, with straight swords drawn, hesitated. The last wilted
like a flower under the harsh afternoon rays of the third cycle King.

She spoke in a soft, deadpan voice. "Do you know who I am?"

They nodded.

"Yet you dare draw your blades?" The fact these pups knew who
she was and still thought they could capture her was insult to injury
enough. Her lips curled into a snarl of disbelief. "Very well, then. The
best way to deal with nobles is to gut them." She sighed. "Let's get this
over with. Who wants to die first?"

The front two exchanged glances, each hoping the other would volunteer. When neither did, the one to her right took it upon himself. Taishi's senses were still sharp even if her reflexes had decayed. No sooner had the man taken a step forward than her arm flashed out, leveling her hollow sword at his eyes. "I guess you do. Step up, boy."

The young man—more a boy—dutifully complied. His straight sword quivered in his hand at a shallow angle, as he raised his guard with his weight on his back foot. A variation of the Far Fist swordplay style. Pretty, but useless. He stamped his feet twice.

Taishi slapped his blade aside. "We're not sparring, son."

"But . . ." Blood drained from the young man's face.

The other three were more than happy to let the young man take the first stab—or get stabbed first. Taishi waited as he lunged. Far Fist, as always, was beautiful and theatrical, full of excessive movements that were mostly pointless. The boy looked like a terrified fawn as he inched closer. The moment the tip of his blade was within reach, Taishi slapped it aside so quickly he almost dropped his sword.

"I don't have all day. If you're going to attack, then attack."

The foolish boy gritted his teeth and charged. At least he was good at following instructions. She moved with an exaggerated flair, stepping aside and rapping the boy on the ear with the flat of her blade as if she were disciplining an unruly child. "You're off-balance. Keep your head straight. Your elbows look like chicken wings."

The young man whirled at her, slicing air. The panic in his movements was obvious.

Taishi continued offering her critique. She turned with him, skimming the edge of her blade against his elbow as they danced. "There goes your arm. Now you're just like me." She jabbed his toe with the point of her hollow sword. "You're missing one foot now too." Then she reached out and tripped him, sending him sprawling to the dirt.

Taishi planted the tip of the sword on the small of his back. "Stay down. The lesson's over." She turned to the others. "Who is ready for the real thing?"

The seconds ticked by. The remaining three averted their eyes. Taishi made the decision for them and walked away. If the group *had* worked together to take her down, she had no doubt about the out-come. Shulan nobles, no matter how haughty and arrogant, were usu-ally suckers for fair fights.

Taishi turned her back to them and then, chin raised, walked past the two in front. "Tell the lord who sent you to bring an army if you hope to capture me."

As soon as her back was turned, she sucked in a deep breath. Even that bit of exertion had exhausted her. Taishi was nearing the end of the block when an armored ducal carriage rolled to a stop in the inter-section, cutting her off. Flanking the transport were two full squads of Shulan elite displayguards.

The door swung open, and a beautiful bald woman in silver glitter-ing robes stepped out. She looked furious as she snapped at Taishi, her voice light and beautiful, clear and pure as arctic water. Her words, on the other hand, were not. "Get in the blasted carriage, Taishi, or I'll have you cut into a thousand pieces and fed to the warhorses."

How lazy did a lord have to be to use a mindseer to arrest or kidnap her? A quick inventory of the twenty armored guards informed her there was no talking her way out of this. She sighed and held up her good arm. "Fine, you caught me. Take me away."

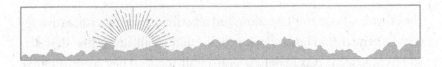

CHAPTER FOUR

THE REFRESHED START

Wen Jian, Prophesied Hero of the Tiandi, Champion of the Five Under Heaven, Savior of the Zhuun, accused Villain of the Tiandi, and *the* undisputed number-one fugitive in all of the Enlightened States—at least on most reputable bounty lists—gnawed at his lips. He studied his big toes poking out from the ends of his sandals as the attractive box girl working at the counter said something nice to him while serving red and green shaved ice in a small wooden cup.

"Third time this week. You must be my biggest fan." She winked, with a bright smile and twinkling eyes.

Technically Hachi, fidgeting next to him, was her biggest fan, which was why the two had frequented her establishment so many times over the past week. Jian just loved the watermelon flavor. His best friend had been sweet on the girl for weeks, but the usually smooth-talking, wit-quipping whipfinger became tongue-tied every time they visited the girl's box.

The city of Vauzan was littered with hundreds of these popular box shops, which consisted of little more than a white-painted wooden

shack with a large front window and a counter to display attractive female attendants. These shops usually sold small items like desserts,
sweets, tobacco, psychedelics, and hand foods. They were popular
places for young people to hang out, snack, and ogle a pretty person.
Times were difficult, but like Master Sohn often said, the business of
ogling was recession-proof. Tiandi monks were often the most popular
customers. The locked box shops were for the women's protection.

Hachi had come across this particular box—more specifically, this
girl—a few weeks back and had been smitten since, dragging Jian
along at every opportunity. The box girl, as they were commonly
called, was very pretty, with large luminous eyes and wavy black hair
that fell past her shoulders. She also had a smart mouth, often bantering with her customers and able to keep up with a variety of topics. It
wasn't lost upon Jian that whenever she wasn't working, she had her
face buried in reading the revered monk Goramh's *Bylaws of a Civilized World*, which meant she must attend one of the city's scholar
universities. Unfortunately for his best friend, the box girl was currently paying more attention to Jian than to Hachi. For some reason,
the box girl had expressed no interest in the whipfinger, which befuddled both men. Hachi was taller. Hachi was more handsome.
Hachi was wittier. At least, usually.

"I lock the box at dusk," the girl was saying. "My mam's place is at
the edge of the Kaleidoscope Gate. Care to walk me home?"

Hachi shrank like a wilting lily. Jian's discomfort grew. After being
in hiding over much of the past five years, excessive attention made
him uneasy. Besides, Sonaya would drown him in a shallow pond if he
ever walked a box girl home. Taishi would probably hang him by his
toes.

Jian side-eyed his friend. Well, if Hachi wasn't going to do it, Jian
would make his friend's intentions clear. Most of the time, being
straightforward was honest, and honesty was good. He had learned
that from Taishi, Sonaya, and Zofi, usually when he had to apologize.
"My good and noble friend is very free. He's also very nice." He kicked
Hachi's ankle. "And usually not so shy."

The box girl offered Hachi an obligatory glance and then promptly went back to ignoring him. "Yes, he's pretty, but I want *you* to walk me home."

"Why me?" he blurted.

She planted her hands on her hips. "Because this gold-tongued rooster walked my friend in Box Fourteen home three weeks ago, my classmate in Twenty-Seven the week before that, and my cousin in Nineteen last month, and who knows how many others. Box girls gossip." She wrinkled her nose. "You, on the other hand, have never asked anyone I know."

Poor Hachi's ears were strawberry red as he slinked out of view of the window. Jian had never seen his friend so deflated or so speechless. He looked as if he were about to turn into a puddle on the ground. Hachi was usually gregarious like his master, Fausan, who was renowned throughout the lunar court as the God of Gamblers. And while it *was* true that Hachi was often outgoing and a known carouser, Jian had never witnessed his friend go any further. What Jian *did* know, however, was that Hachi had been mind-melted about this girl in Box Three since the first time he laid eyes on her and bought a candied fruit skewer.

Jian decided to do something about that. Hachi was about to flee when Jian hauled his friend back to the window before the next customer could step up. "Hey, his name is Hachi and he's a war artist. He's also smart, clever, ambitious, and a stupidly loyal friend. Give him a chance."

The box girl eyed Hachi and squinted as if appraising a rack of lamb. "A war artist? Is he any good?"

"Heir to the famed Whipfinger family style."

That drew a blank look. "But you vouch for him?"

He nodded. "On my name, Lu Hiro."

Her eyes narrowed. "Is he walking any other girls home?"

"No one, I swear on my honor!" Hachi blurted. He would have dropped to a knee if Jian hadn't held him up.

"And mine," added Jian.

The box girl made a show of considering the offer. "There are a couple hooligans who give me trouble every so often on my way home."

"I'll walk you home every day to make sure they trouble you no more, great lady." Hachi almost fell to his knees a second time. It was a good thing Jian's grip was tight.

The box girl noticed his attempt the second time and smirked. "The name's Neeshan. I close when the King is half to bed. Don't be late, whip boy."

The moment they turned the corner and were out of sight of the box, Hachi threw his arms around Jian and shook him like a tree full of ripe apples. "Thank you, little brother."

"Great lady? She's not your aunt, you dud." Jian elbowed his friend in the ribs. "You better treat her well. I don't want to get blacklisted from all the box shops. Come on, we're late for the training yard."

The pair hurried down the street away from Box Three, merged with the main road heading west toward the seedier side of the city, and made their way against traffic along Vauzan's notoriously windy roads.

The capital of Shulan was breathtaking, a true work of art. It was a marriage between architecture and nature, with flowing, curved buildings that began where the hills ended. Streets ran alongside riverbanks, and towers and cliffs leaned against each other for support.

Unlike the other major ducal capitals: Allanto was a meticulous grid that was a playpen for the wealthy, Manjing was one big beach resort, Danziyi an army camp, and Xusan a big round cylinder. Vauzan, renowned as the City of Flowers, was a place of harmony, where the people coexisted with nature and the land, rather than bending it to their will. The entire city was a kaleidoscope of gardens and groves with fields of flowers in every color dotting the landscape.

Vauzan was littered by dozens of steep hills and sharp valleys. Giant columns, not unlike those back in the Cloud Pillars to the west, dotted the city like pins on a map. Between the hills and the basins, the city was divided into neighborhoods known as wards, with every one possessing its own distinct flavor and customs. Some wards rested atop pillars, while others ran along the deep cuts at the basins of narrow ravines. A few wards expanded over lakes with buildings sitting on stilts, while others hung along the sides of pillars hugging the sheer walls. Still others were hidden behind giant waterfalls with curtains of water spouting perpetual clouds of mist.

Jian loved Vauzan, although he had to admit this constant walking uphill and down tired him out. At least it made his legs strong. The two continued through these elevation changes until they reached the tallest structure in the city, the Three Hands to Heaven Tower. That was where they found Hwang Kaiyu, heir of the Houtou style Third Lin Lineage, attempting to climb the side of the tower, having reached some four stories off the ground. A small crowd had gathered at the base of the building, observing the spectacle.

The two friends joined the crowd and waved. Jian cupped his mouth. "Hey, Kaiyu, how goes it?"

Kaiyu glanced down from where he was standing on a small ledge with his back flattened against the wall. "Oh hey, Jian!"

"Everything all right?"

"Everything's great." He looked up and then down. "Actually, I've been stuck here for twenty minutes. Is it time to go?"

"We're already late," Hachi yelled back. "It's competition night!"

Coming down was far quicker for Kaiyu than it was for him to climb up. The Houtou style was famed for its agility. Kasa, the former master, had been called the Sky Monkey within the lunar court, and it was well earned. His adopted son was just as talented as any within their lineage. Kaiyu dropped a story before catching a ledge with his fingers, and then swung like a pendulum a few times before landing on a nearby windowsill. He paused before traversing the curved wall seemingly at a full sprint until he leaped into the air, twisted into a somersault, and landed gracefully in a roll before bounding onto his feet.

"Show-off." Jian grinned, throwing his arm around his friend. "How goes the practice?"

"I can't puzzle out the fourth-to-fifth-floor transition through the inverted slant." The happy-go-lucky young man's face turned toward downtrodden. Kaiyu often wore his emotions like face paint. "It's also getting scary that high. I'm never going to pass the test at this rate."

The final test for the Houtou style Third Lin Lineage required the ascending new master to climb atop the Allanto Temple of the Tiandi and ring the Gong as Large as the World three times. It was a simple task, more a formality and celebration than a real test of ability. A former master three centuries ago had pranked his daughter with the goal to surprise her with her friends once she reached the top, and that was how the tradition was born.

Since then, that celebration became the Houtou way.

That was until the temple burned down during the fall of Allanto. Sunri had also ordered the Gong as Large as the World melted down to repurpose for cavalry armor, which meant the traditional Houtou test was no longer possible. A new test had to be administered, and unfortunately for the Houtou, Master Kasa had left the decision of what that test would look like to Taishi when he passed. So, Taishi being Taishi, she chose the most difficult and treacherous test she could devise by decreeing that all Houtou masters must scale the Three Hands to Heaven Tower free solo. Young Kaiyu had embraced the challenge and for months trained diligently. Leave it to Jian's master to ruin a good party.

"You'll get it," he replied, wrapping his arms around his little brother.

Hachi appeared on the other side of Kaiyu and did the same. "Come on, you can take out your frustrations on Jian tonight."

Kaiyu brightened. "I thought I was finally getting some competition."

Jian's embrace turned into a playful headlock.

The three arrived at the Three Punch of Fury fighting field a short jaunt later. It was one of the larger and more popular fields in the city, known to attract many promising war artists to train and match skills. Vauzan was the birthplace of war arts, and it was a distinction the people of Shulan Duchy wore proudly. Each duchy had evolved its war arts differently. Caobiu had mastered the military war arts style. Xing had the styles best suited for killers, spies, and assassins. Gyian styles had a flare for theatrics and beauty, while most Lawkan styles emphasized fighting in coordinated teams. But it was Shulan that had elevated the war arts to their purest form. For many in Vauzan, practicing the war arts was a way of life.

The Shulan were the first to create the idea of the lineage. The war arts styles in Vauzan were organized by a master choosing every one of his disciples to train in his lineage. It was considered a great honor to be invited to a war arts family. Coin never changed hands. It was taboo for someone to buy their way into a family.

These training yards were where hundreds of war artists from all families and skills and ages mingled. Groups would arrive at dawn to lay claim to the best arena circle, and for the rest of the day hold court, inviting other families to practice, spar, and train together. Children as young as four attended group classes held here. Students from brotherly schools would spar for exposure and reputation. Sometimes an entire family would challenge another for the rights of a particular arena space. It was usually, but not always, done in good nature.

A gaggle of children rushed Jian, saying,

"Hi, Hiro."

"Late start, eh, Hiro?"

"You owe me a rematch, Hiro."

"Hi, big brother!"

They grabbed him and patted his arms and pants. They were definitely trying to pick his pocket. There was an entire war arts family trained to do just that.

Jian offered a friendly smile as he scanned the field for an open arena. He and his friends were familiar faces at the Three Punch of Fury. The people here were those he sparred with regularly, caroused with at the bars and salons, and bonded with over idle talk, spectating matches, or just eating sweet sausages. The Three Punch was like a second home to Jian and his friends.

The three continued up and down the grid of arenas arrayed on the field. Most of the eighty spaces were occupied. Jian and Hachi's little detour to Box Three this morning had cost them prime real estate. They combed the field once and were on their second pass when Jian noticed that the Hoshingyi family had finished for the day and were vacating their arena.

"Over there, before it's too late!" Jian broke into a jog, ramping up into a full sprint. Even though he had a head start, Kaiyu kept up with him easily and soon pulled ahead. Hachi, like his master, wasn't a fan of running, and kept his pace.

Kaiyu had just reached the circular arena when he collided with another who was likely coveting the same space. Both crashed to the floor, although it was Kaiyu who took the brunt of it, being the smaller of the two. The agile Houtou heir managed to stay on his feet, however, as he checked on the other person. "Are you all right? I didn't—"

The other man swatted Kaiyu's helping hand away. "Mangy pup. Watch where you're going. I should beat some respect into you."

"Hey, who do you think you are, talking to my little brother like that?" Jian saw red, especially when it came to Kaiyu. He stepped in between Kaiyu and the larger man. "You owe my friend an apology."

The thug spat, facing him. He was a full head taller. He brought a reed whistle to his lips.

That was when Hachi caught up to them. He stepped next to Jian and swiped the whistle out of the large guy's mouth. "Let's not get too hasty."

Hachi grabbed Kaiyu by the collar and shoved him back. He turned back to the black-and-gray-robed man. "No disrespect. You can have the spot. We'll get another."

"What are you doing?" Jian glared. "He—"

"He's a Today Boy," Hachi muttered. "A stupid arena circle is not worth it."

That only made Jian hotter. The Worst Today Boys was an underground organization known for their pretty-boy thugs who committed violent acts. The information washed over Jian, and he allowed Hachi to push him back.

That was until a new voice carried across the field. "Well, if it isn't Hachi the whipfinger, running away again."

Hachi stopped, his hands clenched into fists. He turned toward the new voice. "What did you say, Xuamio?"

More gray-and-black-robed Worst Today Boys arrived. The lead thug was a brawny man wearing a thick sleeveless vest showing off his muscular shoulders and protruding chest. He stepped up to Hachi until their noses nearly touched. "I called you a coward, Hachi. What are you going to do about it? Nothing. You and your pip friends are going to walk away like a cur with your tail between your legs. Because otherwise . . ." He shrugged as his boys—and three girls—surrounded them.

Anger flashed on Hachi's face. He glared at Xuamio, looked at Jian as if remembering something, and then back at the underworld thug. He sniffed. "You're right. We're going to turn and walk away."

"You do that, you addled egg," Xuamio gloated.

That should have been the end of it, but Hachi hated being called an egg. He sniffed, saying, "You've been making a stink ever since I bested you in that duel."

"You didn't best me!" Xuamio matched his intensity. "I bested myself!"

"You bested yourself six matches in a row?"

"It was an off day!" Xuamio roared. "I'm going to beat you with my slippers!"

A crowd had gathered to watch. Jian was suddenly aware that they were outnumbered five to one, and he was still forbidden to show his true skill. They might still lose even if he did go full effort. Worst Today war artists were not pushovers. Hachi and Xuamio were still jawing at each other like two male peacocks flashing their feathers. It was probably too late, regardless. A fight was inevitable. Jian readied himself.

"What is the meaning of this?"

Everyone, including the adjacent arena practitioners, stopped. The crowds dispersed. There was no crime for gawking, but no one liked being a witness. Snitching was often worse than the crime.

Xinde, wearing a blue robe and a cone-shaped hat, stepped through the two parties. His club on his right hip remained holstered, and the latch for his three-sectional staff strapped to his back was unfastened. The crowds parted before him as he entered the arena. The former Longxian senior looked calm, collected, and cool.

He tipped his cap. "Hello, Hiro."

"Magistrate," said Jian. "Nice to see you've finally shown up." He added, "Sir."

"I had to break up a cat fight."

"Back at the Central Girls' Big Head School?"

"No, two large gangs of stray cats got into a turf war at the intersection of the North Polar Gates. Captain called in reinforcements." He stepped between Hachi and Xuamio. "This is the second time this week I'm breaking you two apart. I'm not doing a third." He crossed his arms. "Here's the deal. You either bury this rivalry between you two or you fight to the death right now. Take your pick."

Both war artists looked taken aback.

"What?" sputtered Xuamio. "You're insane. I'm not fighting to the death. At least, not for free."

Hachi spoke in a muffled voice. "I don't want to fight to the death. I have to walk this box girl home tonight."

"There you go," said Xinde. "Neither of you actually want to fight, so bow and walk away. Stop wasting everyone's time, or I'm going to haul you both into a cell and see which one comes out alive tomor-row—"

A woman's loud cry cut across the field. Jian craned his head and looked toward the east. His mouth dropped as a large flaming ball of fire crashed into a building several blocks away. The resulting explosion sent a column of smoke into the air. It was soon followed by three more flaming balls and then five more. Soon the morning's clear blue sky had become a fleeting memory as Vauzan began to burn.

CHAPTER FIVE

CHOPSTICK

Qisami set off to complete her assignment. Her current boots were on their last threads. She departed Sunxia's office and headed down to the main administration floor. The first thing she needed was a team-up. Qisami the shadowkill could have easily walked into Barrack Twenty-Four and laid waste to the sad lot with little effort. Her arms might have been tired afterward, but she wouldn't break a sweat. The problem was, she wasn't Qisami the shadowkill; she was Chopstick the thug, and there was no way a lowly street brawler could take out fifty heads in a barrack by herself. The inmates at the Happy Glow might fear her violence, but none could know her true nature.

The Consortium would never allow one of their former operatives to languish in a penal colony. The moment they learned about her, a shadowkill cell would arrive on the next supply run to tie up her loose end. She needed to recruit some muscle to maintain the illusion of being a common thug if she planned on roughing up an entire barrack, even if they were a bunch of guppies. Besides, she liked to share the wealth. Several of her buddies could use another pair of shoes.

"Hey, you little gelded hunk," she purred, her voice silky and flirty and loud enough for the entire room to hear. "Where are the Goons today?"

"Why, 1439?" Soy scowled. They were on a formal name basis.

She slapped the warden's marker on the table. "Tell me or I'll clip your other ball."

The former taxlord nearly fell out of his chair to escape her. She had that effect on people. He scurried off and spoke to a few of the other administrators before returning with an answer. "Level forty."

Ugh. Forty was deep in the pits and never a fun place to go.

Qisami hurried back to the main yard of the colony and hitched a ride heading toward the mines. Her fellow passengers—Shulan inmates from Barrack Nineteen—eyed her warily as she sat in the back as they were transported from the penal colony and down toward the valley. She was used to this sort of attention, as if she were a rabid dog. Because she was. The Happy Glow wasn't a large colony, and her reputation was well earned. Fighting and killing had been her only useful skill, and it was one she leveraged to make the best of her situation. She was tempted to glare back, but even she had to admit being mean was tiring.

Qisami instead stared toward the horizon as they continued on their way. The Grass Tundra was bland and empty other than occasional smatterings of rock outcrops and small bunches of brush. The wintry landscape was flat all the way to the mountains in the distance where the land met the flat gray sky with the King overhead, dull and weak. They say that if a person stayed alive in the Grass Tundra long enough, their color would eventually fade until they were an equally gray husk by the time they took their last breath.

Qisami's vision had nearly glazed over when she noticed movement, the silhouette of some creature, with short white hair or fur blowing in the wind, perhaps an arctic bear or wolf, or maybe even a grass tundra bush. Some plants were known to have no roots and could crawl along the soggy, wet earth. Qisami blinked again and whatever she thought she saw was gone, or perhaps it had been a figment of her imagination.

Gravity shifted hard to one side as the tracks made a last sharp turn and then descended into a steep ravine as a massive hole in the earth came into view. The Hope You Get Rich Mine was the largest of its kind in the known world outside of Xing Duchy and was critical to Caobiu's economy and military. It was the main reason Sunri was able to maintain her large, well-trained professional army. The mine had originally been named the We're Filthy Rich Mine by the first explorers who discovered it, due to the large ore deposits found on these lands. They said that the giant veins in the earth practically glowed with gems, gold, sparkstones, and other valuable minerals.

They were followed by massive caravans of would-be rich miners who then promptly grew ill and succumbed en masse to the terrible arctic conditions. Eventually the mine was renamed Hope You Get Rich to reflect its true conditions more accurately. It was also the reason the colony that had been built to support it was named the Happy Glow Retirement Home, since it more often than not became the final resting place for those seeking their fortunes in the Grass Tundra.

The Hope You Get Rich Mine was a swirling vortex of earth, ice, and rock nearly a half mile in diameter that burrowed deep into the earth. Its edges were rimmed with an intricate set of iced roads, ramps, and stairs circling around its edges growing smaller the deeper they went into the darkness-shrouded ground. A tall and thin structure sitting directly above the center of the vortex was the main lift building. It was held together by a network of taut chains staked into the sides of the circular pit. A lone elevator, built decades ago, operated along a long, metal shaft and transported the miners down to the lower levels.

Into the Crack of Hell, as they say.

The rail wagon squealed to a stop at the front entrance of the open mine. Qisami and the Barrack Nineteen inmates stepped out and separated. They continued to the left where the ore washing operations were located, while she headed toward the bridge leading to the lift. She reached a platform jutting out over open air and flashed her warden's marker to the guards at the checkpoint. They didn't bother acknowledging her as they waved her through. Qisami was a well-known person with access throughout the colony. Even if she weren't, most knew not to mess with her.

She continued along a narrow wooden bridge hanging directly below one of the massive chains holding the lift in place. The bridge was called the Pray for Luck Bridge, because the violent winds that often rattled the rickety thing would claim at least one or two lives every cycle. Even Qisami muttered prayers every time she crossed. Unfortunately, it was the quickest way down. If someone were to descend along the circumference of the mine, it would take over half a day to reach the fortieth level, and over twice as long to come back up.

Qisami could never traverse the bridge fast enough, and she always breathed a sigh of relief when she made the last step through the front door of the lift building. She flashed her marker at Three-Chins, the ancient elevator king sitting in a metal cage adjacent to the main lift. In the five years since she first arrived, Qisami had never seen the man outside of his little prison. The gossip was that he was around when the lift building was first built and was the only one who knew how everything worked around here. The problem was he knew how to fix everything but was too addled to pass along that knowledge. Frankly, Qisami could think of no worse punishment than growing old here.

"Hi, sweets," he cackled.

He was sweet on her. At least she thought so. He was also senile.

"Where to?"

"Eight, handsome." She flashed a smile. The operator king wielded a lot of power here in the mines. The elevator was a bottleneck during rush hours, and he was known to let people he liked cut to the front of the line.

Qisami entered the elevator and slid the gate shut. Dozens of chains outside rattled to life a moment later, clanging and banging against one another as they snaked along the sides of the cage, and she began to descend. The elevator moved at a crawl as the contraption lowered her to her destination.

She checked her robes to make sure none of the bits were hanging outside the bars. There had been more than a few instances when a passenger's robes got caught in the chains, and they were yanked out, their bodies pulled through the thin gaps between the bars like a strainer just before the rattling and rubbing chains pulverized their bodies. It was uncommon, but always messy, and a good reminder that there were dozens of ways to die down here in the Hope You Get Rich Mine.

Qisami gripped a metal handlebar until her knuckles turned white as the cage continued to descend. She wasn't afraid of heights—she wasn't afraid of anything, but there was always something unnerving about being lowered into a black pit. The Crack of Hell was certainly an apt name. Qisami had always wondered what it was like at the very bottom but never had the nerve to actually visit it herself. Call it superstition, but part of her feared that if she ever did go that far down, she would never come back up.

Fortunately, the level forty bank of mines was barely halfway down to hell. The elevator stopped abruptly with a bone-shaking rattle, and she stepped out onto yet another wooden bridge that swayed like a fishing boat getting tossed around during a tsunami. Everything was pitch-black here, an oppressive void that pushed against her. The air was eerie, cold and stale, with no wind and only distant sounds that echoed from deeper into the unknown. Qisami's skin crawled as she minced along the bridge. Just like she detested being out in the open in broad daylight, she was equally uncomfortable being in total darkness. Shadowkills needed shadows to maneuver and operate, and vast blackness was abjectly terrifying.

This ring this far down in the pit mine was narrower than the levels above. It was so dark down here that Qisami couldn't see her outstretched hand. After she stepped on solid ground, she sighed with relief, then followed the sound of voices and the chipping of stone. Everything echoed down here, but miners didn't work in the dark, so it was only a matter of time until she found a spark in the distance to follow to where the Goons were working.

Qisami found whom she was looking for when she came across one of the largest, ugliest men she had ever met. The Goons had a bunch of them, but the one standing before her would for sure win the ugly contest. He was twice her height and a mountain of flesh; half of his body had been scarred and burnt to look like a rocky crag. The other half had so much hair on it she couldn't see skin. The man's head was shaped like a watermelon that got dropped and landed on one side, and his legs were so stubby he looked like he was all torso. One of his hands was easily the size of a man's head and the other was missing with his arm lopped off at the elbow.

Qisami thought him rather cute. She waved. "Hi, Hair Bear."

Hair Bear wasn't the monster's real name. No one knew it; no one asked. Asking for real names at the Happy Glow was frowned upon. Everyone went by nicknames, anyway. That or their numbers. The rumor about Hair Bear was that he was a former Hansoo initiate whose transformative growth cancered and deformed. He somehow survived his ordeal and was thrown out of the Hansoo sect. Hair Bear ended up going full brigand and robbing caravans along the Shulan/Gyian border until he was eventually captured.

Now Hair Bear ran Barrack Twelve, or the Goons, as everyone called them. They were usually the biggest and most violent in the penal colony, the men and women considered too uncivilized to mingle with the rest of the general population. Qisami knew them well; she used to be one before she found a way to curry favor with the warden and got herself moved to the plum and swanky Barrack Three.

Hair Bear, leaning against the cavern wall just below a torch sconce, looked up from something he was holding. His face twisted in what she assumed was a smile. His voice was raspy and low. "Chopstick, what brings you here? Did management finally realize their mistake and throw you back where you belong?"

"I need five muscles for a job." She decided to keep an extra pair of shoes for herself. "I'll bring them back tonight, mostly in one piece." She reached into her pocket. "I brought you cookies."

"Much obliged, Chopsticks." Hair Bear knew it was just one stick, but he enjoyed ribbing her about it. The colony's most handsome man plucked a cookie from her outstretched hands, holding it gingerly between his massive forefinger and thumb. He sniffed it as if scenting the notes of fine wine. Then, satisfied, he dropped the cookie into his open-gaped mouth. His eyes fluttered, and a low, satisfied rumble rose from his massive body. He sighed and grinned, baring a set of broken teeth and fangs. "Assume you want Grunt's gang. First turn on the left. Grab any of his boys you want, but not the Lettuce boys or Turtle. Those boys are grounded from perks, and Turtle promised to cook noodle soup tonight."

Qisami flirted with a wink and dropped three more cookies into Hair Bear's outstretched hands. The monstrous man was a straight-up killer—he once tore a man's arm off for swiping his soup—but he was the honest type of murderer, which carried weight in the lunar court, and especially in a penal colony. She also thought he was cute in a unique way, sort of like those yipping Zhuun crested dogs the nobility often kept as pets.

The mines down in these depths had not been as fully excavated as the ones above. The tunnels were still somewhat virgin and unruly, so the ground tended to be treacherous, sharp, and craggy, painful to traverse with shoddy thin prison soles. One had to be careful too because any patch of darkness could end up being a bottomless hole or ravine. Whatever light emanated from the line of lanterns hanging from the ceiling was barely bright enough to reach the ground. It was also annoyingly loud. Water dripped constantly. The earth rumbled and hissed intermittently as if after a bad meal. The sounds of picks on stone and men grunting, laughing, and singing echoed along the walls. Every note was off-key, but at least it made them easy to track.

Qisami saw Cyyk squatting over a boulder, playing knife fingers with one of his clowders. The man squatting opposite was staring into Cyyk's eyes as the tip of a shank bounced between the gapes of his outstretched fingers. This was the exercise she had taught him to work on as training. His skills had not suffered since they were sentenced. Qisami had seen to that. Her former cell's grunt had faithfully stayed with her throughout her incredible fall from the penthouse floor as a diamond-tier shadowkill down to the basement level, and now even lower to hell. Not that he had a choice. His loyalty to her was due more to bad luck and lack of options than anything else, but it didn't matter. He was still at her side, and that meant something. He was the only person left who had not betrayed her . . . yet. The least she could do was complete his training. She owed him that much.

Cyyk looked up and waved with his left hand even as the shank in his right continued its dance. "What's up, Stick?"

"I need five Goons, you included," she replied.

"Back breaking or *back* breaking?"

"The fun kind, but no killing."

"Bah, pillow fighting is such a hassle."

That much was true. Restraint was an exhausting process.

"What's in it for us?"

"Shoes."

"Oh really?" Cyyk perked up and stood, twirled the shaft of the shank between his fingers before disappearing it into his holsters. "All right, Uglies, huddle up. We've got a job."

Qisami stood off to the side as the grunt's clowder dropped what they were doing and assembled around him. The Goons in Twelve were broken down into rival crews that competed against each other not only for jobs but also for earnings. That's how Hair Bear liked to manage his house. It worked out most of the time, save for the occasional brawls and stabbings that broke out. Qisami missed her time down here with the Goons. The scum life was hard and dangerous but fair once a person knew where they stood in the hierarchy, which for Qisami was always near the top. The hard physical labor the Goon squad got assigned tended to be the absolute worst, however.

She watched with pride as her former grunt walked down the line. Her little broodbaby was all grown up now and was running his own little cell. Quan Cyyk might never become a true shadowkill with his blood drawn at the training pool, but it certainly wouldn't be from lack of ability.

Cyyk picked his four. "Fungusfeet, Snoutnose, Big Lettuce, and Badgasgirl—"

"No Lettuce," she interjected. "He's off the line."

"Why, you little twig!" The large, brawny, rotund man with a ghastly skin condition snarled and took three steps toward Qisami, waving a beefy fist.

She wasn't fazed. "Hair Bear's orders, Cabbage. Take it up with him."

Big Lettuce stopped in his tracks and then thought better of it, retreating back to the huddle.

"Chalkface, you're in. Lettuce, you're out." Cyyk pointed to a lanky, pasty-faced man. He turned to Qisami. "Blades or fists?"

She shook her head. "Clubs."

He broke into a grin. "We'll be ready in a few. Going to finish our food first."

Qisami studied Cyyk's select crew. Back when she was a career woman, she wouldn't have been caught dead operating with such a rabble, but that wasn't who she was now. Just a lowly convict—a political prisoner—eking out a living any way she could. These arrow fodders would have to do. "Meet on the west end outside the mess hall. Queen's high. Masks on."

"You can count on the clowder, Stick."

"Whatever." A sigh escaped her as she turned to leave.

Everything was fine. Just fine.

CHAPTER SIX

THE SHULAN COURT

Taishi sat opposite the mindseer as the armored carriage rumbled along the tiled streets of Vauzan. The window shutters were closed and the doors barred, which would have enveloped them in darkness if not for the lantern hanging from the ceiling. Duke Saan had bragged to Taishi many years ago that these carriages were so well put together that they were airtight and wouldn't leak even if one fell into the ocean. That sounded fine to Taishi, but she wasn't sure if she preferred suffocating to drowning. The mindseer sharing the carriage with Taishi was poor company. The woman hadn't said a word since she came in. Hadn't even moved. She just sat there frozen, her eyes wide and unblinking, staring off into the distance.

The ride was surprisingly comfortable. Taishi could usually feel every stone and bump on her bony backside whenever she traveled on wagons, but these ducal transports were on another level. There was obviously more care given to ducal backsides than commoner ones. She noticed that many of the noble carriages utilized several layers of green sponges to soften the ride. Some even used wooden springs.

She knew where they were heading. In Vauzan, the higher the

destination, the higher the station. Also, a luxurious carriage of the nobility cost more than most peasants' lands. Few could afford to own one, let alone send it to fetch an old woman. There was also the matter of the displayguards who had helped round her up. Someone in the military camp of the court. And then there was also the mindseer. All this narrowed her audience down to one of three possible lords.

The first faction was led by Highlady Saku Saku, who was in favor of throwing the gates open and surrendering to the Caobiu. The woman practically dropped to her knees with reverence anytime someone uttered Sunri's name. Her faction was already in favor of shedding their Shulan identity to embrace the Caobiu. Their motivation was not only due to admiration, however. Saku was one of the wealthiest nobles in the Enlightened States, some say second only to Yanso, and held extensive investments all over the Enlightened States. The war disrupted her businesses far more than anyone else's. Taishi thought Saku was naive to think that the Shulan could save themselves with total capitulation. Sunri, above all others, respected strength. The tyrannical woman did not tolerate fools. Taishi called her group the capitulation caucus.

The second faction was one led by Highlord Ayque. They were an idealistic bunch who wanted to end the conflict with Caobiu through marriage, which was a laughable proposal considering this was how Duke Yanso lost his head in the first place. Lord Ayque was a renowned handsome and charming man and a romantic. He believed that he could woo Sunri into marriage because love would conquer all. It was a naive position. There was no noble in Shulan who could remotely be considered the woman's equal, let alone her husband. Sunri would probably gut every man in Shulan Duchy rather than marry one of their mediocre lords.

Taishi called Ayque's group the stupid faction.

The third faction was by far the most honorable and worst of the three powers ruling the Shulan Court. This was controlled by Highlord Oban Ori, the leader of the hardliners who were determined to fight the Caobiu to the death. Oban had been Saan's childhood friend and was at his side when the duke was assassinated in Allanto. He was the only high lord to fight his way out of the city and escape Gyian after the Caobiu had seized the duchy. His faction would rather see Vauzan in ruins than bend the knee to Sunri. They considered any negotiations with the Caobiu not only dishonorable but a betrayal. Taishi understood their position but considered them the idiotic faction.

The carriage's movements transitioned from rolling on stone to wood. The noises of gears and chains grinding and rattling followed, and then she could feel the sensation of the carriage being lifted upward. This likely meant they had entered one of the council arenas or possibly the court palace. Taishi hoped it was the latter; the food there was amazing. After a spell, the door swung open, spraying the interior of the carriage with so much sunlight it temporarily blinded her. Taishi's facade of confidence broke when she stepped out and a large blast of wind nearly knocked her off her feet. She pursed her lips and recovered after a stumble. Her balance was not what it once was. Few people knew that she was alive, but no one could know she had lost her powers. Taishi the legendary war arts grandmaster still had influence. Taishi the old, weak, dying woman did not.

The beginning of a hacking cough itched the back of her throat, but Taishi swallowed it down. She forced her breath to calm and batted the arm of a waiting attendant. She surveyed her surroundings with an imperious expression. They were near the top of a large and opulent tower with tall walls ending in a curved dome. There were four half-moon openings directly in front and back and to the sides, with strong winds gusting through the space. At the far end was a large balcony and wide blue sky beyond. Every bit of the tower was intricately carved with exquisite detail.

Taishi loosed a breath of relief. This extravagance likely meant she was meeting with Highlady Saku Saku. The woman had a reputation for luxury. In a way, Taishi preferred meeting her. It was difficult to talk to the stubborn or the stupid, which was the case with Oban and Ayque. Saku at least would be pragmatic, and that was often what was most important when facing overwhelming odds.

At the end of the day, if the coward's approach saved lives, then she was all for it. There was little chance the city's defenders could win this battle. The bulk of the Shulan army had been shattered back at Allanto, and it had been a slow rout since. The only reason Sunri hadn't marched into the capital last year was because those sand lovers from Xing in the south were gluttons for punishment and kept coming back for more defeats, while at the same time the uppity Katuia were rebelling against the armistice. All this had kept Caobiu stretched thin over the past five years, until now.

The attendant led Taishi down the corridor toward the balcony. Her breath caught as she noticed the intricately carved tiles beneath her feet. Some were translucent, but clear enough to reveal the floor below. Taishi tapped into the nearby currents and found them quick and thin, which was usual for higher elevations.

The escort at the edge of the balcony bowed.

Taishi gawked at the platform. It was a circular, flat disk made entirely from glass, giving the entire balcony an illusion of floating. The Shulan were always artists at heart. Taishi would have preferred if they just added railings. She looked down through the glass floor and realized they were six stories off the ground, on top of a steep and narrow hill. The view from up here was breathtaking, with an expansive view of the city as well as across the valley, blemished only by the red-and-yellow army surrounding the perimeter of the eastern side of the city. A lone figure stood at the far end of the balcony, her robes whipping in the wind. This must be the patron who went through all this trouble to see her.

Taishi stopped a few feet from the edge and bowed. "Highlady—"

"Taishi, it's good to see you again. Thank you for coming." A man turned to face her. "My nephew informed me he had trouble bringing you in."

Taishi recovered quickly. "It was a majestic if not amateur effort, Highlord Oban."

Oban broke into a chuckle. Even that sounded grim. "I'm not surprised he muffed it up. That spoiled boy is green and naive, but his heart is in the right place. He just needs seasoning, or a proper beating."

"Then it appears I did you a service," she replied with a straight face. "You know, Oban the Orderly, you could have just sent me a summons."

"The entire court would know that we are meeting then. Information flows through the court like a sieve. I wish to speak privately and in confidence as fellow loyal subjects to our beloved friend Duke Saan. Besides, would you have answered?"

"Probably not."

Oban nodded. "Exactly. It would arouse suspicion if it ever became public that a commoner had rejected a high lord. I would probably have put you to death."

"You could certainly try." Why were men so insecure? "He tried to buy me off with soup."

"Idiot." Oban shook his head. "How is our young hero coming along, master?"

"He's none of your business, Oban."

The high lord didn't miss a beat. "I am one of five lords in this court who know his identity. It is my liang and my policies that keep you two hidden and safe. It is very much my right as your lord and patron to inquire about the state's ward."

"Enough of these pleasantries. Let's get to business, yeah? What do you want?"

A long sigh escaped Oban's mouth as he stared at the battle line formed along the outer wall. His voice grew soft. "Can you see the future, Taishi? Can you imagine what those red demons will do to our beloved city? All because we didn't stop her three years ago."

Several horns blared from the Caobiu army. Three lines of siege towers, giant war wagons, and catapults were rolling forward. They reached the front and began to spread out, forming an artillery line along the eastern wall. Soon, the first artillery began to dot the city, growing pillars of smoke with each passing volley.

"We didn't stop her three years ago, because you and Saan were too greedy, attempting those negotiations when it was so obviously a trap," Taishi replied. "I warned you not to deal with Sunri."

"Do not throw hindsight at my face, Taishi. That was always beneath you. We saw a chance for peace and seized it."

"It was a fair point, now get to yours."

"We're going to lose the city and probably the duchy," Oban said. "Maybe tomorrow, maybe in a week, a month. Possibly end of the cycle. It'll happen eventually."

"Yes, well, everyone knows that." Taishi added, "My lord."

"Unless we rally the city. Instead of just rolling over and exposing my belly like those other cowards in court, let's inspire the citizens of our great city to rise up in her defense. All we need is a symbol, something to inspire them." He turned to face her.

Taishi shook her head so hard she cricked her neck. "Not a chance in hell, Oban."

"Think about it, Taishi," Oban pressed. "What better opportunity can there be to introduce the resurgent Prophesied Hero of the Tiandi, the Champion of the Five Under Heaven, here in Vauzan, the holy city, during her darkest hour? You can't write a ballad better than that. Fate waits for no man, Taishi. Let him rise to the occasion. His people need him! He could be a symbol of hope and justice, resilience and strength."

It *was* a fairly good script.

"This isn't a fucking song, Oban," she snarled. In more peaceful times, that could have landed her in the stockades. "I will not tie Jian to this catastrophe. He wouldn't matter anyway, not against these vastly superior numbers. Your local populace will get butchered."

"So, what then? We lay down and die? Dig our own graves? Just let her take everything?" Oban's voice grew stern, louder, and more outraged. "That woman butchered Saan—your student, my friend, our lord—under a flag of truce. She took the most important thing from us, and now she's here for the rest. And your boy won't even reveal himself in his people's time of need? Maybe he is a coward."

"Maybe he doesn't need to get involved in your little suicide pact." Taishi turned away. "I'm taking him away from this doomed city tonight."

Oban called after her. "I can order him."

"You could, but that only does Sunri a favor."

"I'm only asking out of respect. I can stop you from leaving."

She shrugged, not looking back. "You don't have three hundred soldiers to spare to take me down."

"It's only a matter of time, Taishi."

"No," she muttered under her breath. "Not if I have anything to do with it."

The Voice of the Court interrupted their spirited discussion, announcing, "High Lord, Dowager Nun, it is my honor to introduce the Oracle of the Tiandi."

That startled Taishi. What was Pei doing here?

The two turned toward the entrance to see a girl of about twelve stomp onto the balcony, carrying a wet, stinky bright-orange fox under one arm. Taishi could just see the silhouette of two Hansoo standing on the other side of the doorway.

Both she and Oban bowed.

Pei glared at Taishi. "Out. I want privacy with this one."

Oban didn't hesitate. "Yes, wise one."

The young Oracle of the Tiandi began spitting at Taishi before Oban even turned the corner. "What is it with you, Taishi? Every time you have a choice, you make the wrong one. It's like you're a bloodhound trained to chase failure." The little oracle's mouth was getting fouler by the year. What were those monks teaching her?

Taishi shrugged. "Isn't free will a bitch?"

"It certainly is. Why can't you knuckle eggs do the right thing?"

"I agree," said Taishi. "Pardon, wise one, what exactly is the right thing?"

"That's what you're supposed to decide!" the tiny girl roared. "Why are you still here? I told you to leave a year ago!"

Taishi raised a finger. "You told me to stay ahead of the tidal wave."

"What do you think that is!" Pei pointed out toward the siege. "For some reason, you and that mule-headed disciple of yours unfailingly keep making the wrong decisions—" The oracle threw her head back and then slowly met Taishi's gaze, her eyes glassy.

Taishi watched, and waited, deeply curious but tinged with dread. It was almost always bad news.

The oracle finally intoned: "When the great lioness approaches, the string boy must go to ground or be torn apart beneath her celestial claw."

A chill swept through Taishi. That was as definitive a prediction as she had ever heard.

"And he'll never reach his full potential if he flees," the oracle continued.

"What?" said Taishi. "What does that mean? So, he's to stay?"

"He'll never reach his full potential within the walls of Vauzan."

What did that mean? If either decision led to a bad outcome, then was there any hope at all?

"Oracle," said Taishi, pleading. "Tell me, how—"

The fox Pei was carrying under her arm squirmed loose and ran back inside. Pei, like many little girls, promptly forgot about Taishi's existence, and ran off after her pet. "Floppy!"

Taishi was all alone now. She muttered and committed those words to memory. "When the great lioness approaches, the string boy must go to ground. . . ."

Taishi broke into a sprint, running back down the hallway to the lift where the carriage was parked. She yanked the collar of the nearby attendant. "Get me back to the temple, right now!"

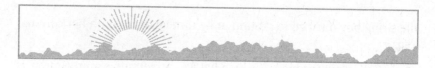

CHAPTER SEVEN

THE TEMPLE OF
THE TIANDI

The streets of Vauzan were a mess as the boys hurried back toward the Vauzan Temple of the Tiandi. The city, usually famous for its clean streets and orderly traffic, had devolved into chaos as more fireballs rained down. Panic spread through the populace like smallpox ripped through poverty wards. Horses—some with riders, some without—raced out of control. Wagons piled up at intersections. Gates became jammed up as panicked people rushed home to their loved ones or fled the city. Unlucky buildings occasionally exploded when the large pitches of burning tar, hay, and stone smashed into them, shooting out rings of concussive fire in all directions. A wagon carrying a full six-pack of giant rain collectors sped down the street, passing buildings on fire to others with higher property values farther down the street.

Jian and his friends descended down a curved road that followed the path of one of the city's many aqueducts. Vauzan was a beautiful city, full of rolling hills, sudden cliffs, and deep gorges. It was described as the City of the Living Rainbow in poems and songs due to its vibrant colors and organic skyline. Today, the splashes of color were blotted out by gray columns of angry smoke rising to hold up the sky, as dribbles of fires scattered across the city.

The group pressed on, avoiding the clogged and panicked main streets, and proceeded toward side streets and less-used paths, pedway tunnels, and the roundabout that took them to the crest of hills and then down to the low valleys. There were many ways to get everywhere in Vauzan. It was one giant maze. However, these detours also meant more stairs. The ground down here in the low valley was dank and wet, with clouds of spray swirling from the plunge's constant mist. They reached the mouth of a cave behind a small waterfall curtain and continued deeper through a tunnel to one of the underground buried wards. This one, the Waterknife, was a small neighborhood popular with the young for aggressive underground poetry battles and its vibrant underground fight scene. Most skyside residents avoided these lower wards and often associated them with the criminal element. The only crime most of these buried wards had ever committed was being poor. The young people, including Jian and his friends, frequented this area because the zuijo and food were cheap and the magistrates were scarce.

They took a short jaunt through seedy Waterknife, and then they exited through the other end to the Jewel in the Eye of the Lotus ward. From there, they would need to take the shorter Hard Climb to Heaven path, the long but narrow and winding route flanked by needle-thin buildings on the Peony Peak side and a sheer two-story drop on the city side, to the Vauzan Temple of the Tiandi.

The boys were halfway up the narrow road heading back to the entrance when one of the Caobiu fireballs smashed into a wooden building several loops of road farther up the mountain. A large cloud erupted, blotting out the sky as a row of wooden buildings shook loose from their supports and began to slide down the mountain. Everyone nearby screamed and scattered as the avalanche of bricks, wood, and dirt sped toward them. Everyone except Jian, who could only stand and gape. Someone ran into him, sending him onto his belly, and then it became a trample. Jian covered up and tried to regain his footing, but more panicked people kicked, stepped on, or knocked him over. It became hard to breathe.

A pair of hands grabbed his robes and hauled him to his feet. Kaiyu shoved him forward. "Get going!"

It was too late. An entire section of the mountain was coming down. Hachi and Xinde had already made it to safety ahead. Hachi had climbed a light pole and was frantically urging him on. The crowds were thick, however, and progress was slow. They weren't going to make it.

Instinct took over. Jian looped his arms around his friend and took to the current, bounding into the air. He struggled with the additional weight but managed, so far. "Be a stick, not sand!" he screamed.

Kaiyu understood, stiffening his body to make it easier for Jian to hold on to him. The two managed to get clear of the path and out into the open air, but then the weight of holding another person became too much. Jian lost his balance and slipped, plummeting like stone to the ground. They crashed onto the roof of a building farther down the mountain. Fortunately, the Houtou were experts at landing, and Kaiyu was able to smoothly roll out of the fall onto his feet. Unfortunately, Jian was not, and he fell flat against the tiles. He grunted as the wind was knocked out of him. The floor rattled while the mountain shook, bringing back his sense of urgency as he scrambled to his feet. He looked up as the avalanche continued to roll toward him.

Kaiyu was already sprinting toward the edge of the long, thin building. He waved at Jian to follow. "Come on, we have to go!"

Jian met Kaiyu a moment later, and the two stepped onto the wooden railing and looked at the shadow of the approaching landslide engulfing the entire block. They still had a ways to go. Jian threw his arms around his friend and was about to jump when he noticed a flash below and heard a cry. It sounded like a baby. He glanced down through the hazy fog of dust and saw movement on the balcony below. A child, perhaps?

"I think we're close enough. You can make it on your own."

"What? All the way there?" sputtered Kaiyu. "I can't fly, wait—"

Jian shoved Kaiyu off the roof and dropped onto the balcony floor below. He landed on a potted plant, which toppled and cracked under his weight, flipping him on his head and temporarily knocking the breath out of him. Pain enveloped him. He groaned as he rolled onto his back. A high-pitched whine reminded him why he had come here. Jian opened his eyes and sat up expecting to find the poor child trapped here. Instead, he came face-to-face with a large fluffy red dog that did not look pleased to see him. It bared its teeth and snarled. He showed his hands to try to calm the creature, and nearly lost a finger as it snapped the air.

Jian's first instinct was to get away. He had only seconds to escape before the building was smashed into bits and carried away by this landslide. The last thing he needed was to deal with an angry, rabid animal. He was the Prophesied Hero of the Tiandi. His life was too valuable to risk, especially to this dog. He put a foot on the railing to save himself but then stopped. Guilt was a strong itch that he knew would keep bothering him for the rest of his life if he abandoned this dumb animal. A cat maybe, but not a dog.

"You better appreciate this." He scowled as he scooped the big dog in his arms. It yelped and whined and squirmed in his grasp. Jian stepped off the side of the balcony and was swept away by a current a sharp moment before the entire structure was washed away by a river of debris. The dog was larger and fluffier than he expected, partially obstructing his vision, and heavy too. It was all Jian could do to keep his arms wrapped around the creature as he veered drunkenly toward safety. The annoying mutt howled and kicked, no doubt panicked that there was several hundred feet of air between them and the ground.

"Don't worry, little guy, I got you." Jian tried to soothe the floppy-eared pooch.

Then the unthinkable happened. The vicious, ungrateful animal opened its mouth and chomped down on Jian's forearm, tearing his robes and skin. Jian screamed and let go of the jerk dog, but it hung off his arm with its jaws. That made things even worse. Jian grabbed the animal and managed to stay upright before finally clearing the ava-lanche's path and crashing into the street. It was a bad landing, sending both tumbling across the stone tiles before finally sliding to a stop. It was only then that the jerk dog released its grip on Jian and scurried off, whining as if it had all been Jian's fault. He sat up and clutched his wounded arm. His sleeves were torn and soaked red. The jerk dog had raked a chunk of his flesh. Several large pieces of skin hung loose on his arm, and blood dribbled off his wrists.

Kaiyu ran to his side a second later. "I can't believe you left me for a dog! I almost died!"

Jian glared at the mutt. "I can't believe I left you for this ungrateful mutt either."

"Did this mutt bite you?" Kaiyu noticed the blood. "Good. You deserve it."

Jian sighed. "I do."

Kaiyu stared at the shaking dog huddled off to the side. "Aw, it's scared and homeless now. Are you going to keep it?"

"No! That thing tried to eat me."

"Can I? I mean, assuming we can't find the owner." Kaiyu didn't wait for a response. He walked up to the jerk dog and lowered to his knee. "Hi boy, are you all right?" Of course the damn dog did *not* bite him and even allowed the Houtou to scratch his ears.

The two found a ladder that was still intact and were able to climb toward the upper levels. Kaiyu was somehow able to convince the dog to sit on his back.

Xinde was waiting for them when they finally reunited back at the mountain path at the other end of the landslide. He rolled back Jian's sleeve and studied the wound. "You're leaking like a sieve. What happened? Looks like you lost a fight with a wild animal."

Jian winced as he held out his arm. "Is it bad?"

"Might need to cut it off here." Xinde made a chopping motion just below his elbow. "You're going to need stitches. Come on."

Jian glowered at the big red dog as it licked Kaiyu's face. "Ingrate."

They reached the Vauzan Temple of the Tiandi twenty minutes later. Fortunately, the main bridge connecting the temple to the adjacent Gold Prayer Mountain was still intact, so everyone above the avalanche wasn't trapped on Peony Peak.

The entrance to the Vauzan Temple of the Tiandi was wide and open with constant traffic passing through. Six Hansoo and ten monks guarded the front double gates, which was already one more than the usual residency here at the temple. This was significant since all Hansoo who took up residency here became celebrities in the city. Children loved the Hansoo, and the temple profited by selling action dolls of them.

The friends parted ways. Xinde left to report to Brother Solum, as was customary for a magistrate entering the temple. Hachi, after quickly checking in on everyone, had hurried off to Box Three to check on Neeshan. The man was in love all right, or at least smitten. Kaiyu, also smitten, went to track down the owner of the dog. The temple kept a registry of every resident on Peony Peak. That left Jian, still bleeding, to seek treatment for his arm.

He wasn't surprised by the large crowds huddled around the temple. Tenth Day Prayers was already a busy day for the devout. That was why Taishi recruited the other women for their breakfast meal, and why Jian and his friends always found excuses to be gone for the day. He could only assume that the venue would be even more popular with the city under siege. The main courtyard of the temple was a zoo. The three lines waiting to pray and tithe before the Mosaic of the Tiandi snaked in every direction. The line for the nobility was full as well. One would think everyone had more important things to do right now than tithe and pray to the Tiandi, but perhaps prayer *was* the most important thing to do for the deeply pious.

The crowded courtyard was eerily quiet. The people looked in disbelief with their heads low and huddled in small groups. There had never been an attack on Vauzan in any of their lifetimes. Jian wasn't sure why people were surprised. There had been talk about a Caobiu attack for years, since the Gyian fell and the Shulan army was routed. The bulk of the army that had accompanied Saan had returned in tatters, and while the duchy had been able to muster three armies since, Sunri had crushed them all. The only positives from those disastrous battles were that each defeat had weakened the Caobiu enough that it prevented them from rolling deeper into Shulan and completing the siege of Vauzan. That had been the difference before. This time, there was no standing army in Shulan left to soften the Caobiu army's advance. This invasion was inevitable.

Jian avoided the milling crowds of anxious devout. He was leaking blood from his arm and the last thing he needed was to cause a panic. He hurried through a false wall next to the gift shop. He followed it down a narrow side street that opened into Monastery Village, which was the main residential area for the monks living inside the temple. It wasn't much of a village, really, just a squat and compact collection of buildings that supported temple operations. This was a modest area where the monks cooked, labored, studied, trained, and relaxed. It was a far cry from the majestic public-facing facade manufactured by the Tiandi temple.

The Vauzan Temple of the Tiandi was self-sustaining with its own gardens, livestock, and forest of fast-growing bamboo trees. If the monks wished to ride out the siege, they could lock the gates and defend Peony Peak almost indefinitely. Siege weapons couldn't reach this high up the narrow mountain, and there were only two ways up to the front gates—the path Jian came up and the main bridge—both of which the monks could destroy at a moment's notice.

Jian passed through the tight spaces, passing by light traffic. Busy monks scurried about. He reached the temple hospital situated at the main square a few moments later. The hospital was the largest building in the village. The life of a Tiandi monk was surprisingly injury-prone, either from too much time spent deep in meditation and study or too much physical training.

"To die is the inevitable state. To live is a bonus" was one of Goramh's popular sayings at the temple.

A young initiate took one look at Jian's arm when he walked through the door and escorted him into a back room for treatment. Over the next hour, a young nun came by to clean his arm, an acupuncturist numbed it, and a hypnotist put him in a relaxed and meditative state. It was a full-service operation. It also took the rest of the afternoon. The Tiandi monks were never in a hurry and never did anything fast.

Jian was in the process of finally getting stitched up by one of the temple doctors when someone burst into the back room. Zofi looked out of breath and was panting hard. Her face was a mix of concern, outrage, and exhaustion when she confronted him. "Hiro, the bald boys at the gate told me you were hurt. Who did this? I'm going to—" She gawked at his arm. "What happened? Did you fall into the zoo pit again?"

He huffed. "I didn't fall in that time. I was helping when some of the animals got loose!"

"What happened then?" Zofi leaned over and poked the top of one of the big fat needles stuck just beneath his elbow, sending a jolt through his entire body. "Does that hurt?"

"Now it does, thanks." Jian gritted his teeth. "A house was collapsing from artillery fire, so I saved a dog. Then it bit me."

She ticked her finger, looking puzzled. "Why would you risk your life saving a dog while the city is under siege?"

"Because at first I thought it was a kid, and then by the time I realized it was a dog, I was already there, so I saved it, and it bit me."

"You confused a dog for a child?" Zofi blinked. "That makes no sense. Why did it bite you if you were saving it? Why didn't you just drop it?"

"I was up in the air riding a current along the side of a mountain and didn't want to drop it."

"So what did you do?"

"What was I supposed to do?" Jian shrugged. "I let it bite me until I could land."

Zofi blinked. "You're an idiot."

"Yes, we've already established that."

"Your aunt is going to murder you."

That was also true. It embarrassed him that this was probably the worst injury he had suffered since he left the Celestial Palace. What did it say about Jian, the supposed Champion of the Five Under Heaven, the Prophesied Hero of the Tiandi, that he was so swaddled that a dog bite was his worst injury? Well, that and the time he almost died due to the death touch a few years back, was kidnapped by one of the lotus factions of the Tiandi religion, and nearly killed by mute men, but those didn't count. This was his most severe injury.

Jian's shoulder slumped. "It was a big dog."

"You'll live." She turned to the doctor. "He'll live, right?"

The woman nodded. "No training or fighting for a few days. Bring him back in a week to take out the stitches."

"We don't have time for that." Zofi's face twisted as she turned back to Jian. "The Caobiu have reached the walls. The eastern line is under siege!"

She was met with stunned silence.

"Already?" Jian gasped. "It hasn't even been a day. It takes longer for me to cut up a watermelon."

She yanked him by the arm. "Come on, we have to go."

"To do what?"

"I don't know yet, but we have to do something!"

That was a very Zofi thing to say.

CHAPTER EIGHT

FINAL AFFAIRS

Taishi raced back toward the Vauzan Temple of the Tiandi as fast as the ducal carriage could carry her. She was usually in a bath by this time. Most of the streets had cleared by dusk. A city under siege didn't have much of a nightlife, at least until their food and water supplies were cut off. It was still too early for the looting to begin, and the Shulan were generally too polite to riot for fun. The best thing every resident of Vauzan could do right now was stay home or flee to one of the buried wards underground. Or better yet, flee the city altogether. At least that was Taishi's plan. She just needed to wrap up her business here and escape out of the city through the west gate. The Caobiu had surrounded Vauzan, but it was an expansive city, and there were always holes to exploit.

The front gates to the Vauzan Temple of the Tiandi were still open when her carriage pulled up. The two Hansoo and four initiates manning the front doors placed their palms together and bowed as Taishi, her dowager nun robes whipping in the breeze, stepped out and continued inside. The temple looked as if it was bracing for a siege as the main courtyard became its own little encampment. Racks of weapons, supplies, command, and triage tents had been set up in neat rows, although Taishi doubted the temple would involve themselves in the fighting. The abbots at the Jade Tower of the Vigilant Spirit had made it a point to remain neutral during this conflict, citing the Zhuun civil war as a secular matter. No doubt they were waiting to see who came out on top. It was a shame. The combined power of the Tiandi religion rivaled that of any duchy in the Enlightened States. If only they would choose a side . . .

Taishi continued past several tents with the flags of a few different sects whipping in the air. Mori must have put out the call to the devout to defend the faith, and many from the surrounding countryside had answered. Some of the monks stopped and paid their respects to the dowager nun as she passed, but most didn't pay her much attention.

Taishi found Brother Solum, the senior Hansoo at the temple, walking across the courtyard. She waved him down. "A busy day, Brother Solum."

He bowed, keeping in character with the status her robes demanded. The war monk was one of four who knew her true identity. The twenty or so rings running all the way up his arm from his wrist to his shoulder jingled against each other. "Perspective quickly changes when death rolls up to one's door."

"Why are people still here? The temple should have closed by now."

"Keeping late hours. Extra tithing goes a long way during war."

"If everyone was smart, they would be fleeing the city right now."

"This temple is a holy place. It is a privilege for the devout to defend its honor."

"It's just a place. A plot of land, Solum, like any other." She pointed off to the side. "Four hundred years ago, the temple was a mud hut at the bottom of the valley, but the devout decided to upgrade their view. There's nothing especially holy about the land we're standing on, and certainly nothing worth dying for."

He smiled. "You are correct. The holiness accompanies the temple, no matter where it is, so as long as it stands here, the devout will defend this place until our dying breath."

Taishi had to strain from not making a face. She hated when someone she disagreed with made a good point. "This temple contains the largest library and the greatest collection of Tiandi relics in the world. You should spirit it away for safekeeping."

Solum looked surprised, as if the thought had never occurred to him. Of course it hadn't. Hansoo were known as the Shields of Tiandi. Defending their faith was the only purpose for their existence.

"At least prepare for the inevitable. Take Mori with you and flee. In a burlap sack, if necessary."

"The templeabbot may be upset if we kidnap him."

"It's better to be alive and upset than dead." She looked around. "What about Hiro? I need to kidnap him for his own good."

"The gatewatch reported that your nephew returned a few hours ago with his friends."

Of course he would keep tabs on Jian. "Good. Lock him down on temple grounds. No exceptions."

"As you request, dowager."

"And Mori's whereabouts?"

"The templeabbot has retreated to his serenity of thoughts, dowager. Unfortunately, the long day was too overwhelming, especially at his age. I told him to retire years ago. His rest is well earned after a lifetime of service to the Tiandi."

"Yes, I get it, he's old." Taishi flashed a scowl. Mori was only a few years her elder. "We're all getting old. You too, graybeard."

Solum temporarily broke character and scratched it. "I forgot to shave this morning. A Hansoo's body hair grows so quickly."

"You look handsome, regardless." Taishi walked past him. "You should take Mori away if you truly value his safety."

"That decision is above my pay grade, dowager nun."

Taishi hurried on. There was much to do if she was going to escape before the Caobiu breached the walls. The city's defenses were stout, but there was no finer war machine than the Cinder Legions. Sunri had built the most terrifying military in history. It was a matter of when, not if, the city's defenses succumbed to Caobiu's might. How much time she had to prepare, Taishi couldn't be sure, but she estimated a week at best before the red army broke through the outer wall and spilled into the city. Any longer would be a heroic victory, immortalized in song and rhyme. Once the walls fell, the real battle for the city would begin.

Taishi hurried into the main temple, skirting past the long lines and initiates clustering around the Mosaic of the Tiandi. Heavy incense layered the air, with the scent of cinnamon, tin, and fire wafting to her nostrils. An initiate hurried past her carrying two vases of red and white incense sticks. Those colors were for victory in battle and continuation of lineage, which would be popular now.

Taishi continued across the length of the main temple, passing dozens of priceless artifacts. If these fools were smart, they would all be packing right now. Many of the relics here at the temple, the oldest in the Enlightened States, carried historic significance not only to the religion but also to the people. The duchess, once she took the city, would be ruthless enough to use these relics and the temple to gain leverage over the entire Tiandi religion. Speaking of old relics that Sunri would use to her advantage, Taishi set off to find Mori. She passed through the main chamber housing the Mosaic of the Tiandi and continued to the back, where a small army of initiates scurried around, making sure the incense vases were properly stocked, the donations were being counted, and the lines were managed in an orderly fashion.

The extensive garden and bamboo forest behind the main temple was one of Taishi's favorite places. Large, intricately designed pagodas and beautiful statues lined one side while a row of willow trees lined the other. Hundreds of small paper lanterns floated in a nearby pond, drifting under a red arched bridge. In a world where everywhere had become dangerous, she still felt at peace here, even with the enemy knocking down the gates. The weather at dusk was cool, with a breeze blowing from the east. Taishi could smell the scent of smoke and burnt wood all the way on the other side of the city. Birds sang from their nests on low-hanging branches while dragonflies and fireflies buzzed overhead. Pink-and-white cherry blossoms floated across the sky. It was a pity the most beautiful time of the year had to be tainted by an army intent on razing the city. It was probably intentional. It was common gossip that the only beautiful thing Sunri tolerated was herself.

Taishi crossed the training yard packed with Hansoo, warrior monks, and battlenuns. There were so many that the lessons and sparring had spilled out to the adjoining fields. Younger monks were practicing line fighting—individual melee along a unified front—in the lotus garden. Hansoo were taking turns weight training, lifting giant boulders and statues. There were rows of archers on one side, spear formations on the other, and shield drills in the center. Even the monk children were practicing basic forms and weapons in preparation to defend the city.

The steady stream of monks and nuns parted before her, bowing as she passed. The largest contingent representing the training yard, who also bowed the deepest to her, were the Black Orchid battlenuns. Although they were considered a minor faction within the Tiandi religion's hierarchy, the Orchid sects were by far the most active across the land. The all-woman sect utilized a short-range, effective war arts style that was adaptable to people generally smaller and less physical. The Orchid sects' purpose was to train women to defend themselves, and they had set up small temples all over the countryside.

Taishi had long admired the Black Orchids. Her dowager robes originated from that sect and were revered throughout the religion. The battleabbess, the head of the Black Orchids, was the third person who was aware of Taishi's true identity. There was no way Mori could have received approval for this subterfuge without the head of the Black Orchids' approval.

Taishi continued down the path and proceeded up the steps leading into the front entrance of the temple, up past the stone statues of the righteous lions. She was surprised to get stopped by a Hansoo, of all people. Solum was not taking any chances today. This one was a baby, barely six feet tall, and wearing only one iron ring around each wrist. He was standing below a torii gate on the path leading up the hill. To his left was a small wooden shack with a crooked door, and another path leading to the bamboo forest to his right.

She stepped up to him and looked into his face. "I need to see Mori."

The young Hansoo, still broad as a bear, looked uneasy. "Apologies. No one is to see the templeabbot without prior approval. Brother Solum's orders." The large boy leaned toward her. "You see, there is an enemy army at our gates. Has anyone told you about that?"

It must be his first day on the job. Taishi didn't have time for this. "Do you know who I am?" She felt bad about playing that card.

He gulped. "Yes, dowager nun."

"Then move aside."

"But Brother Solum said not to." The Hansoo faltered. "Sorry, it's my first assignment. I don't want to mess it up."

"You'll definitely mess it up if you don't let me in."

The door to the wooden shack slammed open, and Templeabbot Mori walked out, hiking up his pants and adjusting his robes. His wiry hair was frayed, and he favored his right knee. He also looked like he had gained ten pounds and sagged more since the last time she saw him, three days ago. "Don't torture the poor boy. Second day on the job and third as a Hansoo. This is his first time away from Stone Blossom Monastery."

"He'll learn quickly, then," she replied. With the enemy at the gates, he'd better.

"Accompany me to the grove?" He offered a hand, palm down.

She accepted, placing her open palm over his. It was an archaic Lawkan sign of affection. Taishi appreciated the gesture, even if it raised eyebrows. They reached the top of the hill and sat on the stone bench in the shade of a giant, old, twisted bonsai tree hanging over a cliff overlooking the temple campus. A babbling brook nearby dipped off the rocks, spraying into a small koi pond below. The spot was known as the Templeabbot's Wisdom; Mori liked to take naps there.

"I gather you came to say goodbye," he began.

Taishi nodded. She realized that her hand was still over his. Bah, they were old enough no one should care.

Mori cared, however. He moved his hand away. Taishi felt a little sad about it. "Jian included?"

For him to even consider that she would not bring her disciple along bothered Taishi more than she cared to admit. She never did trust the Tiandi fully when it came to her ward, even if he was their prophesied hero. Especially then. Her continued silence, however, was answer enough.

"Is that wise? It's dangerous beyond these walls."

"It's true, the entire realm is all the sacks of shits right now. It's chaos everywhere. Wildfires to the south have been raging out of control. There are signs that the Katuia are in the midst of their own civil war. Worse yet, there was a pestilence in Xing that wiped out the entire soybean crop. Can you imagine any time in Zhuun history where there's a soy sauce shortage? It truly is the end of the world. I guarantee some desperate egg-humper is going to try to rob us a day's ride from the city." Taishi took a breath. "All that, however, is still preferable to getting trapped in a besieged city with Sunri and her hell-damned army of flying monkeys!"

"It may not be that bad here," he replied. "As . . . purposeful as Sunri has been, she isn't someone who wishes to rule over a kingdom of corpses."

"That's a very low bar, Mori," she retorted. "If Sunri catches wind that Jian is here, she will raze every building, set fire to every field, and butcher everyone to get to him. Jian being gone is for your good as much as his."

Mori considered. "The initiates' transport carries ten and is fairly sturdy. Its sides are armored because we double it up as a tithe collector to the surrounding farms. I'll have the kitchen load six sacks of rice, three racks of smoked meat, and one—make that two triage boxes. The warehouse can provide everything else you need for travel: cloaks, flasks, blackrock, water gourds, and arrows. Not much in the way of weapons, unfortunately." He spoke like a man familiar with fleeing a city. It touched Taishi more than she could convey to not have to ask for his help. He had always been too good for her. She could almost forgive him for choosing to join the Temple of the Tiandi instead of staying with her. It didn't feel right to have trapped him all for herself.

Still, if Mori was in a generous mood, Taishi might as well press for more. "Can you assign us a Hansoo or two, just for a few months?"

He shook his head. "Our Hansoo brothers are in high demand, especially during these trying times. There's a backlog with the Stone Blossom Monastery that is currently nine months. Our stout brothers of the Tiandi grow as slow as trees."

"I would think protecting the Prophesied Hero of the Tiandi is considered more of a holy mission than protecting a couple old buildings."

"Well," Mori said, his demeanor mild. "You're right. Jian is the most important figure in the Tiandi—no doubt about it—while these temple grounds are just earth and stone framed by wood and cloth, illuminated by candles and prayer. The people from Vauzan come, go, and die. Most will never leave a mark and be forgotten in time." He spoke as if he were a librarian reading to students. "However, no place in this realm has ever had as deep a commitment to the Tiandi than this temple. If Wen Jian is the soul of the Tiandi, then the Vauzan temple is its beating heart."

"My apologies, Mori. I didn't mean to speak unkindly. You have done so much for us already."

"It's quite all right, Taishi." He smiled, squeezing her hand. "Templeabbots do not command the Hansoo. Only the Stone Blossom Monastery can assign one of their own to Jian. I will pass your request along. Perhaps they can send one to meet you. Where do you intend to go?"

"Manjing along the coast. Nice beaches, temperate climate, and it's as far away from Sunri as possible without having to travel across the Ngyn Ocean." Taishi decided to go for broke. "You should come too."

Mori smiled. "The Vauzan temple is my home. It's where I belong. It needs me just like I need it. I'm exactly where I'm supposed to be."

Taishi put a hand on his arm more forcefully. "You're one of the most important and influential abbots in the Tiandi religion. You are an important figure to people. You will become a political puppet if Sunri gets her claws on you."

"If I am so important, then what message does it tell them if I run?" He leaned forward. "In the time of crisis, the devout need their religion more than ever. I cannot abandon my people."

There was no doubt in his words or tone. Taishi respected him enough not to keep trying. "At least send the initiates away. The children and the elderly, everyone at risk."

"And where would you have them go?" asked Mori. "Like you said, war, destruction, and famine ravage every corner of the Enlightened States. Who's to say the violence outside these cities will be any better than when the Caobiu arrive? I am where I am needed." He looked out over the city to where the fires and the flaming arrows illuminated the night like streaking comets. When he spoke, there was an air of finality to his words. "If this truly is goodbye, then Taishi, I'm glad we were able to reconnect one last time before our journeys into the afterlife. It has been a blessing. I treasure our recent conversations. I feel like my life has finally come full circle and can now rest at peace."

"Stubborn ox!" Her blistering words came out angrier than she intended. A tsunami of grief, love, and lost opportunities slammed into her in painful waves of long-embedded memories. She would rather die than weep in front of the only man she had ever loved. Then, on impulse, Taishi put a hand on his shoulder. "I'm sorry."

The templeabbot, her former lover and oldest friend, reciprocated and leaned into her. "I'm sorry too, Taishi. I wish we could relive our youth with the wisdom we now possess. Perhaps the Tiandi will give us another chance in the afterlife."

Their embrace again fell to their old ways and habits, with Taishi resting her head on his shoulder as he caressed her cheeks. Their lips nearly brushed as they faced each other, and she was transported back to the day at a bar near Sunsheng University. Someone had started a brawl, and of course, Taishi partook. Someone else had tossed her off the balcony. She'd bounced off the railing and onto the floor. Picking herself up, she was about to rejoin the melee when her face had nearly collided with a cute guy hiding underneath the table. He had later iced her bruised face and then cooked her congee the next morning. That had sealed the deal.

Taishi could feel tears welling and broke away.

"Taishi, there's something I've always wondered. This may be the last chance to ask." Mori's voice was quiet, emotional. "When I first told you that I was joining the temple, why didn't you say something back? I would have stayed if you asked, but you said nothing. Why?"

Several beats passed before she answered. "Because I shouldn't have to, Mori."

Taishi was about to say her final goodbyes when a massive crack reverberated through the valley, followed by a plume of fire. The air around them immediately became several shades darker as a rising pillar of heavy smoke threatened to blot out the sky. She watched with increasing alarm as a large section of the eastern wall—not too far from where they had dim sum this morning—collapsed in a plume of dust and smoke. Hundreds of small red-and-yellow dots looking like fire ants from afar poured into the city.

"The Caobiu have broken into the city." Mori used to say dumb redundant things when they were together too.

Taishi sighed. "So much for the walls holding out for a week."

CHAPTER NINE

THE LESSON

The doors to Barrack Twenty-Four blew off their hinges, splintering inward as big man Fungusfeet rammed his way through the entrance. The poor sap manning the doors that night got trampled as Qisami and Cyyk's clowder of Goons poured in. Her little crew had met outside moments before, as the faint glimmer of the Queen reached her zenith. The sky was still annoyingly bright and blue since true night rarely touched this part of the world. Fortunately, launching a bust during daylight didn't matter. Few broke curfew since the temperature dropped to bitter levels after dusk. There wasn't much to do after dark anyway. Besides, busting up this barrack wouldn't take long.

The Lawkan held five barracks at the Happy Glow Retirement Home, located in the far northwestern end closest to the mines. The two duchies barely acknowledged each other, let alone bothered to war. Caobiu had the largest army. Lawkan had the greatest navy. The two sides couldn't properly war even if they wanted to, which was also why they were by far the smallest contingent of prisoners here at the

Happy Glow Retirement Home. It was too much effort on both their parts to try to kill each other.

Qisami grabbed a fistful of Fungusfeet's shirt. "Guard the door. No one comes through."

The man with the gross feet stopped. "Why bother?"

"There's four other barracks full of these people residing in the corner lot," she hissed. "If someone escapes to get help, you're all dead."

"You'll be dead too," he shot back.

She turned away. "I'll be fine either way."

The stink of lemon and salt filled her nostrils as did a sudden blast of heat. It was as if she had just assaulted a bakery, which while not unpleasant, raised the question of how a barrack in a penal colony up near the True Freeze could conjure so much heat. Sunxia wasn't wrong. Something was certainly afoot with these pruneskins. Not even Barrack Three, which housed many of the wealthy inmates, could turn their barrack into a sauna.

As she stood at the entrance to Barrack Twenty-Four, feeling such warmth infuriated Qisami. Anger overwhelmed her to such an extent she could feel her control slipping, and she wasn't sure why, but she fed upon it. She charged inside with a feral roar, wielding a club in each hand. Teach them a lesson, the warden had said, so that was exactly what she planned to do. She began smashing tables and chairs and indiscriminately bashing any poor soul who came within reach.

Her training pool teachers used to encourage controlled rage. Rage made them stronger, more savage, more resilient. Rage desensitized them to the lethal and ugly work of an assassin. Qisami had tapped her anger since she'd arrived, fueled in particular by her betrayal not only with Sunri back in Allanto but also with her own shadowkill cell. Those cuts had been deep, and it was all she could do to not let it consume her existence. The only way she had been able to quell that pain was to give in to her anger until she was all numb. A person couldn't feel pain if they couldn't feel.

The first victim was a table and a coat hook standing off to the side. Next it was a bare-chested young man holding a shovel who had dozed off in a chair. She whirled about, cracking an ice chest, sending chunks flying in every direction. The third victim was another man, older and bald, who had managed to roll out of bed when the ends of her club smashed the side of his face.

The rest of the Goons joined in. Badgasgirl and Chalkface were off to the left, yanking bodies out of beds and clubbing them like baby seals. Cyyk was next to her on the right, laughing maniacally as he pinned a woman to the wall and sank his fist into her gut. He tossed her aside and moved on to his next victim, a plump young man who tried to fight back. Many nobles thought they knew how to fight but discovered too late that they didn't. Their instructors had been too worried about their employment to give their spoiled kittens a tough time. This was why the firstborn son of a noble family was often the greatest failure.

That was the opposite with the youngest. Cyyk, a fifth-born—or was it sixth? Everyone stopped counting after four—had a chip on his shoulder about being lastborn. He took out his frustration of being the youngest son upon the young noble, slapping the sense out of the man, twisting his arm at an unnatural angle, and causing him to drop a knife. Her former grunt kicked the fallen knife with the top of his boot as it fell, bouncing it back upward. He snatched it out of the air and was about to slam it into the poor sap's eye when Qisami grabbed her own forearm and scratched it. The bloodscrawl immediately gave Cyyk pause. He looked over at Qisami.

"We're allowed one kill," she hissed. "Save it for the boss in charge."

He snorted, reversed the grip, and then brought the butt end of the weapon down hard on the crown of the chunky kid's skull, toppling him. Cyyk stood over the victim, admiring his handiwork, before stepping on him and then over him, moving to his next prey, whooping and crowing about like the young, confident fool that he was. She had been tempted to rein him in, but everyone needed to find their own joy and happiness here, in prison.

Several Lawkan inmates tried to make for the doorway. Qisami tripped one as she ran past while Cyyk clotheslined another. Badgasgirl followed, bopping each on the head with a club to keep them down. Snoutnose and Chalkface worked in tandem, forming a wall to pull down several more trying to cross the tops of the bunks. Two somehow managed to slip past this gauntlet of beatings but then came upon Fungusfeet at the doorway. The large man with the gross toes sent his heel into any who neared, kicking them back into the brawl.

The assault pushed deeper into the room, leaving a trail of fallen bodies and broken furniture in their wake. By now, the barrack had come alive, but none of the Lawkan so far had been able to mount a resistance. She didn't blame them. An ambush was an awful way to be woken up. When the Goons hammered into them, most were barely conscious and discombobulated, let alone stretched and warmed up for combat.

They neared the end of the first room when a figure stepped into the doorway to block their path. Interestingly, he didn't try to engage them but was content to wait for them to come to him. That gave Qisami pause. Why wasn't the man helping his fellow inmates? What was he guarding?

Upon a second glance, she could tell that there was something different about this one. For one thing, he was fairly handsome, or at least he didn't look like he had experienced the Happy Glow lifestyle for long. He must be fresh fish, having arrived on the last supply run. His face was untouched by snowburn, his luxurious black hair was still relatively kempt, and he still looked healthy and well fed. Not only that, but his gaze was also steady and his posture relaxed as they approached. His movements were fluid. This was a trained war artist, and his wide, balanced stance revealed that he practiced a common Lawkan southern style known as Shout Fist.

"Oh, pig feet." Qisami detested Shout Fist. Hated it with the passion of a thousand needles on a porcupine.

Badgasgirl shot past her and came at the Shout Fist first. Qisami was content to let the woman get the first taste. Qisami wasn't surprised, however, when the Lawkan caught Badgasgirl's swing with his palm. She only had time to blink in surprise before he surged forward with a powerful punch. Qisami waited for the inevitable sound, and then there it was.

"Kiyaaah!" Shout Fist roared as the blow sent Badgasgirl flying across the room like a rag doll. Common underworld thugs like Badgasgirl tended to jump into fights without thinking things through. She must not have noticed that this Lawkan was not the usual baby seal that they'd been clubbing.

Snoutnose and Chalkface followed Badgasgirl, the two tag-teaming to try to batter the handsome guy with their clubs. The Lawkan blocked each, yelling an annoying "Kiyaaah" with every block, and then followed through with another devastating punch that laid Snoutnose flat on his back and sent Chalkface toppling over a stack of wooden crates. Shout Fists were the worst to fight, especially when there was a whole gaggle of them screaming at the same time.

Cyyk was up next, and while he fared better than the others, he wasn't ready to step up to this level of competition. At least he put up a decent fight utilizing his shadowkill training, but Qisami had known before their exchange even started that he was going to lose. Experienced war artists could usually predict outcomes, and she wasn't wrong in this case. She had been tempted to call him back before he suffered too much injury, but she had been curious to see if he could pull it off. He didn't, as expected. It was too bad, but she didn't mind his failure. He had grown too bigheaded lately. There was also something about his recent attitude in battle, the way he gloated and mocked his fallen victims and how he pranced about between exchanges. It was just rude. He deserved a good beatdown. It wasn't lost on Qisami that her former stupid baby grunt had probably picked up his swagger from *her*, but at least she could back it up.

Speaking of that, all that remained was Qisami and the Lawkan war artist.

The man surprised her with a formal bow before raising his guard. "Honor is the way." Pausing to study him had been a giveaway.

"We're in prison, you dork." Qisami spat on the floor. She had never cared for all this ritualistic honor crap.

The Lawkan shook his head. "In a place such as this, honor is all we have left."

"Whatever."

The two war artists squared up, Qisami in her Rolling Boxing style, the Lawkan in his stiff Shout Fist stance. Seconds passed as both waited for the other to make the first move. Qisami could tell that the Lawkan fought at a high level, if not quite a master, and the man likely assumed the same with her. The problem for Qisami, however, was that she could not use her full bag of tricks. She couldn't reveal herself as a shadowkill. That, unfortunately, placed her at a decided disadvantage.

He came at her first, launching his style's trademark powerful straight punch, and of course, a loud and enthusiastic "Kiyaah!" Qisami wanted to rip his tongue out.

Fortunately, the Consortium and many of the training pools were based in Lawkan Duchy, which meant Qisami had spent hundreds of hours sparring against styles from the Shout Fist tree, which meant there were very few surprises. Also, this guy wasn't that good.

Great Batter Fist met Sparrow Flees the Hawk, and then she swung to his side and hit the Lawkan with the shadowkill Rolling Boxing trademark, shooting small sharp fists in rapid succession, landing twice hard on his ribs, cracking one. Two more blows strafed his face, with more snapping his chin. She went low the last few strikes, hitting him one time in the groin and folding the man over. The Lawkan war artist was tougher than he was skilled. He managed two more wild haymakers before the delayed pain of a crushed testicle sank in, wilting him to the floor.

"Honor is *not* the only way, fresh fish," she muttered, stepping over him and into the room.

The back room was dimly lit, and if anything, even warmer than the front. Candles dotted the darkened landscape and across the three wooden beams crisscrossing the ceiling, while not one but two large hearths were lit with flames. The room was deep enough that she couldn't make out the wall on the opposite end. It smelled clean, nice even, with a faint but pleasant odor, like cilantro moss or bleeding mint stones. Rugs woven from straw and hemp lined the sides and ceilings, covering the snow walls, making this room look almost normal.

There was even strange stick artwork hanging from strings over several sections of the room.

A pipe hanging from the ceiling ran water over several miniature aqueducts that delivered several basins lining the near wall and beyond. Two more roaring fires boiled water in three basins lined against the wall to the right. The thought of warm water made Qisami's insides clench with envy. These Lawkan bastards had skimmed off the ore wagons to create a luxurious spa. Her already tilted anger spiked even harder. Worse, she was now confronting the boss of this mine-embezzling ring. And worse even than that, the Lawkan leader was one of the few people Qisami actually liked in this wretched eighth level of hell.

Tawara Issa, known as the Mother of the River, was a kind and matronly woman. A former high-ranking noblewoman who chose the monastic life of a nun, she had united the broken Lawkan inmates and won concessions for the entire colony purely on the goodness of her deeds and conviction of her heart. Everyone at the penal colony respected this woman, even adored her. She was a treasure. Warden Sunxia once commented that anyone who disliked Great Nun Tawara Issa had moral deficiencies.

Qisami couldn't disagree. However, there was no mistaking what was happening here in this steamy, decadent room. There was no way Tawara Issa could deny being involved in this mine-embezzling operation, and she was likely the one in charge. That meant there was only one fate awaiting her.

"Chopstick," said Tawara Issa, "will you hear me out before you continue down this violent path? You don't need to be Sunxia's hound in this matter."

"Nothing you say matters, old crone." Qisami hated this, but she needed shoes, and she didn't feel like joining the Goons for a lifetime of hard labor. She wanted this night to end so she could go back to bed and forget this ever happened. She lunged forward before Tawara Issa could utter another word. The elderly woman did not put up a fight as Qisami wrapped her fingers around her neck. One light kick to the outside of the ankles—she couldn't muster any enthusiasm—toppled her to the floor. She rolled the Mother of the River onto her backside and then straddled her chest as she pulled out her shank. Only one death tonight. Make an example of her.

Qisami faced the tip at the woman's eye. "That was a stupid thing to do, Mistress Issa."

"There are things worth dying for," she replied. "This is one. I have no regrets."

Qisami's fingers were still wrapped around Tawara Issa's throat. She hesitated as the shank hovered close to the woman's eye. Qisami felt the need to get something off her chest. "I'm not thrilled about this."

"Think with your heart, child." If Tawara Issa was pleading for her life, she was doing a poor job of it.

Then Qisami brought the shank down. It was clean, quick, and hopefully not too painful. That was the best she could offer the woman. That old fool. What was she thinking? Qisami used the Mother of the River's robes to wipe the blood off her shank and stood. She wore actual clothes; that was how much the woman was revered here. And now Qisami had killed her.

She caught herself breathing heavily. She muttered, "Everything is fine."

A sudden wail filled the room: loud, shrill, and pained. It was joined by another similarly high-pitched rattle. More soon followed. Qisami scanned the room, confused. It had been a long time since she heard this sort of crying. These weren't cries of men or women, but of babies: four, five, six of them. They were all swaddled in blankets and placed on cradles repurposed from wheelbarrows and wash basins. Those weren't art pieces hanging from cradles; they were crib mobiles. This wasn't a spa. It was a nursery. This was why the Lawkan had stolen the ore. Babies were not allowed at the Happy Glow Retirement Home. Anyone caught with a child would forfeit their life as well as the babe. This was what they had been risking their lives for.

Qisami's hands trembled as the truth set in. A small movement off to the side drew her attention and she noticed another woman. This one was older with spectacularly large, sagging exposed breasts beneath her open robes, likely the nursemaid, huddling off to the side in the shadow of an overturned table. She was staring frozen in terror at the fallen Mother of the River. Tears streamed down her face as pained sobs escaped her covered mouth. She scrambled to her feet when their eyes met. Qisami took a step forward.

The nursemaid placed herself in between Qisami and the rest of the room, her arms spread. "Please, not the little ones," she cried. "Do what you want with me but spare them."

The room swayed and turned red, the darkness almost pulsating as Qisami's chest heaved. Her arm shook, and she squeezed the hilt of her shank so tightly she nearly snapped her finger. Finally, with a hiss, she tossed the shank aside, sending it clattering on the floor. "You stupid pruneskins are trying to hide mewling babies in the barracks? Have your heads gone soft? You're just begging to get drawn and quartered, aren't you, you dumb filthy waterlogged sluts!" She took in a deep breath and continued, "The south ends of the third and fourth tunnels on level three have been exhausted and abandoned. Get these dumb chicklets out of here before you get caught again!"

"Is everything all right, Chopstick?" Snoutnose called from the other room. "What's that sound? It almost sounds like—"

"Stay out!" she screamed.

But it was too late. The man burst into the room. His eyes widened and he whistled when he noticed the crying babes. "The nerve of these pruneskins. The warden is going to eat these little runts—"

Qisami crept behind the chattering Goon. Without hesitation, she ripped her remaining shank out of its holster and rammed it into the Goon's head from the base of his neck. The blow had been so powerful, so furious, that the metal piece snapped in two as it embedded into his skull. She glowered, rage filling her in a hot flash, then finally sucked in a deep, trembling breath. Finally, after her labored breathing threatened to make her lightheaded, Qisami turned and stormed out of the room.

"Hey." Cyyk stopped when he noticed the red-eyed rage painting her face. "What's going on? Is everything all right?"

She continued walking. "Let's go."

Cyyk glanced in the direction of the other room. "Where's Snout-nose?"

"He's dead."

"What? What happened?"

"It doesn't matter. We're done here."

CHAPTER TEN

HOME LIFE

Jian and Zofi hurried out of the hospital and headed back toward the main temple grounds on the public-facing side. It was now well into the evening, and the crowds were finally thinning. The worried devout had prayed themselves out, and the last stragglers were making their way out through the front gates under the watchful eyes of several Hansoo standing guard. The air was tense and smoky as plumes of smoke drifted from the many fires lit throughout the city.

Xinde was still deep in conversation with Brother Solum. The former Longxian senior noticed them and waved. He shared a few final words with the Hansoo and hurried toward them.

"Are you patched up, Hiro?" he asked.

Jian held up his bandaged arm. If he ever ran into that dog again . . . "As good as new. Is it true? Are the Caobiu on the wall?"

"The wall fell a few minutes ago." Xinde looked grim. "The enemy is inside the city."

Zofi gasped. "What happens now?"

"I have to report back to the precinct," Xinde said. "There will be fighting in the streets soon. The magistrates are organizing civilian defenses."

Jian burned with righteousness. "I'm in. Let's go."

"Jian!" Zofi clutched his elbow. "Taishi is not going to be happy about this."

That was certainly true, but he would deal with that when the time came. He shook her loose. "We ran from Sunri back in Allanto. I'm not doing it again. Not in my city. Come on."

The three joined the light traffic and made their way toward the front gates. "Each ward will be forming volunteer corps. The magistrates need to help maintain order if this city is to stand a chance."

To Jian's surprise, the two Hansoo guarding the gates stopped them from passing through. No, stopped *him*. They had no problems letting Xinde and Zofi pass. At first, he had thought it an accident until he tried again. The second time, a beefy hand the size of his chest shoved him backward.

"Hey," he yelped.

The big monk crossed his arms. "Sorry, Hiro. Your auntie's orders, and I'm not crossing the dowager nun. You're to remain inside the temple."

His friends stopped outside the temple and looked back, waiting. Jian's face reddened. "But I have to fight! We need to defend the city!"

"You need to stay put, little man."

Jian made a feeble lunge past the Hansoo, more out of frustration and embarrassment than anything else. This time, the war monk with his five rings jangling around his forearms picked Jian up by his left wrist much like a girl carrying her rag doll. He walked Jian back into the temple and dumped him unceremoniously on his backside. The Hansoo closed his fist in front of Jian's face. "Don't try that again, runt."

Furious and humiliated, Jian jumped back to his feet and nearly shouted, "Do you know who I am?" He really, really wanted to stick it to this oversize self-important war monk.

Fortunately, wiser minds prevailed. Zofi nearly tackled and dragged Jian away. "I see that look on your face. Dumb words are about to come out of your mouth, so you better just keep it shut," she hissed in his ear.

Jian felt this terrible need to get in the last word. He shouted at the Hansoo, "You're lucky this time, war monk. I won't be so nice next go-around."

The Hansoo cracked his knuckles. "I fart out bigger squirts than you, little man."

Zofi smacked the end of Jian's nose. That shut him up. She turned and waved at Xinde still standing at the front gates. "We'll catch up with you later, handsome!"

"But—"

Zofi turned back to Jian. "Now march, before I assign you homework."

Zofi latched on to his arm with a surprisingly strong grip and escorted him all the way home through the main temple, past the rear garden and the practice yard, all the way to the little cottage he shared with Taishi tucked deep in the bamboo forest.

"It's not fair that everyone else gets to fight," he complained. "They're my brothers. This city is my home. I'm one of them. I should be fighting alongside them."

Zofi didn't let him go until he was standing inside his doorway. She looked stern. "No, Jian. You are not one of them. You are the Prophesied Hero of the Tiandi. You will never be one of them. That's why you shouldn't be fighting beside your friends, and that's certainly why you shouldn't be rescuing stray dogs off balconies. The sooner you get that through that gelatinous skull of yours, the better. Now stay put until Taishi comes back, or I swear I'm going to give you a surprise test on the rivers in Lawkan."

Jian deflated. He hated geography. All the stupid rivers in Lawkan sounded the same. "Fine. I hate you."

"I know it's hard. I know what it's like to lose your home and everything you love." She reached over and embraced him, patting his back as if burping a baby. "Is Taishi around?"

He looked around their cottage. "It doesn't seem like it. Didn't you ladies have your breakfast today?"

"That woman has a busier social calendar than most kids." She shrugged. "Taishi wants me to get our supplies packed in case we need to leave in a hurry. Do you promise to stay put?"

"Sure."

Zofi shook a finger in his face. "On your stupid honor."

He scrunched his face like a child caught stealing dried plum candies. "Fine. On my honor."

The cottage was quiet after Zofi left. There wasn't much to the home he shared with Taishi, just a main room and kitchen up front and a bedroom at the back. Jian's sleeping quarters was a lofted space nestled in the corner near the roof. It often got too hot in the summer and too cold in the winter, but it was quiet and peaceful, and the only place in his two decades of living that actually felt like home, just like this city and his friends. He finally belonged somewhere, and there was now a chance that he could lose it.

Jian paced around the main room. He could hear the loud booms and crashes over the background noise of battle in the distance, and the anticipation ate at him. It wasn't that he enjoyed fighting or the thrill of battle, just that he knew his friends were out there, possibly in danger, as were his city and all the places he had grown to love in Vauzan. His way of life was under threat, and it twisted his insides that he was unable to do anything.

And where was Taishi?

It was rare for her to be out this long, especially in her increasingly frail condition. She would never admit it, but he wasn't a koala brain. Her health deteriorated with each passing day. The signs were small and incremental but could be seen in the way she gripped handrails when she walked down stairs and breathed more heavily after a long walk and how long it sometimes took her to rise from bed. Under those years and cracks, however, she was still the terrifying and powerful Taishi the world knew, feared, and respected.

She detested being treated like a fragile orchid or an invalid, and though he hadn't seen her practice her war arts in over two years, he was still sure she could wipe the floor with him if she so chose. Her powers might be greatly diminished, but she still had a long way to fall.

The truth was that Taishi was already living on borrowed time. He was supposed to have killed her to pass his final test to ascend to the mantle of the Master of the Windwhisper lineage. He had refused, against her wishes. How many years that bought her was anyone's guess. It was three so far, and he hoped there would be many more. He had no regrets about his decision, even if it resulted in Jian failing both the prophecy and his destiny. Whatever that meant anymore. Some prices were steep, others had no price. Taishi's life was one of them, cantankerous attitude, ornery temper, and all. Still, it would have been nice if she had lightened up on him a bit after he spared her life. If anything, she was even harder on him than ever. She never did get over not dying that night and had been punishing him ever since.

It was now too late to head to the kitchens, so he might as well fend for himself. Dinner tonight was noodles and overcooked sweet sausage paired with undercooked salted cabbage. He was a terrible cook, and the food was barely enough. The two were living off the temple's generosity, so they couldn't complain.

Jian was still coaxing the fire when there was a knock, followed by the door opening. The scent of lavender and citrus permeated the air, followed by footsteps. Jian's nerves relaxed, melting the day's worries away, yet at the same time he grew excited, feeling a gurgle in his gut. He had to fight the urge to tap his toes.

A moment later, soft but firm arms wrapped around his waist. "Hey, Five Champ. What's for dinner?"

He turned to face Sonaya, a slow smile growing on his face. "I have noodles, sweet sausage, or cabbage left over. Which do you prefer, pretty miss?"

She arched an eyebrow. "What type of noodles?"

"Bamboo," he admitted. There had been a shortage of grain since the civil war started. Gyian lands were the most bountiful in the Enlightened States, but half of it burned down during the first two years of war and now the Caobiu owned the rest. The monks had figured out a way to spin noodles out of bamboo. It tasted like eating wood.

Sonaya stuck her tongue out. "Pass on the noodles, but sausage and cabbage sound delightful."

The drowned fist daughter ate all the time. He had no idea how she maintained such a slim figure. Jian winked. "As you wish."

Jian returned to cooking while the drowned fist told him about her day, how she had breakfast with the club on the wall when the invasion began. How all the shops were closed or swamped by the time she got there, and how she had nothing to wear if they had to flee south to the hot, balmy Lawkan lands. "Taishi wants to leave as soon as possible, tomorrow perhaps. Tonight, even, if she could get her way."

Jian continued sautéing the sausage on a small wok, his back facing her. He pursed his lips, saying nothing.

"Do you have any thoughts on that, Jian?"

Jian had many thoughts on that, but it wasn't his place. He was Taishi's disciple. He did as his master commanded. Although this time . . . There must be moments when it was more important to take a stand. There was no place in the Enlightened States that was safe from Sunri. Might as well make their stand here in the city, in their home alongside their friends and allies.

Jian felt her presence again. She put her hand on his shoulder. He relaxed again yet felt a rush of tingling course through his body down to his toes. Sonaya had that effect on him.

"Do you think I should put my foot down and demand we stay and fight?" he asked.

Sonaya wrapped her arms around his neck. "I think the Enlightened States need someone to believe, if not for the prophecy, then for someone to stand up for them."

Jian held her waist for a few moments, their lips close. Then she pulled away. He didn't know where he stood with Sonaya. The two had been nearly inseparable since they arrived in Vauzan. However, that was it. They were close, spent all their time together, and had twice—no, three times—kissed when both had drunk too much. But every time Jian tried to get closer, Sonaya would shut down the conversation and then avoid him for a few weeks. Then, suddenly, she would reenter his life as if nothing had happened.

Jian knew he should be upset with how she toyed with his affection, flirting and then pulling away repeatedly, but he couldn't quit her. She was his best friend and the one person he knew would bail him out of jail right away if something happened. Zofi would have let him stew overnight, Taishi probably for a week. The worst part about all this was that he had no one to talk to. Every woman—even Zofi—was on Sonaya's side, whatever that meant, while Jian's guy friends were oblivious. Kaiyu was just starting to notice women, Hachi noticed them too much, and Xinde never seemed to notice them at all.

Dinner wasn't a disaster. Sonaya swallowed it. That was as good a grade as he was going to get. They washed up afterward. Zofi never tolerated messes back at the Cloud Pillars, and it was a habit she had beaten into him. The former mapmaker's daughter was now following in her father's footsteps attending Sunsheng University, courtesy of a recommendation by Templeabbot Lee Mori. Her studies barely afforded her the time to tutor Jian, let alone prepare meals. She never was much of a cook anyway. Unfortunately, Jian was far worse.

Jian and Sonaya spent the rest of the evening lying side by side in a hammock tied between two droopy bamboo shoots at the edge of the cottage's yard. The night was quiet, the Cinder Legions likely having retired for the evening. Only the foolish or the desperate tried to take a fortified enemy city at night, and Sunri was neither. They would continue the siege at dawn. The defenders were going to try to shore up the collapsed part of the wall tonight, but the Caobiu would smash through those barricades before breakfast, and then the real fighting would begin.

"You're thinking about the siege again," said Sonaya.

"Are you reading my thoughts, mind witch?"

"Hardly." She ran her hand from his shoulder down to his arm. "You're tense." Her finger reached his forearm. He winced.

She noticed his bandages for the first time. "What happened here?"

"Nothing. I got bit by a dog."

"Why would a dog bite you?"

"I was trying to save it."

"That makes no sense."

"Tell me about it."

The two continued to lie there close, swaying in the wind. Jian turned toward her and took in the scent of her hair. Everything became a little lighter, a little less immediate. Not that defending the city or fulfilling his destiny or his master's failing health matters were any less concerning, just that they weren't so pressing. No one else ever had that effect on him.

He brushed his fingers over hers. "Hey, Sonaya, there's something important I want to ask you."

She rolled toward him and snuggled close, the crown of her head nestling into the crook of his neck. She put a finger on his lips. "There's a fairly good chance we're all going to be dead by the end of the week, so let's not spoil a good thing while we still have it."

That was fair. "Sure."

"Besides"—her voice was almost a whisper—"I already know what you're going to ask. It's hanging all over you like odious perfume."

"So should we talk about it, then?"

"No."

Jian blinked once, twice, and the scenery dimmed as the rhythmic swaying of the hammock, the rustling of leaves, and the warmth of Sonaya's body pressed against his sent him into a contented stupor. The Zhuun believed that the final thing they saw before closing their eyes for the last time would be the only memory that they carried with them into the afterlife.

Jian closed his eyes. At this moment, he wouldn't mind if eternity could begin right now.

CHAPTER ELEVEN

LAWKAN CORNER

After the job at the Lawkan corner was finished, Qisami and the Goons—sans Snoutnose—received their promised pairs of boots, and that should have been the end of it. Everyone should have put that sordid night behind them and moved on with their miserable existence. That's how professionals acted. At least, that's how professional former diamond-tier shadowkill Qisami should have acted.

Fleeting images of beating the Lawkan inmates, the screams in the dimly lit barrack, and the steady gaze on Tawara Issa's face as she died haunted Qisami. The worst part was that awful soundtrack of wailing babies in the background. It was like a bad head cold she couldn't shake. She suffered sleepless nights and discombobulated days as if she had drunk to the bottom of a wine barrel.

To make matters worse, Tawara Issa's death had hit the colony hard. The old hag was universally respected and adored, even by those outside of Lawkan corner. Even by management! Every day was a slow news day at the Happy Glow, so the Mother of the River's death was all anyone was talking about. They held a funeral full of the grieving

Lawkan. It was maddening, and all very awkward. That bastard Sunxia even gave her a eulogy, which was so deeply ironic because Qisami had been acting on *his* orders. It was *his* hit!

There was a saying back at the training pool: Shadowkills opened the doors to Diyu, but never passed through. Qisami wasn't responsible for the old crone's death. *Sunxia was!*

Again, all very fucking unprofessional.

Time heals all wounds, so by the next day, Qisami was able to move on with her dreary life. That is, until the events of that night roared back at her. Qisami was still wallowing in bed one afternoon while the rest of the barrack was away on laundry duty—the rest of Barrack Three knew better than to involve her—when there was a knock at the door. There was no chance Qisami was going to answer. She was toasty warm under six layers of sheets and sacks, and she planned to remain this way for the rest of the day. Her special status afforded her significant latitude with management, while her savage reputation gave her leeway with just about everyone else.

The knocking finally stopped. Qisami closed her eyes and turned her attention inward, back to her swampy maelstrom of malaise and turmoil. She was running out of daydreams. When she had first arrived, they had been revenge fantasies focused on Sunri and her backstabbing cell that had kept her going. After that, she wasted her days on bitterness and resignation. Then it became a matter of numbness and survival, which worked for a spell. After the incident at the Lawkan corner, however, Qisami caught herself feeling things again, and she didn't like it. Now she yearned for that numbness to return.

The front door to the barrack kicked open with a bang, followed by the shuffling of many feet. Someone shouted a phrase she couldn't quite make out, and then there were more pitter-patters of movement. Barrack raids weren't uncommon. It happened every so often. That was why most inmates carried their valuables on their person at all times. Qisami wasn't worried though, more curious than anything else. Her bed was far in the back and high up. It would take a while for these barrack raiders to find her. They better hope they didn't, else they'd receive a nasty surprise. No one was dumb enough to mess with Chopstick. She continued her nap.

Someone spoke a few moments later coming from somewhere just below. "Careful, brothers. Touch nothing. Stay close together. She's dangerous."

That earned Qisami's attention. She pried one eye open, and then the other. This wasn't a random raid. They were actually searching for her.

Qisami pulled her blanket over her head and sank into the darkness. The familiar rush of bubbles prickling her skin crawled over her as the sheet flattened over her bed. She appeared a moment later in the small alcove near the ceiling where the wooden rafters connected. She must be out of practice because that took twice as long as it should have, but it still felt good to stretch that muscle.

She peered over one side of the railing, and then the other, like a cannibal cat on the prowl. The darkened intruders, all wearing padded sacks, were spread between the bunk stacks. There were over a dozen, possibly as many as fifteen. At least they showed her respect. She would have been insulted if they thought to send only a handful of thugs. It didn't take long to identify the leader. He was surrounded by bodyguards, hissing out orders. She recognized Tawara Issa's nephew, much to her annoyance. Sunri must have thrown the entire clan in prison.

Qisami respected a revenge hit but didn't love the idea of killing another in the same family right after burying the first. Not to mention, a dozen or so more dead bodies would certainly push the already short-staffed mine operations even further behind. Management would not be pleased. Maybe there was a way to avoid a massacre. Besides, nobody liked taking a dump where they slept.

Qisami skulked along the crisscrossing wooden beams until she was directly above the amateur hour of Lawkan. They couldn't even thug properly. She picked the order of her targets, whispering, "Three, four, five, six . . ." before she descended upon them like a creature out of a nightmare. She took two out on the way down, one with a sharp kick to the side of the shoulder, sending him bouncing off a bunk post, and the other with a punch to the jaw, dropping her like a sack of heavy ore. She landed low to the ground, her other foot already swinging wide, which swept a third attacker off their feet. She bounded to standing behind the Tawara boy in charge, having snaked an arm around his neck and pressed her shank against his jugular with the other.

"Now, now, didn't anyone tell you it was rude to intrude on someone without knocking first, Tawara Ito?"

The Lawkan leader struggled in her grasp but was too soft to put up much of a fight. The rest of his people surrounded her, but as long as there was no one directly behind her—and as long as she was standing in a shadow—Qisami wasn't worried.

"We, we did knock—" he stuttered. "We just came to talk."

Oh yeah, they did. It didn't matter. Qisami retreated a few steps to keep the group in front of her, dragging the young man along. "You bring twenty armed dogs just to talk?"

"You killed my aunt and battered an entire barrack." His breath became labored. "Please, I can't breathe."

Another good point. "Fine. Tell your people to drop their weapons and sit on their hands. Then we'll chat. You might even get to take a few more breaths." The tip of her shank broke skin. Blood trailed down the length of the shaft.

The young man waved frantically at the rest of his people. They gathered in front of her and put down their weapons, slowly. Some raised their arms as if to surrender while a few crossed theirs. All glowered at her.

"Now we can be civilized. Did anyone bring tea?" As Qisami relaxed her grip on Tawara Ito, she caught one of them stooping to pick up his weapon out of the corner of her eye. The shank flew from her grasp straight into the poor sap's hand just as he reached for his club. He cried out as the sharp tip went clean through. Another shank appeared in Qisami's hand. This time it poked Tawara Ito's ear.

"Let's try this again," she said. "If you're not here for revenge, what do you want? Why shouldn't I kill the lot of you?"

The young man stiffened. He had a reputation in the colony as intelligent but soft. He certainly was not trained in the war arts. "You killed my aunt, but you also spared the babies, and from what we gathered, you didn't rat us out. You even told us where to hide them. We thought the tunnels in level six were a trap, but we checked them out. You're right. It's as good a place as any, and a far safer location for the nursery. We want to make an arrangement. Keep our secret, and we won't seek justice."

Qisami snorted. "Ha. I'd like to see you try."

"We also won't reveal your secret."

"I don't know what you're talking about." Then Qisami noticed the nursemaid from the previous night, standing in the back next to the door. The woman stepped forward. Her voice trembled. "I was born in Manjing. I know of the nightdeath. I saw you emerge from the darkness."

The Consortium was based in the capital of Lawkan. In fact, most underworlds were headquartered there. The city had fantastic weather. Shadowkills were as common there as brothels in Allanto. Qisami released Tawara Ito. He stumbled forward and turned to face her, clutching his bleeding neck. She might have poked him a shade harder than she intended. Qisami really was out of practice.

"So," she drawled. "You keep my secret. I keep yours. Fair enough." She waved the shank at the group. "You didn't have to go through such a production to tell me that."

"We . . ." Tawara Ito's voice faltered. "The Lawkan corner would like to hire your services, shadowkill."

"You want me to *work* for you?" Qisami sneered.

"You didn't betray the babies, or the warden would have appeared in force at our doorsteps the next morning," said Ito. "Management would have rewarded you for such a find. That means something— perhaps that we can trust you. The Lawkan need your help. We moved the babies to the abandoned tunnels like you advised. You're right. It's quiet there, and far from prying eyes and ears."

Qisami cursed. Her and her stupid big mouth. She had screamed at the nursemaid out of sheer bewilderment. She hadn't meant for those stupid pruneskins to *actually* follow her recommendation and hide a gaggle of babies in mining caves. What an asinine thing to do! But then these were the same idiots who decided to have babies and open a nursery in a penal colony.

"We need someone with your particular set of skills, shadowkill," Ito pressed. "Our people can't keep the nursery supplied. There are too many checkpoints at the mine, too many guards. We can't get enough milk and blankets and food for them. We need someone who can get supplies there and back undetected, someone to give the mothers and caretakers safe passage to the nursery. We don't have much to exchange for your help, but we'll offer what we can."

"What could you possibly offer me that I can't just take off you wet noodles on my own?" She sneered. "I want nothing to do with you. Get out!"

"A shadowkill's secret here in the penal colony is worth keeping."

Was that a threat? Qisami was impressed. She didn't think these soft bellies had it in them. She stepped into the nearest shadow and emerged just to the young fool's side. She dug two fingers into the soft flesh under his chin. "What was the body count the other day? Look how easily I thrashed you all today. I suggest you think about your next words very carefully."

"No, it's not that. We just need—"

"I said, get out! Get out, and if anyone else learns what I am, I will make the Mother of the River of you all!"

Qisami shoved the young man toward the door. To drive her point home, she dropped into a shadow and stepped out behind Boobs, shoving her toward the door as well. Before the rest could reset their attention to her, she stepped into another shadow and reappeared on the other side of the room, pushing another Lawkan. The next shadowstep sent her swinging from the ceiling of a first-level bunk and knocking another woman off her feet. Then she came back to give Ito a shove. Qisami was suddenly everywhere, popping from every side, herding the Lawkan toward the front of the barrack. The bewildered Lawkan began to flee, nearly trampling over one another in their haste to escape. The stampede continued until they were in full flight, leaving Qisami standing alone in the doorway.

She stood there, watching them fall over each other while trying to get away. "If you bother me again, I will slaughter all of you!" she snarled, following the last of them from the barrack. She watched as they fled across the yard and around the corner.

After they were out of sight, she returned inside and slammed the door behind her. Qisami stood leaning her back against the wooden frame for several moments, her chest heaving and stomach roiling as fury crawled up her throat. She wanted to tear her hair out. She wanted to stab someone. She wanted to beat someone senseless.

Qisami bent over and felt the air seep unsteadily out between her pursed lips. She felt what tenuous control she had over her sanity slowly leak with every breath. Mentally, she could feel her toes dangle over some intangible edge, and she was teetering, which was peculiar because she never thought she actually *had* an edge to cross. There was no turning back. Now, at this moment, she preferred returning to numbness, but it was too late. "Get a hold of yourself, you lame, soft bitch. Everything is fine. Everything is fine. Everything is . . ."

Qisami's breathing grew more strained. She sucked in, holding it high in her nose and chest before exhaling with force. She repeated the effort several more times, but froze when she felt a single tear roll down the side of her cheek. Stumped, she did what she was taught as a little girl back at the training pool whenever she felt tears wet her face.

She made a fist, changed her mind, and then slapped herself.

CHAPTER TWELVE

EXIT PLAN

Taishi dropped by the cottage to change into her padded cloaks. It was late and she might need some protection where she planned to go next. She added a few knives to her small arsenal alongside the opera sword, and then wolfed down half a loaf of bread before heading out again. She checked Jian's room and was surprised to find his bed empty. Was he not back yet? Where was that fool boy? Probably joined the volunteer corps. Well, no time to worry. She had to trust that he was all right.

She would deal with him later, as long as he was ready to leave.

Fausan, Sohn, and Bhasani were waiting at the front gates chatting with Solum. The massive Hansoo was crouching on one knee, as he often did when chatting with the diminutive drowned fist. He saw her approach and rose to his full height.

"We need to go out."

"Are you sure? The streets are tense tonight. The city can flip to battle, panic, or devolve into a riot at any moment."

She pointed at the other three masters waiting on her. "Nothing they can't manage."

"The four of you look like you belong in a gambling parlor more than a war zone." Solum grunted. "I wish I could assign a Hansoo to you."

"You should. I promise I'll return him in one piece."

"I don't believe you." The war monk chuckled. "However, you're a dowager nun. You don't need my permission to leave the temple. If your group of seniors wishes to venture forth, to danger, then by all means." He shouted at the monks manning the closed gates. "Form up. Gates opening." He turned back to Taishi. "Make it back before the fighting reaches these slopes. The temple goes on lockdown, and the gates won't open no matter what, not even for a dowager nun."

"Understood." Taishi led the group of seniors out through the gates, waiting to speak until after they were out of earshot. "Are your disciples with Jian?"

Fausan shook his head. "Hachi said he needed to head to the other side of town. Something about a box shop?"

Bhasani looked perplexed. "You didn't see Sonaya? She said she was going to visit Jian at your cottage."

Taishi shrugged. "Those kids are somewhere, but not at home."

It was a long way down the path to the base of the hill. Fortunately, there was a lift that could take them down to the lower levels. Some entrepreneurial monks several centuries back had realized that the temple could profit handsomely if they built a lift that carried the devout and clergy up and down the temple hill. Technically, monks weren't supposed to earn and hold wealth, but no one took that seriously. The business became so successful that the temple promoted him to an abbot and then claimed ownership of the lift.

The rides were free for the nobility with a recommendation for a tip, a modest sum for the wealthy, and exorbitantly priced for commoners. The abbot who now ran the lift had explained to her that pricing out the poor and making them walk all the way up the hill was the only way to stay in business. This all sounded backward to Taishi, but then again, she didn't have good business acumen, so what did she know?

Vauzan late at night in the eastern wards was understandably tense while also eerily quiet. The city had never had a vibrant nightlife, unlike Allanto or Manjing, but no capital city in the Enlightened States ever truly slept. Taishi could make out the clashes in the distance, either from rioting or Caobiu sleeper cells. Magistrates moving in pairs patrolled the streets while soldiers erected barricades at major checkpoints and intersections.

Sohn, leading the way, signaled for a stop as they neared Holy Glow Plaza, the main public square at the base of Peony Peak that began the trek toward the temple. This was an important center where six streets converged, making it a critical position to control. The city guard had erected checkpoints at the main intersections, bottlenecking traffic as people fled from the east side of the city toward the west. Most appeared to be families carrying everything they owned on their backs while fleeing the brunt of the attack.

"There's no way around it." The eternal bright light master sighed.

"We can go around or take to the roofs." Fausan looked at Taishi. "Think you can still handle it?"

"Not with that added weight." She looked at his ever-expanding belly. "Congratulations on the happy news. Twins by the look of it. Did you pick out names yet?"

He grinned and smacked his generous midsection. "Don't blame me for knowing how to enjoy my latter years, unlike someone else I know."

That much was true. Taishi had never seen Fausan and Bhasani so happy as they were in their golden years. How annoying.

"It'll take an hour to get through that line," said Sohn. "We better get started."

Taishi held her ground. She crossed her arms. "I am not young anymore. I am not waiting in line for anything unless there's a drink at the end of it."

"I agree," said Bhasani.

"I don't know about that," said Fausan. "Putting soldiers in the infirmary on the eve of an invasion may send the wrong signal about which side we're on."

"How about we just knock them unconscious," said Sohn. "They'll wake up in a few hours refreshed for the slaughter the next day."

"You're all a bunch of stunted eggs. I'll take care of this." Bhasani moved out into the open before anyone could stop her. Instead of heading to the back of the line, she walked up to the guard manning the checkpoint. Taishi and the men had little choice but to follow.

"Cutter rat," more than one person made sure to say as they passed.

Taishi didn't care. Ling Taishi was not a known line-cutter, except for once or twice. Dowager Nun Nai Roha, on the other hand, was an entitled and terrible person.

The soldier waving wagons past the checkpoint spat at Bhasani's feet as she approached. "You think you're going to just show your wrinkled ass and walk on through, eh? Fat chance—"

"It's not wrinkled. It's spectacular." Bhasani's skill with compulsion was unmatched. Her strong jing slammed into the soldier. She had this smooth, silky delivery that seemed so casual at first.

His eyes widened and he stood up taller. He craned his head around to gawk at her backside. "You're right. It's amazing. Absolutely spectacular."

"We need to go through so you can watch my beautiful, smooth, perfectly round ass as we walk past."

"Absolutely, mistress. Thank you, mistress." He waved them through, much to the line's outrage. Catcalls rained down upon them. Taishi barely avoided thrown potatoes. A pear bounced off Fausan's head. He turned and caught it on the second bounce and bit into it. He pinky-waved back, further infuriating the crowd. The guard continued to stare at Bhasani's travel cloak as if it were the best view in the house.

She winked at him. "Be a dear and arrest anyone who is rude to us."

"Yes, mistress," the soldier replied. He turned to face the line. "I want the maggot who threw that apple—"

"A pear," Fausan called.

"—pear at the dowager nun and the fat one!"

"Hey!" the whipfinger replied.

"If he isn't presented to me right now, then I'm closing down the checkpoint and you can get crispy as the city burns." The line gave up the fruit-thrower immediately, shoving him forward and passing him along to the guard.

"Well, that escalated quickly," said Fausan, looking back. "Was that necessary?"

Bhasani put a hand on his arm. "He threw something at you, my love, and that's like throwing something at me. No one gets away with throwing anything at me."

"How did you just turn me getting pelted into something about you?" he asked.

The four continued moving, taking the right fork of the street that curved toward the lower levels leading to the buried wards. They moved at a dawdling, relaxed pace. It was safe to say none of them was enjoying this walk. Taishi's knees didn't respond well to descents, while Fausan was starting to hobble. Bhasani was just lazy, while Sohn's fighting style was designed to stand in place.

Eventually, they reached the Nightrun, the largest of the buried wards, which also housed the densest criminal elements in the city. The streets were little more than needle-thin alleyways. Buildings were stacked upon each other like toy blocks, and everything was squat, from the buildings to the walls to the low ceilings, adding to the feeling of claustrophobia. The walls flanking each narrow street seemed to lean over them. They stopped briefly as a mischief of rats scurried out of an alley across onto the street and then over to the other side.

"I've never been a fan of this place," said Fausan. "Why are we here?"

Taishi turned the corner and pointed at a garish green building with large signage in yellow letters painted above the front doors. She scowled at the long line of people waiting to get inside.

The whipfinger master sighed. "I was afraid you would point there."

Copper Crane 8888 was an infamous restaurant in Vauzan, but not for its cuisine. It was home to the Worst Today Boys. The underworld organization had especially come to prominence over the past three years with the rise of their new, mysterious leader. The Worst Todays also controlled the teamster routes and shipping lanes in Vauzan, which meant they would have to be who she dealt with to escape the city.

"You know we can't just walk in there, war arts masters or not," said Fausan.

"Mori took care of the introduction," said Taishi.

"What could a dowager nun possibly have to bargain with the underworld?" said Bhasani.

"He took care of that too."

Taishi walked up the ramp to the restaurant and stopped in front of a beefy young thug. He looked puzzled. Very few nuns probably wandered down here.

It didn't matter. He gestured for them to leave. "Everyone has business here, not just you. Back of the line, cutter."

"I'm here to see Beautiful Boy."

"Doesn't matter." The guy didn't budge. "What business do you have with the boss?"

"Your head if you don't let me through."

The young meathead sneered, but Taishi's confidence was enough to give him pause. He stood and stuck his head through a curtain-beaded doorway. "There's a bunch of raisins demanding to see the boss. They won't leave. Look, man, I'm not good with punching geriatrics. I draw the line at beating up nanas. What should I do?" He turned back to face them. "Listen, lady, get out of here or we're both going to have really bad days."

Someone else looked out from behind the doorway. This time, it was a young woman with the left side of her head shaved. "Hang on, Jap, is one of the raisins a nun?"

"Yeah."

The woman whacked him on the head with a stick. "Let them in, you boiled egg! Never keep our best clients waiting!"

"I'm surprised the temple deals with the underworld, and the Worst Boys, of all people," said Fausan as the young thug stepped aside.

"The temple's one of the underworld's biggest clients, actually," said Taishi.

"I'm surprised, but I guess I shouldn't be," said Fausan.

The four were allowed into the restaurant and were immediately surrounded by a group of toughs, all looking as if they were auditioning to be Hansoos in a local opera. The interior of the Copper Crane 8888 *looked* like a restaurant, with tables and chairs and a bar running along the right side, but that was as far as it went. The room was thick with smoke that stunk of tobacco, opium, and seaweed. Several groups of burly men, broad-shouldered, clustered around comically small tables, playing cards, tiles, dice, and games of Siege. A few raised their heads and looked their way, but none offered more than a casual glance before returning to their games. Cups were everywhere, sitting on tables, rolling on their sides along the floor, piled into a corner. This place was filthy. Taishi couldn't help but feel disappointed. She'd expected more.

"Do you think we can fight our way out of this alive?" Fausan said to Sohn, not sounding remotely confident.

The eternal bright light master looked around. "We might lose one of the ladies along the way, but I'm pretty sure one of us will make it."

Taishi snorted, noting the gutter trash in the room. "Sohn wouldn't even break a sweat with these house cats."

"I appreciate your confidence in my great ability," he remarked.

"No, they're just that bad."

"This looks like a scene from a bad Burning Hearts romance novel," remarked Bhasani. "At least their clothing was clean."

Taishi had noticed that too.

They passed through the main dining hall and entered a cramped hallway with a row of wooden doors along one side and a wall of weapons hanging along the other. Most were street weapons: clubs, hammers, maces, and chains. All looked cheaply made, disposable gear wielded by disposable henchmen. Underground outfits usually came two ways: small but elite, or large and expendable. The Worst Boys appeared to be the latter. That made sense, considering the amateur display out in the main room. How did the gang manage to gain control of something as important as the mercantile routes?

They entered a large room in the back that was for parties. There was a long, rectangular table running down the center. Flickering candles on sconces diffused the light, hazing the room with shadows that constantly changed shades. There were ten people on each side of the table, drinking and yelling like the drunk thugs they were. Sitting at the far end, on an elevated dais, was a man who must be Beautiful Boy. Taishi had to admit she was disappointed there too. He was decent-looking, but hardly worthy of his name.

"Are you thinking what I'm thinking?" said Bhasani. "Like a solid seven, at best."

"Hardly beautiful," Taishi agreed.

Beautiful Boy was a man in his late thirties with sharp eyes and nose, and hair pulled into a tassel in the back. Tattoos of falling orchids ran along the right side of his face and body. His shirt was plain and open in the middle, revealing more tattoos, this time of a dragon and blade.

Sitting to his left was a woman. Her garb was modest but disheveled. The boy's mistress, perhaps. Sitting at a table at the far end of the room, near the door, was another woman, this one with a handsome face. She looked bored and fixed their group with a deadpan expression. Perhaps the boss's sister? No, they looked nothing alike.

"So," said Beautiful Boy. He chewed loudly. "Temple never sent a nun as a messenger before. Mori must be hard up on able bodies."

Taishi kept it brisk. "This is a personal request."

"Yet the templeabbot is covering the marker."

"That's his business, not yours."

Beautiful Boy's eyes flickered to the side, then he lounged back in the cushions. "What's the personal ask then, nun?"

"I have a wagon that needs to be smuggled out of the city."

"What's the cargo?"

"People."

Beautiful Boy barked a rough laugh. "Ha, don't get cute with me. We both know not all people are created equal. A lord is not gutter trash. A general is not his arrow fodder. A war arts master is not mustered infantries, so come on, give up the manifest if you want a ride: names, ranks, and deeds."

Taishi shook her head. "Just family and a few companions. My nephew, a few old no-ones of note, and their assistants. That's it."

Beautiful Boy considered and then stood. "I don't believe you. Not with the pay that the temple is offering. Who are you really stealing away?"

"I think I am quite of note," whispered Fausan.

"Shut up," hissed Bhasani.

"Shutting up," said the whipfinger.

Beautiful Boy glanced at the woman sitting to his left and then paced down that side of the room. He studied the four gray-haired—or in Sohn's case, no-haired—masters. "Why would the temple pay a gold liang to move a retired nun out of the city?" He stopped in front of Taishi. "Who are you to them, or what are you holding over them? In any case, please convey to the templeabbot that while the Worst Boys usually would love to accommodate the Temple of the Tiandi, these are extraordinary times and we'll be unable to fulfill his request at the usual agreed-upon price. The Worst Boys require a favor, however. One of my sub-bosses has a devout cousin who has answered the calling of the Tiandi. He is now serving the Tiandi at the Jade Tower of the Vigilant Spirit in Lawkan. He has been passed over for templeabbot several times now. It would please us greatly if Templeabbot Lee Mori could see to the promotion he so richly deserves."

It wasn't surprising that the underworld had infiltrated the temple. They probably had people embedded everywhere: in the army, the magistrate corps, the teamsters, probably even the Shulan Court. Of course, they would have seeded someone into the ranks of the Tiandi religion. To have someone elevated to abbot, however, meant that the Worst Boys had infiltrated the highest ranks within the Tiandi hierarchy.

What was shocking, however, was an underworld abbot ascending to the rank of templeabbot. The training to become a templeabbot was rigorous with a detailed vetting process. They took their ideological purity seriously. For an underworld to rise to the position of templeabbot would cause a scandal. There was no chance Mori would accept this offer. The Tiandi abbots would never allow the underworld to sink their claws into their leadership. The templeabbots would root this infiltrator out and brand them a non-person throughout the Enlightened States. That was worse than death. This was valuable information Beautiful Boy had given her for free. It was certainly a clumsy pivot. She was insulted that he even asked.

She caught Beautiful Boy looking over her shoulder. This was the second time. Taishi followed the gaze to the back room. That was when it clicked. Now she knew what was happening.

"Sure," she said aloud. "It's probably just an oversight. We'll have that devout cousin raised to templeabbot, on my word." The stakes were too high to worry about such trivial matters.

"What?" said Sohn.

"Taishi!" Bhasani hissed.

Fausan missed it entirely, having made friends with several of the Worst Boys at the gambling table in the other room.

"This isn't a problem," continued Taishi.

Beautiful Boy seemed surprised. "Well, that's great. You're sure about this?"

"We promote each other for fun all the time." Taishi winked. "Tell me the name and he'll be wearing that ugly bumblebee hat by tomorrow."

"His name . . ." stammered the leader of the Worst Boys.

"I've seen enough." The woman sitting at the far end of the table stood. "She suspects already. Clear the room." She bowed formally in the martial way. Then she touched what appeared to be a hidden door, swinging it open. "This way."

Taishi and her friends had little choice but to follow. "You must be Beautiful Boy," she said, ducking into the next room and following the woman down a set of stairs that connected to a larger room. This area was finer, with tall ceilings, polished marble walls, and tiled floors.

Beautiful Boy answered, nodding. "It's not a well-kept secret, but it still surprises most people."

"Is it to glean information during negotiations?" asked Bhasani.

"More like for assassination attempts," Beautiful Boy replied. She pointed back the way they had come in. "Bak, my man back there, is perpetually food poisoned. It's rather amusing, if not for the fact he has the worst bowels."

"You know," said Bhasani, "if you wanted to sell that ruse, you should get a more beautiful boy. This one doesn't reach expectations."

"He was more handsome when he first took the job," admitted Beautiful Boy. She sat in the chair at the opposite end of the table and gestured for them to sit. Taishi was thankful. The relief of getting off her feet after so much walking today sent a shiver up her spine. She fell into a small fit of coughs, wiping the blood off her lips with her sleeve. This was not a place to show weakness.

Beautiful Boy studied Taishi first and then leaned forward. "You have a very shallow record, Dowager Nun Nai Roha, almost as if you appeared out of someone's imagination one day. Nothing in the temple records, and stranger still, nothing in the Black Orchid rosters."

"I'm from the original temple," said Taishi. "You didn't bother checking with them, did you?"

"No, that's not it," said Beautiful Boy. She had a peasant's face but possessed a strong jaw and determined eyes. She was an observant one. Taishi still couldn't shake her familiar face. "Then it hit me. I don't know you." She pointed at Taishi, and then she pointed at Fausan. "But I'm a big fan of him!"

"Me?" Fausan, who hadn't been paying attention, looked up. "How big of a fan?"

Bhasani slapped his shoulder. "Does it matter?"

"The God of Gamblers is revered in the Underworld. The bulk of our business is gambling and loansharking, and most of our loans are to degenerate gamblers."

"It's like a double-dip," said Sohn.

"You do the Worst Boys great honor by standing in our inner sanctum."

Taishi groused, "You keep this up and his head won't fit through the door."

"And you, Dowager Nai Roha." Beautiful Boy faced Taishi. "There were reports coming from the west about the God of Gamblers sighted with the Queen of Hot Air."

"I'm what?" said Taishi.

"You never heard yourself called that?" Bhasani looked surprised.

"Everyone calls you that," added Sohn.

Taishi rounded on him. "Do you call me the Queen of Hot Air behind my back?"

"Uh," the eternal bright light master stammered. "Of course not. That's outrageous."

"You have the look. You speak with the authority. If the God of Gamblers is here, then I must be in the presence of the Queen of Hot Air, or Grandmaster Windwhisper Ling Taishi."

"I'm going to kill the next person who calls me that," Taishi grumbled.

Still, smart girl. No wonder she ran the operation. "You have your big name now. How much more will it cost to smuggle us out of the city?"

The Worst Boy boss sat in her chair, wearing a fake smile while pretending to think. "Last I checked, you were the second-most-wanted fugitive in the Enlightened States. Imagine what you're worth now." She gestured at the door. "I could hand you in for the reward myself."

Taishi shrugged. "You could try. Maybe you catch me alive—that reward is only good if I'm captured alive by the way—or my fellow masters and I can slaughter every one of you little plague mice and wipe your stain off the ass of the kingdom once and for all."

Beautiful Boy arched one eye, impressed. "Now that is the Ling Taishi my father used to tell me stories about. He claimed he even knew you. I never believed him. Yes, we could try to capture you, and you could slaughter us all, but then you'll never escape the city."

"So name a price. How much to ferry Ling Taishi and her party out of the city?" At this point, Taishi was willing to pay any amount. It wasn't her money, anyway. She would apologize to Mori later.

"That's the thing." Beautiful Boy stood and shook her finger. "I'm not going to charge you anything to smuggle you out of the city. But . . ."

Taishi's eyes narrowed. "But what?"

"I'm going to need you to take someone out for me, Ling Taishi." Beautiful Boy looked her straight in the eyes. "I want you to kill Highlord Oban."

CHAPTER THIRTEEN

THE NURSERY

For the next few days, Qisami couldn't stop seeing the signs of her run-in with those stupid pruneskins at the Lawkan corner. The clues were everywhere, and in many cases, impossible to ignore. That is, unless you were these skull-squeezed prison guards. They missed everything. It wasn't hard to notice the nursery runners. Every Lawkan heading in and out of the mines looked suspect. The guards were finding strange contraband almost daily, anything from stockings to candles to pacifiers. Women were being dragged out of the lines on a daily basis for carrying contraband.

A guard caught a Lawkan inmate one morning carrying a large jug of breast milk to the mines. He convinced them that it was a popular drink back home, and considering the river folk's often strange reputation, the guards bought it and let him through. There was another instance of an inmate caught stashing a bag of dolls and carved stone sailing ships, a man with five gourds of mashed vegetables, and a woman holding a stack of washed but shit-stained diapers. She told the guards that her barrack was so behind on their quotas that they decided to save time by skipping piss breaks. And the guards bought it!

Inevitably, that same woman was caught at the end of the day carrying a satchel of soiled diapers, which they allowed through as well. Qisami happened to be standing in line near the main elevator when that woman had passed by. The stink had been overwhelming.

As a professional, amateurs grated on her last nerve, probably the only nerve she had left. Bad criminals gave everyone in the lunar court a bad name and made it much more difficult for the legit ones to commit crimes. And weren't the Lawkan supposed to be expert smugglers? Then she remembered that smuggling was a lowbrow profession, while the Happy Glow Retirement Home was a prison for court and powerful inmates. Sunri would never bother throwing real smugglers into this high-class joint. She would just lop off their ankles—hands for thieves, feet for smugglers—and be done with it.

After a few dozen times, even the lazy pudding-brained guards began to notice that something was awry. Those bored ninnies began to chatter and share stories of strange incidents. It was only a matter of time before they figured things out. The whole operation was so amateur hour that the insanity bordered on entertaining, like a badly written Burning Hearts romance.

It was later that evening, after she had spent the day with Cyyk and the Goons working on an opal vein on Ten. Qisami had just stepped out of the elevator heading toward home when she encountered Boobs the nursemaid trying to get past the checkpoint. The heavyset woman carried two large burlap sacks, one slung over each shoulder. She was hunched over like an oversize turtle as she struggled to keep them from slipping.

Two guards were having fun poking at her, mocking her size and age. One snatched a sack off her back, nearly causing her to tip over. He opened it and pulled out a stack of neatly folded clothes, dumping them in the dirt. The other pretended to climb onto her hunched back and ride her like a horse before shoving her to the ground. Boobs squawked. Her frail voice broke, causing a new fit of laughter. Many of the guards in management were former court-martials from the Caobiu army, all serving life sentences, so their poor manners weren't surprising. Sunri did not tolerate bad soldiering among her ranks, but they were far from the well-trained Cinder Legions. These guards now felt free to let loose their worst instincts, especially against those from enemy duchies.

Now, Qisami enjoyed a good tease as much as the next person, but only if they could fight back. Otherwise, it was bullying, so watching the two young guards harass big Boobs cut her the wrong way. She was just passing this childish display when her annoyance got the best of her. The truth was, Qisami wasn't the same person anymore, ever since Allanto.

"There you are, Boobs. You were supposed to report to me an hour ago!" She squeezed herself between the two guards and kicked the woman lightly on the ankle. "Now get up before we lose the rest of the day."

The two guards recognized Qisami. One guard stammered, "Is . . . is the pruneskin with you? She didn't have the right marker to take the elevator."

Qisami flashed her marker. "Sure is, Duckface. Supposed to bring drinks and supplies down to the Goons."

The blood drained from their faces. Even the guards treaded lightly around the Goons. These guys might be the management, but they were all prisoners.

"She said she was taking it down to her barrack."

"I don't care what Boobs says," Qisami retorted. "This stuff is for the Goons, or there'll be hell to pay. All the dogs down there are thirsty and pissed. You don't want to get on Hair Bear's bad side, do you?" She jabbed a finger at him. "That was a trick question. Both his sides are bad."

That last jibe broke just enough of the tension. Duckface waved Boobs through. "Thanks for clearing it up, Chopstick. Tell the crone to bring the right marker next time."

"Do I look like a wristwagger to you?" Qisami shot back.

"No troubles, Chopstick," said the other guard. Her reputation was almost as scary as the Goons', which was a bit insulting.

Qisami latched on to Boobs and dragged the woman along in silence until they crossed the bridge and were about to head into the lift
building.

"Thank—" Boobs began.

An elbow to the ribs shut her up. Qisami stepped ahead of the
nursemaid and waved at Three-Chins sitting behind the cage next to
the elevator. "Hi, sweets."

"Back so soon, Chopstick?" The blind elevator attendant squinted.
"You were smaller the last time I saw you. Wasn't it just a small bit
ago? My, the time has flown. It felt like you were just a little turd just
yesterday. Where are you off to now?"

Qisami frowned and craned her head to see the larger nursemaid
overshadowing her. "Level eight."

Boobs interrupted, "Don't you mean level—"

Qisami elbowed her harder, this time in the right boob. She shook
her head. "Don't mind the feeble-minded Boobs here. Eight, please,
sweets." To quicken the transaction, she dug out the cookie she had
planned to snack on later and passed it through the bars.

The two women stood in silence as the cage began to rumble,
clicking loudly and rattling in random intervals. Curtains of chains
snaked up and down as the cage lowered, banging against each other.

Finally, Qisami, more out of boredom than anything else, spoke.
"So." She continued staring straight ahead, watching the vectors of the
cage pass by. "How's your baby incubator coming along?"

"Thank you for helping with the guards." The woman joined her
in watching their descent. "Will you accompany me to where I'm
heading?"

"That was a pathetic display," said Qisami. "You Lawkan are terrible at smuggling things. Isn't that supposed to be your expertise? You're
all so amateur I'm offended." She pointed up. "And with Three-Chins
up there. Why would you tell someone exactly where you're going?"

"Sorba doesn't even remember his name half the time, let alone
where you're going."

"Who is Sorba?"

"Exactly, child." The nursemaid popped a smile. "As for the elevator, you'll understand when your knees get worn down like mine."

"That'll never happen."

"No one stays young forever."

"Shadowkills don't get old."

"That certainly is true." The nursemaid's response was weighted.

The elevator stopped at eight, and Qisami slid the gate open. Boobs reached for the extinguished lantern, but Qisami slapped her hand away. She shook her head. "Let your eyes adjust." Her voice was low and soft. The wind and echoes carried words well down here.

The two women traversed the bridge and then continued up the nearby path that curved toward the upper regions of the mine. Each elevator stop covered two to three levels, depending on the mine, so to get to six they had to walk up approximately seven flights of stairs. The old woman was huffing after the first set and had to take a break after they reached the seventh level. She plopped down on a nearby stone ledge and gasped for breath. For a few moments, it sounded almost as if she was going to keel over, which would have posed a serious problem. Her body was too large for Qisami to push over the side. Corpse removal was the weakest part of her assassination game. Fortunately, it didn't come to that as the nursemaid recovered.

The pair was still resting when the elevator began to click. Qisami yanked the nursemaid's sleeve and dragged her behind a raised lip along the path as the cage carried a group of miners back to the surface. The Happy Glow open pit mine had been operating for over a century. Most of the higher levels had been picked clean decades ago, so the crews had to venture deeper to mine ore. That left the upper levels abandoned but also meant that those coming from below had to pass through on their way back up.

"We need to get away from the main shaft before rush hour," said Qisami, dragging the woman along.

Six minutes later, they reached level six and turned into one of the tertiary tunnels. Qisami was surprised. It wasn't the area she had in mind to place these brats but she said nothing. There could be many reasons for the Lawkan to plant their nursery in any of these caves. It also occurred to her that the pruneskins had been trying to hide the babies from *her* as well, in the event that she betrayed them.

As they wandered through the maze of cave tunnels, it wasn't lost on Qisami that this might be a setup. Perhaps there were thirty Lawkans waiting to stab her to bits. It would be justified, although she doubted these court-groomed limp lilies could muster such an elaborate ambush. Speaking of which . . .

"Hey, Boobs," she asked. "How did you know I was a shadowkill? You said you were born in Manjing, but it wasn't like we advertised on every corner."

That earned a chuckle from the woman. "My sister was a training pool mother."

That startled Qisami, mainly because it had never occurred to her that training pool mothers had family. They had always come across as sterile cold bitches. Besides, the nursemaid was so nice.

"Was she a shadowkill?" she asked.

The nursemaid nodded. "For a while. She was my mother's brood atonement when the Consortium had put a contract on her. She became a shadowkill, but eventually realized she preferred to teach, so retired as headmother of Ba Liu Zhi Wu San Ling Yi pool."

"A seven-tier! Your sister was big shit." Qisami whistled, impressed. She had attended only a four-tier pool.

"A good teacher. Not a great killer," agreed the nursemaid. "My family hail from a long line of educators."

And nobles. Seven-tier training pools only served high-ranking lords. Which meant this woman wasn't just some nursemaid. Who was she?

Qisami was about to scratch that curious itch when she heard the first cry. It was distant, whiny, and grating. The sound reminded her of the sniffling and sobbing of freshies at the training pool, or little Lady Akiya, whom Qisami had been a child companion for during her undercover job in Allanto. That sensitive dear could water fountain on command. Her twin sister, Akiana, was a crier too, albeit for different reasons. That little demon wanted to win so badly at everything that she broke down into uncontrollable sobs with every lost fight or argument. Now *that* girl was meant to be a war artist. The lunar court lost a great one when the twins had drowned in the Lake of Bountiful Abundance back in Allanto, courtesy of Chiafana, Sunri's Minister of Critical Purpose. Qisami adored those hellions. Her hands clenched at the thought of that woman. One day, she intended to square up that balance.

The pair followed the sound of the noise. The lone cry was soon joined by a second, and then another. Their sounds bounced around the tunnel walls until it became a constant chorus of babies wailing. It was harsh and sharp enough that Qisami nearly lost her balance.

The nursemaid pulled out a long rag and tied it around her head from the top to under her chin, covering her ears. She offered one to Qisami too, who followed her example. It was somewhat effective.

Eventually they reached a small, cavernous crawl area. There were a dozen makeshift cribs crafted from various materials stacked close in the center of the room, with the area surrounded by a burlap curtain. A lantern hung directly above, offering some illumination. The cribs were also surrounded by several torches burning down to various states of use. Three of the Lawkan were here. A man had one of the babies in his arms trying to feed spoonfuls of what Qisami assumed was breast milk through a funnel. A woman was changing a baby on a stone slab off to the side. Another man was sleeping on the ground in what looked like a deeply uncomfortable position.

Qisami was underwhelmed by the entire operation. This was what all the fuss was about? For some reason, she thought it would be a bigger production with babies crawling and peeing everywhere, with nursemaids reading books and changing diapers. At least that was how all the nurseries in Allanto had been. This just looked depressing. This cavern was smaller than she thought it would be, with ceilings so low not even Qisami could stand to her full height without banging her head. It took her a few moments to realize why: small spaces were easier to heat and keep warm.

Boobs woke the sleeping man and handed off the two sacks. He whispered into her ear before hurrying off. The nursemaid froze, shaking her head as grief welled in her eyes. She sucked in a long breath and wiped her face. "One of the little ones didn't make it through the night. The runner bringing up the sparkstones was apprehended by management."

Irrational anger sparked in Qisami, and she took it out on the nearest person: Boobs. "That's what you dung cows get for bringing babies into this mess hole. Why, why are you doing this? What's the point in having them if you can't keep them alive?"

What did Qisami care? Why was she so angry?

The nursemaid didn't back down. "Because people need a reason to keep going even if it seems like our lives have ended."

That answer needled Qisami. It struck a chord deep in her soul at her own pointless and bleak existence. She wanted nothing more than to wipe her mind of this revelation, of this place, of what was happening. She felt compelled to dig deeper. Her voice was quiet as if she didn't want to wake the babies. "What happens when these brats grow up? Where will you put them? What will they do? Are you going to just raise a colony of tunnel rats?"

"We'll worry about that when the time comes. For now, we just want to give the little ones a chance. Perhaps, one day, when the war is over, the winner will see fit to free us. It's a risk our people are willing to take."

"Even at the cost of your lives?"

The nursemaid chuckled. "Our lives are worth very little these days." She looked at Qisami. "What do you have to live for, shadowkill?"

That stumped Qisami. Even though she knew the answer, she was too ashamed to utter it aloud. It also enraged her to confront her reality. Her mother had died when she was little, and then her father had given up caring. He became a terra-cotta warrior: cold and distant, removed. That was the cruelest part of her childhood. Qisami had been old enough to remember having a family before having to live with a broken one. And then he gave her away to the Consortium.

Qisami retreated to the corner of the cavern and wrapped her arms around her knees as Boobs finished whatever tasks needed to be done. Now she knew why the nursemaid had come down to the mines instead of sending a runner or someone more able. She was a full-service restaurant, suckling two babies at a time while four more were lined up on a slab like an assembly line until she was fully out of supply. It was as if the woman's breasts were her jing. After that, she did a bit of everything: burping the babies, changing them, bathing them in sand and water, and even playing with them. At one point, she offered one of the larger boys for Qisami to hold, but she had shrunk away. Playing with kids was too painful a reminder of the Aki twins.

Qisami wasn't sure how long they were down here. Time lost all meaning in the caves. She thought she'd known what to expect from her time as a child's companion, but this was strange. These mewling and wailing babies were nothing like little girls. They weren't even people. They were life, blank slates untouched by the world.

This was the strangest thing for someone whose entire professional career was involved in ending life. Now she was not only protecting it, but it made her reflect on all the people who could still be living if she hadn't been so damn good at her job.

"I have to go back," she finally announced. Her stomach was growling. She also had her fill of poop for the day.

"Of course, child," Boobs said, closing her robes. They had deflated since she arrived. She also looked exhausted. "Will you escort me back to the surface? I assume the infamous Chopstick will make the journey less treacherous."

Every step back felt heavier. Qisami berated herself. She *knew* she was going to get wrapped up in these pruneskins' conspiracies if she came. She had turned from a knife into a shield. This was none of her business. Why did she put herself into this situation? If only her old cell could see her now. The two began the trek back toward the mine vortex.

"I can feel the weight of your thoughts," said Boobs.

I think you're raising a bunch of dead babies, Qisami thought. "You are fools. This will not end well."

"Perhaps." The nursemaid was lagging behind again. "Likely, even, but as long as we have a chance, we have hope for a future."

"It's the hope that kills," Qisami muttered.

"The blade of hopelessness is equally sharp and far more poisonous."

At some point, there were bound to be children running about. "It's just a matter of time before management catches on. It may not be tomorrow or next week, or even the next cycle, but they will, eventually. So what's the point of all this?"

"That is likely." The nursemaid looked at her. "But that is a worry for tomorrow. Just like you were a solution for today's problem."

They reached the mouth of the tertiary tunnel and stopped at the foot of the winding ramp down toward the level eight elevator bridge. Qisami looked up. The elevator on five was directly above. The first five levels were used for storing the ore before delivery. Traffic would be too heavy on the main elevator during the day. They'd best take a different route to avoid questions. Qisami looked at the old woman, who was already wheezing and looking unsteady on her feet.

She pointed toward the up ramp. "This way is shorter."

A sigh escaped the woman's lips. "Why is everything always uphill?"

The journey up to level five was mercifully shorter. It was just a short jaunt up one long but gentle slope that curved a quarter of the way around the circular pit, and then a straight shot past a bank of ore wagons ready for delivery come next shipment.

"I've always wondered," said Boobs, passing the silence. "Why Chopstick?"

"Same reason I call you Boobs. No one here needs to know our real names," Qisami answered.

"How do you know where you're going if all you do is try to forget where you've come from? If you wish to know who I am, just ask."

Qisami held up a hand. "Perhaps one day. Right now, I like calling you Boobs."

"Hey, stop right there!" Mubaan Soy and the two guards from the checkpoint stepped onto the wooden bridge.

Qisami played it off coolly and waved. "Hi, Soy."

Soy approached with the other management in tow. "What are you doing here, Chopstick?"

She pulled out her warden's marker. "I'm doing whatever I want, One-Ball. What are you doing here?"

"I'm management," he retorted. "I do whatever I want."

The two guards surrounded the nursemaid. "Guess who showed up on the wrong floor without the proper marker."

"She's with me," Qisami said. "And what we're doing is none of your business."

Soy's eyes narrowed on her. He looked at his associate. "Make a note to send some guards to sweep levels six and seven." His eyes narrowed on her. "There's an unpleasant smell in the air. Must be the warden's pet dog."

Qisami did not appreciate being called that. Her hand drifted to her head, where a lone chopstick was hidden in the tangled nest of her hair.

The nursemaid, standing behind her, shifted. "Let me speak with them. Maybe I can talk our way—"

Qisami shucked her away and kept her eyes on Soy. "Nothing to worry about, Boobs. I'll take care of it." She patted the nursemaid on the arm and then spun around, charging the three management. She jumped up and split kicked, sending the two guards toppling over the rope railing. Then as she landed, she brought her fist vertically downward, stabbing the chopstick into Soy's left eye. He stiffened and threw his head back as a fountain of blood shot upward and she yanked the stick out. His back arched as he cried out, his hands clawing at his face. Qisami stepped up and shoved him, sending him toppling over the side and plummeting down into the darkness. She stood at the edge of the bridge and watched until Mubaan Soy's screams faded into oblivion.

Qisami turned to face Boobs, the bloodied chopstick still in her hand. "You want to know how I got the name Chopstick?" She brandished the bloody stick at Boobs. "This is how."

CHAPTER FOURTEEN

HARD CHOICES

Taishi spent most of the night trying to talk Beautiful Boy out of killing the interim leader of the Shulan Duchy. To consider the thought was ridiculous, outrageous. Assassinating any lord was treason, but certainly high treason during war. She would be vilified by the Zhuun for all eternity, even by Shulan's enemies. Taishi did not spend a lifetime building her reputation just to throw it away like that.

Second, she liked Oban. They didn't agree on much, but she recognized his principle and admired his honor. Oban the Orderly was a good man. His hardline stance against the Caobiu was foolish, but understandable. Saan was his best friend and blood brother. Oban's fight against Sunri was personal.

Third, and probably the most relevant: Taishi couldn't kill Oban even if she wanted to. A high lord of the court would be protected by elite packs of mute men. Attempting to assassinate Oban would be suicide, even when she was in her prime.

"Someone managed to kill Duke Saan," Beautiful Boy had remarked. "I'm sure the great Ling Taishi could figure it out."

And that was the last consideration, more of a minor detail than anything else. There was nothing great about Ling Taishi anymore. She was just a sick old woman wasting away during her declining years waiting for death's final cut. She felt like a dim shadow fading into oblivion.

Beautiful Boy wouldn't budge, however. The price to steal Taishi and her people out of the city was Oban's life. She would accept nothing less, not if Taishi offered to pay double, triple even. Beautiful emphasized the death toll, and the unmaintainable loss of culture and destruction that would befall the city if they allowed Oban to fight to the death.

"It would cost hundreds of thousands of lives, Master Windwhisper," she pressed. "In a useless war of attrition that the Shulan have no hope of surviving. It's not even the people's fight. Those in the buried wards do not care if we call our lord Oban or Sunri. One duke is the same as any other. Both will claim our taxes. But right now, only one side will kill us all. Only a negotiated surrender will save lives."

Of all the times for a criminal to become a patriot. The hardest part of this, however, was that Beautiful Boy was correct. Her position might be self-serving, but she certainly was aligned with the greater good of the city. Assassinating Oban *would* likely tip the Shulan Court toward suing for peace. An early surrender would certainly prevent the city from being razed to the ground.

By the next morning, they were still at an impasse. Taishi could not be swayed from her position. She was not willing to consider murdering a good man, even if it were for the greater good. Righteousness and honor were not something that could be weighed and balanced on scales.

A weary Taishi returned to the others waiting in the main dining room. The restaurant was closed with stools turned upside down on the tables. A lone man in an apron was mopping the floor. None of the Worst Boys were around, save for a few passed out at a table off to the side.

Taishi waved for the others to join her as she made for the door leading out of the restaurant. "We're done here. It's a dead end."

Fausan wrinkled his brow. "They won't smuggle us out?"

"The price is unreasonable."

"Who cares," said Sohn. "Let's just pay it and go."

"We'll have to find another way." Taishi shook her head and told the others about the failed negotiations and Beautiful Boy's asking price to spirit them out of Vauzan. She was met with silence when she finished.

Sohn took the lead across the buried ward. The cobbled streets were quiet save for a pair of drunkards still making their way home and a young boy biking a wagon carrying water jugs. The faint odor of smoke lingered in the cool air even this far below ground.

"I have an idea," said Fausan. "Hear me out. Once the Caobiu get into the city, we jump a few soldiers and throw on their uniforms and walk through the gates."

Bhasani sputtered. "That's the stupidest thing I ever heard, and I live with you."

"What's wrong with that plan?" he asked.

The drowned fist ticked a finger. "First, you're old. The Cinder Legions are a professional army. They don't have geriatrics in their ranks." She ticked another finger. "Second, you're fat. You're not going to fit into any armor unless it's barding." She ticked her third finger. "Lastly, the Caobiu hierarchy is complicated, involving hundreds of ranks with dozens of salutes and titles, not to mention rituals and pass phrases. Even if you weren't caught for being old and fat, you wouldn't make it past three Caobiu officers before they realize you're fake."

Fausan wrinkled his nose. "But you still love me, right?"

"I'm just with you because I don't feel like cooking or cleaning the house."

"Beautiful Boy was being dramatic, right?" asked Fausan. "Killing a high lord cannot be the only way to ensure peace."

"Not at all," Taishi had to admit. "Beautiful Boy's not wrong, but not wrong doesn't necessarily mean right." She looked over at Sohn, who was eyeing a young thug who had been following them since they left the restaurant, no doubt sent by the Worst Boys to see them out of their turf. "Don't even think about recruiting a disciple from these ranks, Bright Light."

"I've given up on regaining my lineage." Sohn sounded mournful. "My terrible brother has won."

She might as well tell him. "I'm sorry to tell you, but your brother Grandmaster Soa Sohi died eight years ago."

Sohn brightened. "Then *I* won!"

"His son Sohnsho runs the Pan family lineage now."

His grin was ear-to-ear. "Who cares about that? Outliving my conniving little snot of a brother is winning enough. Victory is mine!"

The three weaved their way across the buried ward from the cramped underground caverns up the long winding slopes to the surface. The streets were quiet this early in the morning, shortly after dawn. The city was waking slowly with only a few souls about running errands. Most stayed indoors now. Pitched battles could erupt in many of the wards at any given time. Fortunately, most battles were waged after breakfast. No one bothered them as they found their way back through the narrow streets, toward the top side. Unsurprisingly, they could hear fighting the closer they got to the entrance leading out of the ward. Taishi began to cough and sneeze the moment they reached fresh air. The smell outside was tainted by smoke and burning flowers. Her sinuses had worsened with the years. It was bad enough for her allergies with all those blasted plants in the city. Now it was unbearable. Stupid City of Flowers.

"The fighting is moving this direction," said Bhasani.

"The heavy smoke is drifting south from the next ward over." Sohn sniffed the air as they stepped out to ugly streaks of smoke crisscrossing the sky. The acrid stench of char burned her nostrils, the wails of humanity a background crescendo that then lulled.

City fighting was the tenth pit of hell. They were now trapped inside the largest city in the world going up against the largest army in the world. It would soon rain red over the city, soaked from souls on both sides. The army may have already been beaten on the wall, but the Caobiu would find Vauzan difficult to crush. This was a martial city. The invaders would bleed for every ward, every block, every street.

The small group came closer together as they joined the throngs of people milling about. Many, mostly families with children and elderly, were picking their way farther west, away from the fighting, while the young and strong—war artists, volunteers, retired veterans—were heading east to form volunteer corps to defend their beloved city.

Fausan, who once claimed to have led several defenses of keeps and fortified towns during his day, surveyed the streets. "Once the Caobiu commit to fighting in the city, there will be cracks in their blockade. We may have a chance to fight our way out. No need for the underworld to smuggle us. It's risky, though."

"That might be our only option at this point," said Taishi. "Let's round up the children. We need to reach the temple."

Their small party went against the throes of traffic, meeting the gazes of many stone-faced war artists moving in the opposite direction. Taishi admitted there was a part of her that yearned to walk alongside them. A glorious and romantic death for a noble cause was the most any of them could hope for.

They soon crossed into a ward that had become an active battlefield. Several flaming pitches arced by overhead with one slamming into a building just down the block, knocking the walls down. The fire that started jumped to the next building, then the entire street was soon ablaze. Smoke and sweat stung Taishi's eyes as they picked their way through the ward. There were skirmishes between anarchists, thugs, and magistrates, but otherwise the streets weren't too disorderly, just tense. The citizens of Vauzan were not fans of looting. Most loved their city. Even their underworlds frowned upon the act. It was often said that Shulan had the most civil criminals in the Enlightened States.

They passed by a city block with a building at the corner of the intersection ablaze. The four masters watched, anxious and horrified, as the flames leaped from one roof to the next. Bhasani stopped at a broken, ramshackle corner storefront just as the wooden frame sparked like a matchstick.

Taishi urged her forward. "We can't save everyone. Keep moving."

The drowned fist's gaze was locked on the second-floor window. "Taishi, there are people trapped inside."

"If we don't make it back to the base of the temple hill before the Caobiu, we'll be cut off from the children."

"There's children up there right now!" Bhasani pointed toward the second story. "Little ones, Taishi!"

Damn it. "Fine. Sohn, Fausan, make it quick."

Sohn took three long steps, bounded to the second floor, and smashed the window. He disappeared in a thick plume of smoke and then finally reappeared holding two toddlers like a sack of rice over his left arm, while holding an elderly woman by the waist in his right. Meanwhile, Fausan had trotted—that was the fastest he could go—down to the middle of the street. He noted a water collector sitting on a platform on the hill above the endangered row of homes. Fausan shot his bullets—small round iron kill-shot marble balls—striking one of the supports holding the water collector up. The wooden beam popped and splintered as the bullets struck. Fausan's arms were snapping around as if he were conducting a symphony of violence, sending bullet after bullet at his target. It was a good reminder that the God of Gamblers was still one of the most dangerous war artists alive. Within moments, the water collector exploded, drenching the building next to the fire. It didn't put out the fire, but preventing it from spreading was just as important.

The whipfinger master was about to work on the next water collector when a crowd appeared on the other end of the street. He retreated back to them, wheezing, and pointed back to where he came from. "Trouble. Caobiu vanguard."

"We cannot get bogged down with these red rats," Taishi hissed.

"They're forcing the fleeing people back into the burning buildings! Where's the Shulan forces? We have to do something."

"No, this is not important. We'll go around. Find another way."

There was a scream, a little girl. Another followed it. A group of women, children, and elderly that had just escaped a residential building were being herded back in by a squad of armed Caobiu soldiers. Several more of the Cinder Legions joined them a few moments later.

"Taishi!" This time it was Bhasani hissing. "We can't."

Taishi bowed her head. Getting bogged down was inevitable. "Make it quick."

It didn't take long for Bhasani to melt their brains into pea soup. Taishi marveled at the drowned fist master's supple grace and flow as she tied up the minds of an entire squad of Caobiu soldiers and ordered them to charge into their own people. She spewed chaos from her compulsions, sending them into a mindless rage as they hacked and clawed their own people. Within moments, they lay dead at her feet in the same amount of time it took Sohn to get a kill.

Taishi urged everyone on as soon as the last Caobiu soldier fell. There was no time. The larger wave was fast approaching and was about to wash over them. They took to the side alleys, avoiding the pitched battles being waged while at the same time watching the trajectory of the fire raining down upon the city. Masses of soldiers in red and yellow collided into walls of defensive brown and gray. Those from the lunar court ambushed enemy squads leaking from buildings and hidden places. It was sheer chaos as the two sides ebbed and flowed until they mixed, and then it was impossible to tell friend or foe.

The four masters had just come into view of Peony Peak when the ward square they were crossing suddenly became flooded with two opposing groups of soldiers, with Taishi's group sandwiched between them. The Caobiu were three times the size of the Shulan guards. The lopsided encounter was decidedly one-sided until a volunteer corps of war artists joined them. Their ranks were bolstered a moment later by locals spilling out of the buildings wielding shovels, axes, and pitchforks. Their numbers swelled but still paled in comparison to the Caobiu line.

Fausan looked dubious. "Maybe we should get out of their way."

"Nah, I was made for this." Sohn adjusted the spiked buckler strapped to his forearm, and then broke into a trot. Taishi reached forward and tugged at his arm. She shook her head. "We'll go around the pedway and cross underground. We don't have time to fight this."

He pointed at the melee. "Taishi, they can't win without us. Come on, four masters. We can make a difference. Maybe we can't defend the city from the Caobiu, but we can win *this* battle. Besides, it'll be fun."

Taishi's sense of righteousness yearned for battle. It was becoming more and more difficult to do the right thing. "Winning this battle means nothing. We stay the course."

"The city could fall if we do nothing!" Sohn yelled.

"Vauzan has already fallen!" she snapped.

He spat at her feet. "You've lost your edge, Taishi!"

"I'm the only one still with a razor's edge," she snarled. "The lot of you are here itching to fight when the real task is the Prophesied Hero of the Tiandi. These people mean nothing. Everything means nothing if he is captured or killed."

"The legendary Ling Taishi was a righteous woman," said Sohn. "She would never have allowed these atrocities."

"That woman is dead."

Fausan crossed his arms. "No, she's not. She's standing right in front of me still, but she didn't die. She just lost her nerve. She's lost her honor."

That was as straightforward as it got. They were right. She was wrong. Taishi nodded, somber. "You're right. I have."

Sohn shook his head. "Well, I haven't, so I'm going to do something about it."

"This is a terrible time for you to discover your moral compass, Bright Light," Taishi growled.

"I know," he replied. "It's pissing me off too."

Fausan took two steps toward Sohn and turned back to face Taishi and Bhasani. "I'll go with him, you know, because that's what dumb brothers do."

"Men," muttered Bhasani. She turned to Taishi. "The kids will be fine a little longer. I'm going to fight and die alongside my love."

"Fine." Taishi heaved a sigh and drew her hollow sword. "But make it quick."

CHAPTER FIFTEEN

THE RIGHT MOTIVATION

Jian and Sonaya held hands at the northeastern corner parapet of the temple, stone-faced and speechless, watching from atop the walls of the Vauzan Temple of the Tiandi as the Caobiu poured into their beloved city. He had heard hundreds of stories about sieges. They were popular in Zhuun literature. Every great romance began during a siege. There was something so romantic about how Burning Hearts books painted sieges. The vantage point this high up Peony Peak gave them a perfect view of the disaster unfolding below.

The reality was there was nothing remotely romantic or exciting about sieges. It was awful to slowly watch your home burn and everything you cherish be consumed by the fire.

The first breach happened where a massive war wagon rammed up against the battlement and was vomiting soldiers from its cavity along the southeastern corner of the city. The second was a collapsed portion of the north wall near the corner parapet, which had been decimated by concentrated artillery fire. The last, which was still being contested, was a back-and-forth battle over control of the main gates. The Cinder Legions had captured it over the past hour, but the resilient and desperate defenders managed to take it back before the gates could be opened. Jian's stomach churned. He felt helpless and angry. Helpless that his adopted home was besieged and in flames. Angry that the life he had built here in Vauzan was being taken away from him, and there was nothing he could do about it. He felt shame and guilt that his friends and loved ones were out there risking their lives in the city's defense, while he hid here, behind the temple walls.

By mid-morning, the Cinder Legions had pushed deep enough that they were butting up against Peony Peak. The tension roiling in Jian's gut increased as he watched the sea of red and yellow swarm over the square. The Caobiu vanguard had surrounded the Eye of the Luster Ward from two sides and rushed in like a flash flood, quickly overwhelming the barricade. The soldiers at the checkpoint, supported by local war artists, managed to prevent a total rout before regrouping at the road leading up to the temple, at least for the time being.

And still Jian was doing nothing.

His stomach churned as the brown-and-red-clad city defenders, joined by random citizens, struggled to hold back the red-and-yellow waves of Caobiu. His heart beat double time and his breath became labored as his body anticipated the need for violence. He was barred from leaving the temple, and he had promised Taishi—especially after the kidnapping a few years back—to obey her commands. He still blamed himself for the events that led to Hwang Kasa's death and culminated with their surrender to the Shulan. So many of his friends got hurt because of him.

A crowd had formed outside the temple gates as panicked residents of Peony Peak gathered to find refuge. They pounded on the heavy wood of the double gates, pleading to the monks to let them inside. As if anywhere would be safe once the Caobiu broke through these walls.

Jian continued to throw scowls at Brother Solum, who was commanding the monks to keep the gates barred. Why weren't the temple monks defending the city? The giant Hansoos and the hundred war monks and nuns surely could make a difference, yet they cowered like weasels while the city burned.

After hours of watching this mind-numbing horror unfold, Jian had had enough. His heart hurt too much. He couldn't tolerate this pacificism any longer. He cupped his hands around his mouth and aimed it at Solum. "Open the gates, you massive pinky finger!"

"Jian . . ." Sonaya tried to pull him back before he fell over the side, but he shook her off.

"Open the blasted gates! They'll die out there!"

He finally got the giant war monk's attention. Solum looked up and glared, and then he continued as if Jian didn't exist. He hollered a reminder: "Remember, nothing in, nothing out. On the templeabbot's orders."

Templeabbot, eh? Well, Jian knew one person at the temple whose authority superseded Templeabbot Lee Mori's. Their entire stinking religion was based upon Jian. Maybe it was time—past time!—to put his exalted standing to good use. He stepped onto the railing and was about to drop to the ground level when stern hands grabbed his collar and yanked him back like an errant child.

Sonaya held a fistful of his robe. "Don't do this, Jian. It's not our place."

"It's absolutely my place." He glanced across the courtyard and roared. "I'm the—"

The drowned fist daughter yanked him around, her hand clamped on his mouth. "Revealing yourself right now, just as the city is about to fall, would be the worst decision you'll ever make, and I've seen you make plenty of bad ones."

Her grip was shockingly strong. "Like what? Name one."

Sonaya proceeded to tick her fingers, giving his cheek a squeeze with each one. "There was the time you chugged a jug of zuijo and then serenaded every girl at the bar, telling them you were the Savior of the Zhuun. Off-key, I might add."

The color in his face drained. "You knew about that?"

"I was there, pumpkin brain."

"Oh." Shame filled him. He mumbled, "It was Hachi's birthday."

"It's all right, Five Champ. I would have been annoyed if I hadn't been laughing so hard," she replied. "Then there was the time you tried to help that little old lady who had just burgled the Syndicate Underworld."

"She was little and old," he mumbled.

"The time you and Kaiyu put hellpepper flakes into the incense vase and then smoked out the entire main temple on a Tenth Day Prayer."

"Someone told Kaiyu that hellpeppers turned sweet when cooked."

"When you boil it, Jian, not smoke it," she said. "And let's not forget that you tried to rescue a monkey from a tree hanging over the waterfall."

Jian looked sullen. "It looked like a cat."

"Or how about that time you challenged that underworld thug to a fight in front of his fifteen friends?"

Jian crossed his arms. "He was bothering you!"

"I don't need you to save me, Jian." She stuck out her tongue. "I'm a whisper witch. I was going to make him pay for our entire dinner and bar tab until you wasted good beef noodle soup by throwing it in his face." Sonaya took a deep breath. "What I'm trying to say is, your heart is in the right place, but your head is often stuck up your ass. So don't get involved with Solum. He's just doing his duty."

Jian deflated. She was right. "It's still not right. We should be saving others, not just ourselves."

"It's easy to be righteous when you're not responsible for the temple and everyone inside it. You're a good person, Jian. That's what I love about you, but you cloud your goodness with stupidity." She grasped his shoulders. "You're the Prophesied Hero of the Tiandi. There will be times you need to weigh your goodness against the greater good."

He stared at her large luminous eyes. "Did you say you love me?"

She sniffed. "Love *about* you." Sonaya pointed at the left side of his heart. "The rest of you could use work. Seriously, though, leave the monks alone. You're a guest in their home."

"But . . ." Jian felt so lost. What good was it to be the hero if he couldn't do anything? The prophecy spent thousands of pages speaking, singing, rhyming about his arrival. It gave detailed accounts on how to search for him and how to name him and even the shape of his nose! But the prophecy provided no guidance on what Jian was supposed to do after he was found. When was he supposed to fight the Eternal Khan? Where would they fight? How could he hope to defeat this immortal god monster? Should he bring an army or just a couple of friends, or was it a duel?

He was so tired of this legacy. Where were the instructions on how to fulfill his destiny? At least give him some clues! The pressure caused his knees to buckle. Fortunately, Sonaya was there to hold him up.

She wrapped her arms around his elbow. "Come on, this horror opera is doing no one any good. Let's head back to the cottage. I'll brew a pot of lavender tea, and you can rub my toes."

That sounded more appealing than watching the end of the world. "Even your little pinky toes?"

"Leave my little girls alone." Sonaya slapped him lightly on his shoulder, and then her hand slid down his arm until she held his hand. She began to lead him away. "Are you calm now, Champion of the Five Under Heaven, rescuer of feral animals stuck in trees?"

His face flushed. "Calm's not the right word, but I'm feeling something." Their noses touched. It wasn't accidental. A surge of warmth enveloped him. Her face was right next to his, their lips nearly touching. She was using compulsion on him, just a touch. Jian could resist it if he wanted to—his mind had become better fortified during his studies under the two drowned fists—but he didn't mind. He enjoyed it, even. Their lips were almost touching. Maybe sieges were good settings for Burning Hearts romance stories after all.

"Good." Then, as always during intimate moments, Sonaya pulled away, leaving him panting and dissatisfied but mostly confused. If she ever met him halfway, he would be there waiting for her. But every time, she would falter. No, not falter. Ras Sonaya was her own woman. She was fond of him, that much he knew, but not enough to want to be with him, at least not in the way he hoped.

The heat left him, and he felt like he'd taken a cold dunk in the Yukian River.

Jian was still sorting through his chaotic emotions when he thought he heard his name. He looked around and pulled away from Sonaya, following the sound toward the outer wall, and then along its length, heading toward the front gate.

"Is everything all right, Jian?" Sonaya asked, following.

Jian looked over the wall. The walkway along his other side was manned by thirty monks and nuns armed with spears and bows ready to take out anyone foolish enough to attempt to scale the walls. It disturbed him that the Tiandi monks were ready to kill their own people and not the invading army. Directly below where they stood, Solum was still shouting orders. The crowds outside had ballooned, and there was fear that the mob was going to try to break through the gates.

Then Jian heard it one more time: his name carrying in the wind. Someone was shouting his name. He spun in a circle, and then realized it was coming from somewhere outside the temple walls. He leaned over the side and listened. It sounded like a high-pitched cry mostly buried by the discomforted anxiety of the humanity below: "Lu Hiro! Lu Hiro! Please, I must speak to Lu Hiro."

Jian homed in on the sound and pulled it toward him on the wind and then traced back toward where it came. He caught sight of a young woman, an older teenager in fine university robes struggling to push her way toward the main gates.

"Lu Hiro!"

Someone needed him. Jian stepped up toward the edge of the wall.

"What are you doing?" Sonaya reached over and grabbed hold of his arm.

"There's someone down there who needs my help."

"Everyone down there needs help."

"She is calling for me specifically! They need help!"

"Lu Hiro, Lu Hiro!" By now the girl was directly below Jian as the crowd shoved her around, threatening to sandwich her against the wall. "I need to speak with Lu Hiro. His friend is hurt!"

"Hold up. I sense strong compulsion." Sonaya concentrated. "There's another mind witch about. Don't listen. Fight it, Jian. It's a trap. Remember your training." The drowned fist grimaced as if suffering from a migraine.

It was too late. The compulsion, reinforced by his desire to help, was too strong for his already wavering fortitude. Jian shook loose from the drowned fist and then leaped over the edge of the wall, down to the bubbling cauldron of desperate humanity below.

CHAPTER SIXTEEN

FOUND OUT

Qisami promptly forgot about killing Mubaan Soy. Accidents weren't uncommon. People fell over the pit bridges all the time. What was one more rag-brained noble born with a silver spoon up his ass? Soy wasn't well liked anyway. No one was going to mourn him. She had all but forgotten he'd existed, except for one small fatal flaw.

Three missing from management—Soy and the two guards—was not considered a small matter. She had heard rumblings about the warden opening an investigation but hadn't thought much of it. This was a penal colony. Who cared if some lowlife noble disappeared in the pits? It wasn't like anyone was going to go all the way to the bottom of the mine to investigate. But apparently, they found the bloodstains on the bridge leading to the elevator on the fifth level.

Then it all went downhill from there.

Qisami had joined the Goons the next evening after their hard day's work chiseling deep in level fifty-one. One of the spelunkers had uncovered a large vantam vein ripe for excavation. The warden was positively giddy about the find.

Management had also approved Hair Bear's request to hold a memorial for Snoutnose. The Goons had been fond of the piggy-nosed man, although it was probably just an excuse to drink. In any case, Qisami was here for the barrel of zuijo. The bosses stockpiled their supply of alcohol like a pool of koi hoarding coins, doling it out strategically to stave off unrest.

The Goons were by far the most difficult and violent bunch at the Happy Glow, so keeping them content was just good business. They were a loyal, tight-knit group for a bunch of murderers and convicts. The lunar court had their own rules about honor and brotherhood, and that held true even in a penal colony, perhaps especially in a place such as this because that was all any of them had left.

Qisami sat between Cyyk and Badgasgirl as the Goons traded stories about their deceased bunkmate while drinking a cup of badly fermented homemade zuijo. With every round, the Goons poured a cup of water onto the ground. Zuijo, even badly fermented and terrible tasting, was too valuable to waste on symbolism. It surprised her that Snoutnose was genuinely liked by the rest of his crew. Cyyk actually considered him a friend.

Qisami kept shifting in her seat. For some reason, she couldn't get comfortable. It was a weird out-of-body experience, seeing the consequences of her actions. Murder never bothered her before, especially some lowlife as useless as Snoutnose, but here she was, sitting with a group of fools wasting words and soliloquies over someone she had killed.

Fortunately, it distracted her from the consequences of her actions. Qisami and the Goons were halfway toward getting properly drunk when a group of prison guards marched into the common area at the center of the colony's five corners. It couldn't be because of Snoutnose. No one liked him *that* much.

In fact, it looked like the entire garrison had been roused, which was unusual. The last time the warden called every hand on deck was when a group of Xing tried to stage a rebellion at the colony. The warden had entertained the colony with a good old-fashioned drawing and quartering of their leaders for a solid week. Nothing happening these days was as ripe or interesting as an uprising.

Until Warden Sunxia appeared. He signaled to a guard, who shot a red signal flare into the air. Qisami, head heavy, looked up as the bursts of red flowered across the blue sky. How pretty. Maybe Snout-nose was more beloved than she thought. The carousing stopped, if not the drinking, as many pairs of eyes turned toward the warden. Not Qisami, however. She still had her back to Sunxia, burying her face in her foul drink.

Warden Sunxia's voice carried over the biting wind. "Citizens of our illustrious home, we live in this desolate, hostile place where even the land, air, and sky wishes us dead, courtesy of our"—he clicked his tongue—"Duchess of Caobiu." A chorus of boos rained down at the mention of Sunri. Sunxia continued. "Regardless of why we are here—"

"I'm innocent!" someone shouted, followed by rough laughter.

"—we are a community. We persevere and survive by relying on each other. Though many harbor resentment toward those in management, we are your brothers, comrades, fellow victims of circumstance. We are brothers and sisters here in these harsh lands. We depend on each other for strength."

Qisami sniffed. "Your title is literally warden."

Only one group here was sleeping on soft beds and eating roasted duck, crispy dumplings, and ginger cookies while the other sustained itself on gruel. Grumbles and snickers and catcalls erupted around her.

Sunxia ignored them and continued. "So it pains me to uncover a sinister plot that now threatens the delicate balance we've achieved here at the Happy Glow Retirement Home. Bring out the traitors."

Qisami felt a rare sinking feeling in her stomach. The last time she felt this way was when her father had summoned her to his office to inform her that he was paying his brood atonement with her life. A few moments later, she heard the unmistakable high-pitched squeal of Ta-wara Ito followed by the nursemaid's tired, worn wail. They were soon followed by several of the Lawkan as they were herded into the center.

"We have a confession from those within the Lawkan corner that they have opened a breeding farm. Babies, in this unholy place," Sunxia continued. "Weak, useless infants who will do nothing but sap the delicate balance of our colony. More mouths to feed. More resources to expend. Wasting is the gravest crime anyone can commit here at the Happy Glow Retirement Home."

Qisami tried to ignore and tune out the warden. Those silly pruneskins had been found out, just like she had predicted. They were as good as dead. Management was going to throw them into the pit mine or plunk them full of arrows. Again, not her problem. She had warned them! Qisami threw her drink back in one gulp. She gasped as the oily zuijo burned her throat, and then she stood to leave. She didn't need to witness this spectacle.

"And you, Chopstick!" Warden Sunxia said before she could take three steps.

Qisami swerved back to face him. Everything swayed. "Yes, Warden."

"You paid their barracks a recent visit, and had no clue of this treachery, not even an inkling of this nursery? A whimper or a bawling babe or a dirty diaper?"

She shrugged. "I just do what I'm told, boss."

"It's good you follow orders so well, because I have another task for you," the warden spat. "Find the nursery and bring back the evidence. Beat the location out of one of the pruneskins if you must. We'll give those mewling monstrosities a quick and painless death. We are not cruel. That is, unless you animals are desperate for meat."

Outrage erupted from the Lawkans, but everyone was shaken. The rules were explicit about infants. This was too cruel a place to bring life into this world. A quick death was the most merciful option. There was usually one or two a cycle, but this was not just one random child. It was several, many. An uproar grew but then died. The crowd silenced.

Qisami shook her head. "I'm not collecting kids for the slaughter."

"You forget your place, 1439." The warden flicked a hand, and four guards converged on her. "Dogs don't decide what commands to follow."

"Find someone else to do that work."

Sunxia grimaced. "Goon squad, 1439 is returning to your barrack. Her privileged days are no more. She will be joining you underground."

Hair Bear, standing next to Qisami, patted her on the back. "Welcome back."

She offered a thumbs-up and turned her back to the warden. "I'll go get my things."

The warden's eyes narrowed. "Take her in for questioning."

Fungusfeet and Badgasgirl exchanged glances, and then Fungusfeet actually reached for her, that bastard. She was insulted but not surprised. Still, she thought the first of the Goons to come at her wouldn't be from Cyyk's crew. Before Fungusfeet touched her, Cyyk rushed past Qisami and leveled his clowder-mate with an overhand punch.

He then feinted at Badgasgirl, who pulled away, and looked at Sunxia. "I don't think so."

"Take them all, then," said Sunxia. "We'll question them before throwing them into the pit."

"Thanks for getting my back, grunt." Qisami stood back-to-back with Cyyk. It was like old times.

"You didn't tell me about the kids, Kiki," he accused her.

"I didn't tell you I killed Snoutnose either," she retorted.

The broodbaby looked shocked. "Why would you do that?"

"Same reason why you just decked Fungusfeet."

Cyyk frowned. "Dumb loyalty?"

"Something like that." Qisami hated her reasons, but she owed it to Akiya and Akiana. She would forever be pissed about that. Most sins were forgivable, but there was no forgiving murdering those two girls. One day, Qisami was going to find Chiafana, Caobiu's Minister of Critical Purpose, and claw her eyes out with her nails. And then she'd wear the bitch's face like a mask during the Lunar Full Moons.

"Are you all right, Kiki?" asked Cyyk. "You zoned out there for a second."

"Just daydreaming," she replied, focusing on the five guards converging on them. "Guess we fight it out."

"Can we be us?"

Qisami considered. There was no point in cowing to management's threats anymore. "Sure, let's play it back how we used to. Worst thing that can happen is we end up dead."

"That would be an improvement to our current situation." Cyyk broke into a grin, and both shadowkills stepped into different shadows just as the warden's guards tried to seize them. The perpetual day made the shadows weak and small, but it was just enough to work.

It. Became. A. Massacre.

Two shadowkills surprising two hundred management and guards was certainly suicide, but it was a good way to die, noble even. The nearest guards never recovered from their initial shock. Qisami appeared behind one and yanked him backward off his feet. She finished him with a quick punch to the throat. She tripped another charging blindly at her, sending him diving headfirst into a crop of rocks.

Then the shanks came out.

Contrary to common belief, shadowkills fared well in pitched battles. Their kind thrived with chaos. She stayed low, hidden in the sea of flailing bodies and confused guards. The moment anyone got a bead on her, she would find the nearest shadow and slip in. It was an advanced and dangerous maneuver, and far trickier to pull off during a melee. People moved continuously during battles, as did their shadows. If a shadowkill didn't time and execute their entry perfectly, they could get cut in half while attempting a moving shadowstep. She once witnessed one of her training pool siblings lose both legs just below the knee. That was a lesson she had taken to heart.

Qisami continued to wreck guards and former nobles alike. Prison garrisons were never armed with quality weapons because more often than not, those weapons would be turned on management. Lastly, prison guards usually weren't the best stock of soldiers. No officer or elite candidate went into the military to take a post at a penal colony, and the ones sentenced here were the definition of bad soldiers. Right now, a third of the guards in the center were milling about in confusion, while another third were standing frozen in abject terror, leaving the last third to get wrecked by two shadowkills.

Qisami snapped one of her shanks into the knee of one noble, and then swept both legs of another, flipping him heels up as his head crashed on the hard, frozen ground. She skittered to the side and pounced like an alley cat, punching her last shank into the back of another noble with Qisami riding his back like a monkey. She realized her error a moment too late. This guy was tall, and she stood out like a virgin at a brothel. Three guards close by converged on her.

Experience and trickery kicked in. Qisami swung to his front and used her weight to yank him on top of her. She slipped into the shadow beneath him as he fell and came up a blink later using her momentum to shoot out from beneath a large, beefy noble standing off to the right. Qisami had no idea how anyone stayed so plump out here, but his ample shadow gave her plenty of room to maneuver. She rose out of the ground, leading with an uppercut that connected with big boy's groin, lifting him off the ground. The pain from her blow must have short-circuited his brain because he was unconscious—or possibly dead. She had never known a testicle punch to be a killing blow.

"By the Tiandi, a monster!" an inmate cried out.

"Rawr." She hissed and bared her teeth.

"It's a devil." That one dropped to his knees in prayer for salvation to the Tiandi.

"A shadowkill!" At least someone got it right.

The brief lull in the brawl allowed Qisami to check on Cyyk to see if he was still alive. She watched, amused, as he charged a guard wielding double clubs. Qisami patted herself on the back. She had taught her broodbaby grunt well. He was coming into his own as a war artist, even if she would never admit that to his face. Cyyk had even developed his own style alongside the echo striking they used back in his previous Longxian school. Whereas Qisami used her shadowkill abilities to leverage angles, surprises, and quick kills, Cyyk used those same abilities to intimidate and batter his opponents. His style wasn't what anyone would consider shadowkill best practice, but Qisami approved of it, nevertheless.

Her former grunt closed half the distance in three long bounds but then swerved to the side, dropping into a shadow before popping back up in front of the guard. The poor man startled and tried to bat at Cyyk with the club as if he were waving a flyswatter, and then took a powerful punch to the gut that lifted him several feet off the ground before falling flat on his face. Then Cyyk shadowstepped again and came out in front of another pair. This time, his arms blurred as he sparred with the two—courtesy of his previous training back in Jiayi. He disarmed and beat the two men into the wet dirt with their own clubs.

"Kill those mutts!" A voice cut above the din of the brawl. That was Sunxia. Qisami homed in on him. If she couldn't kill Sunri directly, she was going to do the next best thing. There were about ten bodies between them, but that wasn't a big deal. Not with this sad bunch.

The violence had spread. Many in the Lawkan corner had joined the fight, swarming management from behind. By now, the entire Happy Glow Retirement Home had exploded into a riot wavering toward a full-blown rebellion.

Qisami had her eye on Sunxia, however, and methodically picked her way toward the warden, taking out a noble here, flipping a guard onto his back there, and snapping the knee of an unfortunate someone who was fleeing Cyyk and ran into her. That was lucky for Qisami because she had run out of shanks, and this person was bristling with five knives. After that, everything happened quickly. A group of guards jumped on Cyyk to her right, but then he was saved by an even larger group of Goons. A noble stabbed Hair Bear with a spear, and then both men were knocked down by a bull rush of riot shields.

There was an explosion in the building just to the east of them, temporarily stopping the frenetic melee. Everyone paused in mid-killing as they stared at the plume of smoke erupting from the kitchen. That annoyed Qisami. What cracked egg would set the colony's only kitchen on fire? What was the point of winning an uprising if everyone was going to starve after? Well, one worry at a time. She continued to fight her way toward the warden, batting down another guard and two more nobles before finally coming face-to-face with the large man.

Sunxia stared at her, enraged yet bewildered. "A bloody real shadowkill, eh? All this time you were at the end of my leash. If I had only known, dog." He spat. "Wait until the Consortium catches wind of this. They'll pay enough coin, I'll earn my way back to court."

Qisami advanced on him. A sharp twang barked in her left ear, and she noticed a blur out of the corner of her eye. Even in her prime, Qisami wasn't skilled enough to catch a crossbow bolt mid-flight. She had a bag full of war arts tricks but snatching things out of the air had never been one of them. Fortunately, this evening had shown time and time again that management here at the penal colony did not have the best weapons. In this case, she had plenty of time to see the warped bolt warbling toward her like a pregnant dove. She reached out to snatch it from the air. Unfortunately, she was not at her best and she muffed the catch.

The crossbow thunked into her shoulder and shattered, torquing her in a circle before she collapsed. Qisami grimaced and stared at the broken shaft sticking out of her chest. It didn't go deep, nor did it hit any vital organs, but it was awfully embarrassing. She looked up as Sunxia approached.

"You must not have been good at your job, Chopstick," he snorted. "No wonder you ended up here."

Qisami gritted her teeth. "I'm out of practice."

She looked to the side for Cyyk in the slim hope that he could save her. One quick glance showed her that he was overwhelmed. Five guards managed to get their claws on him and drag him to the floor. Too much weight on a shadowkill prevented them from entering the darkness. He might as well be trying to shadowstep with a horse.

Sunxia raised a boot over her as if about to squash a bug. Qisami squirmed and tried to roll to the side, but sharp lightning pain jolted up her spine, momentarily freezing her. What a piss-poor way to die. How embarrassing, and strangely fitting. Such an ignoramus end of a former diamond-tier shadowkill.

Just as the warden was about to crush her skull, something blind-sided him and knocked him off his feet, followed by people trampling him. Someone tripped over her. A boot kicked her in the face. A foot crunched on Qisami's thigh, another on her shoulder right where the crossbow bolt had hit it. A scream escaped her as she curled into a ball and covered her head. A woman shouted over the din of the fight-ing, and the trampling stopped. Several long seconds passed. Qisami pried an eye open and peeked between two fingers. There, standing before her, was the nursemaid, of all people. Her back was turned to Qisami and she had her arms spread. The woman was shielding her from a crowd of Lawkans that had just rushed into the fight.

After the immediate danger had passed, the woman turned to her and offered a hand. "Are you all right, child?" Qisami accepted the help.

"Thanks, Boobs." She considered the woman. All this time she thought her a simple nursemaid, but it was obvious that she carried authority. People listened to her. "Who are you?"

"My name is Tawara Saia, but that's not important right now. You're safe. Our debt to you is paid, as is yours to us. Ito was right to trust you."

Qisami startled. "Tawara? The Mother of the River is your sister?"

The woman shook her head. "Tawara Issa was my wife."

Then it dawned on her. Qisami had killed the woman's lover in front of her. The tension on her face every time she had seen her wasn't fear or trepidation, but grief.

She pointed at the crowd. "You did my people a great service today standing up to management. You were the spark that lit the fire."

The Lawkans, though the smallest group at the Happy Glow, had more to fight for than any other faction. They had united under a com-mon cause and hit the guards from behind, overrunning them and scattering those management had left. The rest of the nobles soon dispersed, and it became a matter of cleaning up. The guards, realiz-ing that they were outnumbered, began to flee or surrender. At first, one by one, and then in groups. The remaining nobles suddenly found themselves without protection and followed suit.

Qisami found Cyyk a few moments later, bruised and beaten, but no worse for wear. He had ended up at the bottom of a pile of bodies, which probably saved his life. She hauled him to his feet.

"You good, broodbaby?"

He spat out a tooth. "I haven't had that much fun since those mute men jumped me back in Allanto."

She nodded. "It's good to feel alive again."

The fighting had died down. The remnants of management had fled and were cornered in the lower levels of the mine. There were still sporadic brawls between management and inmates, but the guards were outnumbered, and they no longer carried superior weapons courtesy of the Shulan breaking into the armory. The leaders of the other corners were meeting at Sunxia's former office, and there were talks about creating a council to manage the colony. The rest of the Happy Glow Retirement Home penal colony had settled into a weary and wary uneasy peace, with each group tending to their wounded.

Tawara Ito found her after the fighting had ended. "Chopstick, my stepmother wanted me to inform you that we've retrieved all the babies from the nursery, and are preparing proper quarters for them in the main building. They'll now have the chance to grow up in a bright and warm building."

Until Sunri finds out what happened and butchers the lot of you. Qisami kept the words to herself.

To her dismay, Ito rushed to embrace her, which probably would have earned him a shank in the gut if she had any left. She pushed him away. Hugs were weird. "Touch me and I'll eat your spleen."

If the young Ito took offense, he didn't show it. "Our people control the colony now. The other groups are larger. They won't listen to us, but they might if you help us. Will you?"

"I still don't like you," she quipped. "I don't want any part of this."

"Listen," pressed the Lawkan boy. "You were the first one to stand up to the warden. People respect you. Will you help us build a new life, Chopstick? A fresh start?"

Fear and respect were different sides of the same coin, but the point still stood. Tawara Ito was trying to recruit her to his side. Others would too. Qisami had to admit that it felt nice to be wanted again, even if it was to be a powerful player in a stupid prison. It was still a drop from her diamond-tier status, but it was better than where she was this morning.

She let out a long sigh. "Fine, I'll help keep the pigs in line until you guys figure stuff out, but I want to move into the nicer digs. The warden's quarters, and better food too."

He ignored that. "With your support, we can finally build a better future for the colony."

Ugh, excessive gratitude was annoying. "Don't get your hopes up. Sunri won't tolerate this once she learns that her prized penal colony and main ore factory just went to shit."

Tawara Ito did not seem daunted. "We can worry about that tomorrow. Today's victory is the first step toward building a brighter future for not only us but also our future children—"

An arrow streaked through the air and punched into the top of his head, killing him instantly. Two more plunked into the ground next to Qisami. An instant later, the sky began to thunderstorm more arrows accompanied by hails of fist-sized stones.

Qisami looked around. Who was attacking them now? It couldn't be the Caobiu. They weren't expected for another two months, at least!

Then an unmistakable high-pitched shriek cut through the air, shattering the freshly minted peace.

CHAPTER SEVENTEEN

CHAMPION

"No, don't go. Jian, I mean, Hiro, wait!" Sonaya shouted, but it was too late. "I can't follow you down the wall, you ass!"

Jian had forgotten about her when he heard the plea for help. By the time he realized his mistake, he had already leaped over the wall, his fingers and feet raking the chiseled stone as he skimmed the slope toward the boiling mass of people trying to batter their way through the closed wooden gates of the Vauzan Temple of the Tiandi.

He homed in on the woman who needed him. She was young, wearing university robes, with a sharp but pretty face. Her headdress revealed her to be a logician-in-training. Jian pushed away from the wall and landed in a small clearing, squirming through the packed crowd toward her. She waved frantically when he neared, and he pushed his voice to her on an air current.

"What's the matter, miss?"

The girl's wild gaze snapped to his. "Are you brave Lu Hiro?"

Why, yes. Yes, he was brave Lu Hiro. He nodded, his chest puffing. She pointed toward the base of the mountain. "One of your friends was injured at Holy Glow Plaza on his way back. He needs help and begs me to send for you."

Every one of Jian's friends leaped to his mind. "Which friend?"

"I don't know," the young woman replied. "He was young and muscular. He had a nice face."

That fit the description of all of his friends. "Handsome nice, smug nice, or cute nice?"

"Does it matter?" The girl wearing the fine robes seemed stumped. "Cute, I guess. He said you were his big brother."

"Kaiyu's in trouble!" Jian shoved past her and began picking his way out of the crowd clustered near the temple gates. He considered taking to the air, but Sonaya's wisdom was fresh on his mind. But what if she was wrong? What if *now* was the perfect time to reveal himself, in the city's time of need? Even if the prophecy was wrong, he was still Wen Jian, the Champion of the Five Under Heaven. Why couldn't he rise to the occasion to defend the city?

The urge was tempting, but something held him back. Was it fear, worry, insecurity? All of the above, likely. Jian stayed on the ground and sprinted down the mountain. It was a short jaunt, but he was out of breath, his chest heaving by the time he reached the main arch leading into Holy Glow Plaza.

He pulled up short and gasped. From high on the mountain, the battle at the plaza looked abstract, two waves of ants pushing against each other like oil and water. Down at the ground level, however, the violence and destruction were devastating. He could only stare in horror at the butchery. It was sheer anarchy, brown-and-red-clad city defenders hacking and dying against red-and-yellow Caobiu invaders. Add in hundreds of plainclothes people wielding axes and broomsticks and even cooking woks, and the pandemonium unfolding was almost too much to take in, let alone discern.

Jian had not been prepared for this. He witnessed a particularly brutal exchange between two soldiers on the ground, each stabbing the other until a runaway horse trampled them both. His stomach churned and his knees shook. He was too terrified to wade into the violence. Jian had to lean against the arch walls to stay upright. He hung his head and promptly threw up.

"Lu Hiro!" The girl appeared by his side. She pulled him away from the wall by the elbow and pointed toward the near corner, fortunately not too far away. "Your friend Kaiyu fell there. Hurry."

Jian squinted. At first, he saw nothing, just two armies of ants butchering each other. Then he saw it, or at least he thought he did. It had been a golden glimmer, there and gone. It looked like Kaiyu's Houtou weapon, the Summer Bow, blurring long arcs on the other end of the battlefield. He couldn't tell if it was the Houtou staff, or if it was just a reflection of the dying light of the King. The fighting masses in that section of the plaza were too thick to allow him a clear view.

His mind brought him back to the last time he saw the Summer Bow in Master Kasa's hand as the Houtou lay injured on the deck of the Lotus ship. The master had rammed his boathouse into their ship in an attempt to cripple it after the Lotus monks kidnapped Jian. Kaiyu's father had died shortly after providing them cover fire from a Lawkan rain ship. Kaiyu was an orphan because of him, and now it was Jian's turn to repay Kasa for that sacrifice.

Jian brandished the Swallow Dances and charged into the square with a renewed sense of urgency. His lips curled into a snarl as he ran into the melee. The terrible sounds of battle became a dull buzz, the fighting around him a fevered dream. Soldiers were rushing left and right, some locked in battle, others tussling on the ground in a general mass melee.

This regiment of Caobiu was the famed Nu Gui, Sunri's elite troops who wore flaming devil masks over banded mail armor with heavy cloaks shorn on one side. Zofi had taught Jian about this during his education, mainly because they were often depicted as the villains in Burning Hearts romance novels.

Jian wasn't looking for a fight, but he didn't shy from it, either. He picked through the masses, making his way toward where he glimpsed the glow of Summer Bow. Eventually, someone noticed him. Several Caobiu archers were standing on a stack of crates, picking shots when

Jian skulked by. He caught sight of a woman casually taking potshots as if target practicing home in on him and loose an arrow.

Jian turned to meet it. He wished he could have snatched it out of the air without looking, as Taishi often did, but that was a matter of confidence, of which he possessed little. He *did* manage to snatch the arrow in flight, however, even if he did have to step to the side in case he muffed the catch. He sent it streaking back toward its source and ended up striking another archer. His aim still needed work.

He continued, knocking off a Caobiu soldier straddling a Shulan defender. Jian whipped the Swallow Dances across the man's back, slicing through wood and leather as if they were nothing. He clasped hands with the soldier he saved and pulled him to his feet.

"Thank you, young lord," the Shulan gasped, catching his breath.

"Stay upright, friend." Jian pushed on.

The Caobiu began to focus on him. They came at Jian in ones and twos at first, from all directions. First was a pikeman. Next were a pair of axmen wielding giant horsecutters, then a small group of archers. He dispatched all of them, save for one of the horsecutters who nearly took his leg off.

After that fighting, however, he had only made a few steps of progress. He was met with two enemies for each five steps he took, and then a tough encounter would push him back three. Time slowed as Jian continued to carve his way deeper into the plaza.

His breathing became harder, heavier. He glanced back the way he had come and was dismayed to learn that he was still close to the entrance.

More Caobiu came at him. The enemy were endless. The Swallow Dances cut through two lines of spears, three, four, five at a time as if flaying wheat. He slipped into Eagle Fans His Wings to break up the spear wall, and then went low with Foal Slips on Ice to close the distance and slip behind their guard. Most of the soldiers were too slow to react with their auxiliary short swords, allowing him to rampage through their ranks with Fox in the Hen House. Those who managed to draw their blades found their pitiful things were no match for the cutting might of the Swallow Dances and the windwhispering style. But as it had been the entire fight, every fallen soldier was replaced by two more.

He had just managed to fight off a trio of spearmen when five more came at him. The first ate two jump kicks to the mouth before toppling over, and then Jian blasted the second in the sides with air, sending him flailing like a rag doll into the roof of the nearby corner store. The rest, however, began to overwhelm him, pushing him back on his heels. He continued to lose ground, first grudgingly step by step, and then quicker until it nearly became a full rout.

Jian's frustrations and exhaustion boiled over. This was pointless. In a fit of impulsiveness without careful thinking, he took to the air. Jian found a low, swirling current and made the decision to unleash his jing. His little brother's life could depend on it. The current swept him up as he leaned on his toe side into the current, curving over the heads of the Caobiu. Spears and pikes nipped at his feet, but the wind was too quick for them. It was almost too fast for Jian as he catapulted above the plaza, higher than he had planned.

It was a clear night with the Queen and the Prince illuminating him for all the world to see. Jian rode the current, slightly out of control, to its zenith at the rooftops of the surrounding buildings, and then an errant arrow zipped close to his ear, startling Jian to lose his balance. He plummeted headfirst, flailing his arms toward the roiling masses of humanity below.

Fortunately, his fall was cushioned by a group of shieldmen locked in close quarters with their Shulan counterparts. He had tried to land by stepping on a Nu Gui officer's helm, but it was shaped like an egg and he rolled his ankle, slipping off and crashing on unsuspecting Caobiu soldiers. It wasn't graceful. Nevertheless, the defenders cheered. People began to shout his name, his legend, his many titles. Word began to spread about him, on both sides. The Shulan must have thought a mighty war artist had joined their ranks.

The Caobiu thought the same, since they sent renewed waves of enemy at him. Jian and the defenders nearby barely withstood the brunt of the first few charges, but they soon found themselves surrounded by longer weapons thrusting at their weakening shield formation.

Seeing no other way to escape, he took to the air again, but this time he was swatted down by a polearm as soon as he cleared their heads. Jian's skill riding currents was still delicate enough that a glancing blow disrupted his flow, sending his legs upward while his head pointed down, and then he crashed. The enemy were upon him in an instant like scavengers on a corpse.

Jian managed to slice an ankle here and knee there, but an unexpected kick to his rib cage sent his sword out of his grasp and spinning away. Panic seized Jian. He was more terrified of his windwhisper master's wrath if he lost the Swallow Dances than an entire army of Caobiu. Taishi was going to kill him, but only if these twenty Caobiu beating him didn't finish him first.

Jian ate a glancing spear thrust to the thigh. A heel crushed his hand, and then a knee to the nose. That was when he stopped fighting and curled into a ball on the ground. The pummeling continued for several more seconds. Jian's consciousness began to ebb and flow. Getting stomped to death was a terrible way to die, and not one poets would write about. Then, just like that, the beatings stopped.

"Jian. Get up. Get up now!" Sonaya's words were sharp in his ears.

He pried one blurry eye open and saw Sonaya standing over him like a guardian phoenix against the backdrop of the Celestial Family. He stood gingerly and stared, puzzled, as the nearby Caobiu soldiers were frozen in place. What happened?

He turned his gaze back at Sonaya and saw that her body was trembling and blood was oozing out of her left ear.

"Are you all right?" He reached for her. "What did you do?"

She held her pose for a moment longer. "You better catch me."

"What?"

Sonaya collapsed. Jian managed to slip an arm behind her head to catch her fall. He dropped to a knee and cradled Sonaya in his arms, holding her close and covering her body with his. Her chest still moved. He could feel air pass through her lips. A deep sense of relief welled in him to know she was all right.

Whatever effect the drowned fist had on the nearby Caobiu evaporated the moment she fell. They blinked, confused at first, and then focused on the two war artists.

Jian prepared for the worst. He was too injured to fight but too weak to run. He wouldn't abandon Sonaya. Taishi would understand if he had died protecting the woman he cared about. Actually, no, she wouldn't. She would call him a pants-less peacock, but this was his decision. Jian closed his eyes and steeled himself for the worst.

He felt the hair on his head blow to one side, but not from the direction he expected. The gust came from behind him. Fresh battle cries followed.

"For Vauzan and the Tiandi!" people roared.

Jian looked up to see a wave of Shulan run past him: soldiers, war artists, commoners, pushing the Caobiu back. Soon the flow of battle reversed. It was the Caobiu who began to lose ground, and then it became a rout. A wash of relief came over him as he rose to his feet. Jian wondered if his display of war arts had anything to do with the tide turning, but he didn't care. Sonaya was safe. That was what mattered.

A soldier with an eyepatch, his face half bloodied by battle and wearing a lord's armor set, stared and pointed at him. "You! You're the Prophesied Hero of the Tiandi. It's him. I swear it."

"Um, what? Oh, no. That's not me." Jian turned to the nearby witness.

"You *are* the Graceful Lord of the Deep Life."

That was a new one. Jian had never heard that title. By now, the chatter had spread across the square. Jian didn't know what to do. Sonaya shifted, regaining consciousness slowly. She blinked and looked at everyone pointing at him, calling him by his title. Some even fell to their knees to pray.

"What did you do, Jian?"

"I don't know!"

It was too late. The Prophesied Hero of the Tiandi, Champion of the Five Under Heaven, was here, they exclaimed, and he had chosen to fight alongside the Shulan! The roars became deafening.

Jian stood there, frozen like a startled fawn. He had dreamed of this day for years, of revealing his true identity, but he hadn't prepared for it to be this very day. Now that the moment had arrived, it felt so sudden, unexpected. At first, he was terrified. He felt naked and vulnerable. Then as his name came into focus from the many shouts merging together, Jian felt a burst of exhilaration as well as embarrassment. There were so many people around, cheering his name. They had expectations of him. Part of him wanted to stand taller for all to see, but mostly he just wanted to run away and hide. He wished Taishi were here right now.

To make matters worse, a fine war wagon flanked by a pack of mute men appeared. The wagon rumbled to a halt before Jian. The mute men broke away and surrounded both him and the wagon. Jian stood alongside Sonaya as the war wagon's door opened.

A man dressed in shimmering golden armor, curved eaves rising up from the ends of his pauldrons, cloak whipping in the wind, stepped out. This was the Iron Moose of the North, Highlord Reevah, the general in charge of the city's defenses. What was *he* doing here?

Sonaya nudged him. He nudged her. They both bowed. "Lord Reevah, it is a great honor."

Reevah stepped closer, his eyes intense. His large, diamond hat had gotten tipped while he stepped out of the wagon and sat crooked. He studied Jian like he was a prized horse. "We haven't met before. Who are you?" He listened to the cheers. "Are you Wen Jian? You're the Champion of the Five Under Heaven?"

It sounded more like a statement than a question. Jian wasn't sure how he was supposed to answer. "Well, actually . . ."

"You are!" Reevah's eyes brightened. "Never did I dream to think that I would live to see the day when the Prophesied Hero of the Tiandi fulfills our people's destiny! He has risen in our darkest hour."

Jian just stood there, frozen, like an opera understudy whose mind went blank the first time they stepped onstage. His entire life had seemingly built up to this. He had prepared himself mentally for this, looked forward to it even. Yet now, at this very moment, with an entire crowd of Zhuun cheering him on, a high lord general was practically in tears crying at his feet.

He was taken aback by how quickly people embraced him as the Hero of the Tiandi. They must really think he was here to save them from the Caobiu, as if he could. One would think they would expect proof or something, yet everyone just embraced him without question. As soon as the high lord proclaimed him as the hero of prophecy, it was as good as settled truth.

Jian honestly wanted to throw up. He wanted to hide, to run away from this attention. But then their attention and enthusiasm slowly seeped in. They were cheering for *him*. They expected him to be their savior. Finally, he did the only thing he could muster his body to do: he waved at the crowds.

Jian gulped as his reception intensified to ear-shattering roars. The force of the cheering caused him to stumble backward a few steps. Fortunately, Sonaya appeared by his side, clutching his hand and keeping him upright.

Her gentle compulsion whispered in his head over the din of the noise. *Steady breath, Five Champ. Look on with resolve. Don't smile like you're at a party. Look determined. Feel intense. Good, now raise a fist.*

He did as he was told and curled his fingers into a raised fist. The cheers became deafening.

Hold your ground. Keep your chin raised. Stop showing so many teeth!

He tried to do as ordered. *Now what?* he thought back to her.

Sonaya stood by his side but kept her attention on him, looking with admiration. *I don't know, Five Champ, but I am quite sure you are in deep trouble now. . . .*

CHAPTER EIGHTEEN

THE RALLY

Taishi was annoyed by the time her group entered the Holy Glow Plaza at the foot of Peony Peak. The fights had taken longer than expected, although she had to admit that it was fun. The old masters still had it and were able to lay waste to scores of Caobiu.

All of them wore out easily. Sohn was leaking so much blood he looked like a devil. Bhasani had practically screamed herself hoarse, while Fausan was so out of shape he threw up his dinner and nearly had a heart attack. Taishi probably had it the worst because she felt useless. Her three friends had defeated nearly a hundred Caobiu soldiers over the course of two hours—stuff of legend—but all Taishi had to show for it was that she knocked down three people and scared another. It was humiliating. She stewed quietly, annoyed, as the others patted each other on the back, laughing and recollecting the events of the battle.

"How did you make those axmen do that dance?" Fausan crowed at Bhasani, his low laughter bouncing off the surrounding buildings. "They were even synchronized like a dance troupe!"

"I implanted the same imagery in each of their heads." She smirked. "My choreography could use a little work."

Sohn stopped and bent over to suck in a few deep breaths, then straightened. He broke into a bloody grin. "I might bleed out, but I'm okay with that. This is a better way to go."

Taishi stared. "You're missing your front teeth."

"I am?" Sohn felt his mouth. "I am!"

"It's an improvement," said Bhasani. "Your oversize front teeth made you look like a beaver."

"I'll have you know that was the fashion in Manjing. A new set will take weeks to deliver." Sohn sounded distraught. "How am I going to bite meat?"

Taishi tuned out their conversation. These old crows should know better. Tonight's fights meant nothing. The Caobiu soldiers they defeated would return with double the numbers tomorrow, assuming the city survived the night. They were only delaying the inevitable. But then, Fausan had accused her of being a cynical downer, so she said nothing.

Her thoughts drifted back to her conversation with Beautiful Boy. She had expected to pay a steep price for their escape—a string of gold liangs or two. Maybe even three. She didn't care. It was all Mori's temple money anyway.

To demand the death of a high lord was unthinkable! It was an outrageous request. But would Taishi be willing to make that kill to keep Jian safe? That answer was not so clear anymore. There was very little Taishi wouldn't do to protect her ward, and while a lifetime of honor and reputation was no small thing, at the end of the day, that was all ego.

The masters entered the ward square and came upon what Taishi could only surmise was the aftermath of a large battle. Bodies, debris, and ruins were everywhere. Tiandi monks walked the plaza grounds among the dead, while nuns and doctors worked to keep the living that way. Men groaned and screamed. Wives and children scoured the area for their loved ones. It was a scene she had replayed many times over her life, and was the main reason she rarely stayed in a battle until the end. It was too depressing, especially when she knew she was a major contributor to the death toll.

The number of Caobiu uniforms on the ground was impressive. It had been quite the battle, easily the largest yet. It must mean the Caobiu had penetrated a third of the way into the city. Anything past Copper Monkey Road was likely enemy territory now. It should be worrying, but the soldiers milling about sounded cheerful despite such carnage.

Fausan must have noticed the same thing. "I think we won this."

Sohn scoffed. "How can a ward's volunteer corps fend off a Nu Gui regiment?"

"I'm as puzzled as you, old friend."

Taishi looked toward the far side of the square where the street leading up to the Vauzan temple began. She pointed. "There's an entire court legion of displayguards there."

"Displayguards so far from court," Bhasani mused. "Why not just the city militia or the army? Unless . . ."

That was when Taishi sighted a court pavilion on the far end. "Look at those flags. Half of the Shulan Court must be here."

Sohn frowned. "This close to battle. That's unusual, and dangerous."

"Why?" asked Fausan. "A commoner bleeds as easily as a lord."

"Too many unknowns and random ways to die during a siege, love," said Bhasani. "And lords dying is bad for morale."

"What are they doing here?" Taishi muttered.

There was only one way to find out. She began picking her way through the packed crowds. Sohn and Fausan weren't wrong. The mood in the square was peculiar, lively even. The aftermath of battle was usually somber. The only thing most survivors could do was sleep or die. Even the victorious would hold off on the celebrations until their fallen comrades were accounted for. It was the only honorable thing to do. In this case, however, the crowds were animated. Most were smiling and joking with one another. Some were holding hands in large circles and hugging. Others were even on their knees praying.

The first time she heard Jian's name, Taishi thought nothing of it. It was a common enough one. Finally, Taishi slowed and looked around. There was *too* much chatter about Jian. It was on everyone's lips. Taishi pulled voices on the breeze to her and listened. Taishi's gut twisted. If they were talking about Jian—*her* Jian—then something big, something terrible, must have happened.

"The Prophesied Hero of the Tiandi came to Vauzan's defense. What a glorious day!"

Taishi rolled her eyes.

"He glided in the wind like the great heroes of legend and destroyed an entire squad of that bitch witch Sunri's elite guards!"

Taishi raised one brow. Jian waddled more than glided across currents, but the point had been made. There were many witnesses. Also, an entire squad on his own, really? She knew his abilities—she had trained him—and she would put money against her own disciple if he were up against three Nu Gui.

Taishi stopped. There was no need to down the boy. She had trained him well. She really needed to have a more positive outlook on life.

Still, Jian taking on fifty soldiers was laughable.

"The sword in the champion's hands shined like midnight, cutting darkness through the air."

That didn't even make any sense. How does a weapon shine like night? At least he hadn't lost his sword yet. Then she'd kill him.

"When all others ran, the champion stood his ground," a soldier chattered to his friends. "The line broke, and you see my donkey leg here, so I fell. Watching death charge at me by those flaming freaks was basically how I expected to die, anyway. But then the hero appeared. He pulled me to my feet and said, 'We fight shoulder-to-shoulder, brother.'"

Taishi couldn't believe what she was hearing. That story was pure plagiarism, pulled out of the last Burning Hearts novel that she had finished not three weeks ago. More outlandish stories filtered to her ears.

This was not good, not good at all.

She grabbed the shoulder of a monk passing by. "Brother, what blasphemous gossip is this I hear about the prophecy?"

The young man's face shone so brightly Taishi nearly had to avert her eyes. He bobbed his head like a weight on a fishhook. "It's true, blessed dowager. It's true! The Prophesied Hero of the Tiandi has returned to his people in our time of need."

"He's supposed to fight the Katuia, not our own people." She scowled.

The young initiate rambled on, citing specific scriptures and passages from the prophecy and stitching them together to fit the narrative.

"Mother!" Sonaya rushed into Bhasani's arms.

"Daughter, what happened to you?" said the drowned fist master.

"Who cares about you! What happened to Jian?" Taishi snapped. She stopped. "Sorry, I mean, of course I care about you, Sonaya. Have you seen my ward?"

"I prefer you just stay your lovely cantankerous self, master," said the girl.

"Where's Jian? What did he do? I'm going to drown him in a tub of dirty dish soap."

"It's not his fault," Sonaya said. She was defending her man. A quality trait, even if they weren't actually together. Taishi wasn't sure what game the Master of the Drowned Fist was playing with matching the Champion of the Five Under Heaven with her daughter and heiress, but she swore she didn't have an angle on this.

"*I prefer to not have my lineage tangled with the Prophecy of the Tiandi,*" Bhasani had sniffed. "*Or yours, for that matter. Nothing personal,*" she had added. "*It's just that your lineage's succession plan stinks and is not something I hope my daughter will have to undergo.*"

That was fair. If Taishi could give up the entire windwhispering style along with all its trappings, she would in a heartbeat if it meant allowing her to spend a little more time with her biological son, Sanso. Her adopted son, Jian, on the other hand, was another story. She might be fine killing him at this point, or at least taking him out to the shed and switching him until his backside turned to whipped gelatin. It was a good thing the bloody khan was dead, because she was going to wring the boy's neck.

"If he wants to die, I'll happily manifest that destiny." Taishi's fury locked on to the court pavilion in the far back of the square. The oversize yellow-and-brown banners with the green streamers in the very center of the flags were a statement. Oban was here, and he wanted the entire city to know. There was a saying in the Shulan Court: Coincidences were for bad planners, and the lord known as the Orderly was anything but that.

"Taishi, where are you going?" shouted Sohn.

She hadn't realized she was stomping toward the tent. Her increasing annoyance and worry guided her now. The crowds of people in the square parted before her. The years might have wasted her body and she might look frail, old, and broken, her jing might have shriveled, and her strength might have abandoned her, but a warrior's will was always the last thing to break. The key to intimidation was to feel the role, and Taishi was in a mood.

Two spears crossed before her as she walked to the pavilion's entrance. "This area is occupied by the court, old one," said the younger displayguard. "Off with you before you are arrested for trespassing."

"Oban!" Taishi snarled, amplifying her voice across the wind.

"Shut it, old bag," the other guard, bearded and more wizened, snapped. He gestured to the first guard.

The younger one, baby-faced, hesitated. "My grandmam wouldn't approve of me knocking around a nun."

She took a step forward and shouted even louder. "Oban!"

The baby-faced displayguard moved to obstruct her way, but Taishi juked him with one fluid motion. She still had *some* agility left. She caught sight of Oban's tall frame hovering over a table at the back of the pavilion. His ample backside, unusually placed for such a lean figure, was on display. The high lord was dictating to a group of his officers standing just outside of eyeshot. Taishi stayed her ground and pulled the sound from the wind toward her.

". . . is the moment," Oban was saying. "We've held the line. Now it's time. We need the breakthrough." He leaned forward. "I want the displays and the imperials to muster near Big Heart Big Riches square at the Prime Ward. Lord Ushmu's men are barely holding it. We break the enemy's spine there with the champion at its head and show the world that the Tiandi is on Shulan's side. If this doesn't rally the city, then nothing will. Sunri will come to the realization that her outnumbered army has a fanatical city to contest with. She'll be forced to withdraw. Then it'll only be a matter of time—"

"I warned you to back off, you old bag!"

Taishi saw the shove coming a moment before the bearded guard reached her. Muscle memory reacted first. Her chest relaxed as it absorbed the impact, offering little resistance as she twisted left. The guard stumbled forward as if he had tried to push loose sand. The back of her hand slapped the guard's forearm to the side, and then her hollow sword twirled between her fingers before pressing against the guard's exposed neck in one fluid motion. The man was lucky her blade was still in its scabbard. Even an opera blade could cut if sharp enough.

The younger displayguard next to him gawked, and then leaped to action like professional soldiers should. The two elite court guards fought with the Shulan military war arts style called Union Boxing. Most on the street called it Hot Pot Fist due to the fact Union Boxing was nothing more than stealing the bits and pieces of dozens of other styles, streamlined for easy training with an emphasis on group warfare. They did not practice lineage nor did the style have roots or heritage, which is why many in the lunar court also called it Bastard Boxing. Taishi hated to admit it—she was a traditionalist and purist at heart—but Union Boxing was a highly effective style, especially to train groups of soldiers into a cohesive fighting force, and the court displayguards were the finest of that lineage.

Mean Beard went high while Baby Face went low. One came with a thrust of his elongated ringed glaive while the other used an oversize shield and short sword. Taishi stepped out of the way as the two soldiers came close, and then she slapped both, one across the nose and one on the side of the head.

"You're dead. You just lost an ear. Now get out of my way."

Two more displayguards were about to join in the fray when one fell flat on his face mid-thrust with his spear as a metal bullet bounced off his forehead. His partner turned to the side in time for Sohn to ram into his shield, sending him sprawling flat on his back. Bhasani and Sonaya appeared next to Taishi and the two drowned fists' presence sent the rest of the guards nearby cowering. More guards swarmed around them until they were surrounded by spears and blades.

Taishi and the rest of her group went back-to-back. She growled. "About time you turtles caught up."

"You could have warned us you were going to charge a high lord's pavilion." Fausan, of course, had caught up to them last. He huffed. "Haven't we already talked about rude manners?"

"Guards, stand down! Show some respect to the dowager nun." Oban's voice boomed across the square.

The guards, immaculately trained, pulled back and came to attention. There was a crash of metal with a synchronized salute, and then another when they dropped to one knee, glaives standing on their end while swords lay across the top flat of the shields.

Taishi looked over their shoulders toward the pavilion and saw Highlord Oban stroll out with his hand resting on his blade, although not like he was actually going to draw it. Wearing it was for show. No one was good at both math and the blade. There simply weren't enough years to master both. Taishi nodded. He offered one back, and then beckoned her to enter.

"We are blessed by the Tiandi, today of all days," he announced, making his way toward her. "We will need the Mosaic more than ever to guide our path through these dark times."

Taishi's sneer deepened before she remembered her place. There was nothing to gain from shaming a lord of the public. She followed Oban into the pavilion. His usual retinue were there: four personal guards, his brother and adviser Obeen, and his personal mind trust, which was a small group of six scholars and mnemonic officials, all dressed in gray and black and arranged off to the side as if to fade into the decor. Two mute women flanked the entrance while a one-eyed lord and young woman in school robes stood off to the side. His daughter, perhaps? Although Taishi couldn't imagine university still in session with the entire city under siege.

She waited until after the tent flap closed before she rounded on him. "This is your doing, isn't it?"

"Whatever do you mean, Taishi?" he replied.

"The Prophesied Hero of the Tiandi announcing himself. Don't tell me you had nothing to do with this."

"He had a little nudge." Oban looked over at the young woman and soldier off to the side. Both bowed.

It was not surprising Jian was being watched. "We had an agreement," she said. "What was the point of asking me if you were going to draw him out anyway?"

"Because I wanted your permission," he snapped. "It would have been easier if you worked with me instead of planning to flee. And because I am a high lord, and you are . . ."

Taishi looked at him. "I am what, Oban, an old woman, a peasant?"

"You are not," he finished. "The will of the court cannot be denied."

"This madness will not see you crowned."

"I have never harbored ambitions for that higher calling." This was the first time she had earned a sharp response. "Saan was my dear friend and brother. This is what *he* would have wanted."

"That's because this is Saan's seat. He had everything to lose. You do not. The people do not. This is not a winnable war. If you do not covet the ducal dais, like you claim, then save the people."

"There is dishonor in surrender."

"There is greater dishonor in allowing your people to get slaughtered for pride."

"How dare you." Oban's eyes flashed, the calm demeanor he wore moments before now gone.

Taishi knew she walked a fine line, especially now that her power was an illusion. However, many lives were at stake, including Jian's—

THE ART OF LEGEND

especially Jian's—so she stood her ground. "There is no dishonor in truth served with a good heart."

Oban shrugged. "You could be right, but how would that look? To see your duke assassinated and then throw open the gates to his murderer."

"Good lords make the hard decisions."

The high lord pursed his lips. "Taishi, we can discuss this all day if you like but the stone's already been cast. The Savior of the Zhuun announced himself, and he has thrown his support behind Shulan. That means something to people. The only question right now is, what are we going to do about it? Will you support the central tenet of the Tiandi?" He swirled a finger at her. "Because all this righteousness is nothing more than mental masturbation." Oban took a deep breath and shook his head. "It would have been a lot cleaner if you had just said yes, Taishi."

"Where's the boy?" she said. "Have you spirited him away and taken him prisoner?"

"That's absurd." Oban sniffed. "The people would never accept a hero who is a tool of a court. I sent him to my tailor at the south end of the square. They do fabulous work, fantastic quality. If you ever need a new robe or even a refresh . . ."

Taishi slapped the flap open and left the pavilion and made a straight line toward the shop. She hadn't realized until afterward that Oban was the lord who owned a monopoly of every tailor shop in the city. It shouldn't be a surprise since the high lord's primary business was thread. The man had somehow monopolized the empire's entire sheep market.

The displayguards had moved to block her egress, but a "let her go" commanded from Oban cleared her way. Her friends, who had waited outside kept under guard, joined her a moment later.

"Where to?" asked Fausan.

"The Blue Steel thread shop." She pointed.

He brightened. "I love that place. They carry the finest robes."

"Oban owns every tailor shop."

"Oh." He scowled. "I hate that place."

Bhasani had told Taishi that Fausan and Oban had once been fierce rivals during their math club days in secondary school and had held on to those grudges since. Oban took his knowledge and served his people, eventually becoming a high lord of Shulan, while Fausan used his math powers to break casinos and gambling rooms.

"Have you heard from the children?" she asked.

Fausan nodded. "Hachi is defending some old woman's plot of land from Caobiu looters. I ordered him to return to the temple and he refused."

Sohn looked puzzled. "Has he been with a girl all this time? He must love her, that fool."

"Oh no," said Sonaya. "They only met the other day."

The God of Gamblers slapped his forehead. "Is she a noble at least?"

"She works at the box shops."

Fausan grimaced. "I taught the boy the best I could, but he just doesn't get it." He threw his arms in the air. "Hasn't he learned anything from being around me?"

"What's that supposed to mean?" Bhasani said.

He looked startled. "No, I didn't mean anything about you, my love."

"Do tell." There was an edge to her voice. "What lesson about women could Hachi learn from being around you?"

He considered. "How to always anticipate all your needs."

She snorted. "Shut up."

"Shutting up, my darling."

Taishi hated them for acting like that in public. It was insufferable.

The door to the Blue Steel slammed open. Taishi barged inside, catching Jian with his pants down as he was getting measured. Fine brown silk with the banner of the Shulan ran across his chest like a dumb advertisement.

He startled like a rabbit when she entered, and turned to see her. "Hi, Taishi."

She stared. He was being fitted for court robes. He had bathed. His unruly hair was combed, and a facemaker had painted his face as if it were his wedding night. Taishi's brows raised, alarmed. That could be the only thing that would make this situation even worse.

Taishi wouldn't put it past Jian, however. "Did you go off and get married?"

"What?" Jian squeaked. "No, of course not. I mean, I don't think I did."

"What?" Sonaya's eyes were large and intense. "How do you not know if you got married?"

"A lot of nobles have been making this vow and that vow," he replied. "It was hard to keep track."

"Did you get any marriage proposals, and more importantly, did you say yes?" Sonaya looked ready to kill Jian.

"I'm pretty sure I didn't say yes to any of the marriage proposals." He looked angry. "At least people wanted to make a commitment to me."

Sonaya was not a woman to lose her composure, but this conversation was about to get bad. Taishi shot Bhasani a look, and the two women moved next to Sonaya. "Let me talk to him," Taishi said.

"I'm going to kill him."

Bhasani turned her. "Come, daughter, let Taishi deal with her idiot ward." She shot Taishi with a glare. "Deal with him or I'm going to poison him with a diuretic."

Taishi kept her eyes on him. "Everyone out."

Sohn and Fausan were the first to move, then Bhasani and Sonaya. Then the tailor's assistant, who was standing by the door. That left only the tailor, a long, hunched-over man wearing thick spectacles. He was bald on top but had a curtain of hair falling down the sides of his head dyed in three different colors.

The owner of the Blue Steel looked puzzled. "Wait, me too? This is my establishment, madam. You can't kick me out. . . ."

She held her gaze.

The tailor blinked and then rose to his feet. He bowed and scurried off. She stared at Jian, bathed with his hair brushed and coiffed, with half-finished robes draped over his shoulders while he stood on a stool getting measured. His face was shaded to accentuate his cheekbones. His thick brows had been plucked and drawn over, and his skin had taken a paler, even shiny hue. The facemaker had done an excellent job. Jian looked almost ethereal, divine. Taishi only questioned the blue eyeliner.

It brought back memories of when they had first met. It was the day the dukes had arrived at the Celestial Palace. She had brought over a facemaker and tailor and others to help prepare Jian to meet them. He had been so proud and excited that day, beaming as they dressed him and painted his face. It was remarkable how much he had grown and matured, yet somehow he was still very much that same innocent boy she had met all those years ago.

"Jian." Taishi tried to keep her voice measured. "I don't know what your thinking was, revealing yourself today, and while I would like to beat you over the head for the rest of your life, it doesn't matter. We need to leave the city."

"But—" he stammered.

"Yes, I know you let that rooster out of the kennel, but that's a mistake you're going to have to live with."

"Won't—"

"It doesn't matter what the people or the court or anyone thinks. This is not something you want to get involved in. We need to leave."

"How—"

"Still working on it. There's an underworld group who can smuggle us out."

"But, Mas—"

"Don't worry about Oban and the court. I'll take care of them." Taishi had prepared responses for just about everything he could say. "You made a blockhead decision, boy, but nothing we can't overcome."

"But, Master Ling Taishi."

He used her full name. Taishi's eyes narrowed. He always used her official title when he planned to disobey. She put her hand on her hip. "What is it?"

Jian looked nervous but met her gaze. "Taishi, I don't want to go. I want to stay and defend the city."

She jabbed his chest with her finger, and then, surprised, brushed her palm against its cool, smooth surface. That silk was really high quality! "I don't care what you want, disciple. We're leaving as soon as I throw you on a wagon."

"Sunri's going to sack the city!"

"Oh, for certain."

"And you're going to let that happen?"

"Absolutely."

"But, Taishi, this is our home. I have friends here. I have a life! I want to stay and fight. I *need* to stay and fight."

"That life you cherish ended the moment you declared who you are." She pointed out the window. "That city is irrelevant. The people are as well. Even the battle for the Heart of the Tiandi Throne is irrelevant. What matters is that you stay alive long enough to fight the fight that actually matters."

"The prophecy is broken," he snapped. "What am I supposed to do, just stand around and wait for something that probably won't happen? What's the point?"

"The point is that *you* get to live!" Taishi was tempted to just drag him out of the shop by his ear. "And you can't do that here in Vauzan, so we're leaving." She reached for his wrist.

Jian pulled his arm away. "I'm not going, Taishi. I made up my mind. I'm staying to help. I don't want to run and hide anymore. I want to stand for something. I want to count for something." Jian's eyes watered. He really did care. How annoying.

Taishi released a strangled breath. "You can't stay here, Jian. You'll die."

"Can't you just believe in me for once?"

"It's not that."

"I'm tired of feeling like a fraud. Let me do this. It's for a just cause. You don't know that I'll die. We could win this, and who knows, maybe this is what will unite our people to fight the Eternal Khan of Katuia."

Taishi snapped. She grabbed the front of Jian's robes and pulled him close. "I know you'll die because the Prophet of the Tiandi told me. When the great lioness approaches, the string boy must go to ground or be torn apart beneath her celestial claw."

He frowned. "Why did she call me string boy?"

"It doesn't matter! What matters is Sunri, the lioness, is here, and you, string boy, are still here as well."

Jian shrugged. "I'll have to deal with Sunri one of these days. Might as well do it here, in the city of my choice, with people at my back and the Shulan Court as my allies."

Taishi wanted to knuckle his forehead. "Did you not hear the part where you die a useless death if you stay?"

Jian looked unfazed. "All I've heard since the day we met was that I was going to get torn apart by the Eternal Khan, so what's another death threat? None of that bothers me anymore. I want to do some good before it happens. Maybe try to live up to expectations for once."

Taishi huffed, sucking so hard through her nose that her face wrinkled, and then she exhaled in a sneer. Her head knew what was right, but so did her heart. Both were right, but for different reasons. In this case, the answer was clear.

She closed her eyes. "Fine. We'll stay and fight. But if the situation appears hopeless, then I call it and we leave. Understood?"

Jian rushed into her arms and squeezed her. "Thank you, master. You won't regret this. I will bring us honor. Everything will turn out fine. You'll see."

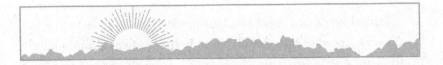

CHAPTER NINETEEN

THE KATI RAID

Qisami looked down at the fallen Tawara Ito, killed by an arrow that punched through his crown, confused. What had just happened? Where did that come from? What was that sharp whiny sound? Another arrow plunked into Tawara Ito's fallen body, and then dozens more began to drizzle the colony like a third cycle winter hailstorm. More began to drop and the crowded field scattered.

A moment later, the eastern near wall that made up the storage pen on the other side of a row of barracks carved from ice blocks exploded as a large metal wagon with disproportionately large, ugly spiked wheels burst through the wreckage. It shrieked once more and then barreled into the crowd, trampling bodies and sending them flying, while several figures hiding inside an archers' nest emerged and peppered more arrows down on them.

"Kati raid!" someone screamed.

The cries rang throughout the Happy Glow Retirement Home, spreading like gonorrhea among the inmates. At first, no one moved. A massacre sounded inevitable, but this was the most riveting thing anyone had witnessed in years.

Qisami herself just stood there, gawking. "No way."

Two groups of cavalry flooded in from the north and south, adding to the panic. Pale riders in white cloaks and feathers wielding long, heavy lances plowed through the crowds riding large horses with hairy elephant-like hooves that cut through the crowds like a hot knife. They were followed by a wave of light cavalry, Kati raiders with their wooden armor, topknots, and shaved sides of their heads, wielding swords that chased fleeing prisoners and anyone not quick enough to escape. The initial shock and awe were overwhelming.

Qisami was no stranger to violence and anarchy. She thrived on it. And while she had participated in dozens of murders, fights, and brawls in her career, this was the first pitched battle she had ever witnessed, or worse, had the unfortunate luck to be involved in. She was usually more of a single or small-group sort of murdering type. Qisami wasn't going to lie; it was terrifying and she nearly soiled herself, gawking at the chaos erupting around her, but she couldn't look away.

That was, until a screaming arrow nearly punctured her eye. She ducked it, barely, her frazzled bird's-nest hair taking a cut. She knocked another arrow out of the air and scrambled for cover, finding an overturned table to dive behind.

She assessed the situation as several more arrows bounced off the stone slab shielding her. The situation was bad. There was no order, nobody taking charge and rallying the Happy Glow residents. It was going to be a massacre. People panicked and bodies were strewn across the ground. Kati horsemen were pouring in from every direction, swords and axes swinging, cutting down anyone in their path. A large group containing the corner leaders were fleeing toward the mine on one side. They would find some shelter from the raid there but then would have to deal with management and the guards.

Hair Bear and the rest of the Goons were forming up and trying to get organized. What were those cracked eggs thinking? Did those idiots intend to fight? Apparently so. Even worse, Cyyk was with them. There certainly weren't enough of them to make a dent against a massive Kati raid. Many of the inmates weren't war artists or soldiers, just soft-shell prisoners: the embezzlers, adulterers, fraudsters, incompetent scholars, and political dissidents. But what else could they do? Defend the colony, or lay down and die. Those were the only options. No, there had to be another way. Did the Kati even leave prisoners?

Qisami chose the only sensible thing to do and saved her own hide, not that it mattered. They would all be dead by dawn, anyway. She made it ten steps from the fighting when she stopped and couldn't force herself to take another step. Only one thing could keep her from abandoning these saps to their fate. One stupid thing. One stupid person, and Qisami hated herself for it.

Everyone else in her life had abandoned her. Everyone, except one. She turned and sprinted across the open field, dodging arrows and horsemen alike, and dove to the ground when an ax nearly cleaved her head off. She rolled to her feet and feinted as the horse reared, its front hooves coming frighteningly close to her face. She dove forward beneath it, into its shadow, popping out beside a collapsed building. She continued sprinting, zigzagging around charging horses and rolling death machines, tripping over bodies and arrows sticking out of the ground.

Qisami miraculously made it to Cyyk, who had managed to find a pike and had joined alongside four other Goons to form the world's saddest phalanx. She grabbed him by the ear like an errant child and hauled him off the line.

"Hey!" he argued. "What did you do that for?"

"I'm saving your life, turdball," she hissed, swatting an arrow away as she dragged him toward safety.

"We can't let them win!" he yelled.

"Win what? What are we winning?" she retorted. "This is a penal colony. There's nothing to win here!"

"Where would we escape to, though?"

The grunt had a point. The Kati attacking the prison didn't make it any less true that the Happy Glow Retirement Home was still stuck in the ass end of a desolate corner of the world. They would die if they left the colony. She pulled Cyyk behind an outcrop of rock. No, that wasn't true. What changed was that they would die if they stayed, so they might as well give themselves a chance.

She watched from their spot as a Kati raider ran down a group of inmates, sending several flying into the nearby snowbank. They were clustered tightly enough, however, that the impact had knocked him off-balance as well, stopping the mount in its tracks.

She stared at the large chestnut. "That's a lot of horse. I bet it can take us pretty far."

"We have no supplies. What happens after it keels over?"

"Then we eat it." Qisami didn't give him a chance to protest. "You take his front. I'll move up the flank."

"Why me?"

"You like attention."

The two attacked together. It had been a while since they danced as partners. She was rusty, her grunt even more so. It was like two virgins giving it their first go, but damn it felt good to flow like a real cell again.

The raider was dicing the rubes in Barrack Nine like raw Happan fish, chopping vertically in tall arcs. He noticed Cyyk stalking forward, making a laughable attempt to stay unseen. Part of it was by design; part of it was the broodbaby generally sucked at prowling and subtlety.

Qisami bided her time until the raider had turned away from her. She was close enough now that the horse's tail slapped her face. She leaped onto its back just when the Kati kicked and reared it to charge. Qisami ripped off the rider's wooden helm and twisted his neck around. The two struggled as the steed lunged in a violent circle. Unfortunately, her opponent was strong, and she didn't have enough leverage to torque him down. Cyyk, after avoiding the rearing horse, finally managed to jump in to help, and the two were able to toss the Kati off. He pitched headfirst to the ground and was converged upon by the survivors of Barrack Nine.

"Come on, broodbaby." Qisami offered an arm and hauled him up behind her. Several other inmates had come to the same conclusion and tried to climb on and hitch a ride as well. "Let's go, horsey!"

She saw an unobstructed route leading out of the colony toward freedom, and possibly death. Probably death, but at this point it didn't matter. She was willing to risk Cyyk's life to take that chance. Qisami grabbed a fistful of the horse's mane and kicked its ribs. She buried her head into it as the horse broke into a wild spring, veering side to side to avoid bodies and projectiles getting thrown into the path before them. Steam shot from the horse's nostrils as it broke into a hard sprint, nearly bucking them along the way. She wasn't looking for trouble or a fight. All they had to do was break free and get clear.

For a moment, it looked as if they were going to make it. Qisami's hope surged as they reached the main gatehouse at the edge of the colony. Before them stretched the vast, open white fields of the Grass Tundra, where likely a cold, painful demise awaited, but at least they had a chance. She was going to die on her own terms. Qisami was almost exuberant.

Then the gatehouse exploded, literally, in a giant shower of splinters and snow. She would have been blown off the mount if she hadn't been clinging to it so tightly. Cyyk certainly wasn't, and was gone the next moment. What was left of the building collapsed into itself, and what stood in its place was the single most terrifying thing Qisami had ever seen.

It looked like a giant platform with structures and siege weapons moving along massive, wheeled tracks. This thing was taller than buildings and larger than ocean frigates, three ocean frigates! The metal monstrosity rumbled and screamed with shrill whistles while sending puffs of smoke and steam shooting into the sky. It was larger and more terrifying than the Caobiu ducal war wagons. How could such a thing exist? Was this one of those famed Kati city pods? This machine had smashed and flattened the gatehouse, crushing it beneath tracked wheels that were as tall as a two-story house. Emblazoned on the hull of this monster was a symbol: a curved dome sitting over a flat line, with two more lines along the sides angling up and outward.

The poor, distressed horse reared, whinnying in panic, tossing her. Qisami felt every rock and bump on the road with her bone-shattering thud as she tumbled and rolled on the hard ice until she came to a stop on her backside. Those dozen or so layers of burlap sacks created a decent cushion. She could only sit there and gape, her arms and legs sprawled as the city pod loomed closer, shaking the ground and threatening to crush her beneath its metal tracks.

She came to her senses an instant later. Getting crushed by a giant metal monster was a lousy way to die, but she was more concerned about the horse. That was her escape. Qisami leaped to her feet and pulled on the horse's reins, trying to coax it back to its feet. But the steed was too large and heavy, and possibly hurt, for it to budge. The city pod swiveled around and rolled closer. She gave the poor steed one more hard yank, and failed, causing her to slip and fall onto her back once more. She stared in horror as the shadow of the city pod blanketed her into darkness.

Then it stopped, even as the tracks continued to churn. Qisami blinked. What happened? Why didn't it crush her bones to paste? A shrill whistle of steam blew from somewhere in its underbelly. She looked to the side. One of the rear tracks had gotten caught in the demolished remains of the gatehouse.

Qisami's heart went double time as a tidal wave of relief washed over her. Her only response was nervous laughter as she scrambled to her feet. She glared at the stupid horse one more time. If it wanted to lie there and die, then fine.

She scanned the area for Cyyk and found him off to the side, picking himself up. At least he was still alive. She staggered toward him, still discombobulated. They could get out somehow. They'd just have to find another way.

She called, "Get up, broodbaby. We have to—"

A long, rectangular ramp slid out from the platform above and slammed onto the ground nearby. Four Kati warriors wielding short spears and tall rectangular shields filed down the ramp followed by a woman wearing baggy pants and what appeared to be an apron. The Kati in charge leading the small group pointed at Qisami. "Towerspears, kill those two and secure the perimeter, while Anja clears the debris."

"Yes, squadlead!" they barked.

One Kati came at Qisami, while the other two went at Cyyk. How typical. They probably thought she wasn't a threat. The tip of the man's spear struck ice, then gravel, and then a patch of mud. Qisami avoided the blows, rolling and shifting, and spread her legs on the third. Then she closed them, scissoring the spear out of his grasp and sending it spinning to the side. She skipped to her feet and threw a punch at the Kati, but succeeded only in banging on the top edge of his shield. She howled, shaking her hand as she backed up. She nearly broke her pinky. The towerspear hid behind his shield and rammed forward, slamming into her body and sending her flying.

By now though, Qisami was finally warmed up. The two were fighting under the city pod, which meant there was plenty of darkness; all she needed was variance in the shade. She found it as she was crashing to the ground and slipped into a shadowstep, feeling the bubbles prick her skin. She emerged behind him within the shadow of one of the metal tracks. She lunged, cracking him in the back of the helmet with an elbow. That hurt her elbow almost as much as it probably hurt him. Qisami dropped low behind him, yanked the two daggers holstered to each side of his waist, and then stabbed inward into the outside of both of his hips. He dropped to his knees, and then a downward hammer with the butt of the dagger cracked his wooden helm and ended his day.

Qisami checked in on Cyyk and noticed he was getting his ass handed to him. Two men with the big shields had boxed the brood-baby against a boulder. Qisami flipped one of the daggers and caught it by the tip. She squinted, stuck out her tongue, and then hurled the unwieldy blade. The large dagger hit its mark, but with the wrong end. It didn't matter since that silly Kati decided to wear a feathered cap instead of a helmet. He crumpled to the ground.

She turned in time to see the guy in charge bearing down on her. The squadlead, older and stronger than his report, was slower, which made him easy prey for a shadowkill. Speed kills, but surprise murders, as went the shadowkill saying.

The man knew how to use his shield more effectively, however, keeping her in front and at bay. Qisami hissed like a cat as she pounced left and right. This Kati was disciplined, unlike the other, or more likely, she had already wasted her element of surprise. In any case, he was still no match for her. It just took her longer than she needed to deal with a lowly warrior. She blamed it on being rusty.

Qisami had rammed his shield and noticed how he braced for it. He planted his right foot to the outside, and squatted. It happened two more times as she probed for a way to slip past that ridiculous wall of a shield. On the fourth attempt though, she put more oomph into her shoulder check. As soon as the squadlead planted his feet, she stabbed with the dagger, splintering his wooden slippers and his leg. To the man's credit, he barely registered a grunt. He dropped his guard enough for her to reverse the grip of her dagger and swing it toward the side of his head.

It should have killed him if it hadn't been for someone interrupting her. Qisami caught the movement of someone dropping from above. She kicked the squadlead away and retreated as still another Kati landed between them. This one was different from the others. Her movements were more relaxed and refined. Her armor was wooden scale mail, not banded or one-piece. There was also something familiar about her flow. A nine-link metal chain whip was looped in her hand. This one was a trained war artist.

"Get the perimeter secured, squadlead," she barked. "We're sitting ducks. I'll take care of this one."

"Yes, viperstrike."

Viperstrike?

That was something Qisami wasn't expecting. She studied this war artist. The woman was younger than that fierce, sexy beast Salminde, whom Qisami had encountered years back. She wondered if they were related. Doubtful. The two looked nothing alike. In fact, they didn't even look like they belonged in the same race. This one looked Happan. There could be hundreds of viperstrikes in the Kati world for all she knew. Still, she couldn't help but ask.

"Viperstrike, eh? Do you know Salminde? We're, like, best friends."

The Kati startled at the name. Maybe there weren't that many viperstrikes. With a snarl, she snapped her chain whip at Qisami, flailing left and right at the ground and air between them. Every once in a while, the chain whip would curl around the Kati's elbow, wrist, and even neck, changing its trajectory as it flayed at her. Qisami's dagger was useless against these things. She could only dodge. It was a good thing this girl was just okay, certainly not as skilled as that sweet hot bun Salminde.

Qisami couldn't help but feel let down by this viperstrike's modest performance. Maybe the Kati gave that title to anyone who could rub their belly and pat their head at the same time. Qisami studied the cadence of the whip swings, and then at the right moment, just as the viperstrike was finishing a swing, she shot forward.

Something weird happened to the chain whip. No sooner had Qisami lunged within range, the nine-linked metal chains stiffed into two batons, which the Kati war artist reversed and used to nearly impale her. Qisami twisted aside and ran her blade along the shaft of the now-sticks. She looped an arm around the other woman's elbow and torqued it in a joint lock. The viperstrike tried to twist away, but Qisami was having none of that. She yanked the girl off her feet and swept her to the ground, still holding her. The two continued to struggle. If the viperstrike won, she would slip free. If Qisami won, she would break the other war artist's arm. Qisami liked her chances. Slowly she cranked, feeling the other war artist weakening by the moment. She looked bewildered as well, as if shocked she was losing a fight to a peasant in rags.

Qisami's lips curled. "You're not that good, sweetie."

She looked up to check on Cyyk and wished she hadn't. He had gotten himself into another mess. He had been fighting only one guy and still he couldn't win. She scowled as the Kati got behind Cyyk and had him wrapped in a choke hold along the shaft of the spear. The broodbaby's face was bulging and purple. He was frantic, pawing at nothing. Oh well, that was the price for losing. Maybe she was not as good a teacher as she gave herself credit for.

Qisami checked on the viperstrike. She should just kill her and be done with it. "Oh, pig feet." She scowled. "Hey you, girl."

It took the viperstrike a moment to realize Qisami was addressing her. "Are you talking to me?"

"Do you want to call a truce?"

The viperstrike sneered. "Like, you let me live and we pull back from our attack? I'd rather die."

Qisami wasn't thinking that big. "No, I mean, I give up and you don't hurt me or my friend anymore. But I wouldn't object if you spared the entire colony. I'm assuming you're here to loot."

The young woman stared, suspicious. "Are you surrendering?"

Qisami bobbed her head. "Sure. The people here look up to me. If I surrender, they will too. Promise! So what do you say? Come on, you owe me. I could have killed you just now. You could say I saved your life."

"What, no! This fight is still up in the air. The result was inconclusive."

"Please. You were done and we both know it." Qisami smirked. "So, how do you know Salminde?"

"Quiet, land-chained. I accept your terms."

Qisami relaxed the arm lock and held her hands up. The other Kati spared Cyyk's life, and slowly the Happy Glow Retirement Home survivors either stopped fighting or stopped running. It wouldn't have gone on much longer, anyway. By the time Qisami, hands up, returned to the main square with the viperstrike following behind, most of the inmates had already been rounded up and were sitting in the center of the open area, guarded by horsemen flanking three sides. Qisami joined the huddled masses and sat down next to Cyyk. Everyone around her looked in shock.

Several of the raiders approached the viperstrike, speaking in muted tones. That youthful girl *actually* was in charge. Strange for one so young.

The woman stepped forward after conversing with her people for several moments. "People of this Zhuun settlement. The children of Nezra claim our earned plunder on the rights of the raidlife. Show us where you store your food, supplies, and clothing, and we will let you live. Hinder us and you will all die."

"If you leave us with no food or clothing," someone shouted, "we'll all die anyway."

The Kati looked unmoved. "Then starve, land-chained, or freeze. It makes no difference to me."

Several of the Goons—Hair Bear leading the way—stood and took several steps forward. A dozen of the Kati stepped forward, their shields locked and their spears pointed at the Goons. They advanced. It was going to be a massacre.

"Hey," Qisami shouted at the viperstrike. "Hey, hey, hey, you, girl. I mean, viperstrike."

The young woman noticed Qisami and raised a hand. The wall of shields and spears stopped advancing.

Qisami stopped waving only after she was sure she had the viperstrike's attention. "Hey, hi, let's make another deal, yeah? I saved your life with the first deal. This one's going to be even better."

"It was inconclusive!" the young woman snapped back.

"You have no idea when you've lost. Don't worry, that comes with experience."

"Are you trying to negotiate for a quicker death, land-chained?"

"You're far from the Grass Sea, Child of Nezra. You didn't come here just to raid our crap prison food, did you? You're here for the ore."

"This is a prison?" The viperstrike looked perplexed. "But yes, we claim everything as ours, by the right of the raidlife."

"But you're here for the ore, right?"

The Kati crossed her arms. "Like you said, not for the prison food."

"What if we give you all the ore we have. The entire storage. We'll even load it onto your scary machines for you. In return, you leave food and supplies for these people so they can survive."

The viperstrike laughed. "By the tits of the beautiful Woman, why would I do that? We already claim everything."

"Then . . ." Qisami raised a finger as if speaking to little cute Akiya. "You can return next cycle, and we'll stock you up with more ore. Imagine, your own personal rare ores mine. Except you'll have to pay us the next time. First time is a freebie."

The viperstrike girl considered this. "You will pay Nezra tribute?"

"Think of it more as a trade deal," said Qisami. "The Caobiu are going to find out about this and send their jerks, so it's certainly in both our parties' interest to arm the colony. So how about some ore for some supplies and weapons or something next time you come back?"

The girl viperstrike looked indecisive. Finally, she shook her head. "I don't have the authority of the Council of Nezra to negotiate this. I'll have to speak to *the* viperstrike about it."

"Splendid," said Qisami. "Have Salminde come by and we'll hash out terms."

"How do you know *the* viperstrike, land-chained?"

"You could say I'm her best friend." Qisami beamed. "In fact, we even went into business together, just like you and I are right now. She'll be thrilled to see me."

"Good, then you two can figure out this"—the viperstrike mulled the term as if not sure what it meant—"trade deal that you speak of."

"Splendid. When do you think you'll arrive next?"

The young woman shook her head. "No, Salminde the Viperstrike does not come here to see you. You go to Salminde the Viperstrike to see her."

One of the Kati walked up to Qisami and bashed her over the head with a hammer.

ACT II

CHAPTER TWENTY

THE VIPERSTRIKE

alminde the Viperstrike, former Will of the Khan, Soulseeker of the Rebirth, Scourge of the Stilled Lands, Blade Daughter of Nezra, and exiled rebel of Katuia, stood on the bow of her speeding warpod. She closed her eyes and inhaled the humid and pungent air, expanding her chest. The scent was sickly sweet, bordering on rotten. It sparked a strangely familiar yet distant memory, like something from childhood that she had lost as an adult. Sali held her breath for nearly a minute before she loosed it, feeling her body soak in the environment outside. It had been three years since the Happan ritualist Conchitsha Abu Suriptika had cured her soul rot, and it felt as if she were smelling the Grass Sea for the very first time. The deep grinding numbness of the rot no longer muffled her, leeching away all her strength and senses.

This was her first trip back into the heart of the Grass Sea since her cure, since she finally severed her connection to Jiamin, the former Eternal Khan of Katuia. After nearly a decade, she was returning home, back to her birthplace as she traveled her former capital city's migratory path. It felt good to travel along these familiar gyres after so many years of running and hiding in the fringe of the Grass Sea. Something was always nipping at their heels, either the spirit shamans, the capital ship Liqusa, bounty hunters, raiders, or some monstrous demon of nature from the wild. Sali moved along the starboard railing of the warpod as it cruised through the tall weeds slicing through clumps of the jungle canopy like a water snake across a still pond.

The last time she was here, she fled a fugitive. Now Sali was back but under completely different circumstances. It was now Nezra's turn to hunt.

Sali had initially intended to christen the warpod *Machete,* for the way it sliced through the jungle, but the crew had overruled her. Apparently, podlife was a democracy, much to her chagrin. The crew had a sense of humor. They all voted, and now Sali was captain of the Nezra warpod *Not Loud Not Fat.*

When it had come time for Sali to bring the fight to the inner capital of Katuia, Malinde, Sali's sister and head tinker of the Nezra clan, had offered Sali her choice of city pods to convert to her flagship warpod.

Sali didn't care which, so she said, "Not a loud one. Not a fat one."

And that was exactly what she received, a slim and swift city pod powered by four engines along two low and wide spiked treaded tracks and outfitted to the gills with ballistic artillery. Sali didn't know what most of these wargear details meant, but Mali and Daewon had assured her that whatever *Not Loud Not Fat* couldn't outrun or sneak past, it could blow up into little bits. The warpod was running dark at the moment, its quiet hum emanating little more than a breeze as it moved stealthily under the jungle canopy like a midnight puma with only the parting of the tall weeds betraying her passing.

Its banners on the mast were green and yellow with three jagged tips: Nezra's colors. Their clan had completed their excavation of Kahun the Elusive, the speed city, a legendary capital city that, until recently, had only existed in fables. It came from a time before the war with the Zhuun, when the Katuia were more technologically advanced. The centuries of war slowly degraded their cities until they reached the poor state they were in today. The ancient wargear was more advanced than anything the tinkers now could imagine, let alone create. So many secrets had been lost because of Katuia's endless conflicts, sunk and forgotten in the waters under the Grass Sea's floating landmasses. The tinkers had finished excavating Kahun from the depths of Mount Shetty a little over a year ago. Nearly three-quarters of the city pods were salvageable, giving their clan a means to travel, defend themselves, and finally, claim a new home.

Sali stared into the depths of the jungle, her gaze locked on to a lone, dim light glimmering in the vast ocean of darkness. It was either a solitary glowbug that had lost its swarm, or the big fat prey Sali was searching for. The pregnant trade barge—long, wide, and slow—was plodding steadily along the gyre, its loud sputtering and gassy engine guiding *Not Loud Not Fat* toward it.

Daewon, her brother-in-law and tinkerchief of the warpod, was manning the helm. He barked behind her, and the Kahun warpod picked up speed.

Anticipation surged through Sali as *Not Loud Not Fat* closed in on their prey, the sharp breeze whipping past the shaved sides of her head. Sali was beginning to wonder if she had made the wrong career choice. She had always enjoyed the raidlife and pillaging Zhuun settlements, but piracy in the Grass Sea was a whole new level of fun. Being the captain of a warpod was far more exciting than raiding a farming settlement could ever be.

Not Loud Not Fat lived up to its name, silently nudging up next to the trade barge. Even though it was one of the smaller Kahun pods, built for quickness and stealth, the ancient warpod towered above and cast a long shadow over the trade barge, its whisper-quiet engines masked by the trade barge's obnoxious track motors. Sali gave the signal, and then stepped atop the pod's starboard railings facing the deck of the trade barge. A row of booms extended out, each with a rope hanging from it like a fishing line. Sali unhooked one of the ropes and raised an arm. Six other sea-raiders stepped onto the platform next to her, including a young woman with a freshly shaven head and richly carved wood-banded armor.

"Stay close, Wani," she instructed.

"I wouldn't dream of leaving your side, mentor," the glib, smart-mouthed lass replied.

Sali had two neophytes after Hampa died at the hands of Katuia back at Hrusha. It was now up to both Marhi, the young woman from the Sun Under Lagoon, and Wani, the talented girl from the howler monkeys, to take Hampa's place and honor his legacy. The two women instantly became sisters, best friends and best enemies, competing relentlessly to earn Sali's favor. Marhi, the former Happan rumblerlead, was older and cleverer. Wani, however, was more talented, with greater physical gifts. Sali hoped they would surpass her one day. Nezra certainly could use both their talents.

"Bicker of my quarrel." Sali snorted under her breath. It still made her chuckle. She raised her voice to the others. "Remember our engagement. These Katuia are not our enemy."

"Unless they choose to be," the sea-raiders finished together. They were raw, but a well-trained bunch, and still had the edgy humor that only the bratty young possessed. Sali, having trained and personally selected every last one of them, adored them all.

She stared down at the deck of the barge. Now came the fun part.

She leaped from the railing with her body fully extended, both hands holding on to the ends of the rope as she swung over the gap between the two craft. The barge's night shift should be a skeleton crew, although even with full hands there were likely less than thirty souls crewing a barge this size, not that it mattered. A trade barge this modest probably didn't have a skilled war artist on board guarding it.

She reached the end of her pendulum swing and then released, floating in the air briefly before dropping onto the pilothouse located just past the center of the barge. The unsuspecting helmsman must have been half asleep. He blinked once when he finally noticed he wasn't alone, and then blinked a few more times as if unsure that she was actually there and not a figment of his imagination.

Sali gave him a moment to make the right choice. The helmsman instead pawed for a bell hanging off a rope just at the edge of his reach. Sali could have ended him right there, but she remembered her own words to her people. This crew wasn't Nezra's enemy, nor was she here to plunder this barge. At least, not really.

Sali flicked her tongue, uncoiling it from its holster around her waist as its bite—the spear-tip at its end—leaped from her grasp and punctured a hole through his hand. He opened his mouth to scream, but she had already closed that distance and looped the tongue's rope around his neck. She squeezed, and within heartbeats the helmsman was unconscious on the floor. At least he still breathed.

The rest of the boarding party landed nearby, each to varying degrees of success and stealth. Again, well trained and disciplined, but raw like Happan cuisine. But then she could say that about Nezra's entire fighting force. Sali had to train them. Some, like Wani, she had to practically raise from when she was a sprout.

Speaking of her neophyte, Sali glanced toward the front of the barge and saw Wani land next to a wandering deckhand with a loud *thunk*. It was more of a controlled fall than a proper landing. Wani was a breath late getting her spearhand to the man's throat, but it did its job. The deckhand clutched his throat and gurgled before she clubbed him across the back of the head. The girl looked over at Sali and beamed. She was rewarded with an admonishing frown alongside a finger to the lips. Viperstrikes weren't stealthy, but they certainly weren't rampaging pandas either.

She signaled to the others with quick finger motions: pair up, end to middle, stay silent.

Wani met Sali a moment later. "How did that look, mentor?"

Sali grunted. She would have to provide detailed notes later. "Follow. Stay as my second."

The two continued down a set of stairs below the pilothouse. Barges of this type kept their cargo on deck, while the engines and crew quarters were below. With some luck, they could seize control of the barge without leaving behind a mess. Unfortunately, the optimal result was pulled off the table the moment she ventured below deck.

Sali opened the door and came face to face with one of the guards on his way up. The poor sap, Tsunarcos by the looks of his glass armor, blinked and reached for the saber hanging at his waist. Wani acted first, planting the bottom of her boot on his chest, and sent him tumbling down the stairs. That was a mistake. His tumble and pained cries against each step on his way down the surprisingly long flight were loud enough to wake the entire ship. His glass armor shattered like an expensive vase once he reached the bottom, echoing throughout the lower decks.

Sali curled her lips at her neophyte. "Really?"

The girl didn't even look abashed. "He startled me!"

"He surprised you, so you kick him down the stairs?" A groan rose from somewhere in the darkness of the hold. Sali took no chances. She leaped down the stairs, covering its entire length in one jump, landing beside the Tsunarcos just as he had pushed himself back onto his hands and knees. She ended his night with a broken nose from her knee.

It was too late, however. The crew was stirring. She could feel the calm down in the hold evaporate. The quiet, creaking hold below deck came alive, filled with shouting in the distance and the rumbling of heavy boots on wood. So much for the element of surprise. Wani joined Sali a moment later, and the two viperstrikes began clearing the corridor. Sali took point and quickly pounced on any crewmembers stepping into the hallway. Once she subdued them, Wani would club them on the head as if she were preparing rabbit for dinner. The two were deadly and silent as they swept through the length of the hold. Things did not appear to be working so smoothly for the rest of the sea-raiders.

Shouts, clashing weapons, and the buzz of battle erupted throughout the barge. They were halfway through the hold when they encountered a man wearing pajamas who looked like he might be someone important. Whoever he was, he quickly threw his hands up to surrender. That saved him from Sali putting a knee in his gut. Wani, however, didn't care and bonked him on the head.

Sali sighed. "This one looked like he could be the captain. We needed him alive, lass."

"Sorry again. I *think* he's still alive." Wani was practically quivering. "I just got too excited. This is *so* fun!"

Sali rubbed her eye and let out a long breath. "How did I go from Hampa the Gentle to Wani the Savage?"

"You always tell me that every new war artist is a blank slate, a puppy who will find their own personality."

"Wani the smart mouth," Sali groused. She wasn't really annoyed. She liked that the girl possessed grit and spunk in abundance.

Sali made sure to keep ahead of her as they continued down the corridor. They really *did* need some of these people alive. The two were nearing the end of the hall when a wrinkled man with a long white beard emerged from a side door. He charged out so suddenly both parties surprised each other. Apparently, he more than they. The older startled when he came face-to-face with Sali. Then he gasped, clutched his chest, and fell over.

Wani held her hands up. "I swear I didn't touch him!"

The two continued across the length of the hold, manhandling any of the barge's crew that crossed their path, knocking them unconscious or breaking bones with equal ease and efficiency. It felt like paddling children. That was the thing with most pod crews. They were not warriors. Most were worthless in a fight, and a low-level trading barge likely couldn't afford to pay to have a staffed war artist.

And just like everything else Sali had predicted tonight, she was wrong. The two had just passed under a thick wooden grate when several spotlights from *Not Loud Not Fat* flared to life, bathing the trade barge with harsh white light.

Sali shielded her eyes. "What is Daewon doing?" She heard a loud, familiar battle cry. Sali took off running, sprinting toward the nearest stairs leading back up to the main deck.

Wani kept up with her easily. Her eyes were wide. "What is that, mentor?"

"A ramshack sect, aligned with the Jomei clan," Sali said. "Possibly a champion, but probably not. I would be surprised if so."

The two reemerged on the upper deck at the bow of the barge. Sali glanced back toward the main hold and saw a large ramshack war artist wielding a twinsword towering over one of her sea-raiders. He twirled his sect weapon, which was a deadly bladed staff formed from two swords attached at the end of the hilt.

So this barge *could* afford a champion after all. Sali's voice carried across the battlefield. "Ramshack!" Sali stepped to the edge of the railing just as her opponent with literal ram horns on his helm was about to bring the pointed end down on her raider.

The other war artist turned to face her. His eyes narrowed. "A viperstrike? I thought I saw the last of your kind."

"Stay out of this," Sali instructed Wani, and then dropped down to the main deck.

The barge champion was a gnarled and twisted old root of a man, ancient by war arts standards. His hair was a mess of curls that made him look like an unshorn sheep. The skin on his face was cracked and scarred, and his posture steep and worn. The war artist's face was red with sunken eyes, but they were alert and sharp, ready for battle even if his body could no longer match his intentions. He certainly carried himself like a big koi in a small pond.

But that answered how this barge could afford a champion. Sali knew many war artists like this senior, men and women who had survived far longer than their calling typically allowed. Some older war artists never knew when to lay down their weapons, walk away from the raidlife, and continue on toward their twilight days. Others simply couldn't retire and pass along their armor and weapons for a plethora of reasons, typically financial. In any case, Sali respected these older warriors and usually offered leniency.

"I offer you one chance to surrender this craft, Ramshack," she said, stalking forward. "Live with your honor blemished or perish with it intact."

The gnarled root sniffed and twirled his twinsword in his hands until he brought it to rest on his shoulder. That was all the reply Sali needed.

The moment the ramshack raised his guard, she sent a jolt through her tongue and stiffened it into a spear. She followed through with a series of sharp cuts and short slashes, whipping the tongue quicker than the ramshack could react with his shorter, more unwieldy weapon. The ramshack managed to parry the first few bites from her tongue before she drew first blood, raking his cheek and adding another scar to his collection. Sali kept the pressure on, and with each exchange blossomed more crimson stains across his body, first the shoulder and thigh, and then the chest.

The older war artist knew he was outmatched. To his credit, he did not retreat or attempt to delay the inevitable. Instead, he pressed against her in a final bid for glory, hoping to slip under her attacks and score a lucky killing blow. Sali appreciated his tenacity. Death by duel was a time-honored tradition, one that she usually was more than happy to offer.

She hesitated this time, however. This man was Katuia and also not her enemy. Her views on tradition and expectations were no longer what they once were. Sali now continually questioned the unquestioned authority and righteousness of the old ways, especially after they had turned their back on Nezra. She offered the ramshack one last chance. "This does not need to be the only way, old one."

The war artist did not hesitate. "Honor is the way!"

Sali shot her tongue forward in its roped state, its bite extending past the ramshack's left shoulder as he juked to one side. Then she yanked it with full force, punching his back. The old war artist stiffened, and his twinsword flew from his grasp as he came at her one last time. He glanced down at the point of her bite protruding from the right side of his chest, thick blood spurting from the fresh gaping wound.

"It is the only . . ." The ramshack collapsed to the floor.

The battle was over. Sali had lost one, a victim to the ramshack, but the rest of her sea-raiders incurred mostly nicks and bruises. Loyo may have broken his wrist, but that was because he tripped over a knot of ropes. The trade barge crew, all twenty-six, surrendered with minimal casualties, save for a scattered few lying about.

Sali walked the line of her new prisoners until she came across that same pajama man Wani had knocked out earlier. She was glad he had suffered no worse than a concussion. "Do you run this barge?" she asked.

The man stood taller and tried to muster as much dignity as one could while wearing a nightgown. She could smell the cumlange on his breath. He spat on the deck. "How dare you! I am Hanus of the Great Deals Galore, yar of the *Honest Run*, and you're making a grave mistake. I have a trade and protection order with the Katuia. You're asking for nothing but pain once the horde comes."

That was the whole reason she was here. "You're on the wrong side of the Grass Sea, Yar Hanus."

"Trade goes where the customers pay, pirate." *Pirate* was a strong word but not entirely inaccurate. He glanced at the large Kahun war-pod casting its long shadow over his barge. "With a beautiful whale like that, I assume I can't just bribe you and send you on your way?"

Sali was amused. "What are you offering?"

The yar took inventory of his situation. "Times are hard. Rebellions are everywhere. I think three billion rooples sounds fair."

Three billion wouldn't keep *Not Loud Not Fat*'s engines powered for a week, not to mention the brutal exchange rates the Tsunarcos charged for their mostly worthless currency. "Which city are you attached to, Yar Hanus?"

"We pay our dues to the wet tulip. This is your last chance to do the right thing, pirate."

Just as Sali expected. Sunjawa was the closest trade port in this region of the Grass Sea, and the largest rim clan in the north just outside of the inner capital city's usual migratory patterns.

"You're not getting your rooples' worth in protection from the Katuia," she said.

"Revenge for injustices comes as part of the payment," he proclaimed. "Just wait, you'll see."

It was common in Tsunarcos culture to phrase everything as an insult or threat. Tsunarcos were shrewd businesspeople, but made terrible friends. They were all bark and little bite. They were also a sensitive group of people who enjoyed taking offense to just about everything.

"I'm going to make you an offer, Yar Hanus." She turned toward Daewon, who had zip-lined down to the barge from *Not Loud Not Fat*. "Leash it up." She turned to Wani. "Sweep the lower decks one more time and escort the crew to the hold. Two guards on watch. No one out, no one in."

Hanus looked outraged. "You're stealing the entire barge?"

Sali ignored him. "Check the stores for replenishment, but no more than a quarter share."

"Hey!" whined the Tsunarcos. "Just take the cargo. No need to take my livelihood as well."

"I don't want your barge, captain. I just want to borrow it for a while," she replied. "Behave and you'll get most of your cargo back too."

"You don't? Why are you pirating my barge if not to rob me?" He looked confused and then outraged. "How dare you think I am not good enough for your thievery! If you don't want my cargo, and you don't want my barge, what do you want, pirate? Did you seize my craft as some kind of sick joke? Is this funny to you?"

"I am amused by this situation," Sali admitted. She tossed him a set of wooden manacles. "Now behave and put these on. I have cargo to deliver."

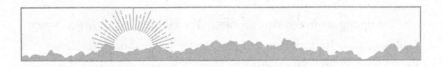

CHAPTER TWENTY-ONE

LIFE UNDER SIEGE

Wen Jian huddled into a ball with his arms wrapped around his knees. He was sitting in a low stream trickling down the bottom of a large stone tunnel that ran under Big Love Big Dowry Road. It was late spring of the second cycle, which was typically the wet season here in Vauzan. The air was nippy as last night's passing storm clouds left behind a lingering morning chill. His teeth chattered and he couldn't steady his shaking. To both sides were two more rows of underground corps with a shallow stream of sewage running between them. This bunch was a mix of soldiers, war artists, and commoners, all looking wary and tired, but determined.

Jian looked across from where he sat. Hachi's eyes were closed. He looked asleep, save for his muttering. His best friend had volunteered to become his shadow at Taishi's insistence. She didn't trust anyone else for the job.

A loud explosion shook the earth around them, drizzling dirt and pebbles over them. A nearby building might have collapsed. The Cao-biu maintained a constant trickle of bombardment on the Shulan-controlled wards as a form of psychological warfare. It worked because every Shulan resident was exhausted, miserable, and in shock, yet everyone endured.

The heavy rumbling of many hooves clopped overhead, which was then followed by a steady cadence of footsteps.

"Now!" barked the captain's sharp voice.

Jian turned to his left and filed out of the sewer tunnel on the short side, while everyone else, save for Hachi, headed to the right. It would leave Jian dangerously exposed for a few minutes. This was by design. While sound tactics were important, good publicity was paramount.

He emerged out of the tunnel at one side of a low bridge passing over a small stream. The King was just setting to the west, casting a long shadow of Jian wielding his blade. The bridge connected the two halves of Diamond Too Small Market, a busy square in a ward currently under Caobiu control. Lines of starving people stretched for several blocks around the market.

Jian stepped onto an air current and launched himself two stories high. He drew the Swallow Dances with a loud hiss at the zenith of his flight and then landed carefully on one of the bridge's corner posts. Every pair of eyes was locked on him. A mutter swept through the crowd. This was also by design.

Soon, every soldier in red and yellow knew that the Champion of the Five Under Heaven had taken the field against them. The blue blade was married to his burgeoning legend. Most of it was due to good publicity. The Shulan Court were experts at that game. It was their national pastime. Everything about Wen Jian, the Prophesied Hero of the Tiandi, was carefully orchestrated by the court.

Everything, of course, except combat. The fighting was all too real, too fierce, and too deadly.

Jian slipped the initial spear charge and sliced the soldier across the back. He parried a pike thrust, a saber slash, and a heavy ax chop. His blood pumped as the nearby enemy soldiers—*candles* as referred to by the city—cornered him. The Swallow Dances was hampered here. Straight swords were not meant for the battlefield, but Oban insisted.

Something, something, image and branding consistency, the high lord had said.

The pikeman came at him next, trying to cleave him in two at the waist. Jian hurdled it with a jump side twist and jabbed the man in the thigh while rolling in midair before landing dramatically on one knee. An incoming ax swing ruined his pose. He almost lost an arm. Fortunately, Jian pulled back in time. The ax wielder was about to split Jian in half again when his body stiffened as a bullet burst through his chest. The man fell, revealing Hachi standing behind him at point-blank range.

The two war artists moved back-to-back as the rest of the enemy soldiers converged on them. There was glory and gold to be earned for any Caobiu who captured Jian. It was rumored that the reward for his capture was a lordship and estates. Greed made men ambitious and careless.

Just when this overconfident candle could almost taste his nobility, the rest of the underground corps emerged from the opposite tunnel entrance. Their charge blindsided the dozen or so Caobiu, cutting down the enemy with brutal efficiency before the candles realized it was an ambush. Half did not see their killer. The remainder who did were then mopped up by Jian and Hachi.

The underground corps rushed to a locked jail wagon sitting in the middle of the street. One blow from the poll of an ax later and the door to the carriage broke off its hinges. A small flood of young men poured out, running to freedom.

The captain of the underground corps looked over at Jian. "Well done, champion."

Jian couldn't muster the enthusiasm to nod.

The next day, the rumors planted on the streets would only re-member that the Champion of the Five Under Heaven took out a conscription caravan along with its security detail and freed many of the city's citizens who had been seized by the Caobiu. The corps scav-enged fallen soldiers, taking weapons and armor and picking through pockets. Jian was surprised to discover that the man who'd nearly lopped off his arm was one-armed himself. That risk must run common in his line of work. As Taishi always said, *"If you can't sword, then you ax."*

The underground corps escaped the crime scene by fleeing down a side alley before returning through a network of sewer tunnels leading to the basement of a building with a caved-in roof. This city block had been decimated during the first days of the siege. Buildings were little more than husks. There were mounds of debris everywhere. The stench of burnt wood lingered in the air. They made it back to a hidden passageway that eventually linked up with a wagon tunnel used for smuggling operations. These underground pedways now served as the primary method of travel for the Shulan resistance.

The corps' captain signaled for a stop after they reached a hub joining three of these tunnels. "You dungshits were sloppy today. Everyone in the Big Rock Ward will know that we freed their people. It's important for them to know that we haven't forgotten them. Now, sleep. One guard at each end of the hub, and one more accompanying the grand lord."

That was the official title bestowed upon Jian by the Shulan Court. The Shulan were sticklers for ranks, and they didn't know where to slot the central figure of their religion within their hierarchy. Being called a lord felt awkward, but Oban had insisted. The high lord was the head of the Shulan Court, and de facto leader of the city's defense. While he possessed little experience in war, Oban was a skilled diplomat and had managed to unite all the disparate groups—the military, underground corps, magistrates, and underworld, among many others—against their common foe. Sunri's Cinder Legions might slowly engulf Vauzan, but they made the Caobiu bleed with every block conquered, all while keeping people's hopes alive by using Jian as their holy symbol.

Jian reveled in his role as the people's champion, while at the same time he reviled it for the false hope it provided. Being a symbol was one thing; becoming that symbol was something else altogether. That meant he had to be seen in the thick of battle and had to at least put up the pretense of leading their war efforts. Most importantly, Jian had to inspire the residents of Vauzan to join the resistance, knowing full well that it would likely lead to their deaths. This fighting quickly grew wearisome. After the initial excitement and bravado wore off, the shock set in, and then numbness. Now, nearly a month into the Caobiu attack on Vauzan, all he felt was exhaustion.

Jian leaned back against the wet wall and closed his eyes. There was nothing artistic about sieges, no honor, no glory. It was just battles in the streets, butchery in buildings, and starvation or pestilence everywhere. He couldn't make sense of why anyone would voluntarily participate in this. Taishi and the other masters had tried to warn him, steel him for the ugly chaos, but nothing could have prepared him for the horror that had unfolded with each passing day. There was no way he was ever going to read those Burning Hearts romances again. Whoever wrote that rubbish obviously had never endured a siege.

If war was hell, then sieges were doubly so.

The captain came by a moment later. "Grand lord, we have orders to pull you back to the friendly wards."

Jian nodded. "When do we leave?"

"You, champion, leave immediately with your shadow. The rest of us are regrouping with the Third Magistrates at the Three Punch fighting field. Caobiu are trying to break up a refugee camp housed there."

Jian made a face. "I used to train there."

"I met my wife there." The captain sighed. "That woman had the sneakiest back leg sweep I've ever seen. Tiandi rest her soul."

Jian wished he could accompany the underground corps, but he understood his role. Every target assigned to him was carefully curated to be real but rarely dangerous. Defending a Caobiu attack on a ward certainly qualified as dangerous.

Soon after, Jian said his goodbyes to the rest of the corps, addressing them with the same canned speech about resiliency and honor and great righteousness he gave every local underground corps he embedded into during these assignments. It was a far cry from what Jian thought he would do when he joined the city's resistance.

He had embedded with them, and now he was being moved again.

Chances were, he wouldn't see any of them again. At least he hadn't seen any of the other nine corps he had worked with so far. He was probably going to go somewhere else, fight some small-scale battle for publicity, and then repeat the cycle all over again.

Jian linked up with Hachi and their escort Puo a bit later. His escort was a few years younger than Jian, and by the looks of his scrawny arms, wouldn't be useful for protection. Puo was attending classes at Sunsheng University. After the attack, he joined his older brother Shum's underground corps. His elder sibling was the sergeant. Now Puo was leading the Prophesied Hero of the Tiandi through sewer tunnels during a siege. Change came quickly during war.

Puo bowed low. "Champion of the Five Under—"

"Just Jian. Jian's fine," he replied. "No need to advertise."

"Of course . . . Jian." Puo sounded uneasy saying his name. "We should head out now that it's dark."

The trip back to friendly wards didn't take long. The Caobiu weren't willing to probe too deep into Shulan-controlled parts of the city. The risks were too high. The enemy's grip on the city was tightening. Fortunately, Vauzan was a massive city, and difficult for the Cinder Legions to consume.

The three traveled through the city's tunnels most of the way and then continued traversing the low fields and gardens before finally reaching topside, sneaking through alleyways and buildings. The few residents who saw them said nothing. They had only one unlucky encounter with a Caobiu checkpoint barring their way.

Jian counted five candles blocking the intersection leading to the neighboring buried ward. The Caobiu had not established a foothold underground yet. Fortunately, Puo had another way. The kid led Jian into an abandoned building and up a flight of stairs. They emerged out of a third-story window and then skirted across the rooftop past the checkpoint. Jian was tempted to take to the air and fly back to friendly spaces, but Taishi had forbidden him. He was an easy target while in the air.

"You move through the air like a clipped chicken," she had said.

She wasn't wrong. He probably was one of those windwhispers who wasn't great at the most important and recognizable aspect of this style.

They snuck past the blockade and crawled along a narrow alley, then finally reached the buried ward. From that point, it was a long jaunt to the other side of the tunnel through the giant pillar, which led to the base of Peony Peak.

"Did you want to come to the temple, Puo?" asked Jian. "You can get a hot meal and a bath."

"I should get back to my corps, grand lord," said the young man.

"Come on," Jian urged. The boy might never get another hot meal. Best he take advantage now, while he could. "You'll have more strength to fight with a full belly and warm bed. The fight will still be there tomorrow."

Puo accepted his invitation. They had to wait for the lift to come down. The pathway up the mountain had been destroyed by the rockslide. The smell of spiced broth enticed the young men. Jian probably should have gone to find Taishi right away, but the food beckoned his stomach. It had been days since his last hot meal.

The kitchen ran nonstop these days. The Tiandi religion had declared their neutrality during the civil war, but that did not mean the temples could not serve the needy. The Caobiu dared not make a fuss about it, lest the abbots officially declare their support for or against any of the dukes.

The three were soon slurping soup on a wooden bench. Hachi was studying Puo sitting on the opposite bench. "You look bookish, Puo. I take it soldiering was not part of your career path. What brought you to join an underground corps?"

The young man was cupping a warm bowl of congee in both hands, practically pouring the food into his mouth. "My older brother Shum's the sergeant of that outfit. Figured I'd be safe with family, or at least have his back in a fight. Our parents perished with most of our neighborhood at the Teapot Ward on the third day from an artillery blast. We're all we have now, Shum and me."

Jian bit his lip. It was a painfully common story, made worse by the fact that Jian took responsibility for each of them personally. The burden felt heavier with each passing day. The Shulan Court had used him to inspire the city and bring in volunteers. How many were here because of him, and how many would still be alive after this siege was over?

"What were you studying at university?" asked Jian.

Puo broke into a shy smile. "You, Wen Jian. I was preparing for my monastic entrance exam."

A small shudder passed through him. It weirded him out that people thought he was some sort of divine being. He used to think he knew what greatness was, but then he left the Celestial Palace and realized how minuscule he actually was in the grand scope of the heavens.

"Well, once this is over, you can tell them that the Prophesied Hero of the Tiandi thinks you are worthy to join the temple." He raised a finger. "In fact . . ."

A robed war artist rushed through the gates into the main courtyard, yelling something Jian couldn't make out. Shouts answered, and then the message began to ripple through the crowds.

He beckoned at a passing blue-robed magistrate. "What's going on, sir?"

The magistrate looked stunned. "Three Punch just fell to the Caobiu. The ward's split open. The Caobiu were ready for our crews. They smashed every defender we had."

It took a moment for the facts to register. The Three Punch field had housed hundreds of refugees and was located in a main area surrounded by several Shulan wards. Now they were all exposed. Jian looked at Puo, whose face had turned white.

"Any news on the surviving corps?" he asked the magistrate in a soft, pained voice.

The man shook his head. "No survivors, son."

Puo began to breathe heavily. "I have to go."

"Hang on," said Jian. "It's too dangerous to go on your own. I'm sure the Shulan are formulating a response. We can join them."

"I have to go," the boy repeated. He looked over at Jian one more time and then ran off.

A wave of numbness washed over Jian. He stood helpless. Bringing him here had at least kept Puo from his brother. Would he blame Jian for this? It shouldn't matter, but it did. Jian probably had saved Puo's life, but it didn't make him feel any better.

He turned and walked past the main temple and continued into the bamboo forest where their small cottage sat, untouched by the outside world. Jian's shoulders finally unclenched. It felt like weeks since he last felt at ease. He walked through the door, suddenly breathing heavily.

"You look terrible," Taishi said, sitting at the table poring over a map. Jian stumbled toward her. Taishi's face grew more alarmed. "What's wrong? Are you injured, boy?"

Jian slipped to one knee and buried his head into her lap, and he began to sob.

CHAPTER TWENTY-TWO

PROGRESS

J ian fell asleep, using Taishi's lap as a pillow for most of the night. She was annoyed and angry, but not because of his pain and grief. She was angry for him. It hurt her soul to see him in such agony. Taishi understood too well the damage that trauma inflicted upon the soul. She would have been disturbed if the horrors of war hadn't affected him so deeply. Empathy was an important trait in a good leader, and that was something Jian possessed in abundance. Too much, sometimes. He was a good egg, that boy, but his shell was too soft.

What really annoyed Taishi was that Jian didn't wash up before he fell asleep on her lap, so now the room smelled like shit, sweat, and unwashed young man. Even worse, her legs had gone numb and she had to pee. When did his head get so heavy?

This charade Oban and the rest of the Shulan Court were conducting by propping up Jian was disgraceful. Putting him in danger so they could show his face to rile up the crowds was a mockery of the Champion of the Five Under Heaven. It was an unnecessary risk not only to Jian's life but also to the Prophecy of the Tiandi. Unfortunately, as she had dreaded, once he was revealed to the masses, his legend had taken on a life of its own. Now he belonged to everyone, not just Taishi, which made him harder to protect and control.

People—the emotional, reactive masses—during times of crisis could turn stupid, greedy, and shortsighted. They might care about the Prophesied Hero of the Tiandi fighting on their side, but not a soul cared a whit about Wen Jian, the young man with a whole life still ahead of him.

Taishi had to finally dump Jian off her lap shortly before dawn. If she lost any more circulation to her lower extremities, they would have to amputate. It was difficult enough being a one-armed woman. What was she going to do if she only had one leg?

She bucked his head off her knee and tsked as tingling pain shot up her body. Jian's head lolled to the side and came to rest on a nearby pillow. His light snoring didn't miss a beat. Taishi could have gotten up hours ago, but she relished that quiet moment. She was spending less time with him lately. Jian was growing up. His world was expanding. She couldn't shelter him any longer. He was once again the Prophesied Hero of the Tiandi, the Savior of the Zhuun. He was the most beloved, hated, desired, *and* most wanted man in all the Enlightened States, possibly even the world.

Taishi had to grit some of her last remaining teeth while she hobbled toward bed. Every step felt like the sting of a thousand bees. It was times like this that she wished she actually had eaten a sword in battle so she wouldn't have to put up with the slow torture of growing old.

She snorted. "You're just too damn good, Taishi."

She passed through the kitchen, stopping by the stove to watch the goat stew from last night. The boy probably hadn't eaten since Tiandi knows when. He had been so distracted lately he might forget to eat when he woke up. Or worse, one of those court vultures might come to steal him away again. Taishi's hand curled into a fist, and she felt an intense need to cook.

She pulled out yesterday's leftover banana leaf sticky rice alongside the previous day's garlic green beans. The day before that was meat. She wasn't sure exactly what, but it was edible. Taishi plated the tray and left it on the table next to the couch. Jian still hadn't budged off that pillow. His body slumped over in what looked like a deeply un-comfortable position, but still he snored. She wasn't going to be the only one with an achy back tomorrow. Taishi looked over Jian. The lines around his eyes were deep. His eyes had been bloodshot. Her nails dug into her palm.

She stormed out of the cottage and made for the front gate, striding from the bamboo forest, past the field where the monks trained. There must be at least forty bodies practicing staff forms. By the looks of the sweat on their brows, they must have been here since dawn.

Taishi entered the courtyard. Even at this hour the temple was awake. Initiates were running about preparing for the day, fetching water and stoking fires, pulling a wagon full of incense vases toward the back of the main temple, or carrying long poles with racks of smoked duck from the kitchen.

Solum was standing at the front gates barking orders when Taishi arrived. He was either up early or hadn't gone to bed yet. The Hansoo, like bears and infants, generally required a lot of sleep. An under-slept Hansoo was as effective as a drunk one.

The senior Hansoo arched an eyebrow as she approached the gate. "Going somewhere, dowager?"

"I'm off to court to beat some sense into Oban."

"The wily Defender of Vauzan may not take too kindly to being beaten so early in the morning."

"There's no good time for a beating, so we might as well get it over with." Taishi bristled at the front gates, still closed. "Open up."

Solum shrugged. "The streets are not safe. Allow me to have an escort accompany you. I don't have the bodies to spare now. Can you wait an hour?"

Taishi shook her head. She was already tired and would pass out if she had to sit around. "I'll be fine. Besides, everyone knows the city is safest before breakfast."

He looked as if he were about to deny her, and then shrugged. "Open the gates."

"Thank you." Taishi paused as she walked past the senior war monk. "By the way, put a guard on Jian today. He's had a hard few days. He needs rest. Don't let any of the garrison or court jackals get to him while I'm gone."

Solum nodded. "I'll assign one of my initiates."

Taishi was soon outside the temple for the first time in over a week, and she rode the lift down Peony Peak.

The streets of Vauzan were quiet this morning. Taishi picked her way across the rubble-strewn streets, passing broken houses and leveled buildings, with the aftermath of the battle strewn across the field: rotting bodies, random pieces of armor and weapons, and the remnants of barricaded positions. She could reconstruct what had transpired. The center of this intersection was where the two sides had fought. To her left were the bodies of a group of magistrate corps near the entrance to an alley. They must have come to help the garrison but found little success. Magistrate and volunteer corps had varying skill levels and disciplines. Magistrates individually might be quality war artists, but single and small-group combat required a different skill set.

The stream of bodies led down one street. That must be the direction where the defenders retreated. Several were aligned in one direction face down with injuries across their backs. Then, once they were past the intersection, the number of red-and-yellow uniformed bodies grew. Several had arrow puncture wounds. Taishi glanced up. Archers from second-story windows had fired upon the attacking Caobiu. By the many types of hunting, competition, and even practice arrows, they appeared to be volunteer corps. The ambush continued down to the end of the block, where another garrison cut off the Caobiu.

Taishi stopped in the middle of the narrow battlefield. This was where the Cinder Legions made their last stand. She studied a streak of blood ending at the entrance to the alley. "They took prisoners." Vauzan won this fight, but by the looks of the Shulan bodies on the ground it was, at best, a Pyrrhic victory.

Taishi reached the fork in the road that either traveled up a slope leading to the front gates of the Court Citadel or forked right down to a valley where a cluster of underground bunkers served as the Shulan Court. The citadel, located near the center of the city, was out of range of Caobiu artillery. As a precaution, the high lords had moved to buried wards, which was where they coordinated and led the city's resistance to the Caobiu onslaught. One lord, however, stayed aboveground. This was the one Taishi needed to speak with tonight.

She rolled her eyes when the Tower of Humblest Modesty came into view. Oban was making a mockery of his political opponents. There was nothing humble or modest about this garish glass tower with its excessive glitter perched on a private pillar that was crossable only by a double-wide wooden roped bridge. She was surprised the Caobiu hadn't taken potshots at this eyesore.

She walked into the tower past four displayguards. No common soldier would dare stop a dowager nun. Any who dared raise an eyebrow was beaten to submission by her pinpoint gaze.

An older, tall woman with a sharp, imperial nose and narrow eyes intercepted her on the way to the lift. "Dowager, the high lord is not expecting you this morning."

"You know who I am. Take me to him."

The woman's face remained neutral. There were few secrets a lord could keep without their Voice of the Court knowing about it. "The high lord is not available at this time, regrettably."

Taishi didn't move, just stared the woman down. The two guards standing near the doorway exchanged glances and then took a step toward Taishi.

"That won't be necessary." The woman's voice was sharp. She offered a stiff bow to Taishi. "This way . . . dowager."

It was good to know her reputation still carried weight. The Voice of the Court escorted her through the large double doors, which led to a flight of curved stairs, and then back out to the large balcony where Oban had last received her. This time, he was having breakfast alone at a small table.

The Voice of the Court stopped at the entranceway. "Grand Dowager Nun Nai Roha."

Taishi stepped forward and bowed.

Oban looked up from what appeared to be battle plans and eyed Taishi. "Close off this floor."

"Yes, high lord," the woman said.

Within a few minutes, they were alone.

Oban looked on. "The fight *does* go well."

"Aye, it does, but you're still losing."

"For now. War is fickle."

"You're using Jian like he is a piece in a game."

He turned to face her. "Aren't we all, though, just pieces in some game?"

"*We* are, perhaps," she said. "The Prophesied Hero of the Tiandi isn't. He's *the* only piece that's important, and you're using him as a recruitment tool."

"That's where he's most useful, Taishi. His presence brings flocks of volunteers to the defense of the city."

"And you're still losing. You're going to get them killed if you don't turn it around." Taishi took a breath and went for it. "I want to take him out of the city. It's too dangerous, and he's far too important to the Tiandi to risk parading about in a war zone."

"He is central to our war efforts, Taishi."

"He's central to all Zhuun. This war with Sunri is a distraction to his greater responsibility."

Oban was about to take a bite of a flaky bun when he stopped and tilted his head at her like an inquisitive cat. "What responsibility could one have that's greater than protecting both home and duchy?"

"You mean, other than saving the Zhuun?"

"From an immortal being who has been dead for nearly a decade."

"If that's the case, why are you dressing Jian up and parading him all over the city?"

"Because he's more useful playing that role than being a warrior on the battlefield." Taishi's eyes narrowed. Her face went sharp. Oban continued, unfazed. "I've watched him fight for weeks now. He's talented and skilled, but even you have to admit his is a dim light next to yours. He will never be the type of war artist who can change the tide of battles on his own."

She was just happy he'd stopped crashing into trees. She tried another tactic. "Now that he's returned, use him to recruit allies from outside Vauzan. Face it, your numbers have plateaued. Anyone who was going to join the resistance would have done so by now. You need help."

Oban snorted. "Like whom? Lawkan won't lift a finger for us. They only have boats anyway. Xing's too far away *and* they won't help us, either." He raised a finger. "No mercenary outfit will sign up for this meat grinder. Most of the underworlds are too busy profiting from this chaos to help, as are the trade conglomerate, the dairy cabal, silkspinners, and just about every lunar court entity. It's a dangerous time, Taishi. Everyone is looking out for themselves."

"What about the Tiandi religion?"

Oban sneered. "What about them? Neutral to a fault." Then he growled, "Smart bastards."

"But if they joined Vauzan, they would make a difference. Jian is the central figure to the Tiandi. He can command them to come."

"Not even the prophesied hero is worth the Tiandi religion breaking neutrality. Vauzan is too small. The templeabbots would never jeopardize their place within the realm by antagonizing the next empress of the Enlightened States. Not even if the Prophesied Hero of the Tiandi ordered them to. They would more likely kidnap him than listen to him. Hand over Jian to them and you will never see him again."

"He's his own man, Oban. They must listen. Let him try."

"Tell you what." The high lord stood. "Wen Jian is invited to send a message to the Jade Tower of the Vigilant Spirit. Send a courier, fly a pigeon, use a mindseer, I don't care. If he has the influence you say, then they will answer that summons. In any case, Wen Jian is not to leave the city. He is one of us. He belongs to the Shulan, and we will not relinquish him under any circumstance. Any attempt to do so will be considered high treason. This will be the last we speak of this, understood?"

Taishi would have killed Oban right there if she could. Jian certainly did not belong to the Shulan. She averted her eyes and bit her lips as she seethed.

"Do I have your word, Taishi?"

She continued to stare at the floor, the lines around her eyes deepening.

Oban put a hand on the hilt of his blade, which was a laughable threat. "Your lord commands you."

Finally, Taishi looked up and bowed. "As the high lord commands."

CHAPTER TWENTY-THREE

SUNJAWA

The trade barge Sali had hijacked, ironically named the *Honest Run*, turned off the main gyre and rolled off the jungle shoreline into a shallow lake that kept the craft buoyant just below the center bore of the barge's eighteen wheels, which continued to spin and operate as paddles.

"Your money is good?" asked the yar.

She nodded. "I have Zhuun liang and Happan chips. Exchange them for rooples on your own if you wish."

Hanus snorted. "Not even the Tsunarcos want to use our currency."

The two sides had settled on an arrangement. Nezra would take control of the *Honest Run* to transport Sali into Sunjawa. In exchange, they would return the trade barge and cargo back to the yar and crew undisturbed. Any supplies acquired from the barge's hold would be compensated at a fair market price. The only stipulation Sali had with the crew of the *Honest Run* was that they would not be allowed to disembark until after the third day the barge was in port. Sali's business should be concluded by then. It was a fair compromise and far more generous than the crew of any hijacked barge could have expected. Sali had misstepped giving Daewon the job of negotiating with the yar on what they considered fair market prices. They were still haggling about it two days later.

This region was a wetland populated by some of the tallest plants in the Grass Sea. Gigaweeds flourished over open water and grew in thick bunches that sometimes reached upward of twenty stories. The pregnant barge entered what appeared to be a maze of weeds as it crawled around bends and turns, many of which were narrow and tight. Yar Hanus took the helm and guided the barge through the tricky passage, narrowly missing a group of boulders sticking out from the water on one side while sliding under a giant green tree branch that skimmed them from overhead. It was nerve-racking, but Yar Hanus steered it with practiced patience.

The city and clan of Sunjawa came into view after the *Honest Run* finally escaped the maze. Sali watched from the back of the pilothouse as Yar Hanus expertly steered the barge into two narrow lanes of floating buoys leading to the city of Sunjawa. It was moments like this that she was glad to have negotiated a fair deal with the yar instead of having to commandeer his vessel. Daewon would never have been able to do that. Trade barges required their own specific set of expertise to operate. Just because Daewon and his crew could operate a Kahun warpod did not necessarily mean they could helm a trade barge. The tinker tended to drive the *Not Loud Not Fat* like a war wagon, just crashing through their surroundings instead of around them.

Sunjawa was located in the center of a circular crop of gigaweeds that sprouted several stories toward the sky. Known as the Blooming Tulip by the locals, they were a living fortification of plants that sheltered the city from both enemies and nature alike. Sunjawa had begun as a small rim clan and served as an important trade outpost connecting the Tsunarcos to Katuia. Over the years, their leaders skillfully raised their clan's standing within the Grass Sea through trade and alliances while at the same time avoiding getting embroiled in armed conflicts. This earned the Sunjawa clan the reputation of being savvy in business and cowardly in war. It didn't help that their clan's war arts sect was known as the gentleways.

What kind of passive war arts style was that? Sali had trained, raided, or warred with just about every war arts sect in the Grass Sea except for the gentleways. Her only explanation for that omission was that they probably weren't particularly good.

The barge waded slowly toward the tulip's imposing walls, which seemed to grow taller the closer they got. Sali wondered if *Not Loud Not Fat*'s artillery weapons could hurl their projectiles at them. That could pose a problem.

Hanus waved at one of the lookouts as the barge passed by. This was the *Honest Run*'s home port, so they were able to continue without hassle. That was why the Nezra warpod had targeted it. Sali remained close to the yar the entire time, just in case. As amiable as things had unfolded between the two parties, a hijacking was still a hijacking. Apparently, Hanus's word was good and Sali's honor still had worth because soon, the *Honest Run* slipped into its assigned berth.

Sali shared last-minute instructions with Wani, and then the two viperstrikes separated. She needed to operate alone on this one. She grabbed a heavy, well-worn, and well-traveled cloak Yar Hanus had sold her for the price of a new one, and threw it over her shoulder and looked into her reflection in the water. Sali looked like a ratty wet rat. Smelled like one too.

Sali disembarked as soon as the barge moored and joined the light traffic moving through the docks. On the other side of the stream was a line of people waiting to petition to enter the city. Sali skipped those, walking through a set of giant rusted doors that appeared to have been repurposed from ship hulls. This was why it was better to stow away among a trade barge crew than as a visitor by land: fewer lines and less paperwork. The gatechecks would never allow a Nezra inside, let alone a fugitive. Ship and pod crews, however, were not screened.

The city inside the walls was a far cry from its exterior. While the outer walls of the Blooming Tulip were green and floral, Sunjawa was an industrial floating city that rested over a shallow lake. Buildings stood on tall stilts and were connected by wooden walkways floating atop barrels and inflated rubber bags, forming a chaotic network of streets. That was only a small part of the city, however.

Sali looked up. The rest of the city was overhead, dozens of floating platforms anchored by ropes staked into the walls of the tulip. They were round or oval, of varying sizes. Some held a few small buildings, others an entire block.

The rim clan Sunjawa had outgrown the confines of the Blooming Tulip several centuries ago. They were not a warrior sect, so instead of risking exposure expanding outside the safety of these natural fortifications, they decided to grow upward, building each level higher than the last until the city now filled the entire tulip.

She was still gawking when she noticed several pairs of eyes on her. The city guards came in two varieties: gray-clads armed with small shields and machetes, and blustering yellow-clads who wielded unbalanced staves. She passed a group of yellows patrolling up the streets and at a nearby open market bobbing over the waters. There were far more yellows than grays.

Standing still for too long also garnered unnecessary attention. Sali moved again, keeping her posture casual as she soaked in the city. The shadows cast by the platform and bridges made the ground dance and sway. Sunjawa was larger than most capital cities, certainly more sprawling, but not nearly as dense. Sali walked along a double-wide wooden walkway that bobbed a few feet above the lake, or "the drink" as the locals called it. She sighted a giant spiral staircase connected to the upper levels at the center of the tulip. A small gondola floated past, carrying several occupants. These small boats were the main method of transportation here. The passengers unloaded off the boat, eyed Sali with suspicion, and then wandered off. At first, she thought they recognized her, then she realized their disdain was broader. Sali was not only inner clan, but from one of the original Katuia clans, with her near-black eyes. Old Katuia were hated outside the heart of the Grass Sea.

That hatred was fine with Sali. She aimed to use it to her advantage.

There had always been friction between Sunjawa and the capital clans. The Sunjawa were large and influential enough to want a seat at the table, but the inner clans loathed giving that much standing to a rim clan. It had been a source of strife between them in the last few years. There weren't many Katuia in the city, for good reason. The Sunjawa traced their lineage back to a Tsunarcos trading outpost several centuries earlier. Theirs was the largest city in the north region of the Grass Sea, whose influence rivaled capital cities, but they were never given the honor of being one of the inner clans, much to the city's chagrin.

The population of Sunjawa Outpost was a mishmash of disparate people, equal parts Katuia and Tsunarcos with some Happan and White Ghost thrown in, but the majority and the leadership were Tsunarcos, and the Katuia would not tolerate allowing those they considered a foreign people to have an equal say in the horde's decisions. It was an issue that had rankled the city and her yazgurs—the leaders of the clan—for several centuries.

Sunjawa had, for decades, been Katuia's angry stepchild. She was ripe for a nudge toward rebellion. Sali was here to push the city off the fence.

Sali continued toward the large spiral staircase in the center of the tulip. She asked directions liberally from several of the scantily clad locals. None looked pleased to see her, but they answered her questions anyway. She passed several roped steps heading to the second level but stayed on course until she reached the staircase and began her ascent. Her destination was the Nest, the platform at the top of the city where the throne room was located.

Sali appeared casual but continued to scan for anyone following her. The crowds thinned with each level she rose. Fish markets directly over water gave way to vendors bunched tightly on large octagonal platforms, which led to modest hemp huts dangling off ropes to even larger, more resilient structures fashioned from wood, and then finally, to the Nest at the top.

Two yellow guards flanked a set of double doors leading into the Nest. Another set of yellow and gray guards leaned against a wall off to the side. Sali loosened her worn travel cloak wrapped around her body, and sniffed; the dead rat smell still lingered. There was nothing she could do about that now. Sali approached the two guards and placed a fist to her chest. "I seek the hearth of your wise ones, brothers-in-arms."

The younger guard crossed his arms. "No one sees the yazgurs without a summons, Kati . . . uia." He almost used the slur but caught himself.

Sali remained in a humble pose. "Your yazgurs will want to see me. I guarantee it."

The other older guard, with an unkempt mustache, chuckled. "Is that so, Kati? And who might you be?"

She looked him in the eye and spoke in a deadpan voice. "Sal-minde *the* Viperstrike, Warchief of Nezra, former Will of the Khan." She hesitated before the final title. "Leader of the Exiles Rebellion." She felt foolish pushing out titles, but she enjoyed the blood draining from the younger warrior's face.

The older guard required more than a haughty name to be impressed. "And I'm the Eternal Khan's harem tester. Move along, woman. Get out of here before we dump you in the drink."

To make his point, he grabbed for her collar to shove her backward. Sali didn't budge. She relaxed and shifted her weight to the side, and the guard found himself missing her completely and tripping forward. Then, without taking her eyes off the younger guard, she gave the older one a nudge in the back, sending him sprawling down half a flight of stairs.

Sali said to the younger guard, "Now, go tell the yazgurs that Sal-minde the Viperstrike seeks friendship and a warm hearth." She pushed her heavy cloak back to reveal her looped tongue resting in its holster. That was enough for him.

"Stay here," he stuttered. "I'll be right back."

The yellow-clad man opened the double doors and fled inside. She planted her feet in the crack before he could shut the doors, and followed him inside. Two more guards closed in on her, but Sali didn't slow. It wasn't lost on her that they were yellow-clad. She ignored them and continued at an even pace. The young guard reached the base of a long set of stairs and faced her again. He looked as if he wasn't sure if this was a good place to make a stand.

Sali assured him it was not. She signaled for him to stand aside. "I ask for a seat at the hearth, nothing more."

She stood at the entrance to the Nest on a large, octagonal wooden surface suspended by dozens of thick hemp ropes anchored into the walls of the gigaweeds on every side. There was a half-moon circle of large seats, nine in all. Behind the thrones was a wooden wall that rose two more stories behind them. Covering the nine seats was a ceiling made entirely from large glass squares.

Two more guards approached them, again clad in yellow. At the same time, the guards behind them closed in, blocking their retreat.

A man dressed in fine translucent silk garb appeared. "Hold. Words can do little harm. Let the yazgurs hear what she has to say."

He was a thin man, emaciated even, but not of the lower classes. His clothing was fine and intricate, and a wooden diadem circlet rested on his crown. He stepped forward to meet Sali and placed a fist over her heart and then on her forehead while staring straight into her eyes: heart and mind. Sali returned the gesture. Both were now honor bound to avoid bloodshed. It was a small custom shared between diverse cultures and languages, but it was these simple gestures that allowed the many clans and people under the Katuia banner to work together.

The man offered an arm. "May I have the privilege of escorting you to the Court of Yazgurs?"

In Katuia culture, escorts were considered insults. This man with such fine garb and obvious high standing must know that. This was a test. He wanted to know how Sali would react.

"Let us proceed together hand-in-hand as friends." She added a warning. "For that is who we are until our ancestors choose a different path."

"Well said," the man remarked. "I am Dai, the Ninth Yazgur. At first, I doubted that you could possibly be *the* viperstrike, but as I see that you are not some blemished reflection, my soul sings at my good fortune."

Sali swallowed her irritation. Great, a fan.

This Ninth Yazgur was a rail-thin young man, not trained in the war arts. His face was long, his nose sharp, and he had a bookish if not wily look to him. Sali thought he was hiding something with a hand tucked in his pocket. As she studied him, she noticed that his shoulders were uneven, with the left drooping unnaturally.

Dai was all smiles as he led her up the short flight of stairs to the upper dais. She watched, fascinated as each step shifted beneath her feet. There was more to this Nest than there appeared. The platform was not carved from one piece, but thousands of small wooden boards linked together.

"The balancing boards help keep the platform from shifting during high winds," Dai explained. The Sunjawa were artisans. This design might not be a city pod, but the engineering required to build this was no less complex. Mali would have appreciated it.

"It is a beautiful arrangement," Sali admitted.

"Is it true, viperstrike?" asked Dai. "Have you raised banners against the inner capitals?"

"I love my people," she said. "I have no quarrel with them. I know the truth behind the Eternal Khan of Katuia, and the power behind the spirit shamans' hold over the entire Grass Sea. I intend to free my clan and my people." She looked over at Dai. "I will free yours as well."

"So it is true," Dai replied. "You intend to claim the mantle of khan."

Sali snorted. "Nobody should want that job."

The two continued up another hundred or so steps before reaching the top. The other end of the Nest revealed a half-moon chamber, not unlike the room where the spirit shamans ruled over Chaqra. It was an open area, with only one wall at the back and the rest of the area exposed to the elements.

The atmosphere in the Sunjawa center of power was different from the stuffy Sanctuary of the Eternal Moor. For one thing, there were small children running around, half a dozen of them galloping about and chasing each other. Toys were strewn across the floor and two kids, a boy and girl, were engaged in a full-on slapping contest, with the girl getting the better of the boy. One end of the dais was sectioned off for a playpen while the other appeared to be a changing station and nap area. The government of Sunjawa appeared to be a family affair.

Sali looked up and squinted. She could see through the covered ceiling above the dais. A leaf had just fallen from a plant and was resting on transparent glass, a truly remarkable thing. Most glass in the Grass Sea and the Enlightened States was stained a color, or at best opaque. Truly transparent glass was a Tsunarcos invention that was slowly filtering west.

Sali turned around and stared at the uneven tops of the tulip rising above the platform, which offered a clear view of the city. *Not Loud Not Fat* was hidden under the thick jungle canopy somewhere. Daewon's orders were to approach undetected, which meant to travel only under the cover of darkness.

The throne room was surprisingly messy. It looked more like a great room where the extended family gathered for the evening rather than the head of government of an entire clan. It lived up to its name, however. There were many thrones lined up in a half-circle along the edge of the platform, eight in all: five large chairs, one rocker, and two swing chairs. *Who uses a swing chair as a throne?*

The two largest chairs in the center were occupied by a middle-aged man and his older wife. The rest were half occupied, with a child snoring on one, a little black dog curled up in his lap. To the right of the two center chairs was a woman nursing a five-year-old. Sali squinted. Directly behind the half circle of thrones was a bedroom hidden behind a curtain of dried leaves.

Sali looked at the man on the main throne and then back at Dai. Same button nose, same large eye folds. "Which one is yours?"

"This room only seats eight," he said. "But I like your idea."

"You don't know my idea."

"You're going up against the spirit shamans at Chaqra. That's a good enough idea for me." He took a step forward and then turned to face her. "Now, allow me to inform my noble father of your impressive appearance." He winked and headed toward the First Yazgur.

Was this young strap flirting with her? Sali would snap him into pieces if they coupled. Break him and leave him drooling for the rest of his days. She chuckled.

Dai was leaning over the First Yazgur, speaking intently into his ear. The first, an older man, face puffy and blemished with age and sun, studied Sali. There was cunning in his eyes. One would have to be cunning to rule Sunjawa, which carried a reputation of being an unruly settlement.

The First Yazgur stood. "I am Huong the First Yazgur. My Ninth tells me you claim to be Salminde the Viperstrike."

"I am who I am. I do not claim," she replied. "You may take my word as it stands or risk testing yours."

"You are an enemy to the Katuia. Therefore, by khanate law, an enemy to the Sunjawa," he proclaimed.

"That is true," she admitted. "But I don't think you care what the khanate says, or have you gotten so comfortable being second class to Katuia?"

An ugly mutter carried in the air around her.

Huong raised an arm, commanding silence, except from the children still going at it on the nearby rug. Then, one hit the other, and both began to cry.

The First Yazgur's eyes narrowed. "You claim to want to share our hearth and then insult us?"

"I am merely stating a fact," Sali said. "Unless you want to do something about it."

"What's there to do?"

Sali sucked in a breath. Here goes. "My clan, Nezra, has been exiled by Katuia, and are hunted by their cities. We intend to break the vise of Chaqra and her spirit shamans. You yazgurs of Sunjawa have always chafed under the heavy boot of the khan. Perhaps it is time we earn our freedom. How would you like to be your own khan again, First Yazgur Huong?"

Huong walked closer to her. "The rumors are true. You are rebelling. What makes you think you can kill the Eternal Khan?"

"I know what he is," Sali replied. "I'm not going to kill him. I'm going to free him. I can free you too."

"Freedom is a strange thing. You can't touch it, smell it, use it, eat it, but is it important enough to risk your clan drowning beneath the black eternal sea? I think not." The First Yazgur paced the room. "The spirit shamans are annoying, yes, but that's all they are. Sunjawa has as much freedom as we need, while under the protection of the Katuia horde. Why should we give that up for"—Huong clicked his tongue— "this silly thing you call freedom?"

The woman sitting next to the First Yazgur spoke up. "Free us or kill us. It's two sides of the same coin. Why don't we capture you now? Send your head in a basket to Chaqra. They will reward Sunjawa for capturing such an important traitor."

A group of the yellows wielding those maces appeared from rope bridges off to both sides.

Sali had expected this. "Four? You didn't bring enough."

They advanced on her. Luckily for them, Sali wasn't here to fight. She reached into her satchel and drew out a brown tube the size of her forearm and pulled the string on one end, holding the tube overhead. A shrill whistle cried out as the flare sent a burst of light across the white sky. The sound and light lingered for a few moments. The guards and yazgurs looked on curiously but made no move to stop her. The whistle continued a little while longer before fading. Sali sucked in a long breath and blew it out. Hopefully, everyone did their job. If not, it could get ugly.

Sali waited. A sigh escaped her. "Oh, bother."

"Was something supposed to happen?" Huong said.

"I'm going to switch that tinker." Sali held up a hand to the yellows, who surprisingly respected her space. More seconds ticked by. Finally, three loud booms erupted from the southwest, sending a flock of starlings into the air. It was followed by three red balls of pitch, flying in formation as they climbed into the sky passing directly over the Blooming Tulip, appearing on one side and disappearing over the other before crashing into the wet swamp. A bell in the distance rang, soon joined by others.

Sali held her breath. One of those flame shots almost grazed the ends of the tulip walls. A few moments later, one of the guards ran into the Nest, his hemp armor rustling as he neared. The yellow-clad warrior put his fist to his chest. "First Yazgur, a large warpod has just appeared on the southwestern horizon trampling through the jungle at attack speed. They missed on their first salvo but are coming in closer."

"My warpod missed nothing, First Yazgur. You're not under attack. This isn't a threat, just a warning. It's a technical demonstration of Nezra's capabilities." Sali raised her hand. "Now if we can quit the chest thumping, let's get down to business, yeah?"

CHAPTER TWENTY-FOUR

THE THORNED GARDEN

Taishi stood at the head of the training yard and yelled, "Goramh Pounds the Earth!"

The ten rows of ten monks arrayed before her at the training yard simultaneously threw their left arms in a looping circle and then smashed the backs of their right fists into their left palms with a shuddering crack.

"Low right block back sweep counter to defend a jump overhead!"

The monks kicked out to an imaginary attack with their left lead feet and then dropped to execute a sweeping right kick. The majority chose to allow their momentum to carry them to the side. Several tried to parry the imaginary attack with their forearms, while a few tried throwing uppercuts.

Taishi walked over and smacked the shoulder of one with her bamboo pole. These were basic maneuvers taught across many styles. She continued pacing. "The best defense against an attack is to avoid it altogether. For those who made the wrong choice, fifty finger pushups, now!" Three monks to her right collapsed with groans. Taishi pursed her lips to mask her smirk.

Mori had asked her to help refresh the monks' fighting abilities. While all were taught in the style of the Tiandi Fist, a rudimentary but effective war arts style, not everyone kept up with their training. It wasn't unusual for a retired dowager to oversee battle preparedness, so Taishi was happy to take the role. It wasn't like she had anything else to do.

Fausan and Sohn sat to the side touching pinkies as a way to seal a wager. Those two bet on just about anything. As usual, Sohn looked grim. She didn't know why he kept trying to wager against the God of Gamblers. Then it occurred to her that Fausan never collected on his bets. The two just enjoyed gambling for the sake of their friendship. That was sweet. Stupid, but sweet.

"Low dragon stance to jump snap kick. Slide into hip toss, have it countered, and then pivot to Mash the Melon and escape to running jump outside!" It was a complicated sequence, which less than half the monks got correct. "A hundred pushups on your fist for those who failed." The groans were audible this time around. Taishi grinned. She hadn't had this much fun in a while.

Bhasani, sitting away from Fausan, looked up from her book. "Taishi, I'm five pages in, and I already know what's going to happen."

"It's a Burning Hearts romance," she answered. "What unexpected complications were you looking for?"

"Whether it's the old groundskeeper's handsome new apprentice or the lost young lord returned from the savage lands, it's all the same."

Taishi held out her hand. "Let me read it, then."

"Not a chance, Great Queen of Hot Air, especially now with the library unavailable."

She hated that nickname. What was worse was that the city's main library was cut off, located behind enemy lines in a captured ward.

Taishi turned toward the monks. "Six punch palm strike your—"

The monks turned away from her to face the side. They put their palms together with a mighty clap, and then bowed as a procession approached from the other side of the field. She spotted two Hansoo first, with their chests towering over the heads of everyone else. Next were two lines of lotus monks, sky lotus by the looks of their crescent moon flags.

She last saw Mori hobbling into the yard. The templeabbot had aged considerably since the invasion. He had worked tirelessly to protect the Tiandi religion while also caring for the city's besieged residents.

Mori offered a smile when he saw her. "Still relentless, even in your old age."

"I don't have time to dawdle."

"I will get to the point, then." He pointed toward a small clearing off to the side. "Walk with me, dowager nun."

Taishi nodded. She looked at Sohn. "Take over."

The eternal bright light master looked surprised that he was called before his face took a devious turn. He clapped. "All right, you tile lovers, listen to this sequence carefully. I'll break it into four parts. . . ."

The lotus monks clustered around her the moment she and Mori walked away. They looked grim. Mori portrayed his usual calm, but the tension around his eyes was obvious. They continued in silence until they reached the clearing. It wasn't lost on Taishi that the sky lotus monks had established a wide perimeter to keep away prying ears or eyes.

"How may I serve the Tiandi, templeabbot?" she asked after they settled to their seats. "You look glum. Did your bosses order you to pick a side?"

That was a sore spot between them and a low blow on her part. Mori had been born in a buried ward not far from the temple. The man loved and bled Vauzan as much as any other, but the Tiandi templeabbots had ordered neutrality among the devout. Over a dozen monks had retired their sashes to join the fight. Taishi knew that Mori would have as well if his responsibilities weren't so great.

The templeabbot did not react to her jibe. "We have a problem."

"We have many problems," she replied. "Which ones do you want to focus on today?"

Mori looked pained. "The magistrates found a message on a Caobiu spy who had obtained information that the Oracle of the Tiandi is nesting in the Black Orchid Convent in the Thorned Garden ward at the other end of the city. We don't know how they found out, but they know. Sunri will move to capture her."

Taishi's face was impassive, but her breath had caught. The oracle would be a prize for the Desert Lioness to possess, almost as great as the prophesied hero. "Why does she live there? Shouldn't she be at the main temple?"

"It was her choice." Mori sounded bitter. "She prefers living with the nuns. She said my monks stink."

"Sounds like Pei, and they do," Taishi agreed.

"Caobiu rabble guards have already infiltrated the Thorned Garden ward and are softening the streets. The area is in danger of falling any day now. We must rescue the oracle and spirit her back here before the convent falls. I can arrange to have her smuggled out of the city."

"Why not send some of those big Hansoo to retrieve her?" asked Taishi. "Why do you need me?"

Mori looked frustrated. "She doesn't want to go."

"She's a little girl. She doesn't get a choice," said Taishi.

"She's the Oracle of the Tiandi." Mori's shoulders slumped. "Temple doctrine says her wisdom is a heavenly pronouncement. Her every word is doctrine. We are not allowed to counter her."

Sometimes, religion was dumb. Taishi shook her finger. "Who cares about doctrine? She's a twelve-year-old girl who still sucks her thumb."

The look on the templeabbot's face told her that she was giving him the same sermon he had already recited to someone else. "I need you to go to the Black Orchid and convince the oracle to come back to the temple, for her safety. Please. She won't listen to the devout. Maybe she will listen to you."

"Maybe is correct," Taishi grumbled. "The little brat hasn't been pleased with my performance lately."

Mori looked pained. "Please, watch the sacrilege."

Taishi was tempted to continue her sacrilege. Temple matters were often as dangerous and twisted as their court counterparts. A nest of holy vipers were still vipers. It would risk too much exposure, especially with her connection to Jian. Bringing the Oracle and the Prophesied Hero of the Tiandi together was too great a risk. All it would take was one leak for the entire Enlightened States to explode. Sunri would stop at nothing to capture them both. No, the smart thing to do was to keep the two sacred relics of their religion as far apart from each other as possible.

Taishi had made up her mind on the matter, but her heart resisted. She owed Mori, owed the temple, really. They had taken her in when she was a fugitive and a refugee. The monks had protected her and Jian. They had hidden them, fed them, and put a roof over their heads. This had meant so much to her, but it meant even more to Jian, who finally found a home and some measure of peace. Refusing this request was shameful. It was dishonorable, and it was wrong. Some debts were more important than doing the right thing.

"When do you need me to go?"

Mori glanced to the side. "A litter awaits you near the front gates. You'll be escorted by the sky lotus. Brother Solum was the first to request the honor to walk at your head." It was a prestigious procession offered to only the highest-ranked Tiandi abbots.

Still . . . "You want me to fetch the oracle right this very moment?"

"The Thorned Garden may still fly brown flags for now, but how much longer? Your task will be nearly impossible if it burns yellow."

Taishi had hoped to renew her search for a way out of the city, but so far had little success. After her last conversation with Oban, Taishi knew she had erred in allowing Jian to remain in the city. She had caved to his emotions against her better judgment. Foolish woman. It was Sanso all over again. Jian wasn't ready to handle this burden, but he had pleaded. And she relented. Just like she had with Sanso.

"Not this time," she muttered as she climbed into the wagon, and then she ordered the sky lotus driver, "Stop by the guest quarters first."

By the time the closed palanquin departed the Vauzan Temple of the Tiandi an hour later, Taishi had wrangled the three other masters and dragged them along for the journey. Fourteen strong sky lotus monks carried the four masters on their shoulders as they headed toward the Thorned Garden ward.

The masters shuffled one by one into the modest palanquin and crammed inside, with Fausan barely fitting through the door. He huffed and wheezed as he squeezed his way next to Bhasani. The God of Gamblers was breathing more heavily these days. Apparently Taishi wasn't the only one to notice. Bhasani had a hand on his shoulder and one on his back. She didn't look concerned, but then a drowned fist would never reveal that weakness.

The palanquin, with its many curtains and pillows, rocked back and forth as the lotus monks struggled to lift it up. The masters immediately began interrogating Taishi about this strange, sudden assignment.

"This better be important." Fausan sniffed. "My wife was about to tantric sex me."

Bhasani looked up from the book she was reading, rolled her eyes, and then buried her face back in it.

"What's going on, Taishi?" asked Sohn.

"Rescue job," she replied. "A little foul-mouthed girl."

Sohn sniffed. "Some noble's brat? All this for a dumb kid?"

"Not quite, except for the brat part." Few were aware of the oracle's existence, let alone that she was in the city. Perhaps it was best to keep it that way.

Bhasani looked up from her reading. "Where are we rescuing the little dear from?"

"Black Orchid nunnery at the Thorned Garden," said Taishi. "The Caobiu are pushing their way in."

"This sounds like fun," said Fausan. "What's the pay?"

"Eternal salvation and a ticket to heaven."

Sohn glared at her. "You didn't even request a fee, did you? Why are we always doing things for free?"

It was a good question. "Because it's the right thing to do."

The eternal bright light master grumbled. "Being a good guy has a terrible career track."

Taishi didn't disagree. The group hurried down the hill quicker than was safe for someone in her condition and was soon moving toward the back of the main temple building. There would be Caobiu soldiers in the streets soon.

"What's the plan, Taishi?" asked Fausan. "Break in, grab the girl, and fight our way out?"

"A simple, straightforward plan," said Sohn. "I like it."

"She . . ." Taishi loosed a long sigh. "The girl might not want to come." They all stared at her as if hornets were crawling out of her nose.

Bhasani snorted. "This sounds more like a kidnapping."

"We have to convince her to come willingly," Taishi explained. "But we may have to resort to rescuing her by force, if necessary."

"How is this different from a kidnapping?" asked Bhasani.

Fausan was more thoughtful. "Who is this girl to the Caobiu? Is she some rich prick's kid, or is she a wanted bounty?"

"Neither, but I can't explain it to you."

"Good enough for me." Everyone should have a friend like him. He yawned. "Well, wake me up when we get there."

Everyone dozed off. Naps were becoming more important to each of them as the years passed. Taishi found herself the only one awake in the palanquin as the sky lotus monks continued to carry the four masters north across the city. Taishi passed the time staring out the small window hidden behind a sheer curtain. It had been a while since she had seen the rest of the city. Other than an occasional visit to court, Taishi had mostly stayed on temple grounds.

The scars of the siege cut deep into the city. Burned buildings littered every block. Storefronts were smashed. Heavy black ash marked the walls. The usually pristine tiled streets were now littered with overturned carts, broken stalls, and the occasional body. Rubble was everywhere. The stink of ash and death filled her nostrils even safely hidden inside the palanquin. An occasional explosion would puncture the air in the distance, followed by sounds of incendiaries and concussive impacts. The Caobiu's artillery barrage on the city was practically nonstop.

There were a few residents walking the streets, scrounging for supplies or carrying buckets of water. Most stopped to stare at the palanquin as they passed, dull-eyed and numb, their shoulders slumped.

It hurt Taishi to see Vauzan like this. She was not a sentimental woman, but this was her city as much as it was anyone's.

They reached the Thorned Garden a long hour later, passing several large barricades and checkpoints before they were finally allowed through. This ward was perilously close to the front line, and the streets looked like an army camp. Clusters of tents filled the alleyways while sharpened stakes and fortifications blocked every intersection.

Taishi caught sight of a girl peering down at her palanquin through the third-story window of a building. She felt deep grief for the pitiful thing. Sieges were no place for children. What was transpiring would traumatize her for life. It was outrageous that Sunri disallowed families from fleeing the city before the siege commenced. It would have been the honorable thing to do, but cities surrendered quicker with women and children still trapped inside.

The palanquin soon veered off the main street and proceeded down a long slope toward a large oval cave. The Thorned Garden was unique in that it was technically half a buried ward, with a portion of the population residing in a giant cave known as the Barberry. Once they passed through the narrow entrance, the Barberry opened into a massive circular cave many stories high. Taishi could just make out the Black Orchid Convent hanging from the center of the ceiling, and even then, its bottom appeared to be at least seven stories above the ground floor.

The sky lotus monks began their long, arduous ascent up a series of winding paths along the sides of the cave walls, zigzagging upstairs and past buildings carved directly into stone. This must be why Mori had ordered a palanquin instead of a carriage for their transport.

They continued along the dimly lit passages up toward the top of the Barberry. Paths and stairs anchored into the side walls soon became passages hanging from giant chains bolted into the ceiling. The air smelled cooler down here, earthy and wet. Most of the buildings cried streams of water, creating small waterfalls dribbling into small pools and channels that drained down to the aqueducts.

The palanquin finally came to a stop at the entrance to an austere stone building. The convent was a larger structure than most buildings on the top side of the Barberry. From afar, it appeared to be a cluster of seven perfectly formed cylinders of differing lengths hanging from the cave ceiling connected by small skybridges. The convent was the home of the legendary Black Orchid sect, an elite battle convent for the devout women who chose to wield the blade for their religion. They were the first known battlenuns of the Tiandi and certainly the most feared. Their long history, born a century after the birth of the Tiandi religion, was the source of many epic poems and tragedies.

Taishi had a long history with the Black Orchids. She had suffered a mortal injury during one of her first campaigns. At least it should have been certain death. A Black Orchid nun, Qinhhwanan, on her first battle pilgrimage, had brought Taishi here. The nuns had saved her somehow. Since then, Taishi had a close relationship with the Black Orchids. The woman with whom Taishi had formed a bond eventually attained the position of sect battleabbess, leading the Black Orchids to many years of honor and glory before finally succumbing to a Katuia champion nearly two decades ago. Taishi had withdrawn from a campaign to travel to the Katuia city of Ankar just to avenge her friend's death. It had been a glorious duel.

The wide doors to the palanquin were removed, and Taishi and the rest of the masters, cramped and stiff from the long ride, were finally able to stand. Taishi stretched her legs and her good arm and winced at her tight back and neck. Even a day trip like this was too much to manage now.

They were inside a small courtyard between the large cylinder building and a low outer wall. A dozen black-robed nuns patrolled that wall walk, each wielding a polearm with a short shaft and a long, curved blade known as a reaping sword. This was the Black Orchids' chosen weapon and was fearsome in trained hands.

Five more black-clad women stood before them in line, reaping swords strapped across their backs. Their robes were plain and uniform, layered with the ends of their shoulders flaring out and curving upward, a stylistic flavor unique to the sect known as the orchid petal.

The one in the center of the group wore an additional spiked head-dress that had two thin black stalks that pointed up.

She touched fist to palm. "Great dowager, you honor us."

Taishi appreciated the war artist's greeting. "Battleabbess Korana-jah."

The current battleabbess was not as impressive as her predecessor. She did not seek to create a name for herself or bring glory and wealth to the sect. Instead, Koranajah was a conservative and pragmatic stew-ard who steadily increased the sect's coffers, influence, and stability, which was all anyone could wish for in a leader. While Taishi did not share the same fiery bond that could only be forged through battle as she did with Qinhhwanan, she valued Koranajah's leadership and acu-men, and considered her a wise and stalwart friend.

Koranajah fell in alongside her, showing her the proper respect owed a dowager as they proceeded through the front doors of the tem-ple. The foyer to the temple was a large, circular room with a low ceil-ing that Taishi could palm if she reached. There were two hallways on both sides and a spiral staircase at the far end.

"I would offer a respite after your travel," said the battleabbess, "but time grows short and the situation dire."

"I understand." Taishi turned to the others. "There's a hot spring that pipes into a pool down that hallway."

"Say no more," said Bhasani, moving that direction.

"You two should go as well," said Taishi. "You both stink. Clean up before we have to crawl back into that coffin."

"Where's the kitchen?" asked Sohn.

Koranajah pointed toward the hallway opposite the spa. "The Black Orchids fast every day until the Queen appears. However, I can ask the cook to prepare something for you."

"I'm not hungry," said the eternal bright light master.

"Remember your place here," Bhasani hissed.

"That is quite all right," said Koranajah. "Unlike temple doctrine, the nuns here believe in sharing a cup of plum wine before and after every battle to calm the nerves and celebrate victories."

Sohn brightened. "I like these ladies already."

The battleabbess turned to Taishi. "The nuns will see to their needs. Now, to more pressing matters."

She descended the spiral stairs, moving deeper into the main building, down six stories to the bottom floor. The interior of the convent, like most, was austere: exposed stone carved with the fine mastery and care that only Vauzan's stonemasons could craft. The Tiandi religion had always been the best patrons of the artists supported by this city.

They entered a circular office at the lowest point of the temple. The floor was made from transparent glass, which allowed Taishi to look into the cave, down to the ground level some seven stories below. It was impressive and more than a bit unsettling.

As soon as the door closed, Battleabbess Koranajah lost the last of her composure. Her stiff back bent, and she hunched backward, falling onto a fuzzy red sheep couch. Koranajah rubbed her eyes. "Taishi, you have to do something. That little stinking brat is going to get us all killed!"

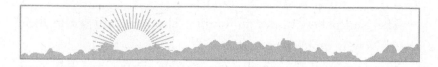

CHAPTER TWENTY-FIVE

DAY OFF

Jian woke the next morning, curled in a ball on the area rug. The King's morning rays swept into the living room, causing him to stir. His eyes fluttered open and then began to water. The constant blanket of smoke and soot hanging over the city had made them red and sensitive to light. It also made them prone to wetness. At least that was what he told himself.

Jian sat up, discombobulated. What was he doing sprawled on the floor? Then he remembered bawling in Taishi's lap. He did cry . . . again. She must be embarrassed by his behavior. His cheeks burned, turning as red as his eyes. He rolled to his feet. His chest, back, and legs ached. His stomach felt queasy, and he was sore everywhere. None of those Burning Hearts romance books ever talked about how someone felt *after* battles. The chapters usually ended with everyone near death, and then the next chapter continued with the characters healthy and ready to face the world again.

"I should write a book one day." Jian sniffed as he lumbered toward the door. "I bet I can do a better job. How hard can it be? Anyone can do it."

The missions he was sent on were dangerous, some of the most important for the defenders. That's why the court sent him. *He* was the Champion of the Five Under Heaven, and only *he* could succeed in these difficult missions.

"Fighting on the front line is how you win the people over," the high lord had said. "You are a shining beacon to all Zhuun."

Being an example to his people was an assignment Jian took seriously. That was another reason he had been so appalled about crying so much so easily lately.

"Damn smoke in my eye," he grumbled. He stopped at the doorway and looked toward her bedroom. Was Taishi already out?

Today was his day off. Taishi had insisted that he still continue his training, and she had negotiated every fourth day of his time. At first, Jian had chafed under that rule, but now he was relieved to rest every few days from the fighting. The only responsibility he had today was a session with Taishi and Bhasani this morning, and then the rest of the day was his to do as he wished.

Jian reached the training yard just as a group of monks was finishing and the next class filling the open spaces. He waved at Solum, who was marching down lines barking orders, enjoying himself.

"Good morning, master. Have you seen my aunt this morning? I have lessons."

The senior Hansoo was one of the few monks who had treated him the same before and after his identity was revealed. Solum was staring down a group in the middle of the cluster of exercises. He bellowed, "That shield wall has holes so large I can drive a cart through it. Huddle closer together. Get intimate, you pig beasts." Solum turned back to Jian. "The dowager, you say? She's off on an errand for the templeabbot. Your day is yours. That is, unless you wish to train with us. It would inspire many."

That was the last thing Jian wanted to do on his free day. "I've taken enough beatings for the week, thanks."

"Beware the cunning fox, prophesied hero. There are those who wish to use you for their own means. No champion should have to fight and dance at the same time."

Everyone appeared to have an opinion about Jian's role in the city's defense. "Master Oban says it's the best way to serve our people, brother."

Solum snorted. "Of course that's what he would say."

Jian ended the conversation as quickly as was polite. While he respected the Hansoo, the senior war monk could talk the day away. "Have you seen my friends, Brother Solum?"

The senior Hansoo shook his head. "I have not seen any of them in a while."

It was the worst thing about Jian's training schedule. It rarely aligned with his friends'. Just because he was free didn't mean his friends were. He had hoped to spend time with Sonaya. The two had barely been together since the beginning of the siege. He had at first excused these long lapses. She was fighting along the front line, while Jian was preoccupied with being sent to various parts of the city. It was a terrible and busy time for everyone. He had seen her so infrequently he was beginning to suspect this was intentional. Kaiyu had joined the same corps, and Jian saw him at least once every few days.

Jian noticed several monks nearby stop their practice and gawk. Jian was becoming used to it by now, but it still made him uncomfortable. It was worse in the temple. Everywhere he went, they stared, as if he were either a leper or a demigod their religion had been built around. Jian couldn't decide what was worse. He didn't blame them. The monks had dedicated their lives to him.

He excused himself from the training field and retreated toward the bamboo grove. He detoured around the edge of the tree lines that circled a few of the small ponds dotting the premises and found his way to the orphanage tucked in a far corner of the temple grounds. The temple had always run an orphanage, but it usually held fewer than twenty young children. Most ended up shaving their heads and becoming monks. Now, due to the war, there were dozens—possibly more than a hundred, most under the age of seven.

Jian found himself here during his free days, more often than not. He liked it here. It was more peaceful, even though a hundred kids made a hurricane's worth of ruckus. It wasn't the noise or the activity, however. It was the attention, or lack of it. The kids knew he was the Prophesied Hero of the Tiandi. They didn't care. Other than a few questions from the older children, the rest treated him like any other playmate. Jian found that relaxing. This was one of the few places he didn't have to manage expectations. He enjoyed just sitting in the shade of the bamboo grove and watching these children—most orphans from the fighting—frolicking like puppies.

He spent the rest of the morning lounging in the yard with a group of the older children wielding sticks and playing soldier. The gaggle of fifteen six- and seven-year-olds were more impressed that he wore a sword than by the fact that he was the Champion of the Five Under Heaven. When the King rode highest at noon, the nuns who ran the orphanage roped him into helping line the kids up for lunch. The four old women, all pushing near a century, also didn't care about who he was. This suited him fine.

Jian was wrangling a cluster of three-year-olds just outside the kitchen when the wooden chimes at the front gates thunked their hollow ring. Jian paused and pursed his lips. He had hoped for a little more time. His respite had been too brief. The grim shadow of reality was pulling him back. He glanced in that direction, dreading who he would see, and was pleased when Hachi and Kaiyu strolled through the gates.

Jian raised a hand. The whipfinger snapped his fingers and beckoned Jian to follow. "We were looking all over for you. Come on, we're going to be late."

Jian frowned. "Late for what?"

"Neeshan's mam's moving today, remember? Did you forget?"

He didn't even remember agreeing to help Hachi move his girlfriend's mother's house. "Of course not."

Hachi tossed him a pile of dirty yellow clothing. "Corpse disposal robes."

Jian sniffed and made a face as he held up the tattered clothing plastered with dark red stains. "These look used. Did you get them from the dead?"

"I don't know," admitted Hachi. "I bought them off the streets. It doesn't matter. No one will bother corpse disposers, or would you rather prance around the city in that ridiculous dress the nobles make you wear?"

Jian loved the battle robe that Highlord Oban had custom-tailored for him. It was a bit on the heavy side and obstructed his peripheral vision just a tad, but he looked so dashing, and the lining was soft. Hachi wasn't wrong, however. His Champion of the Five Under Heaven robes were obnoxiously loud.

Kaiyu fell in beside them. "Jian, I see your face everywhere. You're famous! They have depictions of you at every volunteer office. The devout are signing up to fight in droves."

As if being the central figure of their people's religion wasn't enough.

"Everybody needs to do their part." Jian hated the idea. The fact that volunteers were dying in his name made him sick, but how else would Vauzan defeat the Caobiu invaders? The Shulan ducal army with a body of professional soldiers had shattered over a year ago. As Highlord Oban had emphasized, the people of Vauzan were all that stood between Sunri and the Celestial Throne. Everything depended on them.

"How are you dealing with the responsibilities of your new celebrity?" asked the Houtou.

He was looking straight ahead. He couldn't sleep. He suffered nightmares when he did. His nerves were so tightly wound he was practically numb while awake, but he had to put up a strong face. "I'm great, little brother. Never better. How about you?"

Kaiyu's face tightened. He was always honest. "I killed someone the other day." There was a small silence to allow that to soak in. "I don't like how it feels."

Jian put his arm around the Houtou. "I'd be worried about you if you did."

"Our underground corps keeps churning." Kaiyu's lips quivered. "When I first joined a month ago, I was the youngest guy there. Now,

Sonaya and I are the oldest tenured. They're talking about making us captains."

"You turn that trash down," muttered Hachi. His face was grim. "Tell them you want nothing to do with leadership."

"Why not?" asked Kaiyu.

"You think it's bad, killing a man? Imagine being responsible for getting a whole corps of them killed."

Before he had been assigned as Jian's shadow, Hachi had commanded his own underground corps, the Peony Peak Super Gentlemen. He had been promoted within the first week of service. At first, Jian had been proud of his friend, but he wasn't so sure anymore. Leadership had changed Hachi. Gone was the smug, confident friend he once knew. Now, only a shell of him remained and it was troubled and tense.

Jian threw his other arm around the whipfinger. "What happens to your corps isn't your fault."

"Of course it is." Hachi loosed his breath, his shoulders slumping. "Every wrong decision, missed objective, injury, death, or defeat is your fault. The worst is when you have to leave your people behind."

The friends passed the temple gates and continued on foot down the main road winding around Peony Peak. The path had been closed off ever since the beginning of the invasion. The rockslide from Caobiu artillery had seen to that. The three had to climb through a section of rubble that obstructed their way, but the street was the most direct way to the Undertunnel buried ward, which ran underground east beneath two contested wards topside before reaching the Wailing Duck ward, where Neeshan and her mother lived.

They made a sharp turn inside the mountain as they entered through the underground. They continued down a winding staircase before entering what appeared to be a long labyrinth of tunnels and rooms with crisscrossing passages staggered every hundred paces.

The Undertunnel was one of the largest and oldest buried wards in Vauzan, and it stretched nearly to the eastern wall. It once served as the sewer system for the old city until some enterprising developer realized there was potential for profit down here. He purchased the rights to the sewers from the duke and built an entire miniature city.

The Caobiu had not yet taken over any of the buried wards. The fighting underground had been the bloodiest of the conflict so far, but the defenders were intent on holding these wards. Taking control of some of the major buried ward hubs would allow the enemy to circumvent Shulan choke points and barricades. The underground channels were important enough that if the Caobiu managed to seize the buried wards, the city would fall soon after.

The small group traveled for nearly an hour through the dimly lit Undertunnel. Most underground communities were filled with lamps and spotlights illuminating the way. Some even hung thousands of small chandeliers that illuminated their ceilings like stars. The Undertunnel at this time, however, was dark. This particular buried ward ran beneath an area known as the Death Sleet, which once was a six-lane road that connected the north and south ends of the city. The Death Sleet was a no-man's-land separating the bulk of the two sides. Whole army units had entered the Sleet trying to clear a path to the other side, only to suffer complete attrition. The ghosts of the fallen would haunt that street for generations. The residents of the Undertunnel knew that if the Caobiu ever captured the Undertunnel, then the Cinder Legions could circumvent the Shulan defenses.

"Do you still see Neeshan often, with the fighting?" asked Jian, as they passed the time in darkness.

"Unless I'm in the infirmary, I see her every day."

That sounded serious. "Does her mam like you?"

"Her mother doesn't like that I'm an uneducated war artist."

Kaiyu bristled. "That's rude. Doesn't she know that it's a bunch of lowly war artists coming to her aid right now?"

"Why do you think I'm doing it?"

Jian studied his friend. Hachi was a changed man. His demeanor was more serious, his bearing rigid, and he carried himself with a calm but simmering gravitas. It was as if he had grown ten years in ten weeks. Jian was impressed, and slightly envious, but he also missed the old fun Hachi and hoped he would return after all this was over.

"Have you seen Sonaya often?" asked Hachi back.

"I haven't seen her at all. I think she's avoiding me." It hurt Jian to admit that.

"Why would she do a thing like that?" said Hachi. "Unless you messed up. Did you mess up?"

"Why is it always my fault if something's messed up?"

"Because Sonaya doesn't mess up."

Jian took that as an insult. "It probably *is* my fault."

"Hey, guys." Kaiyu stuck his head between them. "Maybe keep it down a . . ."

"But Sonaya's not as smart as she thinks she is," Jian continued. "Just because everything she says sounds right doesn't make it true. She's just guessing like everyone else. . . ."

Jian startled as the three began their ascent up the tunnel that led to the Wailing Duck. He gasped. "Sonaya, Zofi, what are you two doing here?"

Zofi had her hands on her hips. "I'm going to ask the same of you. I heard on the wind that some baboon recruited the Champion of the Five Under Heaven to sneak into Caobiu territory to move furniture." She took several steps forward. "And I thought, the wind must be wrong. No one's head is that split open."

Kaiyu, for some inexplicable reason, felt the need to confess, which was odd since no one asked. "It was me. I did it. Zofi asked me a question this morning when I told her I couldn't help the nuns with the children's care. After I answered, she asked another question, and then another. Before I knew what happened, she knew everything!"

Jian couldn't be mad at that. He knew what Zofi was capable of. She had a way of asking just the right questions to weasel out whatever it was that she wanted to know.

Sonaya eyed him with her arms crossed. At least she was paying attention to him. He felt forgotten lately, and he didn't even know why. "I'm just guessing most of the time, right?"

Jian held his ground. "More or less."

She walked up to him and wagged a finger in his face. "What matters is not that I'm guessing. What matters is that I'm usually right."

He shrugged. "More or less."

Zofi stormed up to Hachi. "Is it really going to take four war artists, including"—she hissed—"the Prophesied Hero of the Tiandi, to move a bed and a sofa?"

"Depends on how large and heavy the bed," replied Hachi. "Let's say Neehong—that's Neeshan's mam—only has a small cot to sleep on. I could probably do it myself, but say it's a couple's bed or a wedding bed, it could take two or three. Not to mention the mattress is cloth, animal, or marble. If it was marble, we'd have to get a cart."

"Don't get extra stupid with me, Hachi. Is bringing along the Champion of the Five Under Heaven into enemy territory to help *you* score points with Neehong"—Zofi practically sneered—"a smart idea or a dumb one? What do you think, coconut brain?"

He shrugged. "I asked. He offered. That's how it works."

Jian's head slid into view between them. "Honor is the way."

"It's the only way, brother," answered Hachi. The two tapped fists. Jian ducked out again. "It's not my responsibility to make sure he makes good choices."

Zofi fumed. "You two together are stupidity manifested into physical form. I can't believe out of every child in the Enlightened States, the Tiandi chose you dumb spotted eggs to save the Zhuun." Before either Jian or Hachi could get in a word, she threw up her arms. "But fine, whatever. We're here. I just had to get that off my chest. Let's go get Hachi's girlfriend's furniture."

The small group was waved past the final barricade leading out of the buried ward. Hachi's intense eyes and charismatic bearing—again that gravitas!—were all they needed to get by the guards. Jian wondered if that trick would work for him. Probably not. Half of the people wouldn't recognize him, while the other half would probably bundle him up and ship him back to the temple.

They disappeared through a long, dank tunnel that went underneath one of the contested wards. This passage, known as the Little Fist Big Dog, was a difficult and wet trek but was one of the few remaining passages still connected to the eastern wards.

They emerged from a storm drain behind a row of shops an hour later. Morning was in full swing with a clear blue sky. Jian frowned when he climbed out of the tunnel. Other than distant booms near the barricaded streets running along one side of the block, it almost looked like any other day in the city before the war. The streets were clean. Vendors were out hawking wares, and residents strolled the walkways.

He inhaled and realized that for the first time in weeks it didn't smell like choking smoke.

He helped Sonaya and then Zofi out. "Does this place feel strange?"

Zofi caught it too. "Something is off."

"What's wrong with it?" Kaiyu craned his neck. "It feels nice, safe."

"That's exactly what's wrong," muttered Zofi. "Everything looks too normal. There's no specks of war anywhere. Where's the resistance, the fighting?"

Jian spun in a circle. She was right. The Wailing Duck was just one over from the eastern wall. The bulk of the Caobiu army was encamped on the other side. The enemy had swept through here and taken it over on the first night. Yet by the looks of morning traffic—boys pulling supply carts, the elderly walking through a small park, children playing marbles on the sidewalks—there wasn't a war. The only sign of it were a pair of Caobiu magistrates with tall cone-shaped hats and yellow robes patrolling toward them from across the street.

Hachi pulled Jian's sleeve. "Back way is safer. Come on, it's not far."

They followed the whipfinger down an alley that turned into a narrow lane for refuse dumping. Clotheslines hung overhead, many with sheets dangling, obstructing the sky. Hachi turned uphill and picked his way between two rows of buildings packed tightly together. Somewhere ahead, a window swung open and someone tossed a bucket out. The group encountered the output a few seconds later as a stream of liquid dribbled past their feet. Before the invasion, Jian would have been disgusted. Now, after spending hours crawling through sewers, he thought nothing of it.

"Sonaya," he said, slowing down for her as they waded through the garbage.

She looked at him coolly. "What is it, Five Champ?"

Even the way she said his nickname didn't have the usual playful charm. The two hadn't spent much time together the past few weeks, but the last few times he tried to connect with her, she had been demure. Was it something he did? Jian's heart ached. He was desperate to know why she had pulled away.

"I haven't seen you," he blurted.

"I'm fine." Sonaya's hard demeanor cracked. "Long nights, many deaths, and we win every battle, but we seem to keep losing the war."

That was everyone's narrative. The people of Vauzan had fought the Caobiu tooth and nail, blood paid with every step, but no matter how well they fought, they continued to lose ground. Sonaya's beautiful face had the same tired, hollow rings around her eyes that everyone else had.

"After we help Hachi today, can I see you at the bamboo grove? We can pretend the world doesn't exist for an evening."

She shook her head. "I have to get back to the Blades. We have a mission to raid a Caobiu supply warehouse hidden in the trinket ward."

She and Kaiyu had joined a war artist underground corps that operated as an elite unit for the city's defenses. They were often sent on secret missions or allocated to the highest-priority assignments. Jian would have liked to join them, but the court had other ideas.

"Maybe tomorrow, then?"

She didn't even stop to consider his request. "Come on, we're falling behind."

Sonaya hurried ahead, leaving him behind. He did his best to brush his hurt off, but her casual rebuke cut him in a way no knife could. Jian tried to look at their relationship objectively. There wasn't one, technically. She had never allowed it. Besides, these were demanding times for all of them. But Jian had assumed that she would have been the most supportive. Instead, she backed away and kept her distance, only heightening his loneliness.

Hachi continued sneaking them through the back ways, at one point cutting through the kitchen of a restaurant and through the leveled ruins of another building. He raised a fist once they reached a small grove with the tops of trees burned away, and had them wait out a squad of red-and-yellow soldiers marching through. As expected, the Caobiu presence was heavy, but they didn't seem to be watching the populace as they marched toward the fighting.

Jian admired how crisply they moved. Sohn had told him that the Cinder Legions were the only military that spent many hours training to move their feet together. At the time, during his lesson, Jian thought the practice silly. Now he stared in awe. They were more professional than any other army he had seen. No wonder the Caobiu were so feared throughout the Enlightened States.

The ward appeared well run, considering it was occupied territory. The city blocks were clean, especially compared to the rubble- and garbage-strewn streets of the Shulan-controlled wards. There was tension in the air from the many soldiers standing and patrolling, but it didn't feel dangerous. The Caobiu were good at making things appear normal, as if the attack on their city were just some fevered dream.

They moved after the soldiers were gone, waiting for a lull in traffic before sprinting across the street. They entered a narrow but long three-story flat through a doorway in the alley and continued to the top floor along a squat stairwell. Hachi stopped at the entrance and waited until the rest of them arrived at the landing.

The door flew open before he even got two knocks in. Neeshan burst out and threw herself into Hachi's arms, wrapping him in a tight embrace.

Kaiyu leaned in toward Jian and whispered, "Are people supposed to hug that long?"

He made a duck face. "I feel awkward too."

Neeshan pulled away from Hachi. She eyed him and then slapped him on the chest.

"I heard about what happened in the last corps you were embedded in. I was terrified that you were dead. I cried all night." Neeshan sobbed for emphasis and buried her face in his, then she pulled back and slapped him on the chest. "Next time, send word that you're all right."

"Sorry, Nissy," he replied. "It's not easy considering you live two wards behind enemy lines." He added, "I'm sorry I made you cry."

The two came back into an embrace, which probably would have gone on for quite a bit longer if not for Zofi blowing a raspberry in their direction.

"Maybe we should get out of the stairwell," she said.

Neeshan pulled back a second time and wiped her tears, and then she looked Jian's way. Her eyes widened. She shook her head. "I still can't believe it's you, Prophesied Hero of the Tiandi."

He grinned. "I told *you* that you picked the right man."

Neeshan led them inside. No sooner had Hachi stepped through the front door than he was accosted by an older woman who looked the spitting—if graying—image of her daughter.

The older woman put her hands on her hips. "You said you were coming today. The day's already half over."

Hachi bowed formally with his hands at his sides as if he were greeting the empress. "I came as soon as I was able, Mama Neehong."

Mama?

Kaiyu leaned toward Jian. "Hachi wouldn't have married someone without inviting us, right?"

Jian crossed his arms. "Until this moment, I would have sworn it on my life. Especially since, you know, they owe it to me."

Sonaya elbowed him. "Don't take credit for everything."

"What?" he protested in a lower voice. "I introduced them!"

Zofi stepped in last and looked around a barren room with only a small, square table and a stone bed that was cut directly into the ground. She frowned when she saw four similarly older women sitting at that table gabbing away. "Who are these people? Is this a retirement home?"

"This is my tile gaming group." Neehong waddled up to them. "They need to move to the western wards too. I've been on a long los- ing streak, so we worked out an arrangement."

Zofi shook a finger at Hachi. "You said furniture, not people!"

"Would you have agreed if I said they were people?"

"No, because that would be stupid!" She gesticulated. "Extra stu- pid."

Hachi pointed back at one of the women. "See the granny on the left? She lost both sons defending their block when the Caobiu poured in through the southern wall. The one next to her lost her daughter when their home burned down. The last on the right lost her entire family. She has no way of reaching her last surviving niece, except with us. Some people have already paid a high price, Zofi."

Zofi blinked, then looked insulted. "Did you just try to use sympathy as an argument, Hachi? Do you think that will work?"

He snapped back, "Because you don't have any feelings?"

"Because I'm not idiotic enough to ask the Prophesied Hero of the Tiandi to smuggle old women through enemy lines inside a war zone!" The two continued to bicker.

Jian stopped listening and came face-to-face with Mama Neehong. The older woman was studying him as if inspecting a melon. She poked his forehead. "You're it? You're that one they're making such a fuss about? There's not much to you, boy."

If only Jian could earn a gold liang every time someone was disappointed the first time they met him. "I'm a lot more threatening after they paint my face."

She barked a laugh and patted him on the shoulder. "Tell those court fools handling you to stop making you look so bloodthirsty all the time. Every morning, they announce how many Caobiu you've killed as if you were getting paid a copper a head."

"I'll tell my publicity team," he replied.

"Good. You're scaring the young, and nobody likes heroes who scare children." She pointed with her thumb to a pile of furniture stacked behind her. "At least you look like you have a strong back. How much can you carry?"

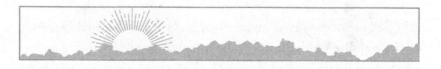

CHAPTER TWENTY-SIX

DIPLOMACY

Sali's offer to Yazgur Huong was straightforward. Sunjawa would declare its freedom from the Katuia khanate and join Nezra and its allies in throwing off the yoke of the horde. In return, Nezra and all five rim clans in this Exiles Rebellion, as they were so named, would support one another logistically and economically and coordinate in the war effort, pledging to come to each clan's defense if attacked. Once they earned their freedom, each clan would be free to form its own alliances or to strike out as a free people, much like it was centuries ago before the rise of the Eternal Khan of Katuia.

"With your control over shipping lanes," Sali said, "we can cut off the north from the khanate. The rim clans that support them will wither on the vine while the ones already ripe for rebellion would declare their independence."

"Until the horde sends a capital city to burn the tulip to a crisp."

"On the word of my ancestors, we will be by your side," said Sali.

"What is our assurance you will come to our aid?" asked the Seventh Yazgur. "Will you leave a hostage?"

"How can we depend on Nezra when their leader betrayed her

oath to the khan's Sacred Cohort?" asked the Second Yazgur, sitting next to Huong.

That was a fair question. The best way to answer it was truthfully. "When it came time to sacrifice my life as the Will of the Khan for the Return, I realized that sometimes honor and justice do not align. I chose to do the right thing."

That answer appeared to satisfy the Second Yazgur, albeit grudgingly.

Sali continued, "And it won't be Nezra who comes to your aid. The Exiles alliance will end Katuia's might. No capital city can defeat us if we unite. Our numbers grow daily. It would require at least two full cities to match our ranks, and there is little chance the Chaqra would dare send two capitals in their current state. This is a generational opportunity, First Yazgur. If you free Sunjawa from the spirit shamans' shackles, every blade within the Grass Sea will sing your name."

"I just want running water," he grunted.

"There is no greater chance to win your freedom than alongside us," Sali pressed, placing a fist over her heart. "We pledge to come to your aid. Nezra's spear will be yours. Horano's hammers as well. Hrusha will coordinate our supply lines with weapons, ore, and food. Unashi to the east can keep trade backchannels open with the Tsunarcos trade routes, while Colandri . . . Well, they'll try."

The Colandri rim clan had little in the way of resources or manpower, or any specific expertise for that matter, but they were honorable and earnest, and the first rim sect clan to join Nezra and Hrusha's alliance after Sali had received dozens of rejections, which meant something to Sali. She had a life debt to the Colandri rim clan.

"What about ore?" asked the Second Yazgur. "Wars require great amounts of ore, which Sunjawa has not been blessed with in vast quantities."

"Nezra is working on sourcing ore," Sali said. "I assure you every rim clan will be well supplied." At least, she hoped.

Dai was practically hopping in place. "First, this could be our chance."

"Silence, Ninth!" the First Yazgur snapped. "You are not one of the eight allowed to open your mouth."

"Noble Dai is not wrong," Sali continued. "Sunjawa's banner flies below no others. Imagine freedom for your clan for the first time in centuries."

She was met with blank faces, save for Dai, whose eyes glistened with patriotic fervor. Rebellion was romantic for the young, but a horror story for most everyone else with a working brain, and in this case, Yazgur Huong was anything but convinced.

A yazgur to her left asked, "Sunjawa numbers five times Colandri and double the Horano clan. Why should their word carry equal weight as ours?"

"Because we are brothers and sisters, not khans or masters."

"We have more to lose than them," said another. He was the Fourth or Fifth Yazgur, Sali couldn't be sure.

"The most we can lose is our lives. There is nothing more you can offer," Sali replied. "Every member of the alliance carries these burdens equally. Just like all we can win is our freedom, nothing more. The future is still yours to write."

In the end, the First Yazgur's response to her offer was inconclusive, which was more than she expected. "You have given the yazgurs of the Nest much to discuss, Salminde the Viperstrike. Return tomorrow and we will discuss further."

A second meeting meant the First Yazgur was open to this alliance. That was more than Sali had hoped for. She placed her fist over her forehead, and then over her chest. Dai appeared at her side and walked alongside her down the stairs and across the length of the longhouse. It felt suspiciously like an escort, but Sali let it go. Perhaps not being so strict on some of Katuia's customs was the first step to show the rim clans that there were better ways.

"I love—" Dai began.

"The idea of the alliance?" Sali said. The Sunjawa clan had the reputation of falling quickly in and out of love. For them, divorce was as common as the changing seasons. Every few days, they married someone new.

"Yes," Dai pivoted. "I dreamed of Sunjawa being free of the Chaqra's heavy yoke." He stepped close to her, his eyes hungry. "I'll do anything I can to help, Salminde."

Sali resisted the urge to cuff him on the head. She could use him. She backed away and squeezed his arm lightly. "Convince the rest of your yazgurs, then. Help me see it come true."

"I'll do everything in my power," he replied, leaning into her space again.

She made a hasty exit before the young lad tried again. He wasn't bad looking, just half her age, which practically made him a toddler. Sali left the Nest and continued down a roped bridge that led to several lower platforms.

Wani fell in line next to her a moment later.

"Your flare was late," said Sali.

"You're lucky I got it out at all. There were guards about. I couldn't get any closer than two levels lower. I had to climb up one of the support rafters to get a good vantage point."

They reached the water level and continued through the floating neighborhood, their footsteps thumping on the damp wooden walkway bobbing over water. They flagged down another gondola and gave instructions to ferry them to the docks.

"Do you see them?" asked Sali in a muffled voice.

"See what?" That girl was oblivious sometimes. "Are we being followed?"

"As soon as I left the Nest. The bald woman with the white feathered travel cloak."

Wani craned her head back at the Sunjawa agent standing at the end of the walkway, and then the gondola turned the corner onto the main waterway leading out of the city. "Wow, I love her outfit. If we have to go to war with them, I'm going to kill her and steal that feather cloak."

Sali side-eyed Wani. That was a tad bloodthirsty. Sali didn't train her that way. Then she remembered how she was once a young, brash girl who dreamed of great victories before she'd even tasted battle. It wasn't until Sali had raided in her first campaign that the brutality of violence tempered her sharp tongue. Wani would learn soon enough. Besides, it *was* a fantastic cloak.

Wani was still ogling the woman when Sali cupped her chin and swiveled her to face forward. Constant staring was another trait of the younger generation. Neither of her neophytes were subtle creatures, but then neither was Sali, nor most viperstrikes. Subtlety and subterfuge were not aspects of the viperstrike war arts style. It also didn't matter that they were being followed. Sali wanted the Sunjawa agent to see what might Nezra brought to the table, even if it was just one city pod.

Especially that it was only one city pod.

The gondola dropped them off at the docks next to the gates. Sali inhaled. The stink of the city had been replaced with the stink of the jungle. There was a brief wait as the outpost guards manning the entrance waved them through. Once they were outside, they continued walking down the exterior harbor where the pods, barges, and other larger craft were anchored.

"You have the flare?" Sali asked.

Wani produced a cylinder tube the diameter and length of her arm. "Pop it?"

Sali nodded, and then flagged a bearded, large-bellied man in gray suspenders barking at a group of laborers. "Dockmaster, I need to anchor a craft."

The man turned to face her. His eyebrows rose when he saw her scale armor and weapons, but his tone remained the same. "Is that so, Kati? Did you book a slip?"

Sali shook her head. "First time visiting your beautiful outpost."

"Then we're out of spaces. You're looking at a four-day wait. Book in advance next time." He turned his back to her, having already moved on.

Sali pointed to the two spaces at the end of the dock. "What about those two?"

The dockmaster stroked his beard. "That's reserved for large freight and pods."

"Just for a few days," she replied.

"That spot opens up in two weeks, woman," the man snapped. "Like I said, all spots are taken. I'm not about to bump you up the list just because you're wearing shiny armor. You can go camp in the jungle until then. Watch out for the baboons. They like to throw shit at the ships that disturb their homes."

Sali refused to back down. "We'll just take these spots for now since they're not being used."

A shrill whistle punctured the air as a green flare shot into the evening sky.

She turned to leave, ignoring his protests, and caught the tail end of the flare as it died in the sky. A few moments later, the edge of the grass began to stir. A small swarm of bats took to the air as clusters of tall grasses in the distance parted. The needle point of *Not Loud Not Fat* soon came into view as its tracks rumbled mostly submerged into the shallow lake. These city pods were supposed to float anyway.

The dockmaster who had caught up to Sali stared, open-mouthed. The Kahun pod was likely the grandest city pod he had ever laid eyes on. It was certainly the most alien compared to the other capital cities down south. The docks they stood on undulated as the city pod slowed. The front ramp lowered with a clatter at the end of the wooden walkway.

She said to him, "Like I said, we'll need both. Oh, and we're on official business with the yazgurs. You can send the bill to the Nest."

Nanka, another former howler monkey who had promise, was waiting to ambush them with questions the moment they came on deck. "How did it go? What did their elders say? Did you see that flaming pitch? I wonder if it hit anything on the other side."

"Patience, lad," said Sali. "These discussions take time." The boy was too young to train, but he had begged her until she accepted him as a squire.

"Marhi's raiding party returned."

"How was their haul?"

"Four wagons, two laden with quality ore, the rest substandard quality weaves, some shoddy Zhuun tools, and some salt and serpent grease." Nanka scrunched his face. "She brought somebody back."

That caught her attention. Sali frowned. "We don't take slaves or prisoners."

"Marhi was saying something about a trade. They insisted on seeing you."

"Insisted?" Sali snorted. "Typical of the Zhuun to demand."

"They claim that the two of you are close friends."

"I have no friends, and I certainly do not have any that are landchained."

Nanka shrugged. "Maybe they're a fan."

Sali was tempted to cut loose this person Marhi had brought back and let the jungle swallow them, but they *did* come all this way. "Fine. Move them to the spare storage room. I'll speak to them when I get around to it. Where's Daewon?"

"Down in the guts, still working on the track that keeps slipping."

Nanka and Wani took off in opposite directions, leaving Sali as she walked the length of the pod to talk to her brother-in-law. She passed several of her warriors. The older veterans offered friendly waves, while the younger ones jumped to attention and placed their fists over their hearts. Most were barely twenty years of age.

She passed two rows of artillery—catapults and ballistae—flanking both sides of the city pod. Kahun the Wind was renowned as the fastest city among all capital cities. She was one of the least armed and armored, but she more than made up for it with her speed. Sali had already notched several battles under her belt simply by outmaneuvering enemy settlements and fortifications. Still, she wished her pods had double the number of ballistae. What they had right now was sufficient for these rim clans, but it would be a different affair once a capital city rolled up on them.

"Worry about that when one of them corners you," she grumbled.

Sali reached the administrative building near the center of the pod and greeted the two guards standing watch. Both placed their fists over their hearts. Sali did the same and spoke to the one on the left. "Did Hoquo pull through?"

The young man lowered his gaze. That was all Sali needed to

know. One of his injuries had become infected after the battle. "I'm sorry about your brother."

"It was the honor of his life to join you on this raid, Sali." He failed to hold back his tears. "All he wanted to do was make you proud."

Now it was time for Sali to temper her emotions. These were also her children. She placed a hand on his shoulder. "Go mourn. Send for another to take your place."

The guard wiped his wet eyes. "My brother wouldn't approve of that and neither will I."

"Then perhaps a gathering tonight on the deck to celebrate his life."

"Hoquo would disapprove of all this fuss."

Sali leaned in. "It's not for him."

The guard blinked as if it was the first time the thought crossed his mind. "I would like that, chief."

She found Daewon with two other tinkers trying to reattach a large sprocket on the side of the engine powering one of the tracks. This set had been a constant problem since she had accidentally clipped *Not Loud Not Fat* against the side of a stone pillar. She watched as he worked with furious intensity with his assistants, patching up the damaged pod with as much care and urgency as a field doctor in triage. It took fifteen minutes before the cluster of cogs attached in their correct places. It formed a harmonious pattern. Sali rarely came down here because the underbelly of the pods was loud, claustrophobic, and disorienting. It also smelled like animal guts, sweat, and sulfur.

Daewon wiped his greasy hands. "Give it a spin, Weigo."

The tinker on the other end of the walkway pulled a large handle, and the engine sputtered to life. The cluster of circular metal parts squealed and shifted. The cogs on one end of the track came to life, wheels and levers churning, a kaleidoscope of lights blinking like the stars. A shrill whistle blew, and the entire system began to move and turn, cascading along a complicated and mesmerizing dance of moving parts. Until it reached the sprocket that they had just reattached.

A shrill shriek followed by a thunderous crack nearly blew Sali's eardrums, and then the symphony of metal crashed to a sudden halt. A soft ringing echo continued for a few moments, and then the jarring silence took over.

Daewon's shoulders slumped. He took every damage these city pods received like a personal affront. A muffled groan escaped his lips. "All right. Take her apart. Reset that alignment and—"

Sali grabbed a fistful of his collar as he passed. "Not tonight, tinker."

He noticed her for the first time. "Oh, hey, Sali. Didn't see you come. I'm just—"

"—going to bed." She turned him around facing away from the engine room. "It can wait. We'll be parked here for a few days. You look like a corpse and smell even worse."

Daewon didn't resist when she pulled him along. Sali walked him through the winding catwalk below the main level of the city pod that ran parallel to the pod's giant tracks. These unsteady, narrow walkways unnerved her every time she traveled in the belly of the pods. It made her feel as if she were being buried alive.

"How are repairs?"

That roused Daewon. "Nothing's a total salvage, if that's what you're asking, although can we avoid hitting heavy objects in the future?"

"Probably not," she admitted. "Do you need anything?"

"Three more tinkers." He paused. "And maybe some pangolin tendons for some of the joints. Whale tarp; need several bolts. Blackrock if we can nab some. Did we get anything from that barge?"

"No," said Sali. "I gave them my word."

"How about some oil? Whale or seal. Heck, I'll even take their sludge. We're low on lubricant."

She shook her head. "My word. Marhi supposedly brought supplies back."

The tinker grew animated. "We should have taken the *Honest Run*'s supply."

"The captain insisted it wasn't for barter. They barely had enough for themselves."

"What is the point of pillaging a barge if we don't actually get anything from them?" the tinker complained. "This is nothing like the raiding stories everyone used to tell."

"Raiders usually have nothing but time to make things up," she agreed. "Come, off to bed with you, tinker." She escorted him to his bunk at the far end of the crew quarters known as the tinker row. He collapsed onto his hammock. His sleep space had an extra table at the end. Everyone used it mostly for meals and playing games of Anklebones and Family Home.

Though he was a grown man, Sali tucked him in anyway, much like how she used to tuck in Mali when they were children. "I don't want to see your hairless face tomorrow morning. Can't have you passing out or dying. You are family now, understood?"

Daewon didn't answer. He was already asleep by the time his head hit the pillow.

Sali stood over him and, for a moment, saw a glimmer of what Mali loved about him. Daewon was honest and hardworking, intelligent and inquisitive, and considerate to those around him. He was still physically inept and cowardly, but he stayed true to himself and embraced his many other strengths. That earned him Sali's respect.

She left the smelly crew quarters and continued down the belly of the pod toward her private quarters on the opposite side. As the warchief, she was the only one who had her own space, but Sali hated these arrangements. Kahun pods were not designed for living and comfort. Everything about the city was engineered for efficiency and speed. It was in many ways the opposite of Nezra's former capital city, which was bright, airy, and spacious, with buildings shaped like trees and greenery everywhere, even the lower decks.

She opened the door to her quarters and stared at the barren, squat space inside. It was barely larger than a bathing tub and offered privacy, but Sali was more comfortable with the raidlife, sleeping under the stars next to many bodies. Her tiny living quarters here were an isolated, claustrophobic tomb. They also stank.

Sali decided to retire under the sky and headed topside. Wani caught her on the way up. "Mentor, I couldn't sleep so wanted to bounce some ideas off you on my blade work. Do you think I'm more suited for—"

Sali raised a hand and cut her off, lest the girl talk all night. "Ask me tomorrow."

Wani didn't miss a beat. "I'll hold you to that, Sali. Hey, I'm leading first watch tonight. Do you think four guards in two shifts is enough?"

The girl still second-guessed herself far too often. "It's a new port in unfriendly territory. Half of the crew are working resupply, so we're half-staffed. Eight on patrol in half shifts should be sufficient."

"Yes, mentor."

The pod's quartermaster sought Sali afterward. "We're barrel dry on citrus." He then lowered his voice. "We're also out of chili oil."

The hackles on the back of Sali's neck raised. "What?"

The quartermaster gulped. "All dishes are bland until we can source more."

Sali quickly gave him permission to head to the city tomorrow to barter for their needs.

She next stopped to exchange words with a repair crew when she reached the surface, and then chose to help a work crew repair a shattered spotlight that had clipped one of the dock posts when the pod came into harbor. The amount of work on the warpod was endless. A full hour passed by the time Sali made the short jaunt from Daewon's hammock to the bench in the tree grove on the west end of the main deck.

A sigh escaped her as her head touched the hard wooden deck and she looked into the glittering night sky. She didn't realize how long she had been holding her breath all day until now. A long sigh escaped her as her chest deflated. Why anyone would want to rule anything was beyond her. It was the worst job in the world.

"Only a true fool. Give me the freedom of raidlife any day," she muttered, her eyes growing heavy. Sali shifted to her side. She had forgotten to remove her armor, but she didn't care. There was still so much to do and so many concerns to deal with. She closed her eyes and tried to bury those thoughts, checklists, and urgent matters, with little success. A small voice in the back of her mind called to her, something about a person she was supposed to check in on and see tonight.

She had forgotten about it, but it didn't matter. It probably wasn't important anyway.

CHAPTER TWENTY-SEVEN

FORGOTTEN

It took some time, over a month, for Qisami to feel like herself again. The last five years had been another life—so much so, the idea that she was a deadly assassin felt like a fever dream, a wild tale someone as pathetic as Chopstick would dream up. There had been days when she had doubted her identity.

But as she had traveled with the Katuia, leaving the frigid gray of the Grass Tundra, to the mushy swamplands, and then into the Grass Sea, Qisami's sense of self slowly returned. Chopstick had shed a layer of her identity alongside each discarded burlap sack as the frigid snow melted into boiling humidity. She should be ecstatic to be free, to be out of prison, to be herself again, but she was indifferent. Something in her was broken.

She had time to dwell on this as she sat trussed up at the wrists atop a donkey for nearly three weeks. This was torture worse than any punishment she had suffered at the penal colony. She had spent a good portion of the journey muttering her own name over and over, partially to get reacquainted with herself, but mainly because it distracted her from the numbing pain of her sore backside.

At least she had a scrawl buddy. Qisami inched herself up to a sitting position and dug a nail into her left forearm. *Hey little blood pal. Are you still alive?*

Cyyk's scrawl came nearly two hours later. Bloodscrawls took longer to receive the farther the shadowkills were apart. *Barely. In the middle of a blizzard going into the third day. I'm about to eat someone.*

You can't be my grunt if you turn cannibal.

Who says I'm still your grunt?

That gave Qisami pause. That was certainly true. Their bond as shadowkill master and grunt had disintegrated when she was betrayed by her cell, stabbed in the back by Sunri, and discarded by the Consortium. The reason Cyyk had been sent to the penal colony was because of her. The only bond the two shared now was . . . friendship.

That sent a shudder through Qisami. The pathetic baby grunt was her only friend in the world. She scrawled back, *Sucks to be you. It's sweltering where I am.*

Qisami detested humidity, but she wasn't about to admit that she was miserable.

We should have escaped when we had the chance. Now you're probably dead, and I'm trapped here forever. Cyyk could never let go of this stupid issue.

I'll be fine. You should worry more about yourself.

The Kati will probably eat you for dinner. At least he was supportive.

Don't be ridiculous. The Kati don't eat people. At least she didn't think they did.

These short exchanges took place over the course of an entire day. This abduction by the Kati was the most interesting thing that had happened to her in years. She was glad she had been captured, and he wasn't. If Qisami somehow earned her freedom, she would go back for Cyyk. He certainly wouldn't last on his own. Besides, she might get to meet that Salminde the Viperstrike again. How exciting.

She replied, *Try not to die before I come back for you. I would hate to travel all the way to that ice pick for nothing.*

The next message arrived nearly three hours later. *They built a nursery in the Lawkan corner. The babies are aboveground.*

Qisami had nearly forgotten about those babies since she had been captured, but it brought tears to her eyes upon reading this bit of news. She didn't know she still cared, and was frankly annoyed she did. But in this case, Qisami was glad.

"Good luck in life, you stupid kids," she muttered. "You're probably better off dead. But I'm glad you get the chance to find out how much life sucks."

It also gave Qisami another reason to succeed with this outlandish plan she had concocted while on the trek to the Grass Sea. She had hashed out the details with the rest of the penal colony's leaders, using bloodscrawling with Cyyk as their main method of communication. Qisami was ready to function as an emissary between their two settlements. The Happy Glow would offer the Kati a fair deal: Give the colony a chance to protect themselves against the Caobiu when they arrive, and in return, the colony would send an equal number of wagons laden with ore. The two sides would meet at the shallow of the Swirl Snow Pits where the tundra and sea meet.

She had even discussed the coordination with the viperstrike Marhi. The young woman seemed receptive to the plan. Both the colony leaders and the viperstrike had decided that Qisami would serve as the middleman between the two due to her unique shadowkill talents and her relationship with Salminde.

Qisami suspected the penal colony was pleased to get rid of her. No one at the Happy Glow would shed a tear if the Kati lopped off her head. She was fine to play along, though, and was looking forward to seeing that hot pepper Salminde again. She hoped the woman had changed nothing about herself since last they met. No need to mess with perfection. Salminde's was one of the faces among about a dozen that kept Qisami warm in bed during cold nights.

The rest of her raiders had broken away some days back to hit a Katuia settlement near the border of Zhuun lands. That left the viperstrike and three of her spears to drive five wagons and a prisoner deep into the Grass Sea.

After many weeks, they arrived at their destination at nightfall. Qisami deeply missed the night. She had not experienced the sun setting and the land draped in darkness over almost five years during her time in the Grass Tundra. The first dusk she saw, she wept.

Qisami had fallen asleep tonight deep in the thickets of the jungle and now woke to the sound of a ramp lowering from a platform overhead. They were entering the outskirts of a Kati moving city, and her anticipation grew.

She had expected Marhi to take her to the woman of her dreams the moment they arrived at this rolling Kati base. Instead, she was left trussed on the ground for another hour. Eventually, some of the towerspears came for her. Qisami was blindfolded, hauled up a metal ramp, and tossed into a small, dank room barely larger than a closet with little more than a bench and a window slit near the ceiling.

"Stay here," a towerspear said, locking the door with a definitive click.

With nothing else to do in this boring, barren room, Qisami caught up on more sleep. She didn't realize how little of it she was getting in prison. The hard wooden floor in this temperate room practically felt like a private spa compared to some of her frigid, public sleeping arrangements back at the Happy Glow.

She found a clean and relatively dry spot on the empty floor and was soon curled into a fetal position. If anything, she slept even better now that she wasn't getting tossed around in a wagon.

Hours later, she woke and realized that she was still in the same room. No one had come for her. She was still locked in the small, cramped cell but now she was famished. Worse, she had to pee, and there was not enough floor for her to go without soiling her shoes. She gritted her teeth; her bladder failing was inevitable.

Qisami looked for a way out. Should she try to escape? Where would she go if she succeeded? She was trapped in the middle of a jungle without food, supplies, or weapons. She was probably better off just staying here. She slapped herself lightly. Chopstick would have stayed in this cell indefinitely, but not Qisami the diamond-tier. There was no jail that could hold a shadowkill.

The room had no light sources save for a box of moonlight shining through a small window near the ceiling, just enough to keep the room from being dark and losing all form. Shadowkills needed a tiny light to give shadows structure. She stretched her achy joints after so many weeks tied to the wagon.

Qisami scanned the ceiling and measured the distance to the window. Then she sucked in two long breaths to work herself up and took the plunge, slipping into a corner on the floor. Qisami entered a swirl of darkness. Black rushing currents swept her away like a rushing river, pushing and tugging her in every direction. Up became down, and then all sense of direction disappeared. It took her several moments to right her mind as she held on to her focus. She welcomed the comfortable nausea boiling in her bowels as she stretched herself into the darkness. It had been too long. She missed the thrill of the nightblossom, a creature of surprise and an ender of lives. Most of all she missed the freedom of flitting through shadows. Qisami shadowstepped out from near the ceiling a moment later. The moment she emerged, she gripped the walls with her feet while her hand pressed against the ceiling, creating a delicate balance in her equilibrium that allowed her to defy gravity. She had always loved hiding in corner perches.

At least that's how it was supposed to work.

Qisami wasn't her usual sharp self these days. Her left foot slipped on the wall and her hand missed clutching at the bars on the window because she had botched the attempt and shadowstepped out far lower than she intended. She squawked and plummeted to the floor. Her bony backside took the brunt of the injury as she bounced off the wooden deck. She nearly soiled herself from the impact, but managed to keep it in. If this pain and pressure in her bladder was anything like giving birth, then she would happily leave the mothering to others. The twins, Akiya and Akiana, came to mind. It infuriated her to know she might never fulfill the death mark on that witch, Chiafana.

Qisami picked herself up and tried again. She fell headfirst to the floor on her second attempt. On her third, she finally shook off some of that rust. Muscle memory never fails. She planted her feet successfully but still ended up skidding down the wall. Her next attempt was executed perfectly, allowing her to rest in the corner like a black widow spider.

"I'm an apex predator," she cooed as she pushed off from the wall toward the window. She missed it by a handspan and smashed into the wall, falling on her backside again. She felt as if she were back in the training pool again. Qisami shuddered. She was glad no one was watching but felt embarrassed anyway.

Finally, Qisami made it to the window. Her fingers strained as they gripped the ledge. She pulled her way up the wall until she could rest her elbows on the ledge. Outside of the window was the side of a building with a narrow alleyway between them. Her feet pedaled on the wall to push up a little more. She could probably touch both ends with her outstretched hands. All that mattered was she had a clear way out.

She shadowstepped to the other side in an instant, slipping into the dark area under the window and on the other side. Again, she failed to clutch a solid handhold and footing against the wall as soon as she emerged. She squawked and plummeted, bouncing between the walls until she crashed to the ground.

Qisami sat up, rubbing her achy back. She was out of practice. The small jumps were easy, but the tricky pulls just felt sluggish, like a musician playing a dulcimer after many decades. It would be best if she could get the kinks out before she had to face live blades. She looked at the window three stories above. The initial escape was always the worst part. It wasn't like she was going to fall again.

Something cracked beneath her.

She looked down and realized she had fallen atop what appeared to be a long, wooden grate. She furrowed her brow. What was this for? A louder crack followed, echoing across the narrow alley. Then the wood beneath her gave way, and Qisami squawked and plummeted weightless into darkness alongside fragments of wood. Her foot caught onto something hard, which flipped her headfirst. Then she bounced off something else, then finally crashed into a cold, wet surface.

This was so embarrassing.

"Not my best work." Qisami groaned. She was sprawled on what felt like a metal floor, which was unusual. This floor was also swaying from side to side. She sat up, rubbing her ringing head, then noticed the chains suspending the walkway in the air. Qisami crawled to the edge and peered over the side. She could just make out the ground some three stories below, but she couldn't tell what was down there. She grunted as she pushed against the cold metal catwalk, struggling to get upright.

Qisami pawed her way into a sitting position and scanned her surroundings. She felt like someone had tossed her inside a giant furnace. The ceiling was all metal with dozens of pipes routing in every direction. On her left was a wall of dials, while to her right was some sort of large machinery, currently half taken apart with pieces lying all over the floor.

Finally, Qisami looked at the other end of the room and realized that she wasn't alone. Sitting on their knees next to one of the large machines with big circle disks stuck to its side were two Kati wearing funny brown dresses with an enviable number of pockets. No, not dresses, but aprons.

The two had paused whatever they were doing and stared at her with their mouths open, like spooked fawns. The two eyed each other and then turned their attention back to her. One raised his hand as if to ask a question. "That was a big fall. Are you all right?" He squinted. "Do you need to see the medic? Wait, who are you? You're not—"

Every instinct in Qisami's body screamed to get her grubby hands on those two and twist their necks until their heads popped off, and her body moved to do just that. Shadowkills were trained to follow their instincts. She rolled over the side of the railing of the walkway and dropped into the shadows, stepping out onto the other end of the room right behind the two limp, stick-armed wristwaggers. She swept the first off his feet with a sharp kick to the side of his ankles and then wrapped her arms around the second, dragging him down with her knee pressing on the first Kati's neck.

"Still got it." She smirked, pleased.

Qisami was about to administer the double killing blow when she hesitated.

What was the point of killing these pathetic, soft plushies? They were both puppies, not worth anyone's time. It wouldn't even be fun.

"Oh, pig feet," Qisami muttered. "I'm turning into a wet rag. How embarrassing."

Besides, killing Kati would not reflect well upon her to Salminde. It certainly was not the best way to kick off a reunion. Qisami wondered if the viperstrike remembered her.

"Of course she does," she muttered.

"What did you say?" said the Kati stuck in her choke hold.

"Can I get up now?" asked the one on the ground.

Qisami snapped out of it. She'd better kill them quickly and escape. Maybe go back for Cyyk. Maybe not. Bah, who was she kidding? Of course she was going to go back for baby grunt. She had no one else.

Qisami gritted her teeth and shifted her weight to the knee on the Kati's neck. His feet and hands kicked and pawed like an overturned turtle. At the same time, she pulled her hold tighter. The standing Kati went limp, and she let him go, dropping him to the ground. She then punched the remaining Kati in the jaw, sending his mind to the ether.

Qisami stood and loosed a breath. She should have finished the job. Her training pool instructors would have disowned her if they'd witnessed this.

"Bye, kitties," she purred. Now, for the dramatic escape. She took off, speeding to the end of the walkway just as someone turned around the corner and came in.

"Guys, I figured it out. I know Sali said to sleep, and I tried, but I had a nightmare that the entire track exploded and crippled the pod. Woke up in a cold sweat, I did. Then I realized; the axle for the sprocket must have gotten bent during impact. . . ." An aproned Kati stepped before Qisami. The Kati stumbled, startled like a wee rabbit. "You're not—what are you doing in my engine room?"

So much for avoiding confrontation. Qisami pounced on him, bowling him over onto his back. She straddled his body and towered over him. The wristwagger's eyes were filled with terror, and for a moment he looked as if he'd fainted. This wasn't fun. She smacked him with the palm of her hand on the ear, causing the Kati to seize up into a fetal position—it would stun him for a few moments at best—and continued on her way. Better for him than the alternative.

She hated this nicer, gentler version of herself.

Qisami fled through a cramped burrow of underground metal passages. She was running along a floating catwalk suspended by metal chains. There was a dizzying two-foot gap between the metal walls with pipes, dials, and levers at both edges of the catwalk. Over the side of the railings, about three stories below, was the swampy Grass Sea earth. She continued to skulk through the cramped passage. Sounds of steam hissing filled her ears as she turned the bend to an encased chamber. Dropping down into the jungle below wasn't a great option either. The darkness was too uniform. With no shape, it was impossible to shadowstep.

It wasn't long before she became hopelessly lost. This was the worst escape plan she had ever concocted. So much for reconnecting with Salminde. Qisami had gone from nearly reuniting with her best friend to breaking out of jail and beating up a bunch of peasants. It was fairly typical for how many of her nights fared on a job, but this time she was trying not to make things worse.

Qisami stopped at an intersection to collect her bearings. With everything being dark below and metal everywhere else, she had no idea which direction to face. Then she felt the slight tickle of a breeze on her left ear. Qisami did not hesitate, taking off down that walkway. Her hunch was correct, as the airflow grew stronger as she sprinted down an even wider floating walkway. This path must cross the length of the pod. She reached another intersection and continued to let the wind guide her. She soon found herself crawling up a steep ramp leading up to the main deck.

"Wow," she breathed. The pod was a settlement. It had streets, buildings, and sidewalks and—Qisami looked to the other side—a row of large siege ballistae.

No matter. She was this close to freedom. Now what? The night was young, with the Queen strutting across the sky, her glow bathing the deck of the pod with an intense blue hue.

Qisami began prowling. She didn't make it far, however, barely creeping twenty steps before a boy, whistling to himself, stepped directly in her path. It was too late to avoid bumping into him. He was lucky she was so small, though she still knocked him off his feet. Qisami grabbed him by the collar and hauled him up to eye level. The kid couldn't be allowed to cry and wake people. She had to silence him.

Qisami raised her hand to smack him across the face, and stopped. "Oh, pig feet." She put her hand down. "Just be quiet, kid. We'll call it even, yeah?" Seriously, what was her problem?

Something smashed Qisami from her left, or was it right? It didn't matter. Whatever struck her hit her so hard her entire body rattled. She spat blood and turned to lash back, powered by adrenaline and instinct, only to come face-to-face with a tall, beautiful woman with a wild mane of hair and glowing green eyes. Just like she had remembered.

Qisami's breath caught, and she squeaked, "Hi, best friend."

CHAPTER TWENTY-EIGHT

ORACLE OF THE TIANDI

"... and then, she stood in the center of the ranch and refused to leave until Sister Surratoo bought her the pair of damn ponies."

Battleabbess Koranajah had spent the past few hours getting drunk and regaling Taishi with the adventures of a young Oracle of the Tiandi's antics during her stay at the Black Orchid Convent. Three empty gourds littered the small table between them. Some of it had been surprisingly fine stuff.

While the Tiandi religion banned all forms of alcohol and drugs among their monks, the battlenuns of the Black Orchid sect were not as stringent. The women of the Tiandi often tended to be more pragmatic about doctrine.

Taishi, lounging on the settee opposite possibly the most powerful woman in the Tiandi religion's hierarchy, refreshed her own glass. "And did you?"

"Did I what?"

"Buy a pony?"

"Of course. We had to. We bought both of them. The Oracle of the Tiandi's every word is sacred to the devout." She covered her face. "I swear, Taishi, I became a nun because I hated children. I was tired of my parents demanding that I give them grandchildren. And now not only did a stupid child follow me here, but she also happens to be the only child in the world we aren't allowed to discipline, or even refute. It's madness!"

"Dumb religion, eh?" This felt strangely familiar. Taishi pursed her lips to smother her growing grin. "I feel your pain."

Koranajah continued to rage, waving her goblet about, sloshing bits of dark red wine all over the stone floor. "And get this. When we returned to the convent, the oracle demanded we house those smelly creatures in a guest room and paint them blue."

"Why would the oracle want to paint the room blue?"

"Not the room! The smelly tiny horses shitting all over the place! Pei demanded we paint the ponies blue!"

"Well, did you?"

"Yes." The battleabbess looked deflated. "Eventually, but only after Sister Surratoo got fed up and threatened her with a switch."

Taishi brought her drink to her lips, mainly to hide her smirk. "You were going to spank the Oracle of the Tiandi? A bold decision. How did that work out?"

"The Oracle of the Tiandi excommunicated her."

She spat her drink out. "She did what?"

"Excommunicated her nanny right there. Sister Surratoo had stood by the girl's side for years. She was practically her surrogate mother, and that power-hungry little tyrant plucked her soul out of the Mosaic of the Tiandi without a second thought." Koranajah drained her goblet for the tenth time and muttered, "Cold-blooded little bitch."

That didn't sound like the Pei that Taishi knew. The precocious oracle had always been overactive and impulsive, but never intentionally mean or spoiled. One could only blame puberty to a degree. There was no excuse for such monstrous behavior.

"It's not healthy, giving a child so much power," exclaimed Taishi. "You have to give them boundaries. Didn't you learn anything from what I had to deal with concerning Wen Jian?"

The battleabbess pawed for another gourd. "Some doctrine is unbending. The Supremacy of the Oracle's Voice is chief among them. Her words, which bore the prophecy's birth, cannot be questioned. It's not like we could just lock up the bloody girl in the corner tower." Her eyes widened as if the thought had just occurred to her.

"Hopefully she's grown up a bit since," Taishi said. "Some children are slower to mature than others."

"This happened last week!"

Taishi sighed. "I thought I was done taking care of spoiled holy relics." She placed her drink aside and rose to her feet. "Very well, then. It's a good thing I don't have any problems punishing our religion's holiest relics. Let's go smack some sense into our dear oracle, shall we? Why does she want to stay, anyway? It's not because of those stupid ponies, is it?"

"The brat won't say why, just that she won't go."

"We'll see about that." Taishi stared out the window. "Do you have a bag?"

Koranajah handed her a small woven bag. "I used to have terrible fear of heights too. I was ill for months when I first came to the convent."

Taishi made a face. "I'm a windwhisper. I don't need a vomit bag. Do you have anything larger?"

The battleabbess's eyes narrowed as she handed over a laundry sack. "What do you need this for?"

"Nothing." Taishi gave her a blank look and then left the room. It's easier to beg forgiveness after the sin has been committed.

Koranajah fell in step alongside her. "If she stays, the Black Orchids will remain as well. It'll be a matter of time before it leaks to Sunri that the Oracle of Tiandi has a residence in the Thorned Garden. The duchess will storm the convent to seize the oracle. The Black Orchids will die defending her."

The two seasoned women continued down another set of spiral staircases, crossing through several somber stone hallways. They passed by a few stained-glass windows, where Taishi could see the ground several hundred feet below, reminding her that this convent was hanging from the ceiling of a massive cave.

"Why don't your sisters clear out?" asked Taishi. "If the girl wants to stay and her capture is a foregone conclusion, why risk needless lives?"

Koranajah looked outraged. "If my sisters and I were to abandon the Oracle of the Tiandi in the face of a secular attack, then the Black Orchid name would be cursed among the Tiandi for an eternity." She looked indignant. "It is better to die with honor."

Was it really? Ten years ago, Taishi would agree with the battle-abbess. Now, nearer to death's door, she could think of a thousand better ways for a hundred elite warrior nuns to live their lives than to futilely throw it all away. She cracked her knuckles and tried to put a positive spin on the conversation. "Or we can convince the girl that she *has* to come with us."

"I don't relish the sect getting excommunicated."

Taishi shrugged. They continued descending yet another flight of stairs. How a building this tall didn't have a lift was beyond Taishi. It was almost criminal. They finally reached the top—or bottom—of the tower, which was traditionally the battleabbess's private sanctum. In these strange times, however, this was the Oracle of the Tiandi's personal quarters.

There were six Black Orchid initiates standing guard at the entrance to the sanctum. All were in full black armored battledress complete with their sect's curved sword polearms. They all fell onto one knee when Taishi and Koranajah approached.

"The steel serves the Tiandi," they recited. Now that was a professionally trained group of war artists.

Koranajah touched each young woman on the shoulder. "Rise, sisters, and be relieved."

All six rose like a team of synchronized water dancers and marched in rhythm, their footsteps echoing as one. Even Sunri, famous for her armies marching in step, would have been jealous.

The two stood before a set of large wooden doors. A muffled yell came from the other side. "About time you got here!"

"I wish I'd brought the plum wine," said Taishi.

"We drank it all." The battleabbess put a hand on the door. "Shall we?"

Taishi waved the sack in her hand. "Let's go."

Koranajah swung the large door open, and the two entered a wide room with the traditional low ceilings, stone walls, and plain wooden furniture. The room was plusher than the rest of the convent, however, with thick rugs hanging off every wall and cushions everywhere.

The first thing that caught Taishi's eye was the wall-to-wall glass floor that revealed the cave below. At this height, so far above the ground, even Taishi clenched her lower extremities during her first few steps inside. The rest of the walls were plain gray stone. There was a closed curtain to the bedchambers to their right. Toys, dirty clothes, and crumpled papers marked by chalk littered the floor.

Taishi wrinkled her nose at a line of ants crawling over a plate of half-eaten buns. "This place is unseemly."

Pei, the Oracle of the Tiandi, was on the balcony at the other end of the room. She was leaning over a low table playing a game of Siege with Floppy sitting on the other side of the board. The fox glanced their way and growled a curious, high-pitched shriek. That thing never had liked Taishi. The room smelled like wet fur and fox droppings.

"I hate that filthy animal," Koranajah muttered even as she portrayed forced pleasantness and stepped forward, stopping at the doorway to the balcony. She bowed, showing proper reverence to the little brat. "You have a visitor, holy one."

Taishi kicked a piece of fox poop, sending it rolling across the room. "Did you excommunicate your maid, too?"

Pei glowered at her. "I expected you two weeks ago. You kept me waiting."

"I didn't even know I was supposed to come until this morning, girl." Taishi took a seat on a torn cushion at the table and studied the game board. "Floppy seems to be poor competition. May I play a game?"

The oracle gestured to the seat. Floppy, realizing he was about to get evicted from his perch, hissed at Taishi before scurrying away.

She sat opposite the oracle and reset the Siege board. "You know why I came, right?"

The oracle nodded. "I'm a bad girl."

At least she was self-aware, which was more than what Taishi could say about Jian half the time. "That's an understatement." She leaned in. "I know you, Pei. You throw tantrums and have mean moments like any other child, but sneaking out in the middle of the night to dance around bonfires? Intentionally flooding the bathing tubs? Excommunicating your caretaker? This isn't you."

"I wasn't sneaking out to dance with boys."

Koranajah looked alarmed. "What boys? The Oracle of the Tiandi cannot—"

The oracle glared. "Get me some freshly squeezed lemonade."

Taishi frowned. "You can get your own lemonade, child."

"Now, you old hag!" Pei shrieked, her high-pitched voice cutting.

Koranajah was only a few years younger than Taishi. The battle-abbess's faced turned pale and her jaws clenched. Her fingers clenched into fists, and then she regained control, slowly relaxing them. "As you command, Holiness." She bowed and retreated, slowly backing out of the room.

As soon as they were alone, Taishi rounded on the oracle and slapped her across the cheeks. "How dare you act so terribly to the women who have dedicated their lives to you? What has gotten into you?"

Pei looked at her without any hint of surprise. She knew this scolding was coming, even if Taishi had not. The oracle made her next move on the Siege board. By the looks of it, the girl did not know the rules of the game either.

"I wasn't sneaking out to the bonfire to dance with boys," she insisted.

"Why sneak out at all?" said Taishi. "We're in the middle of a war in a ward that is about to fall. What is this nonsense of refusing to leave when you know your life is in danger. Sunri knows you're here. I understand teenage belligerence, but excommunicating your nanny? Refusing to flee the convent when the Caobiu discovered your whereabouts? This is madness, girl."

"I know. I'm the one who told Sunri of my whereabouts." The oracle gave her a flat stare. "I sneaked out at night not to go to the bonfire, but to get captured by the Caobiu."

Taishi was stunned. It took several tries before she finally found some words, and even then, those weren't the ones she had planned. She had to fight the urge to reach over and spank the girl. "Why in the name of the Tiandi would you do that, you dumb egg?"

Pei stood and walked to the edge of the balcony overlooking the sprawling Thorned Garden cave floor below. "Remember what I said to you that night Wen Jian spared your life?"

"You said many things to me," Taishi grumbled. "Most of it wasn't what a respectable holy relic should say."

"I said everyone was going to die." Pei turned and stared at her. "Right now, still, everyone is going to die. Everyone you know, the Tiandi religion, and most of the Zhuun empire, will perish. This is the road we walk because of *your* inability to manage blubber-brain Jian. Great job."

"You're blaming me for this?" In hindsight, the girl was probably right. Taishi probably was more at fault for their predicament than most.

As if by some mental bond, Floppy left his perch and jumped into Pei's arms. She squeezed the fox tightly and scratched him behind the ears. "I've spent almost every moment since that day trying to find a way to unravel that knot, the mistake you and Wen Jian stupidly made."

"I tried my hardest to get him to kill me," said Taishi. "The boy's too dumb and too big-hearted for his own good."

"I finally found it," Pei said. "I found a way to save everyone."

It was a strange thing to hear from a little girl, even if she was a holy oracle. "Does it involve painting a pony blue?"

It was then that Koranajah returned with a pitcher and three cups on a platter. She bowed and then placed the tray at the small table. "Lemonade for your holiness."

Pei didn't even look her way. "It's not freshly squeezed. Take it away."

The battleabbess looked about ready to explode.

Taishi cut in and gave her a knowing look. "Obey the oracle. Go find a tree somewhere and squeeze some lemons."

Koranajah's jaw dropped, but Taishi's gaze was intent. The battle-abbess rose stiffly and retreated back the way she had come.

When they were alone again, Taishi spoke. "Is that why you excommunicated your caretaker?"

Pei nodded. "The Tiandi have reached a crossroads. I cannot allow anyone else to deviate off the only path we have left."

Taishi looked around. "So, this is all a test?"

"Sister Surratoo failed. I need everyone to obey my every word."

"Why can't you just order the Black Orchids to take you to the Caobiu then?" asked Taishi. "More importantly, why would you want to do that?"

"Because it is the Black Orchids' sacred duty to protect the oracle. A direct order creates conflicting temple doctrines." She paused as she moved a piece on the Siege board. "You would be surprised how many of our sacred texts contradict one another. A third of them, at least. It's aggravating."

"It wouldn't be a religion if anything made sense," muttered Taishi, moving one of her black pieces in response. "Explain to me, Pei, why you feel you must go to the Caobiu, and how doing so will conflict with the nuns' sacred duty to protect you."

"During my fuzzy moments, I say things I don't remember. Once, my stupid oracle mouth informed the sisters that if I go to the Caobiu, I will die before the first cycle returns. The Black Orchid has pledged their lives to my safety, and going over to Sunri is considered a death sentence. Their honor and duty demand they keep me safe at all costs." The girl shrugged and made a move on the Siege board, chaining three attacks and cutting behind Taishi's defensive line. "That's a breach, you lose. Want to play another game?"

Taishi gaped. "That makes no sense. No wait, that makes perfect sense." She glanced up. Fear and worry gripped her heart. "You want to hand yourself over to Sunri, don't you?"

The oracle remained stoic. "I need to. It's the only way everyone wins. Everyone but me, which I don't think is fair."

A tremor passed through Taishi as she watched the girl. Such a heavy weight rested on those small shoulders. Taishi had watched Pei grow from the little precocious brat she had first met to a much bigger brat, but she had always been *Taishi's* bratty little girl. For the first time, Taishi sensed the Oracle of the Tiandi's jing. It felt immense, ancient, like the King at high noon searing her on a hot day. It also felt weary, as if wanting to close her eyes and sleep. What was going on with the girl?

"So," said Taishi slowly, "you need to hand yourself to Sunri to save the Zhuun. But in doing so, you'll force the Black Orchid nuns to stop you, because you accidentally blabbed that you're going to die if you fall into Caobiu hands. However, in upholding their honor, they will all get massacred. Is that correct?"

The immensely powerful and ancient, weary girl bobbed her head. "The ladies don't stand a chance. That's why I summoned you."

"You summoned me?" scoffed Taishi, taking one of Pei's Siege pieces. The tide was turning. The girl was a skillful player.

"I'm here. You came to me. That's called a summons." Pei scoffed with greater vigor. "So now that you're here—fix it."

"I'm still not clear on what I'm supposed to fix, Oracle," said Taishi, taking another piece. The girl was losing both focus and pieces at a quicker clip.

"Deliver me to the Caobiu without getting the Black Orchid battlenuns killed." Pei clasped her hands together, once again the image of a concerned and innocent little girl.

Taishi snorted. "You have mistaken me for a student if you think that drivel works on me. I don't think you should go either. I won't stop you though."

"Good, then I won't excommunicate you." Pei made a mistake pushing one of her flank pieces up.

"I won't help you either." Taishi shook her head. "I refuse to lead you toward death."

"I can still excommunicate you."

"You won't because you love me, and I am fond of you. I have no interest in sacrificing your life for any reason." Taishi knelt next to the girl. "You are more than just an oracle, Pei. You are a fiery little street urchin who will live a full life. You will experience love and heartbreak, great joys and deep sadness, all the things that make you who you are. You deserve that, no matter what burden the Tiandi places upon your small shoulders."

The Oracle of the Tiandi looked grumpy and crossed her arms. "I knew you were going to say that," she muttered, and then spoke more authoritatively, which was surprisingly effective considering her diminutive person and high-pitched voice. "I tried to ask nicely, Ling Taishi. Now you're going to get a mean oracle." She straightened, to negligible effect. "I, Oracle of the Tiandi, Wisdom of the Zhuun, the Great Child of Light, order you to kidnap me and bring me to the Caobiu. Refuse at the risk of excommunication."

Taishi shrugged. "Getting excommunicated won't be the worst part of my day."

"Auntie, you must, for the good of all Zhuun." Pei picked up a Siege piece and shook it at Taishi for several seconds before placing it back on the board.

Taishi promptly took it. "There is no such thing as a greater good if it involves sacrificing a child. The sisters would be right to disobey your outrageous request."

A long silence passed between them. The Oracle of the Tiandi glowered at her while Taishi relaxed. It was laughable if this little runt thought she could intimidate Taishi with her stare. Taishi had made grown men soil their pants with passing glances.

Pei finally spoke. "Your move."

"I didn't know we were still playing." Taishi made her move. By now the outcome of the game was evident. It was just a cleanup job. The oracle made Taishi grind down her defenses with each laborious move, forcing the game to continue for another hour. It was a waste of time, but Taishi enjoyed spending it with her.

Eventually, all games must end.

Taishi was about to breach Pei's inner sanctum with her pieces when the oracle spoke. "I'm disappointed in you, Taishi. I thought it wouldn't come to this."

"Beating you in a game of Siege?"

"No, I had predicted that there was an even chance that you would agree to kidnap me and save the Black Orchid nuns' lives."

"Free will is a bitch, isn't it?"

A loud crack reverberated through the Barberry. Taishi bolted to her feet and hurried to the edge of the balcony. Specks and debris drizzled toward the cave floor, flurries of tiny dust storms. Another impact followed a moment later, this time in the distance. Alarms began to ring throughout the ward.

The oracle remained seated. "Now it's too late. The Caobiu broke through. They will have me by tomorrow, and there is nothing anyone can do about it."

Taishi looked at the sack she had brought with her. There was still something *she* could do about it. An escape plan had already hatched in her mind. It wouldn't be easy, but with the other three masters here, it was possible to smuggle Pei out of the buried ward during the chaos. She took three steps back into the room to retrieve it.

"I know what you're thinking, Taishi. Don't even consider it," chirped the oracle. "If you whisk me away to safety, Jian will be dead by the end of this cycle."

Taishi froze in her tracks. "You're lying."

"Oracles don't lie. We predict the most likely outcome."

That was one of the only things the oracle could say that would have stopped Taishi from stuffing the girl into that sack. She was stricken with a rare indecisive moment. Her heart felt like it skipped a few beats, or maybe it was a heart attack. The weight of consequences pressed down upon her. Sometimes, it felt as if she had to make the same terrible choice over and over again. There were no acceptable outcomes here, which meant . . .

Another sharp crack reverberated through the air, this time followed by a plume of smoke rising from just outside the entrance. The cave began to fill with smoke.

A small hand touched her arm. "It's going to be all right, Taishi. I promise."

Taishi turned to face the little girl, her eyes brimming. "I can't just leave you, child."

"You must. It's for the best." The Oracle of the Tiandi was stoic. Brave, even. It felt wrong that it was the wise young child comforting the distraught old lady. "Take your friends and go. Don't try to convince the Black Orchids. It won't do any good. Their destiny is now sealed among the heavens. They will die with honor."

Taishi fell to one knee so she was looking into Pei's eyes. "What happened to free will changing fate?"

"Once the choice has been made, there are only consequences left." The oracle offered a small smile, and then ran into her outstretched arms. "You made the wrong choice, Ling Taishi, but it's all right. You made your decision out of love. I can appreciate that."

Taishi became overwhelmed. She felt it within the deepest depth of her soul. "I'm sorry, little one" was all she managed to say. "I failed you."

Pei smiled. "You did, but the only way to have prevented this was for you to die, so I forgive you."

That broke something inside Taishi. It wasn't fair. Little girls deserved to grow up. She wept, her body wracked with sobs as she squeezed the girl close. They were interrupted by an urgent knock on the door. Koranajah entered with several of her battlenuns. All were armored and armed, with their hoods covering their faces save for their eyes and those loud orchid-petal shoulder pieces. Trailing behind them were Taishi's elderly friends, also fully equipped and ready for battle. All three of the masters' faces looked grim; it must be bad out there.

"Oracle," said the battleabbess, dropping to one knee. "The ward has been breached. This is our last chance to get you to safety."

Pei broke away from Taishi. "I'm sorry I was so mean to you, Koranajah. It was necessary."

The nun's gaze wavered. She glanced at Taishi in confusion and then suspicion. "Our duty is to you and the Tiandi, oracle. Please, this way."

The girl didn't move. "Nothing has changed. I'm staying here."

Koranajah set her jaw. "I see. This pains us greatly. My convent has communed. We have each our honor as women and warriors to gladly accept the consequences to our eternal souls if it means saving the Oracle of the Tiandi's life. Take her!"

Something finally caught the oracle by surprise. Pei blinked. "I did not believe for a second you were going to make this choice." She threw up her arms. "I hate all your free wills!"

The nuns moved on her anyway.

Pei reached for Taishi. "You know what's at stake. The greater good!"

Taishi stood mute; her skin felt as if it were being pricked by a thousand needles. If she said nothing, the Black Orchids would escape with Pei to a friendly ward, and that would be the end of it. This girl and these nuns would live, prophecy and honor be damned. But at the cost of the end of their people as well as Jian, if the oracle's predictions were true. Not only that, saving Pei's life was against the oracle's wishes.

For the greater good.

"Stop," Taishi muttered, her voice hoarse. The consequences of what she was about to say rattled her, but she focused on Pei's decision. She had made the painful choice, a decision that every one of her elders refused to accept. Either you believed in her divine wisdom, or you didn't. Taishi dug deep and found new strength from within, no matter how much it hurt.

"Stop! The Oracle of the Tiandi has spoken!"

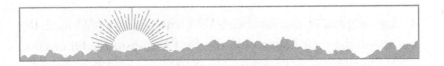

CHAPTER TWENTY-NINE

REUNITED

Sali was upbeat. Today, the Exiles Rebellion was going to add a new clan to their alliance. The past several days of negotiations had been fruitful, if also tedious, but they were nearing the end, and she was optimistic about their conclusion.

Her conversations with the other five rim clans in the alliance consisted of: "Do you feel oppressed by Katuia? Do you detest the spirit shamans of Chaqra? Good, let's kill them." And that was all that needed to be said. Then the chief of each rim clan invited her to their hearth and everyone got drunk. Theirs were simple arrangements based on trust and honor.

That wasn't how First Yazgur Huong operated, however. The man was shockingly meticulous and detail-oriented. He wanted to discuss every aspect of their arrangement, from shared supply lines to trade deals to manpower contributions to the command hierarchy during the war with Katuia. Not only that, but he insisted on discussing the future *if* they won. Like who would have a seat at the council, the land rights for each clan, and who would have authority in the new world.

Sali didn't think that far ahead. Why would anyone? Winning this war should be their priority, but the First Yazgur insisted they cover every contingency in their agreement, so that's what they spent the past several days doing. The two basically formed an entire government. Mali and the rest of the council would be upset with her for not discussing it with them first, but recruiting the Sunjawa clan to their cause was worth a few upset houseplants. She would beg for forgiveness later.

Sali had initially been annoyed at the glacial pace of their discussions. She had other, more important things to do: alliances to forge, battles to win. She shouldn't be stuck at a table drinking tea all day. Everything felt trivial. Who cares about access rights to the main travel gyres during the second cycle? What did it matter that the Hrant River, flowing from the southeast, was overfished by the Sheetan clan during the first cycle of every year? And why was it important that the Fushand clan *not* be allowed to export their specialized breeds of butcher cats to the Crazh region of the north? They were exceptional hunters, and the endangered cactus tree-rats were important to the local ecosystem there.

Sali couldn't make sense of many of these issues, nor did she care about a silly rodent. These discussions were more suited to the likes of a candle sniffer like Supplychief Shobansa, not a warrior. Sali was no diplomat. After the first few days, however, she began to appreciate Huong's diligence. He led the influential Sunjawa clan *because* he was so thorough. The man was sharp and clever. He saw the gray in the black-and-white matters and constantly sought every advantage for his clan. He was a pain in her ass, but their negotiations gave Sali more confidence that Sunjawa would make a powerful ally in their fight against Katuia.

This morning, however, it was finally time to come to an agreement and get drunk. The First Yazgur had sent a messenger with some last-minute questions and one final demand: full control of all trade lanes in the northern gyres, effectively making Sunjawa the trade capital of the north Grass Sea. Sali had no issues with that. None of it mattered if they lost, anyway.

She was about to head for the outpost when she ran into Marhi. "Mentor," said the viperstrike. "It's been three days."

"Three days since what? Never mind, walk with me. I need to pretty myself up for today's negotiations."

Marhi didn't move. "It's about the prisoner, the land-chained. She's been locked in that shed guarded by four spears at all hours. You ordered us to lock the door and leave the assassin there until you had time to deal with her."

"And?"

"It's been three days. She might be dead by now."

Sali blinked. "You're . . . not feeding her?"

Marhi shook her head.

"Did you at least give her drink?"

She shook her head again. "You said to lock the door and leave—"

"Since when did you start following orders?" Sali made a sharp turn and hurried toward the shed.

Marhi looked flustered as she followed. Qisami was the neophyte's responsibility. Within a brief span of time, the shadowkill had managed to escape her jail cell, damage an engine and three walkways, and injure a dozen people, including several tinkers. The fact that she had knocked Daewon unconscious had simultaneously infuriated and made her envious. She had wanted to rap that tin-brained brother-in-law's skull many, many times, and that blasted creature had beat her to it.

"Did she break anything or hurt anyone else since that night?" asked Sali.

"No, mentor. Either Wani or I have personally stood watch the entire time." That likely meant Marhi had stood there for three days straight with Wani only spelling her long enough to get some sleep.

"Did you hear anything? Any signs of life?"

"She snored constantly. Loud for such a tiny thing, mentor. She would have tasted my blade if she tried to escape."

"You wouldn't be standing here if she did. The shadowkill is far more dangerous than you realize." Sali signaled. "Open the door. Let's see if you're guarding a corpse."

The Zhuun did indeed look dead when Sali walked into the storage shed. She looked peaceful, laid out on her back with her hands over her chest as if in her final resting position. Marhi, looking dismayed, bent down to check her pulse.

Just as she was about to touch the shadowkill's neck, Qisami's eyes popped open. She grabbed Marhi's wrist, twisted it at an awkward angle, and wrapped her hands around the neophyte's neck and throat. One sharp twist would snap her neck.

"Oh, bull's balls," squeaked Marhi, squirming ineffectively.

"Release her," said Sali.

Qisami looked at her and beamed. "There you are. I'm famished. Did you bring anything to eat?"

"Have you been asleep the entire time?"

"More or less." The shadowkill jiggled Marhi's head in her hands. "It's a good way to conserve energy when someone forgets to feed you."

"I didn't—" Marhi shot back.

Sali wasn't surprised. Hibernation was a war arts technique common among many families. "I'll have some food delivered. Release my neophyte." Sali pulled out a flask from her belt and tossed it to Qisami, who plucked it out of the air and threw her head back dramatically to down it in one gulp.

The body craved hydration, even when asleep. After a minute, Qisami put the flask down and burped as a contented sigh escaped her. Her gaze met Sali's, and her unhinged smile returned. "I knew you would come see me eventually. Couldn't stay away, could you?"

"Tell me why I shouldn't tie a lead weight to your feet and toss you into the nearest pit," said Sali.

"Hang on now," said Qisami. "Bloodthirsty is usually my thing. I could have kept my head down when your cute assistant raided my colony, but I wanted to see you."

"You escaped from your holding cell."

"I had to pee." She shrugged. "I was hungry, too. You are terrible at keeping prisoners alive. You must be awful with pets."

"You attacked several of my people, including my brother-in-law."

"No one died." Qisami huffed. The diminutive Zhuun rose to her feet, reaching only as high as Sali's chest. "If I had wanted to kill anyone, you'd be throwing funeral parties for the next week. You know that. Which limp lily was your brother-in-law, the wristwagging skinny one with the panicked eyes?"

That was certainly an accurate description of Daewon, and it was true that her people were at the mercy of this shadowkill. Sali remembered just how skilled and deadly she could be. "Enough of this chatter. You have my attention now. Why are you here, assassin?"

"Like I said, I wanted to see you." Qisami added, "I also didn't want your people to slaughter the entire colony. I've grown attached to some of the babies. We can make a deal. A good one that will help both sides. You and the Happy Glow can come to a beneficial agreement for both our people."

Everyone was trying to make deals these days. "My neophyte tells me it was a penal colony. What happened? Did you get caught running one of your murders?"

"I'm retired." Qisami batted her eyes at Sali. "I figured, now that I quit the killing business, I should visit my favorite Kati."

"Do not lie to me. What are you really doing here?"

"Ah, why hold grudges? It's bad for your complexion. Look, I suddenly have all this free time." Qisami paused and added, "I also have nowhere else to go."

"Well, you can't stay here. You're an outsider."

"Why not?" Qisami shot back. "It took your raiders weeks to hit my colony. What if, instead of both sides trying to kill each other—" She furrowed her brow. "I can't believe I'm saying this, but instead of both sides killing each other, let's trade. Doesn't that sound fun? We can be partners."

"Your penal colony is not an equal to the Nezra clan," Sali spat. "Why do we need to talk about anything if we can just raid you again? From what I heard, your defenses were nonexistent when my raiders happened upon your people."

"My people can bring you ore. You'll save time. The mine is rich enough that it can keep your cities powered for a lifetime."

"And how would you make these deals and relay this information to your people?"

Qisami rolled up her left sleeve and raised her arm. "I can blood-scrawl with my guy back there. We can keep the lines of communication open at all times. It takes a bit longer over vast distances, but he'll get my messages. Maybe we can even meet your people halfway at the Grass Tundra's edge, so you don't have to plod through all that snow and slush. Just give us the supplies we need to defend ourselves, and you'll have a dependable trade partner in the Happy Glow."

It was a tempting offer, one they could sorely use right now, but allying with a Zhuun settlement—a prison colony at that—was something the rest of the alliance would not tolerate. "That is impossible. The land-chained enslaved Nezra. Your kind cannot be trusted."

"Hey, that's not fair. The Zhuun are as trustworthy as anyone else." Qisami huffed and then reconsidered. "Except for the Gyian. Those people are rotten inside and out."

The viperstrike crossed her arms. "Last time I took your word, you betrayed me when we had just defeated Ling Taishi. Once trust is shattered, it is not easily mended."

"I'm half Gyian. I blame it on my ba." Qisami offered a weak grin. "But while I stabbed you in the back then, it was for your own good. I was trying to make both of us rich!"

"How do I know you won't do it again?"

"Because this time," said the assassin, opening her arms as if trying to show that she was letting down her guard, "I want to help you."

"You are the enemy, Maza Qisami. You've been here a few days and have already injured half a dozen people. I cannot risk my people around such wild animals. I'm leaning toward putting you down so you do not hurt anyone else."

"I gave you your weapon back the last time we met. You would have lost it forever if it weren't for me," Qisami said. "You owe me, and your person over there owes me too. I saved her life as well."

That last part was true. The shadowkill had returned Sali's tongue back to her when their paths first crossed in Jiayi. It was a greater debt than Sali cared to admit. There was no personal relic she treasured more in life than her tongue, which meant she also owed a heartdebt to this Zhuun assassin.

Sali raised her voice. "Marhi!"

Her neophyte appeared next to her. "Yes, mentor."

"Do you owe this little stink-rat a heartdebt? Did she save your life?"

"More like spared it, mentor," Marhi admitted. "She refrained from the killing blow."

That was even worse. Mercy was the greatest honor a warrior could bestow on an enemy. "You'll vouch for her?"

"I'd rather not," Marhi said. "But I would not be standing here if this Zhuun hadn't shown mercy, much to my shame. She also did not cause any problems on the journey here."

Sali considered. She wavered over allowing this Zhuun to join them. Sali knew this rebellion she was waging would likely send them all to a grave beneath the Grass Sea. A skilled shadowkill could certainly sway the outcome of the war. Qisami would be a valuable asset.

But then how would the other rim clans and prospective allies view it, to see a land-chained fight among them? They would assume Sali was a Zhuun puppet. Most importantly, Sali had a responsibility to her crew, her clan, and her people. It would be irresponsible to invite a rabid hyena into their camp.

"Hoisannisi Jayngnaga Marhi of the Viperstrike sect," Sali intoned a tiny bit more formally, "under the watchful eyes of the Xoangiagu, the spirit guardians of Hrusha, will you place your honor and act as witness upon the good name of . . ."

"Maza Qisami," the shadowkill chirped helpfully.

Sali had learned from Ritualist Suriptika back on Hrusha that this was the most severe oath any Happan could utter. Sali used it ruthlessly on Marhi to keep the headstrong young woman focused.

Marhi considered, staring at the assassin, and for a moment looked as if she would refuse. Then she muttered with her lips upturned, obviously not confident in this matter, "Fine. Under the gaze of the six

Xoangiagu—the beautiful Woman, the pure Child, the wise Scholar, the giant Bull, the sharp Owl, and the staunch Warrior—my good name for her good name."

Sali nodded and turned to the shadowkill. "Because of the debt Marhi and I have to you, Maza Qisami," said Sali, "we will not kill you. You are free to go. You will have seven days' rations, two sets of clothing, and a horse."

"I'm not going to last a day out there in the jungle!"

Sali turned to leave. "That is not my concern."

"Come on, Sali honey. I can help you. You know I can."

"Don't call me that, and we don't need your help. You staying as far away from my business as possible is what's best for both of us, Maza Qisami. Goodbye."

"How about weapons?" Qisami called. "I need to protect myself or hunt or something."

"Marhi will see to your needs."

Qisami rattled off a list that would have armed an entire squad. "A short sword, two long daggers, eight throwing knives, and caltrops, if you have them."

Sali snorted. She drew her oldest and rustiest dagger hanging at her hip and tossed it at Qisami's feet. "Because once you returned my weapon to me, I shall return yours to you."

"One knife?" Qisami's voice went up an octave. "I need at least five."

"You only have two hands."

"Four, then. Come on." The little shadowkill put her hands on her hips. "What am I supposed to do after I throw my one stupid blade?"

"Walk over and pick it up."

Sali left the shadowkill. Whatever awaited her was not Sali's concern. Right now, she had an alliance to forge.

CHAPTER THIRTY

HONOR AND RIGHTEOUSNESS

"Stop!" Taishi's voice rang a third time, the last the loudest of all. It finally had its effect, freezing the nuns from advancing toward the startled young Oracle of the Tiandi. All eyes focused on Taishi. "Stop," she repeated. This time her voice was more measured.

"What is the meaning of this, dowager nun?" said Koranajah.

"Release her." Taishi blinked, feeling suddenly weary. "Have faith in the wisdom of the Tiandi religion. Just let her go."

The battleabbess's focus narrowed. Taishi recognized the glint in her eyes. The woman was ready to kill. When she spoke, her tone was challenging. "I have dedicated my life to the Tiandi, dowager, but I will gladly pay with my soul to save the lives of the oracle and my sisters." She directed the other nuns. "Let's go."

Taishi's sword hissed from its scabbard, its ringing echoing throughout the room. That stilled everyone.

"You dare draw steel against a Black Orchid?" Koranajah said sharply.

"Um, what just happened?" called Sohn from the back of the room.

"Taishi, what madness is this?" Bhasani asked.

Taishi stood her ground and stepped between Pei and the six nuns. "You will respect the Oracle of the Tiandi's wisdom. I will not tolerate this sacrilege."

The battlenuns' reaping swords came off their backs, and Taishi faced a row of long deadly blades to her one opera sword. The black-garbed battlenuns huddled, their reaping swords, with their long shafts and curved blades, arrayed in formation, looking like a giant black panther with its claws extended standing against a lone old woman with a fake theater sword and her three equally old war arts master friends.

The odds hardly seemed fair.

"Step away, Ling Taishi," growled Battleabbess Koranajah. If her real name surprised the other battlenuns, they did not show it as they moved to flank her. Taishi's friends standing behind them had no choice but to follow, sweeping aside to confront the nuns.

"I don't like this!" Fausan yelled. "I hate killing clergy."

Taishi leveled her blade at the nuns. "You violate your holiest oaths with this action, sisters."

Koranajah and two of her nuns turned to face them. "You are on holy ground, masters. Stand down!"

"*You* stand down!" snarled Sohn.

The battleabbess aimed her blade at Bhasani, standing between the two men. "Drop your weapons!"

"Don't point your stick at my wife!" Fausan stuck his hands into his ammo sack and came out with a bullet between his fingers.

"Everyone, calm! There's no need for violence," Koranajah said, though Taishi could barely make out her voice over the shouts.

The shouting continued. A fight appeared inevitable, although no one wanted to make the first move. Several of the battlenuns began looking unsteady as Bhasani hit them with a heavy dose of compulsion. "Stand down and surrender."

"Stop this madness, Koranajah." Taishi turned toward the battlenun to her left. "Put your blades down unless you are prepared to die betraying your sacred vows!"

It was too late. The younger nun, maybe even an initiate, strayed within Taishi's range. The long, curved blade of the reaping sword had swung too close to her face. Intentionally or not, a response was necessary. Taishi snapped her opera sword, slapping the reaping sword off her angle.

Another of the nuns moved on Bhasani, which immediately elicited a response from Fausan, who sent two bullets into the woman's chest.

"Taishi, look out!" Sohn's voice cut above the din.

She was trying to move her useless ass across the melee field to safety when out of the corner of her eye she noticed a battlenun charging directly at her, the nun's reaping sword aimed between Taishi's shoulder blades. In no position to dodge or deflect, the best she could do was fall to the side to glance the blow. She steeled herself to manage the pain.

There was a thunderous crack, and the attacking battlenun's head tilted to one side. She collapsed. Blood poured from a bullet lodged in her temple, and she looked on with unblinking eyes.

The shouting stopped. Time froze as the room looked on in stunned silence. Taishi glanced at Fausan, standing on the other side of the room, one arm extended after shooting the bullet from his fingers. His mouth was agape, his eyes widened in shock. "I didn't have a choice . . ." he uttered before one of the battlenuns screamed a pained war cry. She was joined by several more.

"No, stop!" Taishi reached out, but it was too late. Her voice was swallowed by the terrible chorus of agonized cries.

As Taishi had predicted, the odds were hardly fair. As skilled as these Black Orchids were, they were no match for three masters. One battlenun charged Fausan, no doubt seeking revenge for her fallen sister. Her reaping sword was about to poke the whipfinger's generous midsection when she was obliterated by Sohn's giant shield. Taishi had witnessed the eternal bright light's shield ram through stone walls before. The poor Black Orchid never stood a chance.

Another sister tried to come to her rescue, but then Bhasani stepped in front of her. The look on the drowned fist's face was focused to a point on the battlenun's forehead. The woman's head snapped back. Then, with a scream, she ran onto the balcony and fell over the side. Her screams lingered in the air, growing fainter as she plummeted to the ground level far below. The three masters made quick work of the Black Orchids, killing or disabling them in short order until only Battle-abbess Koranajah remained.

Koranajah sought out the oracle during the fracas. One of the nuns had picked her up and was trying to move her out of the room. Taishi had attempted to intervene, but the battleabbess had swept her aside with ease, nearly toppling her off her feet. Instead, she fell backward onto the couch.

The battleabbess shoved the oracle into the corner and turned to face them. "Stay back. I will not allow death to choose her as a bride tonight."

Taishi held out her hand. "There's a lot more at stake than you realize. I've known you for forty years. Let's talk this through. This has been a terrible mistake."

She shook her head. "There are things I can live with and things I cannot. Saving this child's life is not up for debate. My sisters are dead, Taishi. You'll never leave this convent alive. The . . ." Koranajah staggered forward, slumping over and reaching for her back. She took two steps and then fell to one knee. Embedded deep in her spine was a dagger, the blade halfway into her flesh. Blood dribbled down her leg to the floor. Standing behind her body was Pei, her hands shaking.

Taishi rushed forward. "Why, child?"

The girl blinked, and the motion sent tears streaming down her cheeks. "This was the only acceptable way at this point." She fell to her knees. "I'm sorry, Mother Koranajah. I really am, but there was no other way. This is the only path forward."

The battleabbess looked stricken as her breathing became labored. Blood trickled from the corner of her lips. "Forgive me . . . holy one, for doubting your wisdom." Only the truly devout would apologize to her killer.

Taishi knelt beside her and clutched her hand. She fought back tears. "The sin is mine, old friend. I didn't mean for this to happen."

"I know. My younger battlenuns were quick to temper and react. It was a killing attack. I am to blame for their lack of prudence." She wasn't, but the battleabbess was being kind to the very end. Koranajah's breathing became labored and unsteady. "Promise me that you'll look after Pei and see her safe."

Taishi closed her eyes as tears collected along her wrinkles, tiny rivers of sorrow. "I cannot, but I swear upon my ancestors and my lineage that I will do what I believe is right."

Battleabbess Koranajah coughed. Her lips broke into a bloodied smile. "You were never the reassuring type, Taishi. I always admired that about you." Her head lolled and then she was gone.

The room went quiet. Every nun, every war artist, and the only child stood watching as the life left the Battleabbess of the Black Orchid's eyes. Pei stood over her, eyes blinking, hands bloodied. She sniffled, and then the tears of an inconsolable child were set loose. Pei sobbed, throwing herself on Koranajah's body.

Taishi looked on in disbelief. The remaining nuns around them looked equally stunned. What was there to say about the Oracle of the Tiandi killing one of their own?

Taishi snapped out of it first. She moved forward slowly toward the crying little girl and prodded her gently. "Pei?"

Pei rounded on her, hissing and jabbing a little-girl finger into Taishi's chest. "This was the only path we had left. Jian should have killed you."

"What is she talking about?" asked Fausan.

"Not your business, God of Gamblers," Taishi snapped, not taking her eyes off the girl.

"Your time here at the convent is ended," Pei urged. "You wait a moment longer and you will not leave the convent alive. If you do not head straight for the Undertunnel, we will all enjoy Caobiu hospitality together."

Taishi's mind was gripped with indecision. She blinked and embraced the girl. "I'm sorry. I don't know what to do. I don't know how to save you." A choked sob escaped her lips.

"Some people aren't meant to be saved." Pei hugged her back.

"Nothing else needs to be said. Wish me good fortune. Now go, Ling Taishi."

Taishi wiped away tears as she turned and left the room, stepping over the bodies of fallen nuns. The masters followed as they left the massacre in the sanctum. Everyone was stone-faced, except for Fausan, who looked positively distraught.

Bhasani looped her arm around his elbow. "Keep it together, love."

"She was charging Taishi," he mumbled.

They slowed to a brisk walk once they moved to the higher levels, passing by Black Orchid nuns walking in pairs and small groups. A few splashed them with curious gazes when they noticed the bloodstains on their robes, but no one stopped them. The sparring at the convent between these warrior women could sometimes be brutal.

"Where are the sky lotus monks?" asked Fausan.

"We're not escaping a ward under invasion by a palanquin carried by clergy," snapped Bhasani. "We'll look like assholes."

"Most everyone who rides in palanquins *are* assholes."

"That's true," said Sohn.

Taishi agreed. Only obnoxious lords traveled in palanquins. "We need mounts."

"There are no horses here. There are no stables on convent grounds."

She stopped. Actually, there were horses here, sort of. "Come, follow me."

Ten minutes later, the four masters emerged from one of the rooms in the Worthy Guest Hallway with two ratty but well-groomed ponies led on leashes with yellow bows tied to the ends of their manes. Both animals were a dirty blue, although their gray undercoats were starting to show.

"We're going to ride out of the Thorned Garden on ponies," Bhasani mused. "That's our escape plan."

"Through the front door like we're off for a stroll," replied Taishi.

Two armed battlenuns, faces covered, one with hair flowing down her back and the other bald, appeared before them, blocking their progress toward the door. "A thousand pardons, dowager," the nun on the left said, "but it is not safe outside. The Caobiu have broken through the barricades and are now inside the ward."

The other nun standing guard stared at the two blue ponies, who were looking completely unperturbed munching carrots with loud, squelching sounds. "Isn't that the Oracle of the Tiandi's holy creatures?"

"She asked us to walk them," said Taishi.

"There's fighting and rioting in the streets, dowager." The two battlenuns exchanged glances. "Perhaps it's best we speak with the battle-abbess."

Bhasani stepped forward. "We'll make it quick."

The drowned fist master's heavy compulsion battered their minds quickly into compliance, and they stepped aside. Taishi pulled at the leash of her little steed as they continued past. Fausan and Sohn had just opened the large, curved exterior doors when a bell tolled in a nearby tower. Every ring caused other bells to ring until the entire convent was alive with their song. Taishi didn't know what it meant, but the two nuns did.

"That is the crisis alert," said the bald one. "Close the doors. The convent is going on lockdown."

Sohn, holding the other leash, looked over at Taishi, and then hurried out the door, yanking his pony even harder. Taishi was only a step behind.

"Stop!" yelled the long-haired one. She took a step and fell, clutching her knee.

"Keep moving," said Fausan, one arm extended. He turned to the bald one and flicked a finger.

She was ready for it, drawing her reaping sword just in time to block the shot with its shaft. Fausan fired twice more. The battlenun dodged the first bullet and sliced the second in half with the sharp edge of her reaping sword.

"This one has talent," said Bhasani. "Perhaps I should take . . ."

"No, no, my dear. I have this." Fausan shot three bullets at the nun with one hand and then threw his right arm out to the side, curving the last bullet through the air in a wide arc. The Black Orchid managed to defend against those first three bullets but was too late to catch the fourth as it grazed her head, sending her face-first toward the ground.

"She'll have a headache but will be fine." He sounded apologetic. "Come on, let's get out of here before we have to kill more clergy."

CHAPTER THIRTY-ONE

GOOD TALKS

It took Jian and his friends the rest of the day to smuggle Neeshan's mother and gaming group from the Caobiu-occupied territory to the friendly wards. The old ladies tried to bring all of their belongings with them. One wanted to bring her sewing loom, another her dishes. Neehong went as far as to demand that Hachi carry her game table. The ladies finally agreed to leave the furniture and unnecessary luxuries behind, but they drew the line at kitchen tools. One of the ladies had brought a massive wok that was almost as tall as she. Hachi muttered a sheepish apology when he handed it to Kaiyu, who ended up wearing it like a turtle shell the entire way back.

The trip wasn't dangerous, just long and exhausting. The group took no risks leading Neeshan and the old ladies. That meant they had to take a long roundabout heading through the Undertunnel as well as several other buried wards. Two of the women were nearly blind at night so their progress had slowed to a crawl once they reached deep underground.

It was well into evening by the time they made it to the Holy Glow

Plaza at the base of Peony Peak. Hachi had hired several rickshaws to ferry the ladies the rest of the way to their destinations. Jian was impressed. He had thought of everything. Jian and Kaiyu collapsed under a tree, both huffing and drenched in sweat. Being a pack mule was arduous work. Sonaya and Zofi came by after dropping off their satchels and bags of clothing. Zofi had the added task of having to carry an urn filled with cooking spices, or possibly one of their husbands' ashes, she couldn't tell. Jian didn't care. He hadn't eaten since breakfast, but he was too tired to feel hungry. The four friends huddled together with their legs splayed and watched as Hachi and Neeshan embraced.

Hachi laced fingers with Neeshan and pulled her close. "I have to report in, but I'll check up on you as soon as I can, Nissy."

"Stay safe, my love. I don't know what I would do without you."

It was all terribly awkward. Jian caught himself—Kaiyu as well—shifting uncomfortably at their naked love shining for everyone to see. Zofi cupped her cheeks with both hands, eyes wet. She let out a long, breathy sigh.

Sonaya had placed one hand over her heart and one over her mouth, clutching herself hard as if trying to squeeze a wet rag dry. Her eyes glistened as she watched the lovers' embrace. She never hugged *him* like that. Jian needed to prove that he could be romantic as well. He reached for Sonaya's hand.

The tips of his fingers had just brushed the back of her hand when she noticed him and recoiled. Literally, recoiled. "What are you doing?" she asked.

"I . . ." Jian's face turned red. It couldn't hurt him more if she had slapped him as hard as she could. "Never mind."

Hachi and Neeshan were still whispering romantic nothings to each other when Neehong came to them. "You did good, my young hero. Come by for dinner tonight. We'll have a hot pot in your honor." She turned and walked away before he could respond.

"She called you a hero, not a street performer or thug," said Neeshan after her mother was out of earshot. "That means she's warming up to you. She is in your debt, my love. I'm sure now she will overlook the fact that you are a war artist. You should come tonight. It would mean a great deal to her and to me."

Hachi looked torn. "I can't, Nissy. I have responsibilities to Jian and the war effort."

Kaiyu, staring at the ground, suddenly looked up. "Go to the hot pot, Hachi."

Sonaya was studying the young Houtou war artist. She moved next to Neeshan and linked arms with her. "Come with me for a moment, I want to speak with your mother to make sure she has everything she needs." A moment later, the two women were gone.

Hachi waited until Neeshan was out of earshot. He lowered his voice. "Neehong's cooking tastes like snorting ghost peppers. I'd rather eat army rations."

"Go to the dinner." Kaiyu's voice cracked this time.

"How does someone ruin hot pot anyway? It's just boiling things in water," Jian mused. Then he noticed the somber look on Kaiyu's face and realized that this conversation had nothing to do with food. "Oh, you should go, though."

Zofi added, "You don't know when you'll get the chance to see her again."

Hachi craned his head and looked in the direction Neeshan had gone. His heart certainly wasn't with them anymore. He shook his head. "Jian's back on duty tomorrow. I have to shadow him."

Jian stepped forward. "Don't worry about me, brother. I'll be fine without you for a day. I already checked with the captain. Tomorrow's assignment is a patrol through a friendly ward we recently reclaimed. The Shulan Court just wants the residents there to know that they have our support. You know, greet the locals and pretend to pray. Lots of holding babies and looking brave for the cause. It'll be nothing. Bet we won't even see any of those Caobiu candles."

Hachi looked uncertain. "I swore an oath to Taishi. I promised I wouldn't let you step onto a field without me shadowing you—"

Jian put his hands on his friend's shoulders and turned him in the direction Neeshan had gone. "Take the night off. Your box girl needs you more than I do."

Hachi put on a face as if he were about to argue over a restaurant bill, but his legs were already moving. "You know she's studying to pass her Goramh Scholarly Administrative Wisdom Exam at Sunsheng University. She's going to run a commandery one day."

Zofi appeared next to Jian, grinning. "He's so proud of her."

"He really is," Jian agreed.

She bobbed her head. "You have no idea what your assignment is tomorrow, do you?"

"Not a clue. I don't even know what day tomorrow is."

"That's irresponsible, Jian." Zofi opened her mouth wide and yelled, "Hach—"

Jian was on her, wrapping a hand over her mouth. "Let him have this night. Hachi's been close to cracking for days. He needs this."

Her voice came out muffled. He released her. She exhaled. "I don't like it. You're too important to risk." She sighed. "But he's my friend, too. Just be careful. Have the captain put two shadows on you tomorrow."

Sonaya appeared. "I'll do it."

"What?" This was unexpected.

"I'll shadow Jian tomorrow," Sonaya repeated.

"Thanks," he said.

"I'm doing it for Hachi."

And just like that, the warmth of the moment was snuffed out.

They continued up Peony Peak until they reached the gates of the Temple of the Tiandi. The once-panicked crowds had dwindled to a makeshift refugee encampment filled with mostly elderly and children. The people knew that they would be the first the temple admitted inside whenever the fighting came too close.

The Vauzan Temple of the Tiandi was no less busy, even at this hour. Several hundred Shulan displayguards were resting in formation in the main courtyard. Some were polishing their blades, others praying or conversing with their neighbors. All looked ready to move out at a moment's notice.

The makeshift medical tent was lively with the screams of the injured and dying. A twelve-ringed Hansoo barked orders at the scores of monks manning the walls.

Jian noticed a large, colorful war wagon on the far end of the courtyard near the cherry blossom trees. A high lord was present, which was odd. Jian and his friends continued to pass through the courtyard. They were halfway across when the doors to the war wagon opened.

Oban stepped out and stared Jian's way. "There you are. We've been looking all over for you. Where have you been, champion?"

"None of your business," muttered Zofi. She disliked anyone from court. Nevertheless, she bowed just as deep as anyone else when the high lord addressed them.

"What's wrong, Highlord Oban?" Jian asked.

"We have a chance to deal the Caobiu a great blow," said Oban. "My whisperlord received news that Highlord Akai Hujo is crossing the Death Sleet on his way to assume command of her southern flank. He'll be vulnerable while traveling. This could be the opening we've been waiting for. Killing one of Sunri's most trusted generals will strike a terrible blow to the Caobiu. I want you to lead the attack, Champion of the Five Under Heaven."

Jian didn't know what to say. This sounded like an assassination, and he didn't know how he felt about that. "Have you spoken with my auntie about this plan?"

"She's nowhere in sight, champion, and our time grows short. We must strike before it's too late. I will deploy my most elite displayguards to ensure our victory." Before Jian could utter another word, Oban turned away and pointed at a group of armored soldiers standing in formation. "Come, I will introduce you to Captain Huakt."

"This is not what I signed up for," muttered Sonaya once the high lord was out of earshot.

"Definitely not a patrol," agreed Zofi. "I'm going to chase after Hachi. I'll be right back."

Jian grabbed her sleeve before she could get away. "He probably just sat down to dinner. Leave him alone. We should be fine. We're just going to go to the Death Sleet, where no one survives, to assassinate a Caobiu general. That doesn't sound difficult."

"Every lord in the Caobiu court is a war artist," warned Zofi. "You don't know who you're dealing with."

"I have Sonaya and Kaiyu." Jian gulped. "I will be fine. I think."

CHAPTER THIRTY-TWO

THE ALLIANCE

Sali spent the rest of the morning preparing for her meeting with the yazgurs. It annoyed her to admit this, but most of that time was spent doing her hair and selecting a wardrobe. She had let her image go over the past few years. Between her desperation to save her people and the soul rot killing her, looking the part of a war artist and chief hadn't been a priority. Things were different now that she was speaking with rim chiefs and forging alliances with warlords. Appearances were important. No clan leader wanted to share their hearth with a disheveled, smelly vagrant.

Sali returned to her quarters to get her hair braided. There was only one person on this pod whom she trusted to touch her wild mane of hair. Daewon had exquisitely graceful fingers that were perfect for braiding. He was phenomenal at it too, probably due to his extensive tinker training.

"Do you think the First Yazgur will sign today?" he asked, teasing her long strands of hair.

"I hope so, assuming he doesn't dream up another demand," she replied.

"Is he stalling for something?" the tinker asked.

Sali had wondered about that too. Huong had intentionally slowed their talks, but mainly because of his cautious and detail-oriented nature. She respected that. The First Yazgur approached their negotiations much like a warchief approached preparing for a battle, planning out all contingencies.

Daewon finished with Sali a few hours later. Her hair was now comprised of fifty thin braids with the sides freshly shorn to reveal her warrior's skin. A black horizontal streak ran across her face, covering her eyes.

Sali admired herself in the mirror. Satisfied, she turned to leave. "You have a career in hair weaving if this tinker thing doesn't work out, tinkerchief. Keep the furnaces half stoked while I'm gone, just in case."

"The sooner I can speed home, the better. This is the longest I've been away from little Hampa." This was another way Sali had been able to honor her former neophyte. Her nephew certainly had Hampa's gentle nature.

She hurried from the room and emerged onto the main street of *Not Loud Not Fat*. Several of the crew working on deck noticed her and clapped their chests as she passed. She shot them stern glares before breaking into a good-natured smile. The crew had grown lax lately. There wasn't much for them to do while the warpod was docked. The respite was welcome, but Sunjawa was still technically khanate territory. She touched the side of her eye and swept her finger across the deck: *Stay vigilant.*

All nodded, except for the youngest crew member, who placed a fist over his forehead, then his heart, and then both palms over his eyes. Sali masked her smirk. This boy was a try-hard. She should keep an eye on him. He was a focused lad who took his responsibilities seriously. Marhi would be ready to receive her own neophyte in a few years.

Sali's next stop was the armory. She checked the sun and then hurried toward the stern of the pod.

Her thoughts drifted to Maza Qisami. She looked like the past five years had been hard on her. She certainly appeared rough around the edges. The quick and sharp tongue was still there, but there was also something else. Like hesitation or consideration, or dare she say, prudence? There was certainly a weight to her now. Gone were the juvenile impulses, replaced by a wariness that only hardship could have brought on. It suited her. Not that it mattered. The assassin was no longer her problem.

In the armory, Sali found her scale armor half assembled on the floor. Wani was whistling as she polished each piece.

Sali eyed the mess. "I gave you this task two days ago. I need to wear this now, lass."

"You asked for perfection, big sister, and like you always say, perfection is never fast." That girl had a glib retort for everything.

Sali knelt next to her and began to assist with the reassembly of her armor, relinking the individual scale pieces to their hooks. She had spent just as many years as a neophyte as anyone else, so repairing, cleaning, and putting armor back together was second nature. While they worked, she noticed that her neophyte's weapon was not close at hand.

Sali furrowed her brow. "Did you switch weapons again?"

"I wasn't feeling the trident anymore, mentor."

"You can't keep switching weapon specialties. You'll never master anything if you try to use everything."

"The net was stupid." Wani sniffed. "It kept getting caught on my rings."

The net *was* stupid, but it had been her choice, just like when she tried the double whip, or the season before that when she had been bent on making cloth-fighting a thing. Sometimes, Sali was tempted to grab a spear and shove it into the girl's hands, but weapon specialization was a deeply personal choice, one that only Wani could make.

When they finally finished putting Sali's scale armor back together, Wani helped put it on and strap it around Sali's body, being careful not to muss her hair. Sali had to admit, the girl was slow, but Wani's work was solid. Marhi, on the other hand, would have done a slipshod job of it.

Sali held out her hand. "Give me the cloak."

Wani looked flustered. She picked up a pile of crumpled clothing and held it up. "I was going to do that next."

Sali masked her annoyance and turned away. "It's fine. Cloaks are dumb, anyway." Sali left the armory with Wani in tow, and together the two viperstrikes proceeded toward the front of the city pod, where Marhi was waiting. "Is the assassin gone?" asked Sali.

Marhi nodded. "The land-chained took the clothes and rations we offered and left the pod without another word. She didn't even say goodbye."

"Why do you sound bitter?" asked Wani.

Marhi shrugged. "I owe her a heartdebt. I don't like loose ends."

"You carried her out of a penal colony in the Grass Tundra," said Sali. "She's free now. The debt is repaid as far as I'm concerned."

Marhi didn't look convinced, but then, debts of honor were always personal, and Marhi had greater pride than most.

"Where do you think she went?" asked Wani. "Into town?"

"Who knows, as far as the sharp Owl can fly." Marhi shook her head. "She's probably sprinting toward Zhuun lands as we speak."

"I'll bet my two favorite battle whips she is sticking around," said the younger viperstrike.

Marhi gave her a light shove. "Stop trying to offload those whips. Nobody wants them."

"How about my favorite spear tip, then?"

Marhi considered and then nodded. "I have a bucket of blue paint."

Wani brightened. "Really?"

And a wager was struck. Sali was sure that Marhi had obtained the blue paint to give to Wani anyway, but that was for her two neophytes to work out. Sali did not take sides, nor did she care where the shadowkill went next. If the assassin was gone, then that would be one less item on Sali's extensive list of things to worry about. Sali masked her smile as she led the two squabbling neophytes down the ramp.

The three viperstrikes strolled down the wooden docks toward the tulip walls. A few dockhands stopped what they were doing to stare, but most paid them no attention. Their novelty had worn off after a few days. The guards at the outer gates eyed their weapons but waved them through. Sali had come to the city so many times over the last few days that she recognized most of the guards by the state of their tattered armor.

The three Nezra passed through the outer wall of the tulip and entered the city proper, walking through the mazelike floating streets over the drink. The street this morning was crowded with travelers who had just arrived or were about to leave. The third cycle was upon them, so this was their last chance to travel to or from Sunjawa for the next few months before it became too dangerous. Regardless, traffic was thick.

Marhi had pointed out the increased Sunjawa militia presence, standing on corners, patrolling the main streets, and manning check-points at the harbor gates. The clan's military strength was modest, just adequate really, if not quite respectable. Their warriors were well armed and well trained, if not mighty. War wasn't their clan's specialty or focus, and they were far richer because of that.

They reached the main spiral stairs at the heart of the city and began the long trek up toward the Nest at the top, taking their time ascending the eight stories of winding stairs and roped bridges into the spiderweb levels, where the air was markedly cooler. The big Uhna had come, the mighty breeze blowing from the south that ushered in the third cycle spring. Some of the roped bridges rattled so hard that Sali ordered her two wards to link hands. She wasn't worried about Marhi, but the last thing she needed was for little Wani to get blown off one of these rickety platforms. There were currently only three viperstrikes in the world. This would be a devastating way to lose one of them.

They were just halfway up to the Nest when she gazed at a gap between two tulip stems that was bleeding mist. A heavy fog had rolled in this morning and was leaking its haze through the gaps in the tulip stems, giving the landscape surrounding them a hazy feel to the air.

"Do you think Daewon can spot the flare through that?" asked Marhi.

"It won't be necessary," Sali replied.

There were no guards at the set of steps leading up to the Nest. The viperstrikes invited themselves in and continued up the floating staircase as it curled up to the last platform at the heart of the Blooming Tulip. The floors beneath them rattled and shook as the breeze blew through. It was quiet here, unlike the previous time. Gone were the yazgur broods running up and down the stairs and through the web-like wooden passages.

Now there was only the First Yazgur, sitting on his throne. He was flanked by the usual four warriors standing at his back. He smiled, waving for them to approach. "Salminde the Viperstrike. I am pleased to see you again."

Sali pulled up short of the half-moon of chairs. The rest of the yazgurs not being present for this raised questions. Why wouldn't they be here? They had been present at every step of the negotiations. "I had hoped to see the rest of your wise yazgurs for this momentous day, First Yazgur."

He pointed toward the sky. "It's the wind. Too dangerous for the little ones, and too chilly for the old ones."

That was her first clue that something was wrong. "Please convey my regrets for not sharing the hearth with them this day."

Huong pointed at a small circular table placed between them. "Sit, sit. Share a cup of airag with me. This is from our finest batch of mare milk."

"Are we celebrating?" asked Sali.

"We are celebrating our mutual respect and honoring your time at our hearth."

The yazgur's words were strained. That was the second clue. Sali lowered both hands to the cup and lifted it off the table with a flourish. At the same time, she tapped her right foot twice, and then twice more. She smiled at the First Yazgur.

Marhi noticed it first and took two steps back. Wani was not far behind. Both Sali and Huong touched cups. She brought the cup to her mouth and inhaled. Sali had drank her fill of good airag during her many years, and this brew certainly did not qualify as such.

That was the third clue. Sali set the cup down without touching it. "I had hoped for a different ending."

"We considered"—he shrugged—"but the prosperity of my city comes first."

"There is no prosperity without freedom," she argued. "Think of your future."

"There will be no future if there is no present. Unfortunately, the reward is not worth the risk. Joining a rebellion is not in Sunjawa's best interest."

"I see." Her optimism had been crushed, but this decision was out of her control. She would not dishonor or debase herself begging. There was little else to do but salvage her dignity and depart. "This is regrettable, but your wisdom will be respected. If you change your mind, Nezra is always willing to listen. If nothing else, we will depart and not waste any more of your time."

"But what *is* in our best interest," the First Yazgur continued, cutting her off, "is if the Sunjawa clan is raised equal to that of the other capitals."

Sali hesitated. Were they still negotiating? Perhaps there was an opening here. She forced a smile. "As we've spoken of earlier, Nezra intends to see all clans free. There will be no capital cities or government ruled by a council of shamans. We will all be equal beneath the endless sky."

Huong spoke in a muffled voice. "That is true. Under you, there are no rulers. Katuia had not raised a clan to capital in over a century. With the recent destruction of five of her capital cities five years ago, perhaps it is time to refresh their ranks."

Sali scoffed. "The inner clans will never consider a chained clan—a rim clan, at that—as one of them."

The First Yazgur paced around the center of the dais. "That has been true, yes, but the past does not necessarily dictate the future. Times change. Sunjawa just needs to bring to the spirit shamans a prize worthy of their consideration."

The rumbling of boots grew louder from all sides. The half dozen webbed entrances to the dais were suddenly blocked by oar-wielding Sunjawa warriors.

"You would betray the hearth?" Sali was shocked. There were few more sacred things among residents of the Grass Sea than hospitality, even to enemies. Sometimes especially to enemies.

There was a saying among the Katuia: If you keep your word to your enemies, then your friends will sleep soundly as you keep watch.

"I assure you, it was a decision that weighed heavily on my heart," the First Yazgur said.

"Mentor," Wani glanced around, her voice alarmed. "There're a lot of them."

Her neophyte wasn't wrong. Sunjawa weren't known for their military or war arts prowess, but overwhelming odds were overwhelming odds. Sali wasn't worried, however. "All you had to do was decline the offer. No need to rouse your entire garrison." Sali glanced around the platform. "I don't think you brought enough warriors."

The First Yazgur raised an arm. "We have ten to your one, viper-strike. Chaqra does not care if your body is warm when I hand it over."

"The quality of the war artist matters more than the quantity," Sali said. "Do you want to know why the inner clans would never raise you to capital? Other than the fact you are land-chained, that is."

"Your Katuia biases are known," Huong sneered.

"They'll never raise Sunjawa," said Sali, "because your clan is not strong. Your war arts sects are pitifully weak, your warriors are mediocre, your city never birthed a khan, and your history is plagued with defeat after defeat."

Because she had desperately hoped for this alliance, Sali had to try one last time. "You won't need to be a great warrior city if you join us, First Yazgur. Sunjawa is renowned for its trade and craftsmanship, as well as one of the Grass Sea's most important tourist destinations. That is as worthy as any great war arts sect, even more so."

"How dare you!" The First Yazgur threw his cloak back and raised his palms into a guard position. It was then that Sali remembered that he was the head of the . . . she had forgotten the name of his sect, the gentleways.

"You forget something, Huong," Sali said, keeping her gaze on him. "Marhi."

Her neophyte drew a flare and aimed it toward the darkening sky. She pulled a string and watched as a long green flare shot up, its light muffled by the miasma in the air.

Thankfully, Daewon and the crew were paying attention. A moment later, *Not Loud Not Fat*, still parked at the docks on the horizon, came to life, belching a sputtering column of smoke. One of the ballistae on board the warpod replied, launching a flaming bolt over the city, nearly intersecting with the flare's deep rainbow arc.

"Not a threat, just a warning," she said. "Now, perhaps I've interpreted your words incorrectly, First Yazgur." Her tone turned serious. "I'll offer you one more chance, Huong. If you break the sacred hearth, Sunjawa will burn, and all the people of the Grass Sea will know the brittleness of your word."

Huong didn't seem bothered. "Surrender peacefully, and I will guarantee the safety of your neophytes."

Sali countered, "How about you let us go and I won't slaughter every soul in this room, and my warpod won't bury your city under the dark tears of the Grass Sea?"

"Ah, the famed confidence of the viperstrikes, and the even greater arrogance of Nezra," the First Yazgur sneered. "I was glad when I heard that your capital city was destroyed. Your clan was always one of the first to look down upon us. Your people deserved everything they've received."

"Sunjawa will suffer a similar fate."

"We are well aware that our defense will not match an inner clan warpod, that is true," said the First Yazgur. "That is why we sent for help."

Sali looked toward where Huong was pointing, and she noticed for the first time a cluster of lights in the distance. The fog obstructed the details, but there was no mistaking what that was, especially the eerie gray spotlights sweeping over the land.

"It's the Necro Citadel," Wani hissed. "*Liqusa* is here."

Sali's mind raced instantly to the safety of her pod. *Not Loud Not*

Fat was currently pinned at the docks, and with no chance for Sali to warn them. Daewon and the rest of the crew had their attention on Sali and the platform and were not likely to be on the lookout for the enemy creeping up their rear.

"This was a trap all along, and I fell for it." Sali scowled. The Sunjawa rim clan likely had never intended to ally with Nezra. The protracted negotiations were a ruse to buy the Bone Clan time to arrive.

"Now that I neutralized one idle threat," said Huong, "let me neutralize the other."

More warriors appeared, crowding the already packed platform. *Now* it was ten to one, easily, and numbers would always defeat skill. Sali would keel over from exhaustion before she could kill all of them. Besides, Sunjawa's war arts sects weren't *that* laughable.

The Sunjawa warriors began to crowd in, wielding their long oars like clubs or staves. Sali felt her two neophytes on either side of her.

"What's the plan, mentor?" asked Marhi.

"We need to get back to *Not Loud Not Fat* and warn the crew," said Sali.

"How do we escape?"

Sali was at a loss. She glanced to both sides and then over the railing. They were ten stories up with every path packed with warriors. Sali alone might be able to leap down to each level to escape, but Marhi and Wani didn't have that ability.

Marhi must have been thinking the same thing. "Mentor, you should go. We'll cover you."

Not again. Never again. "Not a chance."

"By the sharp Owl's droppings, don't be so stubborn, Sali," her neophyte said. "There's no point in all three of us going down. At least if you escape, you have a chance to warn the crew."

It would be a lie if Sali didn't admit the thought had crossed her mind. Escaping on her own was a smart tactical decision. A wise chief would heed Marhi's advice. Sometimes, a lesser sacrifice was necessary for the greater good. She looked at her two neophytes. Wani was shaking but maintained her composure. Marhi was all concerned about Sali's welfare but did not care a whit about her own. They were good lasses, brave and honorable.

Unfortunately for everyone, Sali was not a wise chief. Leadership was never black and white. Some situations existed beyond logic and reason. In her case, she had no intention of outliving any more of her neophytes.

The platform was becoming more crowded. The gentleways had surrounded the dais, with the fat ends of their long oars pointed at them.

Sali, fingering the hilt of her tongue, spoke in a steady but loud voice. "Stay in contact, shoulder to shoulder, and move as one. Head toward the corridor to my left. If any of you manage to get close enough to the ground, dive into the water. At least you'll have a chance. Try to shed your armor first."

And of course, both neophytes obeyed immediately, looking straight at the corridor leading to the next platform. The two guppies telegraphed their intention. Marhi pulled her pair of batons out and twirled them in her hand. To her other side, Wani drew two chain whips and stiffened them, turning them into two short, curved swords. So she was giving double sabers a shot again, eh?

There were eight Sunjawa warriors manning the entrance when Sali had first gestured at it. A moment later, there were twenty as more gentleways followed their attention and moved into that space. The Sunjawa closed in until they were just outside of melee range.

"Go on my mark," Sali instructed, looking ahead.

Marhi saluted at the enemy line, lifting a baton into the air and then banging her fist over her heart. Wani raised her swords. Sali tensed, as did both her neophytes. The gentleways warriors tensed as well.

"Now!"

Both Marhi and Wani charged toward the enemy. The gentleways charged back. Sali seized the moment and turned the opposite direction, plowing through the startled ranks of the enemy standing between her and the First Yazgur. She stiffened her tongue and speared the ground at the foot of the enemy line, using the flexible shaft to pole-vault over the first line of Sunjawa. She landed amidst the third line, who weren't able to react quickly enough as she lashed out, knocking two and three at a time with her flexible spear as she cut a path toward the First Yazgur.

"Surrender," she snarled, pressing the tip of her blade into the First Yazgur's exposed neck.

Huong was unimpressed. "Murdering me changes nothing, viperstrike. There are twelve yazgurs in our line of succession. It is the tradition of the Sunjawa clan to kill our leaders if they perform poorly." He shrugged. "We go through leadership changes every few years. I was the twelfth many years ago. The second will take my place without missing a step. All they have to do is resize my robes. You see, death isn't a threat to us. We are all replaceable. Can you say the same, Salminde? Are you ready to be the last of your sect?"

One of the gentleways had come up from behind Wani and put her in a choke hold, pressing his oar to her throat. Five others were piled on top of Marhi, pinning her down as she thrashed like a rabid animal.

What would a wise leader do in this situation? More importantly, what choice would she make for two people she loved? Sali snarled and dropped her blade.

"I thought as much," he crowed. "The other yazgurs would certainly have voted for my disembowelment if today's plans had gone awry."

"Day's not over," snapped Sali as a dozen gentleways seized her, their hands pawing at her until they forced her to her knees.

"I wish to make a trade with you," said Huong. "Your life is already spoken for. You're getting shipped to the spirit shamans. However, you can still save your two neophytes. They could continue your lineage. The viperstrikes won't go extinct. All you need is to tell me where the rest of your clan is located."

This was an easy decision. As much as she loved Marhi and Wani, their lives were drops in the ocean when compared to Malinde, young Hampa, and the thousands of Nezra back in their city.

Sali opened her mouth to tell him to hang by his intestines when the ceiling shattered, raining large sharp shards of glass upon them, striking many of the Sunjawa warriors, cutting several down. Sali hunched over and shielded her head.

A dark figure dropped from the ceiling alongside the rain of glass. They landed softly in the center of the dais, where several of the gentleways had fallen, and were wearing a dark green body suit with their face covered by an oversize hood.

One of the Sunjawa warriors still on one knee batted at the new intruder with his oar. The new intruder ducked the first swipe and charged forward, ducking a weak second swing, then drew a long, sharp, and familiar rusty dagger and plunged it into the gentleways's eye.

Maza Qisami threw back the hood and eyed Sali. "And *you* said you didn't need my help."

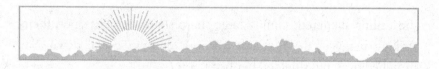

THE TEAM-UP

Qisami snuck into Sunjawa shortly after she was unceremoniously thrown out of the Nezra ship. She had hoped to book passage home and had spent the morning trying to get someone to speak with her. No one gave her the time of day. She was about to give up and look for some quiet back alley to call her bed for the evening when she noticed Sali's unmistakable mane of hair and her two pubescent grunts trailing behind.

Qisami had to admit she was jealous. She had always wanted girl grunts but somehow ended up with two useless boys. Well, not useless. Cyyk had been strangely loyal to her since he'd joined her cell, and that, in many ways, was more valuable than the ability to do laundry and maintain their armory. But still, girls would have been nice. Girls always stick together. Except for Koteuni, that bitch. She was going to have to hunt her former second-in-command down after she figured out how to get home.

Bored, Qisami had followed them, moving quietly within the many shadowed areas created by the weakened rays of the King overhead as the three viperstrikes hiked to the platform at the top of the tulip.

Trailing half a level below, she had followed them from bridge to platform to bridge, slipping through cover as she climbed. It had been a long time since she shadowstepped so much. She jumped through the shadows and scurried around like a rat. She was about to catch up to Salminde and her brats when the staircases and bridges suddenly filled with green-clad warriors moving up the levels behind the viperstrikes.

Now Qisami had to make a choice: leave the viperstrike to her fate or do something about it. Part of her wanted to punish Salminde for tossing her aside this morning, but she had also been curious about the unfolding. More importantly, Qisami sensed opportunity. She was forced to move more methodically, biding her time for when she could skirt from shadow to shadow up the remaining levels. She had to go wide around the perimeter before she could go upward, and once she did, she realized that it was even easier to go around and above all the Sunjawa soldiers, which is how she ended up on the roof of the platform. She was surprised to find it mostly made from glass, and even more so to discover that it was transparent. It was there in the corner, where wood touched glass, that she stayed safely hidden, watching the events below her unfold.

Salminde was surrounded by at least a hundred baddies, not to mention the dozens more manning every bridge and path around the upper platform. The viperstrikes would have to fight to go down every level unless they decided to take their chances plummeting to the shallow waters below.

Qisami was tempted to leave. It would serve Salminde right. Why should she intervene? Not even *she* would stand against these odds.

Or would she? Qisami continued to stare as the silly grasshoppers jumped the three viperstrikes. She felt strangely tempted. There was something addicting about coming to the rescue. She had felt it when she saved those stupid babies at the nursery and she was feeling it now.

Her thinking brain was telling her to just get out of here; it was stupid to intervene, but her feeling brain was fiending for that high of saving the day. But the moment those grasshoppers seized Salminde and drove her to her knees, Qisami acted purely from instinct.

Qisami sprinted onto the center of the glass ceiling. She drew the rusty dagger and slammed it down, sending fractures spiderwebbing in every direction. Heavy crackling sounded all around. She jumped into the air and stomped down again and again. The pane finally gave way on her fifth try, sending a shower of shards onto the people below.

Qisami's landing could have been more graceful, but it didn't matter. Broken glass and bodies were everywhere as a thousand tiny knives sliced the many unfortunate bodies below. One jagged edge punctured her crummy rubber shoes and was jabbing her big toe. She winced as she stepped on one of the bodies.

Every set of eyes was trained on her, even the three viperstrikes'. Qisami preened at the attention. Here was her chance to save the day again, her feeling brain crowed. Her thinking brain was pretty angry that she got involved, but it was far too late for regrets.

"Qisami, what are you doing?" asked Marhi.

Qisami stood at the mouth of a narrow wooden side path leading off the platform. The eight grasshoppers guarding that end of the platform had suffered the worst of the fallen glass, paving the way for an escape.

"Are you kittens coming?" Qisami shouted.

Salminde twisted around, shucking off several green soldiers and elbowing a few more in the face. She took two steps forward and shot her tongue directly at Qisami. She barely ducked in time as the heavy spearhead of the tongue shot past her right ear. An instant later, someone screamed. Qisami looked over her shoulder and saw the bite punching into the chest of a grasshopper.

Sali ran past a moment later. "Why are you following me?"

Qisami caught up quickly. "'Wow, Qisami, what a spectacular entrance. Thank you for saving our lives. We owe you everything. Yay'?"

Salminde ignored her as she ran down the roped bridge. A grasshopper tried to block their way, but the viperstrike barely slowed as she struck him three times with her open knifehand palm and then tossed him over the side. They were near the next platform half a level below when a large number of green guards appeared. Even more were swelling up behind them, trapping them at the center of the crossing.

"That's an awful lot of them," said Wani. "I can't even count that high."

Salminde held up a fist. "Marhi, clog up the rear. Wani, take my left angle. Shadowkill, just stay out of trouble—"

Qisami couldn't make out the rest. She leaped over the side of the bridge and swung beneath it, darting into the shadow of a large bridge. She appeared on the other side hanging from several girders woven from some sort of stiff grass. One more shadowstep dropped her onto the platform behind the entrenched grasshoppers. Qisami barreled into them, knocking them out of their formation. She didn't have the heft to knock anyone down, but her disruption was an effective distraction, allowing the viperstrikes to slip past the shields and oars and penetrate their ranks.

Salminde and Qisami, along with help from the two kittens, cleared out the Sunjawa warriors in short order, killing four and throwing the others over the side. Qisami assumed they were dead from the nine-story fall, but she was taught never to count the dead until she saw the bodies.

As soon as Salminde finished the last grasshopper, Qisami turned back to the bridge they had just crossed and kicked its two attaching beams, separating it from the platform, sending another six grasshoppers plummeting to their deaths while also cutting off the viperstrikes' pursuers.

Sali turned to her. "I spoke hastily a moment earlier, shadowkill. You have our thanks."

"See, very useful," Qisami replied. "I bet you regret making the wrong choice earlier, eh?"

"No." Sali shook her head. "Once trust is broken, it cannot be so easily mended."

"I just saved your life!"

"I had it under control."

"Liar!"

"Excuse me, mentor." Wani cut between them. She glanced at Qisami. "Old auntie, can you two talk about this later? The gentleways are still coming for us."

"Did you just call me old?" Qisami glowered at the teen. "I'll have you know I'm barely twenty-nine, I mean, thirty—"

Sali pulled them both along. "You can lie about your age later. We have to go."

Qisami looked around. It seemed as if the entire Sunjawa garrison was converging on them. Most were coming from above, stuck in a traffic jam along the bridge as they pushed toward their platform. There were more grasshoppers coming from below as well, but they were scattered in bunches.

An arc of red burned across the sky over the tulip's opening. Qisami frowned. How could they keep missing? How could the Nezra war machine be such an awful shot? This was like hitting the side of a mountain.

"We have to warn *Not Loud Not Fat* about the incoming Liqusa warpods," shouted Sali. "They might still be able to get away if we can get to them soon enough."

They met another group of grasshoppers three-quarters of the way down the next bridge. The three viperstrikes took them head-on, Sali's tongue flanked by the girls' with their sticks and blades. Qisami hit them from their blind spots, leveraging the many dark regions in the middle of the tulip to get a drop on them from an unsuspecting angle.

Qisami leaped over the railing and dropped into a darkened spot below three crisscrossing bridges overhead. She emerged just off to the side where they were previously, using the momentum to fling herself across and over the bridge. She grabbed a grasshopper's cloak and dragged him over the side as they both fell. She abandoned the poor bug and entered another shadow as they plummeted, emerging behind the mass of warriors blocking the viperstrikes' path.

She hit them from behind, shoving two over the side before they even noticed her. She jammed her blade into the exposed armpit of a green-clad warrior, and then kicked the legs out from the next. Two of the Sunjawa turned to face her and Marhi cracked them with her sticks. The remaining two grasshoppers, realizing their plight, chose to jump over the side rather than die quick, honorable deaths.

Qisami followed their descent. One managed to land on a platform two levels below, while the other bounced off the side of one bridge and then off another and got clotheslined by a wooden support beam before plummeting all the way down to the drink. Qisami flinched with every hit on the way down.

"Should have taken a knife to the gut, coward." She whirled around as a grasshopper charged her blind spot, hammering down with his big oar as if he were trying to smash a bug. The shadowkill's house style, Rolling Boxing, did not put much emphasis on defense. Qisami attacked the incoming blow, the heel of her right foot shooting out and snapping the shaft of the Sunjawa warrior's weapon. She followed it up with a jab that sank the blade into the soft flesh of the warrior's belly between the chest piece and the skirt. Except she missed, glancing the rusty dagger off hardened wood plate and snapping it in two.

"Are you kidding me?" Qisami didn't have the luxury to be surprised. She blinked and watched as the broken end of the dagger flicked into the air, then ate a punch to the jaw and a boot to the midsection. Unfortunately for the grasshopper, prison toughens a person. She absorbed the blow and spun, looping her heel around and connecting with the boy's jaw, snuffing his consciousness.

She sneered, holding the broken hilt. "What trash equipment."

"Keep moving," Sali remarked as the viperstrikes finished off the last of the Sunjawa. "We can't stay here."

They continued moving, now toward the seventh story. The path toward the ground level was getting crowded, while an even larger group of warriors were convening from above.

"Hey, if I help save your stupid clan," Qisami shouted, "can we start over? I mean, maybe reconsider working together."

"You would have my gratitude but that is the extent of our relationship."

"Holding grudges is bad for you," said Qisami. She should know. "Can you at least give me a ride back to Zhuun territory?"

Marhi intervened. "Are you two negotiating right now?"

The platforms at the mid-levels were larger and more tightly packed with even more wooden bridges connecting them. By now, several residents had joined the fight. Like most of their kind, these war arts hobbyists had inflated egos and were easily dispatched.

"We won't make it at this rate," said Wani.

"Can we cut through the green wall?" asked Marhi.

"It'd take hours." Sali looked over the side, toward the ground. "It's a long drop to the water. If you brace yourself and keep your body vertical, you might survive the fall."

"No, they won't," snapped Qisami. "None of you will survive that fall. I mean, I'll be fine, of course, but you three won't."

"Why are you so disagreeable, old auntie?" asked Wani.

"Call me 'old' one more time and I'll spank you with this broken dagger." Qisami waved it around. "Why do you own such a shit blade? And then give it to me?"

"I thought it was funny," admitted Salminde.

Qisami stopped, and considered. That *was* funny. Something Qisami would have done. She never thought Sali had a sense of humor. It made her feel closer to the viperstrike. "Can you at least give me something that won't break so I can finish rescuing you?"

"Here. This one I want back." Salminde pulled another dagger from her hip and tossed it to her. "It's not a rescue."

"Like hell it isn't—"

A figure sprinted up behind them, trapping them at a dead end. All four women rounded on them, Sali's tongue already shooting toward where they stood. A well-dressed young man came into view a moment later. "Salminde the Viperstrike, at last I've found you."

This was a suitable time to try out the dagger Sali had just given her. Qisami leveled it at the man's face.

"I can help you escape!"

Qisami considered that he might be telling the truth, but decided that she didn't care, and rammed her new blade toward the man's eyeball anyway.

CHAPTER THIRTY-FOUR

DEATH SLEET

T hings at the Death Sleet for Jian and his friends were, in fact, not fine. They were far from fucking fine. It was supposed to have been easy. Highlord Oban had told him that this would be a straightforward mission.

It all made perfect sense when the high lord first laid it out: attack a Caobiu general and his retinue as he crossed the Death Sleet. The Shulan forces were going to throw two full units of elite displayguards into the ambush. Kill or capture the general, Lord Akai Hujo, while having Jian's face leading the attack. Earn the gratitude and worship of the battered locals in the eastern wards, and then disappear back to the safety of the buried wards.

That was it: a lot of prestige earned with negligible risk. Everyone won, except the dead general.

"Your victory will give strength to the city's defenders," Oban had exclaimed, patting him on the back.

The plan had a promising start. The day market was filled with people. Lord Akai and his retinue of a hundred elite cinderblossoms had just turned the corner down the main stretch crossing the Death

Sleet. Jian had Sonaya and Kaiyu with him, as well as twice the enemy's number of displayguards. The overwhelming numbers should have been sufficient to win the day, not to mention they held the element of surprise. It was shocking when the Shulan forces were cornered, all because of one bad oversight.

Akai Hujo, known as Longsleeves, was a master war artist. A real one. Not a fake like Jian.

Neutralizing the general had been Jian's responsibility as a showcase of his prowess and skill, and it wasn't going well. By the time the Shulan realized their mistake, it was too late. Jian had engaged Hujo, and things took a bad turn.

He narrowly dodged a whipping slice from one of Hujo's long silk sleeves, getting clipped in the jaw as he ducked. Off-balance, he jabbed blindly with the Swallow Dances and struck air.

A long bolt of cloth wrapped around the blade near the hilt. He pulled. The cloth tugged back, and then it ripped. That entanglement had been the only thing keeping him upright. Jian managed to stay on his feet until a second bolt of cloth punched him in the abdomen, throwing him back twenty feet through the air until he landed hard on his belly on the cobblestone road.

Jian was losing a fight against a shirt. His stomach spasmed from that hard impact, and he felt the boiled beans he had for dinner surge back up his throat.

Taishi's words rang in his mind: "Vomiting in front of your enemy makes *you* the puke."

He bit his lip, swallowed his bile, and clawed back to a standing position. Hujo was expressionless as he bore down on Jian. The lord wasn't wearing armor and instead was covered by long flowing robes with many cloth streamers, and a wide hat that looked like a whale with legs. His long sleeves, which moments before were longer than a spear, were now tucked neatly at his wrists.

The general walked forward, punishing Jian with the intensity of his gaze. He looked contemplative before he spoke, his voice low and gravelly. "Is this a joke? Did they swap some tenth-day hobbyist for the Prophesied Hero of the Tiandi?"

Those words hurt Jian more than his freshly cracked ribs. He tried slouching to dull the pain, or standing tall, or shifting his weight to one foot. It didn't matter. He hurt all over. He held up the Swallow Dances. Taishi had always told him that bolt fighting, all thirty styles of it, was gimmicky and impotent and required a lot of laundry. Jian had trusted his master's opinion and had joined the ambush believing that bias right up to the moment Hujo began kicking his ass. At least he hadn't dropped his sword yet. He was proud of—

Longsleeves attacked again, his arms shooting out two bolts of cloth. Jian ducked the first blow and barely avoided the second, and Hujo followed it up with Fool Harvesting the Sea, whipping his sleeves in a figure eight, each blow from the cloth on the road kicking up a plume of debris.

Jian held his ground and tried to scatter the shrapnel with a spray of air currents. He managed to deflect most of the dust. All but a few of the larger pieces made it past his currents, cutting up his face.

Hujo shot forward, giving Jian no time to recover. The master's hands were somehow fast and clever and slow and smooth at the same time. Jian found his blade continually out of position. He was just a breath too slow to stab with his sword, too slow to react to the master's feints, and too slow to block an attack. Jian's face began to redden and swell as their exchanges continued. The master imposed his presence, forcing him onto his heel before overwhelming him. Jian fell, performing a rather ungraceful backward roll onto his backside.

Two arrows streaked toward Hujo. He batted them out of the air without taking his eyes off Jian. Kaiyu, perched on a lamp post, launched several more arrows with Summer Bow in rapid succession.

Hujo dodged them easily. The man looked like he could dodge raindrops during a thunderstorm. Some of those arrows came closer to hitting Jian than their enemy, which was unusual because Kaiyu was a good shot.

The high loom master countered the Houtou by shooting one of his namesakes back at him. Instead of trying to hit Kaiyu, however, he wrapped the end of the sleeve around the base of the lamp post and, to Jian's shock, ripped the entire thing out of the ground.

Kaiyu lost his balance as the pole he was standing on was pulled from under him, and he plummeted headfirst toward the ground. He managed to recover in midair and land somewhat on his hands and knees but was disoriented and slow to get back on his feet. Jian watched in horror as the sleeve snapped the post and smashed down where the Houtou had fallen.

Jian moved without thinking, summoning a swell of jing that only desperation could muster, filling his belly and lungs, sending tingles to his extremities. He launched toward his friend on a current of air with shocking speed as he barreled into Kaiyu. The two smacked into each other and crashed to the ground. Fortunately, the momentum from the impact carried them both out of the way of the lamp post. Jian groaned, having nearly knocked himself unconscious from smashing into his friend. He scampered back onto wobbly legs and faced the high loom master.

At least Hujo had the decency to wait until Jian got back to his feet. He sneered. "Is this the best the Shulan have to offer?"

"You're not that good. You just have long stupid sleeves. My master could take you on, no problem!" It was admittedly not a good retort.

Hujo nodded. "Aye, I know Taishi. I have fought alongside her. I have fought against her. My well of respect for the master windwhisper is endless. You, boy, are an embarrassment and a tragic end to her lineage. She would be rolling in her tomb if she saw you now."

This guy wasn't just mean! Those nasty barbs cut so deep Jian had to choke back tears, which would have been more embarrassing than throwing up. Jian recalled what Taishi instructed him to say whenever anyone challenged his position as her heir. He stood tall and faced the high loom master. "I am Wen Jian, master of the Windwhispering School of the Zhang lineage, now of the Wen family style, and I will defeat—"

Jian had to cut it short and dive to the side as the shaft of the broken lamp post crashed into the ground where he had been standing. Long sleeves wrapped around the end of the shaft and flung it at Jian. He rolled to his feet and tried to skip into the air on a current, but those punching bolts of cloth could fly far quicker than Jian ever could.

The lamp post flipped into the air and crashed down again, narrowly missing Jian as he jumped aside. He dodged a looping horizontal swing that would have shattered his spine and then dove aside to avoid another. The one time he tried to close the distance, the end of Hujo's sleeve punched him in the gut so hard he nearly began crying. Even worse, he dropped the Swallow Dances. Jian dropped to all fours, pawing the ground under a vegetable cart as he looked for his blade. There was a good chance he wouldn't survive the next thirty seconds, but all he could think about was how relieved he was that Taishi didn't see him drop her beloved sword.

Jian banged his head on the cart, overturning some of its contents. It began to rain potatoes. He noticed the glimmer of the blue blade off to the side. He stretched out his arm. Longsleeves stepped on the back of Jian's palm the moment his hand touched the hilt.

"Now, runt," said Hujo. "You're lucky the empress wants you alive, else I would have twisted your neck and popped your head off the moment we met."

"You're an unpleasant person, aren't you?" Jian winced, biting his lip. His crushed hand made him want to scream, but he wasn't going to give this bully the satisfaction.

Hujo snorted and brought a fist down on his head. Jian raised his guard, expecting the master to shatter it. Their forearms met, jing clashing with jing. The impact of the master's weight threatened to crush Jian. He steeled himself and prepared to be obliterated.

Except he wasn't. Jian held his own, matching the high loom master in strengths. He blinked, surprised most of all that he was actually keeping up with the master.

Jian would cherish the shock on Hujo's face for the rest of his short life. "You yappy, impudent dog. How dare you try to stand against me—"

An arrow punched into the Caobiu general's shoulder. Hujo staggered backward and then lashed out, knocking two more arrows out of the air. Then his eyes bulged as he touched his temple. Sonaya stood off to the side, bloodied but determined. Her mind attacks were causing a substantial distraction. This thankfully gave Jian the opportunity to break away from his clash with Longsleeves. His arms and legs shook from weariness, and his muscles ached when summoned. Jian wiped his drenched brow, and his mouth squeaked every time he sucked in a long, deep breath. Not a moment too soon. His strength was about to give out.

Sonaya and Kaiyu stood to either side of Hujo. Both looked battered; the three had to fight through several ranks of cinderblossoms to get to the high lord. The drowned fist spoke again, her silent words attacking Hujo's mental fortitude. At the same time, Kaiyu circled away opposite Sonaya, pelting the high loom with arrows. When Longsleeves hit back with his long bolts of cloth, the Houtou would unbend Summer Bow to its staff form to counter. They continued for several exchanges, neither able to seize the advantage.

Sonaya stepped between Hujo and Jian, her two bladed fans, the Truth of Dreams and Truth of Lies, opened wide. Bhasani had given her cherished fans to her daughter on the eve of the invasion, declaring that Ras Sonaya was ready to assume the mantle of Mother of the Drowned Fist. Sonaya had bawled her eyes out that night and then got drunk. She had hugged those two fans close to her bosom even as Jian carried her home. Sonaya had actually said she loved him that night, although he wasn't sure if she was talking to him or the fans. She wouldn't let go of her prized possessions, even passed out. Now Sonaya was using the drowned fists' treasured heirloom to defend Jian's life.

The usually joyful and exuberant Kaiyu was grim as death as he wielded his late father's Houtou family weapon. There were few war artists in the lunar court as skilled with the longbow staff as the Houtou. He thrust and swung the weapon in a blur, attacking with both ends and slamming it down, creating lines of cracked stone.

Longsleeves danced between the two younger war artists like an old master leading children in a demonstration of complex forms. Except it wasn't intricate choreography. This battle was real and turning deadlier by the moment. Hujo caught Kaiyu first, punching out with his sleeves as the Houtou vaulted in the air and tried to shoot an arrow off. The impact sent Kaiyu crashing like a rag doll through a wooden awning and into a row of vendor stalls.

The high loom master turned his attention to Sonaya. She slashed at him with the bladed edges of her fans, occasionally catching cloth. The drowned fist's lips were a stream of words and phrases as if she were a madwoman muttering to the invisible. Sonaya certainly looked mad as her gaze locked on the high loom master. The high loom and the drowned fist waged two fights, one with their hands and the other with their minds. The famed Longsleeves was stalemated for a few moments before the more experienced war artist gained the upper hand, forcing her back.

Snap of the Whale Dragon met Minnow Snakes Upstream. Sonaya followed through with Skyward Death by Torture, which was two downward slices of her fans aimed to decapitate both arms at the shoulders at the same time.

Hujo had half an eternity to study her attack as she descended upon him. He stepped away from Truth of Dreams's and Truth of Lies's paths, and then he launched a crushing kick that lifted her off the ground.

Jian staggered toward her, nearly falling on his face. His legs were noodles. He could only stare as a kick rocketed toward her face.

To both men's surprise, Sonaya twisted out of the attack, landing low on her hands and feet, and darted forward, slashing Hujo across the thigh. Both war artists fell to the ground, Sonaya crashing into a log roll while Hujo fell to a knee. She was on her feet an instant later, pirouetting into her guard stance, sans one fan. She must have dropped it somewhere.

No sooner had Sonaya refocused on their enemy than Hujo slipped a white sleeve around her midsection. She struggled with the cloth constricting her waist, and then the high loom flicked his arm, sending the sleeve snapping out and smashing Sonaya into the nearby stone wall with a heavy thud.

"No!" Rage blurred Jian's thoughts as he rushed the high loom master. He chopped a bolt of cloth in two and ducked another, but that was as close as he got to the high loom master. In his hurry, Jian had overextended too far forward and was slow to recover. He countered a slap with a slash of the Swallow Dances, but then a sleeve slipped around his neck and constricted. It likely would have popped his head clean off as the master had claimed had Jian not sneaked two fingers beside his neck as the cloth cinched. He gasped for air and desperately swiped with his blade at the cloth even as his throat constricted, sending him to his knees.

Hujo, holding the cloth with his hand like a leash, leaned in. "I would be embarrassed if I were Taishi."

Jian's eyes watered even as he slowly died. Those sharp words cut deep because he believed it, too. He tried to kick the high loom master, one last defiant gesture, but even that was too weak and sad as his body flopped side to side like a mouse caught in a trap. The blue sky dimmed.

Jian's head slammed against the stone road, and then he could suddenly breathe again. Long, painful gasps of air flooded into his lungs as he croaked. Spasms shook his body as he finally vomited. Strong hands hooked under his armpits and raised him up. It took a few more long, deep breaths before the blinking stars in the black sky receded to reveal their surroundings.

Jian was flanked by a pair of displayguards as they half carried and half dragged him away. A displayguard sporting a long purple plume of feathers on his helmet appeared by his side. "Move underground faster. Get the champion to safety! Kill anyone who gets in your way." He barked even louder, "Defensive formations."

"What's happening?" Jian asked.

Huakt, the captain of the displayguards, only gave him a cursory glance. "The battle took too long, champion. Cinder reinforcements are coming. Our position is about to get overwhelmed. We're pulling you out of the Death Sleet."

Jian looked back to where he had fought Longsleeves moments earlier and saw that ten more displayguards had taken his place, surrounding the high loom in a desperate bid to hold him back.

At that moment, Hujo's and Jian's eyes locked. The Caobiu general snarled, reaching for him. Jian's eyes widened. He froze.

The high loom master snatched a spear from a nearby displayguard and stabbed the man. He hefted the weapon in one hand. "Prophesied

Hero of the Tiandi!" Hujo roared for all to hear. "You cannot run from me, Shulan scum."

Jian had only a moment to see the spear rocketing across an impressive distance to puncture his armor. He sucked in one last gulp of air and tasted blood. He looked down at the fountain of blood spraying from his chest, and was fairly sure he was dead.

CHAPTER THIRTY-FIVE

ESCAPE FROM THE TULIP

Qisami's blade was about to rupture the Sunjawa's eyeball when the ends of a metallic rope swung around her wrist and snapped it aside, changing the trajectory of her blade just enough to miss his face and graze his shoulder.

The man screeched, voice high and panicked. That was when Qisami noticed his shriveled arm.

Salminde came between them, putting a palm to her chest. She smelled like fresh bladed grass. "Let him speak."

"You're the boss," Qisami replied. "Right?"

The viperstrike ignored her. "What are you doing here, Dai? You're not made for battle."

"That is certainly true," he replied. "Please, Salminde, hear me out."

Qisami nudged Wani. "Who is that?"

"The Ninth Yazgur," the neophyte replied. "One of the rulers of Sunjawa."

"Nine? How many are there?" Qisami twirled the dagger around her fingers. The weight was all in the hilt, which was annoying, but it was otherwise a well-crafted weapon. Finally. "In any case, want me to pull out his guts or keep his spleen intact?"

Sali shook her head.

"Fine, I'll just break his brain."

"Hold," said the viperstrike.

The young yazgur held up his arms in the universal sign of surrender. Qisami could tell he was untrained in the war arts by his soft, pink hands. "I ordered the garrison to sweep the other end of this level. I can get you down to the lake."

Salminde didn't budge. "Why should we go with you?"

"You have trust issues, don't you?" Qisami quipped.

Dai looked agitated. "Look, viperstrike, not everyone agrees with the First Yazgur's decision. Many want to be free of those bloody Kati but don't want the risk."

"But *you* are willing?" replied Sali. "Willing to risk your seat for this cause?"

Dai nodded. "I may be ambitious, but I live for Sunjawa. If the good of the clan aligns with my personal gain, then it means that my claim is the most righteous among the yazgurs. I have languished as ninth long enough."

"You're doing it for the promotion." Qisami nodded.

"The yazgurs aren't related? You're not one big family?" asked Wani.

He shook his head. "Huong was the gentleways sectchief. I was a schoolteacher before wading into politics."

"How long have you been Ninth Yazgur?" asked Marhi.

"Six months."

Qisami was taken aback. "Six months? I've had pubic lice for longer. How often do you change leaders?"

"Someone gets dethroned every few months," he admitted. "The people are fickle about our leaders. Any yazgur can call a vote of confidence. If the vote is more than two-to-one, the yazgur is thrown out of court and flogged, and every yazgur behind him gets promoted. If the vote is unanimous, then their life is given to the office."

Wani stopped in her tracks. "You kill them?"

He nodded. "With great power comes great consequences." He nodded. "If you run for yazgur, you better try to do a decent job."

Wani's eyes were wide. "That's terrible."

"That's amazing." Qisami's eyes were wide as well.

"The only one who has never been dethroned is Huong. The First Yazgur has been in his seat for ten years. The old man is too entrenched."

"He must be doing something right," said Qisami.

"Why in the pure Child would anyone want to be yazgur if it inevitably leads to death?" asked Marhi.

"Hubris." Dai shrugged. "Because every ambitious man thinks they can do it better than anyone else. I actually will when I become First Yazgur."

"Sure you will," Qisami mused. "Be a good leader or we kill you. I love your system."

"Of course you do," said Sali.

Dai stopped at the end of the stairwell. "This door leads to the floating streets. From there, it should be a straight shot to the docks."

"You have my thanks, Ninth Yazgur," said Sali, putting her fist over his chest.

He returned the gesture and spoke more bluntly. "If I become the First Yazgur, you will have your alliance."

Sali's face tightened. "Then I wait eagerly for your ascension."

Dai led them to a wooden building tucked against the edge of the platform sandwiched between two large buildings. "It's a family warehouse." He closed the door behind them.

Qisami stared at a room with a crooked table and rickety chair at the far end, and a ratty rug taking up the floor. "In my line of work, we call this a kill room."

Dai looked flustered. "No, of course not."

Sali scanned the room in a slow pivot. "Why are we here, yazgur? This looks like a dead end." She stomped on the rug and stopped at the hollow sound.

The Ninth Yazgur reached to the edge of the rug and pulled it aside, revealing a circular wooden hatch cut into the floor. He pulled it open, revealing a dozen wooden hooped rings lashed together by thick netting. Dai pulled a lever and the bottom swung open like a trapdoor, allowing the rings to fall, forming a body-sized tube down to the water level.

"Nice smuggler's ring," Qisami observed.

"Even yazgurs need privacy," said Dai. He knelt beside the opening and offered a hand. Marhi and Wani went in first, disappearing down the long tube netting.

Sali was next. Before she climbed down, the yazgur leaned in. Qisami couldn't make out what words were exchanged but heard "waterwheel" and "blue balls." The viperstrike dropped into the ring, and then it was Qisami's turn.

Qisami finger-waved goodbye as she stepped into the tube and dropped half a story before her right toes found a footing on the rope. She clutched the netting to get her bearings and then dropped again, falling past Wani, and then Marhi, and reached the water ahead of Sali.

Qisami clung to the end of the tube and waited directly over the lake.

"You haven't lost a step," said Sali, catching up, keeping her feet on the bottom hole of the tube as she curled her finger into the mesh ropes.

"Prison keeps you sharp," Qisami replied. "You're spryer as well."

"I had a weight lifted off my shoulder" was the cryptic reply.

Qisami scanned for a way to land without getting wet. "See a boat?"

"No boat." Sali pointed at the closest pier. "There's a pile of bamboo shoots leaning against the wall. Can you reach it?"

Qisami squinted. The nearest point on the pier was too far for one shadowstep, and there were no jump points she could leap from. She looked up. She could use the many dark spots cast by the bridges and platforms above, but she still needed a launching point. Then she noticed a stained spot off to the side. She began to throw her weight side to side, causing the bottom of the netted tube to sway.

"What are you doing?" asked Salminde.

"Help me." To her surprise, the viperstrike did not question her further. She joined Qisami as they rocked from side to side. The two neophytes joined them moments later, swinging from the tube like a pendulum above the open water. The edge of their swing brought them into the shade of a platform directly overhead. Qisami timed their momentum, and on their fifth swing, she let go, dropping toward the water.

It was barely enough to shadowstep. The darkness felt like muck, as if it were about to expunge her. She felt more friction going into the usually cool, bubbly sensation, as if she were smacking wet mud. It felt like every part of her body was being pulled and pinched by a hundred forefingers and thumbs, with a painful added twist. The world blinked black, and Qisami came back out again, using her momentum to catapult her from the other end of the shadow over the water to the very end of the pier.

She still came up short, her stomach taking the brunt of the impact as she bounced off the end of the pier, her legs dangled over the side while her fingers pawed at the wet wood, the ends of her toes kicking water. She was fortunate not to fall into the drink and managed to claw her way onto stable ground. She gave herself only a second to catch breath before getting up and limping—she had banged her knee pretty hard—toward the bamboo poles. Qisami grabbed a handful of the poles and toppled them into the water, using her toes to nudge them toward the viperstrikes still hanging off the net. She watched them as, one by one, they swung off the tube just as it oscillated, landing on the floating bamboo poles and running along them until they joined Qisami.

Wani gave her best effort, launching through the air as far as her little legs could power her, but she fell comically short, barely making it halfway across the water before plummeting into its depths. Sali expected it, however, and her stiffened tongue was waiting for her neophyte to grasp as Sali hauled her back to shore.

"Well done, shadowkill," said Sali.

"You're welcome." Qisami practically preened.

The four emerged behind a row of buildings floating over the water near the tulip wall. Qisami moved to the lead and signaled the others to flatten against the wall.

She shadowstepped to the other side of the street to get a better vantage point and waited for a hundred counts before waving for the others to follow.

"We don't have time to crawl around," snapped Sali. "The warpod is about to get caught with her furnaces cold and leashed to the docks. We have to warn them before it's too late."

"You're not warning anyone if you get mobbed by that plague of insects scurrying overhead," Qisami snapped back. Indeed, the web levels above were swarming with those grasshoppers.

Qisami continued sneaking the three viperstrikes through the floating streets in the general direction of the warpod, hopping on boats and scampering on roofs. They turned off several more streets to avoid Sunjawa patrols until they were able to join a crowd heading toward the docks. Qisami was beginning to feel like she was trapped inside a fishbowl, with this city's tall walls narrowing to a small opening pointing at the sky.

"Come on, kids," she said to the two neophytes.

They had just made the last turn toward the outer gate when Qisami stopped short. There was a heavy barricade set up at the entrance to the harbor. A glance identified fifty-some oars raised like incense sticks. "Far too many grasshoppers to take on, especially behind a fortification. We're going to have to sneak around somehow. Maybe hop on a junk and sail through the harbor?"

Marhi shook her head. "Bull's balls, we're too late. The chains are likely up. No ship is sailing out. The city's locked down."

Salminde stared at the heavily barricaded checkpoint. "We have to warn Daewon about the Liqusa pods. We don't have a choice."

"I might be able to sneak through," said Qisami. "I can warn your tinker."

"Daewon won't listen to you. You assaulted him the other day."

"I was being nice! I could have slit his throat and saved myself the trouble."

"Choking someone out isn't a good way to establish trust." Sali shook her head. "One of my neophytes will need to accompany you."

Marhi looked alarmed. "What about you, Sali?"

"I'm going to draw those oarsmen away. Once I do, crash into that checkpoint and break through to *Not Loud Not Fat*. You must not fail."

Marhi's nostrils flared as she stepped forward. "Let me do it."

"I will draw the most attention." The viperstrike shook her head. "I'm depending on you and the shadowkill to make it."

"Good to be part of the team," Qisami quipped.

This time, she was rewarded with a nod. Sali loosened her cloak to expose her shoulders and her coiled tongue at her waist. She turned down the main floating street heading toward the ten rows of five warriors guarding the narrow gates. Qisami wasn't thrilled with the plan. The garrison was on alert. Two layers of barricades had come up, as had three—no, four—archers manning a tower nest hanging from a set of chains.

They would have to cut through many bodies to get through, but Salminde was right. They had only minutes, if that, to spare before it was too late for the warpod to pull out of the docks. If the enemy pods got to it first, then there went her ride back to civilization.

Salminde broke into a jog. Marhi and Wani followed close behind. Qisami let herself drag a bit, watching their surroundings. She still had a half block to cover before reaching the barricades. The Sunjawa were going to see them coming.

Qisami spied one of the grasshoppers staring at the jogging viperstrike. The tall Kati with the mohawk and scale armor wasn't subtle. Instead of moving to confront Salminde, the warrior turned to flee.

Qisami shadowstepped into the shadow of a moving cart and emerged a few feet in front of the grasshopper. He pulled up, startled when she emerged from the darkness, and wasn't able to raise his guard before she gutted him like a piggy. Qisami fell on him as he toppled over, gripping the heavy handle of her dagger. This was made for people with long fingers, which Qisami decidedly did not have.

She picked herself up. "I had to do a little housecleaning." They were gone. The three viperstrikes had kept going. She noticed Sali's beautiful mane and her two shorter neophytes several steps behind, halfway down the street.

"Hey, wait for me!" Qisami took off after them.

Sali smashed into the warriors with a crash. Her tongue whipped about, smashing shields and breaking formations, sending bodies hurtling through the air. More guards spilled from the guard house. Sali was overwhelmed when the Sunjawa warriors formed and countered. Then, to Qisami's surprise, the viperstrike fled in the opposite direction, fighting but giving ground as the garrison chased after her like a pack of mastiffs.

Qisami herded the neophytes toward the gates. "Keep going, you dumb kittens."

"But Salminde—"

"She's buying you time," Qisami snapped, shoving the two viperstrikes. "Get going before they catch her."

"They aren't going to catch her," Wani shot back. "Are they?"

"Did anyone tell you that you're awful at following orders?" said Qisami.

The checkpoint had emptied. A few of the Sunjawa warriors stayed at their post. The two viperstrikes crashed into them. Marhi's batons blurred as she fought two at a time, striking her opponents multiple times in quick succession.

Qisami checked on the other viperstrike and had to do a double take. Was that silly girl fighting with a rake?

A few more grasshoppers rushed from the gatehouse. The first charged them at spearpoint. Wani stepped in front and flicked her rake, trapping the shaft as the man closed in. The young viperstrike flicked her rake again and sent the wooden warrior tumbling forward and skidding on the ground to Qisami's feet. She looked down and kicked the man's consciousness out of him, then stepped over his head. Wani had just finished off a warrior and knocked him over the railing when she noticed Qisami staring.

Wani stopped. "What?"

She shrugged. "Nothing. Your double whip chain is stupid, but you're good at it. It suits you."

"Why does that compliment sound like an insult?"

"I had a terrible upbringing, so I can't say anything unconditionally nice."

They broke through the outer gates a moment later and managed to make their way on board *Not Loud Not Fat*. All three were gassed, barely able to breathe as they stumbled onto the deck.

Daewon appeared. "What happened? Where's Sali?"

"You have to power up the warpod and go, master tinker," said Marhi.

Daewon's face turned thunderous. "We're not going anywhere without Salminde."

"It's Sali's orders. This was a trap," said Wani.

"The yazgurs were stalling." Marhi spoke at the same time.

Qisami reached over and yanked at the tinker's collar. "One of your Katuia cities with a bunch of pods is closing in on you right now. They're going to flatten you the moment they get here, and then probably run you over again for fun."

Daewon's face paled. "Which clan?"

"Liqusa, master tinker," said Marhi. "Coming from all sides. I saw it with my own eyes."

Daewon had already turned away, barking orders. "Fight stations! Flame the furnaces. Prep Kahun to run!"

CHAPTER THIRTY-SIX

THE REALITY

The getaway from the Barberry Cave back to friendly territory was tense, hectic, and slow. That's what you get when you're relying on a pair of stubby-legged miniature horses. Camp ponies, with their short, stubby legs, never worry about going anywhere in a hurry, even in a war zone. It made the slow escape from the chaotic moments when the Thorned Garden fell all the more comical as the last semblance of order vanished. Bhasani had remarked that they could probably leave the ward quicker if they continued on foot. The thought of walking never crossed any of their minds.

Pitched battles erupted as waves of Caobiu candles flooded into the ward's main square just outside the Barberry. They were met by an equal and opposing wave of residents, underground corps, and army in an assorted mishmash of bright colors. No one wore any red or yellow, however. The two sides collided with a thunderous clap, and the square became a boiling soup of violence and death, threatening to bubble over and spill into the neighboring streets.

Even then, the two beasts took their time, whining, snorting, and farting the entire way as they carefully stepped over bodies and debris alike. If there was a pitched battle, the two fearless ponies nuzzled their way through. If the area was getting bombarded with artillery, they just put one foot in front of the other.

Most combatants ignored them, two mangy ponies carrying four wrinkled seniors who already looked like they had one foot in the grave. . . . They had better-armed combatants to bash their brains in. A few hassled them, however, probably seeking easy prey. That was a mistake, which no one lived to repeat. Fausan made short work of any who came close, his fingers flaring dramatically as if he were conducting a symphony.

The side wall of a row of buildings at the end of a block exploded from a ballista's hail of buckshot and collapsed, causing a cascade of attached homes to fall over one by one. A moment later, another barrage—burning oil this time—slammed into the buildings across the street, erupting in a ball of flame that shot toward the heavens. The fire jumped the alley and was soon racing down adjacent blocks in every direction.

Taishi's heart ached as she navigated past the destruction along the narrow streets of the Thorned Garden. She'd spent many a sordid and debaucherous night during her misspent youth down in the dregs of the Barberry back when it was more an industrial rather than residential neighborhood. The massive cave carried a seedy reputation back then and was popular with the denizens of the lunar court. Then people with families began moving in and cleaned everything up, dispersing the seedy vibe.

Her gaze was drawn to the flames running alongside them as they fled. The fire had reached the end of the block but soon found a clothesline to run across the street to continue feeding its hunger.

"Fausan," she called, pointing at the burning rope overhead.

The whipfinger knew what she meant. He eyed the thin line three stories up and flicked both hands, launching a pair of bullets at his target. He must have missed because the fire was still crossing over. A snarl escaped his curled lips. Taishi had rarely seen the whipfinger master miss twice, but the rope was a nearly impossible target so far away. Fausan was determined. He squinted and tried again, this time hitting his target on the third try.

"The smoke was making my eyes water," he muttered. The old man always played it cool, but under that casual exterior was a perfectionist who worked hard to appear relaxed.

That small act might have delayed the spread of the fire, but the ward's destruction was inevitable. There were no winners in a siege when the smoke cleared. At this rate, the two sides would soon be fighting over the corpse of this once great city. What was the point of this? Ducal patriotism? Pride? Maybe this was Oban's vendetta against Sunri.

"I should have let Saan toss me in jail when he made me an emissary," she grumbled.

They soon reached a tunnel entrance leading into a buried ward and passed through a Shulan checkpoint, a heavily armored and well-defended barricade manned by a garrison of underground corps. Only after they were trudging through the sewers did Taishi feel safe enough to let herself breathe. She hated having to depend on others.

Today was humbling. She thought of the Oracle of the Tiandi, little Pei and her fox, making sacrifices for the good of all Zhuun, and in a private manner refusing accolades or explanations. Taishi's eyes became wet at the thought. Those thoughts had weighed her down the entire way home. She questioned her judgment. Should Taishi have refused the oracle's demands?

No, she couldn't.

Koranajah was right. If you were devout, you either believed in the oracle's wisdom, or you didn't. There was no gray area. The devout were not allowed to pick and choose which parts of the oracle's wisdom to follow. Yet Taishi had let a little girl choose to walk to her death. What did allowing this atrocity say about Taishi? It was as much her choice as Pei's. Taishi wept openly. Guilt struck old hearts differently than with the young.

Taishi was in a dark mood by the time they returned to the Vauzan Temple of the Tiandi. She was famished and exhausted. Her legs ached, as did her back, shoulders, and just about everything else. Her feet were swollen.

The day was a disaster. She had gotten one of her oldest friends killed and doomed her convent, the only one in all Zhuun that forged female war artists. And somehow, that wasn't the worst news. Taishi had lost the Oracle of the Tiandi. No, Taishi had given her to the enemy. All in an afternoon. She bowed her head. At least they were home now and the day was near its end.

Night had settled in by the time they passed through the front gates. The courtyard was lively for this hour: monks, soldiers, a triage, and many sprawled on the ground where once they waited in line to offer Tenth Day Prayers. There was panic in the air.

Taishi turned to Bhasani. "Hey, do you feel—"

The drowned fist master waved her off. "Yes, I sense it too, and I don't care. Whatever is causing this stir can wait. Defer it until morning. Don't wake me unless breakfast is being served."

Fausan raised his hand. "I will happily take breakfast, good or bad."

"Come on, you dope." Bhasani nudged her steed, and the two rode off. She gave one final order, as usual. "Send my daughter my way if you see her."

Then they were gone. Taishi looked over at Sohn. "And you?"

The eternal bright light master carried the look of haunted bewilderment. He had worn this expression for most of the day. "Did we really send the entire orchid sect to their deaths?"

"Well, no," said Taishi. "We did no such thing. The Black Orchids chose to honor their vow to the Tiandi and defend the oracle with their lives."

"But," said Sohn with a low drawl. "But if we had brought Pei with us, then all those nuns would be alive, right?"

Taishi shrugged. "Some might not have survived the journey here, but it's safe to say they had a higher chance of survival here than remaining at the Thorned Garden."

He stopped. "So, uh, why didn't we bring her with us?"

"She didn't want to come."

Sohn exploded. "Who cares what that stupid little brat wants! She probably wants a nice doll and sequin dress. Just toss her into a bag and be done with it." He pretended to throw something into an imaginary bag. "Bam, saved a bunch of nuns. We all get to go to heaven."

Taishi eyed him. "I could have, but she's the Oracle of the Tiandi. You either believe in the prophecy or you don't."

Sohn sucked in several deep, shaking breaths. "I'm sorry. It's late. I'm tired and not thinking straight." He rubbed his eyes. "I have two nieces and some distant relatives who are Black Orchids. It's a tradition among my family to send one woman every generation to the Black Orchid sect. I could have just led a fifth of my lineage to slaughter. That little girl is not human. She's a monster."

"She certainly isn't human," Taishi said, although not with the same meaning as Sohn. She stood before her old friend and met his eyes. "I'm sorry about your family. I hope they find a way to survive."

Sohn pulled out a stoppered gourd and headed down the path leading toward the meditation hill near the back. They were on temple grounds, but he didn't care. No one else appeared to either. Everyone had bigger problems to worry about than fundamentalist Tiandi laws. "The night is young. I cannot pray unless I'm drunk, and I have many ancestors I need to apologize to tonight."

She watched her old friend disappear behind the main temple. That man was not going to meet a peaceful end. He would die either by war or by wine. She hoped for the former; for all his faults, Soa Sohn deserved an honorable and noble end to this mortal realm. She turned away, saddened by that thought.

Taishi cut across the courtyard, taking care to step around the many wounded scattered across the ground. She made a slow turn as she walked. The triage was much more crowded than usual. The injured were abundant, while the number of healers and monks caring for them very few.

Taishi saw a familiar face sitting among a group of injured packed tightly together. She stopped to greet their leader. "What are you doing here, Beautiful Boy?"

"Here for the same reason as everyone else. I have a dozen injured, and the temple is one of the few places still accepting wounded." The leader of the Worst Todays underworld looked like she had taken a swim in the sewers. Her hair was plastered to her head. Ash smudged across her face. Blood and mud caked the rest of her.

"What happened to your healers?"

"Taken by the Caobiu. Every bloody one," Beautiful Boy said. "Healers and smiths."

One of the first things the Caobiu did when they took over Sunsheng University was conscript or lock up every student studying to be a healer. They hunted the rest. It had become an epidemic.

"Have the Cinder Legions attacked the buried wards yet?"

"They're trying to cut off the Undertunnel. We all rose up to meet them." Beautiful Boy nodded. "The fighting's been bad. We're holding but for how much longer I cannot say."

"Do what you can and then leave. Survive. You got that, underworld boss?"

"Not this fight." She shook her head. A nun finally arrived to see to the group. Beautiful Boy's attention pivoted toward the care of her people. "Now, if you'll excuse me. I have lives to try to save, and a few to end."

Taishi continued on, stepping around a group of injured displayguards. Then she noticed the line of ducal carriages, including the court doctor and the magistrate. Those were Oban's flags. His presence made no sense. He couldn't fight, so he would serve as a distraction for his forces. She chuckled, imagining the soft potato of a man wearing tin decorative armor and nearly falling off his horse while leading a charge. That would have been a sight.

Taishi was about to head down the path leading to the training yard and then back to her cottage in the bamboo grove when she caught sight of Sonaya sitting off to the side against a building. She had her arms wrapped around her knees. Her head was leaning back and her eyes were closed.

Taishi changed directions toward Sonaya. She got a better look at the drowned fist's face as she got near. Sonaya looked asleep, if not for the wrinkle in her brow and the redness around her eyes. Her hair was matted, and she was wearing her battle garb, bloodied. That was when the hairs on the back of Taishi's neck rose. Her fingers began to sweat.

She hurried over to the drowned fist. "Girl, what happened?"

Sonaya opened her eyes and that was all Taishi needed to see.

The girl looked devastated. Her eyes were bloodshot. Her face was covered with bruises and cuts. "The infirmary. We were on a mission . . ."

Taishi heard nothing else. She took off toward the infirmary, moving as fast as her tired and already beat-up legs could manage.

"Calm yourself, stupid woman," she growled under her breath. "You're going to burst your heart at this rate." But she couldn't help but imagine the worst. What was that ass brain heir of hers thinking, running a mission without her approval?

Taishi wasn't sure which building was the infirmary—the monks didn't label their buildings—but she found it easily enough when she spied four displayguards standing at attention around a plain building with an ugly green door. This must be the right place. That was when she noticed some twenty other displayguards standing along the block.

She stared contemptuously as they lowered their spears at her. "Get your sticks out of my face before I rip apart your spleens."

As expected, the threat did not earn a reaction.

The infirmary door opened, and a familiar face looked out. "I can hear you through the door, dowager nun," said Oban. "Come in."

Taishi didn't wait until the door was shut before she snapped at the most powerful man in Shulan. "Where's Jian? Take me to him."

The high lord looked haggard as if he hadn't slept all night. "He's still in surgery. He's under the care of the court's best doctors. We have no less than two moxibusts, three acupuncturists, two energy healers, as well as every Tiandi monk doctor in the temple working on him. He is young and strong. They believe Wen Jian will survive."

"They believe?" Taishi barely suppressed a scream. She vented her rage at the next best thing. "Tell me what happened!"

"Wen Jian led an operation to target a high-ranking Caobiu general whose goal was to cut a corridor through the Death Sleet. It would sever the southeastern corner from the rest of the city's defenders. We couldn't allow it to happen."

"Why not? It's insignificant," said Taishi. "Those are residential wards. As long as we hold the buried wards, it doesn't matter if they control the Death Sleet. It's a resource sink for whoever controls it anyway."

"The Peace Abundance Highway has always been the heart of the city. Retaking it is a symbolic victory for the city."

"You risked his life to cheer people up?" Taishi was about to break his spleen, with her bare claws if she had to. She wanted to throw him off the nearest tower. It was all she could manage to mask her rage. Taishi knew a thousand ways to kill a man, and she couldn't use any of them right now. Oban was still a high lord. If she pushed too hard, she could lose the support of the Shulan Court.

"It couldn't be helped, Taishi." Oban was not fazed by her wrath. "The mission was too important. Jian needs to be seen leading the city at our darkest moment. The Champion of the Five Under Heaven fought well, until . . ."

"What happened?"

"Until he came face-to-face with Lord Akai Hujo."

Taishi was dumbfounded. "Hujo, that rat bastard Longsleeves? That's the general you sent Jian to kill? That filthy mouth Hujo? Are you koi-brained? Where was Hachi?"

"The whipfinger was attending to personal matters today."

Taishi wanted to scream. "Jian went into a pitched battle without his protector?"

"From the reports of the survivors, Jian fought General Hujo to a standstill long enough for the rest of the soldiers to retreat after they were caught in cross fire. The reports from witnesses say it was heroic. The young man had a good showing."

"Who cares about his showing!" she roared, swinging a fist in the air a little too close to his face.

He stared at her coldly. "Get a hold of yourself, Taishi. Remember whom you are addressing."

"Forgive me, my lord," she said. "I'm trying extremely hard to resist the urge to rip your spine out of your body. You have him chasing a lord general, in public, in broad daylight, *in* the Death Sleet." She was yelling again. Oban could probably count on one hand the number of people who raised their voices at him. Taishi didn't care. "Against fucking Longsleeves! Are you *trying* to get Jian killed?"

Oban's expression darkened. "Watch yourself, Taishi. You are revered for your legend, but do not mistake your reputation as a shield for your actions. We are friends, but I am still your lord."

Taishi lowered her eyes even as she clenched her good hand into a fist. "Forgive me for overstepping, high lord, but I do not understand the significance of putting the Prophesied Hero of the Tiandi into such danger for so little gain. Also, if Jian dies, I'm going to crack open your head and drain your brains out through your nose."

"How is he supposed to defeat the Eternal Khan if he can't beat a guy fighting with his sleeves?" Oban said it like an accusation.

"*I* used to have problems with Longsleeves." She wanted to wring his neck. "We had a deal! No missions without clearing it with me first."

"You weren't around to consult," he snapped. "This was an emergency. I sent for you when we arrived. The templeabbot said you were on an escort mission. Sounds beneath you, Taishi."

"That depends on who is being escorted," she shot back. "By the way, Thorned Garden fell today. The city's center is now exposed."

Oban looked battered. Of course he knew. He certainly cared more about it than she did. "I was made aware a few hours ago. I'm pulling remnants of the Fifth and Ninth Winged Axes to shore the new border. Rest assured—"

"You have to consider a negotiated surrender, Oban. While you still can. At this point, you have little other choice."

Anger flashed on his face. "I will not surrender the greatest city in the world to that bloodthirsty witch."

"Use your head, not your balls," she replied. "The people of Vauzan, capital of Shulan, have risen up as proud and loyal citizens to their duke. They fought with courage and vigor, inspired by hope and patriotism. Your honor is not in question, but it is time to look toward saving lives."

"Sunri will raze the city if she wins," said Oban. "I refuse to die on my back."

Taishi's temper flared. "*You* don't do anything. You're not the one fighting. You're not the one dying. You have no sons and your daughter has witnessed only six cycles in life."

"Saan was like a son to me!" Oban roared. The two mute men in the room with them came to life and advanced on her. Taishi had been so focused on the high lord that she had overlooked them.

"Love is a bad excuse to rule poorly." She held her ground. The worst they could do was kill her for disrespecting the high lord, which she couldn't do anything about. However, she understood his mind better because of this, and tried a different tactic. Berating the man would more likely send her to jail than win the high lord over. "Jian is like a son to me too, Oban."

"Sunri butchered him in front of my eyes, in his own pavilion, in front of his own men!" His voice broke. "The dishonor. The people of Shulan need justice!"

"You *need* revenge," she corrected. "And at what price, the death of thousands of innocents? People need to live. Don't throw their lives away for a lost cause."

Oban's face twisted. He looked as if he were about to strike her down with his words but then closed his eyes. The lines cutting across his face relaxed. For a moment, Taishi thought she had reached past his anger. A few quiet seconds passed, and then he spoke in a clear voice. "Your concern for the Champion of the Five Under Heaven is appreciated, dowager nun. The court has the matter well in hand. With respect to your position, a courier will inform you when Wen Jian is awake. You are dismissed."

"Don't cut me out, Oban." She had intended it to be more a threat than a warning, but the results were the same.

Oban turned his back, and the two mute men moved between them, ending their conversation. Taishi stood outside the closed infirmary doors a few moments later. She stared at the thick fire-tempered wooden doors and seethed. A few years ago, she could have shattered them with one blow. Now the only thing shattering would be her wrists. She hated feeling so impotent. All she could do was wait and pray.

Taishi looked toward the main temple. It had been years since the last time she prayed, but now was as good a time as any. If it could help Jian's odds of survival even a little, it would be worthwhile. She changed directions and walked up the stairs, past the offering vase, and to the Mosaic of the Tiandi hanging prominently against the back wall. Only one monk was here at this late hour. He bowed to her as she plucked two incense sticks from their vases off to the side, yellow and white, health and longevity, and lit them over the soft flame. Taishi fell to one knee and raised her right palm over her chest, the incense sticks burning fragrance that smelled like spring flowers and honey.

A rush of déjà vu swept over Taishi. She had done something similar a long time ago, on her knees, praying. Back then, she was praying for Sanso to survive his final test.

Would her prayer now come to the same conclusion as before?

If only there was a way to stop the fighting . . .

Taishi's head snapped up. She blinked. Maybe there was. She clambered back to her feet and broke into a slow sprint.

CHAPTER THIRTY-SEVEN

DOWN IN THE DRINK

S ali sprinted across the floating docks of the first water level of Sunjawa, her arms pumping. She hated running. She made a poor decision to look back to see that all of Sunjawa had risen against her. It started with the oarsmen, these grasshoppers, as the shadowkill called them, chasing her. Then the rest of the settlement got in on the fun, joining the guards in the chase.

The wave of determined residents nipped at her heels. She tripped over the hitch of a courier wagon, and then plowed into a stack of wooden barrels. Sali stayed on her feet; viperstrikes were trained to have exceptional balance. She hunched forward, her chest heaving.

This day was not going the way Sali expected. She had woken full of optimism, believing that Sunjawa would come to terms by day's end. It would have been a coup for their rebellion. The northern rim clan was important and held considerable influence over its neighbors. The new alliance would have created a legitimate military force to oppose Katuia. All her hopes had been dashed by noon as she ran for her life with half the city howling for her blood.

A young lad with a dumb death wish stepped in her way, his fists curled around his oar's shaft. She didn't slow. He swung as she moved within range. She pounced, darting close to his face. The oar smacked her shoulder. Sali shoved the lad gently to the side, and he fell with a splash into the drink. Sali checked on him to make sure he wasn't going to drown in his father's armor.

A rock flew past her, as did half a head of cabbage. She sensed a flood of people closing in and threw a looping kick that connected with two bodies. Sali bobbed and weaved, slipping out of people's grasps. She kept fighting, hacking and punching. The crowd engulfed her, but she moved with the fluid grace of a master. Soon, the attackers dwindled. The fighting became less fierce until finally, Sali stood alone.

She hunched over, labored, huffing deep breaths of air. "Damn hobbyists."

The pause in the fighting bought her a few seconds to catch her breath. More were bound to be on their way. Sali had participated in more than her fair share of mob attacks, but it was rare to see a group so enthusiastic as the one pursuing her right now. They were relentless. What was in the water here at Sunjawa? Either the people wished for a glorious death, or they were deeply Samaritan. It was then that a teenage girl ringing a bell walked by, calling out in a loud voice: "Attention Sunjawa, housing elevation opportunity to lower third level for the capture of Salminde the Viperstrike, fugitive, traitorous Nezra agent and cannibal."

Four street vendors farther down the path stepped in front of her. Two were unarmed, a third wielded a large cooking wok, and the last a fishing pole. Four fools with a death wish trying to take down a viperstrike. This was madness.

"Move, you limpweeds!" she barked before barreling into them.

Their feeble attempts to stop her went as expected. Sali didn't slow down as she smashed the bravest—and probably dumbest—of the four. He was the only one still standing in her way. She dropped him with a sharp elbow swing that likely cracked his cheekbones.

The fisherman whacked her across the head with his fishing pole and had only a moment to look startled that she was still standing, and then she slammed him low with a hip check that sent him somersaulting. The third tried to crack her with his wok. The thing was so large, unwieldy, and slow that Sali had all the time in the world to react. She gave the man a light shove as he finished the attack, sending him sprawling onto his belly. That left the last of the four Samaritans, an elderly man dressed in rags who looked more skin and bones than flesh. What was he thinking? Then the thought occurred to her; this guy could probably use a house.

Sali didn't have time for this. She put her hands on her hips. "Stand aside."

The old man, wiser than the rest, did as instructed. Sali checked. The mob was less than thirty paces behind and gaining ground.

Sali hurtled away from the rumble, pushing past bodies as she went in a random direction at each turn, getting twisted around and lost, but hopefully losing the mob as well. The tall walls of the weed made the sun difficult to spot and so made it harder to navigate. She tried to follow the shadows that traveled from the opening of the Blooming Tulip.

She looked up and could see that she was still heading south. She lowered her gaze a few degrees and saw a large wooden wheel in the distance scooping up troughs of water and raising them to higher levels. That contraption certainly looked like what she was searching for.

Sali kept the spinning wooden wheel as a visual anchor and made her way toward it. She was nearing the edge of the settlement butting up against walls of the gigaweeds. This part of the tulip was wetter than the rest of the settlement. Dozens of small streams splashed down to the drink from above. The ropes and platforms around this space were smaller and more numerous, casting shadows on the bottom level. Pretty bunches of flowers and colorful weeds rose from the water's surface, giving this area a garden-like feeling.

She glanced forward and realized her mistake too late. The floating wooden docks came to an abrupt stop, ending at a small lake of the drink. There was a gap of roughly five body lengths to a platform on the other side, but there was no other place to go. The mob made sure of that.

Sali weighed her options. She could probably take out ten people before they overwhelmed her, or she could try to make the jump. She might be able to clear it without armor and on a good day, except she was fully armored and definitely not having a good day. Desperation gave people strength, however. She looked back at the mob and made a decision. Better to leave this world with your body and armor intact than be torn apart by a pack of rabid dogs.

She had only a few seconds to strip off her scale armor. She didn't have time to take it apart, so three quick cuts with a blade along the six straps to her sides cracked her open like a watermelon. She gripped the handle to her tongue and sprinted forward, pacing herself so she could leap at the edge. She felt like a turtle outside its shell without her armor, but against these numbers, it was more important to move lightly and be maneuverable.

Sali knew the moment she pushed off the docks that it was a good attempt, but death didn't care if you almost survived, as her mother had often said. There was no chance that she was going to clear the gap. She barely made it past the halfway point. Luckily, there was a rock that projected above the water. She rebounded off it for another jump, and still somehow didn't make it all the way across. Sali splashed a half step away from reaching the next wooden platform, getting soaked up to her chest. The water was slimy and gross, with many bits of rotting debris clinging to her body. Sali clawed at the planks of the platform with her nails, trying to avoid falling in. She made it, somehow, swinging her legs onto hard ground.

Sali didn't have time to rest. She sat up after catching her breath and looked back at the way she came. The mob stood at the edge of the docks glowering and shouting impotent battle cries. Sali got back to her feet and gave them a formal bow. Someone threw a rock at her. Sali knocked it out of the air. Someone threw a shoe. She tilted to the side and let it pass. Someone else threw a grapefruit. Sali caught that one and bit into it. She hadn't eaten today, mistakenly assuming the yazgurs were providing meals.

"Not even lunch," she grumbled. She made a fist and placed her thumb between her fore and index fingers and flipped it at the crowd as she walked away. A chorus of boos followed along with more debris, but nothing struck her.

Sali had entered the industrial corner of Sunjawa. To her right was a row of steam factories and a large manufacturing plant to her left. At the far end was that wooden wheel, tall and wide as the building it was attached to.

A figure appeared from behind one of the buildings. "I watched from afar. I was worried you weren't going to make it, Salminde."

Sali buried her annoyance. This was the man who was getting her out of the city. "Ninth Yazgur Dai, your people try too hard."

"A rich reward for your capture. We live over open water. Real estate is at a premium."

She pointed. "You could have provided better directions than 'head *that way* toward the waterwheel.' I nearly got lynched."

"You made it here, didn't you?"

"Did my people make it out?"

He nodded. "Past the checkpoint and out to the harbor."

It would have to do. "You have a way out?"

Dai pointed at one of the curved smokestacks. "There's an unused stack that comes out the other end of the gigaweed walls."

"How many smuggling runs do you own?" she asked.

He smirked. "All of them. The yazgur throne sells the schedule through a private front. Those who want to move merchandise, exotics, or people can pay their fee and book their time to use the run."

"But smugglers tend to move illegal things that the local government either wants to tax or forbid. . . ." Sali's brow creased. "But *you're* the government. Why give criminals a way to skirt your decrees?"

"Smugglers are going to smuggle one way or another, so we might as well take a cut. On top of that, sure, we allow everything through, but then at least we get to keep an eye on it. If it's important enough"—he shrugged—"we nab it later to not arouse suspicion."

"I hope you booked this time to smuggle me out then."

"No need. The smuggling runs occur only at night. We should be all right here."

Sali followed Dai down a set of stairs, past a shallow waterfall that led to the stream that powered the waterwheel. The steam factories here rested on large barges arranged in rows, all moored to the wooden docks at half a dozen points. It must have been years since these things last anchored.

"Dai," she said, "you're risking a lot and asking for nothing in return. Why?"

He smiled and raised his withered arm. "When I was a sprout, I dreamed of fighting alongside you and the other wills of the khan."

"All terribly embellished, I assure you," she said.

"I lived through my imagination with you."

"The greatest warrior I have ever met, other than the Eternal Khan himself, was a one-armed woman," said Sali. "You're one of the twelve yazgurs of Sunjawa. That is as great an accomplishment as any arm can achieve."

He placed his fist over his chest. "I used to imitate the warrior's salute during my play. Right now, it feels like I'm reliving a childhood fantasy with *the* Salminde the Viperstrike. It is even more fortunate that we share a belief in the same cause. If so, I would be honored to call you a raidsister."

Sali smothered her chortle with a cough. The only way to earn *that* title was to live the raidlife. There were no substitutes. Any other time, such a declaration would result in a challenge, or at least a brawl and beatdown. True raiders took that distinction seriously.

They reached the front entrance to one of the larger barges. Dai unlocked the door after sliding a set of Tsunarcos-styled tiles around on a small grid. The yazgur apparently wasn't exaggerating when he said he owned all the smuggling runs.

He swung open the door, revealing a dark passage. In the distance, a bell tolled. Dai gestured for her to enter. "Opening any door summons the factory watchman. I'll talk him down. Go inside, avoid any contact with the workers, and head toward a corner room on the right.

The smuggling run begins inside the smokestack. Get there first. I'll catch up."

Sali wasn't keen on splitting up with Dai just when she had found him, but this was his city; he was the yazgur. He had gotten her this far; she was just the visitor. She touched her finger to her temple and focused. She glowed as her vision changed to different depths of green.

The steam factory was typical of its type. Large cylindrical boilers two stories tall were arrayed in between thick blackwood beams. Pipes snaked in every direction, running along the edges of the floor, up the walls, and crisscrossed all over the ceiling. It reminded Sali of the subterranean gear level down in the city pods' lower decks. In the center row of this cavernous building were steam turbines. She watched as blue electricity sizzled between two metal rods. She had to look away from the piercing light. Her nighteye made even dull sources of light painful to see.

"Blue balls," she muttered, picking her way through the building. It appeared to be a loom factory with rows of colored boiling vats lining the floors. Sali knew enough about gear to know not to mess with it. Much of what Malinde and the other tinkers worked on was dangerous to the ignorant.

There were a few tinkers around, but they were easy to avoid in this dimly lit place. Sali stayed in the shadows, keeping her distance from some of the large machines spitting out blue light. Fortunately, the paths were wide and clearly marked, with railings cordoning off some of the larger, more intimidating machines that cracked and buzzed.

She made her way to the floor until she found a metal gate leading to a dye room. On the far side was a large box-shaped unlit furnace.

She stared inside. It was dark except for a small bead of light at the far end of the tall stack. This must be where the smugglers' run originated. Sali slid the gate open with a creaking hiss and stepped into the room, one hand on the hilt of her tongue.

"There you are," said a new but familiar voice. She had spent the past week negotiating with this man. "How dare you keep me waiting? Now what is it—*you!*"

A spotlight lantern flooded the room with a harsh yellow light that blinded Sali. She released her nighteye but had to blink away the stars and spots obscuring her sight. When her vision cleared, Sali was surprised to find herself standing face-to-face with First Yazgur Huong.

By his vapid, startled expression, the leader of Sunjawa appeared equally stunned to see her here.

CHAPTER THIRTY-EIGHT

DIFFICULT DIPLOMACY

Taishi watched the soldiers form up from a corner of an alcove on the second-story catwalk as the high lord's retinue assembled in the front courtyard of the main temple. She had come to observe the carriage pull up. It was followed by the servants and escorts, then a squad of displayguards on foot. Other lords' carriages came after with their own sets of guards. The procession continued to build over the course of a few hours until everyone who was supposed to depart the Vauzan Temple of the Tiandi had arrived.

Everyone, that is, except for the person who mattered.

The entire procession, along with Taishi, had to wait another three hours before Oban finally showed up in the main courtyard. She would have fallen asleep hours ago if a few of the monks hadn't come to check up on her every once in a while. It must be nice being a high lord.

The minutes ticked by. Taishi pursed her lips. She felt like she was always just a step behind her desired outcome: Too late to save Jian. Too late to save Saan. Too late for Sanso. Too late for her mother.

Probably too late to save herself. She closed her eyes. It was too late for most of her regrets, but not for Jian. Not yet.

Oban finally appeared just as the King was beginning to set. As expected, the image-conscious Oban walked past his retinue and continued to the main temple to pray at the Mosaic of the Tiandi.

She watched as he approached with a smaller escort of eleven displayguards, ten alongside their captain with the green plumes. Fortunately, there were no mute men present. The quiet death was too unsettling to parade about in public, especially on holy grounds. Two lines of initiates awaited the high lord as he was greeted by Mori, who also probably had waited for several hours. Every candle in this drafty building was also lit. All this for five minutes of fake praying.

Taishi waited until Mori made a show of kneeling before the Mosaic of the Tiandi before rising from her perch and retreating deeper into the temple. She moved to a seldom-used room in the back that was barren save for a small marble table with two chairs and the back opening leading out to the stone garden.

She tapped the shoulder of a passing initiate. "My child, please enter the prayer room and request an audience with Highlord Oban to meet with Nai Roha."

The poor young monk gaped. "Me, dowager nun, to a noble? I can't. I've only been here three weeks. I still can't tie my laces. I—"

"Tell him it is a matter of importance to the health of prophecy." Asking an unknown and unprepared initiate at the very last second was intentional. It gave them no room to question her order and no time to bring it to someone superior.

Taishi sat at the table and poured a cup of tea. It had long gone cold, but the act helped calm her nerves. There was much riding on this meeting. She took a breath and relaxed. The next few moments could determine the fate of the entire duchy.

Oban walked into the sitting room a few minutes later, looking irritated. "You couldn't have come to me yourself?"

She held up her pot. "Tea?"

He nodded. "Fine." Then he realized he had to sit, so he did. As she poured his tea, he leaned in. "What's this important matter regarding Jian?"

The man would be given three chances to change *her* mind.

"The senior healing nun at the temple says Jian's injuries are grave. He is young and strong, but his survival is not guaranteed. With the situation in Vauzan, she recommends we move the boy to the Stone Blossom Monastery. They have the best healers in the Enlightened States. The monastery is fortified and the monks there will lay down their lives to protect him." Taishi's thoughts returned to the Black Orchids. Was she setting up the Tiandi religion for another massacre?

"Out of the question," said Oban. "The Stone Blossom is in Lawkan lands near the Caobiu borders. It's too dangerous of a journey, especially for the injured. You'll need to cross rivers infested with the Alabaster Armada, and likely have to traverse pitched battles between the two duchies, and possibly even the Xing."

"Wen Jian's life is at stake."

"The Shulan Court healers are as skilled as any the Tiandi offer. They will be at your disposal. If they can see to dukes, they can see to the Champion of the Five Under Heaven." He stood, which was the universal signal of dismissal from a lord.

"You are risking the prophecy with your stubbornness, Oban."

"I'm not giving up the Prophesied Hero of the Tiandi on a plate to Dongshi!" His face was red with fury. "Just like I'm not going to give up my one advantage against Sunri."

"Then send a retinue with us there and back."

"Vauzan cannot afford to lose even one of my elite guards right now. They are too important to the war effort."

Taishi closed her eyes. "The city is lost, Oban. It's time to salvage what we can. You know Sunri. She is all business, no feelings. She'll forgive you if you pledge your loyalty. Sue for peace. It will save lives."

"That will spell the end of the Shulan Duchy."

"That died with Saan. You've been maintaining a corpse."

"I'd rather the city burn to the ground than submit to her!" Oban slammed his cup on the table, cracking it. His face was red, his chest heaving. The displayguards at the edge of the room went as far as to put a hand on their weapons and stepped toward her. His breathing slowed after a few seconds and the mask of the steady politician returned. Oban wiped his hands on a silk napkin, soiled from the spilled tea. "Speak no more of this treasonous talk of surrender or of sending the boy away. We are finished here."

There went two chances.

Taishi allowed her thoughts time to gather. Oban ruled with his convictions if nothing else. But strong convictions didn't necessarily mean they were smart convictions. Better to live through a mistake than die being right.

"I can't accept your decision, Oban." Taishi rose to her feet and placed her hand on the hilt of her fake opera sword. That was the signal.

Oban looked surprised and then hurt. He pursed his lips and stared at the hand on her sword. "You're not carrying the Swallow Dances."

"I would not taint that blade with such a sordid task." That was a lie, but an honest one.

He studied her as if looking at her one last time. Finally, he turned away. "So be it. Kill her."

There went his third chance. Now it was too late.

The high lord's displayguards drew their sabers, raised their shields, and closed in. They moved cautiously, one at a time. Taishi maintained a calm facade as the tips of their blades neared. She drank a sip of her cold tea and counted the seconds. Worry gnawed at her. Where were—

Several loud bangs filled the air as the doors off to the side banged open and waves of combatants from both sides poured into the room. Except they had come too late. The Worst Boys were supposed to storm in the moment she had sipped her tea. Now she was surrounded and there was no way for her to escape. Part of her wondered if this was by design. The underworld was not trustworthy.

The Worst Boys were wearing flashy, colorful undergarments that exposed skin and muscles. Most were unarmored or wearing only leather padding. They wielded clubs, maces, and bats, typical of young, half-trained yolks in their line of work. They screamed the worst battle cry she had ever heard.

"Let's get ugly!"

The displayguards formed two rows along both sides of Taishi and Oban. They met the mob without conceding a step. Their large circular shields, each painted with a tiger, locked side by side like a wall. The odds were ten to one, a hundred Worst Boys against only ten displayguards. Still, the outcome was in doubt. The displayguards were some of the best soldiers in the Enlightened States while the Worst Boys were some of the worst. A professional soldier was easily worth two or three civilians. An elite soldier like a displayguard was worth ten, making the odds relatively even.

Taishi caught a glimpse of Beautiful Boy leading from the back, barking at her captains and shoving them forward. She caught sight of Taishi and acknowledged her with a dip of her head. Taishi looked away. Just because this was the right thing to do didn't make it any less shameful. She couldn't help but approve of these elite displayguards who kept their discipline against such overwhelming numbers.

The Worst Boys advanced into the lines of displayguards with a mighty crash that reverberated throughout the tall ceilings of the main temple, sending a flock of turtledoves flying around the rafters. The displayguards soaked up the charge without conceding a step, and then the killing began as they methodically hacked at the boys, driving them back and batting them around like rodents. The unarmored Worst Boys looked small next to these heavily armored elite ducal guards, but even a mighty lion could be dragged down by a plague of rats.

"I did not think treachery was in your blood," yelled Oban, drawing his blade.

Taishi kept hers sheathed. It was pointless. There was no chance she could defeat the captain of the guards standing by the high lord's side. Instead, she bluffed, staring contemptuously at the high lord. "Put that away before you hurt yourself."

Oban looked uncertain. The captain of the displayguards made no move. He was even more wary of her. As long as everyone still believed in her legend, Taishi was safe. That is, until someone tried to actually fight her; then her lie would be revealed.

"What did Sunri offer you, Taishi? A lordship? An estate?"

Taishi scoffed. "You must think little of me if you think that will win my loyalty."

"What is it, then?" Oban sounded anguished. She would have been disappointed if he hadn't. The two had known each other for over three decades. It was he who had first summoned her to the imperial court to train the younger son of Emperor Xuanshing, may his greatness ever last.

He deserved the truth. "You aren't fit to rule anymore, Oban. Your pride has blinded you. You've lost sight of your duty."

"I'm defending them, their homes, their freedom, their lives!"

"You're sacrificing them for revenge."

A displayguard slumped over, the first casualty. There were over half a dozen Worst Boys lying at his feet. Soon another fell, and the line broke, the battle disintegrating into a general brawl. It was a messy way to war. The fight soon spilled into the adjoining hallways and rooms, and out to the main prayer hall. The captain couldn't stand by Oban's side any longer as the random violence quickly engulfed him into its chaotic melee. That left Taishi and Oban standing quietly facing each other, strangely serene, two eyes of the storm.

"I can't beat you," he said.

"So don't try."

"I can't believe you would work for these vultures."

"I don't work for anyone. I'm doing this for free."

That gave Oban pause. "You must really despise me, then."

"On the contrary. I admire you greatly. But in this case, you're simply wrong and you refuse to turn from this path you've set."

A hush fell over the melee as a stampede of war monks crashed through the side doors. Nine Hansoo would wipe the floor of this entire rabble with ease.

Oban waved at them. "I am the High Lord of Shulan, Protector of Vauzan. Traitors have ambushed me. Defend your lord!"

The lead Hansoo acknowledged Oban with a nod, wading into the thick of the fight and swatting aside any Worst Boy who came within reach. The casualties began to grow even quicker. A ripple of panic passed through the thugs. Criminals were often the most pious, and none of them had signed up to fight clergymen, especially the giant ones.

"Taishi! Taishi!"

She looked over and saw Beautiful Boy cupping her hands over her mouth, shouting. When she was sure Taishi had noticed, Beautiful Boy pointed toward the Hansoo. "You have to call off your dogs! They'll slaughter everyone and we'll lose Oban."

"What am I supposed to do? I can't stop them," Taishi shouted back. "They won't listen to me."

"You're the dowager nun. Do something, hurry!"

She *was* a dowager nun. While largely ceremonial, she was high in the temple hierarchy. She watched as a tidal wave of Hansoo plowed through the thugs and displayguards alike.

Taishi yelled over the din. "Halt, Hansoo, uh, by order of the Grand Dowager Nun of the Black Orchids. The devout of the Tiandi must remain neutral in this conflict."

Oban sputtered. "Are you mad? A bunch of criminals attacked a high lord on temple grounds, and they're just going to stand there?"

"That's exactly what they're going to do," Taishi barked. "I am a dowager nun, the highest of the Tiandi faithful."

"And I'm the bloody ruler of Shulan." He roared back, "She's not even a real dowager!"

"Blasphemy!" one of the Hansoo growled. Taishi wasn't sure whom he was aiming his anger at.

"Are you going to allow such disrespect thrown upon the Tiandi?" Taishi was as good at sounding indignant as any opera performer.

"You fraud!" Oban attacked her. He drew his straight sword and charged, hacking like a child the first day they're given their wooden blades. Taishi deflected the first few swings easily enough, guiding each vertical chop to either side. She forced herself to remain stoic, which expended even more energy. It was harder for Taishi than she cared to admit.

After a few futile attacks, Oban pulled back. He slouched, huffing and puffing, and watched as another displayguard fell. Then he charged her, wildly swinging, face contorted with desperation. The blade came at her at an awkward angle, catching her in mid-step. Taishi didn't have time to dodge or deflect it, so she parried.

The two blades met. Neither budged as their strength canceled each other out.

No one was more surprised, however, than Oban. "How is this possible? You're not the real Ling Taishi. What wretched spook are you?"

"Don't be a soft egg, Oban."

"How can you be so weak?"

"I'm dying, you lummox. What's your excuse?"

The high lord surprisingly gave an honest answer. "I find the practice of war arts boring. Force is nothing more than solutions for the feebleminded."

"I don't disagree." Taishi had to try at least one more time. "Allow Shulan to negotiate, Oban. That's all we ask."

"It is beyond me, Taishi. My oath is my word."

Another two displayguards fell. It was turning into a rout. The Worst Boys crowded in, while off to the side, the nine Hansoo stood along the far wall. Their arms were crossed and faces impassive. Oban was beginning to realize his precarious situation. He began looking for an escape.

It was too late. He turned to flee but came face-to-face with Beautiful Boy. He backed away and tried to flee the other way, only to see Taishi, or one of the Hansoo, or another of the Worst Boys. He was surrounded. Taishi had hoped he would surrender, even though she knew he would not. Oban might not have the ability or strength of a war artist, but his honor was no less strong. He swept his gaze across all, but then settled on Taishi.

"Honor is the way." Oban stabbed his sword into the ground, and then drew a dagger. There was only a brief moment of hesitation before he swung the dagger up and jammed it into his throat. Blood seeped from his mouth as he staggered, stepping unsteadily side to side.

"It is the only way," Taishi echoed, sadly.

Oban's face twisted as he labored for breath. "I go to the heavens with a pure heart. May Shulan stand for an eternity." Oban fell to his knees and collapsed.

"This is for all the fallen Worst Boys," said Beautiful Boy.

There were only three displayguards still standing after Oban fell. All three pulled away from their melee and raised their weapons as a sign of surrender. Then each turned their blades on themselves, slicing open their exposed abdomens in the gap just below their chest plate.

"No!" Taishi tried to save the nearest one. Shulan could always use more honorable warriors. But it was too late; elite killers were also efficient killers. All three were dead before anyone could stop them.

Taishi bowed her head, suddenly feeling very tired, very old, and very ready to lie down in the family tomb and call it a life. Footsteps approached. "Are you satisfied?"

Beautiful Boy stopped at her feet. "I already have a messenger en route to Lady Saka. She can notify the Caobiu. There may be a temporary ceasefire by tonight." She sounded assured, optimistic even. "I can't remember the last time I slept through an entire night."

"Don't get your hopes up, girl. The Shulan Court will not let this go unanswered. Oban wasn't wrong, either. The Caobiu are decidedly unfriendly toward the underworlds."

Beautiful Boy shrugged. "If his death saves thousands, then there is no price too high."

"Now hold up your end of the deal."

She nodded. "We can box you up and ferry you out tomorrow night with the weekend smugglers' run."

Taishi shook her head. "It has to be tonight. Jian needs to be out of Sunri's reach before negotiations with the Shulan Court begin. Otherwise, she'll use him as a bargaining chip."

Beautiful Boy considered. "It'll cost big boy coins."

Taishi remained adamant. "Then pay it. I just saved your city."

Beautiful Boy tapped her chin with her long finger and then nodded. "Very well. Meet me at the restaurant tonight. We'll take care of the rest." She looked around the room. "How are we going to explain this to the magistrates?"

Taishi shrugged. "There's nothing to explain. If there is peace by tonight, like you say, then no one will care."

"Best you leave right away," said Beautiful Boy. "The magistrates' hounds will be here any moment."

As if summoned, the beaded curtain leading to the prayer room parted with a clatter as a pair of cone-headed figures squeezed between the Hansoo. The first magistrate looked at the carnage in the room, his eyes went wide, and he promptly threw up. The second, obviously made of tougher stuff, drew what appeared to be a three-sectional staff and charged into the room.

"Surrender by order of the ducal magistrates." The conehead pulled up to Taishi and gawked. "Tai—I mean, Grand Dowager?" He looked over at Beautiful Boy and squinted. Then his eyes grew even wider. "Sasha? Guanshi Sasha! Is that you?"

"Xinde?" Beautiful Boy squinted back. "When did you become good-looking?"

CHAPTER THIRTY-NINE

SCHEMING

"You!" First Yazgur Huong spat at Sali as they stood in the barren dye room with the unlit furnace at the back of the loom factory. "What are you doing here? How did you know about this place?"

"Me?" Sali couldn't tell if this was a trap. It sounded like one, but it didn't feel that way. By the look on the First Yazgur's face, he was probably thinking the same.

Huong spread his legs as if about to pounce. The old man unclipped the pendant around his neck and loosed his heavy cloak, letting it drift to the ground. He rolled his shoulders and cracked his fingers. "Did Dai put you up to this?"

"Don't be absurd." Sali paused. "Actually, I'm not sure."

"Dumb buck, always scheming to get ahead instead of just doing his job. Kids these days have no patience. Always want to skip the line without doing the work."

Sali thought about her neophytes, Hampa, Marhi, and Wani, and shook her head. "No, that's just your kids. Mine learn and grow and will one day surpass me."

The two masters stalked each other. Sali's tongue was still coiled around its holster while Huong's fancy gem-encrusted oar stayed strapped behind his back. Sali had no intention of being the first to draw her weapon.

"Honor is the way," the First Yazgur intoned.

"It is the only way." Sali stopped and raised a hand. "Actually, no, it isn't. First Yazgur, you can step aside and let me pass. I have no desire to bleed you."

"Perhaps, but legacy is a heavy burden. Our ancestors see all." Huong lowered into an offensive stance with his left leg in front and knees bent as if he were sitting on an invisible chair.

Sali crossed her arms, unimpressed. She knew little about the gentleways style other than the fact that it was forgettable. By the looks of Huong's wobbly base, their mediocre reputation was well earned.

She tried once more to talk Huong away from certain death. Bad blood did not need to exist between their clans. "Legacy is just your ego seeking immortality. It has nothing to do with what's good for you or your people."

"Enough talk. I will not be swayed." Huong attacked, moving like someone his age who spent most of his time sitting on a cushioned chair. He charged her, throwing several looping fists, none of which had a chance of connecting. It was obvious those wild swings were just to close the distance as he dove in to grasp at her clothing.

Sali would have laughed if she hadn't been trying to show respect to an elderly person who called himself a master. Sali dodged the exchange by shifting her weight from one side to another. Knocking away one of his grabby hands, she sidestepped the other, then nudged him with an arm, sending him stumbling.

Huong righted himself and came at her once more, throwing several punches and a snap kick that didn't have much snap, or kick, for that matter. Once again, he hit nothing as she shifted out of his range.

This was a pathetic display. She couldn't believe anyone fighting like this could consider themselves a war artist, let alone a master. Such callous disrespect for the mantle of every master leading their sect irritated Sali. She dodged another roughshod flurry from the man and then stuck her foot out, tripping him and sending him tumbling to the hard floor.

Huong's face contorted and he was slow to get back on his feet. For a moment, the old man looked as if he had thrown out his back. He tried to unbend his back and grimaced. "Ugh."

Sali stood over him. After a moment, reverence for the elderly won out. She offered a hand. "If I may, master."

"You're a sweet girl, lass." Huong accepted her offer and clasped her hand.

Sali realized her error too late. The old man's grip on her hand was like a vise.

The gentleways master bounded to his feet as if gravity no longer touched him. Sali had only a moment to register her surprise as he torqued his body into her, slamming his hips into her gut. He threw her arm over one shoulder and tossed Sali onto her back. The impact rattled her bones.

She tried to roll aside but discovered that her hand was still attached to the First Yazgur. He dragged her along the ground, swinging her like an enraged little girl swings her rag doll, and tossed her into the stone wall. Sali's jaw struck the jagged stone first, setting the right half of her face aflame. She crashed to the floor with a thud and pulled away, but the First Yazgur still held on. The harder she tried to free herself, the harder he squeezed, until a shock reverberated up her arm as the bones in several of her fingers cracked.

Sali couldn't stifle her groan as she fell to a knee. She gritted her teeth. This hurt worse than the time Mali ran over her hand with a warsled. Sali launched a punch with her free hand, but Huong was ready. As soon as her other fist was in motion, the gentleways pulled her in the opposite direction and then cranked her hand again. Pain coursed through her body as her arm twisted like a wet rag. He threw her again, sending Sali crashing headfirst to the floor.

"Just because the gentleways do not participate in your chest-thumping sect games does not mean we are weak." His face appeared near hers. "Winning games does not make a sect strong. It just reveals your vanity."

Sali wasn't paying attention as she struggled to unravel this trap. As long as the gentleways master controlled her hand, he controlled her movements and could anticipate them. She tried to break free, twisting one way or another, throwing punches and kicks when the narrow opportunities arose. Every time, Huong would manipulate her arm to throw her off-balance.

Sali tried to punch him in the face; the gentleways master torqued her elbow at an awkward angle, flipping her onto her back like a fish. She tried to sweep his legs. He moved to the side, forcing her to roll with him. Next, Sali tried to scramble to her feet, but a quick yank slammed her face against the ground. Every time she regained her balance, he knocked her over again.

"Any other arrogant opinions on Sunjawa's war arts sect?" He cranked her wrist and sent fresh pain up her arm, then kicked her legs out from under her. This time, Sali nearly lost consciousness.

"I stand corrected," she admitted through grunts. "There's nothing gentle about the gentleways."

"Ha!" It was the First Yazgur's turn to brag. "You would be surprised how many times I've heard that." He twisted left, flipping her onto her back. "Ending a life makes you their killer." He twisted right, forcing her back to her feet, then he shoved her against a wall. "Controlling someone, however, makes you their master." The First Yazgur took several deep breaths before continuing. "I met your father once, back when he was a neophyte. He was even more brash and haughty than most. So arrogant, all you inner clans. Thought you 'true' Katuia were too good for the rim clans."

Huong paused his narrative long enough to pick her up off the ground and flip her over his shoulder like he was tossing a sack of grain. He pressed a knee against her chin, forcing her head to turn sideways. He paused. "Where was I? Yes, it was the Eternal Khan's birthday or wedding or some trite ritual. The spirit shamans demanded every clan, large or small, send a champion for some competition.

The gentleways creed disallows games, so Sunjawa sent me to concede every match."

Sali tried to buck him off, and partially succeeded due to her brute strength. She reached for her dagger at her waist. To her chagrin, the gentleways master now had control of both her arms. She had tried to twist away several times, but he stayed with her, countering her movements in a smooth dance. He wrapped her elbows in an intricate joint lock she couldn't even mentally untangle, giving him even more leverage. He took in a breath. "The viperstrikes didn't send just one champion. The entire sect arrived with their shiny green armor and perfectly shaved faces. They all sneered when I conceded to your father during our match. Instead of honoring my sect's creed, your father called me a coward and came at me with disrespect."

Sali knew her father well. That sounded like something he would have done. He was a good but narrow man, relentless and exacting with his perception of honor.

Huong leaned in. "And now your parents are dead, as is your sect. It will be the gentleways who bury the final viperstrike."

So much for sympathy. It was then Sali realized: Huong could not fight and talk at the same time. The old man's breathing was labored.

"The worst of them all, however, was the Khan." The old man huffed. "Have you seen a more puffed-up peacock than that entitled man-child?"

"Why are you fighting for Katuia if you detest them so much?" Sali stammered.

"Because your arrangement is no better than the Katuia and will likely get many more of my people killed."

She couldn't fault that logic.

Huong took another deep breath and was about to begin his narrative again when a movement off to the side caught his attention. He scowled. "You!"

Sali followed his gaze and saw Dai standing at the doorway. The Ninth Yazgur was staring down at them looking shocked and stricken, his eyes wide and brow furrowed. All the blood had drained from his face. He bowed. "First Yazgur, I . . . I . . . how . . ." He bowed a few more times. "I did not—"

"I'm going to have you quartered and torn into pieces, you ambitious wretch. I'll pluck your nails out with sharpened reeds and feed your fingers to rats." Huong sucked in a breath and prepared for another assault.

Sali twisted and slammed her left shoulder into his arm, breaking his grip on her. Before he could recover, she push-kicked him backward and sent her tongue snaking out. She stiffened the shaft and punched it into the gentleways master's shoulder.

"Yield, Master Gentleways," she intoned. Sali held the spear of her tongue firmly as the First Yazgur fell to his knees.

Blood spurted from Huong's wound. His face had turned white as he sagged. He stared at her with resignation. "I almost defeated you, viperstrike, even at my overcooked age."

"Aye, you did," she conceded.

"I would have ten years ago."

"Perhaps," she admitted, "but I wouldn't have offered a hand ten years ago."

"That is fair." The First Yazgur's long breaths grew steadier. "Your reputation is well earned, Salminde the Viperstrike."

The First Yazgur was older than her father. There was no honor to be earned here today. Respect, however, costs nothing. "The Sunjawa sect war art is underrated, Master Gentleways. For that, I offer my apologies. Now, please, surrender and let me pass peacefully."

"Very well, viperstrike, the fight is yours." Huong gripped the shaft of her tongue and slowly extracted the bite. Pain flashed in his eyes. "Honor has been satisfied. We are still enemies on the field but with a clean slate. Our honor is intact."

"Your honor still stands clean," she recited.

That was the best Sali could hope for from this encounter. She loosened the shaft of her tongue and snapped the coil back into her hand. It hurt. Three fingers were broken. She tapped her fist over her heart and bowed from the hip.

Before she could take a step toward the furnace stack, however, Ninth Yazgur Dai crept behind Huong. Sali wasn't sure what he was attempting at first, until she noticed the glint of a blade in his hands. Who was his target? She had no idea. Then Dai pounced. He looked at first as if he were lunging for Sali. Then, at the very last moment, he reached over and slipped the knife under the wounded First Yazgur's chin.

"No!" Sali yelled. "You don't have—"

Dai dragged the blade across Huong's face, spraying a fresh fountain of blood. After a few moments he let go, pushing the slumping body forward onto its belly.

"No! What have you done?" she cried.

Dai wiped the blood off the blade with the back of the murdered man's robes. "I had no other choice, Salminde. My life was forfeit the moment Huong survived this encounter. He would have boiled me alive as soon as you are gone."

Cold realization set in as a wave of numbness passed over her. Few things cut deeper into her soul than knowing she had been deceived and used. She leaped forward and wrapped her uninjured hand around his neck. "You set me up."

"I—" He choked. "It was for the greater good. Now Sunjawa can join your alliance."

That was when she realized. "The shock on your face was because you were surprised that I was losing. You set us up. You wanted the First Yazgur's death."

"I wanted Sunjawa to join your alliance," said Dai. "The First Yazgur refused to see this as an opportunity. I had to take the chance to free our people. Now that the first is gone, I can assume leadership of the clan. You can have a government friendly to the rebellion. Think of the good it will do both our clans."

Sali continued to restrict his breathing. A twist of her wrist would snap his neck. This conniving administrator who had dishonorably murdered his chief now wanted to ally with Nezra. What did that say about Sali if she agreed? But then, Nezra needed Sunjawa. It would give them a chance against Katuia. Her clan, her people, her family might yet survive.

Her grip around Dai's neck eased. "You're only Ninth Yazgur. There are still many ahead of you."

Dai rubbed his neck. "Don't worry about them. Numbers Two and Three are his wife and toddler. Four is too old and senile, and Five is only there for the housing benefits. He's a jellyfish. The rest I can manage. Our clans can be friends."

Sali was beginning to see the man in a new light. The hairs on her arms rose whenever he spoke. There was an oiliness with his words, slippery and hard to pin down. She had underestimated Ninth Yazgur Dai's skills in the court. Still . . . "Think of the greater good," she muttered. Perhaps there was a way to salvage this trip after all. "That would seem the practical choice."

"Agreed." He walked toward the furnace. "Come, I'll walk through the stack and see you to safety."

Dai turned a large, rusty metal wheel and opened the gate to the furnace's mouth with a squeal, revealing a long but low, dark passage. He pulled a latch from a nearby shelf and proceeded inside, with Sali close behind as they ascended toward a speck of daylight at a far point. The passage was cramped, half path, half steps, and enclosed by tempered wood. They were walking up the factory stack, out of the city.

"Was this your plan all along?" asked Sali.

They walked two flights in silence before Dai finally spoke. "The thought crossed my mind but I had not considered it. Not seriously, at least, until I learned of the First Yazgur's plan to betray you. I knew I had to stop him. I will do what is good for the clan."

It sounded plausible, but there were too many twists here in Sunjawa. Sali was beginning to doubt these yazgurs' words *and* their honor. "Shall we renew our talks then, future First Yazgur?"

"Of course," he said. "But not right this moment. Give it a cycle. Let the First Yazgur's death and his succession run its course. Return next year when things have calmed, and we will have a grand display of friendship pledging each of our clans' support as equals."

Sali grunted. Her old Nezra arrogance itched at the thought of calling a rim clan her equal. Bad habits were hard to break. Old Huong hadn't been wrong about her people. The reborn Nezra, however, should be relieved to have one more clan stand by their side.

They neared the end of the stack. Dusk approached, painting the sky purple and green. A fresh breeze flowed through the crown of the stack, carrying a refreshing chill. The stack had burrowed through the gigaweed walls and ended at an angle about thirty feet off the ground.

Sali stood at the rim of the stack and turned to her new ally. "Dai, I wish to convey my gratitude for supporting the rebellion, and I swear upon my hearth and my ancestors that your loyalty will not be misplaced."

The Ninth Yazgur, and possibly future First, stopped at the lip of the stack. "Head out. Circle around to your right. I don't know where your people are, but at least you'll be out of the city and free to search for them."

"May our hearths be warm and welcome," she replied, stepping out of the chimney stack.

"For you as well," he replied.

Sali spotted a point on the ground and stepped off, plummeting down to the wet, swampy earth below. She landed softly with her knees bent, just past the massive plant walls surrounding the city. She stood slowly, taking in her surroundings. The symphony of the jungle was quiet here. She could hear explosions in the distance. Was her pod battling the Liqusa? She hoped not. Daewon should be far away by now.

"Let's go find my quiet, skinny pod," she complained, stepping toward sunset.

Something struck Sali on the side of the head, staggering her. A body slammed into her from the back, sending her sprawling on her belly. More blows pummeled her face, body, and legs; each hit a ringing wave of numbness, pushing her further and further away from consciousness. The blows stopped hurting after a while, until finally, only a sliver of her mind remained, slowly sinking into oblivion. The last thing Sali saw was a blurred vision of a cloaked figure approaching. Sali closed her eyes and the world went momentarily dark. She flirted with the abyss before blinking her eyes open once more.

The blurry figure was speaking. "You have fulfilled your end of the bargain, yazgur. The spirit shamans will keep ours."

"Thank you, great one," Dai replied, still standing up above. "I look forward to a new age of cooperation between our two great clans."

Sali blinked, sinking back into unconsciousness once more. She shifted. No, she was being moved. This time she was barely able to open her eyes more than a sliver.

The figure grunted as he knelt down next to Sali, examining his catch. "Bind her well. Mystic, slumber weed for our guest. Alert Liqusa to prepare for the journey back to Chaqra."

"Your command, Will of the Khan."

ACT III

ACT III

CHAPTER FORTY

REACQUAINTED

M aza Qisami woke from her restless nap and nearly fell off her yellow dun mare. Shadowkills usually weren't horse people. She recovered her bearings, however, something shadowkills were exceptional at. She shifted in her seat and wished she had tied herself to her saddle so she could drift off again.

Instead, she took stock of her surroundings. It was drizzling this morning, or was it evening? She couldn't tell. This part of the world, where the Grass Sea and Grass Tundra met, was always gray. The last month had been absolutely miserable with cycles of thunderstorms, boiling humidity, and unpredictable howling winds. This was why most sane travelers stayed home during the third cycle.

Qisami glanced over at her small party. Marhi the Viperstrike was leading point. She had taken over the role of warchief ever since Salminde was captured. The young woman was trying her best; that was the best Qisami could say about her performance as interim warchief of Nezra. She just needed more seasoning.

Qisami craned her neck. Behind the three was a line of ten wagons with bulging beds laden with supplies. The caravan had left the rest of the clan two hours earlier, winding toward the lake plateau leading to the start of the Grass Tundra. The sequence of events leading up to this moment felt strange. Qisami had initially come to the Grass Sea because it was the only way to escape the penal colony. But she had also been curious to see Salminde the Viperstrike. No sooner had they connected than Salminde kicked Qisami off her vessel and promptly got herself captured.

Not Loud Not Fat was a stupid name for a boat or pod or whatever it was called, anyway.

By the time Daewon and the rest of the crew realized what happened to Salminde, it had been too late. They managed to track her down to the enemy city, a clan named Liqusa, but were too outgunned to mount a rescue operation. They had watched from a distance as the ugly, armored jerks paraded Salminde up the ramp and into one of their massive bone-shaped pods before rolling into the sunset. The viperstrike could be anywhere by now.

Marhi, riding a few paces in front, slowed and raised an open hand. "This is the spot."

They had just reached the plateau. In front was a large frozen lake. Sloped steeply to both sides were long descents that ended in a heavily forested valley. The other side of the lake was the beginning of the vast, barren tundra. Shobansa brought up the rear. The old man was miserable, shivering while riding a small white donkey. Nobody cared much for him, but he controlled the purse strings and supplies. The last two were on the council that led the Nezra clan. Qisami had met them a few days ago when they had rejoined the rest of their clan.

Qisami scratched her left forearm. *We are close.*

The reply came immediately. *You are not close! You are three days late.*

I am happy to see you, too.

No, fool! We do not have enough food and oil to make it back to the Happy Glow!

Qisami blew a raspberry. When did Cyyk get so mouthy? Her former grunt had been laying it on thick about their desperate plight during negotiations with the Exiles Rebellion, no doubt trying to sway the Nezra council. Shobansa, their chief negotiator, was a savvy businessman and not swayed. In the end, Nezra got the better deal. Both sides were desperate, but the penal colony was starving *and* freezing and now had many young mouths to feed. Qisami had on more than one occasion become offended on behalf of the penal colony, and had threatened to break off negotiations, causing a panic on the Happy Glow side. In the end, it worked out to everyone's mild dissatisfaction.

And weapons. The words scratched along her arm. *We can't keep fighting off both Caobiu and wild animals with shovels and pickaxes!*

After food, arms was the most pressing matter. Since she left, the Caobiu had attempted two supply-collecting expeditions to the colony. Both had been slaughtered, but the next one would certainly come in force. Cheap labor and abundant ore were two of Sunri's favorite things, and essential to powering her war machine. She would not let this mine go easily.

We got you, baby grunt. Don't you worry your ugly grunty head. Big sis is here. Qisami joined the front of their procession on top of a low bluff overlooking the frozen lake. This was the meeting place. The flurry pelting them was a mix of rain and sleet, or ugly snow as she called it. Visibility was poor past a few hundred feet. *Where are you? I don't see you.*

Took shelter in woods on the south end.

It took Qisami a few seconds to figure out which way was south. She pointed. "We go there."

Shobansa furrowed his brow. "That's not where we agreed."

"We didn't agree to be three days late either."

"I'll concede that point," he replied. He rode to the front with his little white donkey and signaled to the procession to follow. It was obvious to Qisami with the way his ass was sore that supplychiefs spent as much time on horses as shadowkills did.

They entered the wooded area full of short, gnarled trees. They looked to be in pain, with twisted branches that intertwined overhead. They passed a few downed trees, stumps recently chopped, which formed a straightforward path wide enough for a mining wagon. They continued deeper, following several lines of wheel tracks freshly disturbed in the snow.

They came upon a small clearing where a cluster of covered mine wagons formed a protective circle. It was quiet and still, save for the light flurries dancing through the woods.

Qisami rode deeper into the forest and appeared beneath the low forest canopy only *fairly sure* that she wasn't walking into a trap. The thought had crossed her mind that either Sunri or the Katuia might have gotten here first. It wasn't too difficult to fake bloodscrawl. Heck, Cyyk might be doing this willingly. She knew she probably would in his circumstances.

The bigger targets would be the Nezra clan leaders. Maybe Qisami was a tool for them to capture the Exiles Rebellion's leaders. The thought of selling out the Nezra chiefs for a quick score entered her mind. It didn't get far. She wasn't that type of bloodthirsty killer anymore.

She was still musing about the possibilities when she entered a small clearing where a circle of wagons huddled together. As she neared, a shirtless Cyyk, so skinny he was now all bone and tendon, emerged from under a tarp. He sported a terrible haircut with matted, clumpy hair. He certainly looked older. Prison life would do that to someone. He stretched his arms toward the sky and twisted to the side. Then he noticed her. "You're late."

Qisami waved. "Hey, grunty-baby."

"Like, really late." He looked her up and down. "You look well fed. Care to rub some of that off on the rest of us?"

She patted her belly. "We eat bugs all day. It's the Kati way."

He shrugged. "Bugs, rodents, worms, it's all the same to us at this point."

"That bad at the penal colony?"

"We don't call it a penal colony anymore. It's just home now, but yeah, it stinks." He lit a smoke stick and exhaled. "After we ate the first two supply caravans, the Caobiu brought a patrol, and then an entire company."

A company was a lot of soldiers. "How did you survive? You're not *that* good, baby grunt."

"Blizzard swept in and got a tenth of ours, but most of theirs." He chuckled. "The rest we clubbed to death with our mining tools."

"The Tiandi must favor your lucky ass."

"Nothing lucky about it. The Happy Glow is a terrible vacation spot. Did you bring the stuff we need?"

Qisami nodded. "Fifty sets of armor and spears, a hundred bows, and twenty barrels of fletching. The bows are Kati versions—small as a kid's bow—but that's all they make. You're also getting five catapult kits, twenty-five fire twigs, and one bixi track pod. All that's up the hill. No need to unload. We'll just swap wagons."

He nudged the nearby wheel with his toe. "Good, because the ones we brought probably wouldn't make it back."

There was a rustling coming from behind her. Shobansa and his donkey arrived at the clearing. Cyyk didn't give the man the chance to announce himself. His arm shot out in the newcomer's direction. Shobansa, definitely not a warrior, sat on his steed, looking startled as a rusty knife streaked toward him.

Qisami's arm flashed out as well, sending her own throwing star spinning through the air. She had been a breath behind Cyyk to react, but her weapon was quicker, and she was stronger. The two projectiles collided, sending both their trajectories safely into the woods.

Cyyk cursed. "That was my last good knife."

Qisami blew out a sigh of relief. "It would have been your last good life if you killed a Nezra chief."

"That crusty old candlesniffer?" He blinked. Cyyk looked confused. "I always thought a Kati chief would be more, I don't know, fearsome?"

Shobansa joined them. "I did not expect the Happy Glow's leader to look like a mangy puppy."

"I didn't expect the terrible rebel Kati leader to be a shriveled, shorn, seedless stick," he retorted.

"That's because your head is an empty sack," Shobansa shot back. He looked over at the furred people from the colony huddling against the frozen bite of winter. "Come, we'll meet at the hill to complete the exchange. We have a camp there. You'll be warm and well fed."

Cyyk raised his voice. "You hear that? They have food!"

Silence answered him. Finally, someone spoke. "Is it really bugs?"

"No, of course not," he replied.

Qisami stayed silent, but there were a fair amount of Katuia dishes that *did* involve bugs, usually as a garnish or flavoring. She kept that to herself, not that these spoiled kitties could complain. Qisami had reeled at the thought of eating bugs, but they were rather tasty once they'd been toasted over an open fire.

Several heads popped out of hiding places around the wagon. She recognized Big Lettuce and Badgasgirl, but not the other half dozen. Had she been gone that long? It had hardly been more than a cycle, but it already felt like a past life.

"Break the camp," Cyyk instructed. "The sooner we hit, the sooner we get food." He left Qisami to help.

"Hey," she said. "They can manage it. Come with me."

"But I'm the boss. I have to boss them around."

"They're driving wagons, not building a bridge. Come on, this is important." Qisami offered her hand.

Cyyk looked conflicted but allowed her to haul him over. They fell in next to Shobansa and continued back the way they came. Cyyk craned his head, staring back at the wagons until they turned the corner and were out of sight.

Once they were out of earshot, the supplychief pulled up next to Qisami. "Cyyk, I trust you have fulfilled your side of the agreement?"

He pretended to hedge. "Most of it. Maybe not the full mix but close, good enough."

Shobansa's narrowed eyes indicated that he did not think being close was good enough.

"We'll be able to ramp up the next shipment now that you've brought your supplies and armaments," Cykk continued. "We won't have to worry as much about starving or getting slaughtered for now, but we'll need you to up your quota by half on your next shipment."

Shobansa rebutted. "Can you up yours by a half as well?"

Cyyk blew a raspberry. "We all know how badly these scales are off. You have room to come down."

Qisami stared the supplychief down until he spoke. "We can do it for a quarter."

"Splendid!"

The three were still negotiating as they began their return route out of this low-hanging forest and back toward the plateau lake. The moment they emerged from the forest, the winds picked up, snapping at them from every direction. Qisami wrapped an arm around Cyyk's waist and buried her face into his back, feeling his rib cage protrude from his taut skin. He was a shadow of his former self. Qisami wasn't the feeling-guilty type, but his condition worried her.

"Does anyone else at the Happy Glow know how to run these shipments, or is it just you?"

"Big Lettuce is my second," he said. "Svent and Amara from the council back home are coordinating with the rest of the workers."

"Svent." Qisami snorted. She sensed some weight in that last sentence. "I need to know that if something happens to you, I dunno— you get mauled by a wayward polar bear—that the colony can still function. Nezra needs to know that their new supplier of ore is a dependable trade partner."

"Nothing will happen to me."

"That's not what I asked."

"Big Lettuce will know what to do. Did you know he used to be a professor at Sunsheng University?"

"What's he doing at a prison colony?"

"Yanso's daughter tried to seduce him."

Qisami rolled her eyes. Big Lettuce had a face that only a string of copper liang could get someone to love. "I don't believe you."

"He's a fine poet."

Marhi and the head of the caravan were still waiting as the small group began their ascent of the hill. Qisami kicked her steed and hurried ahead. There was another more pressing reason she wanted to get Cyyk alone.

"Do you have all your gear, grunt?"

"Piss me," he grumbled. "I forgot to get my last good knife."

"Don't worry about that. You're coming with me. I have an important job lined up. We're going to rescue Nezra's leader, Salminde the Viperstrike. It's going to be difficult, and we'll probably die, but it'll be so much fun. After we finish, we can go back to Zhuun lands and start a new life. Maybe go into the private contract beatings or rabbleguard work. Maybe even debt collection. That's always fun."

Cyyk stiffened. He must be thrilled to finally leave that hellhole. "What's the job? Listen, Kiki, I don't know how . . ." Her former grunt's mouth dropped when they reached the top of the hill overlooking the wet weed fields on the other side. He slid off the horse and stepped forward, eyeing the four large city pods grazing along the watery plains.

"See that skinny toothpick ship?" She pointed at *Not Loud Not Fat* parked in the distance, half hidden in a clump of weeds. "That's ours."

"Kiki . . ."

"Come on, I'll give you a tour." She offered a hand.

Cyyk didn't accept it. "Qisami."

She swallowed her annoyance. "What is it now?"

He hesitated. "I think I should go back to the Happy Glow."

"Nonsense. That hole is a waste of your talent. We're trained shadowkills, you basic lug."

"The colony is in the middle of the Grass Tundra. I'm the only way they can communicate with the outside world."

"It's just hauling ore. There's nothing to coordinate. We'll carve the colony a road after this is all put to bed, okay? We're in a hurry here." This time, she urged her yellow dun forward without him. If he wanted to walk the half mile down the slushy slope, then by all means, he could probably use the training.

"Qisami, you're not listening to me." Cyyk still hadn't moved. "What I'm trying to say is, I don't want to go."

"Very funny." She snorted. "Wait, you're serious. You want to stay at a penal colony in the Grass Tundra? You'd rather live in this stupid land than go back to civilization and running water and frost that doesn't freeze your nipples off? Do you really want to live the rest of your miserable life out there lost in some desolate corner of nowhere?" She was dumbfounded. "Why would *anyone* choose to live in a prison?"

Cyyk averted his eyes. "I met someone."

"What?" Qisami wasn't sure she heard that right.

"After the rebellion, the corners began to mingle. Her name is Huyyi from the Xing."

"I know Huyyi," said Qisami. "She's a slut, but that's what I like about her."

"Well"—he shrugged—"we've all lived different lives in the time before, but we're who we are now at the Happy Glow, and I prefer to live the way I am now. I didn't like myself that much before."

Qisami hated to acknowledge that she knew exactly how he felt. A grunt's life was forfeit if they refused the command of their cell. It was rarely enforced—grunts were hard to come by—but was often used as a threat to keep them in line. Not that she would ever do that to him. Cyyk knew where he stood with her. Besides, they weren't in a cell anymore. They weren't even shadowkills. They were discarded killers. Qisami bet the Consortium had probably raided all her accounts at her money holders.

She needed him. "One last shoot, baby grunt, come on. Do it for me."

"You're probably not coming back from this job, and you're okay with that." He shook his head. "I'm not anymore. I have someone to go back to."

Upon reflection, she probably wouldn't have taken it personally, but in the heat of the moment, she did. Qisami hissed, "Fine, you go live with your whore. See if I care! You'll never amount to anything more than a stupid baby grunt anyway!"

Before Cyyk could retort, Qisami slid off her steed and threw herself into Cyyk's arms. She held him tight. He was surprisingly gentle. Qisami hated to admit it, but she was feeling weepy. How pathetic. She pulled back. "Treat Huyyi well. Make lots of babies. I'll miss you, baby grunt."

Cyyk's face turned crimson. "She's already expecting. Found out the morning I left to see you."

Her former grunt's words affected her more than she cared to admit. Something about the idea of a little baby Cyyk running around sparked a sizzle in her heart. She broke into a grin and smacked him on the back. "Congratulations. Are you sure it's yours?"

CHAPTER FORTY-ONE

A SORT OF RETURN

Sali should have seen the double cross coming. The signs were all there. Dai had played his role perfectly. She would have been more suspicious of him had he not worked so hard to betray both sides. She had falsely assumed his patriotism was real, and that he had been powered by more than just ambition.

Sali was paying for that mistake by spending her days in darkness. She had been blindfolded, doused with slumberweed, locked in a box, and hooded over dozens of times since her capture in Sunjawa. She had lost track of how much time had passed, or in which direction she traveled. At one point, they must have reached the capital city, Liqusa. She could tell by the long, deep tones of the city's horns, the squeaking sounds unique to the Bone City's engines, and the way the pods swayed as the city traveled. Every capital city had its own cadence and rhythm.

After that, Sali was moved again, always blindfolded, unconscious, or locked up but never mistreated. The Katuia were not kind to their prisoners. Their culture did not believe in imprisonment. They usually just let people go or killed them. Imprisonment was just more mouths to feed.

Sali had prepared herself for the worst, a slow death or possibly torture. The spirit shamans certainly had cause to make her death as painful as possible. She had caused them a bit of hassle, yet no punches, kicks, or blades came. They even bathed her once, although it was more a dunking than anything else.

Sali spent many days dwelling on these heavy thoughts as her captors transported her several times over the course of many weeks. Much of her journey was spent lying prone inside a long, rectangular box. It was a tomb, albeit a surprisingly comfortable one, with soft hemp lining, a cushioned floor, and even a little pillow for her head. She had resorted to taking long naps.

With little else to do, Sali spent most of her time meditating, communing with her ancestors and making peace with what little time she had left. The best-case scenario was if the spirit shamans quickly eliminated her as humanely as possible. The worst would be if they made an example of her in the most public and humiliating way. That was the likely scenario, since breaking her would be the best way to shatter her legend and reputation and squelch any future rebellions. At least that was what she would do in their shoes.

The last leg of the journey felt different. It was something in the air. Her captors had drilled vents in her tomb, so at least they weren't explicitly trying to murder her. There was little moisture here, and the slight breeze that penetrated these vents held a distinct odor, earthy with floral notes, unlike the heavily fragrant and spoiled scents of the Grass Sea. Sali had raided the land-chained for many years and knew when she was breathing Zhuun air. What was she doing in enemy lands? Had she been sold to the land-chained and sent back to Caobiu to pay for her crime of freeing Nezra from slavery?

Her prison was constantly on the move until this morning, when it stopped altogether. It had been set down roughly on a firm surface, and then there was nothing. Sali could still smell the hot breeze. She rubbed her fingers together, feeling the dust in the dry atmosphere. Everything became still. The small rays of light poking through the breathing holes faded with the night. No meal arrived when it should. No one let her out to stretch her legs.

Sali was beginning to feel forgotten.

She spent the rest of her time mentally getting her affairs in order. She had long overcome the fear of dying, but embracing death was a whole different matter. She tried to make peace with her life, putting to rest the unfinished matters in her heart that hopefully would not continue to haunt her in her next life. The first loss was knowing the viperstrikes would end with her. That failure would be her legacy with her sect ancestors. Marhi and Wani were not ready. Sali hadn't gotten around to cutting a new sect totem yet. To allow the name of the viperstrikes to sink beneath the waves of the Grass Sea under her stewardship would be her eternal shame.

The next loss was even greater. Sali worried for the future of her people and her clan. She had served as their shield, saving them from slavery and leading them into exile. Her work was incomplete. Nezra was not out of danger, and they certainly were not free. Their enemies were still too many and too strong. The next generation of leaders and warriors she had trained were not ready to take her place. Sali wished she could have more time to prepare them for what lay ahead.

She had little else to do but meditate, not only to pass the time but to ward off the slowly mounting claustrophobia and insanity. The last mindful and most difficult bit that she struggled to find peace with was her family, or what little of it that was left. Sali had been born to the blood of hundreds: parents and grandparents, uncles and aunts, as many siblings and cousins as the stars in the sky. Now she was reduced to two: Mali and baby Hampa. Three if she included Daewon.

Malinde was the sister of her heart. She was so proud of her Sprout; the lass had come far. Sali just wished she could have spent more time with her. Ever since the exile, the two had been overwhelmed with their duties to their people. That was one of the main reasons why she had chosen to accept her fate instead of seeking a cure. Those last few days together would have been precious.

Baby Hampa changed that. Now Sali had a reason to live, not only for Mali or her people, but also for the future. She had intended to begin his viperstrike training the moment he came of age. She knew she could forge a great war artist out of him, one who would make her ancestors proud, even with Daewon's blood coursing through the lad's body. She had come around to Daewon. The young man had proved himself worthy of Malinde, and then some.

Eventually, Sali ran out of stamina to meditate and patience to stay still. Her body had stiffened from staying still for so long, and her empty stomach ached with hunger. Worse, her body had been shriveling due to dehydration, especially in this dry heat. Sali had resorted to drinking her own sweat, but it was only a matter of time.

She was dying.

After what certainly felt like days, Sali couldn't take it any longer. She banged her fist against the cover of her tomb, hoping to attract attention. The heavy wood rattled with each *thunk*. She hit it three times, and then three times more. There was no response. Sali had grown so weak during the course of her captivity that even that effort caused her to become short of breath.

After several repeated attempts of knocking followed by silence, Sali's frustration boiled over. She tucked her knees up to her chest and pressed her feet against the lid and kicked with all her might. She had intended to strike the heavy wood loud enough to attract someone's attention. She was surprised when the lid exploded from the box, flying several feet into the air and then landing with a clatter on the ground.

Cool air swept over Sali, rushing into her lungs as if she had just nearly drowned. She had not realized how labored her breathing had become in that sarcophagus. Her mind dizzied as she choked on the large gulps of air. She pulled herself into a sitting position and hung off the side of her box, gasping. Her body was starved for breath as much as it was for water.

Sali stopped. Had this stupid lid been unlocked the entire time? That was impossible, or was it? She hadn't bothered to check.

She looked around. Her tomb had been placed on a table in the center of a circular room. No, it was octagonal with black walls. The ceiling was low and oppressive. Black stained glass windows lined the walls near where the frame touched the sloped ceiling rise to a midway point. Sconces dotting the walls were the only source of light. There was only one way out, an open door leading to more dimness.

Sali's joints ached when she pulled herself over the side of her tomb and rolled into a sitting position on the table. She paused. A sharp pain shot up her leg with the first step, followed by another on her second. Straightening her back felt like she had just snapped it. A shudder seeped through her as she hobbled, swaying side to side as she took one slow step at a time.

That's when she smelled it. Off to the side, on a long rectangular table, was a spread of food. Real Katuia cuisine, the sort available in capital cities. Sali's stomach nearly forced her to it. She grabbed a pitcher of water and tipped it to her lips, pouring most of it down her chin and neck. Next she fell to a knee and pawed at a pie of fried bread, bending it in half and stuffing the flakes in her mouth. The dried meat came next: sweet barbecue and orange strips. She skipped over the cubed cheese. Even starving didn't make her that hungry. There was a cup of fermented mare's milk for good measure. It went straight to Sali's head the moment she sipped. She continued down the table, picking at the foods that brought memories of her former life. She wasn't ashamed to be wistful for that ignorant existence. She could never go back, but that didn't mean she didn't want to.

Sali reached the end of the table, where a rack of cooked goat waited. It was still somewhat warm. Sali picked up the long meat cleaver and was about to hack at the slab when she stared at her hand. This was a strange weapon to just leave around a room where a prisoner was being kept. What sort of trap was this? Then she smelled the cooked meat and forgot her worries, cutting slices and stuffing them into her mouth. She stopped to grab a pitcher to wash down her food. Iced mandarin tea. It was her favorite growing up.

She stuffed a few more bites in her mouth and then hefted the cleaver in her hand. It was time to escape.

Escaping the city pods shouldn't be too difficult. There were always dozens of places to drop. She just had to get out of this building and to the street level, then it was a simple matter of biding her time for the right moment. Sali picked up the cleaver and crept through the entrance.

Sali could feel her strength return with each step. She continued down the dimly lit tunnel to the next room, under an arch that was so black she felt like it sucked her in as she stared at it: vantam glass. Sali averted her eyes. She continued into the room, where a small fire crackled in a glass hearth at the bottom of a depression.

"Three days, Salminde," a deep voice rumbled from the side. "I was wondering when you were finally going to break free. I have to say, I'm disappointed."

There was movement out of the corner of her eye. Sali's hand shot out, flinging the cleaver at the source. This was the enemy stronghold. Kill first, ask questions later.

To her surprise, the figure caught the projectile in a large hand mere inches from his face. He held on to it briefly and then tossed it aside. The large mountain of a man stepped into the light, the muscles under his loose shirt rippling. His hair was long and luxurious, while his goatee was pulled to a point. Most intimidating were his eyes, sunken and intense, but familiar.

"You . . . it can't be . . ." Sali's mouth dropped open. Her body became numb, and her hands began to tremble uncontrollably.

"Hello, Salminde," said the Eternal Khan of Katuia. "It is good to see you again, my old friend."

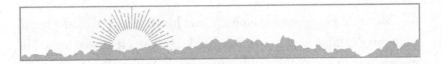

CHAPTER FORTY-TWO

RECOVERY

Jian woke up in a cold, strange place. His head felt like a crushed melon and his throat like a dried lake bed. He groaned, rolling side to side like a turtle rolled onto his back until he noticed the hundreds of small needles sticking out of his arm. He frowned, wondering where he was. His body felt heavy and unresponsive. His vision slowly came into focus and settled on a gray-robed figure slumped over a table. It was a small woman with long, curly hair pulled up in a haphazard way, with her face half buried in her arms. On the table next to her were several water jugs lined up in a row.

Déjà vu washed over Jian. A dull pain throbbed in his chest. For a moment, he was taken back to when he saw the flash of a spear blurring through the air. Then his body went into shock and shut down. He blinked and recalled another, similar pain, a death touch to his heart. That too had sent him into darkness, where he had awoken to his body full of needles at the Longxian war art school's infirmary. He had awoken thirsty and had called out. . . .

Jian squinted at the woman snoring lightly at the table. No, that can't be. It was impossible.

"Mee . . ." He opened his mouth, and his gaze locked on the jug of water on the table next to her. Survival kicked in. He pawed for it. His tongue was so numb he couldn't properly formulate the words, so he moaned.

The figure woke with a start and turned to him. "Jian, you're awake!"

His sight was still hazy. He could barely make out a pair of big spectacles over large moon eyes. There was no mistaking that squeak in her voice, however. "Mee-hayyy!" he slobbered.

Meehae rushed to his side. Their embrace was decidedly one-sided. Jian couldn't lift his arms, so he flopped them. His friend expertly embraced where there were fewer needles in him. She passed a hand over his forehead, stuck a finger in his ear, and another over his wrist. Then she squeezed his cheeks to force his mouth open.

"Tongue's still too hot," she muttered.

Several long needles, each a finger's length, appeared in her hand. His eyes widened. These were bigger than the ones she used the last time he saw her. She plucked them one by one and pushed them into the soft flesh of his hips just above the kidneys. Jian somehow felt pain through the numbness. He opened his mouth and wailed like a yawning bear.

"Make me numb again," he whined.

"I'm pulling you up slowly," she said, stabbing the side of his head with three more needles. Then she pinched a needle embedded over his chest and began to spin it between her fingers as if turning a knob. The numbness gradually faded, which was unfortunate, because his chest began to throb in its place. His breathing became painful. Jian struggled to sit; that hurt too. He reached for the jug of water on the table. Raising his arms *really* hurt.

Jian bit back the discomfort as he grasped at the jug.

"Oh, right." She rushed over and brought the pitcher. He snatched it from her with his lobster hands and brought it to his lips. Jian's tongue was so numb most of it dribbled out of his mouth. Bit by bit, the sensation returned to his dried and cracked lips. The first thing he noticed was the ice chill of the water, so cold it felt like thin blades slicing his throat. He shuddered with both agony and pleasure. He finished the first pitcher and gestured manically for another, which Meehae promptly obliged.

"Slow down, coconut tree," she murmured, "before you get sick."

The warning came too late. Jian had just tossed aside his third pitcher and was about to bring the fourth to his lips when his stomach rebelled and sent the liquid back up, which met the water going down, causing him to lean over the side and spew everything into an empty wooden trough next to the bed.

Meehae waited patiently. She brushed her splattered robes. "Gross. I just had these washed."

Jian spent several more long moments dry heaving. When there was nothing left, he raised his head, exhausted again, his tongue hanging loose. He looked at the other six pitchers remaining on the table, then at the trough, and then back up at Meehae. He was breathing heavily. "Why can't I stop drinking?"

"I had to put you to sleep while you healed. You've been out for over a month," she explained. "Your body slows during hibernation, but it still requires sustenance. I can only put a few drops into you at a time, else you risk choking. The needles are so strong, your body doesn't know to spasm or contract when it needs to."

His mind slowly cleared. He glanced down at his chest, noticing the bloodied bandage. That was where every breath hurt. His memory returned to the moment the spear struck him. He shuddered.

"How am I alive?" he asked.

"You almost weren't," she admitted. "You were near death when you arrived at Skyfall Temple. The court healers could only do so much, but they managed to keep you stable until you arrived. I've been tending you since."

"You saved my life? That's twice now."

Meehae beamed. "Maybe becoming a master healer to save you is my destiny."

"You're a master now?"

"Not in experience, but certainly in skill." She sniffed. "At least around here."

Where was here, exactly? Jian looked for a clue. They were in a small room with tall ceilings framed by nearly white wood. The furnishings were plain but crafted with care. The lacquered bedpost he was holding on to was finely sanded smooth and had a shine. There was one large window on each wall, all shuttered but not tight enough to prevent a breeze from passing through. He noticed droplets forming on his arm where a few of the needles were stuck. Everything felt . . . moist.

"Come on, let's get you moving and loosening those joints," the apprentice acupuncturist—sorry, the *master* acupuncturist—said, looping her arm around his waist. Meehae helped Jian swing his legs off the bed. He planted his feet gingerly on the ground. The atrophy in his body was real. Everything hurt, as if his joints had rusted shut. His knees nearly gave out as he put weight on them. He would have fallen if Meehae had not been there. The two walked ten careful steps before Jian needed to catch his breath. Then they walked five more before he needed another break. The only thing keeping him upright was his friend.

Jian noticed her iron grip as she held him up. Studying his friend more closely, he realized she was not the same person he last saw leaving the Cloud Pillars. They were both teenagers when they met in Jiayi. He had arrived as a dying fugitive, while she was a freshly anointed apprentice. Both were trying to find their place in the world. That was probably why they had grown close. Meehae was a woman now, with strong, callused hands and weathered stone in her demeanor. Gone was the impulsive and sometimes girlish apprentice acupuncturist; she was a woman confident in her art and in charge of her responsibilities, including Jian.

Jian smiled. That hurt too. "It's good to see you. How long has it been?"

She considered and then shrugged. "I've lost track. I remember the world felt sane when I fled Jiayi with you to the Cloud Pillars. When I returned to the world, however, the land was at war. The world has been on fire since."

He wrapped his arm around her and squeezed. "It's a good thing you're here to heal it."

"And you to put an end to it."

"That remains to be seen," he muttered.

The Mosaic of the Tiandi had spoken often about the peace that would sweep across the Enlightened States after the prophesied hero killed the Eternal Khan of Katuia. How that would come to fruition was still a mystery. Jian didn't feel any closer to fulfilling that destiny now than he had when he left the Celestial Palace what felt like a lifetime ago.

It took them five minutes before they reached the ten steps to the doorway. A curtain of humidity blasted him as they left the room and entered a covered walkway outside. The bellowing wind filled his ears even as the air, weighed by wetness, swirled around him. The sky felt low with fat, dark clouds hovering just above the tops of several pointed towers.

"Where are we?" he asked.

"You don't know?" Meehae sounded surprised. "Well, of course not, you baby chick. You probably slept the whole way here." She led him to the edge of the stone railing overlooking a vast green land that stretched below for so far the horizon was shrouded by mist.

Jian's mouth dropped. This was the most magnificent view he had ever seen. They were in a fortress halfway up a mountain. Before them unfolded a wide expanse of green grasslands and winding rivers that stretched as far as the eye could see, all the way to the edge of a gray mystical haze. To his left was a sheer cliff that began on the ground level far below and rose into the low clouds above. On the side of the flat, gray stone was the unmistakable carving of the Mosaic of the Tiandi some five stories tall and so wide that Jian had to squint to see the edge of the mosaic.

The architecture was understated but elaborate, with heavy lacquered frames, tall arches, and curved lines adorned by exquisitely detailed statues and paintings. The paths running along the ground revealed gardens, both green and stone, as well as beautiful, twisted bonsai trees and meditation circles. The most striking, however, were the waterfalls. They were everywhere, hundreds of them plunging from towering heights to long aqueducts to cascading steps. A low roar rumbled in the background as the falling water sprayed a constant mist, giving the scenery a mystical if not mythical ambience. There was something about the mixture of the King's rays and the haze surrounding the mountain that made water from the falls appear to be falling upward, thus this mountain's namesake.

"Am I dead? Is this the Heaven's Gate?" Jian murmured. For an instant, he wasn't sure, because he was too awestruck to believe a place so beautiful could exist. He looked at Meehae. Wait, if he was dead, then . . . "Are *you* dead?"

"Don't be absurd." Meehae giggled. She reached over and booped his nose with her finger. "This is Skyfall Temple, home to the High Seats of the Tiandi in Lawkan. This is the beating heart of the religion built solely around *you* and *our* salvation. You're finally home, Wen Jian."

CHAPTER FORTY-THREE

HENGYEN

Taishi sat at the window of the Limp Stick, a cozy noodle shop on one of the side streets of Hengyen, a small village nestled at the base of the edge of Skyfall Temple, watching the closest intersection. Half the people were locals while half were clergy, with a few travelers sprinkled in.

She scooped two more unenthusiastic spoonfuls of soup into her mouth and leaned back. Taishi never cared for Hengyen. It was a weird place. The village felt sterile, almost artificial. The streets were neatly arrayed to form squares, the foliage was regularly manicured, and the village magistrates made their rounds with the steady drips of a water clock. Everything here felt fake. At least the streets were clean. They were eerily clean, actually. Not a piece of trash or vagrant in sight.

The wealth of the Tiandi religion was stored in a vault deep within Skyfall. The monks were fabulously rich, which they used to generously subsidize the needs of the settlement. The villagers lived leisurely and generally wanted for nothing, which meant there were many idle hands and minds. Work was, for the most part, optional.

Furthermore, Lawkan rested on blessed, fertile lands and abundant resources, so everything was cheap. Taishi's lunch cost only half a copper. She was fairly sure the restaurateur was working for fun. It was unnerving. Not only that, but the food was also awful, the entertainment scant and amateur, and it seemed like every piece of artwork was the damn Mosaic of the Tiandi. That thing was everywhere: from that monstrous carving along the side of the mountain to every wall facing the streets to the side of the wooden cup she held in her hand.

To make matters worse, she was drinking squeezed dragonfruit juice. Because this was a dry village, alcohol was forbidden in the settlement.

Not being a fan was an understatement; Taishi hated Hengyen village.

She sniffed, turning her attention back to her bowl of noodles. The food was bland, mushy, and salty. The Lawkan loved to heavily salt their food. They doused salt on everything, even their candy. She scowled at a six-wing bug that landed on her salt-rimmed cup. Even the insects were alien.

The journey from Vauzan to Skyfall had been uneventful but at the same time, harrowing. Taishi had remembered the oracle's last words to her and had planned the treacherous journey to bring Jian to Skyfall Temple. That meant sneaking past tight Lawkan blockades and entering a war zone. An army entering Lawkan would have invited pitched battles, so Taishi opted to sneak past the naval blockade with a small group.

The journey took two weeks by cart, barge, wheelbarrows, and junks. They were fortunate to have made it without incident, but her nerves had been on edge the entire time. One encounter with a Lawkan patrol would have been the end to their journey here. Taishi was relieved that she had prayed for luck before she left the Vauzan temple, because that luck held.

She eyed a large group of blue-robed university students when she sighted a familiar face. The boy, around twelve, wore apprentice robes and had his face partially covered by a round bamboo hat. She recognized his gait, however, as he crossed the street, stopping to bow to every monk who passed. That was another reason Taishi disliked the village. Not bowing to a monk was considered poor etiquette. The problem was there were so many damn monks it would take all afternoon just to cross the street.

The boy finally made it into the shop. His gaze swept across the room, locking on to her. Then, with forced casualness, he passed by where she sat and placed a folded note next to where Taishi had spilled some of her soup.

He continued walking.

Taishi unfolded the note and squinted at the soaked paper. The ink had smudged, blurring the small Zhingzhi words running up and down the page. It didn't help that her vision had deteriorated to the point where she had trouble seeing things up close. She looked over at the messenger boy and pulled one chopstick from the wooden cup on the table. Holding it up like a throwing knife, Taishi flung the chopstick, spinning it through the air, clipping the boy in the shoulder. Fausan would have had a field day mocking her with that poor throw.

"Hey, what did you do that for?" the boy yelped, spinning back to her. He must have realized his outburst too late because his face turned crimson. He pressed his palms together and bowed. "I mean, is there something you require, mistress?"

Taishi waved the wet note between her fingers. "Ink's smudged, boy. Pull up a chair and tell me what it says."

He looked like a startled rabbit. "I'm not supposed to talk to you."

"Come on. I'll buy you lunch."

He at first looked tempted, then reconsidered her offer and took off sprinting down the street. She grimaced as the boy disappeared around the corner. Trying to bribe someone with food here in Hengyen was like trying to bribe them with air. The food might taste like grimy ocean water, but it was hard to beat free.

Taishi's reading level had never been high. She had just enough literacy to enjoy a Burning Hearts romance novel. The words in this note by now had diffused into black blotches. It took her several passes.

One set of words indicated the "patient," which was obviously Jian. Then there were three blurred lines that ended in the word for . . . death.

Taishi's heart stopped. She looked up—death. Knocking the plate over and sending the rest of the contents onto the floor, she took off running, darting onto the street and shoving her way through the crowds. The crowds in Hengyen were usually orderly. The monks led by example, shuffling down the streets in neat lines.

She personally preferred her traffic more chaotic. Here in Hengyen, however, she found herself bowling people over as she shoved her way through the crowds. Finally reaching the main road leading to the front gates of the temple known as the Gaping Mouth of Refreshing Bliss, she began the long trek up the winding path. She didn't make a hundred paces before she became winded. Every time she had gone to the temple, she had done so in a conveyance. Only peasants walked.

Taishi approached the front of Skyfall Temple, which was made up of three double-wide wooden gates that swung inward. When closed, they revealed another painting of the Mosaic of the Tiandi. Of course. There were at least six Hansoo always standing guard at the entrance. It was an ostentatious display, given the rarity and value of the Hansoo ranks, even if they were only initiates with one ring on each arm. The six were still strapping young men, each easily over six feet tall with shoulders twice her width and arms as thick as her torso.

She passed through the outer wall and into a long tunnel, which was gold-plated on the sides with still another tiled mural of the mosaic running along the ceiling in case someone forgot what it looked like. The temple's public square was a replica of the one at the Vauzan Temple of the Tiandi. Or more precisely, the Vauzan temple's public square was modeled after Skyfall Temple's. In fact, every public square of every major city used the same blueprint. Familiarity comforted the masses, which in turn meant larger tithings, as the logic went among the temple management.

She reached the main temple stairs and began her long ascent. The infirmary was on the sixth level and required navigating some forty separate flights going every which way. Taishi couldn't believe

there weren't any lifts. It was practically criminal. Of all the technolo-
gies the Tiandi religion chose to forbid, this one would have been the
most useful. She reached the wing on the sixth level overlooking the
western end of the village. By then, her legs were as wobbly as a new-
born foal while her right foot hurt like she stepped on a caltrop. Taishi
pushed away the aches as she half ran and half limped down the long,
covered stone bridge to the entrance.

Thinking nothing of the two five-ringed Hansoo flanking the doorway, Taishi stormed toward the door. Large beefy Hansoo hands moved
to block her way. She nearly ran into a dirty palm. Taishi looked up at
the man twice her height. "What are Hansoo doing here, brother war
monk? This is beneath you."

He grunted, obviously agreeing. "The infirmary is under watch.
The Tiandi Dawn has arrived. No souls may pass through without the
blessing of the Seats."

The High Seats of the Tiandi were the council of the highest abbots, which ruled the Tiandi religion. Someone at that table had ordered this.

"The Seats were thrilled when I brought Jian here." Taishi tried to
push her way through. "He is my ward. Stand aside."

The two Hansoo did not budge.

"Remove your hands or I will tear your arms off at the elbow."

The two remained unfazed. Taishi had to know what happened to
Jian. It was pointless, however. The two handled her easily, pushing
her back gently but with enough force that she nearly lost her footing.

A surge of desperation catapulted her forward. "Let me pass!" she
screamed. "Jian! Meehae!"

One of the healers walking by stopped and admonished her. "Show
some respect. There are sick here!"

Taishi managed to slip around the Hansoo's left big thumb and
squeeze past him toward the doorway. For a moment, it felt as if she
could break through. Then one picked her up by the back of the collar
like an errant toddler. Taishi's strength flagged, and her voice became
hoarse.

"What is the meaning of this?" Meehae stormed up to the two

Hansoo. "Release her at once. How dare you disturb the peace of my hospital!"

Meehae had developed some toughness since the last time she saw the girl. Taishi was impressed.

"Apologies, master acupuncturist," said one. "Seats' orders. Ling Taishi is forbidden from entering the Sixth Level West Wing."

"Why?"

He bowed. "The Hansoo do as commanded."

"This ward is my responsibility. My word is the law here."

"The Seats would disagree."

Taishi rubbed her temples. "Just shut up, both of you."

"Perhaps," a voice chimed in from somewhere behind her, "I can clarify the situation here."

Taishi watched as Meehae and both Hansoo dropped to their knees and prostrated themselves on the floor. Only one person in Skyfall Temple would elicit such submission from two Hansoo and a senior healer.

Taishi's mouth dried and her stomach dropped as she followed suit, turning to sit on her knees and folding forward as far as her creaky body allowed. She had not expected encountering such stakes today. "Voice of the Tiandi, you honor me."

This particular voice was a tall, stern nun, the scariest kind. She stared down at Taishi. "The High Seats of the Tiandi will have words with you."

There were few people these days to whom Taishi would show deference: the dukes certainly, the Prophet of the Tiandi, the Eternal Khan of Katuia, the Chief Executive of the White Ghosts, the Super Fire Guys war artist band she worshipped as a girl, and probably the author of those Burning Hearts romances. That was it. No one else within the Enlightened States remotely warranted such deference.

The Voice of the Tiandi swept her disappointed gaze across the group. She stopped at Meehae. "Master acupuncturist, we shall have words as well." She spun around and left.

"She's a battlenun, in case you're wondering," said Meehae, "from an extinct convent. She's the high seats' personal protector."

"I like her already."

"You want her on your side when you deal with the council."

"Good advice." Meehae fell in step alongside Taishi as they trailed after the voice. "What do you know about the high seats?"

"High Seat Galen," Meehae muttered through the side of her mouth, "is the sixty-fifth in the line of high seats since the inception of the organized Tiandi religion, and the eighth in the past decade."

"What happened over the past ten years?"

"Oh, you know, a certain Prophesied Hero of the Tiandi getting kidnapped or killed and then missing. The Eternal Khan of Katuia meeting his end on a common soldier's spear. The five dukes of the Enlightened States starting a war for the throne." Meehae paused. "Oh yes, the religion's slipshod rebranding efforts to discredit Jian, and then his recent reemergence as the Champion of the Five Under Heaven rising up with the Shulan to fight against the most hated woman in the Enlightened States, and now you bring him here while he's at death's gate."

In her shock to see the high seat, Taishi had forgotten why she was here in the first place. "What happened to Wen Jian? Your stupid apprentice tossed your note in water. I couldn't make out your message."

"Oh, Avi." Meehae shook her head. "You didn't yell at him, did you? He's a sensitive child."

"I threw a chopstick at him and then tried to buy him lunch, but who cares." Taishi sighed. "Is Jian alive?"

"Jian woke up this morning. He will be fine. He's weak as a panda cub right now but he should recover in a few months."

"Months?" Taishi frowned. "This is a precarious time, Meehae. Is there anything you can do to heal him faster?"

"The kid took a spear to the chest," the young woman replied. "What the healers here have accomplished so far is already a miracle."

"Forgive me, Meehae. You have my thanks." Up ahead, the Voice of the Tiandi turned up a wide flight of stairs toward the Eye Touches Heaven Chamber, where all the high abbots meet to rule over the religion. "Tell me about Galen."

"Old guard from the conservative faction of the abbots. Assumed the role of high seat after that rebranding fiasco with Jian being the villain of the Tiandi. He's a tyrant, but his heavy hand guides the devout through these turbulent times."

"A fair man, then?"

"I wouldn't go that far." Meehae kept her voice low. "Let's just say he has little tolerance for disruption."

They entered the chamber for the Seat of the Tiandi, which was the towering building at the head of Skyfall Temple looking down on the rest of the world. This elevation was nearly halfway up the mountain, but still within range of heavy ballistae.

They were met by initiates at the front entrance, who escorted them past the front facade and into a chamber that spanned three stories overhead. They were led at once to a hallway to their left, down a series of narrow passages. At one point, Taishi wondered if this was an assassination attempt, but eventually there was a light at the end of a tunnel that opened to the sky on the other side of the mountain. The blast of humidity soaked Taishi the moment the initiates stepped onto a small landing that overlooked a row of sharp teeth lining the horizon: the Jagged Peaks. On the other side was Caobiu Duchy.

"I stare at those same mountains every night."

Both Taishi and Meehae turned to see a tall man with a long, rectangular head and sunken features matched by broad shoulders. Meehae's round, wide eyes were even rounder and wider than usual. She was standing at attention as if she were a new grunt in the Caobiu army. Taishi found herself standing frozen like a fawn caught in a spotlight. She usually wasn't a fan of bald heads, but the High Seat of the Tiandi was a handsome man. She pressed her palms together and bowed.

"Master Ling Taishi, it is an honor to finally meet you." His voice was a strong but low baritone, resonating around the chambers.

She bowed again for good measure. "The honor is mine, high seat." She hated that her voice had become so breathy.

"It is my understanding that you were the one who returned the prophesied hero to the devout."

Again his word choice. Returning something usually means you had to take it in the first place. "I was the one who brought Wen Jian to Skyfall for treatment."

"Yes, after you kidnapped him from the Celestial Palace," he said. "I assume to train in the ways of the war arts. He was lost to the Tiandi for many years after."

His statements ended Taishi's adulation of him, or more specifically of his position. Galen was not friendly toward her cause and did not view her favorably. He likely had never trained as a war artist and seemed to look down upon the field as many academics did. More important, however, was that the high seat had offended her, and Taishi was too old and too tired to let that pass. This was her son's life that he spoke of so casually.

She lifted her chin. "The five dukes of the Enlightened States had just voted to kill him. I had hoped the Tiandi religion would have had the wisdom to prevent that atrocity from happening. When none of the devout presented themselves to do their sworn duty and protect the Prophesied Hero of the Tiandi, I took it upon myself to save his life."

Galen brushed aside her challenge. "Things had moved too quickly. The Seats of the Tiandi were still discussing the wisest path forward when the unfortunate event occurred. The dukes had demanded ultimate authority over his situation due to the exorbitant cost of his upbringing."

It always came down to money. "You declared him a villain to the very religion that is based upon him!"

"Mistakes were made by my predecessors."

"Mistakes?" She stepped toward the man and then remembered her place. "I appreciate your wisdom, high seat. What does our meeting now have to do with—"

There was an explosion coming from the direction of the Jagged Peaks. A cracking boom reverberated throughout the valley, shaking the ground, the trees, the buildings. The sky, blue and orange moments before, turned instantly gray and ashen.

The high seat stared into the horizon. He nodded. "I was expecting you sooner, old friend."

"What is that?" Meehae looked like a rabbit with a hawk approaching.

The high seat pointed into the distance. "There is a geyser along the Xing border that erupts wet sand every spring during the third cycle. Large plumes of wet sand clouds blot the sky for two, sometimes three days. It is a terrible and beautiful sight, a testament to the miracles of the Tiandi." He placed his palms together and bowed his head.

"Where does the wet sand come from?" Meehae asked.

"I was waiting for you to ask, master acupuncturist." Galen beamed, flashing many white teeth. "The geologists in the Tiandi thought trust believe there is an underwater tributary coming from the Sand Snake. The pressure mounts each year and the land must have its release. That is why the surrounding regions rumble every spring third cycle."

Taishi cut to the chase. "High seat, why have I been barred from visiting my ward?"

Galen's eyes narrowed but he kept his cool demeanor. "You, Ling Taishi, have served your people well. You saved Wen Jian. You trained him. You kept him safe. Most importantly, you prepared him to fulfill his destiny. For that, the Tiandi religion is grateful.

"However, you are now advanced in age, and your care has been worrisome. You brought him to us near death. Fortunately, the skill of our great healers"—he nodded at Meehae, who preened—"was up to the task. We may not be so lucky the next time. Therefore, it is the decree of the High Seats of the Tiandi to free you from your obligations to the Prophesied Hero of the Tiandi for those more suitable to see to his needs and development. You have brought him far, Ling Taishi. For that you are honored. The Tiandi religion will guide him the rest of the way."

Taishi had feared this. The thought of being cut off from her son was a spear through the heart. The only thing she feared more, however, was his death. "Wen Jian is a grown man but still young. The task ahead is great. He will need all our wisdom. Let us work together."

Galen bared his teeth. "Unfortunately, there are those in the high seat who fear that too many advisers could muddy the waters."

Taishi snarled. "Like hell you will. You will not take my son!"

The Voice of the Tiandi darted forward like a swooping hawk, planting herself between Taishi and the high seat, a slithering kris dagger in one hand half drawn from its sheath.

Galen continued, his tone mild as he turned away. "To avoid further confusing the prophesied hero, you are barred from all interaction with him. While your service to the Tiandi is appreciated, it is no longer necessary. We expect your business at Skyfall to be concluded at once. Thank you for your service, Ling Taishi." The high seat stopped at the doorway and glanced at her.

Then he was gone.

Taishi felt as if her heart had been ripped out of her chest. She could only stare, numb, as Meehae shot her an apologetic look and then hurried after the high seat.

CHAPTER FORTY-FOUR

NEZRA RIDES

Qisami had spent the past week bloodscrawling with Cyyk, at first trying to change his mind, and then venting her annoyance at him. The farther south the Nezra fleet moved, however, the longer it took for each to receive the scrawl. The downtime between messages allowed her to reflect on their circumstances. The white-hot anger and humiliation of his rejection cooled. She eventually came to accept his decision, if reluctantly.

Their conversation changed. The insults and threats became less sharp and more sparse, and in the end, disappeared entirely. Instead, Qisami asked Cyyk how he knew that little slut was the right person for him. She joked about how mortified his parents would be if his noble father learned about his new peasant wife. She even offered to gut General Quan Sah for Cyyk, as a favor.

Worry about killing your own ba, he bloodscrawled back. *I am taking a break from the lunar court.*

Going limp? Don't be absurd. But she understood. She felt the same. She just didn't have his courage to admit it.

Loneliness set in after a week when it began to take longer than a day to receive a bloodscrawl. Cyyk was the last link to her old life, and it felt like he was fading. They must really be far apart. That, or he had better things to do, like spend all of his stupid time with that little trollop.

Qisami felt smaller with each passing day. The last thing she had was gone: no Consortium, no shadowkill cell, no friends. She was all alone now. The silence hurt. It stabbed into her like a dull blade. She felt untethered, floating in the vast sprawl of the ether without knowing where she was or where she was going. What would she do with her life now? She had nothing to live for.

Sure, her father was out there somewhere, probably still alive and fuddling around some small, petty existence. Who knows, she might even have brothers or cousins. Maybe there was a chance she could reconnect with her family. In some ways, it hurt Qisami more to know she still had blood out there. Her family had long ago disowned and forgotten about her.

Not Loud Not Fat and the three other pods accompanying them returned to the bulk of the Nezra fleet a week after the ore exchange. One moment they were cutting through thick jungle and the next they emerged in what looked like a swamp.

These city pods, big floating boat cities with wheels, looked like they were from the same family of craft. They were beautiful structures with long curves and sloped lines to better slip through the wind, Daewon had said. These things looked organic, almost like living creatures. She could imagine them being brown-and-white land whales grazing in these shallow waters. Wani had told her that their pod was once part of a city called Kahun, but now it was Nezra.

"Why not just call it by its old name?" she had asked.

"Because we are Nezra," the viperstrike neophyte replied, puzzled.

"You can still be Nezra."

"Not if we're Kahun."

Qisami let it go.

Several smaller pod-boats converged on their craft, each sending flashing lights from their upper nests. The largest pod at the center of the fleet sent up a flare that exploded overhead. The *Not Loud Not Fat* began making its way toward the already dying sparks.

It wasn't long before *Not Loud Not Fat* joined a dense cluster of pods. Within minutes, ramps from all directions connected to their pod. Dozens of these Katuia came aboard. The crews greeted one another like long-lost siblings, full of hugs and laughter, and then they got to work unloading the cargo. Qisami and Daewon were on the main deck watching workers scurry like ants when a large procession joined them.

"Father!"

A child of around four years nearly got trampled by one of the mine wagons being offloaded as he sprinted between Daewon's legs. The tinker barked with joy as he picked up his son and tried to toss him in the air.

"When did you get so big?" Daewon's eyes were wet.

"You missed a great deal, heart of my heart."

Qisami looked over to see a familiar face approach. She had not been allowed near Malinde the tinkerchief when the *Not Loud Not Fat* first returned to the fleet, and for good reason. Qisami was a Zhuun *and* an assassin after all, and the clan was protective of their tinkerchief.

This small woman was obviously Salminde's sibling. She was a miniature version of her older sister. Their faces were nearly identical, but that was the extent of their similarities. Malinde ran the whole operation in her sister's absence.

She went to her husband, kissing him. After a loving reunion, Malinde turned to Qisami. "You are the one responsible for this arrangement with your colony?"

She nodded.

"It was a fair trade," Daewon interjected.

"Hardly," Qisami grunted. "The street price for this ore is twenty times the crap you gave the Happy Glow. We'll need to revisit the arrangement next cycle." She admitted, "Everyone wins though for now, so there's that."

"In any case, you have my thanks, Maza Qisami the Shadowkill," said Malinde.

"Former shadowkill," Qisami muttered.

But the clan leader had already moved on. Malinde had refocused her attention on the hive of activity on *Not Loud Not Fat*'s deck, overseeing the unloading of the ten wagons of ore. Qisami stood aside and watched as she greeted each crew member, addressing them personally. It was easy to see why she had risen to become their chief. The woman was soft and approachable most of the time, but could turn hard like marble when necessary, which she did at one point when a group of laborers were careless loading one of the rail cars leading to the next pod over. Malinde's response was sharp yet even. She did not raise her voice nor was she demeaning. She simply expressed her disappointment and reminded them to be more careful.

As Malinde was leaving, she signaled Qisami. "Why don't you come to my pod, the *Nezra Rides*, to share my hearth? We'll have zuijo, or tea if you prefer. I would like to get to know my first landchained friend."

"Sure." Qisami wasn't sure what to make of that invitation, but she might as well get to know this fellow diminutive woman. At least she was offering free booze.

Qisami watched, fascinated, as the Nezra fleet formed up in its battle line and began rolling south. These mechanical beasts were marvels. Sprawled as far as the eye could see was a veritable fleet of these city pods, forty-six in the attack armada, including nearly the entire clan of Nezra. The city pods looked like rolling citadels, each unique but all sharing the same design aesthetics. They were gigantic pods with three-story buildings cluttered together atop massive tracked wheels. There were other long, thin pods with short one-story shacks lining the perimeter. One squat, wide pod had no buildings. Instead, racks of artillery lined the top. Some pods were on tracks while others rolled on large black wheels. A few seemed to use some sort of paddle-wheel system while one looked as if it were resting on inflated balloons woven together with animal skins.

The Exiles Rebellion's intention was to surprise their enemy from behind and shatter their control over the Grass Sea. The five clans together made a formidable force, but it remained to be seen if they could defeat any of the Katuia cities. Usually, only fools traveled during the third cycle of each year, but this was also the time of year when every capital city was spread out to the different corners of the Grass Sea. The fleet intended to take advantage of this.

Qisami thought it sounded like suicide, but most rebellions were. Their intention was to hit Katuia while their capital cities were stretched thin. Daewon had offered her the choice of leaving, going as far as to offer to drop her off in Caobiu lands. She had declined. She was happy to tag along, because there was nothing left for her back in the Enlightened States. There weren't many career options for former shadowkill assassins. It wasn't like she could work as an independent or open her own murder school, so she might as well become a revolutionary.

Evening came quicker than she realized. Qisami had spent most of the day on the top deck watching the land float past. The days in the Grass Sea during the sweltering third cycle summer were unusual. Light shined most of the day and then the curtain of night dropped almost instantaneously. One moment she was at the bow of *Not Loud Not Fat*—linked up with four other city pods parting the clumps of tall weeds swaying to fierce winds. The top of the jungle canopy sped below the deck of the pod, giving it the illusion of being the surface of a sprawling green ocean.

Irritants in the air stung her eyes, causing them to water. She blinked several times. When Qisami opened them again, night had curtained. One by one, a vertical spotlight shone directly upward like a pole—probably to prevent the pods from crashing into each other, especially the ones linked by bridges.

Qisami remembered her invitation and headed toward the bridge connecting *Not Loud Not Fat* to the *Nezra Rides*. She was glad to see small lights turning on to illuminate her path, especially on the shaky bridge connecting the two pods. The street level of the tinkerchief's pod was two stories higher than her pod, so she had to hike uphill. Once she was on top, she knew why this was considered the flagship city pod. The *Nezra Rides* had four times the girth of *Not Loud Not Fat* and was far grander. The structures and layout in the clean, well-maintained streets wouldn't be out of place on the streets of Duke Yanso's estate in Allanto. The buildings were huddled together, each circular with differing girths. They all wore large, round caps on top, resembling a troop of mushrooms.

It wasn't hard to locate Malinde's workshop. It was the one with a giant tin statue slumped on its side next to the doorway. Qisami stepped over it and studied the metal figure. There was some sort of hatch opened at its back, like a little sitting area. She was tempted to climb inside but thought better of it. The boss of this clan wanted to chat with her.

Qisami entered the large mushroom building, passing through a thick, curved metal door. The thing looked heavy but opened easily with a soft hiss. She was surprised when she walked inside. Because of how pristine the streets were, Qisami had expected the buildings' interiors to be equally tidy, especially for the leader of a clan, but that was not the case with Tinkerchief Malinde.

The place was a sty, with piles of junk everywhere, hanging on the walls, parts scattered across the floor, and piled in stacks lining the walls. She couldn't even see the floor in most places. A large, square worktable stood at the very center of the room directly under a flower head of spotlights. It too was brimming with metal parts and tools. Qisami noticed another one of those metal statues near the back, again piquing her interest. What were they for? Whoever was the metal worker must be an amateur. The statue looked basic and plain, an embarrassment to anyone who thought it was art. This one stood upright, at least.

"Ah, there you are." Malinde had come out of the back room. Her hair was pulled up in a tight knot while her face had been smudged with soot and oil. She wore a baggy apron with a dozen pockets, each bulging. A tool belt hung across one shoulder and large spectacles covered half her face. She looked more like an academic blacksmith than the head of a savage Grass Sea cannibal tribe, as they were often painted back at home.

Qisami studied the woman, unsure what to make of her. Malinde certainly came from the same womb as Salminde. The two shared the same face with the moon eyes and sharp nose. The sisters shared the same mannerisms and expressions, often waving their hands the same way. They even had similar sharp laughs. However, Malinde was a scrawny, thin wristwagger. Her face was often scrunched. Her hair was a matted mess that clung to her small head. She spoke in a thin voice. There was a stillness in her movements.

Salminde, on the other hand, was nearly her opposite in almost every way. Whereas the tinker often looked like she had just woken up, the viperstrike looked like she spent half the morning on her appearance. She was tall and statuesque, body stone-hard yet supple, a warrior goddess with a perfect mane of hair. The viperstrike carried an air of leashed violence.

Malinde must have sensed her watching. "Something on your mind, friend?"

Most of the other Kati had avoided Qisami as if she were a demon from one of the ten hells. Malinde had so far greeted her so graciously, with kindness and respect.

Qisami shrugged. "I'm just fantasizing about your sister."

"I miss my sister weed dearly as well." Malinde looked Qisami over. "Did you really fight my sister to a standstill?"

"I mean, more or less." It was probably less, but close enough.

"Then," the tinkerchief declared, "Nezra could use someone with such talent."

That was another thing about this particular diminutive Kati. The entire clan looked up to her: the children, the people, the warriors, even the elderly. The tinkers especially treated her as if she were the fiftieth coming of Goramh himself.

"Goramh without a cock," she muttered.

"What was that, friend Qisami?"

"Nothing." She was so damn nice, too.

Malinde held up a bowl. "Would you like some boiled meat?"

Qisami couldn't remember the last time she had a good hunk of meat. It was considered a delicacy back at the Happy Glow and was rationed on the *Not Loud Not Fat.*

"Sure."

"And zuijo." Malinde brought two cups over after pushing a bowl of brown soup across the table.

"Even better."

Qisami attacked it at once, slurping the soup like a parched lioness dying of thirst. Then she gagged, her nose aflame. Her eyes watered, and for a minute she thought she had been poisoned. The cluttered, squat room began to grow taller, as if stretching. Then, just like that, the pain in her sinuses receded. Her vision cleared, and she could breathe again.

"You need to sip the ayahuasca soup slowly," the boss girl explained. "Otherwise, that happens."

The Kati zuijo came next. At first it tasted just like the swill back at home, albeit with a minty flavor. The kick came several moments later, well after she had swallowed. Something bit her stomach from the inside and then shot straight up her spine to her head.

"Distilled from krait poison," Malinde explained, taking a sip.

The two women enjoyed their strange soup and drank their poison while sitting opposite each other. Malinde studied her and hiccupped. "You were the one who fought my sister back in Jiayi. You don't look that intimidating. My husband is positively terrified of you."

"He is? Aww, thank you. That's a nice thing to say. I'm good at scaring babies. I will say, you don't look terrifying for a boss girl, but here we are."

That earned a grin from Malinde. "Here we are, Scare Baby."

Both women broke into grins.

The two shared their stories for the next hour over mind-altering soup and poisoned beer. Both were the youngest in their families and shared many of the same youngest-child angst even on opposite sides of the continent. Both had their worlds destroyed as girls, Qisami given to the training pools to satisfy a brood atonement, while Malinde's city was razed beneath the Grass Sea, and then their survivors sold into indentured servitude. For once Qisami had to admit that someone else had it much worse.

From there, Qisami told her about the penal colony while Malinde regaled her with the tales of hiding in the lava tunnels of a dormant volcano. Again, Qisami wasn't sure who had it worse. That was when she also learned about Sali's sickness and how she had traveled across the Grass Sea to find a cure, succeeding only after traveling to Hrusha in the Sun Under Lagoon.

"But she's healthy now? She defeated this disease?"

"So it appears. May the ancestors look over her." She nodded. "And you may call me Mali."

Qisami leaned in. "Does Salminde have a partner, a man?"

Mali considered. "Not now, and rarely ever. It was never important to her."

Qisami went for it. "Does she have a preference? Does she have a type? Like a handsome man, or a brawny man, or possibly a brainy one, or a warrior man?" Qisami added, "Or woman."

"She's rarely shown interest in a man. She was always with Jiamin when we were sprouts, and then she shaved her head for the raidlife and never took on a serious lover since. Why do you ask?"

Qisami batted her eyes. "Could I be her type?"

The startled look of disgust flashed only briefly on Malinde's face, but it was unmistakable. An honest face does not lie well. Her revulsion was clear. Then she laughed.

The mockery stung. "You don't have to be rude about it."

Malinde laughed even louder, her voice tinkling off-key. "Oh, it's not that. The Katuia trade partners of all sorts as often as there are seasons in a cycle. It's just that you're Zhuun. Laying with a land-chained is probably the most outlandish thing one would ever expect Sali to do, but it's possible, I guess."

"So you're saying there's a chance," Qisami cooed.

The tinker sipped her drink. "I always assumed she'd marry another war artist."

"I'm a war artist," Qisami blurted.

"Everyone in the clan thought she was going to be the khan's consort, but she was having none of that."

Before Qisami could answer, there was a knock on the door and Daewon burst in. He looked surprised that both Qisami and Mali were red-faced and giggling with their heads together like little gossiping girls. "Howlers in the vanguard just sent a bird. We found Liqusa. The capital city is two days to the south moving at speed along the Corsac Gyre. We found Sali!"

Mali was alert. Whatever giddy drunkenness she had shown moments earlier had evaporated as she jumped to her feet. "Do they know we're here? It doesn't matter. Prepare for city-to-city battle." She turned back to Qisami. "Do you believe in our cause?"

Qisami was on the edge of drunkenness, which often meant she was stupidly honest. This case was no exception. "I mean, not really, but that never stopped me before."

"Liqusa was the last clan known to hold Sali. Will you help us find her?"

"Sure, why not? It's not like I have anything better to do." Qisami drained her drink and leaned back in her chair, tipping it onto the two back legs. "I don't suppose there's pay, is there?"

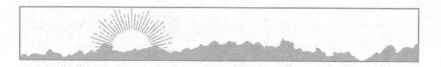

CHAPTER FORTY-FIVE

PRISONER

"I will not take the khan's bait."

Sali watched the row of bells hanging off the ropes lashed between two buildings just outside the Sanctuary of the Eternal Moor, each chiming its tone at its leisure. Somehow, amidst the choir of competing sounds, a beautiful chord resonated throughout Chaqra, the Black City. Sali stood on the second-story balcony of the Sanctuary of the Eternal Moor, studying the landscape. A sharp breeze blew past as the Black City's fleet rolled along the Xing desert in scattered formation.

After she had gotten over her shock that the Eternal Khan of Katuia had returned, Sali had to spend considerable willpower resisting falling back in line with the rest of Katuia who were eager to serve him. Ever since she was a seedling, she had been conditioned to worship the khan and heed the wisdom of the spirit shamans. To fight against those instincts was almost counterintuitive to her identity.

But things were different now. Her world had changed, and there was no going back to that life. It was impossible to wipe away the betrayal that had been inflicted upon her clan and people. There was no way to remove the stain upon their honor. Sali could no longer continue this charade.

Sali still did not understand why they were here. Chaqra was not a raiding city. It was a battering ram, supposedly, because despite being one of the most heavily armed capital cities in the horde, Chaqra held the distinction of being the only capital city that had never seen battle. The spirit shamans had always steered their clan away from danger and conflicts. Except for now. What was the Black City doing in the Zhuun lands? At the very least, they could have entered the Zhuun lands farther north where it was more fertile.

Sali was still a prisoner, of sorts, but was now given free rein to walk about the pod, which was an improvement over being locked inside a box. Sali stared at the side rails of the pod. Why hadn't she tried to escape? She had been given so much freedom she could disappear any time and it'd be a day before they realized she was gone. She had survived in Zhuun lands before. It would have been difficult to survive in this arid place, but it was possible.

Sali hung her head. She hated the truth. Salminde the Viperstrike was still here because the khan was here, and this was the largest horde incursion into enemy lands seen in her lifetime. Something momentous was happening, and her ego wanted to be part of it.

She closed her eyes. Jiamin had somehow won her over without even trying. No, that man, the new host of the Eternal Khan of Katuia, was no longer her friend, regardless of his familiarity. She sucked in a breath. "I will not take his bait," she repeated for the hundredth time.

"Salminde the Viperstrike." A young spirit shaman approached. "The khan requires your attention."

Sali looked over and nodded. "Of course."

She fell in behind the messenger, already chastising herself for being willing to come along so easily, almost eagerly, to obey the khan's demands. Within a few short days, Sali felt as if she had fallen back into the old ways of being at the khan's beck and call. Part of her welcomed it, much to her disgust. Generational conditioning was a difficult habit to break. She also knew what life with the khan would require. Every other way led to uncertain waters. That familiarity held its own allure.

She followed the shaman through shiny black obsidian hallways. The sanctuary was large and opulent, but it wasn't comfortable. The walls were cold to the touch and full of sharp edges. The ceilings were often low and the hallways claustrophobic. The worst thing, however, was what was directly below it. Due to the size of the structure, the engine of the city pod carrying the Sanctuary of the Eternal Moor had to be immensely powerful. It was certainly the largest within Katuia. The monstrosity directly below in the lower decks was always emitting strange, sharply pitched sounds that reverberated throughout the pod. There was a reason none of the shamans actually resided in the temple. Sali still hadn't slept through the night during her stay.

The young spirit shaman led her to an open pit at the center of the sanctuary. Known as the Khan's Peaceful Fury, it was a circular meditation spot with the stones raked into a spiral that met at the center at a raised circular platform. The pit was surrounded by a larger black-rock chamber with a domed ceiling. Directly above it was an opening to the sky. It was a place Sali had frequented as a child. This was where Jiamin had been tested by a soulseeker.

Speaking of which, Sali stopped the moment she caught Jiamin's— no, the khan's—eyes and bowed. She was a prisoner, but there was no reason to be rude. Besides, she performed the bow automatically. Sali was annoyed.

The Eternal Khan of Katuia was shirtless with his hair pulled back in a ponytail. His sides were covered by face-framing strands that looked like long saber fangs. The khan looked strong and was taller than her by two heads and easily half a body wider. His face was chiseled, with high cheekbones and a sharp nose and chin. His eyes were sunken and covered by wild, thick eyebrows. The man's body was crawling with muscles, thick knots that rippled with every movement. He was tanned and lightly marred with cuts, but otherwise stood as a supreme specimen of a warrior.

Except he wasn't, not really. Sali knew the truth.

Nine people surrounded the khan: two spirit shamans, two female attendants, three dressed like wills of the khan, and a cupbearer. The last, a pretty woman wearing little except the barest modesty, was lounging at a small table off to the side. All of this was cliché, like a scene out of an ancient Katuia fable.

The khan was working through open-hand fighting drills with his two wills, taking on both at once, their feet kicking up sand with their continued exchanges. Sali studied him as he split the air with a lightning first step. His arm swings were powerful yet soft, like a rushing ocean wave. One such strike smacked one of his wills in the chest. There was a delayed reaction, and then the will flew backward as if launched from a catapult. He fell far outside the pit and nearly landed on the hard obsidian floor. His momentum was too great, however, as he lost his balance a second time, skidding along his backside until he slammed into the far wall. The other will of the khan launched a series of quick snapping kicks.

All three war artists fought in the house style of Chaqra, known as Eight Limbed Art. It was an aggressive and straightforward war art, focused on battering an enemy down with aggression and strength. The outcome of the melee was never in doubt. As soon as her partner was knocked out, the female will of the khan gave it her best effort, but she was easily dispatched by the khan's superior power. There was nothing elegant about the sparring session as the khan cracked down upon her with a large forehand. Within moments, he drove her to her knees and then gave her a haughty shove to the side, sending her falling on the sand and gasping for breath.

Sali's eyebrows furrowed. Jiamin had never been this rough with his Sacred Cohort. Sali would have been the first to dunk his head in a piss trough if he had been so hard on any of them like that.

The khan noticed her and gestured for her to approach. "Salminde, I'm recollecting many things about you. I wish to know if it's true."

"All you had to do is ask." She had to bite down on her lip to keep from saying "my khan."

"What I wish to know cannot be told," he replied.

The cupbearer approached and sank to her knees, holding up a long wooden box. The khan reached in and pulled out a coiled rope. Her gaze intensified. The man had her tongue. She had mourned its loss, assuming it was gone forever. Sali remained calm, not allowing her face to betray her emotions. The khan held the tongue in his hand and tossed it over. Sali plucked it out of the air and placed it in its holster.

He pointed at her and then beckoned. "Let us test these memories I hold of you."

Sali's heart sped up even as her arms and legs relaxed. Her body sank down as she settled into a defensive stance of the Serpent Fang with her left spearhand held forward. Her right drifted down the loop of the tongue, caressing the cold, familiar diamond links until she felt the carved handle.

The khan stepped forward, his guard still down, his pace relaxed. In the world of the Katuia war sects, it was the higher caste or senior who initiated sparring as a sign of respect and reverence. Combat would not begin until he chose.

At least that was expected. That was custom.

However, customs be damned. Sali attacked the moment the khan stepped within range. Her arm drew forward, launching the coiled tongue and aiming a killing blow to his neck. The way she saw it, she might as well try to end it now if given the chance. The worst he could do was kill her, which wasn't a bad way to go.

The tongue bit closer to her mark than she expected. The khan didn't look surprised, nor did he react poorly. As always, his movements remained casual, as if he were putting forth little effort. The khan raised a finger to his face as if about to scratch his nose. And somehow caught the bite of her tongue in mid-flight inches from his throat.

He smiled. "Little Sali always wanted to win practice."

It was true. She hated that this man had access to Jiamin's memories.

The khan closed his fist around her bite and yanked. The force of his jing combined with his strength tore her off her feet, nearly dislocating her shoulder. Sali barely held on to her handle, flying out of control before she twisted to strike at him with the point of her steel-tipped boot.

The two collided, Sali kicking his chest. The khan took a step back as he absorbed the blow. She sent a jolt to her tongue, stiffening it and launching up and away from him, and then he struck back. She landed on a knee, her spear in hand.

"Are you still *the* viperstrike, or is that warrior a memory?" He raised his guard. It wasn't lost on her that he chose to fight her spear with an open hand. She intended to make him question that confidence.

Sali came back at him, twisting and bending the flexible shaft of her tongue, alternating spear thrusts and sharply angled slices, hitting from low to high and from the side. Sparks exploded around him as the bite raked his metal armlets. Then he lunged with a punch that was blindingly fast and covered more ground than she thought possible. She raised her arms in time to block the hit, but it still threw her halfway across the room, nearly toppling her off her feet.

"Or perhaps you were just a figment of my imagination."

The khan attacked and was on her in an instant, throwing elbows and punches, kicks and knees, each an attack that sent a wave of force like a swinging hammer. The Eight Limbed Art emphasized extending power past the body. The greater the surge of jing, the more powerful the force. The Eight Limbed Art required a practitioner to have an immense fountain of jing, which very few war artists possessed, which was why this sect never became a dominant style. In the hands of the Eternal Khan of Katuia, however, the immense well of jing he wielded was devastating.

Interestingly, there were no hints of other styles within the khan's movement. While all khans fought with the Eight Limbed Art as their base style, most were influenced by their past life. Jiamin often mixed his Eight Limbed Art with Nezra's own Serpent Fang style. This khan so far had not revealed any parts of his past. He fought strictly with the Eight Limbed Art, with no excessive movements or outside influences. He simply chopped and hacked at her with overwhelming force. It was effective, if not elegant or beautiful.

The outcome of the fight was never in question. Sali took as many hits as she could handle. Her flesh turned crimson with each impact until her face and body were red and purple. She managed a few hits, three spear gashes along his arms and left knee, and a downward smack with the butt of the spear that should have concussed him. She also landed blows to the ribs that would have crippled a normal person and slipped a spearhand in that would have punctured a hole into the side of anyone else's face.

The khan took the hits without so much as flinching. He wrapped his two large hands around her head and brought his knees up: the first slammed into her gut, the second into her chest. The first blow sent her body into shock, while the second made her lose consciousness. Then, still holding on to her skull, he swung around and tossed her like a child angry at a stuffed doll.

Sali screamed as her neck stretched to the point she thought her head would separate, and then sank into the gravel. She groaned and tried to stand, but the moment she got to a knee, the room turned sideways and she pitched forward, face-first.

Sali lay sprawled on her belly with half her face submerged in the sand. Her heart hammered as time slowed. She blinked once, watching the khan approach, his feet crunching on the rocks. This had been a lesson. He had beaten her to prove that she had no chance, that rising up against him had been futile. Sali pushed herself up and sat on her knees in the sand, then looked up and stared defiantly as he towered over her.

A small smile appeared on his lips. He barked, "Leave us."

The speed with which the room cleared was impressive. The cohort around this khan must be well trained. Jiamin had always kept lax surroundings, but these two were not the same men.

The khan continued to study her long after they were alone, with only the sound of dripping water to break the silence. Finally, he offered a hand. "This has been illuminating. The opinion I have of you is well earned."

Sali wasn't sure how to react. This was someone she had sworn to slay. However, her parents had taught her better. When in doubt, lean toward honor. She accepted the khan's offer, and he hauled her to her feet. "How so? You beat me worse this time than in your previous life."

His hands were surprisingly gentle, another difference. Jiamin had trained alongside Sali to be a warrior since they were both sprouts, and they both shared the rough hands and thick calluses to show for it. This khan only had hints of calluses at the tips of his fingers.

There had never been a khan not raised from the warrior caste. While the man standing before her was certainly mighty, it raised more questions about his desires.

She remained guarded as she followed him to the table. Her odds had improved but there was still a chance she wasn't walking out of this room alive. He sat at the table and waited until the cupbearer hurriedly returned to the room to pour their drinks. He gestured for her to join him as the girl scampered away. That was another difference; Jiamin rarely bothered with servants unless necessary.

"And what have you learned, great khan?" He certainly wasn't *her* khan.

He brought his cup to his lips, draining it quickly. He made a face that had the look of someone new to strong drink. "You are still formidable and resolute. You hold on to honor and the old ways, but you are not rigid. You are willing to take advantage." He motioned to the room. "Most importantly, you are still Katuia."

That was where he was wrong, but there was no need for her enemy to have unnecessary information. "You've brought me here against my will. What is your intention?"

"Straightforward as well. I respect that."

He spread his arms out and motioned to nothing in particular. "In our long history, Chaqra has never crossed the Grass Sea into Zhuun lands. I am forging the future of our people at this very moment. I do not intend to rest upon the laurels of my ancestors. I shall be the catalyst for change in this world. The Katuia will cast a storm across all lands. The Zhuun are only the beginning. Tomorrow we will assault the shores of the Tsunarcos. The day after, the White Ghosts. The Katuia's moment to ascend has arrived.

"But not even I can accomplish this on my own. I will need other great men and women to stand beside me." He set his cup down. "So, I have an offer, viperstrike, a chance at redemption. Swear your soul to the Eternal Khan of Katuia as you once did and reclaim your place as a Will of the Khan. Nezra will be forgiven and will again be a capital city among our people. It would be as if nothing had changed. What say you, Salminde the Viperstrike? Sali, my old friend?"

Sali was stunned. She had come here expecting to die, not to be raised back to the Sacred Cohort, a place just below the khan himself. This arrangement would save her people and guarantee their future.

But she could never go back. She knew too much about who and what the khan was, and how the spirit shamans had manipulated their people.

Sali opened her mouth to refuse his generous offer, but the right words wouldn't come out. "My . . . I mean, great khan . . ."

He held up a hand. "Call me Visan. It was my name from before, and the one that I would be pleased to hear come from your lips."

CHAPTER FORTY-SIX

PROPERTY OF
THE TIANDI

The monks at Skyfall Temple gave Jian a cane with four small wooden wheels at the bottom to help him limp about the hospital. He refused to use it at first, his pride getting in the way of common sense. Having the Champion of the Five Under Heaven hobble around was a bad look. It made him feel self-conscious and weak. But mostly self-conscious. The monks here practically worshipped him. He was the face of the entire religion, and felt the immense pressure of always putting up a good front. It was a terrible burden. It wasn't until after Meehae introduced him to an injured fourteen-ring Hansoo recovering from a broken hip after tripping and falling down a flight of stairs that Jian got over himself.

He could hear Taishi chastise him. "Big muscles mean nothing." She would then poke him in the chest. "Strength comes from within, as does weakness. Never presume." She was a shining example of inner power in a frail-looking shell.

Several hospital healers checked in many times a day. There was an entire staff assigned to him, given his stature within the religion. He received around-the-clock care from a surgeon, spiritualist, acupuncturist—Meehae, in this case—a jing master, masseuse, herbalist, cupping mender, and even a midwife. Jian wasn't sure why he needed one of those, but he soon found himself preferring her company. She was more motherly.

He spent his days puttering about the recovery ward, moving between his bed, the urinal, and the small pebble garden just outside the hospital entrance. Eventually, he felt strong enough to brave the stairs. That opened the rest of the hospital wing to him, but even those added spaces quickly grew too small and quiet. There was only so much stupid rock and fungus and the weirdly tight-lipped but judgmental healers that he could bear. These stuffy monks were awful company compared to the ones back at Vauzan. All were respectful, but few were friendly.

Jian's restlessness grew with his strength. He eventually tried to leave the hospital but was rebuffed by the two big Hansoo guarding the door. It was for his safety, they said. He needed to be close to the healers in case anything happened. They would happily fetch whatever he needed from the outside. What Jian really needed was to go for a walk, but no matter how much he pleaded, he was not allowed to leave.

Even worse than not letting him out was that no one could tell him what had happened to his friends. What happened to Taishi and Sonaya and Zofi? What about his other friends and the masters? What disappointed Jian the most was his oldest friend, Meehae. He had been so happy to see her, and she had seemed happy to see him as well. But she treated him like an acquaintance, not a friend, which hurt more than he cared to admit.

No one seemed to know what happened to any of his friends, or about Vauzan's fate. Did the Cinder Legions emerge victorious? Was Vauzan still standing? Had the city been razed and the ground salted? They couldn't even tell him how he got here. Even Meehae turned cagey, changing the subject every time he begged for answers.

He thought about Taishi a lot. Her birthday was around this time of year. She needed warmer robes during the third cycle winter. She had lost her beloved llama slippers during the siege. He wasn't sure she would survive this year, although that was the same conversation they usually had every year. Did she make it out of Vauzan alive? His breathing grew heavy. The wound in his chest throbbed.

The gardener, who was raking a green bed of java moss nearby, looked over. "Is all well, holy one?"

Jian waved him off. "I'm fine, Haiksong."

The gardener had been one of the first here to speak to him. Unlike most others at the hospital, the older monk was not as impressed with Jian and so treated him like anyone else.

"Very well, son. Watch your step to the left. The rock's slippery from that fresh bed of moss." The kind man nodded and went back to his work.

Jian winced as he rose to his feet. He grasped his stick-on-wheels and rolled back to the hospital.

Haiksong walked past with his two rakes slung over his shoulder. "Are you on your way back to the shack? Mind returning these for me?"

"I'm just going to the acupuncture ward," he replied.

"That's all right, then." The gardener waved and turned away toward the equipment shack.

Jian found Meehae tending a young monk with an angry gash across his shoulder. Leaning against the wall beside him was a horse-cutter blade. Dozens of needles were stuck near the wound as she sewed him up. The young monk was oblivious as he babbled on about how many battles he had waged. It was obvious to Jian that with the angle of his wound, it had been self-inflicted, likely accidental, but he kept that to himself. Let the boy keep his pride.

Meehae noticed him. "Is everything all right, Wen Jian?"

"I need to know what's happening in the outside world. You can't just keep me in the dark. You must know something."

"Like I said, we've been so busy—"

"What happened to Vauzan, to Taishi and my friends?"

Meehae stared, her eyes fixed on him for several moments. She put the needles in her hand back on the tray and stood. "Cici, please finish this suture."

"Yes, master." The girl, who looked only a few years younger than Meehae, rose and took her place on the stool next to the monk.

"Now, what's the matter?" asked Meehae, putting her arms around him. "Do your bandages need refreshing?"

"Of course not," he sputtered. "That's not why I'm here."

She squeezed him harder once they were out in the hallway. Her lips brushed his ear. "Jian, keep quiet," she whispered.

Why would he do that? Why was she whispering? He wasn't asking her for anything he hadn't loudly asked dozens of times. What was the use in keeping quiet unless . . . unless Meehae was afraid someone was listening. Jian looked around and saw no one about, save for Haiksong the gardener pruning a potted plant in the adjacent hallway.

That was when he noticed the strange man who followed them out of the room. He hadn't seen the guy until he moved. The man was dressed in plain brown robes with an unusual high collar that rose past the sides and back of his head. He also wore dark spectacles that hid his eyes.

"Who is that creepy man?" he asked.

Meehae patted his shoulders, leaning in. "Listen closely, Jian. If you want to keep me around as your acupuncturist, keep quiet and stop asking questions." Her face brightened. "Now let's see about fresh bandages."

Jian had to undress and remove the old wraps and reapply his salves and ointments and strange creams. It was a whole process, but it worked. He was recovering quickly. After that, he had to bake his wound over a focused funnel from a burning fire.

He was still putting in his bake time over the wound when Meehae retired for the evening. She took pride in her long hours and small army of apprentices. The war had been a terrible knowledge drain within the medical community. A whole generations of healers had perished or been conscripted into one of the armies, leaving their ranks tending to the common people stretched thin.

Meehae gave him final instructions before leaving the room. "Don't fall asleep if you don't want your face melted. Remember, for the wrappings, you want the spongy side against your flesh. Try to sleep on your back tonight."

Jian was soon alone, sitting next to the small burning hearth funneling the heat toward his chest wound. The lights had dimmed, and the hallways cleared. He sat in silence as night blanketed the last light shining through the windows. Then Jian did the one thing that Meehae had told him not to do. His eyes closed and he drifted off as the concentrated heat continued to cook his chest.

Fortunately, someone woke him. Jian opened his eyes with a start, grimacing in pain as he touched the burnt spot. That was going to blister. He pushed the heat funnel away with a loud creak.

"Meehae, is that you?" said Jian.

"Hey, Meehae," said the newcomer at the same time.

Both men were startled by the other.

It was a Hansoo by his massive frame, a far cry from the diminutive acupuncturist. This one, like most, was large and bald. His face appeared more disheveled, which meant he wasn't holding patronage at a temple. His robes were tattered and stained. He must have just returned from outside and seen real battle. This Hansoo had ten rings to an arm. A herd leader, then.

"Master Meehae has retired for the night," said Jian. He caught the Hansoo staring. He probably recognized Jian from the pictures of him everywhere.

The Hansoo tilted his head, still staring at him. "Jian, is that you?"

"Do I . . ." Jian tilted his head the same way as well. "Pahm? Pahm!"

He hobbled into his old friend's embrace. "What are you doing here?"

"Me?" The Hansoo laughed. "I'm at Stone Blossom Monastery, which is only a boulder's throw away. What are *you* doing here?"

"I don't know." He pointed at the Hansoo's stained robes. "What happened to you?"

"Brigands along the Xing passes near Wugong. It's a mess out there. I take my orphans on patrol."

"Orphans?"

"My squad or herd. We call them orphans." Pahm waved his arms in a grand way and gestured to the nearby table. "Come, come, I have wine. Let's drink and follow each other's tales."

Wasn't Hengyen a dry settlement? And when did Pahm start drinking? Not that Jian was complaining. He decided not to ruin a good thing and accepted the invitation. This was the first fun thing he had done all cycle. He studied his friend. Pahm certainly looked how Jian remembered, just bigger in every way.

It wasn't his body that had changed the most. This Pahm was talkative and gregarious compared to his old, shy friend who used to avert his eyes and barely utter sounds louder than a mumble.

Pahm pulled out a gourd and uncorked it. He swished it between his beefy thumb and forefinger, gently pouring its contents into two cups without spilling a drop. He nudged one toward Jian. "To old friends."

Jian touched cups. "Old friends."

The stuff was strong. Jian was prepared for the worst but he didn't brace hard enough. His knees went wobbly and he would have pitched over had Pahm not grabbed his head with that same thumb and forefinger.

"It's great," he hissed, not selling his enthusiasm.

Pahm laughed, his chest rumbling. "We Hansoo need the strong stuff. Otherwise we end up having to piss all night."

That made sense. Still, Jian couldn't help but stare. "What happened to you? You seem to have come out of your shell."

"I *was* a quiet, righteous, fanatical prick, wasn't I?" Pahm grinned, bringing his cup to his lips.

"I prefer to think of it as earnest and gentle."

Pahm continued to chuckle. "I resumed my training at the Stone Blossom Monastery after I left the Cloud Pillars. It was there that I began my official seminary training as a Hansoo. There, I learned something that changed everything." He leaned in. "Do you know what the Hansoo's primary duties to the Tiandi are?"

It didn't sound like a trick question. "You're the Shields of the Tiandi. You protect the devout."

"That's what I thought too!" Pahm skipped the cup entirely the next time and swigged directly from the gourd. He passed it to Jian. "But our real job, the thing the Tiandi religion wants out of us, is to stand by the offering vase every Tenth Day Prayer to attract more donations."

That certainly was where most Hansoo stood every time he saw them. "I assumed you were there to guard the pot of coins."

Pahm shook his head. "That's how it's sold, but really the Hansoo are popular with children and families. We're puffed up show dogs to attract attention, a spectacle to drum up revenue."

"But you can fight." Jian was indignant on his friend's behalf. "I've seen you fight. You're great war artists."

"It's all part of the marketing plan." He took a swig, slapping the gourd on the table. "I learned that mopey, sullen Pahm did not have much of a future as a Hansoo. I needed to change how I presented myself to the devout, so there you have it. Five years of cracking that dour, righteous exterior. Drinking helps." He shot Jian a grin showing all his teeth, then his tone darkened. "When war broke out between Lawkan and Xing, I begged the blossomabbots as well as the high seats to defend the villages around Skyfall. It was the least we could do, as Shields of the Tiandi. Their protection was made more urgent because these neighboring settlements are the temple's primary source for food, supplies, and labor."

"Sounds reasonable." Jian shouldn't try to match his friend drink for drink, but he tried.

"I was denied," Pahm continued, "because the Hansoo were needed next to the offering vases. Revenue was down because of the war. We needed to drum up more offerings. So it was more important to the high seats that we act like the Shields of the Tiandi instead of actually being the Shields of the Tiandi." His giant shoulders slumped. "I tried to stay out of it until they started burning villages. Then I couldn't any longer."

"What did you do?"

He shrugged. "I gathered a band of my like-minded brothers and we began to patrol the surrounding regions. First, we fought off the bandits. Then, it was the Xing army and sometimes the Lawkan fleet.

Any of the powerful who terrorize the helpless meet our wrath. No one makes a fuss when we come back to resupply, either."

He held out his gourd. Jian touched it with his cup, and the friends drank. Every subsequent shot of the hard liquor went down smoother than the last. He had to clench his cup and squeeze his eyes shut to force it down. But after that, it went straight to his head. Jian chuckled, and then giggled, which only hurt his wound, ending with a grimace.

"What happened to you, Jian?" Pahm asked, looking him over.

"Spear to the chest."

The Hansoo's eyes widened. "Here?"

Jian shook his head. "I was in Vauzan with Taishi when the Caobiu attacked the city."

Pahm shook his head. "Terrible stories have come out about that siege."

"Do you know what happened?" asked Jian. "I've been out for the better part of a month."

Pahm poured them both a cup. "Caobiu controls three duchies. The Xing and Lawkan have allied, but is it too late? Who knows. Sunri has the biggest army, the most land, the most everything, really, but she's stretched thin and her new holdings sit on wet sand. Lawkan and Xing are pressuring her in every way."

"What about Vauzan?" Jian pressed. "Have you heard what's happened to them?"

"Negotiated a surrender, I hear," Pahm continued. "Not a great deal for the Shulan Court, but at least they saved lives."

"Do you think the people there are all right?" Jian asked, his voice growing softer.

"It doesn't matter if they're all right," said Pahm. He breathed a body-deflating sigh. "Fate comes, regardless."

Jian drained the last of his cup. The room was beginning to blur. "Why does everyone get a pass on making bad choices except me? I feel like I have to be perfect and do everything right. It's the worst."

"You think you've been perfect?" Pahm's laughter echoed through the long stone tunnel. A certain glint appeared in his eye. "My friend,

I hate to tell you this, but only someone as blessed and holy as you could make *so* many mistakes in such a brief period of time and somehow still come out intact. That's why *we're* here to help you."

That was the moment Jian realized that his old friend Pahm did not just happen to run into him this night.

CHAPTER FORTY-SEVEN

THE FIRST PLAN

Taishi walked the rooftops along the row of buildings across from Skyfall Temple, scanning the parapet of the outer wall on the other side of the wide street. Guards were stationed at thirty-foot intervals, all young initiates by the looks of their fresh faces. Standing watch was valuable training for young monks, even if they couldn't fight. When Mori was a Tiandi initiate, his teachers used to make him memorize the details of tree bark. The fact was, being a monk was often tediously boring. Using initiates as guards was a useful source of cheap labor.

Taishi pointed at a gap between where two of the monks stood. "See that groove next to the rock jutting out from the wall? That's the perfect spot. Can you tap that mark in that corner shadow, Fausan?"

"Don't be insulting, Taishi." The whipfinger master sniffed. He picked a pebble off the ground, glanced over at his target, and then looked back at her. He flicked a finger. A moment later, there was a soft but audible crack as stone struck stone. "I can tap anything."

Bhasani snorted.

"What?"

"Let's just say, the problem isn't hitting your mark," the drowned fist master exclaimed. "It's staying on target for more than five minutes."

He stayed unfazed. "But it's a spectacular five minutes."

She patted his arm. "You *do* try your best."

These two were too old to act like fresh blossoming flowers. Taishi continued, "Moving on, Xinde was able to get a job as part of the night watch."

"Why do they need Xinde?" Bhasani mused. "Isn't everyone in the temple a trained war artist?"

"That's a false stereotype," said Taishi. "Studying the war arts is an elective. It's my understanding that tree pruning is the most popular course. Training in the war arts is near the bottom."

"Besides, my love," said Fausan, "guard duty is soldier work, and war artists make the worst soldiers. Someone has to teach them how to stand still for hours on end."

"That's the truth," Sohn huffed. "War artists stink at fighting in formation. They're like dogs chasing balls. A great war artist can defeat ten soldiers. However, a thousand soldiers will defeat a thousand war artists."

Taishi pushed that discussion aside. "Anyway, Xinde is joining the night shift. He'll cover that section of the wall. We'll get Meehae to sneak Jian to the wall one night, have him rappel down, and be out of Hengyen by dawn."

No one looked confident in her plan. "What if we're discovered?" asked Fausan.

Taishi waggled a finger in his face. "Nothing. Stops. Us."

"There's a problem with your plan," a new voice announced.

The group turned to see Zofi emerge from the stairwell onto the roof.

Taishi looked over. "I thought you were fetching Meehae to talk over the plan."

"She wouldn't come, even when I said I was taking us to a girls' night reunion. She apologizes for not being able to make it and"—she paused, musing—"she said she had to be careful what she says or who she is seen around, or they'll take her off Jian's shift. Skyfall Temple has increased scrutiny since several of their monks were threatened."

"Who threatened the monks?" asked Sohn.

Zofi made a face and stared at Taishi.

"*You* threatened the monks?" Fausan sounded scandalized.

"Not really," Taishi said. "I may have told a few Hansoo I was going to break their arms."

"What do we do now if we can't draw Jian out to us?" asked Bhasani.

"This changes nothing," Taishi said. "If we need to go in and bring him out ourselves, that's what we'll do."

"What if we encounter monks inside?" Fausan asked, worried.

She fixed him with a stare. "What about it?"

"I have a delicate palate regarding killing clergy, Taishi."

"I"—she shrugged—"don't care."

Fausan glanced at Bhasani, and then at Sohn. "Actually, there's something we wanted to discuss. We've made a mess of things. Jian nearly died back in Vauzan. We barely managed to bring him to Skyfall Temple in time. Have you thought maybe . . ." He made a face. "Have you thought that perhaps we're not suited to this type of work anymore?"

Taishi arched an eyebrow, her voice sharp. "What's your point?"

"I'm just saying, perhaps it's time to let the Tiandi religion step in and fulfill their purpose." He sounded apologetic. "Maybe here is where Jian belongs, with the Tiandi religion and the monks who worship him. Maybe it's time you let go."

"Taishi," said Bhasani, stepping between them. "You've done everything you could for Jian. You saved his life. You trained him. You've sacrificed everything for him. Let him stand on his own now. Maybe it's time you take care of yourself, especially during your final . . ."

"My final what? I'm not dead yet." Taishi's face tightened as she rounded on the others. "You want me to abandon Jian?"

"Don't lump me in with them. I think that's messed up." Zofi crossed her arms and glared at the others. "I'm with Taishi. You're terrible people."

Taishi's good hand contorted into a claw that she hid inside her robes. Too old, too weak, and now they were telling her to abandon her son. Hearing these words from her close friends—her brother and sister in the war arts—hurt her more deeply than she would ever admit. The only thing betraying her fury was her locked jaw as she glowered. Inside, though, she was shattered glass and screaming.

Sohn was the voice of reason. "Taishi, the last favor I did for you got me thrown in jail. This time was even worse. But we stuck by you this far. We're not young anymore. We've done all we could for Jian. It's time to let him find his own way."

"I will *not* leave my son to those vultures!" Taishi spat. She leveled her rage at Bhasani. "You, of all people, should know better. Would you abandon your child if they were still alive?"

The blood drained from the drowned fist's face. Zofi gasped. Sohn's mouth dropped. Taishi had crossed a line. Bhasani would have every right to challenge her to a duel for her insult. But she didn't care. She would burn the world to ash to see Jian safe.

Taishi covered her shame by turning away. "Fine. All of you can crawl back into your holes and hide for the rest of your lives in some remote corner of the world to waste your final days. I'll save him myself." She walked away, making it halfway across the roof before a fit of coughs overtook her. She bent over, gasping for breath as each spasm shook her. Zofi was there an instant later, her hands supporting Taishi's elbow.

Taishi tried to wave her off. "Leave me alone, girl. Like they all say, I'm old, dying, and useless. I might as well go lie down on my death-bed."

She locked gazes with Bhasani, and then stormed away, out of the building and into the main street. She could use a drink, but of course Hengyen was a dry settlement. The busy, narrow streets parted before her, no doubt due to her angry demeanor. That and possibly the dowager robes she still wore. They were now ragged and torn, but still comfortable and cushiony. It also made life much easier in this religiously fanatical place.

Some silly people even fell to their knees as Taishi passed, which made her uncomfortable. It was one thing to disguise herself as a dowager nun. It was entirely another to falsely claim the honor and trappings of one. Taishi was so preoccupied that she didn't notice when she reached an intersection and smacked into another monk who had just turned the corner, falling over. She cursed her weakened body and looked up to see a monk wearing senior initiate robes.

The young man blinked in horror when he recognized her garb. He pressed his palms together, bowed his head, and at once dropped to his knees. "Forgive me, dowager. Please allow me to serve penance!"

"Just help me up, oaf," she muttered.

The young man blinked, grabbed her forearm, and helped Taishi to her feet. Her rump ached, but not as much as her pride. "May I aid you further, dowager? Can I escort you to your destination? I can serve as your page and mule, as penance, for the next three days."

The man was too earnest. Taishi waved him off. She dusted off her shoulder and chest. "Just be careful next time. Off you go."

He slapped his palms together and bowed.

Taishi sucked in a breath and considered. "Excuse me, initiate."

The young man turned and tried to do the whole bowing and dropping to the ground ritual. "My name is Pengzo, dowager."

"Stop bowing so much."

He stopped mid-bow. "Yes, dowager. How may I serve?"

Taishi leaned in as if she were about to sell state secrets. "Do you know where I can get some wine?"

The initiate looked scandalized, and then his expression became worried, as if he were wondering if this was a test he was about to fail.

Taishi pointed at her chest. "I am a Black Orchid battlenun. We like to . . ." She made the motion of tipping a cup to her lips. "I just came here from Jiayi after months of battle, so spit it out. I know you know."

He gulped. "The Nine Regrets. I can lead you to it."

The two kept a low profile as Pengzo led Taishi off the main street, into one of the many zigzag alleys that ran across the settlement. Hengyen had few main roads and far too many side streets, which made getting around confusing and cumbersome. Their path dipped beneath a low bridge. Taishi would have missed it on her own.

The two continued to a door at the underbelly of the bridge. He knocked on the rusted iron door. The eye slot slid open. "Who's that?"

She stood taller and turned so he could see her robes. "I just want a drink."

The door swung open.

Taishi turned to the initiate. "Thank you, young Pengzo. I trust you will honor my discretion?"

He nearly fell to his knees. "I would never dream to betray the Tiandi so, dowager."

Taishi watched him scamper to his feet and flee, but she turned her attention to more pressing matters. The interior of the tea shop known as the Nine Regrets matched its title. Taishi had entered a small bare room with low ceilings partitioned by white paper walls. Small lanterns hung from the ceilings above, bathing the tight space with a warm glow and creating silhouettes through the translucent paper dividers. The place was eerie, the shadows barely moving.

A thin woman, body covered from neck to ankle in heavy robes, wearing a face piece that looked like a curtain of small white pearls, walked past carrying a tray with one gourd and one cup. She stopped at the table next to Taishi and sank to her knees, presenting the drink as if this were part of a sacred ritual.

The damn place felt like a murderers' confessional. The monks and nuns present—their numbers unsurprisingly skewed toward the latter—looked miserable, hunched over their tables, exuding guilt. No one met her gaze as she walked past. Taishi couldn't stop staring at the shame porn until one of the masked servants approached and bowed.

"You honor us with your presence, holy lady. Please, this way."

Taishi nodded, refusing to hang her head. She was led to one of the empty tables. The moment she sat down, two more servant girls came. Both sank to their knees and hung their heads as one held a menu toward her. Taishi looked it over.

"Chilled rice wine," she said before handing it back.

There was the whole ritual again of getting back to their feet, and then the two disappeared, leaving Taishi to study the silhouettes on the other side of the paper wall as well as the monk sitting across the aisle from her. It was all a bit much. These clergy were here to drink alcohol, not the blood of virgins.

The two servers returned a moment later, one carrying a drinking vase and the other a cup. They repeated their ritual before pouring her a drink and then departed, finally leaving her alone.

Taishi held the cup between her forefinger and thumb. For some reason, she felt the need to dredge up her past. "To Yinshi and Munnam, mam and ba, Sanso and Jian, my two boys, and Zofi, because why not. To my hearts and hated, my lovers and enemies, I drink to you this life." She drained her cup in one gulp.

A different server from the three she had met so far appeared as if by magical summoning and refreshed her drink. "You made a mess of things, old woman," she muttered to herself, tossing that back as well. "Why didn't you throw Jian on the first cart out of Vauzan the morning of the invasion?"

Taishi had made more than her share of mistakes, and now she was running them all through her mind. She held up the next drink. "I'll figure a way to get you out, Jian." She threw that back too.

Still another server appeared. Taishi shooed her away before she could fall to her knees. There was too much bowing in the world. "I still have one good arm. I can pour my own drink."

Taishi drained three shots before the liquor made its way to her head. She closed her eyes and again felt the need to speak her thoughts, as if expunging them from her body. "You made a mess of things, you old hag. So many decades, and you still haven't learned to hold your tongue. Now you've acted like a fool to the only friends you have left in the world. Face it, Taishi, you need them."

She held the drink up and wondered what she should toast to next. "I spoke rashly, Bhasani. I will make amends tonight."

The past few months had been overwhelming, from the invasion of Vauzan to Jian revealing himself to the world to his near-death injury and now to losing him. It was as if she had squeezed a hundred terrible lifetimes into one compacted, terrible year. All her worries and woes spilled from her mouth and, surprisingly, she felt better, like a drunk purging last night's revelry. It felt good to finally get it all out. She was so exhausted with life. Some part of her ached for the peace of a cold slab. She didn't want to die, but she wouldn't have minded it either. She was just so tired.

Taishi wallowed a while longer, sipping her drink at a more measured pace. She studied the slightly yellow liquid in her cup, swirled and sniffed it, feeling it bite the back of her throat. She looked up, now understanding why this establishment was called the Nine Regrets. Taishi had gotten it wrong all along. These monks weren't ashamed to have snuck in here to drink. They were here to confront their remorse.

She had not expected to have to deal with her emotions. She had just wanted to numb her pain, and this had always been the easiest way. Now, however, the alcohol was affecting her differently, and it was not fun. Still another masked server arrived with a new drinking vase. Taishi plucked it from the tray before the server—an older boy this time—could fall to his knees.

Taishi held her cup and was digging deep in her wallow when there was a commotion at the door. She leaned to the side from where she sat to see a figure storm inside. The Nine Regrets was dimly lit, and her vision wasn't what it used to be, but that looked like . . .

Taishi squinted. "Bhasani? How did you find me?"

The drowned fist's eyes scoured the room. Her gaze locked on Taishi, and she stomped over, her face twisted with fury.

Taishi rose to her feet. "Listen, about earlier," she said, once Bhasani was within arm's reach. "I want to say I'm sorry for being a bitch. That was a shit thing I said—"

Bhasani reached out and gripped her fingers around Taishi's neck. "How dare you!"

Taishi struggled with the drowned fist's firm grasp. What was going on? Surely her insult hadn't escalated to a duel, had it? "Bhasani, stop. You're choking . . ."

Still holding on to Taishi's neck, Bhasani backhanded her with a slap that spun her body. The left side of Taishi's face stung as she reeled backward. She tasted blood and her vision swam. She was already precariously close to losing consciousness. A few more hits would finish her.

Bhasani raised her arm to strike her again. Taishi managed to twist out of the drowned fist's iron grip to block the attack. She threw a low and then a high kick, her foot shattering and ripping the thin paper walls. The two exchanged several more attacks. Taishi's bones rattled with each impact, but she managed to stand her ground. At one point, both women threw punches that met halfway between them. The collision sent them both stumbling. Taishi gasped several deep breaths. Everything hurt, but this was the most fun she'd had in months. In fact, she was doing well, all things considered.

Taishi stopped. That was impossible. She was doing *too* well. That meant Bhasani wasn't actually trying. She was putting on a show, but for whom? She rubbed her jaw. "Why did you hit me so hard?"

The drowned fist's voice boomed inside her head, between her ears. "I had to disrupt your mind patterns."

"Why?"

Bhasani looked around. "Have you felt the sudden urge to confess everything?"

"What a strange thing to say. Of course . . ." Taishi's breath caught. "Oops."

Bhasani homed in on one of the paper dividers, which still hid a silhouette. The other monks had already fled when she had started the ruckus. The drowned fist punched through one of the paper squares and pulled a man through. He was dressed in strange Tiandi garb with a high collar and darkened eyepieces bound around his eyes.

"A truthsniffer," Taishi hissed. That was the lunar court's name for the Tiandi religion's secret police. They were a small sect that held authority over every sect and reported only to the high seats. It was said that they could smell the truth. Everyone hated them, especially within the lunar court.

Bhasani punched the man in the gut, doubling him over. She looked up at the ceiling. "Forgive me, my love." A quick chop to the back of his neck put him down for good. "I don't know what he was able to glean from you."

Taishi understood. She had been careless and allowed herself to fall into a sniffer trap. "Come on, we'll get out through the back. How did you find me?"

Bhasani led her behind the counter and then into the rear of the building. "I followed you. Was going to give your bony ass a good beating for insulting my parenting. I saw your encounter with that young monk. It was such an obvious trap, I couldn't believe you fell for it."

"I just wanted a drink," Taishi mumbled. "How did they find us?"

"Maybe when you waved at the guard this morning, I don't know." They burst out into a needle-thin alley with those zigzagging turns. "But probably because they've had a tail on you since you barged into the hospital, which means they've identified everyone on the roof." They reached the end of the alley, which opened back up to one of the main streets. "Come on, head toward the edge of town. The men are returning to the inn. We're assuming everything's compromised. The Tiandi will be on the lookout for us. They'll have our faces on bulletins all over the settlement tomorrow. It'll be difficult to escape Hengyen, let alone break into Skyfall Temple."

Taishi pulled up short. "I'm not leaving Jian."

Bhasani stopped and faced Taishi. "I wouldn't have abandoned my baby either. You were right to point that out. More often than not, the smart and easy thing to do isn't necessarily right. I promise, on my honor, we will not leave Hengyen without Jian."

Taishi hadn't been ready for that response. She almost had to blink back tears. Almost. She reached out to embrace her old friend, her old enemy. "Thank you, Bhasani."

"The men aren't wrong either," added the drowned fist. "We can't attack Skyfall Temple to get him out, especially now that they will be on the lookout for us. Fortunately, I have an idea."

"Care to elaborate?"

Bhasani offered her best knowing smirk. "Our heirs are good for other things than doing our laundry."

Taishi was taken aback. "You trust yours to do laundry?"

CHAPTER FORTY-EIGHT

WAR PRELUDE

Qisami stood at the observation nest of the *Nezra Rides* and watched as the two fleets, the Exiles Rebellion and the Liqusa clan capital city, lined up and charged each other. She did not know what to expect, so when the attack began before dawn, she found a prime seat at the bow of the *Nezra Rides* and watched with morbid fascination as two Katuia clans in their big moving cities lined up to slaughter each other. The *Nezra Rides* happened to be in the middle of the action, being the city at the heart of the Exiles faction.

The other city pods were arrayed in loose formations that stretched out to both sides, with the *Nezra Rides* at the center a few rows back. The massive city pods, while impressive and threatening, moved at the speed of a comfortable jog. So watching the front lines of giant machines crawling toward each other in the tall weeds of the Grass Sea was anticlimactic. It took almost the entire morning before the vanguard of each fleet reached artillery range.

Then the first arc of the flaming artillery took flight and hell was unleashed.

The jungle foliage they rolled through was tall and dense. The larger pods rose above the grass, but many of the smaller lancer pods were hidden. The only way to track them was to detect the wake of the parted grass as they slithered through the giant weeds.

In hindsight, Qisami would have recommended against anyone taking part in one of these pitched battles. She had had her share of wild fights and violence, but what unfolded on this battlefield was sheer chaos. Thousands of people riding giant metal monsters lobbing death at each other was the craziest thing she had ever seen, which was saying something.

Red and gray streaks began to cut through the open sky as the land around them exploded. The ground shuddered as a concussive burst of flaming pitch just missed the *Nezra Rides*, exploding on the ground and sending plumes of smoke and sprays of water everywhere. Some parts of the Grass Sea caught fire, spreading to the land around it.

Qisami stared, wide-eyed, sometimes squealing with exhilaration and fascination as the foremost pods traded projectiles and arrows as they advanced. Once they were close, the two pods would circle each other, closing in until they finally locked horns. Then they unleashed their warriors. That was when the real dying began.

Qisami couldn't look away. As the city heart of the fleet, this pod was too important to throw into the first few waves. *Nezra Rides* had stayed nearly at the edge of the enemy's artillery range as the rest of the fleet's pods rolled past.

Nearly, however, still wasn't good enough.

An explosion and a withering wave of heat hit her from behind, causing her to stumble forward. She caught the railing before the force sent her toppling over the side. Qisami dropped to a knee as a section of *Nezra Rides* erupted in flames. She looked through a charred hole on the main deck to the gear level below. Something down there had caught fire, sending a gray column of smoke drifting out. Dozens of clan members rushed to put out the growing fire. She noted how most of the volunteers were not crew or warriors. They were the ones who would otherwise hide below deck during battles: the young and the old, the laborers and the peaceful folks. Everyone took part in some way.

Daewon stood at the control platform, screaming at the top of his lungs. She had the impression that he was the one steering the ship. Several crew and tinkers worked their stations in a frenzy of activity. Malinde, on the other hand, was at the foremost building near the front, a few feet away from Qisami. She could hear the woman's voice as she directed artillery.

"Find out who just spat on my house!" she yelled.

A lookout on the port side pointed toward a giant pod in the distance that looked like it was wearing a rib cage for a hat. A woman next to Malinde who Qisami recognized as the clan's calculator yelled out new angles, and then the catapult crews pushed the spokes of a circular platform, turning a catapult to their desired angle. Malinde gave the order and sent a hail of head-sized rocks flying through the air, with about half hitting their marks.

The battle continued for several hours. The action wasn't fast, but it was frantic. At one point, Qisami had to step away from the railing to catch her breath, but for what reason she wasn't sure. Just watching the battle made her tired, and she hadn't even gotten to her part in it yet. The battlefield was vast and the pods far apart. Every time the *Nezra Rides* focused on a Liqusa pod, it would take five minutes for them to change direction to line up. Then it would take five more minutes for the artillery to turn their platforms, and then five more minutes to fire. And most of the shots would miss! It was an inefficient way to kill people.

Eventually, the pods waded deeper into battle, intermingling as they fought on all sides. If the *Nezra Rides* was approaching on its tracks, focused on one target, there were certainly at least two more enemies taking potshots at it from the sides. After an hour of watching these exchanges, Qisami decided that she was bored and went to the lower gear level. She found a private nook and was soon curled up like an alley cat taking a nap. That was one of her special abilities; she could sleep anywhere, through just about any situation. It was what made her stay at the Happy Glow so bearable.

It was midday, at least six hours into the fighting, when Marhi and Wani found her. Qisami woke and waved at them the moment the girls got within ten paces. "You two look so fancy and pretty. Do you have a special place to go?"

The two young viperstrikes were in their birthday best. Marhi's wooden banded plates looked like they'd been given a fresh coat of paint. There were carvings of each of the six Xoangiagu on her armor. Wani's hair was freshly braided and her face had so much paint on she looked like she was attending her own wedding.

Wani beckoned. "We've been looking all over for you. We're late."

"Late for what?"

"We're nearing Liqusa's city heart," said Wani. "We have to join the boarding party at the insertion point."

"What are we doing again?" Qisami grumbled. She had been distracted by a mango lassi drink during the debriefing.

Marhi tossed her an arm buckler that was easily large enough to cover her body.

Qisami stared at the shield with disdain. "What's this for?"

"You'll need it."

"Really, I don't."

Marhi pulled out a knife and flicked it to the shield.

Instead of blocking the throw, Qisami snatched the blade out of the air with her free hand. "Like I said, I don't."

The older viperstrike wasn't impressed and took the buckler back. "If you want to be the Warrior without his skirt, then suit yourself."

Qisami followed the two down the corridor and began heading up the stairs toward the main deck.

"No, this way," said Wani, continuing down the gear level corridor. "You don't want to go topside."

Qisami hated being told not to do something, so of course she went topside to check it out. She just managed to stick her head out from the top of the stairs when she stopped. It was sheer pandemonium. The battle had reached a fever pitch. There were several Liqusa bone-ships within a hundred yards of the *Nezra Rides*, each tossing everything they had at the Exiles flagship. Qisami ducked back under the deck as a drizzle of arrows pelted the stairs.

She surveyed the current battlefield. Several enemies and a few

Nezra pods had sunk or were in the act of sinking into the ground.
Malinde had explained that these pods had to keep moving or their
weight would send them into some underground ocean. The whole
thing sounded outlandish. They had both been drunk at the time, so
Qisami wasn't sure if Malinde's story had been a fool's tale.

Now she was watching as the land swallowed these shattered pods,
the ground seemingly pulling them into its depths. It was terrifying.
Now Qisami understood why these Grass Sea hordes had fought the
Zhuun for so long. They wanted to get to a place where the ground
was solid.

Qisami hurried back down to the viperstrikes. "It's madness up
there!"

Wani smirked, offering the buckler.

"Why do I need that stupid thing?"

She shrugged and tossed it aside. "I tried."

Marhi picked it up off the floor anyway. "Let's go."

The three joined a stream of heavily armored warriors pushing in
the same direction. Some carried spears and swords, but most carried
axes. Marhi had two shield bucklers strapped to her forearms and
wielded an iron baton in each hand. Wani carried an oval shield bigger than hers on her arms, and had the round buckler strapped to her
back. She looked like a sandwich.

"What are you using?" Qisami asked Wani. "You forgot to bring a
weapon."

The younger viperstrike grinned. "You'll just have to see."

Before them, a crowd of warriors faced a dead end.

Qisami nudged Marhi. "What are we doing here?" This reminded
her of the hazing she received during her first days at the training pool,
when a bunch of her older sisters put copper coins in their socks and
beat her until she had lost consciousness. She was fairly sure that
wasn't the case here this time around, but old traumas died hard.

Most of these kids looked green. Hands were shaking; half looked
as if they were about to piss themselves. She didn't see a whisker among
the babyfaces. The girls looked even younger.

"Viperstrikes coming through," someone called.

The warriors' focus turned to the three. A path opened before them. Marhi waded through first, followed by Qisami, and then Wani brought up the rear.

The fear drained from their faces, replaced by a feverish determination. "Viperstrike," some said.

"Viperstrike."

"Marhi, Wani."

"For Salminde."

"Viperstrike," the quiet but firm calls continued.

Qisami even got a few catcalls, which she appreciated.

"Assassin."

"Land-chained."

Someone patted Wani's shoulder. "We'll get her back."

"We won't let you down."

"I love you, Marhi."

Marhi snapped at the young man. "By the beautiful Woman's tit, not now!"

Qisami marveled at how enthusiastic they seemed. Salminde must be withholding their pay. That, or these people genuinely loved that sexy snake woman. Marhi turned to face the crowd of cheering warriors, her eyes nervous and downcast. She waved, then spun away, turning her back to them.

Qisami startled. "What the hell was that?"

"Nothing," Marhi mumbled. "I'm just getting ready to fight."

"No, I mean your cheering squad there. You can't just leave them pep-talk crumbs. Say something to rouse them to violence!"

"I waved," she replied. Even *she* knew that wasn't enough. Marhi sighed and sucked in her breath. "I don't like giving talks. It makes me nervous."

"You're about to go to battle. Isn't that more nerve-racking?"

"I'd rather go to battle than speak in public."

Qisami understood that. "Hey, listen, I get it, but these little wooden dummies are about to follow you into battle, and they're going to go fight and possibly die for your boss, so the least you can do is address them. Say a few nice things. Inspire them!"

The viperstrike squeezed her eyes shut and nodded. "All right. What should I say?"

"Speak from your gut."

Marhi sucked in a deep breath and turned to the large mass of Nezra warriors crowding the corridor. More were joining by the second.

"My sister and I humbly thank everyone for—"

Qisami turned her around. "What was that lame drivel?"

"I was thanking them! That's what you told me to do." She shook her head. "Why am I listening to a land-chained anyway?"

"They're going to rescue Salminde, not attend her wake."

"It's not a speech. I really mean it."

"That's even worse. Here, repeat what I say."

Marhi turned around. Qisami whispered into her ear. The girl pulled back, offended by Qisami's opening line, but then after some prodding, began to repeat her impromptu speech. "Hey, you wooden blockheads, don't die."

The crowd's reaction was confused. Qisami blamed it on a shoddy delivery.

Marhi continued after a couple elbows into her ribs. "You don't get to die because that would be embarrassing." She faced Qisami again. "Are you sure I should be saying this?"

"Have you ever led anyone into battle? I didn't think so. Trust me."

Marhi coughed and addressed the crowd again. "Your ancestors would think poorly of you because your enemies are terrible. They're sheep! They're bad like last week's potatoes."

"What's a potato?" someone asked.

Marhi continued, "Like gangrene on a chicken leg. Losing to them would be terrible for your self-esteem, and your ancestors would think poorly of you."

Qisami whispered, "They might even disown you."

Marhi shook her head. "I'm not saying that."

"Tell them they would live an eternity being a disappointment and destitute, every child's worst nightmare."

"No, that's terrible." Marhi threw her hands up. "Forget it. I'll just say it myself."

The viperstrike nudged Qisami away with her elbow. She addressed the warriors again, this time using her own voice. "Your ancestors will think poorly if you die because you are lions! Lions do not fall to sheep. Lions do not cower when they are on the hunt. Lions take what they are owed!"

The crowd was more roused with this change of tone.

Qisami was modestly impressed. Where was this little cracking whip all this time?

"And what are we owed?" Marhi was screaming now.

"The viperstrike!"

"We're going to bring her home! We will *not* be denied. The Bone Clan will fear the name of Nezra. We will be victorious and bury their clan under the Grass Sea!"

The packed crowd of warriors cheered.

Marhi yanked the lever to the side and turned back to face the wall. "Gangrene on a chicken leg," she muttered. "You almost made me choke on my drink."

Qisami smirked.

The metal wall before them began to fall away slowly, as if forming a platform, exposing them to the outside elements. A strong gust of wind slammed into them, whipping Marhi's cloak directly into Qisami's face. She was momentarily blinded as she slapped at the fluttering cloak, nearly losing her balance when the city pod suddenly shook and rumbled, likely from an artillery blast.

Qisami finally brushed it off and looked outside. By now, their city pod was in the very heart of the battle. The Kahun-designed pods were quicker than the enemy's and were able to avoid much of the slow-hitting artillery. At the same time, however, the enemy pods were larger. The *Nezra Rides* shook as more artillery crashed into it. The pod was taking a beating, but the enemy looked equally damaged.

She squinted in the distance. "Is that a balloon?"

"Liqusa scout lantern," said Marhi.

There were arrows and rocks flying between pods. A spray of moderate-sized rocks clattered against the hull, shot from a small, tracked vehicle near the ground level while someone from those stupid balloons was taking potshots with fire arrows at them.

Wani offered the shield again. "Last chance."

Qisami took it. It wasn't hard to identify which pod was her target. The *Heartbone*, as the pod was known, was nearly upon them, barely more than a stone's throw away. It was easily the biggest and ugliest of the bunch. Liqusa's command heart was a massive city pod with large black ribs forming a cage along the edge of the platform. At its center was a squat tower that was shaped like a heart, and they were heading straight for it.

"That thing is ugly."

"The Liqusa have eclectic taste," said Marhi, pushing her way next to them.

Qisami now appreciated her big shield. "Where are the ropes? How are we going to get on board?"

The viperstrike chuckled. "That would be funny."

"Why is that?"

Marhi shouted over the rising excitement. "Ramming speed! Brace for impact."

CHAPTER FORTY-NINE

SECOND CHANCE

S ali remained in a state of stunned confusion for several days after her conversation with the Eternal Khan of Katuia, or Visan as his dead name went. She had traveled in captivity for nearly a month, blindfolded, tied up, and boxed, and had been ready to face her end, either publicly for treason, or privately by the spirit shamans. The least imaginable outcome had occurred: a way back to the horde. Even more important, back to hope and a potential future.

Back to civilization. To culture, music, and community. To tasty food. Flavorful, intense Katuia dishes that scorched the tongue and drenched your brow but kept you begging for more. Spice was the one thing Sali missed so much it nearly moved her to tears. Even at their cultural height, Nezra was not known as a culinary clan. The reborn Nezra was bereft of food, supplies, and talent. No one knew how to cook. Sali's stomach certainly wanted to accept the khan's offer.

"It will be as if nothing had changed over these past few years," he had said.

But that was impossible. Things could never go back to how they were before, at least not in the same way. Much had changed. *She* had changed. But that didn't mean things couldn't begin anew.

The possibility weighed heavily upon Sali. Visan had lifted her confinement to the temple. She spent her newfound freedom wandering the streets of Chaqra, with its vast network of interconnecting pods. At this time, only four other pods were currently linked to *Aracnas*, the large, circular city pod carrying them to the Sanctuary of the Eternal Moor. The others had spread out like a vast armada across the expansive savanna that formed the eastern edge of the Xing Duchy. They were moving at a rapid clip, rolling over the clustered patches of shrubs and small trees with their heavy tracked wheels.

Sali had rarely ventured this far south during her raidlife. The dry heat did not agree with her. Fortunately, one of the pods linked to *Aracnas* housed Chaqra's book-storage house, which was insulated and kept cooler to preserve the written texts. It was the largest in the Grass Sea, and by decree of the spirit shamans, housed a copy of every book ever written in their tongue. Sali spent many hours in the shamans' records house poring over recent papers to learn about this new khan.

Visan had been a neophyte right here in Chaqra when he had been discovered by a soulseeker. It occurred quickly, mere days after Sali had been cured of the soul rot. Usually, it would take years if not decades before a new khan was found.

"How lucky for them," she muttered, "and within their own ranks."

Young Visan had been an excellent student, at the top of his year, excelling in every category within his shamanic studies, from history to ritualistic casting to the Eight Limbed Art. It was rare for someone to be so naturally gifted. It had been a joyous occasion, if not entirely surprising, that Visan had been discovered to be the reincarnation of the Eternal Khan of Katuia. The glowing reports continued for several pages, chronicling his many accomplishments.

Sali flipped through more pages of accolades for the lad. Visan must have been a savant to have accomplished so much. She finished going through the record and reached for the next volume, then held the two sets of documents side by side. The one she had just finished was noticeably fresher than the next, with its withered yellow pages.

"Of course," she muttered. They had lied about the history of all the old khans back at the Grand Monastery of the Dawn Song. Why would they be truthful about the new one?

Hours later, as she was perusing birth records, she came across another interesting bit. The young little overachiever's uncle just happened to be Brother Vanus, one of the ruling spirit shamans belonging in the Circle.

A suspicion bubbled in Sali's mind. If there was any time for a new khan to return so quickly, it would be now, at this moment, considering the upheaval in the world. Sali did not believe in coincidences.

The constant whir from the engines below shifted, taking on a higher pitch. Gravity shifted too, tugging her in one direction just enough to notice. The lamps tilted overhead at a slight angle. The city pod was gaining speed. A loud chord strummed, resonating in the wind. The shamans working at the table at the front of the book-storage house stopped what they were doing and drew sabers from the weapon vase beneath the table. All six were soon armed and hurried outside.

The last one leaving stopped at the doorway and glared at Sali. "You cannot stay here alone, traitor."

So much for nothing changing. Chaqra was going to view her as a traitor, regardless. Sali nearly snapped back at the boy but decided she was curious about what was happening outside anyway. She followed the young shaman outside, into the late evening. She looked over at *Aracnas* across the bridge. It, too, was running dark. She looked the other way over the railings to the other pods rolling nearby, all dark. Sali looked up. The sky was blotted with clouds. None of the moons or stars could throw their light down on these lands. The engines, however, were running hard. The stacks rising near the bow were burning hot. There was no mistaking the pod's intentions; a battle was brewing.

The bridge connecting this pod to *Aracnas* made a loud clicking sound as chains supporting the network platforms began to rattle. The bridges connecting the pods were about to disengage. This cluster of pods was separating. She glanced up and could just make out the silhouette of Visan, standing at the forward balcony, near the top of the sanctuary tower, as a sliver of moonlight penetrated the clouds.

Sali made a quick decision and took off, sprinting down the street toward the port side of the pod, reaching the foot of the bridge just as the center hooks unlinked. The two platforms began to retract, pulling away from each other. She continued sprinting, reaching the edge of this half of the bridge just as it was a good ten feet from the other half. Sali attempted the jump, partially because she wanted to be on *Aracnas* to get answers directly from the khan, but also because she just wanted to try the jump.

She made it, barely, with her heel hanging off the edge as she landed on the other retracting bridge. She teetered before catching her balance, and grinned. Bridge jumping was one of the riskier games she had played as a youth. It was always a dare to see who could make the most risky jump. Sali never won, because she wasn't a fool.

She waited at the edge of the bridge until it had fully retracted, ignoring the tinker scowling at her as she hurried back to the sanctuary. She passed several more shamans and city residents. All were armed and moving to their war stations. Every city pod inhabitant, from elite towerspears to the youngest weed, knew their assigned stations. She reached the Sanctuary of the Eternal Moor and continued up the three flights to the top, where she found Visan.

He stood still, studying the darkness. "You made that jump. Not bad. I wasn't sure if you still had it in you." Jiamin had always bested her, but he had always been more reckless with his life.

"I'm older, not ancient," she replied. "What is going on, Visan?" From this vantage, she could make out the silhouettes of the other city pods lining up in a row on both sides of *Aracnas*. "Why is Chaqra lined up in a shock formation?"

The khan continued looking forward. "Have you considered my offer, Salminde?"

It was almost the only thing she had thought about since they spoke. "The spirit shamans abandoned Nezra. That is an insult and crime not easily forgiven."

"If you hold on to the past, one day it will be too heavy for you to walk into the future."

"Keep my father's words out of your mouth." He also had a point. Sali hated that. Was a grudge worth her people's safety? Was turning down the khan's offer a principled stand or foolish ego? Sali was unsure what was the honorable choice anymore, let alone the right one.

Silence drifted between them. The warm rustling air around them was a choir of singing sands squeaking as the *Aracnas* rolled on. Sali felt the soft vibration of the engines even this high in the tower. Chaqra's city pods had always been technological marvels. The tinker sect's main academy was located here. Just three pods over to her starboard, actually. She had walked with Mali to that place many times during their childhood.

"He loved you, you know."

Sali turned to the khan. "Jiamin was the brother of my heart."

"It's not too late. He's still here." Visan placed a palm over his heart. "The two of you can still make up for lost time."

Sali shook her head. "Those moments in time have passed, nor is the Eternal Khan of Katuia part of the natural world. We can never return to the world we once lived."

"I do not have control over being the Eternal Khan of Katuia any more than you do as a child of Nezra." Visan did not sound offended. "I am no more unnatural than the winds that blow through the gyres. Judging me for my existence is no different from judging the birds for flying or the land beneath our feet for moving."

Sali hated this argument because she knew it was true. The khan couldn't help but be who he was. Visan was just as much a victim as Jiamin had been. To pass judgment on him for being the khan was like judging someone else for being short, bald, or old.

"You still have a choice." But did he?

"Just like a snake only knows how to be a snake and a wind horse only a wind horse, a khan can only serve his people as a khan." Visan turned to face her. "The real question, Salminde, is what you plan to do with what little years you have left. Do you plan to place your name among the stars or are you content withering away in peaceful obscurity?"

"If my name is with the stars, then where is yours?"

"I would be the sun, of course. My actions today will be praised for generations."

"And what would those be?"

Visan turned back toward the darkness before them, his smile growing as he stared into the abyss.

Her answer came a moment later when a lone light on the horizon appeared. At first, it looked like a star that had fallen to earth or perhaps a bonfire. Below, four large siege platforms began burning as the pitches of the large siege catapults were set on fire. Moments later, a line of flames stretched to both sides of the pod.

Sali turned to Visan. "What is happening?"

Visan's lips curled. He nodded and continued staring ahead at that lone light in the distance. A few seconds later, he raised his face and bellowed, "Loose!"

On command, every catapult from Chaqra's pods launched their pitch, sending hundreds of fireballs high into the night, illuminating the landscape as they soared overhead. Sali gripped the cold, black stone of the temple balcony and watched as the fireballs converged on that light in the distance. A moment before impact, the shine these flaming pitches illuminated revealed the target.

"A border watchtower," she whispered. That meant Chaqra had ventured deep into Xing territory. That also meant . . . Sali turned to the khan. "Your target is Xusan. You're going to raid the Xing capital?"

"Not a raid," he replied. "You should thank me, Salminde the Viperstrike. We will do to the Zhuun what they did to Nezra. Justice rides tonight."

CHAPTER FIFTY

CITIES BATTLE

Qisami did not recommend fighting a pitched battle.

She had watched, mouth agape, as the *Nezra Rides* cut through the thick clumps of the jungle, its giant tracks plowing the weeds across the low but thick vegetation. The pod's target, the *Bone Soul*, was the command heart of the Liqusa capital city, housing their terrifying rib cage fortress, the Necro Citadel. The enemy pod was easily three times larger than the *Nezra Rides*. Fortunately, the quicker and more technologically advanced Kahun pod had other ways to compensate for its diminutive size.

The *Nezra Rides* circled the *Bone Soul* like a porpoise around a whale. The quicker ancient city pod, with its pointed teardrop front, slipped to the side of the Liqusa pod and gashed the hull with hooked, protruding blades, slicing its metal flesh open with a shriek, exposing the pod's metal innards. The collision had been spectacular, teeth shattering as if the world had just come to a sudden stop. Qisami would have been knocked off her feet had she not clung on to Wani's leg for dear life when she did fall.

The *Nezra Rides* bumped against the wound of the injured pod. A wall of vertical boarding ramps lowered, serving as a bridge between the two hulls. A roar erupted from around Qisami and then the mob surged forward.

The distance between the two pods may have been only about fifty feet, but it was the longest fifty feet of her life. The moment she stepped into the open space between the two pods, the sky began to rain arrows, rocks, lukewarm oil, corpses, and other gross things. Qisami got splashed by dark liquid that she was fairly sure was feces. The downpour grew worse the closer they neared the entry point. Their progress stalled, forcing Qisami to stand out in the open while getting pelted. She raised her tiny buckler and lowered her head like everyone else, hoping not to be one of the unlucky ones getting killed while waiting for their turn to fight.

Many of the warriors who began this attack alongside her were no longer standing. She blamed her good fortune on being short. Everyone taller served as a shield. Some unlucky warriors were killed by projectiles. Others were knocked off the ramps. They really should build some railings on these things.

In most cases, the secret to surviving battles was to be lucky. A rock could fall on your head. A random arrow could punch you. An artillery shot could explode you into tiny bits. There were so many ways to die on the battlefield. The worst part was it was all random. Almost none of it was in your control.

It was one of Qisami's greatest fears growing up in the training pool. No amount of skill could account for a giant rock falling out of the sky and smashing your head like a bitter melon. There were few things more annoying than training a lifetime for battle only to eat an arrow fired by some peasant archer who was shooting them into the sky.

The best student in her training pool had died on her first job because lightning struck the rooftop she was sneaking across. Come to think of it, that girl also preferred metal armor, so maybe she was not very bright. Certainly not lucky.

The truly skilled, like Qisami, could make their own luck. She was usually the best war artist in the room. This appeared to be the case as she unleashed herself at the Liqusa like a badger in a chicken coop. She took advantage of the dark, crowded hallways, stepping in and out of small spaces of blackness. Her fighting style had changed over the years. She no longer went for every killing blow. She was older and more calculating now, content to make longer but surer deaths.

Part of Qisami questioned why she was so stupidly loyal to these people. She didn't owe them anything. That greedy voice inside her was still encouraging her to jump over the side of the ramp and disappear into the jungle. Just forget all this clan-on-clan violence. This wasn't her fight. They were less than three days from the Zhuun borders. She could make it if she tried.

The truth was, Qisami had come to the Grass Sea because it was the only way to escape the Happy Glow. Then she didn't escape at her first opportunity because she was curious about Salminde the Viperstrike. After Salminde was captured, she stayed because they were heading the same direction—toward Zhuun lands—as her. Then Qisami met the rest of the Nezra clan, and she stayed because she liked Malinde. She had grown fond of most of these Nezra Kati. But did she like them enough to eat an arrow for them? If there had been an easier way to worm out of this with her pride intact, she might have done so.

Much to her annoyance, fighting inside the cramped tunnels of these pods was far worse than fighting up top. Qisami led the charge through the breach point into the gear layer inside the enemy pod, through the twisty metal tunnels under the pods. The *Bone Soul's* passages were wider than the *Nezra Rides's*, but also the ceilings were lower, forcing even a shorty like Qisami to have to squat. It made for cramped, ugly, claustrophobic fighting.

Qisami swept forward with the other Nezra warriors. The two sides charged, slamming shields and hacking. This wasn't fighting but dumb luck. When faced with a wall of Liqusa spears, Qisami would drop through a shadow behind them and wreak havoc, breaking up their defensive line, giving the Nezra a chance to break through. Most of the enemy carried kris spears with their wavy blade ends, far too cumbersome to wield against a shadowkill. She dodged those, moving within their guards and sticking her short blades with precision thrusts into the flesh between armored pieces. Again, it was more chopping wood than carving a figurine. Half the time she had to use the same two techniques: Nun Shakes Her Finger No followed by Viper's Appreciation for Being Stepped On. Qisami must have killed a dozen Chaqra that way.

Then, much to her chagrin, Qisami lost one of the baby snakelets. One moment, Wani was fighting by her side, then the girl broke ranks and chased after a fleeing enemy towerspear. Qisami at the time was busy helping Marhi fight off four enemy warriors. She had taken her eye off Wani for only a minute, just enough time to score two kills, when she turned back and the silly girl had disappeared.

Qisami momentarily panicked. Then she saw Wani farther down one of the side passages, surrounded by what appeared to be a bunch of those tinkers armed with metal sticks and clubs. Qisami broke into a sprint, shoving friend and foe aside, shadowstepping when necessary or just elbowing anyone who got in the way as she fought her way to Wani's side.

The girl had been oblivious to her danger. She brightened when Qisami appeared next to her. "Hey, Qisami. Isn't this fun?"

Qisami deflected a spear thrust and cut a Liqusa towerspear across the back of his knee. "Stay close, kitten, or I'm going to drown you in a shallow puddle after we're done here."

Both neophytes were actually decent, especially for young women only a few years into their craft.

They were enthusiastic hobbyists, try-hard amateurs. Qisami had expected more from Salminde's heirs until she learned that this was the viperstrike's second litter of students. She remembered the first boy, Hampa or Bimbo or whatever his name was. She had captured him back at Jiayi and slapped him around. Tough kid, loyal, stubborn. She appreciated that about him even as she had nearly beaten him to death. Perhaps Salminde had a thing for strays. In any case, these two kittens were Salminde's wards, so they were now Qisami's problems as well.

The two young viperstrikes had annoying habits. Wani, of course, kept wandering off like an eager puppy. Marhi, however, posed an even greater problem. Although she was the more skilled and experienced of the two, Marhi's confidence outweighed her modest abilities. The young woman would charge headlong into a Liqusa, knock them down, and move on to the next enemy before finishing the job. Then Marhi would find herself surrounded by her beaten foes who'd returned for a rematch. Qisami was certain neither of the women would have survived the first hour of the attack if she had not been running around like a panicked mother bitch herding her wayward puppies.

The fight eventually wound through the gears and made it onto the main deck of the enemy pod. The problem they had to deal with now was things thrown out of windows from the buildings on the main deck. One Nezra warrior fighting alongside Qisami died when a cooking wok crushed his head. She was about to avenge him when she realized his killer was an eighty-year-old grandmotherly type on the third floor of a building. There was little chance Qisami was going to run up all those stairs just to murder an octogenarian.

Six Nezra were shredded by a ballista bolt that ripped through their ranks as they advanced down a corridor. Three more perished when they turned the corner and were pin-cushioned by arrows. Then half of the remaining group fighting alongside Qisami were cut down when two waves of enemy surrounded them in a pincer attack. Still, they fought on.

Qisami stayed near Marhi, huddling under her shield as if sharing an umbrella. The taller viperstrike looked down and frowned. "What happened to your bucklers?"

"I lost them saving your dumb asses. How did you think you got past those four skull-faced ax-wielding black deaths back there? Did you think you took them out by yourself?"

"Yes," Marhi said without hesitation. "The staunch Warrior is fighting by my side today."

Qisami swallowed her frustration and attempted to speak more diplomatically. "We're going to have to talk about your hubris after this, assuming you survive."

"Why wouldn't I? I am in better shape than you. There's barely a scratch on me."

Qisami felt the deep urge to grind her teeth to their nubs. She wanted to reach over and strangle the lass. Thankfully, the two snakelets were more or less fine. Marhi might have broken her arm; at least it wasn't her good one. Wani broke her nose. Her unusually high bridge now looked like a lightning bolt. Other than that, the two were as good as new, at least for now. They were still two blocks from the Necro Citadel, and there was a whole lot of dying to be had.

Fortunately, their dwindling group was soon joined by other Nezra. They joined forces and pressed on. The attack on the Necro Citadel had been messier than they anticipated, but they had the numbers to break through the last line of Liqusa defenses.

Qisami pointed at the ugly, squat, skull-shaped building. "Salminde is in there?"

"That's where she would be held . . ." said Wani, her expression downcast, "assuming she's still alive."

Qisami hated trying to cheer these kids up, but here she was. "Of course she's still alive. The spirit shamans wouldn't waste this opportunity to kill her in public, so as long as we haven't heard about it, she's probably alive."

The three led a crowd of a hundred assembled warriors, mostly Nezra, some Happan, and a smattering of their other allies, through the narrow streets, splitting down different curved paths before intersecting again. They pulled up at the entrance of the Necro Citadel, where three rows of Liqusa warriors guarded the front gates to the fortress. They weren't the regular variety, however. They carried the haughty air of a war arts sect.

"Coldshatters," hissed Wani.

"What's that?"

"Liqusa's war arts sect. Sali fought them before, killed one of their leaders."

"I guess talking our way out of this is out of the question," said Qisami.

"They'll demand a duel. I must represent my sect." Marhi grimaced as she stepped forward, holding her injured arm close.

Qisami yanked her back. "Not a chance, duckling. Even if you weren't hurt, that woman looks like she could bake you for biscuits."

"It's my duty as the champion of the sect in Sali's absence."

Qisami spun Marhi around. "You honor nothing by acting a fool. Salminde's in there, waiting for you. Go ahead."

Marhi looked relieved. The young woman's pride didn't swallow her common sense, at least.

Qisami focused on her opponent, who looked suspiciously like a strange bog hag she had heard about in romance books—that or stepmothers. The woman was ancient by war artist standards and had a long white mane of bushy hair and a crazed air about her, as if she cooked children in a pot. Her eyes were milky, her skin like a dried prune. She had a haunted look about her. She spoke in a lilting gravelly voice. "Is this some sort of Nezra insult, sending a filthy landchained as the viperstrike's champion? I will not tolerate this disgrace."

"Very well, I accept your forfeit," Qisami shouted.

"I am Zowna, first of the coldshatters, a matriarch of Liqusa." The woman hissed like a strangled cat. "You will not desecrate this holy temple with your shameful presence, land-chained."

"Well, I'm not beneath beating grandbitches, either. Don't worry. I'll make it quick. That is, unless you want to drag it out."

"I've spent the last few moments of my dwindling time in this world having to deal with the likes of you, and none of it was pleasant. What makes you think I wish to waste more time on you?"

"You don't have to be so mean about it." She leaped forward to bury a blade in this woman's eyeball. Qisami moved low to the ground, shifting left and then right, and then just as she neared Zowna, she dove into a shadow and emerged flying upward just above the woman's back shoulder. She drew two blades from their sheaths and slammed them down on the back of Zowna's neck. It would have been a spectacular one-hit killing blow, except for the fact that the coldshatter master suddenly vanished in a puff of white mist. One moment the target was exposed, and the next, Qisami's arm passed right through her. The mist swirled and dissipated, leaving Qisami standing there, grabbing at nothing. She looked around, confused, and then startled when the mist coalesced back into human form.

"How did you do that?" Qisami gawked. "Can you teach me?"

The hag bared her crooked teeth. She reached out and slapped Qisami clean across the nose. Half of her face immediately went rigid. She stumbled back as cold pain seeped into her bones. The coldshatter master smirked, exposing more rotting teeth, and attacked, hungry fingers reaching for any part of Qisami's body.

The coldshatter was deadly to the touch. Now Qisami really wished she still had those bucklers. "Damn viper-kittens," she muttered.

The coldshatter master had blurring hand speed despite her age. She attacked several more times, her swings and thrusts blinding quick, since she did not have to put any force behind her attacks; her mere touch was damaging enough.

Fortunately, her technique's advantage worked both ways. While her touch was deadly, it also meant the coldshatter master was fighting without weapons. That left Qisami free to slash with her Kati daggers. The two canceled each other out as they exchanged swing hands and blades, even as they attempted to keep their distance.

Qisami hated to admit that she was getting tagged more often than she gave back. Zowna had only suffered grazing blows along the shoulder and thigh. She took a deeper cut right down the middle, between her sagging tits, but was otherwise coming out of these exchanges mostly unscathed.

Qisami was getting worse than she gave, and in front of an audience, no less! She was sporting half a dozen purple blots across her body that tingled like blisters, likely frostbite. The damage aggregated, causing her joints to lock and slowing her with every hit. This woman was truly a master war artist.

The real problem with Zowna wasn't her attack. It was her annoying ability to mist her body whenever Qisami's blade was supposed to hit. Killing slices slipped right through her suddenly incorporeal body, which would then solidify just as she countered. The few times Qisami managed to tag her were when she had been caught off guard. The master was too old and savvy for that to work too many times, however.

Their battle became one of mist and shadow as the two fought before the Necro Citadel. Qisami eventually managed to draw their fight into an alcove and for a moment seized the upper hand, gashing the side of Zowna's raisin head and slicing six inches of white thinning hair off before disappearing into the darkened corner close by, emerging out of arm's reach.

They traded fists for several more exchanges, with Zowna getting one or two touches in. The two pivoted and spun like dance partners, popping into shadows and puffing into mist throughout the courtyard so often the darkness and mist began to swirl.

Qisami had made it a closer match than she'd anticipated, but there was no mistaking who was the better war artist. Short of luck, an experienced war artist knew when a fight was lost. The difference between a highly skilled war artist and a true master was that the master made fewer mistakes. As the fight continued, both women slowed.

Qisami suffered from the cumulative effects of the coldshatter master's touch. Every frozen purple welt shot tweaks of pain up her arms and legs every time she moved. Every joint ached whenever they bent. It was as if she could feel parts of her system slowly shutting down.

As for Zowna, she was just an ancient woman. The coldshatter master had dropped her hand and was noticeably wheezing as the fight progressed. She just wasn't getting tired fast enough.

It wasn't long before Qisami made that fatal mistake. She juked to the right to avoid the coldshatter's attack, but mistimed their distance. No sooner had Qisami exposed her head than Zowna's curled fingers reached out and clasped around her neck.

Cold enveloped her. Qisami's legs gave and her breath became labored. She pawed at Zowna's arm to no avail. Damned old hag had strong fingers! The freezing shock was moving into her brain. The room dimmed and was about to go full black when a large round shield crashed into the coldshatter master. Qisami dropped to her knees, gasping. Her throat constricted as she tried to suck air into her lungs. She looked up at Zowna, still standing. It was her attacker— Wani in this case—who received the worst of the impact.

The younger viperstrike rolled to her feet and tucked her body behind the shield. Then the strange tube sticking out in the middle of the shield shot a jet of flame. The burst of pyrotechnics initially startled Qisami, and then she was quickly underwhelmed. "That's it? That's all it does? What kind of piss-ass Tiandi limp-lily weapon is that?"

"This limp lily just saved you, assassin."

Qisami shrugged. The girl had a point.

Zowna waved a hand and the fire went out. The coldshatter master swooped in and knocked the girl down. She raised an open palm and was about to smack the younger viperstrike's face when it hovered.

She stood. "How the viperstrikes have fallen, depending on a slip of a girl and a land-chained to serve as their champion."

Qisami took advantage of Wani's diversion to slip behind Zowna and press a dagger to her throat. She tried to speak and failed the first few times. Her mouth was still numb. "Pathetic enough to get a blade on you, old woman."

Zowna was not bothered by her imminent death. "I do not kill children. My soul is satisfied with this journey's conclusion."

Qisami shrugged and began to drag the blade across the coldshatter's neck, and then stopped. There was no such thing as cheating in war, but it didn't mean there weren't moments she felt guilty. She glanced over at Wani still prone on her back, wide-eyed and looking as if she were staring death in the face, and then back at Zowna, chin raised and awaiting her fate. Qisami cursed and relaxed her dagger. "Fine. It's a draw. We'll both retire from the field."

Zowna turned to face Qisami. Her look of surprise was as great as Qisami's annoyance and was soon replaced with a small smile. "Honor is the way, land-chained."

"Yeah, yeah, whatever, you old crone." Qisami, irritated with herself, turned and walked away.

CHAPTER FIFTY-ONE

THE SECOND PLAN

J ian sat on a bench at the edge of the kidney-shaped pond at the center of the pebble garden and tried to meditate. It wasn't going well. He never got the hang of it back at the Cloud Pillars. Water trickled down a narrow stream emptying into a small pond at his feet, its babbling sounds echoing around the cavern. The lantern next to him hissed in the moisture-laden air every now and then. He had spent the past few hours here, partially because it was calm and cool, but mainly because Jian was bored.

His recovery under the care of the Skyfall healers had progressed well. The wound to his chest was now just an ugly star-shaped scar with some tightness every time he breathed in too deep. His other injuries had scabbed over or healed. He still could only hobble around, but his strength was returning. The healers at Skyfall Temple were skilled.

In many ways, his stay reminded him of his days back at the Celestial Palace. He was an especially important person, after all. Back then, he didn't mind being a caged bird, but Jian was not that silly, spoiled boy anymore, and the idea of having to stay on the temple grounds was driving him crazy. Skyfall Mountain was beautiful, but there was surprisingly little to do. At the Vauzan temple, there were always monks training, giving tours, teaching classes, and running the prayer halls. The Vauzan temple's main purpose was to attract the devout and their donations. Templeabbot Mori ran an efficient operation that not only engaged the city's residents but made them repeat customers.

Skyfall's purpose was not to serve the people, but to serve the religion itself. It was here that monks were trained to be abbots, where the high seats ruled, and where administrators determined policy and managed the dozens of religious sects, hundreds of temples, and thousands of monks and nuns. Skyfall was not a place where monks trained in the war arts. Commoners were not even allowed on holy grounds except for major religious events. Most of the monks who walked the grounds were older, while the only Hansoo Jian had seen—other than Pahm—were the ones guarding the entrance to his hospital wing.

Jian shifted in his seat, his backside growing numb against the hard stone. He might as well put his time here to use. He closed his eyes again, attempting to recenter himself, focusing on his breathing. Jian's mind wandered, first sensing the cold touch of the stone seeping through his thin garments. He listened to the lapping of the pond's waves, which harmonized with the rustling weeds and the soft plunking noise of water dripping down from the stalactites. A low whistle reverberated every time the wind tickled the back of his neck. Jian sensed it all, although he still had difficulty keeping his mind grounded. His thoughts tugged him in every direction. How long was he supposed to stay here? Where would he go next? Where was Taishi, and Sonaya, and the rest of his friends? Why wasn't anyone telling him anything?

As for Meehae, she was acting weird. Jian had missed his old friend since she left the Cloud Pillars and had been dismayed that she kept their conversations professional, as if he were only her patient and not her old friend. Every conversation they had focused on his health. The few times he tried to catch up with her, she fled. He couldn't understand why, and she refused to tell him. That really hurt.

Lastly, Jian thought about the prophecy and his role in fulfilling it. He had never experienced a day without the weight of that awful burden and Jian was tired. He had finally made a life for himself in Vauzan. He had friends, a home, activities, and a social life. No one was trying to kill him! It was great!

Now Vauzan was probably gone, and Jian could never be himself again. He felt a hole in his soul. For those brief happy years, he had been himself, Wen Jian. He had lived a normal life, and he had loved it. Those were days he would never experience again. That very public reveal saw to that. From now on, he would only be the Prophesied Hero of the Tiandi to the rest of the world, not Wen Jian.

Jian, eyes closed, shook his head. "Stop spiraling, you fool."

But he couldn't help it.

Jian.

He looked to both sides. He was alone in the garden save for the gardener raking gravel on the far side and that strange man with the high-collared robes and black spectacles standing in the archway. The man rarely spoke, only offering a deep bow whenever Jian tried to strike up a conversation. One of the healers had bowed when he passed, calling him an inquisitor, which Jian assumed was some sort of Tiandi religious magistrate. He could certainly sense strong jing in the man. The old boy was probably here to protect him.

Jian *was* an important person.

Wen Jian, the weird voice in his head spoke again. He was definitely not imagining it.

"Who is this?" he said aloud.

Inside voice, Five Champ.

Jian gasped. *Sonaya? Is that really you? Are you here at Skyfall Temple?* He craned his head. *Where are you? What are you doing?*

You're making a scene right now, aren't you?

I miss you so much. What happened to everyone? Is Taishi with you? Is she all right?

Later, love. Xinde took a job with the local garrison shepherding the monks. He's smuggled me into the temple. I got as close to you as I can. Can you make your way to the lower levels?

Jian glanced at the gardener, and then his guard. *I have babysitters, but I'll try.*

All right. Just, just don't overact. That's what you do. There was a pause. *I'll contact you soon.*

"I do not . . ." he grumbled. He stared at the gardener. The old man had his back turned toward him, humming a song as he raked the gravel. Then Jian stood and faced the inquisitor, walking as casually as he could muster. He waved at the stuffy-faced man as he passed. "I'm going to go for a walk. I'll be back soon."

"Kindly remain on this level, great hero." The inquisitor was a man of few words.

"I've already walked this level a hundred times. I'm just going to stretch my legs." Jian raised a foot onto the railing and went through the motions of touching his toes. Was this too much, or not enough? He wasn't sure.

The inquisitor stared at Jian for several moments, his nose flaring. Finally, "Very well, holy one. Be sure to stay within the confines of the temple."

Jian nodded as he passed him toward the stairs. "I'll be back soon."

That was easy. He kept his head up and continued down the stairs. He whistled, trying hard to act relaxed, and congratulated himself for only sneaking one peek back at the top of the stairs. The inquisitor was watching. That was no problem. He only had to walk a few more flights down the exposed face of the mountain, and then he could disappear in winding streets mostly covered by awnings. It would be easy to get lost in that maze of nooks and alleys.

He poked his temple with his finger as if pushing a button. *Are you there?*

There was no response. He waited at a tiny intersection, trying to get his bearings, and called her again.

Sonaya?

Still nothing.

There was too much traffic passing by. Standing around looked too conspicuous, so he picked a direction and walked.

A few minutes later, *Jian, are you at the first level?*

I was there fifteen minutes ago. Why didn't you answer when I called you?

You don't have an open line in my head, Jian.

Why not? You have an open line to mine.

Such is life, Five Champ. Hang on. Are you being followed?

Of course not.

There's mental jing clinging to you.

He wasn't sure what that meant. *I was with several healers today. Could that be from their work?*

Perhaps. Head to the barracks at the south end of the grounds. There's a white building behind it. Stay inconspicuous.

Jian picked up his pace even as he lowered his head. Many might not recognize who he was, but more might. The last thing he needed was for someone to throw themselves at his feet. The last time *that* wasn't awkward was when he was allowed to leave the Celestial Palace to Hengyu, the settlement nestled at its base. So many of the locals flocked to him, it nearly set off a riot. He had been nine years old at the time, and it was the last time he had set foot outside the Celestial Palace. Until Taishi kidnapped him, anyway.

The cobbled streets were organized and neatly marked. Everything was so clean. There were no vagrants along the sides of the buildings, no garbage strewn on the ground, and he swore every tree and hedge he passed was freshly manicured. Even the dogs and cats looked bathed and well groomed. This place didn't seem real.

Jian had to stop and ask for directions a few times, but he was careful, asking only the guards from the garrison and not any of the monks. He figured the devout were more likely to recognize him, while the guards were only looking for suspicious individuals, which he certainly was not. Finally, he made it to the barracks and remembered to head around the back. The armory looked like a little house, complete with its own garden wall. It was quaint, with a lacquered bridge that spanned a pond in the front yard leading to the entrance.

"They treat their weapons here better than they did their hero back in Vauzan," Jian grumbled.

He looked around and bolted across the bridge, then yanked the door handle and was surprised it opened so easily. The interior of the armory looked the part. It was lit only by the shine from the King through its many windows. A solid block of light shone through a window near the roof and illuminated a small workbench. The rest of the room was filled with racks of weapons. Three rows of pikes lined several racks on his left. Several more spears lined the right. Shields were on the far right wall, and an assortment of whips, chains, and catchpoles lined the right wall. Sword hilts stuck out of barrels in the back.

Jian didn't make it three steps inside when the door shut behind him. A sharp point touched his lower back, then the edge of a bladed fan slid across his neck just below the chin. He felt a prickly pain across his throat, and then wetness as a small stream of blood poured down his neck and stained his shirt.

His arms shot up. "I'm sorry, I didn't mean to come in here. It's not a good idea to kill me. I'm sort of important."

Strong hands turned him around, revealing Sonaya. "You're sort of important?"

"I . . ."

Sonaya threw herself against Jian, her arms wrapped around him, squeezing as she buried her face in the crook of his neck.

"Gentle," he stammered, caught off guard. His wound throbbed. "I missed you. I thought—"

She covered his mouth, first with her hand, and then she pulled his head down for his lips to meet hers. He was startled at first, and then warmth blossomed and surged through his body, reaching the tips of his fingers and toes. Her tongue touched his, probing and hungry. He inhaled her scent.

Sonaya pressed into him again. This time, he lost his footing and stumbled backward into one of the racks. The edge of a pike nicked the top of his head, but Jian didn't care. He felt heady, his thoughts intoxicated. Tears welled in his eyes. He missed her smell, like the last bloom of the screaming nightdrake flower before dawn's first light burned it away. He missed her touch, her fingers digging into his flesh, her body wedged between his thighs. All of his worries and loneliness and affection for her bubbled to the surface. He thought he'd lost her when he was hurt. Now she was here, holding him, and he was holding her, and the relief was palpable.

And soon out of control.

Jian's emotions overwhelmed him, and he began to sob. His face went crimson as he tried to regain his control.

Sonaya pulled back, startled. "It must be you, because I'm a great kisser."

"No, it's . . . I thought I would never see you again, and it was too much—"

Sonaya jumped him again, pressing her lips against his wet cheeks. Jian gasped, and then lust pushed every other thought out of his mind. Their lips hungered as they fell to their knees and then to the cold tiles below. He appreciated that the floors were swept and clean, even here in a weapons storage room. Jian's hands ran up her side until he touched the hardened leather of her breastplate.

Then he remembered where he was and stopped. "What do I do with that?"

She sat up. "Take it off?"

"But we're in a Tiandi temple. I don't know. It feels like sacrilege."

She smacked his chest. "You're their religious golden boy. You're their whole reason. You can't sacrilege yourself."

That felt true. However . . . "But aren't we trying to escape? Where's Xinde?"

"He said he'd be back to get me in an hour. Why are you trying to ruin the moment?"

"I'm not. I mean . . ." He looked around, alarmed. "What if someone comes in?"

"I've been hiding here for two hours. All this stuff is auxiliary gear. Not one soul has come by. No one is going to come—"

Someone came in. The door latch twisted with a heavy *thunk*, followed by muffled voices, and then the heavy wooden door began to swing open. Two monks, chatting amiably, walked in and stopped before them. Jian wasn't sure who was more surprised. It certainly wasn't Sonaya, who leaped to her feet.

The drowned fist hissed, "Exhaustion is setting in. Now, sleep."

The two toppled over, falling flat on their faces.

Jian stared. "When did you learn how to do that?"

"Sorry, I slap the compulsion on a little harder when I'm aroused or frustrated." She looked pointedly at him. "Or both."

The door twisted and opened again. This time, Jian was ready. He was closer, so he threw a punch right. To his surprise, whoever came in caught his punch and trapped his elbow in one smooth motion. Jian's reflexes took over. He was about to break the guard and throw an elbow when both men stopped.

"Hello, brother," said Xinde.

"Hello, big brother." Jian grinned back.

They embraced. Jian nearly fell apart again.

"You're early," said Sonaya.

"Something's happening." Xinde glanced outside before shutting the door. "Orders came down to stop the flow of traffic and bar the main gates. You weren't planning to stroll out the front door with the Prophesied Hero of the Tiandi, were you?"

"It would have been the easier way," Jian grumbled.

Sonaya frowned. "How do we get out now? Everyone is waiting for us just outside the walls."

Xinde studied Jian. "Do you think if I threw you from a catapult you could use your windwhispering skills to land safely?"

"*That's* your idea?" he sputtered.

"Just an option." Xinde looked at Sonaya. "Maybe we'll get lucky at the front gates."

She sneered. "You want to publicly kidnap the Prophesied Hero of the Tiandi, the whole blasted point of their religion, and walk him out the front gates of Skyfall Temple? I have no desire to be the most wanted person in the Enlightened States. I don't care how big my bounty is. I don't love that sort of attention."

"Fine, what do you propose, then?"

Sonaya looked around the room. "Dress us up as guards and send us out."

Xinde's mouth dropped.

Jian blinked, wide-eyed. "That's a good idea."

The three quickly threw everything together, finding old chest plates and tunics and a stack of straw hats in the corner. They armed themselves with a large shield and spear. They looked like kids playing at guards, but it would be sufficient as long as Xinde, the barrack commander, was leading them.

That struck an odd chord. Jian crossed his arms. "How do you automatically become an officer no matter where you go?"

"I guess I just have that leadership presence." The handsome man with the perfect face shrugged. "Stay close. I'll say I'm sending you on an important retrieval."

Jian and Sonaya flanked Xinde as he led them out. Jian stuck his chest out, walking stiffly as he imagined soldiers would, while Sonaya slouched with her head down and used her spear like a walking cane. He didn't know why she acted that way until they passed a group of guards. The three saluted Xinde, but then their eyes wandered down to Sonaya. Female guards were uncommon, and the few there often received extra attention. Sonaya slapped them with light compulsion to turn away as they passed.

She shook her head at Jian. "You still have that mental jing on you somehow."

"Fine, I'll bathe tonight."

"That's not how it works." She leaned close. "But I'd appreciate it."

They made their way to the front gates without any problems. Xinde's rank was enough as he walked up to the two guards attending the inner gate. "Open the gates. We're on an important errand for the high seat."

"But the high seat ordered the gates closed for the night."

"That decree obviously excludes those on a mission for the high seat. Open up."

They didn't need much more motivation. Soon, one of the gates was slightly ajar and Xinde ushered them through. "I'll catch up" were his last words.

Jian and Sonaya were left standing in the short tunnel between the two gates.

"Open outer gates!" Xinde's strong voice cut through the noise.

Jian's breath was uneven as he waited for the outer gates to open. Every second felt like ten. What was going on here? Were they found out? Was it too late? This had to work. This was their only chance. Suddenly, a series of deep, hollow *thunks* and chains rattling reverberated overhead. Counterweights were being dropped. Pulleys rattled as ropes slithered through the grooved wheels. The gates were finally opening. Jian's near hyperventilation switched to relief, and it came out of him in a nervous laugh. Then a pair of giant doors finally began to grind open.

Except it was the set of doors behind them, leading back into the city.

Jian shielded his eyes as the King's light hit him. The opening gates revealed a crowd of armored bodies. It was many soldiers, monks, and a few Hansoo.

"Oh no." Sonaya pointed at Xinde standing off to the side with his wrists manacled. She hissed. "Truthsniffer."

Then Jian noticed the man standing next to his friend. The plain-robed man with the high collar and black spectacles walked forward. "Take these two to the high seat. As for the traitorous guard, hang him at dawn."

CHAPTER FIFTY-TWO

THIRD PLAN

Taishi stood inside the stable on the opposite end of the south gate of Skyfall Temple, under the tiled awning. She stared outside through the row of vectored windows. This was taking too long. Xinde and Sonaya were supposed to be back by now, with or without Jian. They had been told to play it safe. This was only the third time Xinde had smuggled Sonaya in to search for Jian. They had time to fish him out. There was no need to risk capture. She closed her eyes, her arms trembling, and not just from her illness.

Sohn was even worse, pacing in circles next to her. Fausan was snoring next to a sleeping cow with his arm draped over her neck. He wasn't worried, and neither was Bhasani, who had stepped out to get something to eat. Truth be told, it wasn't a bad idea. They had already missed lunch, and Taishi was getting irritable.

Zofi, Hachi, and Kaiyu were sleeping in the corner. The children had taken it upon themselves to survey the front gates.

Sohn appeared in front of Taishi, his face lighting up as if he had just been smacked with an epiphany. "I think I have it."

"Congratulations. After sixty years, you got it."

"No, hear me out." Sohn gesticulated wildly, which was one of his ways of conveying gravity and presence. "What if I made Xinde the heir to the Eternal Bright Light lineage?"

Taishi chewed on a reed and cast a lazy eye. "That's pretty high up on the list of dumb things that have come out of your mouth."

"No, it's brilliant. It solves both our problems. Xinde is a noble young man. He deserves a noble old lineage."

"Why would Xinde want to join your lineage? He is a proud Longxian and a fine one at that."

"Sure, but the Longxian name is middling." He thumped his chest. "The boy deserves an old, venerated, prestigious lineage."

"It doesn't bother you that Xinde's never held a shield in his life?"

"He can learn."

"You think he's going to just ditch Longxian at his age and start over with Eternal Bright Light?" Taishi snorted. "You're sounding desperate."

"Well, you're not the only one dying."

Taishi raised an eyebrow. They were two warriors who had long conquered their fears of death, but it was still sad news. She empathized as only someone who was already dying could. "It doesn't matter, but how long?"

"What matters is who you plan to stand beside and what you plan to do with the time you have left."

Taishi reached over and embraced her old friend. "You're a good man, Soa Sohn. The mortal world has still not seen the best of you."

Fausan, lying in the hay patch, sat up. He clapped his hands. "Masterful performance, my talented friend. You certainly deserve the win."

Sohn pulled away from Taishi. He beamed. "I thought so too."

Taishi momentarily seethed. "Did *you* just pretend you were dying to win a bet?"

"Oh no, I would never do that." Sohn shook his head emphatically. "I actually am dying. Fausan was the first person I told this morning. He said there was no way I could coax a hug from you."

Her indignant scowl slowly evaporated. "Pay the man, Fausan."

Something moved near the front gate. Sohn sank under the vector window. Taishi slipped behind a pole, while Fausan disappeared into the haystack. Bhasani appeared a moment later, in a rush. One of her eyebrows was significantly larger and darker than the other.

Taishi's eyes widened. "Were you getting tweezer work done in the middle of a mission?"

"We've been sitting in this stinking stable for three days, and my face needs love too, Taishi."

Fausan crawled out of the hay and brushed his robes. "What's wrong, my love?"

"My daughter touched my mind, but only briefly. She had moved to the edge of our link, and then she was gone."

"What did she say?" asked Taishi.

"I couldn't tell, but it wasn't good."

"We should go," said Fausan.

Bhasani was pacing the room. "I can't sense my daughter. Some-one may be masking her from me."

"That means the monks might be onto us," said Sohn.

"We can't leave Xinde and Sonaya," said Bhasani.

"Rouse the kids. We'll come back for the others later." Taishi turned to Bhasani, who was obviously conflicted about leaving Sonaya behind. "We will return for both our children, sister. I swear upon Sanso."

Bhasani didn't hesitate as she hurried to one of the horses. "If these filthy monks so much as injure one hair on my daughter, I will spend the rest of my life making sure they yank their own bits off in their sleep."

That was oddly specific, which made Taishi wonder how many times Bhasani had enforced this threat.

A few moments later, the masters sped out of the stables on horse-back with Taishi riding double with Zofi. That girl was a klutz on anything four-legged. She certainly could not be relied on to stay up-right during a ride, let alone on a hard-charging horse. Taishi preferred it this way. She had lost too many children; she preferred to keep her last one close.

The group kept their steeds moving in a tight line as they sped down the narrow streets of the temple grounds. Fausan, leading the way, was being too careful picking his way around the sparsely filled streets. A pair of nuns walked in front of them at an intersection. Fausan had to yank the reins hard to the side. One of the nuns — an elderly crone — fell in the mud, crying out with terror. The big soft heart would have dismounted to help her up if Bhasani hadn't been behind him screaming to keep his fat ass on his saddle.

Bhasani grabbed the reins to Fausan's horse and urged her own past him to the front. "Follow me."

The group didn't have a choice but to follow. The eternal bright light master was less concerned about the safety of the monks as he plowed through the crowds haphazardly. Their line continued weaving along the narrow streets through crowds and people, knocking over several monks, overturning a cart, and releasing several crates of caged chickens. Then they passed by a large herd of Hansoo armed with giant hammer maces.

The head of the herd, a seven-ring Hansoo, stared perplexed, and then recognition painted his face. He leveled one of his hammer maces at Taishi. "It's the windwhisper assassin!"

"Assassin?" Taishi sputtered. "Are they still parroting that old lie? How dare they peddle—"

The herd charged, lumbering like a stampede of rabid gaurs. Taishi had been involved in more than her share of battle charges, riots, and panics, but a mass of Hansoo bearing down on you was a unique sort of terrifying.

"What are you waiting for? Get going, you clown cakes!" Bhasani slapped Sohn's back.

That woke him up. He sputtered out of his stupor and took off, leading the way for this last stretch of the temple grounds to the front gates. The massive set of double doors, some three stories tall, required an extensive network of pulleys, ropes, and manual labor to move. It was supposedly a rite of passage for monks to go on pilgrimage to Sky-fall Temple and assume a cycle of Heavenly Gate duty during their initiate period. The gates were still in the process of closing, their joints squealing and snapping like tiger pistol shrimps. Ten long ropes, five tied to each door, were being pulled by ten heaving monks.

"If that gate closes, we're dead men, or even worse, excommunicated."

"How is that worse than death, master?" asked Hachi, riding along-side Sohn.

"You can't go to heaven if you're excommunicated, and I dearly miss my mam."

This time several monks tried to stop them, much to their detriment. Several struck at Sohn's horse with their pikes, horsecutters, and spears, but they were brittle twigs against the shield jing of the eternal bright light. Wood shattered and metal bent as Sohn's jing expanded past his shield. At the same time, Fausan and Hachi took out the archers and guards charging in from all sides. Bhasani looked to both sides, causing several of the monks to drop their ropes and flee. The gates stopped closing. Only a narrow gap remained, barely wide enough to walk a horse through.

"Come on!" Sohn reached the opening first, jumping off and patting his steed through. He turned to face two of the gate monks and made short work of them, his powerful shield charges blasting through the monks with ease.

Fausan tumbled off his horse and rolled to one knee, flicking out several bullets and striking a few monks. Bhasani rode through next, followed by Taishi and the children. Sohn and Fausan emerged last, following them out the front gates.

"We bought a few seconds. The Hansoo can't fit through that gap." Fausan huffed, face flushed. "We can escape in the woods just beyond the settlement."

Bhasani led his horse back to him while the rest remounted. Hachi was by his master's side, helping him back on his horse. There was a heavy *thunk* and then the gates jerked, opening wider. Taishi looked back and saw the fifty Hansoo inching them farther open. The Hansoo streamed out a moment later and avalanched downhill toward them.

She kicked her horse, now taking the lead. "Go, go!"

The rest followed, racing through Hengyen's main street. The sounds of heavy galloping filled the narrow path. Taishi's speeding mare nearly bowled a vendor over as people jumped out of the way. Luckily, the crowds were light, though still they had run over a few people by the time they reached the settlement's edge.

"Taishi," yelled Zofi over the sound of their flight.

"What is it, girl?"

"You're squeezing me too tight."

No sooner had she spoken than their group was swarmed by a group of temple soldiers. One managed to reach in with a crescent-blade pike and hooked the reins of their steed. He yanked, pulling the horse to one side, threatening to separate them from the rest of the group.

Another came from their other side and yanked at Zofi, nearly causing her to fall. Taishi couldn't hold on to the girl much longer. She whirled the horse around, bowling the man over. Taishi drew an iron dart with a feather flight and flicked it at the guard. She had been taking lessons from Fausan for her technique and used what little jing she could manage to help guide the iron dart to her target.

Her aim was close, but Taishi still needed more practice. She had aimed for the soldier's eye but succeeded only in hitting the bridge of his nose. His head snapped back and he screamed, pawing at his face with one hand. Taishi pulled out her opera sword and whacked his arm, causing him to drop the pike.

Taishi righted Zofi on the saddle and kicked the steed's hindquarters, urging it through the thickening crowd. There was a noticeable gap between them and the others now.

"Sohn!" Taishi screamed, but he was already out of earshot. She did the next best thing. *Bhasani.*

You know I don't appreciate screaming, Taishi.

I need help.

The drowned fist looked back her way. *How did you fall so far behind?*

Bhasani pulled her horse around and plowed through the crowd, forcing the quick to jump aside and the slow to get trampled. One battlemonk wielding a saber in his right hand grabbed the reins of her horse with his left. Bhasani's head snapped toward him. The man blinked and then brought his saber down upon his own wrist. He stared at his bloodied stump for a moment, confused, and then screamed.

Others tried to stop the drowned fist, including a Hansoo, but Bhasani whispered into the ear of her horse, enraging the roan and sending her rearing and kicking any unfortunate soul who got too close.

The three managed to rejoin the main group. Taishi rode to the front and took the lead, speeding along the road leading east. The Hansoo and soldiers were a few hundred yards behind. Taishi should be able to shake them loose once they reached the mountains.

"Keep going around that turn," yelled Fausan. "We'll lose them in the forest."

Taishi looked back. They were pulling away. The Hansoo should tire long before the horses. Taishi looked forward as they neared a sharp bend. She drove her horse hard, his nostrils flaring. Just a little bit farther. Once they put enough distance between them and their pursuers, they should be able to trot the horses a bit. She was fairly certain Hansoo could not keep this pace up.

Taishi led them past the turn and pulled to a sudden stop, gawking. Facing her was the unmistakable red-and-yellow armor of a Caobiu officer. More serious, however, was what was behind this vanguard patrol. Coming up the long, winding hill was an army carrying a line of Caobiu Duchy flags. The Cinder Legions had found them. *Sunri* had found them.

Taishi pulled her horse around. "Back to the temple!"

"But why?" said Bhasani, right behind her. The drowned fist stopped abruptly and then was soon riding just as hard alongside her.

A few moments later, they came across the pursuing Tiandi monks, who stopped and looked confused as Taishi and the masters charged toward them.

Taishi tried to wave them out of the way. "Turn around and flee, you fools! Go!"

The nose of the Cinder Legions appeared a moment later.

The monks turned and fled alongside Taishi back to Skyfall.

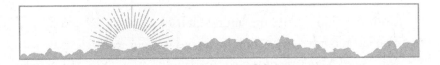

CHAPTER FIFTY-THREE

IDENTITY

Sali huddled at the end of a round table carved from the trunk of a black grimtree, flipping through the many seaweed manuscripts bound by hemp. The Sanctuary of the Eternal Moor had the most extensive book-storage house in Katuia. The spirit shamans also kept detailed records of every clan's genealogy. They had records of every marriage and cross-clan union, of every child born and adopted, and most importantly, they steered each child toward a particular calling from an early age.

She never realized their callings were so intentional until she found her own records. She had been marked for a physical calling at the age of three, marked again for the path of the warrior at seven, and then placed in the raiding reserves at ten. She had been invited to join her first raid at twelve, and the rest was history.

After several successful years in the raidlife, Sali was recruited by the Viperstrike sect. A few years later, she became Jiamin's Will of the Khan and joined his Sacred Cohort when he was raised to the Eternal Khan of Katuia. Sali had walked their script to perfection, following their predetermined path like a leashed hound.

Until she didn't. Until the hound bit back.

The last recorded entry in Sali's record was her exile.

Sali found Mali's records next: marked for mind at three, marked again for mental acuity at five, and reached a fork for tinker, shaman, or leadership at nine. Leadership was removed from her branch at eleven, and then she was recruited for her tinker apprenticeship at fourteen. Sali flipped through several pages. Sprout's records were more expansive than hers, likely due to the rigorous education required to become a tinker. That and the fact there were no records kept during her raidlife save for the spoils she brought back. There were no entries during her neophyte days with the Viperstrike sect, either.

All of this was irrelevant. This was a diversion for her as a prisoner here in Chaqra, a way to pass the time. At least she wasn't in chains. Visan had so far been a gracious jailer.

Afterward, Sali stepped outside onto the main street of the giant black city pod *Aracnas,* upon which the Sanctuary of the Eternal Moor rested. She leaned into the railing at the bow and studied the lifeless brown land. They were deep in Xing territory now. Sali's raidlife had rarely brought her this far south.

This was a dead place, so barren and desolate. The dry heat was oppressive while the dusty air constantly itched her nose, making her eyes irritated and watery. The fleet of pods that formed Chaqra moved as a wedge, with *Aracnas's* heart at its center. Dry wind carried dust and pollen. Shrubs, cacti, and small trees dotted the otherwise barren landscape. The sun was relentless, beating down upon the land until deep into the evening.

Sali was staring into the formless nothing of the land, her thoughts swirling like the sand, when she heard the familiar voice. "Hello, heart-daughter. May we share this hearth?"

Sali kept her gaze outward, her fists clenching before turning to face her former heart-father, godfather, and friend, a man she once held in esteem only third after her father and mother. "Jhamsa."

"My dear Sali. It is good to see you again." The high-ranking spirit shaman looked more wizened and frail since the last time their paths crossed. His graying hair had turned white and sparse. His once strong and tall frame was gaunt and bent. His wide and expressive smile had once brought her joy and comfort as a child. All she could see now was the small conniving man who had betrayed her clan and sold them out to the enemy and then refused them shelter when they returned during the time of their greatest need.

Behind the face paint and false smile, under the layers of ritualistic garb, feathers, and fur, was a shameful coward. It wasn't just him. The spirit shamans had sold Nezra to the land-chained for peace. That betrayal would survive in song for a millennium. Some crimes could never be wiped clean.

She looked around. "Are you sure it's safe for you to be seen with me?"

He offered a small smile. "My people know you are a person of honor. My standing among them will not be sullied by your company."

She considered putting her hands around his neck and tossing him over the side of the railing. "I meant, are you sure it's safe for you, because I am considering killing you right now."

He responded, unfazed, "That would not appear honorable for Salminde the Viperstrike."

"One thing I learned," she continued, "during our many years of exile, was that certain people's opinions of my honor are meaningless."

"I doubt you believe that. I didn't raise you this way," he replied. "Nobility runs through your veins. It is a way of life, a philosophy, not something easily discarded."

The old bastard was right. The urge to strangle him grew. She willed her fists to unclench. "My honor requires that we share the same hearth this day."

"You were always rigid, even as a child." Jhamsa smiled. "But I am not here to reminisce with my old heart-daughter about the past. I'm here to talk about something greater than both of us." He leaned on the railing and stared at Sali. His voice shrank to a hiss, his words spoken with a sharp, spitting edge. "What are you waiting for, Sali? Take the deal. Accept the khan's offer."

She crossed her arms and sneered. "Really? Did the council really think sending *you* would persuade me?"

"I come on my own, and I say this with sympathy for Nezra."

"The last time I heard the name of my clan on your lips, you had exiled us, and sent other clans to hunt us down."

"Let the past stay buried, Salminde. Be grateful that exile was your punishment. The others in the council wanted to hang you from your ankles until the pterodactyls pecked out your intestines."

"You sent Liqusa after us. The Bone Clan hounded us relentlessly for many cycles."

"That was your clan's fault for refusing to leave Katuia lands. Their orders were to chase you out, nothing more. But then you had the audacity to return and kill Chief Surumptipa's son during one of the raids, and then it became personal."

"They raided *us*!" Sali hissed. "I didn't even know his son fell in battle. Which one?"

"The third, who was his favorite, but that's not important." Jhamsa leaned against her, as if expecting her support to keep him upright.

Yet Sali couldn't help but offer an arm. She was annoyed with herself at that very moment. "Jhamsa. There's no coming back from this between Nezra and Katuia."

"That's where you're wrong. This *is* the way back. Back to the lush lands in the heart of the Grass Sea. Back to your clan's respectability and back to your old way of life! As if that black mark upon your clan had never happened. Imagine, Nezra again a capital city among Katuia as the horde rises to greater heights under this new khan!"

Sali stared out into the horizon. The scenery after nearly an hour was still unchanged. The sun cooked them mercilessly. There was a river to their distant left, but Sali couldn't make it out in the hazy heat of the scorching third cycle summer.

Jhamsa's message had been clear. Accept the khan's offer and save her people, too. That was the price of her honor. Could she make that sacrifice for the future of her clan? It was a good trade.

"As if it had never happened," both Visan and Jhamsa had said.

Sali struggled to mask her emotions. It was as if everything she had lost over the past several years was now being offered back to her, and to her chagrin and shame, she realized that it was the one thing she wanted so deeply it hurt. But she also knew she couldn't accept it anymore. It would be dishonorable to even consider it.

Several seconds ticked by as she grappled for the right words to say.

"You are a selfish fool to your people to keep the khan waiting," Jhamsa continued. "He has been magnanimous so far, but patience is not an attribute gods carry in abundance."

Sali ground her teeth. "I know the truth. I know about the khan, the Xoangiagu. Where they came from. What they really are. What *he* really is. I know what they did. What you're all still doing. The khan is an unnatural creature who possesses the young men and women of Katuia and leeches their jing and consumes their soul. He is a parasite!"

"You speak as if that's some great revelation," Jhamsa replied. "All you had to do was ask. Where he came from doesn't matter. It only matters that he returned. The khan is here now, and this one is ambitious. This is the way back for Nezra, Salminde."

Sali's nostrils flared, and her heart rate quickened alongside her growing indignation. "The truth is a betrayal to everything our people stand for!"

Jhamsa wasn't backing down either. "You speak of things you have no understanding about, viperstrike. What the Eternal Khan of Katuia and the spirit shamans strive for is the good of all our people. Now, if you truly honor your clan as well as our people, if you want to protect them and see your loved ones walk toward a brighter future, then you will graciously consider our khan's magnanimity."

She closed her eyes, knowing that the spirit shaman was not wrong. This was the best way to protect Nezra. To refuse this offer was as great of a betrayal to Nezra as Jhamsa's had been.

A small stampede of footsteps snapped them out of their intense conversation. Sali looked behind her to see Visan, flanked by several of his wills of the khan, approaching. The khan's eyes were intense, aflame. He did not look pleased.

"You!" Visan thundered, stomping toward her.

Sali placed a fist over her heart. "Khan."

He shook a rolled green leaf parchment in his hand. "We just received word that the Exiles Rebellion razed Liqusa clan."

"No," Jhamsa said. "When?"

"During the Solstice Gyre and her tertiaries. Pitched battle in the seaweed swamps."

Sali was surprised. This wasn't part of their strategy. She smiled. "Good. Clan Liqusa attempted to prey upon Nezra when we were weak. They nipped at our heels even as we starved and sent us underground, but they never could finish the job. Now, for their failure, the Bone Clan's name is no more."

The khan made a fist and held it toward her. Sali raised her chin. Now his true self was showing. Now it was time to see who this Visan was beneath the skin of the Eternal Khan of Katuia. This man was not Jiamin. She saw that now. This was a boy in a god's body, quick to anger and lose control.

Visan stopped just short of striking her. "Your people are coming for you. That is a mistake. I will show them no mercy if we meet on the battlefield. I will hunt them until every pod and every member of your clan is buried deep within the abyss."

Sali shrugged. "If you can, you should. My people will do the same."

Visan was furious in a way Jiamin had never been as the khan. His face was red, his expression twisted. The veins on his neck bulged. Sali would not have been surprised if he struck her dead on the spot. The khan lunged at her, his chest heaving and his fingers curled into claws.

Sali held her ground. If death was inevitable, then she would meet it on her feet, defiant. His breath smelled of black licorice and chocolate mixed with mud, likely ayahuasca, or maybe he had a sweet tooth.

"You will tell me everything there is to know about the Nezra clan if you value your life: their location, their pod fleet makeup, the number of warriors and tinkers, everything!"

Her expression remained unchanged. She raised a hand slowly and lowered it to her right hip, where her longer dagger was sheathed, conscious of the many wills of the khan eyeing her every move. She gripped the handle and yanked it out. Holding it in a reverse grip, she presented it to the khan.

"Do it then, because you will never hear a breath of betrayal from me."

For a moment, Visan glowered. Then he swiped the knife from her grasp with blinding speed and swung it at her neck, digging into the soft flesh of her throat.

Sali challenged him with stillness. The two were frozen for several beats, their eyes locked. She thought quick prayers for her loved ones: Mali and little Hampa, Wani and Marhi, and the rest of her clan. This was a good way to die, if not in battle then at least in defiance.

"You owe your loyalty to your khan," he growled.

"I owe my loyalty to my people, not its enslaved god."

Visan's eyes widened with confusion, and Sali was surprised to realize that, perhaps, the khan did not know about his nature. He probably viewed himself as an all-powerful god. That's what Jiamin used to say shortly after his ascension. Except Jiamin said it mournfully.

A hesitant voice spoke. "Great khan, we have arrived."

Visan's gaze never left Sali. "You say your loyalty is to your people. Prove it." He walked to the front of the ship and leaned over the railing, pointing at a tall cylindrical structure jutting out of a distant tower. A chill ran down Sali's back. That structure was unmistakable: Xusan, the Column City, the Pedestal That Lifts the Sky, and the seat of Xing Duchy.

"You're really going to attack a Zhuun capital," Sali muttered. "You're mad."

"If your loyalty is with your people, then today should be a glorious day." He held the knife out to her. "Show that you still are Katuia. Will you seize this moment and fight for Katuia? Will you fight by your khan's side and burn your name among the stars for eternity?"

Sali's soul howled to join the battle. Every shred of honor she possessed demanded justice and retribution against the Zhuun. They were the ones who enslaved her clan. They killed her mother and father. They nearly destroyed the Viperstrike sect. Her heart demanded justice.

But she also knew Visan was trying to manipulate her, to entrap her. Still, sometimes the instincts were too strong.

"I'll fight," Sali growled. "I'll always fight for my people, but this means nothing between us."

Visan nodded. "However you wish to feel, viperstrike." He turned to one of his wills of the khan. "Hwashi, prepare Chaqra for victory."

CHAPTER FIFTY-FOUR

THE CONQUEROR

J ian watched from the sixth level of Skyfall Temple down to the ground level. The front gates swung wide open, and the Duchess of Caobiu's long procession entered in a parade of red and yellow that slowly ate up the gray cobblestone road leading up the large central steps. By all accounts, the entire Caobiu Court had arrived: the Cinder Legions, the mind trust, the nobles, and probably the entire estate staff as well. Sunri had insisted on bringing a thousand soldiers for her honor guard.

Skyfall Temple didn't even have a thousand monks and guards who could put up a defense. The rest of the Cinder Legions encamped outside Hengyen were already well within artillery range of the temple mountain. Any siege would be a massacre. The temple stood no chance. Even if the Stone Blossom Monastery down the road sent every Hansoo, it would mean that three generations of Hansoo would have perished for naught.

Why was she here? The temple was alight with chatter. Everyone had their guesses. A woman surely could not shoulder the burden of the empire, so she must have come to consult the high seats for their wisdom. Perhaps she came to raze the temple or broker a marriage alliance. Both were equally feasible when it came to Sunri. Some believed she was here to announce her celibacy and convert to a nun. Nobody took those dumb eggs seriously.

Jian had told everyone who would listen that he didn't care about Sunri. He hated her with the passion of a thousand twinkling stars. She was a terrible person, but also beneath his notice. Who did she think she was, strolling through this sacred place as if she were important?

"Jian," said Meehae, "the high seats summon you to chambers. They want you there when Sunri arrives."

He crossed his arms. "I don't want to see that witch. She killed Saan, and almost killed Taishi, and she was trying to kill me. So no, she doesn't get an audience with me."

Meehae shot him the same look she used back at the Longxian school when he would whine about needles. "She's probably going to be the next Empress of the Enlightened States, so you should get over yourself."

"But . . ."

Meehae leaned close, wagging a finger. "There are truthsniffers sniffing down every hallway. Keep your mental fortitude strong and stop with all those errant thoughts. Do breathing exercises or something."

"She also can't be trusted. She broke a banner of peace and then betrayed the Shulan army."

"Hey," Meehae snapped. "No one is asking you to kiss her. And definitely no one is going to ask you to be diplomatic. The high seats just want you to look like the Prophesied Hero of the Tiandi while keeping your mouth shut. Can you handle that?"

Jian didn't know if he could. "Fine. But I don't have to like it. I'm not going to smile."

Meehae scrunched her face. "What's wrong with you? Why would you even think of smiling at Sunri? We all hate her. No one's asking you to marry her." She perked up. "Do you think she's here to marry you?"

"What?" Now it was Jian's turn to panic. "I can't marry her! She's twice my age."

"Really? You're worried about the age gap?"

He frowned. "I feel like we're arguing on the same side."

"No, we're not." She looped her arm around his elbow. "I missed you, you little bitter snowflake. I'm sorry I couldn't tell you earlier. The inquisitor was already sniffing my every breath. I didn't want to risk being taken off your care. They're all focused on Sunri's delegation now."

They crossed the bridge toward the staircase leading up to the high seats' chambers. It had never crossed his mind that *he* could be considered a candidate for the duchess's consort. His importance to the prophecy would guarantee support from the Tiandi religion for the Celestial Throne.

"I would be emperor consort then," he muttered.

"What was that?" asked Meehae.

"I mean, if I was married to Sunri, I could order the high seats to release my friends."

"I just saw them this morning. Sonaya told me to give you this." Meehae leaned over and kissed his shoulder.

Xinde and Sonaya had been separated from Jian the moment they were detained. He had begged the senior abbots to release his friends, but so far had been rebuffed. They were in the hands of the inquisitors, and as far as Meehae could determine, had been treated well. Sonaya's mental jing was so strong she wore down many of the inquisitors' mental fortitudes. Her captors, Meehae had reported, were fascinated with the drowned fist. Sonaya, in turn, made friends with her captors. They became like thought buddies. Jian wasn't surprised by this turn of events. Sonaya had a way with people.

Xinde on the other hand was in a whole heap of trouble. Sonaya may have been an intruder, but Xinde was a temple guard, which made him a traitor. The universally accepted penalty for treason was death. They were going to hang him the next morning had Jian not pleaded and threatened the high seats. They had declared that they would schedule his public execution for after Sunri's visit but before the Strawberry Festival. Currently, Xinde was chained in the dungeon awaiting his fate.

Meehae stopped before the door leading to the high seats' circle. She adjusted his collar and frowned. "Everything is a little short on you." Her face darkened. "They did this on purpose, didn't they?"

"I thought that was the style here," he said.

"You look like a little boy."

The Voice of the Tiandi met them at the gates into the high seats' chambers and then led them down a hallway off to the side that curved just outside the main chambers. "Your place is standing just to the left flank of High Seat Galen. Your wisdom is not required today, Prophesied Hero of the Tiandi. You need to remain still throughout the proceedings and acknowledge the duchess with a bow befitting her rank." She stopped. "Do you know how to do that?"

"Not confidently," he admitted. Sohn had taught him years ago, but he had more important things to remember than the forty-seven different bows within a court.

"Then do this." The voice offered a lilting bow with clasped hands at a subtle side angle. "This will keep you neutral throughout the proceedings."

Jian did his best to copy the motion.

The voice made a face. "It'll have to do."

Jian didn't like feeling as if he were a prop. He turned toward Meehae. "Maybe—"

"Master acupuncturist, you are dismissed." The Voice of the Tiandi had an edge now that was not there previously.

Meehae stiffened, bowed, and took mincing small steps backward out of the room.

Jian didn't want her to go. "But . . ."

"This way, great hero."

Something about the authority in her voice made Jian stand a little straighter. He stood in his assigned spot. There was even a dot on the ground showing where that was. High Seat Galen was within arm's reach, seated at a low table. Ten abbots were seated on either side, and then thirty more lined both walls, each facing the open center of the room. Jian remained standing for several more moments. The abbots were preoccupied. Some were meditating, others working with calligraphy brushes on parchment. Every once in a while, an initiate would walk in from one of the side doors to retrieve a finished document or bring the abbots a drink. There were also a few nuns dispersed through the line, perhaps a mere ten among the hundred monks present.

A dozen inquisitors flanked the walls. Jian remembered to slow his breathing and protect his mind from intrusion. He inhaled and exhaled several times, allowing his breath to circulate his jing through his body to create the mental shield, just as Master Bhasani had taught him.

The gong rang as the high seats waited for Sunri to arrive. A few minutes passed, and then ten, then twenty. Jian began to fidget at thirty and was ready to find a chair at the passing of an hour. Some of the other monks were shifting in their seats as well.

Finally, after three hours had passed, the Voice of the Tiandi appeared and announced in a clear, imperial voice: "Announcing Sunri, the Empress Consort to the Enlightened States. The Desert Lioness. The Duchess of Caobiu and Gyian and Shulan."

The doors that spanned the far wall slid open, to reveal a foyer packed with Caobiu nobles and soldiers arrayed in a tight formation. They looked like monstrous insects with their ceremonial armor. Jian shifted his weight. Even after all this time, he grew tense whenever he saw the red-and-yellow flames of the Cinder Legions. He wanted to make a face, to scowl or sneer. He wanted to spit in disgust. Sunri was the reason some of his friends were dead. She was responsible for Vauzan's destruction. It was her war that had caused so much suffering. All that for what? She already controlled more land than she could ever visit in one lifetime. What more did she need? What was this for? Rage and indignation swirled inside him as he watched Sunri approach the high seats.

She looked spectacular. Jian admitted that even though he despised her. The duchess looked every bit the empress. Her presence had a gravity all its own. None could remove their eyes from her, including Jian. She wore an expansive flame-colored dress with imperial gold along the trim. Her sleeves fell nearly to the ground as she floated across the floor. Her headdress was intricate with beads curtaining half her face while flaring out like a peacock's feathers. The other half revealed her perfectly painted porcelain face with deep crimson eyeliner and blood-red lips.

Her movements were as graceful as a dancer's and as predatory as a serpent's. She reached the base of the high seats and bowed, not just the bow of the devout, but one of presentation and announcement. The Duchess of Caobiu presented herself imperiously in every sense, as if the woman was born for this very moment.

"Great and wise abbots of the Tiandi," she intoned. "I, Sunri, Duchess of Caobiu, Conqueror of Gyian and Shulan, Stewardess of the Celestial Palace, Grand Marshal of the Armies of the Enlightened States, and the rightful Empress of the Enlightened States, now stand before you with the opportunity to heal all Zhuun and unite our people once again to fly the gold-and-lavender banner that once spanned the six corners of this great kingdom belonging to the blood of our beloved emperor, Xuanshing, may his greatness ever last."

"May his greatness ever last," came the reluctant chorus among the monks.

Even Sunri's smile was majestic. "Now is the time, High Seat of the Tiandi, to unite the people. Legitimize my claim to the Heart of the Tiandi Throne and put an end to this miserable war. In doing so, every one of the high seats in this chamber, with the full support of the empire, will be elevated as saviors and future saints for all time."

It took Jian a moment to realize that was Sunri's opening offer for a bribe: sainthood.

High Seat Galen slapped a large stone on the table. "You forget yourself, duchess. It is not the throne's wisdom that bestows sainthood on the worthy. It is the high seats of the Tiandi who decide the holiest of our people. This was a matter your late husband had trouble understanding as well."

Sunri ignored his comment. "Your support will save the lives of thousands."

"Your withdrawal will elicit the same effect. Do not attempt to pass fault when you are most responsible."

"The unification of the empire is long overdue. This succession must be seen to its conclusion. The people need an inspiring leader with a strong hand to guide them to prosperity."

"If you are that person that you speak of, then conclude your work," said Galen. "If you can unite the Zhuun, then show that you are worthy. The Tiandi devout, as is our way, will not get involved in the secular realm. Return to us, Duchess Sunri of Caobiu, once your banners fly across all corners of the Enlightened States."

To her credit, Sunri's face remained neutral throughout High Seat Galen's announcement, save for the glint of her eyes and the tightening of her jaw. That was likely as close to a rebuff as the duchess had ever received.

Jian had mostly tuned their conversation out, but something Galen said resonated in his mind. There was a strange moment during that last exchange; Jian couldn't quite put his finger on it. It reminded him of Sohn's lessons, something about powerful emperors and weak Tiandi high seats or weak emperors and powerful Tiandi high seats. The imbalance always led to bloodshed and chaos, like the Straw Hat Rebellion and the Worship the Tiandi or Die Movement. Both had to be brutally suppressed.

Then the puzzle came together. The most powerful lords did not rule over their court with an iron fist. No, they weighed each faction as if on a scale, intertwining them delicately to keep them all balanced.

That was it.

This era had been one with a powerful high seat and fractured power among the dukes. A strong leader like Sunri would change the dynamic of power in the Enlightened States. High Seat Galen did not want a new empress to challenge his authority.

This was all a game to them! At the cost of prolonging the war and thousands more deaths. How could the Tiandi monks want this? Jian broke form momentarily. He felt ill. His chest throbbed and stomach churned. He wanted to vomit. They were playing with people's lives.

Thousands died in Vauzan because of ducal politics. Now, tens of thousands more would die because of imperial politics.

He looked up to see Sunri looking back, studying him. Galen's voice faded into the background. It was just Jian and Sunri. The high seat's voice trailed off. Slowly, everyone stopped and took notice.

"Is something notable, duchess?" asked Galen.

"Enough of your many empty words, high seat," she said. "I want to know what the Prophesied Hero of the Tiandi thinks. What is on your mind, great Champion of the Five Under Heaven?"

"I—" Jian stammered.

"Pay the young man no heed," said Galen. "He is here to observe."

"I wish to understand what he has observed," said Sunri.

"I . . ." Jian froze. He was stupefied. He had spent the past few years hiding from the world. Now it felt like everyone in the world was focused on him. He blinked. "I . . . don't think . . ."

"However, as the leaves and trunk and roots serve a tree differently, each of us must serve the Tiandi in our own unique and necessary way," Galen interjected. "The Prophesied Hero of the Tiandi holds an esteemed and honored place among the Tiandi, but it is his strength we need, not his wisdom."

The high seat's tone dripped with dismissiveness. It sounded like Galen had just called him stupid. Jian wanted to snap back at the high seat, but was far too intimidated by the presence of two of the most powerful people in the Enlightened States. Who was he to stand up to them? Still, he simmered, smarting at the insult.

"I'm the Prophesied Hero of the Tiandi, that's who," he mouthed silently. It didn't make him feel more courageous, though.

"I would like to hear the young great lord's thoughts," said Sunri. "He certainly built a reputation during his defense of Vauzan. His opinion has a profound influence. Why doesn't the great champion of our people share his divine insight?"

"As you know far too well, Duchess Sunri, the affairs of governance are too nuanced for our young warrior, who must spend his time focusing on fulfilling his destiny. Rest at ease, the prophesied hero will not be your concern. He is well attended by the devout, where he belongs."

It sounded like Galen called him ignorant as well.

Jian began to boil even as his self-esteem sank to his toes. The High Seat of the Tiandi had just called him stupid in front of the entire room. Jian wanted to defend himself; shoot back a witty retort, say something wise and insightful. Anything but stand there gawking like a hapless fool.

His nervous gaze continued to sweep between Galen and Sunri. The high seat fumed, his face red and twitching with fury. Sunri's was the opposite: stern and measured, yet there was something in her eyes that dared him to stand up for himself.

One of Taishi's lessons echoed in Jian's mind: Always find two buyers before you make the sale. Multiple parties fighting over a product raises its value. In this case, the parties were High Seat Galen and Duchess Sunri, and the product was Jian. Before, he had no leverage with the Tiandi religion. He needed them. He had been at their mercy. But now Sunri was here. Jian now had two interested parties. He glanced between them.

Jian found his voice. "Perhaps it wouldn't be a bad idea if the duchess hears my wise counsel, maybe even in private."

Those present broke into loud, indignant rumbles. Words like "disgrace" and "outrage" and "insulting" were flung about. Also mutterings of "marriage" and "seduction" and "temptress."

"Out of the question," Galen thundered. "You overstep protocol, duchess. The responsibility of the prophesied hero belongs to the Celestial Court, not to the courts of man."

Sunri bowed. "My apologies, high seat. I did not realize I was speaking to a puppet of the Tiandi."

That topped off Jian's roiling boil. Did *they* know who he was? Of course they did! This made this entire display all the more insulting. He stepped forward and roared, "I am no one's puppet!" His voice cracked at the end. "I am the Prophesied Hero of the Tiandi, given the Mandate of Heaven, and the Savior of the Zhuun. I am the binding that keeps these people bound. I am"—he paused for dramatic effect—"the most important person in this room. My wisdom and requirements demand respect."

High Seat Galen eyed him with new hostility. "Perhaps this is a good time for a recess. You look pale. An afternoon nap might do you some good."

"Maybe right now would be a good time for an audience, duchess," Jian shot back. "Or perhaps I should get some rest first, check my busy schedule. Oh, high seat, I order my friends freed from jail. Bring them to my chambers immediately, understood?"

Galen did not look impressed.

Jian turned to Sunri. "We can take the audience now."

A lengthy silence passed. Finally, the high seat spoke, his words dripping with malice and outrage. "They will be freed at once and brought to your service, Great Hero."

Jian smiled. "Great." He stretched. "I'm tired. I better go get some rest."

CHAPTER FIFTY-FIVE

TOGETHER

T he Hansoo came for Taishi and the other masters late in the afternoon. The temple had not bothered imprisoning them on account of the fact that they were all imprisoned at Sky-fall, with the Cinder Legions just beyond the walls. Still, it had been startling when a large figure squeezed under the low doorway in the already run-down inn.

Taishi and Sohn had been drinking tea while passing a gourd under the table between them. This settlement being declared dry of alcohol was preposterous. Dumbest thing she had heard any city do other than when this one settlement in Shulan tried to prohibit prostitution. Now *that* was a stupid mess. Riots for weeks. An overthrown local government. The mayor had been hanged. All for trying to shut down the one brothel, which was on land he had been trying to acquire.

The young Hansoo, face unblemished as a baby's ass, was sporting only one ring around each wrist. He stomped his way to them and jabbed a beefy finger at each of the masters. "You, you, you, you. Out of the shop, and into the wagon."

"We haven't finished our drinks yet," Taishi remarked. She wasn't going to let some mid-tier Hansoo ruin her nightcap. It was the only thing she looked forward to these days.

Fausan put his feet on the table in emphasis. Taishi was impressed that he could still stretch that high. No one else moved. The rest of the room was frozen, waiting for the hammer to drop, figuratively and possibly literally as well.

The Hansoo looked annoyed. "You can come willingly or I can drag you to the street by your ankles."

Fausan cracked a pistachio and flicked a half shell across the room, bouncing it off the Hansoo's forehead, right between his eyes. The Hansoo put on a performance, swinging his arms wildly in reaction. "How dare you attack one of the Tiandi! That is a crime punishable by heavy fines."

"You threatened us first." The whipfinger shrugged. "Besides, we're broke. Can't flay the flesh off a skeleton."

Bhasani turned her nose up. "What does that even mean?"

"It means, my love, that—"

"I know what it means. I just think it's a trite and silly thing to say."

"The important thing is that you understood the reference."

Taishi snatched the gourd from Sohn's hand and raised it to her lips. The zuijo was putrid, but it was this or rubbing alcohol. "Listen, One-Ring, why don't you get going before the God of Gamblers here decides to start throwing knives?"

The Hansoo growled and took a step toward them. Fausan flicked the other half of the pistachio shell, bouncing it off the same spot as the previous one.

Another Hansoo ducked under the doorway, this one larger. "What's the holdup, Guiman?"

"These insolent dogs attacked me, big brother."

The larger Hansoo stood, his head nearly touching the building's rafters. "Taishi, there you are!"

"Pahm, is that you, my boy?" Taishi's eyes widened.

Zofi squealed and threw herself into his arms. Pahm scooped her up.

He held up his ten-ring arm and embraced both Taishi and Zofi at the same time. "My friends, it's so good to see you."

Zofi poked his massive arms. "You've grown in every direction since the last time we saw you."

"More rings, too," Taishi pointed out. "You are now the same rank as Liuman. Your elder brother would have been proud."

"He guides me to this day." Pahm put his hands together and bowed. He signaled behind him. "Speaking of brothers, I see you met my new ward. Little brother Guiman, come here. I want to introduce you to my friends."

The young Hansoo blanched. "They're your friends? Then why did you tell me to bring them in?"

"Bring them in as guests of the temple. High Seat's orders." He stared at the two confrontational sides. "What seems to be the problem?"

"Guests?" stammered Guiman, looking offended, as if these old bags of bones weren't worthy to be guests of Skyfall Temple.

Fausan launched another pistachio off his forehead.

Guiman roared. "Stop flicking me!"

"The pup has a temper," said Bhasani. She plucked the gourd out of Taishi's lap and took a swig.

"Don't mind little brother. All young Hansoo are emotional," Pahm admitted. "It's a result of the drugs we receive for our transformation. I was a wound-up bag of prickly scree at his age, too."

"Aye, you were, though always the sensitive, weepy one. Not a raging little pup pissing all over the floor," said Taishi. It was wonderful to see how much Pahm had matured over the years.

"Were you really going to try to arrest Ling Taishi and her comrades?" asked Pahm, amused. "I have a mind to let you try."

"You didn't tell me they were guests," Guiman grumbled.

Pahm offered a hand, which Taishi accepted. "Come, this way, master."

Kaiyu and Hachi were waiting at the wagon outside with another Hansoo. At least it wasn't a jail or meat wagon this time. It was a legitimate transport carriage with cushioned seats and handrails. Most importantly, it did not reek of piss or corpses.

The old masters dutifully filed into the carriage, squeezing in next to each other, shoulders rubbing. The children came in next. Zofi got a cushioned seat, but Hachi and Kaiyu were relegated to the floor.

"Do you think they're going to hang us?" asked Kaiyu. Taishi could tell he was trying his best to hold it in, but the boy was both devout and nervous.

"Why would they do that?"

"Well, you tried to kidnap the Prophesied Hero of the Tiandi, and the gossip in town was that they were going to hang a spy who masqueraded as an officer. They're talking about Xinde, right?"

"As long as they don't excommunicate us," Fausan grumbled for the fiftieth time.

The ride from the tea shop at the settlement square of Hengyen was short and uneventful. Most of the residents had cleared out, fleeing either into the temple or out to the countryside. The walls were heavily manned, but it was more for show than anything else. If the Caobiu army could break through the Vauzan outer walls within a day, that pathetic outer wall wouldn't even serve as a speed bump. The temple walls might delay them a bit longer, but even that would only stall the Cinder Legions for a few hours, if even that.

"Do you think our summons has anything to do with Sunri visiting the high seat this morning?" asked Zofi.

"Without a doubt," said Bhasani. She leaned toward the center of the carriage like a conniving cat. "I hatched an escape plan to save the children."

"What escape plan?" Sohn snorted. "There's only one way out of the temple, which is guarded by several hundred monks in all shapes and sizes. And if we manage to get past them, there's thirty times that number in the world's most elite army, which is encamped just outside."

"That's easy for you to say. It's not your lineage heir locked in their jail cell." A flash of pain tightened Bhasani's face. She patted his shoulder. "Apologies."

He looked thoughtful. "You know, that Guiman boy doesn't look happy with his lot in life. Do you think—"

"You are *not* stealing a Hansoo pup from the Tiandi." Taishi shook her head. "The reason you don't see Hansoo who wash out of the program is because they don't allow it. Once you've joined the sect, you're either in or you die trying."

Sohn shook his head. "Shame. A Hansoo would make a formidable eternal bright light."

"Let it go, my friend," said Fausan. "You're better off apologizing to your family and asking to be let back in. You're still one of the strongest in your lineage."

The eternal bright light master brightened. "Do you think I should challenge my way back in?"

"You're too old to be head of your lineage anymore. Just accept being the emeritus and enjoy the status with none of the responsibilities. Best of both worlds."

"It never occurred to me to not have to kill some family to get back in, which is why I never tried, to be honest." Sohn frowned. "Do you think they'll do it?"

Taishi shrugged. "I don't see why not. War arts lineages like to keep their families intact, especially the ones who are powerful, even the black sheep. Sometimes especially the black sheep."

"Besides," Bhasani added, "everyone who knew you is already dead. It'll be a fresh start. You just have to behave. You can do that, right, you old, dumb bull?"

Sohn looked deep in thought. "Do you think they'll say they are sorry for what they did to me?"

"Not a chance in hell."

He sighed. "I guess it'd be good to see the rest of my family, but what would I do then?"

Taishi clapped her friend on the shoulder. "You would be their strongest practitioner. Your legacy is to pass on your powerful secrets to the worthiest eternal bright light in your lineage."

He racked his brain. "I guess it'll be sort of like passing it along to an heir."

"An heir is nothing but ego," said Taishi. "Passing your knowledge and power to your lineage, on the other hand, is legacy."

"But it feels like I surrendered."

"That's just your pride talking, old friend."

She leaned toward the group. "Bhasani isn't wrong. There's a possibility we may need to fight our way out. If so, this could be our only chance to free Jian, Sonaya, and Xinde. We don't leave here without our kids."

Everyone nodded, likely knowing that their odds of escape and survival were slim but that abandoning them was also out of the question. Every war artist who valued their honor within the lunar court understood this. The only exception was . . .

"Zofi," said Taishi. "Consider staying back."

"Not a chance, old witch."

Their conversation ended when the carriage pulled up to the bottom of the main stairs leading up to Skyfall Temple. Two more Hansoo were waiting for them, as well as a squad of lotus monks. This was as close to a protective escort as the Tiandi religion offered. That or an armed guard. At least no one tried to confiscate their weapons.

The group, led by an even larger number of guards, began the long trek up the many stairs toward the high seats' chambers. Kaiyu, the always thoughtful young man, offered Taishi an arm to hold on to, which she gladly accepted.

The group's mood was somber as they were escorted upstairs. She had been around her friends enough to recognize the signs that they were all on alert. From Fausan's open bullet pouch next to his chest to Bhasani lightly cooling herself by flapping her bladed fans to Sohn always keeping one arm limp at his side, giving him quick access to the giant shield strapped at his back, everyone was prepared for battle.

Taishi was relieved when they continued past the second floor. Turning left at the intersection led to the temple prison, so at least they weren't going to jail. The Tiandi religion had a surprisingly large prison population for a religious organization, especially since they weren't supposed to be a government.

She was winded by the time they reached the fourth level. By now they were higher than the walls, and it was only here, halfway up the mountain, that Taishi could see the sprawling encampment outside the settlement walls. It looked as if Sunri had just finished mopping up Vauzan and marched straight here. How did an army this size get past the Lawkan Alabaster Fleet?

"That clever, conniving bitch," Taishi muttered, impressed.

Taishi was huffing by the time they reached the eighth level. As was their custom, they had to stop as every monk, and Fausan, pressed their palms together and bowed their heads in meditation for several minutes. Taishi waited respectfully, if impatiently. When you're dying, standing around is the last thing you want to do.

The door to the chambers opened, and the stern-faced Voice of the Tiandi met their small procession. Her eyes focused on Taishi and then swept past her. She met Pahm at the base of the stairs and spoke to him quietly. Then, without a word, she turned and stormed back inside.

Taishi was surprised when, instead of going up the last set of stairs leading into the high seats' chambers, Pahm turned toward the east wing. She caught up with him. "Where does this lead, boy?"

"Imperial guest quarters."

It occurred to her that perhaps they had been summoned to be forfeited to Sunri, but why? Four retired masters were hardly worth the effort, and the bounty on Taishi's head had been long canceled. She never could raise her bounty above Jian's. Still, second only to the Prophesied Hero of the Tiandi wasn't a bad place to make her mark in the lunar court.

Sunri was famous for her temper. Perhaps this was revenge for defeating her back in Allanto. Out of habit, Taishi began looking for a way out, or at least which direction to fight and flee. She knew that escape was not an option. She could hardly manage going up and down stairs, let alone brawl her way through hundreds of Tiandi warriors. A few years ago, she could have ridden a current off the mountain, but that would have meant abandoning her friends, and that was never going to happen.

Two Hansoo guarded the door, which opened into a foyer that was suitable for a duke. The room was decorated with red vector screens and calligraphy art lining the walls. A sun mirror near the ceiling infused the space with soft light, while dozens of paper lanterns illuminated every corner, likely to ward off nightblossoms looking to spy or assassinate those inside. These quarters were designed to protect the most important guests. They also made escape more difficult.

Taishi entered a small busy courtyard filled with soldiers standing guard at every corner. A cluster of Tiandi initiates were maintaining a rock garden under the watchful eye of an elderly gardener. A line of servants were moving in and out of the kitchen building off to the side.

Taishi continued scanning the space until she saw Jian standing just inside the doorway in the building on the opposite end. He was surrounded by several high seat and Caobiu officials, and looked as if he were getting fitted for new robes.

Her eyes locked on him as she soaked in his appearance. The last time she laid eyes on him, he had been near death and was kept alive only by acupuncture needles. Now his face was flush with health, and he was standing, moving, and speaking. Her body finally released all the stress and worry she had locked tightly to her heart ever since he was injured.

Taishi broke into a sprint, shoving monks and servants aside. Two Cinder Legion soldiers guarding the entrance looked at her uncertainly, unsure if they should be protecting their responsibilities from a charging nun. Both lazily threw out an arm to block her way, but she slipped past them, shoving a poor tailor measuring Jian's leg out of the way as she threw herself into Jian's arms.

Jian only had a moment of surprise before he squeezed her back. "Taishi!" His voice cracked. Poor boy sounded like he was never going to get past puberty. "I was so worried about you."

She held him, afraid to let go. Within moments, the rest of the group had surrounded him and Taishi was forced to share him with the rest of the world. Bhasani and Zofi completed the embrace, while Fausan and Sohn patted him on the back. Hachi and Kaiyu, like most other young men, touched clenched forearms with him. Jian looked overwhelmed and then relieved, and then watery-eyed and overwhelmed again as he tried to embrace all of his friends at the same time.

After they finally settled, Bhasani asked, "Was it you who summoned us?"

Jian tried to sound modest but failed miserably. "I told Galen that I required my people if the Tiandi wished to have my cooperation."

Taishi noted the way he worded that. Her eyes narrowed. "Something is different. What happened?"

He caught them up on the events since he awoke from his injury all the way to this morning with Sunri in the high seats' chamber. Just about everyone else gasped when he told them how he stood up to both the high seat and the duchess, with only slight bits of exaggeration. There was another round of pats on the back as he continued to regale them with his exploits at the temple. The mood turned somber when he said he was weighing aligning with Sunri and the Caobiu over the rest of the Tiandi monks.

"You're not seriously considering it, are you, Jian?" Hachi and Kaiyu were outraged.

"You can't make a pact with that devil," added Zofi.

Fausan and Sohn looked stone-faced.

"No, of course not," huffed Jian. "I mean, I don't know . . ."

"You'd better not!" came a shout from across the room. Sonaya and Xinde walked in.

Jian nearly lost it. "What took you so long? I ordered you freed hours ago!"

"We had to take a bath first," said Xinde. "We stank."

Sonaya, glaring, walked up to Jian. "You better not side with Sunri or there'll be hell to pay." Then she threw her arms around his neck and hauled him close. "I'm sorry. It was my fault." She burst into tears. "I should have stopped you back at the Vauzan Temple. You wouldn't have gotten hurt." The two melted into each other.

Taishi looked at Bhasani. "I blame you for this."

"Me? My daughter was fine before she fell for this walking corpse over here."

Jian looked over. "What?"

"The khan's going to crack him into fifteen pieces. And then I'm going to have to deal with Sonaya's broken heart. It'll be unbearable."

"If the people and the Tiandi religion band together, then we can raise a force as powerful as Sunri's," said Xinde.

Jian didn't look convinced. "But that just keeps everyone fighting."

"Better to keep on fighting than to surrender," said Sohn.

"Why is it?" Taishi barked. "Why is it better to fight than to surrender?"

"And allow Sunri to be empress?" Bhasani sounded offended. "She sacked Vauzan!"

"Yes, that's what armies do after they take a city. It happens all the time."

Hachi spat. "She's a monster!"

"Sure she is," Taishi said. "But no more so than any of the other dukes. They're all assholes. But she's the best of these assholes, the most competent. She's taken out two, and she's three days' march from a third. Face it, Sunri has won the succession war. She earned her achievement as the next Empress of the Enlightened States."

Jian nodded. "If we align with her now, then we'll have the support of the imperial throne under a unified country behind us, not this raging storm of civil war. We could work together. That's how we defeat the khan."

"You'll make a permanent enemy of the high seats, though," said Sohn. "This is a humiliating betrayal for them."

Jian considered and then nodded. "If it'll save lives, then I'm happy to live with it."

Taishi's eyes watered as she looked at her ward, now grown-up. Jian was finally ready. She signaled to Pahm. "Send a message to the Duchess of Caobiu. Inform Sunri that the Champion of the Five Under Heaven requires her presence."

CHAPTER FIFTY-SIX

SHADOWKILL HOMECOMING

The two viperstrikes tried to creep up on Qisami, stalking her from above, one atop the balcony off the second-story artillery tower, while the second—the larger one, breathing heavily—crept up from behind the stack of siege ammunition. It should be obvious that viperstrikes, contrary to what their name implied, were not a stealthy bunch.

Qisami, hands stuffed in the front pouch of the tinker outfit—she loved pockets!—hummed a tune as she padded around the main street of this long, sleek boat with wheels. The one above leaped. That was their first mistake. Qisami waited until the last moment and stepped to the side. Her ambusher squawked as she crashed to the floor.

Qisami looked down and nudged her fallen attacker with her shoe. "That looked like it hurt."

Of course the other viperstrike attempted to make up for the botched ambush by charging at Qisami. The mouth breather tripped over her friend and stumbled forward. She went for it anyway, flashing her batons at Qisami, who rolled her eyes and tilted to the side, letting the batons pass overhead harmlessly. Just as her body was about to hit the ground, she shadowstepped through the ground and emerged on the opposite side of the path, using her momentum to execute a perfectly timed flying kick that sent Marhi flying like a rag doll.

Wani picked herself off the floor and tried to spearhand her. Qisami slapped the hand away and then slapped the girl across the face. She snarled and tried again, launching the same attack at the same angle at the same speed. It was adorable, really. Qisami caught the attack in midair, clutching the viperstrike's pinky and ring finger. Then, with a wicked snarl, she clenched and yanked to the side, causing the viperstrike to flip onto the floor.

She waited for both Marhi and Wani to pick themselves up. Qisami turned to face her audience of small children for the first time. "What were their mistakes?"

Many small hands shot into the air. A little Nezra boy's cries were slightly louder than his brethren. "Wani jumped too late."

"That's not it." Qisami shook her head. "There's no crime in missing. A war artist is not going to draw blood with every strike. You will miss more than you hit. That doesn't mean you still shouldn't be murdering every enemy you find."

One of the clan elders frowned. Qisami didn't care. "Anyone else?"

Another boy raised his hand. "Marhi made it worse!"

"Close! Good boy." She waggled a finger at him. "Once Wani missed, Marhi tried to make up for it by attacking. She not only ran into and tripped over her cellmate, what else did she do?"

"Lost the element of surprise!" the choir shouted back.

"Lost the element of surprise. That's right!" Qisami waggled her finger at the others. These kids were sharp. Give her a training pool, and she could make her own shadowkill operation that could challenge the Consortium.

The tall weeds of the dense jungle they had been traveling through parted before the sharpened point of the *Nezra Rides*. The shaded, swampy ground suddenly opened to a sprawling brown river. Qisami, alongside the children, hurried to the railing of the starboard side of the *Nezra Rides*.

The Sand Snake.

The *Nezra Rides* was nowhere near the head of the Exiles fleet. A dozen other pods were already half covered in the sand as their tires and tracks spun, kicking up spray in their wake. More Exiles pods emerged from the jungle thicket, sliding down the Sand Snake dunes and paddling forward. The *Nezra Rides* was halfway across the narrow expanse when the first of the vanguard pods made it to the other side.

Qisami watched with professional interest as the advance pods formed a beachhead and waited. Her gaze went to a small but clearly visible structure in the distance, standing atop a needle-shaped spire. It was daylight with perfect visibility. Why was the watchtower still silent?

This wasn't some small raiding party sneaking past the towers in the middle of the night. This was a whole blasted fleet, dozens of giant pods. A blind person couldn't have missed this. Qisami was still pondering when a small detail caught her eye, something about the tip of that tower. Every Xing watchtower had a wide, circular platform at the top for surveillance. This one had been shorn off. Someone had come here before them.

The change in the climate when the Nezra fleet passed from the Grass Sea to Xing Duchy was immediate. What had been a vibrant green jungle an hour ago gave way to an arid desert with deep dunes that undulated and shifted with the breeze.

Qisami breathed in deeply as the first familiar scents of the desert swirls passed her. Hints of cinnamon and cacao. She knew exactly where they were passing, just to the south of Dragon's Maw Pass. The Nezra fleet had crossed into Zhuun lands.

Qisami was home, and once again a criminal and fugitive. She couldn't catch a break these days, could she? Well, at the bottom of every beautiful waterfall was a drowning victim, so she was just going to have to roll with it.

"So this is the home you keep blabbing about." Wani appeared next to her on the bow of the pod. She looked out. "This place sucks."

"The Xing desert is like an ugly courtesan. Underestimate her at your own risk." Qisami grinned. She was a softie when it came to her favorite duchy.

That was when it finally hit her. After all these years, she was home again. By the King's shriveled balls, she missed this dry heat. After nearly ten years—five of them in prison—she was finally home. This was where she began her career. Xusan was where she had carved out her reputation, where she earned diamond-tier status, and where she could command top coin. Xing was the largest market for shadowkills, and certainly the most fun region in which to operate. The Xing Court in Xusan was filled by a bunch of madmen. Sometimes, Qisami and her cell would get double-booked.

She had been so lost in thought she forgot Wani was still chattering about something.

". . . so it doesn't matter which way. We understand the need to return home. There aren't any sour feelings if you decide to do that, all right?"

Qisami frowned. "You think I'm going to dump you sorry lot the moment I get twisty sand beneath my toes?"

The younger viperstrike blushed. "I would like it if you stayed with us a little longer. Your training is fun."

"Don't worry. I'll still be here when you find Salminde."

"It's just that we would understand—"

"Got it." Qisami elbowed her hard enough to stumble. "Do you want to go over the three-prong counter?"

"Yes, please!"

Why the hell not? Qisami swung her leg over and landed on her feet. "Peel those brats away from the railing and let's get back to work. Tell the mouth breather to meet us back on deck."

"Marhi!" Wani called. "She's staaaaaaaaying!"

Qisami watched as the girl ran off. She couldn't help but feel weird about Wani's reaction. It was good—warm, even—but awkward. Qisami spent the next hour teaching the brats how to properly slash someone with a knife. Everyone's follow-through was terrible. She had never pegged herself as a training pool mother, but she was finding fulfillment when she passed her knowledge to these little brats. Maybe she was getting old.

The evenings were spent at a small settlement that looked like it had been flattened by giant pods. The residents had hidden in sand crates when they arrived. It was only with Qisami shooing the city pods away and walking up the stupid stretches of dunes that she managed to lure one of the locals out in the open. Like most remote desert settlements, supplies were often buried in the sand. It took a bit of convincing, cajoling, and only a few threats before she managed to persuade these dirty eggs that she meant no harm, which was a lie. No sooner had they finally opened up to her than the bands of Nezra appeared. Qisami felt guilty for betraying a fellow Zhuun, but only a little. In the end, the fleet received a fair barter of oil, blackrock, and cooked cactus in return for several barrels of food and water. Everyone won, sort of.

More importantly, Qisami was able to extract what happened here from the locals: a large group of black Kati pods had come by a few days prior, followed by a cluster of red-and-green pods. The settlement had only minutes to stow their supplies.

They had stared at Qisami while she hammered out their trade. They recognized a nightblossom when they saw one and panicked when a city pod arrived to pick up the supplies. The thought of robbing these peasants blind *did* cross her mind, but now—she wasn't sure why—she watched with satisfaction as the barter was completed without incident. The Exiles Rebellion received some much-needed supplies to continue powering their fleet, while these Xing settlers wouldn't starve or freeze to death tonight.

The most vital information they learned was that Chaqra had veered west, toward Xusan. That surprised Malinde and the rest of the Nezra leadership. They had assumed that the Black City would continue to head south to pillage the many smaller settlements and minor towns that were plump with ore and weaker fortifications. There was even talk that Chaqra could target Sanba, the unofficial southern capital of the duchy. Hitting Xusan directly, however, was unthinkable. The Katuia had never directly threatened a ducal capital before. Qisami was impressed. Whoever was leading these spirit shamans was brazen.

They only realized the extent of the Katuia attack into Xing a few hours later when one of the lancer pods scouting ahead came across one of the watchtowers that had been leveled by artillery fire. The report back was that most of the Xing soldiers had been massacred inside the tower. Many had attempted to flee but were hunted down. Their bodies were found half covered in sand several hundred yards to the west with wounds on their backs.

The Exiles fleet passed by three more towers and two more settlements on their way to the heart of the duchy. The settlements had been sacked while the watchtowers had been leveled, although it appeared the third tower at least put up a stiffer fight. That meant the watchtowers were able to get off the signal fires. It also meant Xusan would be ready for the attack from the khan's fleet. It gave Qisami hope. She would be pissed off if someone busted up her hometown.

This time, she accompanied the lancer pod to investigate what was left of the third watchtower, known as the Crane Tower. This was halfway between the Grass Sea and Xusan. The Crane Tower was far larger and more fortified than the previous two, but it appeared to have crumbled easily, which was astonishing. Entire wars had been fought to a standstill at the Crane Tower.

Malinde stood next to her and made an uneasy face at the bodies strewn about. They were three days baked in the hot sun and were thoroughly dusted by the constantly shifting sands. But the story of the attack, based on where men died, was clear. This had been a quick battle.

"Chaqra's fleet must be large. Easily a hundred pods, maybe more, to our forty-two." Malinde sniffed and wiped her nose on her sleeve. "Those are pretty bad odds, right?"

"I don't think you have to be a master tactician to know that being outnumbered two to one is a bad bargain, but that's where we go if we want to save Salminde." Qisami paused. "Are you sure it's worth it?"

"Worth the effort of saving my sister, Salminde the Viperstrike? Absolutely."

Qisami said the quiet part aloud. "I mean, risking your entire clan for one person."

Malinde looked even more determined. "These Kahun pods are

faster than anything Chaqra can roll at us. Besides, the enemy is now deep in Zhuun territory. We should be able to catch them."

Qisami nodded. "'Let your enemy stab your other enemies and then stab the survivor.'"

"What is that?"

"It's a saying from the training pools. Basically, what it means is—"

"Oh, I get it. You don't have to be a master tactician to decipher it," said Malinde. "The battle still has to make sense, understood? Our entire clan is here. The risk has to be worth the reward."

"Why are you bringing your kids into war anyway?"

"The *whole* clan is here." The master tinker huffed. "It's not like we can gather all our children and drop them off with a neighboring clan. 'Here are our lads. Please give them back after we're done going to war.' Everyone has a role in our battles. Even the sprouts."

"Madness," Qisami muttered. She stepped over an older corpse. The watchtowers were often garrisoned by soldiers finishing their last few years on contract before retirement. Hardly elite. Perhaps that was how Chaqra smashed through them so quickly. That sounded as plausible as any other excuse. "Bunch of fat white whiskers padding their pensions."

The lancer pod returned to the main fleet a while later. Daewon had decided to keep the fleet moving through the night to avoid the sandstorm that had been nipping at their heels for the past two days.

"It'll take two days to clean out the sand," Daewon proclaimed. "You don't want your steeds to pull up lame out here in enemy lands."

That was good enough for Malinde, so they pressed on. If the fleet continued traveling through the night at their current speed, they should be able to see Xusan, the Column City, by morning.

While they traveled, Qisami did what all good professionals did during quality downtime: she caught up on her sleep. Qisami spent so much time here aboard the *Nezra Rides* that Malinde had offered her quarters near the children. She still thought it was outrageous for the clan to pack them on a warpod, even if this was the safest one, but that was their way.

No sooner had she closed her eyes than she found herself looking out at morning. Streams of light were poking through a window off a porthole. Qisami heard shouts from above. She leaped out of bed and into the hallway, picking her way against traffic until she reached the staircase leading up to the main deck.

Qisami hurried to the bow of the pod. She didn't need anyone to point her to where to look. Off in the distance was a magnificent tower standing alone in the midst of a sprawling plateau.

Xusan. The capital of Xing Duchy.

And it was burning, billowing a giant spray of black soot. The Pedestal That Lifts the Sky was now stained black.

CHAPTER FIFTY-SEVEN

UNIFICATION

Taishi was already annoyed with this new arrangement.

The tailors had put a stunningly beautiful but unwieldy robe on her, complete with small glass beads hanging from her shoulders and elbows. She looked like a silly tree with the rest of the participants waiting for their turn to be announced. Taishi would get called early as the less important always went first. She didn't have any rank or importance, but her presence would be missed if she did not attend a ceremony with the dukes, the high seats, and most importantly, the Prophesied Hero of the Tiandi. Jian would be announced second to last, with only Dongshi after him.

Which was absurd. In more peaceful times, Taishi would have contested that arrangement with her blade. It was an insult to put some duke higher than the Prophesied Hero of the Tiandi. Now, still inching closer to death, she thought it hilarious that she had cared. She was never good at holding her tongue, which was a necessity among lords. Today was going to be a trying day.

She moved to her place in the queue beside a group of Black Orchid nuns. Taishi averted her gaze. She wasn't sure if word of the con-

vent's destruction had reached Skyfall Temple yet, and she didn't want
to be the one to pass along the news. A thuggish group of bald Tiandi
battlemonks glowered as they took their place next to her in the queue.
Many of the devout still believed that Taishi kidnapped Jian from the
Celestial Palace and held her responsible for every catastrophe that
followed.

If only Taishi wielded such power in her one good hand.

The Skyfall Temple had been a hive of activity. It began on the
morning of the second day after Wen Jian, the Prophesied Hero
of the Tiandi, the Champion of the Five Under Heaven, the Savior of
the Zhuun, appeared in front of the temple with Duchess Sunri of
Caobiu and declared his support for her as the next Empress of the
Enlightened States. It wasn't a long event. Jian had workshopped a
speech with Zofi for days, but then he learned something as he was
about to give his remarks.

Jian had stage fright. He looked out at the sea of gaping admirers
watching his every move. Before, he just had to wave or look brave.
Now they expected him to talk! He blinked. "Uh, ba . . ."

Taishi had to usher him away, and then Sunri took over. The newly
endorsed future Empress of the Tiandi declared martial law and then
ordered Dukes Waylin of Xing and Dongshi of Lawkan to appear at
this temple in three days, or risk dismemberment for this dishonor.

The chamber emptied. Dozens of monks scrambled down the
stairs and poured out of the temple, pushing back out of the square
while demanding a stop to this. Others tried to bring Jian back inside
Skyfall's walls.

Sunri did not allow that. Her guards locked shields and drew
swords, forming a protective wall around Jian. It looked like a conflict
was brewing between the new empress and the Tiandi religion. That
would have been a scandalous disaster, especially with the Champion
of the Five Under Heaven taking the duchess's side over his own religion. The news had spread as fast as light could flicker. By night, it had
reached every capital within the Enlightened States. By the next
morning, both Waylin and Dongshi messaged Skyfall Temple through
mindseers that they were on their way.

That was two days ago.

This morning, a massive nine-linked serpent barge appeared, nine ships connected by flexible tunnels with a water dragon head up front. The majestic craft snaked down the river with its many white masts pointed straight up and to the sides like a caterpillar. Taishi had joined the rush to watch the spectacle from the eighth-level balconies. It was a spectacular sight as massive six-mast ships glided toward shore like a bevy of floating swans performing synchronized swimming. Dongshi certainly knew how to make an entrance.

The lead ships docked in Hengyen's harbor and then extended a bridge to connect to the next ship over. Then that ship would extend its bridge to connect to the next ship farther out. This continued until the Lawkan Alabaster Fleet formed a floating fortress.

Dongshi's actual entrance from the ships to the main road through Hengyen and then to Skyfall Temple was not nearly as impressive. The duke and a mob of sailors poured onto the street. It looked like a riot more than a procession, but whatever it was called, it got the job done. The Lawkan were famously relaxed except when it came to sailing. They treated sailing like a second religion, if not the first.

Now that the Duke of Lawkan was here, it was time for their meeting, which was how Taishi ended up wearing this silly robe. The queue lines were crowded. A small stir passed through the crowd. Taishi craned her head and caught sight of the procession: the Duchess of Caobiu leading the way. Sunri was wearing a glittering gown crafted from gold and diamonds with plum-colored trim that lined her shoulders and a high arc around the collar. There was no questioning her imperial designs.

Sunri led a contingent of thirty attendants. Standing at the edge of the path near the queues, mute men eyed the spectators with suspicion. Many around her fell to their knees, which was overkill. Taishi had considered it, but then she would have to get back up. Instead, she stayed standing and bowed respectfully as the procession passed by.

The duchess's procession had nearly passed when it came to a sudden stop. The attendants collectively twirled into a seated position, revealing only Sunri in all her shiny madness. The duchess, wearing a golden headdress that looked like a cross between a bat and a head of broccoli, slowly pivoted to face her. The procession was silent. Finally, she spoke. "Grandmaster Ling Taishi, walk with me to the high seats' .circle."

Taishi noted the respect even as she bowed and fell behind the duchess like a servant. She imitated one of the attendants walking next to her, head bowed, her good arm tucked close to her body, and her footsteps mincing along the cold stone floors.

"I must have you to thank for these recent developments." Sunri led the slow but steady procession up the stairs, toward the eighth level. "Wen Jian is loyal to you, grandmaster, which means he would not have supported my claim without your approval. I'm glad we've reached a place of mutual respect, considering the circumstances of our last encounter."

Taishi decided to give her thoughts voice. "You mean when I beat your ass in the duel?"

One attendant gasped. Another stumbled.

"It was a fair fight," Sunri conceded. "I had a lot on my plate, though. I was busy conquering Gyian province."

"Then you shouldn't have challenged me to a duel, duchess."

"Let's put that behind us. You were the better woman that day."

"I was."

"I will need to keep Wen Jian close. The Champion of the Five Under Heaven will be a valuable ally. I look forward to collaborating with you in renewed friendship."

Fifty steps passed in silence before Taishi spoke again. "If I may, your grace, we're not friends."

Another round of gasps erupted from the attendants.

Sunri smiled. "The term can be applied so many ways."

"I don't even like you. I think you're a terrible person." Taishi was starting to enjoy speaking her mind, even if it would probably get her killed. "There are few worthy of my friendship, and you certainly don't qualify."

"I'm glad you got that off your chest, grandmaster." Sunri eyed Taishi for several moments before turning away. "I certainly hope you give Wen Jian sound advice."

They reached the top of the stairs leading into the high seats' chambers. Sunri gave her a pointed look and then walked away while an usher corralled Taishi toward another, where she was shuffled back to her place waiting in the queue. She was eventually announced two hours later. Once admitted by the Voice of the Tiandi, Taishi was then placed two steps away, flanking Jian's position, which in turn was to the side of Sunri's elevated throne. It was carefully choreographed.

Dongshi eventually joined them, sauntering his way into Skyfall Temple. He was larger than the last time Taishi had seen him, and his shoulders sagged. Ten years, the weight of rule, and a costly civil war would do that to a man. His long hair was knotted and disheveled, and his shirt was only half tucked in. He looked like a vagrant but walked with the fluidity of a duke and bellowed, "Sister, well met!"

Sunri was sitting at a makeshift throne set tallest in the room. Dongshi acted as if no one else was present as he plodded up the curved staircase wrapping around the back toward the throne. She arched an eyebrow. "Duke Dongshi, you've made it on time. Regrettably, it appears Waylin will not."

"Be reasonable, Sunri. He has to travel by land. The only way he was going to make it here in three days was to jump on the next horse and ride it to death, and he has a bad back! You know he's not coming without his army."

Sunri snorted. "I already destroyed his army."

"Yet you can't complete the conquest."

"Because it's bloody Xing with their bloody big desert! It's not worth the effort."

"Not even for all their ore and minerals?"

"The Caobiu do not need to rely on anyone."

"My little spooks tell me otherwise. I hear that a certain mining colony of yours had a burp in its operations. Something about a prison rebellion?" Dongshi, the former emperor's whisperlord, had a spy network that was rivaled only by the silkspinners. The Ten Hounds, as his spy network and secret police were named, were better than the silk-spinners because they functioned to serve one man. This made him one of the most dangerous in the empire.

Dongshi whirled around and locked his gaze on Jian. "So that's the mouthy little runt you got leading around like you have your tit in his mouth, eh?"

"Maybe he likes winners, Dongshi."

"You haven't won yet." He shrugged. "You still have two more duchies to knock out. We're not rolling over. You've already said you can't take the bloody desert, and we both know there's nothing your big, ugly army can do against my big, beautiful navy." He plopped in his seat. "Besides, that's not even your biggest concern."

"What, pray, would that be?"

Dongshi grinned and leaned forward. Beneath that relaxed demeanor was a calculating mastermind. "I've seen your ledgers, Sunri. You were always a spendthrift, but your . . . loose ways appear to have caught up with you. My, how the coins slip through your fingers. You have, what, six months left before your coffers are dry?"

She raised a cup to her lips. "Spend little, gain little. That's no way to build an empire."

He smirked. "Your books are a bloodbath, sister duchess. You're hemorrhaging, bleeding out. The more land you conquer, the deeper into debt you fall. Have you considered that perhaps the solution to your financial problems is to stop trying to conquer everything? Your government is two cycles away from bankruptcy. The moment your soldiers' rations dwindle and they miss payroll, Sunri's mighty Cinder Legions will snuff themselves out."

All ears in the chamber were riveted to the duke's every word. The two continued to ignore them.

"I froze your Allanto accounts!"

"I broke the dam at Hsube River and flooded the rice fields in western Caobiu. Your entire crop has been wiped out. Prices per pound have tripled now, and we're going to have a healthy market for Lawkan grain."

The two traded barbs several more times. Taishi was glued to their conversation. The two verbally sparring dukes were beginning to paint a clear picture of the situation in the Enlightened States. Each side was accusing the other of being close to defeat, and strangely both were correct.

"... and it is an indisputable fact that the realm will be more stable when a man sits on the throne. Your position is unsustainable, Sunri. We both know that. Aren't you tired of all this bloodshed, sister duchess?"

"Why is it that only Duchess Sunri bears the entire responsibility for peace?" Taishi said. "Why do you not bear any of the burden, your grace? What have you done that is worthy of the imperial throne?"

"Who is this old woman who dares to speak out of turn in my presence?" Dongshi spat. "If the crone is one of yours, Sunri, I suggest you flay her as a personal courtesy to me. . . ."

"I am Grandmaster Ling Taishi of the Windwhispering School of the Zhang lineage of the Ling family style. I am the greatest war artist of this generation."

Doubt flashed across Dongshi's face. He bobbed his head as he spoke. "You're the actual Ling Taishi?"

"You and your retinue are welcome to test my blade, but half will be dead before you take ten steps."

It was a silly boast. No one could kill two dozen skilled war artists in five seconds. It would take at least five minutes to kill that many.

He stared, as if considering his odds in a fight. When Sunri made no movement to temper either of them, he shrugged. "Very well, grandmaster. You have spoken. Share your great wisdom with the imperial court. All I have to do is wait Sunri out. Once her duchy implodes, there will be no lord stronger than I. Tell me, why should I *allow* her to be empress when the crown is at *my* fingertips?"

Taishi continued toward dumb truthfulness. "Because she's the most qualified. Of course her purse is tight and her strings of liang dwindling. She's surrounded by enemies, fighting wars on every front. All four of you ganged up on her, tried to squeeze her out, but that woman kicked your asses up and down the Enlightened States, all while making plenty out of little. Sunri defeated you on the field and outflanked you in court. She took out two other dukes while you did nothing. Waylin lost every battle against the Caobiu while you hid behind your fleet trying to do nothing all the way to the Celestial Throne. People do not respect that. More importantly, the lords and generals will not respect that."

"Yet they will respect a conniving, bloodthirsty woman for the throne?"

"You paint her as conniving, you say she's bloodthirsty, but are you any better? You all scheme and murder. Even the supposedly good ones. The difference between all of you and Sunri is that she's a woman and you all lost. The best duke won. So kowtow, bend the knee. It's over. There's nothing else to do. Just save some lives."

Taishi caught Sunri staring at her out of the corner of her eye. Dongshi was too. They all were.

He finally spoke. "Lawkan Duchy recognizes the Duchess of Caobiu's accomplishments and her temporary control of Gyian and Shulan. However, holding an empire together is not a task we have seen her accomplish. Therefore, Lawkan Duchy will wait three cycles, one full year, before determining how to proceed. If the Duchess of Caobiu is as savvy with the ledgers as she is on the field, then Lawkan will bend the knee."

A weak answer from a weak man.

"Now, if you will excuse me . . ." Dongshi made a show of getting up. "It's been a long day, and if we can't come to terms between us quickly, then we might as well wait until old Waylin arrives."

A courier ran into the room, pushing his way past the Voice of the Tiandi, who made a half effort in stopping them. The courier ran up the steps leading to where the dukes sat and fell to his knees. "Duke Dongshi and Duchess Sunri. I bring news from Xing!"

"About time," said Dongshi. "Has Waylin arrived yet?"

"A thousand apologies, great duke. Xusan, the capital city of Xing, was attacked by a Katuia horde and destroyed! Duke Waylin is dead."

Both Sunri and Dongshi bolted to their feet. Sunri was already on the move. "How could this happen? Are there survivors? I need a full report immediately. Alert the generals and muster the Cinder Legions."

"Duchess," said the courier. "There's more."

"What is it?"

"Witnesses say the Eternal Khan of Katuia personally led the attack."

A gasp flooded through the chamber. Several of the high seats stood. The tension in the chamber became thick, verging on panic.

"That's impossible," sputtered Dongshi.

Taishi's mind reeled at the courier's words. She was still processing everything when she heard a strange squeak, like a squealing cat that had its tail run over. She looked over and noticed Jian wavering on his feet.

"Boy, are you all right?" she said.

He turned toward her, his face white. He opened his mouth and closed it, and then his eyes rolled into the back of his head. Then, Wen Jian, Prophesied Hero of the Tiandi, Champion of the Five Under Heaven, Savior of the Zhuun, pitched forward, falling flat on his face.

Taishi should have tried to catch him, but that would have sent them both to the floor. Instead she remained standing, staring down at the heir to the windwhispering lineage lying unconscious on the floor.

At least he didn't throw up this time.

CHAPTER FIFTY-EIGHT

TO THE VICTORS,
THE SPOILS

ali woke with a start. Her head pounded. It felt like someone had spiked a stake through the back of her skull. Her body ached like she had just fought a three-day drawn-out battle. Every muscle was sore, everything hurt, but it was a good hurt. She was nauseous too, her stomach churning, but that had nothing to do with the battle.

She was still wearing her armor, half of it now torn and the other half fallen into disrepair, with scale mail dangling off broken links like a knotted-up curtain. Hampa, the older one, would have been horrified at this tangled chain mess. Sali sat up and the room swooned. Her vision blurred. Lights pierced her eyes. She rested her face in her hands as she rolled to a sitting position from her bed. Her stomach threatened to send its contents back up her throat. At that moment, Sali desperately wanted to die.

Such was the price for victory.

And then the party afterward. There was a proverb in the raidlife: If the battle doesn't kill you, the after-party should.

This one almost did.

From predawn this morning—yesterday morning, actually—when the last of Xusan's defenses fell, to now—whenever now was—Sali had mostly drunk, partied, had random intercourse. Sali was fairly sure she nearly died more times playing drinking games than during the battle. It reminded her of the old days, when great warbands would celebrate after great battles. And the Siege of Xusan was a great battle indeed, worthy of history and remembrance, to be enshrined in the songs and legends for future generations. After the surrender, the Katuia partied, as was their custom, and no Katuia partied better than the Eternal Khan of Katuia.

And Sali had been an important part of it.

Xusan's defenses were formidable. The siege had lasted three long days and nights of nonstop artillery and massacres. The artillery from the city pods quickly broke through the siege. The interior fighting in the Column City was terrible and unrelenting as the Katuia painted it with blood, floor after floor.

It was Visan, however, who broke the stalemate. The Eternal Khan of Katuia was a whirlwind of death, slaughtering dozens as he led the attack. Sali could tell he was raw in many aspects of his fighting and lacked the tactical awareness that most seasoned warriors possessed. No amount of reincarnation and knowledge could replace experience.

Sali staggered to her feet and shuffled. She had been fortunate to avoid any major injuries during the battle but *had* taken a beating. Most of her cuts had dried, but some would need to be stitched. The rest she could endure.

Most importantly, Sali had had fun. An unexpected, savagely exuberant time. Visan had seen to that, putting her with other elite warriors and in prime battle positions where the siege was thickest but still manageable. The khan led the attack; Sali fought by his side. The fighting was intense and constant, but there had never been any threat of being overwhelmed or in tactical danger. The wills of the khan saw to that.

Sali knew what babying the Eternal Khan of Katuia was like. She had run similar operations dozens of times during her duties serving

Jiamin. Visan was more difficult to manage than his predecessor, that much was certain. This new host was more aggressive and less disciplined. He was also younger.

Still, she appreciated how well the khan's Sacred Cohort operated. They were skilled and efficient, which she admired. Sali knew that the khan was wooing her to pledge her allegiance back to Katuia. Wooing her with tradition and familiar trappings and the glorious days of the past, when causes were simple and straightforward. Back to a time before Sali had learned about the Xoangiagu.

That had changed everything. Sali didn't know if she could come back from this knowledge. That didn't stop the khan from continuing to woo her.

She hated to admit it, but it was working. Part of her, steeped in culture and reverence, wanted to return to the way things had been. Her resolve wavered. The last few days of being back in the horde, back in the raidlife, back in positions of influence and change, had been alluring. She missed the power, privilege, and status of her old life. She missed after-parties as well. They gave the warriors an opportunity to celebrate and feel motivated to achieve something.

"Sali, viperstrike, Salminde," several of the wills of the khan called out in passing. They were already treating her as if she were one of them. This was usually what happened when someone joined the Sacred Cohort. It was the greatest honor and most exclusive sect within Katuia.

Sali offered a lazy wave in greeting and continued to walk heavy-footed and bleary-eyed through the outer gates of the Sanctuary of the Eternal Moor. That was when she first noticed the rumbling under her feet. Chaqra was on the move, but why? They had only conquered Xusan just the other day. It would take an entire cycle just to properly sack the city of its resources. The capital of Xing Duchy was a massive city filled with hundreds of thousands of people. Just to restock necessary supplies would likely take two weeks. The Black City should be digging in and feasting upon the corpse of its fallen enemy. Occupations were not a Katuia tactic.

Chaqra's victory here was heroic, the greatest victory Katuia had ever inflicted upon the Zhuun, but victory had come at a steep price. It would take weeks if not longer to repair the damage and replenish their ranks. Convalescing at Xusan made perfect sense. They could sit out the entire third cycle within the confines of the city. So what was happening? More importantly, where were they going?

Sali stepped out of the temple and onto the main street atop *Aracnas*. The roar of the engines at the lower levels was deafening. Chaqra had never been a quiet city. Its shrieks, as if everything needed to be oiled, cut through the ears as it rolled at a walking pace across the arid Xing landscape. She sniffed. There was something else: smoke and burnt wood, rot and corpses cooking under the sun. Buzzing filled the air, like locusts, but if she listened carefully, she could make out words.

Sali walked onto the observation deck, which was just below the control deck. Her mouth dropped. There, in an open field, used previously as a battleground for Xing soldiers, were hundreds of lines of captured land-chained, a mass of disheveled and broken humanity walking through the fields to the side of the road, bound at the wrists, getting loaded into large wagons.

She turned to the nearest towerspear standing guard. "What is happening? Where are those land-chained being taken?"

The question, of course, was above a simple guard's standing. He simply stared ahead. "Apologies, great viperstrike." Then he stood more at attention. Sali sensed immensely powerful jing approaching from behind, like the sun's searing burn on a hot, wet day.

"Salminde, you've recovered from the well-deserved revelry." Visan grasped her shoulders as if they were comrades, strangely closer than Jiamin had ever done after he had been raised to the khan. It just showed how each host's personality was still prevalent in each khan.

"What is happening here?" she asked.

He beamed as their pod slowly squealed past the field. "When the Zhuun last killed me, they didn't seize the land within the Grass Sea or its abundant resources. They did not demand our tinker technology, or attempt to integrate our people with theirs. No, they seized the most valuable thing we have to offer: our blood, our strength, and our endurance. They stole our labor and paid us with nothing except removing the threat of annihilation, yet they continue to kill us. We've watched as the Enlightened States grew fat and wealthy from our labor, blood, and tears. It is now the slaves' turn to reconstitute our people with the labor of our former masters."

"Human chattel is anathema to our people," Sali hissed, shaking through the wave of shock and disgust that had passed through her. "It is against everything we stand for. We *are* noble people. To act in any other way is not Katuia. It will be a black mark on your soul for eternity." The emphasis she placed in her words would have been worthy of a challenge for her disrespect in most cases.

Sali half expected him to lash out at her, but instead, the khan nodded. "You would not be honorable otherwise, but times must change. The old ways have not brought our people victory. A new strategy is necessary. While the Zhuun are busy fighting for their empty throne, the Katuia will be rebuilt to become the mightiest horde this world will ever see."

Sali hated that the man's words made sense. Her soul knew it was wrong but also true. Never-ending war, death, and destruction over the centuries had stagnated their civilization's growth. Something had to change if her people were to rise out of this quagmire, but slavery, or indentured servitude, as the Zhuun called it, could not possibly be the answer.

"We would be no better than the enemy," she said.

"We would have no enemy then," said Visan. "What is peace worth to our people?"

She had to admit that ending this conflict was tempting. She once said she would have paid any price to provide calm seas for future generations of Katuia. Now, seeing the price Visan was trying to extract not only from the Zhuun but from her people's honor, Sali was no longer sure.

One of his eyebrows raised at her. "If you disapprove, then change my mind. Show me a workable solution that is more palatable for your delicate honor."

"Sometimes, there are no good solutions to complex problems, great khan, but there are certainly terrible ones."

"And doing unto the Zhuun what they did to our people would be one such terrible idea?"

Sali nodded. "We would be no better than the land-chained. What has set us apart from them has always been our righteous ways and elevated reasoning. If we wallow in their muck and shit, we will end up indistinguishable from their filth."

The khan considered. "And these righteous ways and elevated reasoning, what good is it? I cannot touch it. It does not nourish me. It will not slay our enemies. It cannot feed troops or power cities. It cannot be melted and forged into armor, nor will it keep people warm." He waved a finger in the air. "It is an idea, nothing more."

"But it is the idea that leads the way. If you lead our people down this dark path, it will be a scar that will echo for generations. Is the weight of this sin something your legacy is prepared to bear?"

He studied her before turning back to the fields of endless Zhuun prisoners. "Your wisdom has merit, Salminde, and I am a willing ear. I welcome it, but it appears none of these sycophants possess the courage to say what is necessary."

Sali stepped next to him. "Would my counsel stop this tragedy before it happens?"

"It'll depend on how persuasive you are. What say you?" When she didn't answer him, Visan added, "You are free to leave anytime, Salminde the Viperstrike. But where would you go? I am the center of the Katuia's world. The sun and moon orbit around me. If you hope to make change, the best place to do it is by my side. I will even forgive your rebellion and the sin Nezra committed on Liqusa."

It pained her to think about it, but this was an offer worth considering. It would be the best way to guarantee the safety of her clan, but would betray everything she had led them to believe about this rebellion. Sali would have to renounce the beliefs that she had instilled in her people. The shame would destroy her legacy and her standing in the afterlife. But would it have been worth it?

Sali closed her eyes. She knew the answer to that. There was another thing she couldn't let go. "I know your true nature, Visan. Who and what you are, twisted to the spirit shamans' selfish aims. I cannot serve someone while knowing that."

Visan snarled, rage flashing on his face. "You've been listening to the Happan again, haven't you? They've always felt so possessive of me, as if I were theirs to own. I am my own being. No one controls me."

"Not the spirit shamans?"

"You mistake the order of things, Salminde. They are my most loyal believers."

"After all these centuries, can you distinguish between your followers and your keepers? The spirit shamans dictate your every decision, your education, your policies, even what you eat. Are you sure it's *you* who are free?"

The khan's chest swelled as he surveyed the spoils of their victory. "I allow it. As long as they serve my purpose, it matters not what you call them. Now, it is time to prepare. The fleet is moving to full churn once we reach open desert."

Sali suddenly realized they were heading west, deeper into the Zhuun lands, and uncomfortably far from the safety of the Grass Sea. "Where are you taking us, khan?"

"You'll see, Salminde. You will see, and you will believe! You can still leave us if you choose. I won't stop you. There will be a stallion and a month's supply for you to journey in any direction. But here, in this spot and at this moment, you're in the epicenter of change. If you wish to leave your mark on Katuia, then you will remain and see our people's destiny to its end." He began to walk away.

Sali called after him. "Was sacking Xusan and enslaving its people the Eternal Khan of Katuia speaking, or the spirit shamans' command?" She couldn't qualify her thoughts, but his answer mattered.

Visan turned to face her with a new expression, not one of confident charm or rage, which had been typical up until now, but introspective. His tone was softer, more hesitant. "The Chaqra clan and her allies, Nezra included, were an existential threat upon Hrusha.

The Katuia had set a blockade around the Sun Under Lagoon. The Happan faced extinction. Half of Hrusha was a burnt ruin. Diseases were rampant. The city was starving. The other Xoangiagu had fallen, the pure Child had disappeared, and I was left alone to protect the Happan." He moved closer. "I was given a choice. Serve the spirit shamans to save my chosen people or be buried alongside them."

A wave of numbness swept over her. Sali had never viewed the khan's—the Warrior's—situation under this light. It also hit close to her current situation. "You knew, and you accepted it, for noble reasons. But that was centuries ago. Why do you still fight for those who threatened to destroy your people and enslaved you?"

"Because, as you said, that was centuries ago. Those Happan I cared about are long gone. Those on Hrusha now are strangers. My kind has disappeared. I have nothing left. So I do what I must to survive. Now, many centuries later, the cycle has returned full circle. The Katuia are the closest thing to a family and people that I have left. They are now my people. In this cycle, it is the Zhuun who are the existential threat and Katuia who face extinction, and I am again the solution, so I will do what must be done." Visan began to walk away from her. "That is my burden, and my choice to make, just as you will have your own burden to shoulder and your own choice to make."

Sali's thoughts were frozen. Her body tingled from her toes to her fingers. At that moment, she understood his sacrifice and loss. She realized his intentions, misguided but pure, made from a place of deep nobility. Mostly, Sali felt the khan's loneliness. The last of the Xoangiagu still trying to find a purpose and will to survive.

The Eternal Khan of Katuia stopped at the doorway to the Sanctuary of the Eternal Moor, and turned to her. "You know, you had Jiamin wrong. You were the reason his harem went unused. Did you know that?"

Sali looked up, hearing her old friend's name. "What do you mean?"

"He loved you more than anyone else in the world, but you were too preoccupied trying to make your own name to notice. Jiamin understood that. Never once did he attempt to tame you. He respected you for forging your own way, even if it broke his heart. He waited until his dying breath for you to reciprocate, but you never did."

Each of his words slammed into her. Her knees weakened and her breath grew labored. "That can't be true. Jiamin has been my heart-brother since we were sprouts. I would have known."

But Sali *did* know. In her heart, she did, even if she had buried that knowledge. She had loved him in her own way. Jiamin had become the khan! It was impossible! The khan did not take wives.

"That poem he once dedicated to you was his last words when the Zhuun spear pierced his heart. He died with you on his mind. It's not too late, Sali." The Eternal Khan of Katuia, the Lord of the Grass Sea, the Scourge of the Enlightened States, and the first man who ever loved Sali, studied her for several more moments before disappearing into the Sanctuary of the Eternal Moor.

Sali was still reeling from this revelation. It had shocked her but it wasn't surprising, if she was to reminisce about her younger days with Jiamin. The signs were there, and she had intentionally overlooked them, especially after he had been lifted to become the khan. It wasn't that she didn't love Jiamin; she did as a brother and possibly more if she hadn't been so focused on her own glory. Now, Visan wanted to pick up where Jiamin had left off.

It was a startling revelation. What shook Sali the most, however, was that she didn't outright reject the idea.

CHAPTER FIFTY-NINE

BEGINNING
OF THE END

Jian. Was. Freaking. Out.

Fainting in the middle of the high seats' chamber wasn't great. It was not the best look for the Prophesied Hero of the Tiandi. When he had come to a few moments later, upon remembering why he fainted in the first place, he had fainted again.

Finally, Jian found himself back in his chambers a few hours after the meeting of the dukes. Taishi and Bhasani were there by his side. The two masters were taking turns babying and disciplining him.

"You need to learn how to faint subtly, boy. It's all in the knees," said Bhasani. "The moment you feel dizzy, relax your knees and lower down to your ass. Don't pitch forward like you got punched. That's embarrassing."

"I'm humiliated," he admitted, gingerly touching the knot on his forehead.

Bhasani snapped at Taishi. "Didn't you ever teach the boy to fall properly?"

Taishi snorted. "Windwhispers have little use for that skill. We rarely lose."

"It's a good thing your style is single lineage. There's not enough ego in the world to go around."

Taishi offered him a cup of warm black tea. "The thought witch isn't wrong, though. You're the head of a religion and expected to lead a nation. We can't have you passing out like a fat uncle all over the place. It's lousy for morale."

"But . . . he's back." Jian's words were hushed, as if calling the man's name too loudly would summon him here. "He's alive again? How is it possible? Did he come back from the dead? Maybe he can't be killed." His eyes widened. "Is that why they call him the *Eternal* Khan of Katuia?"

"You . . . just noticed that now?" Bhasani glanced at Taishi, who covered her face.

"I'm just saying." Jian gesticulated furiously. "I'm not ready to fight him yet. I'm still recovering from my injury. It's not fair. He's cheating!"

"Slow down, boy," said Taishi. "Just because the khan has re-emerged doesn't mean you're fighting him tomorrow. We always knew this day would come. It could be many years before the two of you stand on opposing fields."

A gong outside Jian's quarters began to chime, sending vibrations through the walls and floors, rattling the shelf and the lamps hanging from the ceiling.

"General alarm," said Bhasani, moving toward the door.

Jian and Taishi followed her outside at the seventh-level balcony. Others had gathered on different floors overlooking the temple grounds below. All eyes were focused on the bottom of the serpentine stairs. Finally, a courier emerged, wearing the traditional blue and white of their calling. The man—long and lanky and wearing a blue turban—yelled something. Jian couldn't quite make out the words, as the courier was too far away, but whatever he had said sent everyone within hearing into a tizzy.

Jian frowned. A sinking feeling plopped into his gut. He froze, listening as the courier's voice grew louder, until eventually, the words became clear. "Katuia army heading toward Skyfall. Only a day's ride away! Katuia army heading toward Skyfall! Less than a day's ride away!"

"Well, is it a day's ride or is it less than a day's ride?" Bhasani sniffed. "Details matter."

Jian felt the world sway again. He tried to remember what the drowned fist master had said to him moments earlier. Bend what knee?

Bony fingers clasped his elbow. "Back to the quarters. Bhasani, summon the others," Taishi snapped into his ears. "We have to be off temple grounds within the hour and heading on the road toward Manjing by dusk."

"But what would happen to Skyfall?"

"It doesn't matter."

Jian stopped. "I can't."

Taishi tried to pull him along. She stopped when he refused to budge. She threw her arm around his shoulders and pulled him close. "You're not ready, boy. You're just not. I didn't save your hide and raise you right just to have you throw your life away."

"He razed Xusan. He'll raze Skyfall too, won't he? Tell me the truth."

"Yes, Jian, he will."

Jian's mind went down a dark path. "It feels like every city I visit burns to the ground: Jiayi, Allanto, Shulan, and now Skyfall."

"You visited Sanba, and that shithole didn't burn down," she said.

Jian frowned. "That's a strange thing to say. It's not exactly comforting."

She flicked him on the nose. "The point is that you created a narrative for yourself when it's simply correlation."

"I'm the Prophesied Hero of the Tiandi," he said, feeling defensive. "Of course it's my fault. I was the reason those cities burned."

She grabbed a fistful of his collar. "Jiayi burned because of the Katuia Nezra uprising. I just happened to drop you off there. Allanto burned because Sunri sprang a trap on Saan and Yanso. You just happened to get captured on the other side of the Enlightened States because *I* surrendered to a garrison of supply wagon guards. Finally,

Vauzan burned because everyone knew Sunri was going to target the city next in her conquest. I just happened to be too tired and lazy to steal you away from there before the Cinder Legions arrived. That and we had free housing at the temple where my former lover is boss."

"Sounds like it's all your fault then."

"Blame me all you want. You're alive, aren't you? Now hurry and pack—"

The two stopped at the entrance to the guard quarters. Staring at them was a little red fox.

Jian locked big moon-eye gazes with the creature. "What the . . ."

Taishi snapped, "Pei! Where are you, you little brat?"

The diminutive Oracle of the Tiandi, mouth stretched in a grin, stepped into the open from somewhere to the side. "Hi, Taishi."

"You're supposed to be dead!"

"I lied. I had to get you to deliver me to Sunri."

Taishi's voice went up another octave. "You're the blasted oracle. Your word is doctrine! You can't lie. That defeats the whole purpose of being a prophet if you lie!"

"You mistake my relationship with the truth, Taishi," said the girl, sounding far wiser than her years. "I don't see truth. I see possibilities. I choose one and strive to make it reality."

"What happened to the Black Orchid sisters?"

"Even the best outcomes require terrible sacrifices." The oracle bowed. "They were good souls. The sisters did what the sisters felt they had to do. I am responsible for their deaths, but the fault is not mine. It was their free will to choose."

Jian had never seen his master so furious. She stomped toward the little oracle and looked as if she were going to strike her. Instead, Taishi brought a side hammer fist down upon a small end table, shattering it. Jian was surprised she had the strength for that display.

Pei remained stoic, unmoved. "The events that unfolded in Vauzan had to happen because Sunri needed to be here, and I was the only one who could have convinced her. It is reflected in the stars."

"What about dying under her custody before the year is over?"

"The year is not over yet, Ling Taishi," said Pei. "What happened had to be done for this to unfold."

"The bloody khan is less than a day's ride away," Taishi stormed. "They will burn this temple and every person in it to the ground. If they capture the Oracle of the Tiandi, our people will fall!"

"Which is why I am here." Pei nodded at Jian. "And why he is here. We both need to be here for the last good outcome that will last the next four centuries."

"And what outcome is that?"

"You will see."

Jian, standing between them, raised his hand. "Um, what happens if that good outcome doesn't happen?"

"Then it's fourteen generations of famine, disease, and petty warlords until the fates align once more."

That felt like a lot of pressure. "What am I supposed to do?"

"The same thing you're always supposed to do. Try your best." She smiled sweetly at him. "Now prepare yourself."

"For what?"

Pei looked toward the door. "Fate has arrived."

The emergency gong began to bang relentlessly.

"They're already here?" Taishi fumed. "That's not even remotely close to a day's ride away."

CHAPTER SIXTY

TWISTED LOYALTIES

S ali gripped the railing of the *Aracnas* with the claws of her long
fingers as she watched green fields of vast, terraced rice paddies
slide past, the land carved out and submerged according to its
masters' design. It was obscene for these Zhuun to bend nature to their
will. The land-chained always harbored crazed obsessions to control
everything around them. It had always been their way. Still, she admired the beautiful geometric patterns curving along the earth. It
could be sacrilege and beautiful at the same time.

One thing could not be denied, though. These enslaved lands
were plentiful, full of life and sustenance. It was by these designs that
they could cultivate so much food. Sali understood that, but was it
worth the price of domesticity? There was enough food here to feed
the horde for years. There would be no need to raid if the land-chained
shared their bounty. Instead, the two sides raided and warred over
scraps, while their plentiful fields burned and rotted.

Her eyes flitted upward. It had been days, and the Chaqra fleet
continued to move west. They were now deep into Zhuun lands, as far
as any raiding party had ever dared. But what were they doing here?

There were dozens of settlements to the north and south that the Katuia could have struck, easier targets as well as a closer retreat back to the safety of the Grass Sea. Even then, with the defeat of Xusan, there were enough spoils that Chaqra could have laden their stores for a decade from this one victory alone.

Yet the fleet pushed west, past the end of the desert lands and into lush farmlands. The strange thing was, Chaqra didn't bother resupplying. They could have raided scores of unarmed settlements, fat for the picking with stores of food, ore, and jewels. Yet they pressed on.

The fleet was now deep within enemy lands, surrounded, cut off from supplies, with a long, nearly impossible journey back to friendly lands. One poorly waged battle could destroy Chaqra forever. Sali was conflicted by this, her loyalty torn between the sin the spirit shamans had committed against her people and her deep-rooted loyalty to them. It bothered her that Chaqra had embraced enslaving the Zhuun. Slavery was anathema to the Katuia. No person can own another, but she had also recognized that the stalemate they had waged for centuries only led to generations of death and war, while defeat had led to their own people being enslaved by the Zhuun.

Was it truly evil to do unto their enemy what their enemy had done to them?

The answer was clear in her heart, but the justification in her head gave her pause. Which evil was the lesser?

None of the pod crews knew their destination, and the spirit shamans weren't talking. All they knew was that their orders were to head west and six degrees north of the setting sun, through the hot third cycle of sweltering heat. Fall was around the corner, too, which meant harsh rains would arrive soon.

Visan had been too preoccupied to spare her his valuable time, which was understandable. This was the largest army Katuia had ever raised for raiding Zhuun lands. No, this wasn't a raid; it was an invasion. The khan was after conquest, which was not the Katuia way. Land was not something that could be owned by any person. Visan had already shown that he cared little for spoils and treasure. So what were they doing?

Sali closed her eyes. The only logical answer was revenge. The Eternal Khan of Katuia carried with him a decade of their people's fury at their indentured servitude. Capturing Xusan had already cemented him as one of the greatest khans to ever exist. But to risk the Black City itself was foolhardy. She was shocked that the spirit shamans allowed such an attack.

Then Sali remembered his words. "They are my loyal believers."

Could it be she had it wrong all along? That the khan was not a captured, twisted victim, as the Happan believed, but a being with its own agency, one who had accepted this path?

A young spirit shaman appeared. "Viperstrike, you are summoned to the control room."

"By whom?"

"By one who demands your attendance."

That could only mean Visan. The khan had been indisposed lately, too preoccupied to deal with one wayward warrior. Sali pushed away from the railing. "Lead on."

She followed a step behind the spirit shaman, observing his gait. There was something different about him today. Then she noticed what it was. The young man was wearing his battle robes, heavily padded to protect him while traveling or in battle. Something was afoot.

Visan was waiting in the control room conversing with his generals, all of whom were spirit shamans, and none happy to see her. The group parted for her as she approached.

Sali put her closed fist over her forehead and heart. "What is your will, great khan?"

"My hope was to have you consecrated as a Will of the Khan by now, Salminde the Viperstrike. Unfortunately, it will have to wait."

"I have not decided if I shall accept this honor yet, great khan."

He grunted. "You speak as if I had just offered you a job cleaning the stables. You should be honored."

"Kidnapping me to offer me a job isn't the honor you think it is, Visan." She followed his gaze as *Aracnas* plowed forward, moving toward what appeared to be a large lone mountain along the horizon. "What are we doing here in these wetlands, Visan? We are too far from the Grass Sea. Retreat will be difficult now, if not impossible. All for what? Spoils, slaves, and revenge?"

A smile cracked on the khan's lips. "Is that why you think we're here? Your opinion of me is so diminished." He pointed at the mountain. "There is a reward far greater than any worldly possession. It is both true immortality and an end to everything."

"You're speaking nonsense, Visan. We should return home before disaster befalls Chaqra."

"We're not heading back to the Grass Sea. This journey ends one way. That mountain is called Skyfall, and it is the seat of the Tiandi religion, just like Chaqra is the heart of ours."

"What about it? If you destroy it, the Zhuun will just rebuild."

"It is not their earthly world I wish to destroy, it is their legend. The Prophesied Hero of the Tiandi is on that mountain."

"How do you know this?" she asked.

"I know not how, but my heart pulls toward it. It is a voice I only hear in deep slumber, and it calls to me. My heart knows this to be true," Visan admitted. "Something pulls me there, whispers in my dreams. I know the Hero of the Zhuun is there. Once I kill him, I break their religion, and the will of their people, in one defining blow. That will be my legacy. I will tear apart and bury their Prophecy of the Tiandi once and for all, starting with their hero, whom I will rip apart limb by limb."

Sali acutely remembered her own failure in capturing and killing the boy. If Visan succeeded, his name would be etched in the stars for an eternity just as he claimed. She was standing next to greatness, if so. Or madness.

Visan faced her. "Will you fight alongside me in this final battle?"

Sali only stared back. She had participated in more than her fair share of important moments in her lifetime, but never had she anticipated this one would come. Ever since she was a child, Jiamin had roleplayed as the khan while she played one of his wills, and not once did the story have the khan hunting down the Zhuun hero. This felt strange, unnatural and unsettling. Sali didn't know what to make of it.

In the end, however, she was Katuia, Visan was the khan, and the

Prophesied Hero of the Tiandi, a young man she had tried to kill once already, was their mortal enemy. Every fiber of her being screamed for that man's blood.

She nodded. "My spear will stand with Katuia today, khan."

He acknowledged her only with a raise of his eyes, and then he bellowed, "Raise the Mark of the Serpent!"

A long red flag ran up a pole at the bow of the pod, fluttering in the wind. Moments later, the adjacent pods followed suit, and then the ones next to them, spreading the Mark of the Serpent. The pods increased speed, the wind picking up an edge as they whipped by.

The control deck was a hive of activity as the khan's Sacred Cohort stood by, ready to do his bidding as they prepared for battle. From this distance, they were still at least two hours away from the temple. The land-chained would have seen their approach by now.

The lookout from the nest above shouted down: "Zhuun army to the west! It's the banner of the Flames!"

"The Duchess of Caobiu is here?" Sali's worry grew. "Visan, a battle in the open field against the Cinder Legions is unwise. They outnumber us, and their war wagons will put up a struggle against your pods." She almost said *our* pods. She might as well, considering she was about to fight alongside him.

The khan studied the horizon, in the direction of the Caobiu army. "Ahbiduval and Horsaw."

Two of the wills of the khan stepped forward.

"Take your group to deal with the Cinder Legions. Circle around and hit them from the far flank. Harry them and keep them out of my way."

They barked their assent before hurrying away.

He turned to Sali. "We cannot afford to get bogged down fighting the Cinder Legions so close to the shoreline within range of the Alabaster Navy. If we punch into the temple, we use the mountains' fortifications to defeat the Caobiu."

"The city pods would be exposed."

"The city pods can be rebuilt."

"No, they cannot." What was he thinking?

"They are irrelevant then."

Sali could barely mask her shock at his flippant words toward their sacred pods. "You would rather hide behind still walls than maneuver out in the open?"

The khan grunted. "Once I kill the Prophesied Hero of the Tiandi, it won't matter." He beckoned to another of his wills. "Bhusui, lock down the river to the south. Prevent the Alabaster Fleet from reinforcing the waterways."

The will slammed her fist into her chest. "Yes, my khan," she said, and hurried off.

"Tinkerchief, how far until siege range?"

The spindly old man looked through a gauge. "With the *Aracnas* moving at twenty-three feet per beat, an hour until we are within range of the catapults."

Visan nodded. "Maintain gallop speed until the first volley and then raise the Mark of the Stallion."

"Yes, great khan."

The khan continued leading the fleet, barking orders and demanding information and feedback from the advisers around him. He was a far cry from Jiamin, who had never cared much for the details of strategy and tactics. More commands followed, and more of the khan's Sacred Cohort departed to go about their assignments. This continued until only a handful remained. The anticipation grew among the crew as the Chaqra fleet neared the settlement's edge.

The tinkerchief studied the temple through a monocle. "The settlement has a minimal wall, but the temple's mountain walls are formidable. It will take hours to break through. Many of our pods will be torn to shreds by then." That had always been one of the main reasons why the Katuia never engaged the Zhuun's larger settlements.

Visan shook his head. "No time for that. Send terrapin pods to each of the three main gates." He considered. "*Ronsu, Quiman,* and Ao."

The tinkerchief paled, his voice tinged with outrage. "Great khan, terrapin pods play a critical role in the city's health. Mounting a charge against land-chained fortifications utilizing all three of the city's terrapins is risky. Attacking such strong fortifications could cripple if not destroy all three pods."

Visan's face didn't change. "Fly the Mark of the Terrapin. All colors."

"Are you certain?" the tinkerchief blurted. At first, he looked alarmed, and then he bowed. "Your will, great khan."

"Salminde." Visan did not look her way. "You will lead the Ao on the eastern flank."

Shock filled her. This offer—no, this command—was not entirely unexpected, however. What better way to test someone's loyalty than to order them to lead a suicidal attack? It's what she would have done in his place. If the Ao succeeded in breaking through the eastern gates, then Sali had proved her loyalty. If it failed, then she was likely dead, and that proved her loyalty as well. The only way Visan wouldn't get his way was if she refused, but a khan's request was never a request.

Any answer other than the one he expected was certain death. Sali placed her fist over her heart. "It would be my honor, great khan."

"Bring five squads of spears. Take and hold the gates until the rest of my Sacred Cohort relieve you. If you can, disrupt their artillery, but the gates are the only things that matter." The khan turned away and began exchanging words with Thuaia, another of his wills of the khan. Sali had already been forgotten.

Joum, one of the younger wills of the khan, approached and placed his fist over his heart and then forehead. He bowed. It was awkwardly formal. "Salminde the Viperstrike, I am to accompany you on the honorable command. The Ao is already docked with the Aracnas to receive you. They await your leadership." He offered her a sturdier plate of armor, more suitable for such a heavy attack. It was full heavy-banded armor forged from actual bands of iron instead of the usual flame-tempered wood. Visan had had her participation planned for some time.

Sali stared at the black-and-white colors of the Chaqra clan painted like zebra stripes on the banded armor. She politely pushed the offering away. It was every Katuia's duty to slay the land-chained. That did not mean they were Chaqra. "I'd rather die than wear that," she muttered too loudly.

She *did* accept a large black-and-white swirled buckler. It was foolish enough to wander into a siege without armor. Only an insane person would refuse a shield before a battle. One of the worst ways to die was by arrow. Sali shuddered.

The city pod *Ao* arrived shortly after, pulling alongside *Aracnas*. It was a terrapin pod, used primarily for warehousing and storage for the city's uses, but also as a troop transport. These pods were heavily armored, fire resistant, and had the open space needed to house hundreds of warriors. It was oval-shaped, low to the ground, with only one-story buildings, not unlike the shape of a sea turtle.

Sali stepped onto the deck and was met by dozens of curious and suspicious eyes. No doubt word had spread among the crew that the viperstrike was arriving. Most probably viewed her as a traitor, yet here she was taking command. She was going to need to earn their trust.

Joum and Sali stepped onto the control deck a few minutes later. Unlike most other pods, the control decks for terrapin pods were positioned at the stern on a lower level beneath the main deck. The six others on the control deck, including the pod's tinkerchief, eyed her with open hostility as she stepped up the short flight of stairs to join them.

Sali's eyes locked on the captain of the pod. She was an older woman with her thinning hair pulled tightly back. The sides of her head were shaved. Someone from the raidlife. Sali kept her gaze level as she approached. The captain stepped up to her, eyeing Sali before finally speaking in a rough voice. "Captain Chikara of the Hosep sect, viperstrike. I captain the *Ao*."

That was where the hardness came from. The crew had likely considered her an enemy just a few days ago. It must be difficult to now ask them to follow her commands. Sali's stomach tightened. She felt that it should be the captain in command of the attack, not her. She certainly wasn't as qualified as the captain here.

"The khan's will above all others." Chikara removed a thick black-

and-white shawl draped around her shoulder and presented it to Sali.
"The *Ao* is yours, viperstrike."

Sali stared at the large command strap in Chaqra colors. She might
as well drape their clan's banner over her body. There was no chance
in the abyss she would ever consider wearing this filth. Sali looked
over and noticed the rest of the crew waiting expectantly. She blinked.
She was the captain for this battle. These souls were now her responsibility. What other choice did she have? Her ego was not worth the
price of these Katuia lives.

Sali accepted the shawl and donned it, feeling its soft, cool fabric
against her warm skin. She now wore the chains of the enemy, willingly.

Joum looked at her, approving. "Now you are dressed for the part,
viperstrike."

"Let's just get this over with." Sali raised her voice. "Ao, break away
and take point at the lead of the right flank."

Sali watched the helm operate, with its many levers and buttons
spread across several consoles. Mainly, though, she noticed the large
turning wheel. Chaqra's pods were from a similar era of gear as Kahun,
Nezra's new home city. A team of tinkers were still excavating for more
city pods buried down inside Mount Shetty.

Sali signaled. "Battle speed. Prepare for—"

Chikara stepped in front of Sali. "The fleet has just received new
orders. An enemy approaches from the flank. The khan orders that
they be destroyed so they cannot interrupt his divine task at Skyfall
Mountain." She turned to Sali. "On your orders, of course, viperstrike."

"Who is this new enemy?" she asked.

The captain shrugged. "It doesn't matter. We face it either way."

"What do we know about this enemy fleet?" asked Sali. "Is it a
Zhuun army, an approaching navy?" Then she saw the first of the
enemy along the horizon on the other side of the vast, flat plains. They
were neither Zhuun armies nor navies, but Katuia city pods. Not only
that, Sali recognized the familiar teardrop shapes of the Kahun city,
with the striking design of the *Nezra Rides* leading the way. Her clan
was here, but how, and why?

Captain Chikara stepped up to the platform next to Sali. "Will you do the honor, Salminde, and order the attack?"

These weren't new orders. This was a setup. No, a test. Sali's gaze shifted from the captain to Joum, the will of the khan behind her. His hand rested on the hilt of his saber. He leaned forward, ready to pounce. A test that she would pass or die.

Chikara spoke in a soft voice. "The Eternal Khan of Katuia informs you that greatness always requires sacrifice. Are the orders understood?"

Sali's fingers trembled as they drifted toward the handle of her tongue. Everything she had considered over the past few weeks had coalesced and reduced to these two choices: betray and attack her own clan, or die here and be forgotten.

Sali closed her eyes. Sometimes honor was enough. Sometimes, it wasn't. She sucked in a long breath and raised her voice. "Signal the pods in the grouping. We turn to meet the new threat head-on!"

CHAPTER SIXTY-ONE

THE PURSUIT

Q isami couldn't look away as the pods of two cities collided. She'd had her first taste of city-on-city violence a few weeks ago, and she wasn't a fan. This time not only was she participating in it, but she was leading the attack. Qisami wasn't even sure who they were fighting. The rest of the crew had tensed when they learned who their target was, but they were speaking quietly amongst themselves and no one bothered to update her on her assignment, not like she had been paying much attention.

"Artillerychief, range on the lead pod?" said Malinde.

"Five hundred yards for the main siege batteries," Daewon replied.

"Time to range."

"Three minutes," someone else called out.

"Increase to flight speed. Fire at will. I want first hits."

"Yes, Warchief." Daewon leaned down and spoke into a pipe cover. "Flight speed!" He stood and raised a red-and-green banner, waving it in a set pattern.

It was soon acknowledged by the adjacent pod. The already quick collective of Kahun pods picked up speed. They were smaller than the

Chaqra pods, but far nimbler. This time, the *Nezra Rides* was leading the attack, and as the largest and most symbolic pod in the fleet, they were the obvious target. But that was necessary to allow Kahun's smaller pods to close in on the larger pods. Then they could practically run circles around them.

Skyfall Mountain reached high up to the evening sky. She studied its jagged edges, its sharp peaks and rock faces, and that giant, goofy painting etched into its cliffsides. It would be majestic if Qisami had been the sightseeing type. Which she totally was. She loved to go to new places and see expensive, rare things, and then, usually, break them. Her father had fancied himself quite a golden egg collector. He had six rares and one unique ruby-encrusted egg in his collection. As a girl, Qisami had broken one of the rares one afternoon while taking it out of its nest and playing catch with it. It had slipped out of her hand and cracked on hard stone tiles. She had always assumed the eggs were boiled before donning the artwork. She had assumed wrong. Her ba had been furious. He had beaten her silly for one hour a day for seven straight days. Six months later, he sold her to the Consortium.

Did her breaking his stupid egg have anything to do with him giving her to the life of a nightblossom? She was going to have to ask him when she next got the chance. Qisami snorted. She had always had the chance. She just never took it, even when they were in Manjing at the same time. She should have gone back then, but she was too busy being young and drunk to care. Now that she was older, she wanted to gut that man before it was too late. For closure, of course.

"Incoming fire!" one of the crew cried.

The rose-colored evening took on a darker cast as streaks of small black hail peppered the sky. Arrows and stones began to spray the deck. Qisami jumped behind cover, in this case in the shadow of a lawn chair she had dragged up from below deck. It wouldn't do much against the bigger rocks, but the tough pachyderm hide should protect her against the smaller stuff.

Rapid pitter-patter began to hit the deck as arrows plunked into the main deck. Louder *thunks* and cracks dispersed as rocks and other objects clattered against the pod. A boulder the size of a horse smashed into a nearby building, collapsing it. Another the size of a fist crushed one of the crew running rigging, killing him instantly.

Qisami could just hear Malinde's yells. "I said I wanted first hits!"

"Bigger pods. Bigger artillery. Better range," Daewon replied.

"Then get me more speed!"

"Yes, Warchief." Daewon played second to his wife well. Qisami liked that about the young man. The tinker bellowed into one of those metal flower stalks sticking up from the ground: "Ramming speed!"

Qisami couldn't tell the difference between the different speeds. Ramming speed was still pretty slow. She continued sitting behind cover, her arms crossed and legs splayed out as her mind wandered from thought to thought, all while more arrows drizzled the nearby decks. She glanced up. Getting killed by projectiles was one of the worst ways to die. Sure, death was usually instant and painless, but no one who spends an entire lifetime training for battle wanted to die from some doe-eyed farm boy playing bowman five hundred paces away.

The Kahun mangonels finally retaliated, launching several heavy boulders arcing through the air. The rocks weren't as big, and they were set afire, and they didn't fly as far, but Kahun pods didn't need any of that. These minnows slipped up close and personal and were now broadsiding the larger whale-shaped pods with their own artillery at point-blank range.

The mangonel next to her launched several rocks, each as large as boars or giant bitter melons. She watched as the pile dispersed in flight and punched a dozen small holes into the hull of one of the Chaqra pods, exposing its gear layer. A follow-up ballista bolt shot perfectly into the hole. An explosion followed seconds later, sending fire and smoke shooting from the pod's gaping wound. The large track gears of the Chaqra pod slowly ground to a halt.

"Shadowkill!"

Qisami glanced at Malinde, then at where she was pointing. Two varieties of the enemy were dropping down from above. Most were uniformed soldier-types wielding tall oval shields and short spears.

They looked like the garden-variety fodder and appeared to move in squads of five to eight. Those who made it onto the deck were immediately met by less-well-geared and far less imposing Nezra crew, which looked positively ragtag next to those put-together enemies.

Those guys weren't the ones that caught Qisami's attention, however. Sprinkled among the several dozen enemy that had descended upon the *Nezra Rides* were two others, dressed even more sharply in shiny black armor, extravagant headdresses, and flaring black cloaks to match.

"Wills of the Khan," a Nezra crew groaned. "That must mean the khan is here."

Qisami wasn't sure what that meant, but she didn't care. All she needed to know was that those two someones were special and worth killing. She studied them as they quickly and efficiently cut down two of the Nezra warriors. They were not terrible, which was the best she could muster about their performance. Qisami perched like a cat in the shadows, waiting for the right moment. At the very least, removing these threats would save some Nezra lives. She had grown fond of these Katuia weirdos, especially the kids. They were so damn earnest. She watched with increasing alarm as one of the *Not Loud Not Fat* brats crept up on one of the cloaked wills of the khan. The boy was going to get himself butchered in the worst way. That little hatchet in his hand probably couldn't even crack their armor.

Qisami moved without thinking, A black blade materialized in her hand. She had lost her favorite set long ago. The Katuia had given her another to use. They were all right, rather substandard for an artist like herself. Her old black blades had been black, so she had this new Katuia set painted while she was doing her nails. She thought they turned out quite well, save for the fact that they were still shoddy blades. At least they were somewhat balanced. She stepped into the shadow of the raised helm and out behind the bush on the other side of the pod just a few feet behind one of the wills.

Qisami pounced, streaking out with her blade extended. The will must have noticed her from the corner of his eye. He drew his curved saber and tried to pivot toward her. The drag caused by puffy cloaks made turning more difficult. Qisami passed her mark just as he was about to face her. Her daggers flashed, raking him twice along the back, across the thick cloak. That was another thing about puffy cloaks; they make for surprisingly sturdy armor.

The will of the khan hacked at her with classic swings. Qisami could have dodged these in her sleep. Then she almost missed and paid for her mistake as the will of the khan morphed one of his sword slices into a swinging elbow. She narrowly dodged getting cracked in the jaw. He followed up with a sequence of elbows and knees, tight thrusts packed with power. Qisami's feet had been set and she danced around them with only mild effort. She hit back with two quick slices, both raking him across the chest but scraping off the dark, banded armor. This guy was a lobster. Her thrust at his chest was deflected, and then she retreated. Just when she lurched out of the way of his latest upward elbow strike, the will threw out a punch that nicked her in the chin.

His extended arm gave her the opening she needed as she stabbed her blade upward right between pauldrons and vambraces and into the tendon and bony flesh of his elbow. The man stiffened, his mouth contorting in pain. Qisami yanked the dagger out and stabbed once more into his exposed armpit. Then she swung with her other hand, ramming the blade into the soft flesh of his throat. With a snarl, she yanked out both blades, spraying blood across the deck in a wide radius as she glowered and reveled in her primal fury.

That was when she noticed she had an audience; Chaqra and Nezra alike gawked as she stood over the body of the will of the khan. Qisami smacked that howler monkey boy on the nose. "Who said you can come above deck? Get back down where you belong. Do you hear me?"

"Hey, I'm on your side, black cat," the boy whined as he tried to escape her slaps. That's what the Katuia children called her.

"Get below deck before I flay your skin off for undergarments!"

Qisami sensed attention from the side. She stared at the other will of the khan. This one was a young woman. Now that she thought about it, the man was young too. The woman raised a spear and settled behind her shield. An enemy pod nearby passed behind her. Two clusters of projectiles were launched. Qisami tracked their trajectory before jumping for cover. The will of the khan noticed what she did and followed suit. The ground they'd stood on moments earlier was suddenly littered with rocks and oil pitches. The subsequent volley contained fire bits, one that lit the deck aflame. Half a dozen Nezra, including that howler monkey boy—he was supposed to go below deck!—scrambled to put it out.

One of the crew trying to put out the fire scrambled a little too close to the will of the khan. The young woman shot him a look of disdain and stabbed her spear out, striking him in the gut.

Qisami snarled. "No one gets to beat up my friends but me!"

She drew a knife and chucked it at the will of the khan. It stuck into the shield all the way up to the hilt. Qisami snarled and threw another. That one went wide. The will of the khan knocked it out of the air, and the next one bounced off the shield.

The woman retaliated, tossing her spear at Qisami, and another, and then one more in rapid succession. Qisami kicked the first, dodged the second, and snatched the third mid-flight. Her lips curled. She was about to hurl it back when a large shadow loomed over their pod. Qisami looked up and gawked. A large black pod with bone-shaped protrusions was moving close. The city pod was easily three times the size of the *Nezra Rides*. Malinde was barking off to the side, hopefully trying to prevent them from getting run over by this monstrosity. The *Nezra Rides*'s tracks were grinding toward a sharp turn, but just as it looked as if they could slip out of the way of the Chaqra pod's path, another of their pods appeared from the side, cutting off the *Nezra Rides*'s escape and boxing them in. Trapped between two larger enemy pods with no room to utilize their speed was a deadly situation.

Daewon was trying to line up their artillery but there was no pretense about which side would win going up against these two larger and heavier city pods. The first pod, with the bone spikes, was closing in from behind while the new pod, shaped a bit like a squat turtle, was squeezing them from the other side.

"Are both pods going to try to board us?" Qisami asked.

Daewon nodded. "If we're lucky. They'll probably just try to crush us."

"Which one is worse?"

"Oh, crushing, for sure. It's not even close. Imagine falling into a burning pit of sharp nails."

The two enemy pods were getting closer. Qisami scanned for a way out of the inevitable. The only escape was over the side. It was a three-story drop but she had dealt with worse before.

The new pod in front was cutting in close. Malinde was trying to steer the *Nezra Rides* away, having their pod turning sharply starboard, the Chaqra pod was too wide to avoid. The head-on collision seemed unavoidable. At best the larger pod would only clip the *Nezra Rides*, hopefully causing just minor damage.

To their surprise, it was the Chaqra pod that turned away, giving the berth they needed to avoid each other. Then, just as it passed the *Nezra Rides*, it headed straight for the other Chaqra pod. The bone pod was ringing all its bells and flashing all its lights at the other pod, but the turtle pod was silent as it continued on its path. The bone pod was still trying to blare a warning at their ally when the two pods crashed with a mighty crack. Their frames crumbled, seemingly imploding into each other before exploding in a squealing cry of fire and debris.

Just before the explosion, however, a figure could be seen running along the side of the turtle pod. They dove off the side near the port-side of the *Nezra Rides*, and then were lost in the thundering explosion and billowing smoke. The shockwave from the initial explosion would have knocked Qisami off her feet, if she had not had catlike balance. That, and she held on to the railing.

Qisami scanned the chaos, when she caught sight of the silhouette approaching. The remaining will of the khan hadn't moved. She too was staring at the new figure approaching. When they were nearly upon the two battling war artists, the will of the khan called out: "Ho, Sa—"

A spearhead punched through her chest and out the back. Attached to it was a taut rope. A sharp pull retracted it, and then the will of the khan fell to the ground.

Salminde the Viperstrike strolled up to Qisami and Daewon—Malinde was staring from the helm. Salminde looked around and nodded. "Finally, you're here. We have a khan to kill, and the Prophesied Hero of the Tiandi too."

"Both?" Qisami blurted. The other two were too stunned to speak.

"What are you doing here?" Malinde finally spoke. "How did you get here?"

Sali dismissed her sister's concern. "Save the reunion for later. But yes, both need killing. We have work to do."

CHAPTER SIXTY-TWO

LAST CONTRIBUTION

Taishi watched from the eighth-level observation deck as the big black Katuia city pods got pulverized trading artillery fire with Skyfall Temple's formidable defenses. The enemy had appeared a little over an hour ago, and without parley or bothering to establish a camp or perimeter, the Katuia Black City of Chaqra launched itself at Skyfall Temple in what appeared to be a suicidal frontal attack. She had never seen the Katuia so blatantly disregard their cities, especially Chaqra, their capital. The Katuia were supposed to revere their city pods, yet the wreckage of dozens of these warpods in Hengyen settlement and at the temple walls told another story.

Only one thing came to mind that was valuable enough to warrant the destruction of an entire capital city.

How did the Katuia know Jian was here? They had no such thing as a spy network. Then came the scattered reports from Xusan refugees trickling in about a giant man in gleaming silver armor laying waste to entire squads of soldiers. He had even slain several reputable war artists, including the respected Master Kuolong of the Tea Bears.

Could it really be the Eternal Khan of Katuia, and could he be here at Skyfall?

More pressing, what should Taishi do with Jian? Should she attempt to spirit him away? Was she willing to risk allowing the prophecy to conclude? Did Jian have a chance? Taishi shuddered. That was her answer. But then, would there ever be a good time for Jian to face the Eternal Khan of Katuia? Perhaps if he had killed her in the final test and taken her power as the master windwhisper, but he did not, and now it was too late. Or as the Oracle of the Tiandi had moaned, "Everyone is going to die."

Her concern grew as the large city pods, rolling laterally before them, pounded the temple walls with thunderous explosives. Some of the artillery went over the wall, raining boulders, scree, and flaming pitch onto the temple grounds, with some reaching as high as the fourth level of Skyfall Mountain.

The Katuia outgunned them in artillery, and while the temple walls were thick and strong, it was only a matter of time. That occurred a few hours into the attack when a tower on the eastern end of the wall exploded from a perfectly aimed blackrock barrel, sending a thick crack down the length of the wall. The Katuia focused on that weakened point, and a few minutes later, the east end collapsed. The newly formed opening wasn't large, and was quickly plugged by the defenders, but it was the first of many breaches.

Jian and his friends appeared from his quarters a moment later. He was wearing armor suitable for the occasion: effective and well constructed, but also handsome and slightly immodest without being gaudy. He *was* the Champion of the Five Under Heaven, after all. He should at least look the part. He looked like he'd come out of a legend. A smile curled her lips. Perhaps they were writing it now. Pride swelled in her as he walked by. She waved. "Come here, son."

Then he ruined her proud moment by opening his mouth and whining, "Taishi, I'm not running away again. You can't make me this time."

"Stupid boy." She pursed her lips and brushed his shoulder with her hand. There was a finality to this moment. Taishi didn't know why, but it frightened her. "Listen carefully. Stay with your group, especially Sohn. Don't chase anyone. Always look to retreat and cover. Do not allow yourself to get trapped. The victory today is irrelevant if you do not survive, understood?"

Jian looked surprised. "You mean, you're going to let me fight? You're not going to stop me?"

It was her turn to look surprised. "Do you want me to?"

He gulped. His brave facade cracked. She could see the terrified boy hiding there. At least his back was turned to his friends. Taishi leaned in. "I can arrange it, if you wish."

Jian hesitated. She could see his resolve waver. Then he shook his head. "I won't abandon these people who depend on me. I have to be ready this time."

Taishi knew she couldn't fight this. She embraced him. "Don't worry about the consequences. Just do your best."

He wrapped her in his now-strong arms. "What if my best isn't good enough?"

"Then you will know that there was nothing more you could have done. You had no further responsibility in this prophecy."

He nodded. "I'll make you proud, Taishi."

"You already did."

Sohn appeared from behind them wielding the biggest shield she had ever seen. The obscene thing was larger than him. "Don't worry, Taishi, I'll be at his front."

"And I'll guard his back," said Fausan.

"And I, his mind," added Bhasani.

"Come on, Jian," Sonaya called at the top of the stairs, waiting alongside Hachi and Kaiyu. Zofi was there too, but the girl was wise enough to say her goodbyes.

Taishi detested feeling so powerless while everyone else joined the fight. She was left up here, with the old, the young, and the invalids. The dead weight. At least she was still alive to witness this momentous occasion if the Prophesied Hero of the Tiandi met the Eternal Khan of Katuia. Or better yet, if they didn't meet and everyone rose to see the next dawn. Taishi would prefer that. She intended to die before either Zofi or Jian.

Speaking of the two, Zofi ran up to her, tugging her sleeve. "Taishi, while I'm sure this is all very exciting, we should seek shelter deeper in the mountain with the others."

"I want to see what happens, how things unfold. I *deserve* to bear witness to the consequences of my actions."

"Don't be so dramatic, you old witch." Zofi put an arm around her elbow. "That's all anyone can ask of you."

Taishi's gaze trailed after Jian as he continued to snake down the stairs leading toward the ground floor. "I could have done a better job preparing him."

"You took Jian as far as he needed to go. The rest is up to him."

"Fool boy should have just finished the test, killed me, and taken my jing. Then he would have stood a fighting chance. If they meet now, he's pulverized meat."

"Oh, get over yourself, you old bag. You've been muttering this same tired fart for Tiandi knows how many years now. Ever since you two asses faked your death." Zofi squeezed her arm tighter. "By the way, I still haven't forgiven you two for not clueing me in on your ruse. I'm hurt you didn't trust me."

"Of course we trust you, stupid girl," said Taishi. "It's just that you're such a good crier. The chest-heaving, snot-nosed sobs at my funeral were masterful. We didn't want the public to miss that."

Zofi glowered. "I could have pretended!"

"You're also a terrible actor. What makes you think you're going to pull off a convincing sob? You can't even lie well."

The young woman, wise beyond her years, reconsidered. "Fine, but you should have told me after and not waited until the next morning."

"If I recall, you had cried yourself to sleep and snored through the entire night." Taishi patted her back. "You needed the rest, dear."

The two walked down a flight of stairs to the seventh level, where a long and wide roped staircase ran up to a lookout lantern floating several hundred feet higher in the sky. A dozen ropes lashed onto the lantern-shaped balloon kept it from escaping into the heavens. The lantern's basket was a large bamboo platform with railings and a glass floor in the center. An encapsulated blackrock furnace provided the fire to fill the balloon. There were even two racks of incendiary liquid fires if the lantern needed to be called into duty.

The lantern had launched at the first sighting of the Katuia horde and had fed Skyfall with important logistical information. From this vantage, a lookout could see for miles. Right now, however, Taishi only cared about what was happening below. She watched as the Katuia pods formed a bombardment line against the wall, while their smaller wargear vehicles ravaged the settlement. The enemy pods, shaped like giant crawling black beetles, were terrifying.

Taishi had become even more alarmed when only a few of their pods managed to cut off the entire Caobiu army, preventing them from coming to the temple's aid. When the city pods reached the outskirts of Hengyen, the sky began to rain artillery. That was when Taishi knew that the fight was lost, even if the defenders hadn't realized it yet. Overwhelming odds rarely fail. But then the clergy were always an optimistic, delusional bunch.

Still, it was a shock when the city pods appeared and blasted the wall with overwhelming strength. These metal Katuia monstrosities seemed like the old behemoth monsters of lore, found only inside Daleh, the Pit to the First Hell. They belched black smoke and left crushed devastation in their wake. Their siege weapons battered Skyfall Mountain's staunch walls until the stones crumbled or in some places completely melted into liquid. It would be impressive if it hadn't been so terrifying. Even with such a powerful display, Taishi had expected the walls to hold for several days, if not weeks. So of course she was not terribly surprised, but disappointed, when one of those large black pods rammed through the closed front gates, destroying both the massive wooden doors and the entire city pod itself.

Now the main fighting was down in the vast courtyard below, where the defenders were being pushed back by an ocean wave of Katuia spilling in from the shattered entrance, and it wasn't even dinnertime yet. Skyfall Temple was going to fall in a day. The observation balloon drifted to the right, giving them a clearer view of the battle. They looked like warring colonies of ants from so high. In many parts, she could only make out what was happening by the colors of their banners. They were two waves of competing colors ebbing and flowing across the open field.

The guard ranks had crumbled shortly after the city pod crashed through the gates. They were quickly shored up by the battlemonks and nuns as well as several Hansoo wading taller than the rest of the crowds. The survivors of the Black Orchid sect, recently extinct, had been given the honored position at the head of the fight.

Taishi continued scanning the battlefield, searching for one group, or one person, rather. She finally found Jian after methodically scanning the ranks of temple defenders. More specifically, she found Fausan and his garish battle robes. They were impressively hideous, yet he insisted on wearing them at every major point of his life, including his wedding to Bhasani, twice! Those bright yellow and green glittery swirls splattered over an orange background on his body made him look like a giant parrot.

In spotting him, Taishi also located Bhasani and Sohn, and Hachi, Kaiyu, Xinde, and finally Jian. The high seats had placed her people in an important central section of the fighting, but with rows of buildings and narrow streets to prevent them from being easily overwhelmed.

Taishi squinted through the monoscope. Jian was too tense. She could tell by how he held his fight stance. It wasn't a problem now, fighting these regular Katuia warriors, but he would be exhausted by the time he met stiffer enemies. Unlike formal duels, challenges in the field were often a matter of attrition and stamina. How spent would the two war artists be when they encountered each other?

Bhasani, tell Jian to loosen his shoulders.

Are you bloody serious right now, Taishi?

Just do it. There's a Bixi and a good fifty Katuia rolling up on the street off to your right.

Thanks for the heads-up.

He's too tense! Tell him to relax!

Bhasani did not look Jian's way, but he relaxed. He paused and took a deep breath and lowered his shoulders, and then looked toward the lantern. He couldn't see her, but Taishi raised her arm and waved.

The Katuia wargear shrieked into view, its steam engine puffing dirty smoke trails in its wake. Its body was shaped like a tortoise shell with an archery nest sitting on top. The Bixi turned down the street and raced toward a crowd of guards, crashing through their shield and saber lines and shattering their ranks.

Tell Xinde to watch over Kaiyu. The boy's getting pushed too far away from the others and seems to be in trouble.

Bhasani didn't answer, but she did wade into the battle to yank Kaiyu away from whatever mess he had gotten himself into. *Anything else?*

Taishi thought about it. *I'm sorry I didn't believe in you back then when we were young. I should have known that something was wrong. I should have trusted you, given you the benefit of the doubt.*

There was a lengthy silence.

Yes, you should have. I appreciate the words, regardless.

Two more tracked Katuia wargear moving your way.

And that was that.

Taishi spent the next hour watching, relaying information to Bhasani, who did the same to Sonaya. The two drowned fists were so preoccupied that neither threw a punch the entire time. The defenders were doing surprisingly well once the Hansoo rolled into the mix. The Katuia only advanced half a block. There were even hopeful murmurs about possibly turning the tide.

Taishi had been so focused on keeping Jian out of danger that she nearly missed hearing Zofi scream. She looked away from her looking glass. "What is it?"

Then she saw it as another ballista bolt shot past their basket, narrowly missing the balloon of the lookout lantern. Taishi hobbled next to Zofi at the corner of the nest. It took another missed shot, this one closer, for her to track its trajectory back to one of the enemy city pods just outside the walls.

"Why would they shoot at us?" she groused. "We're only spying on them. They didn't have to get so angry about it."

"What happens if one of these big arrows hits the lantern?" asked Zofi.

"I'm guessing we die."

"Why are we still standing around under the lantern?" the girl pressed.

That was a good point. Taishi turned and moved across the net to the wooden roped bridge still swaying in the howling wind. The other two monks, lookouts for the high seats, were already halfway down the roped steps. That was when another ballista bolt punched straight through the link, shattering the wood and severing the lantern's connection to the temple, and sending the two monks tumbling all the way down the mountain.

Zofi yanked Taishi back as the wooden staircase collapsed. The wind scooped up the lookout lantern and tried to carry it away. The ropes went taut as they strained. One snapped, then another, and then another until the lantern lookout was free from its restraints and began drifting higher.

Taishi's eyes widened and her stomach sank. If the lantern escaped into the heavens, who knew where they could end up. They could be hundreds of miles away by the time they landed. The thought alarmed Taishi, and she nearly panicked. The idea of being forcibly swept away to safety and leaving Jian to suffer his fate was terrifying.

Thankfully, in a way, the Katuia quelled her fears. Before their lantern could escape, a ballista bolt shot at a steep angle, nearly punching through the nest as it punctured the lantern's hot-air balloon, sending it deflating and shriveling into a bunched mess.

The heavy hemp ropes holding on to the basket went slack, and then gravity abandoned the lookout lantern as the heavy canvas balloon fell over the nest and they began to fall. Zofi held on to Taishi as if she were a parachute and screamed into her ear. Taishi was fortunate she was already half deaf.

"We're going to die!" Zofi screamed. Somehow, even her screams sounded off-key.

"That would appear likely," Taishi replied, more perplexed than anything else. Falling out of the sky to her death had long been one of her favored ways to die, so in a way, she owed the Katuia thanks for shooting their lantern down.

She looked over at Zofi, and all thoughts of a graceful death abandoned her. The girl still had a full life ahead of her and Taishi intended to deliver her those future days. "Come here, girl."

Zofi fell into her, clutching her waist, gripping her tightly. "I'm sorry for all the times I was mean to you, Taishi."

"Good, you should be," Taishi muttered, studying the visible currents of the howling wind. The currents were too strong to rein in, especially in her pitiful state.

"Hey, I'm baring my soul trying to end things nicely here!" Zofi yelled. "The least you could do is pay attention!"

"In a second, after we're dead." Taishi looked over the edge of the nest. The courtyard was rapidly approaching. From this angle, it looked like they were going to plummet into enemy ranks. Maybe they could get lucky and squash some Katuia.

Whatever jing Taishi had was a trickle. She likely couldn't save both of them, but she might have enough to save Zofi. All she had to do was time this disaster perfectly. She counted her heartbeats as the ground loomed larger. This was *almost* like flying again. Perhaps she could fulfill her final wish after all. The lantern fell below the eighth level, then the fifth, where the main staircase forked to either side, then the third level, which was the height of the outer walls.

Taishi seized a fistful of Zofi's robes at her neck. The former mapmaker's daughter, *her* daughter, startled and grabbed Taishi's forearms with both hands. "What are you doing?"

Taishi, with all her strength and the jing she had left, threw the girl directly upward just as the nest crashed to the ground. Taishi's final gasp of jing, powered by desperation, was stronger than she expected as Zofi screamed, falling toward the sky. To her chagrin, the girl held on to Taishi's sleeves, yanking her off her feet. Her jing became instantly spent, disconnecting her feel and control of the current.

And then the lantern crashed into the ground. Both Zofi and Taishi landed roughly. The impact rattled Taishi's body, shaking her every bone. Some of these frail old things probably might have broken for all she could tell. She was in too much pain to notice. Her vision went dark. Then something was shaking her.

She wanted to sleep but forced herself to pry an eye open. The world was sideways as she stared among the wreckage of the nest. Shattered wooden beams and loose ropes lay everywhere. Something shook her again. Her vision came into focus.

Taishi could just make out Zofi, face bloodied, hovering over her. The girl shouted something, but all Taishi heard was silence. Then the pain came rushing back. Taishi opened her mouth and screamed, falling into a fit of coughs, spitting up globs of congealed blood. She spasmed, curling her spine in an unnatural way. Perhaps her back had broken, or maybe her heart had given out. She wasn't sure.

Zofi was shouting gibberish. Slowly, the roaring echoes of whistling wind quieted until she could make out the words. "Taishi, I need you to get up. We're surrounded. Please. We need to go now. Taishi, can you hear me?"

Taishi finally found the moment between coughs to realize that they were surrounded by frenzied Katuia warriors. A circle of spears jabbed at them from just outside the perimeter of the wreckage.

"Play dead," Taishi hissed as Zofi slowly rose to her feet, holding up her hands. "What are you doing standing up?"

"It's too late! They already saw me alive."

Well, if this silly girl was going to die standing on her feet, then by the Tiandi, Ling Taishi, the greatest war artist of her generation and grandmaster of the Windwhispering School of the Zhang lineage Ling family style, was going to die on her feet as well.

"Hey, Taishi," said Zofi as they stood side by side. She pawed at Taishi's arm until their fingers laced. "Thanks for letting me come with you from Sanba. You didn't have to."

"Your sand sleigh was the only transportation we had." Taishi squeezed Zofi's hand. "I'm proud of you, girl. You came a long way, but you would have done it on your own. You were too bright for the lot that life had given you."

"You showed me the bigger world, Taishi."

The sound of fighting crescendoed and then the right flank of Katuia spears collapsed. Each advancing Chaqra warrior fell one by one in a neat row. Fausan's voice rang out over the cacophony of battle. "Back, you black toads!"

The whipfinger master's arms were a complete circular blur as he sent bullet after bullet at his marks, decimating entire enemy lines in rapid succession. Several Katuia tried to close the distance on the whipfinger master. One warrior dual-wielding short spears lunged at Fausan's blind side, but Bhasani was there to defend her husband. Each thrust was countered by each of the closed fans in her hands, and then she flicked them open, cutting the Katuia warrior's throat with one and disemboweling him with the other. The next one that attacked she stopped dead in his tracks with just a look. He shied away and dropped his weapons, and fled screaming as he clawed his eyes.

Katuia reinforcements soon joined the attack, and were immediately met by fresh waves of temple guards and monks. The two sides collided in a resounding crash. The battlefield seemed to have taken on a life of its own, churning into an ocean of violence.

Taishi held on to Zofi, trying to shield the girl from the serious danger of getting trampled by these heavily armed warriors. A large metal body bumped into her, easily knocking her back down to her hands and knees within this chaotic ebb and flow. A large cluster of fighting was spilling their way when Sohn barreled into them, sending half a dozen bodies flying backward like bowled-over pins. He raised his gigantic shield in the air and hacked with its bladed edges left to right, cutting down any who stood too close.

There were still too many. No sooner had the eternal bright light master made space with his charge than a group of black-clad Katuia war artists appeared. These were a different category of warriors compared to the ones they had been fighting.

"Wills of the khan," Taishi shouted. "The big handsome bastard must be close."

One of the black-clad wills landed a few feet away. His armor was black-and-white banded, and his thick cloak whipped in the wind. He looked down at Taishi and raised his saber, hacking it down at her neck almost offhandedly as he walked past.

There was a flash off to the side and the edge of the will of the khan's saber clashed against the wooden shaft of a staff. Then, the end of the staff twirled on a chain link and smashed the will in the face.

Xinde shifted to shield her front. "Master, are you injured?"

"I'm fine, Xinde." Taishi really wasn't, still feeling dazed from her fall.

A group of Katuia warriors tried to fill the gap Xinde held, and he countered, swinging his three-sectional staff in large and small circles around his body and limbs. His Longxian abilities blurred his movements, making his arms and legs seemingly multiply, with each taking on a life of its own. A half dozen Katuia with spears and shields tried to pin him down, but the Longxian's quick and confusing movements disrupted their positioning, and then his three-sectional staff would swing over the tops of shields and strike the enemy's heads behind cover. Still the enemy numbers grew.

"We're too far behind enemy lines!" Bhasani yelled from off to the side. "Get Taishi out of here. We'll hold for as long as we can."

Kaiyu appeared a moment later, helping both Taishi and Zofi to their feet. "Come with me!" he yelled, leading the way through the moving maze of bodies. When there was no clear path, Summer Bow made one.

The three managed to pull back to the main battle lines that the Skyfall defenders were tenuously holding. Taishi looked back in horror toward where they had come as the overwhelming numbers of Katuia overtook her friends. First she lost sight of Bhasani and Fausan, and then Xinde was swallowed up. A dozen Katuia warriors tried to smother Sohn, but the stubborn bastard refused to fall. Like the others, the churn of the battle swallowed him up.

And then just like that, all of her friends had disappeared.

The blood drained from Taishi's face as she sought within the fighting any signs of her friends. They had all charged behind enemy lines and risked their lives to save her, and now they all might have paid the price. Taishi's heart fluttered. The sudden pain in her chest was sharp, as if it had been torn asunder. Why did they do this? She was a dying old woman! This was a terrible exchange. Taishi took an involuntary step forward.

"No, Taishi," Kaiyu shouted, rebuffing her. "Get back to the upper levels of the temple where it's safe. I'll go look for the other masters."

Taishi just stood there, dumbly, until Zofi came and wrapped her arms around her. "It's not safe here. We have to go, now!"

A pair of triage nuns met them as they reached the first flights of stairs up the mountain, trying to spirit them to safety, no doubt deeper into the mountain, where all the women, children, and elderly were hidden. Taishi was still reeling. She was a liability here. Her friends could be dead. She might be the one responsible. They should hurry to safety before anyone else got killed protecting her.

They joined a steady stream of traffic moving both directions, monks coming down to join the fight while the injured and residents fled upward. They had just reached the third-level stairwell when Taishi heard the strange voice. It was either in her head or ethereal in the wind. Or she had imagined it.

Ling Taishi, it is time.

Taishi stopped her slow shuffling and stared at the servant tunnel off to the side. What was that sound? Probably her concussion talking, but something about that hallway pulled at Taishi. She took a step toward it, and then another.

Every river ends, Taishi. You have carved a mighty legacy. Now see it to its end.

"Taishi," Zofi called. "Where are you going? We have to go!"

It is the only path we have left.

Taishi stared down the tunnel leading into darkness. She wasn't actually sure if she heard the voice or imagined it. She snorted and tried to turn away. It was about time she went crazy. Frankly, she was surprised it didn't happen years ago. Taishi only made a few steps back toward the main group when she felt the invisible leash, yanking her back deeper into the tunnel.

It was a strong compulsion, incredibly powerful. Taishi knew what it was; she knew she should look away and fight against it, but she was powerless to do so. Finally, the immense pull of the compulsion yanked her forward like a puppet, causing her to lurch and stagger deeper into the tunnel, one awkward, forced step at a time.

The future is now set.

CHAPTER SIXTY-THREE

REVENGE

Qisami had to hand it to Salminde. Business was *all* business today. The entire Nezra fleet had come to save her, at significant risk and expense. By some miracle, they found her after first venturing into the Grass Tundra, destroying a Katuia capital city, and then traveling deep into Zhuun lands. And what do they receive for their happy reunion after this long, incredible trek? More work.

There were no hugs or pats on the back. No congratulations or thanks for risking everything coming all this way to find her. Nope, there was none of that. The moment Salminde the Viperstrike stepped onto the *Nezra Rides*, she began barking orders.

Apparently she was back in charge, because everyone on board fell in without question, even Malinde and Shobansa and the other members of their council. It was impressive how smooth and neat the transition was.

The orders were simple. The bulk of Chaqra's forces were pulled in two separate directions. Destroy as many of their city pods as possible. As for the *Nezra Rides* . . .

"We will go to Skyfall and slay the khan," Salminde had proclaimed.

She was met with confused silence.

Wani raised an arm. "You mean the prophesied hero, right? We're supposed to kill him."

Marhi raised her hand as well. "We came all the way here to rescue you, and we have. Shouldn't we turn around and let our enemies kill each other? That makes a lot of sense to me."

Daewon nodded. "I like her plan. We should just—"

Salminde turned away. "We press on. I want to be inside Skyfall Temple by sundown."

And that was that.

The first thing they did was summon the *Not Loud Not Fat* to ramp with the *Nezra Rides*. It was too risky a plan to ride to Skyfall Temple in the *Nezra Rides*. The *Not Loud Not Fat* was smaller, sleeker, and quicker. The *Nezra Rides* was a plodding cow beside it and too valuable to risk.

Qisami soon found herself standing next to Sali and the two viper-strike initiates as the ramps between the two pods were pulled. Daewon had wanted to come as well, but he had greater responsibilities than to join their suicide mission. Qisami was excited. She had never attempted a coup before.

The *Not Loud Not Fat* was escorted by two other city pods as the battle between the Chaqra and Exiles fleets spread. One of the pods soon peeled away, swept up in a running battle between several city pods and smaller wargear. The second managed to get them nearly to the fringe of the settlement outside before a blast tore apart its starboard tracks, causing it to sputter out. Salminde left the injured pod without batting an eye as they pressed on.

They were soon inside Hengyen, or what was left of it. Within a short few hours, half of the settlement lay in ruins. Chaqra city pods were rolling up and down the streets. At the same time, groups of soldiers and monks had formed throughout the city, ambushing and often devolving into running battles with the pods.

The *Not Loud Not Fat* was low enough not to stand taller than most of the buildings, unlike the Chaqra pods that were all at least one story taller. It allowed them to sneak somewhat undetected through this haze, smoke, and chaos most of the way to the walls. The problem, however, was the Zhuun. They had retreated into their buildings, sniping from hiding places. The *Not Loud Not Fat* took half a dozen casualties before Sali ordered the deck cleared. That was ill advised, however, since Zhuun boarding parties dropped in next. They jumped from windows and rooftops onto the decks in the gear layer and wreaked havoc.

Qisami had volunteered to patrol the lower levels. The many shadows in those darkened passages made her especially deadly. She ended up dispatching a dozen of these half-baked groups on her own. Most were fodder, locals and lowly guards. No wonder they were put outside the walls. But these guerrilla groups were still trouble, no matter how inexperienced. It was challenging work to hunt them down before they could do too much damage. One group managed to kill one of the tinkers and nearly exploded the main furnace powering the portside tracks.

The *Not Loud Not Fat* continued without soaking in too much damage, however, until they made a wrong turn near the base of the temple walls and came face-to-face with one of the larger Chaqra pods.

"We need to get past that thing," said Salminde.

"The *Not Loud Not Fat* isn't large enough to run over buildings," said the captain, as if he had read her thoughts. "We can't outgun that monster pod, viperstrike."

Sali nodded and turned to Marhi and Wani. "Initiates, you're with me." She looked at the rest of the crew. "Keep the pod safe. It has served us well and deserves a long life for its resilience."

"Yes, viperstrike."

"Hey, what about me?" Qisami chirped, raising her hand.

Sali looked at her. "What about *you*?"

Qisami sputtered, "You can't be serious. After all I've done for you, you're not going to bring me?"

"Killing the khan is a clan matter. You are an outsider."

"I'm the outsider that got your clan the ore they needed to get here. That led a battle to victory over Liqusa."

Marhi made a face as if she smelled something sour. "I think I was in charge—"

Qisami pushed on. "I taught a couple hundred of your weed-chucking little kids how to fight. Don't you call me an outsider. Not after what I've been through for you."

Salminde did not appear moved. Wani stepped forward. "Mentor, Maza Qisami has been as loyal and helpful as any in the clan. She took the measure to train me while you were away. I am a stronger viperstrike because of her."

Qisami was so stunned by the girl's words her eyes nearly leaked. She blinked them away. *Think violent thoughts.* "Well, the girl needed the work. Someone had to step in. You've been too preoccupied to train her." Qisami wilted slightly against the viperstrike's stare. "I mean, on account of you being kidnapped and all."

"Mentor." Marhi stepped forward as well. "I will also vouch for the shadowkill, under the gaze of the six Xoangiagu: the beautiful Woman, the pure Child, the wise Scholar, the giant Bull, the sharp Owl, and the staunch Warrior, my good name for Maza Qisami's good name. She has proved herself to me many times over. Give her this honor and she will not let you down." This time, unlike last, Marhi's voice was confident and her words firm in her vouch for the shadowkill.

Sali shrugged. "Fine. Let's go then."

And she really meant right this instant.

Qisami didn't even have time to celebrate joining the team before she and the three viperstrikes were dumped on the ground as the *Not Loud Not Fat* pulled back and fled from the attacking Chaqra pods. The four landed behind part of a crushed building, sprinting along half a shell of the outside walls. The attackers had broken through the main gates but it appeared as if the defenders were still holding the wall. That made things easier for them to get inside, but then they would have to contend with two armies.

Qisami had always thought she'd die doing what she loved: a

botched job, failed assassination, or getting stabbed by her cell. She never thought she'd die fighting a coup for a bunch of Kati, in a pitched battle, no less. Her life had certainly taken a stranger turn of late, and she hadn't even thought about her time in prison.

Sali was in the lead, followed by Wani and Marhi, with Qisami bringing up the rear. Sali stopped at the husk of another building and fell to one knee along one of the standing walls. The others followed suit and watched. Farther down the field was Skyfall Temple's main entrance, with the front gates splintered into several large bits hanging from the side. There were Chaqra warriors there, all over everything like ants on syrup. By the sounds of it, there was heavy fighting on the other side, which meant Chaqra had broken through the front gates, but had not taken control over it yet. She glanced at the windows and the tops of the parapets. Neither side appeared to have taken the wall.

"The wise Scholar knows we'll never sneak past that crowd," Marhi whispered.

"I have an idea," said Wani. "What if we ambush a patrol and strip their armor? Then we can pretend to be Chaqra spears and just walk through."

Marhi clipped her little sect sister. "This isn't an old fable told by curio tale spinners around the hearth. That silly stuff never happens in real life."

Wani clipped her back. "Of course it does. Every one of those lessons starts with 'This is a tale as old and as true as the light,' so that means it must be true."

Sali appraised the situation at the gate. "The front's no good, and we're not jumping a Chaqra squad. Their armor is etched with the spear's name on the shoulders. Besides," she added, "I'll never find armor that fits me."

"Nor me," said Qisami. "That and on account of I'm Zhuun. They'll notice that I have beautiful eyes and a cute button nose." That earned her a withering glance from the other three. Katuia eyes were nearly black, while their noses tended to be flatter and wider, not to mention her tan complexion compared to the Katuia's usual bluish gray. And she was shorter. Basically, there was no way she was going to pass for one of them.

"We could pretend she's a prisoner," said Wani.

Marhi snorted. "That won't work either. You're just going down the list of stories now."

"Why not?"

"Because we don't take prisoners. Chances are, someone will just walk up to Qisami and stab her in the gut."

"I don't see you coming up with any big ideas," Wani shot back.

Sali closed her eyes and rubbed—or pinched—the bridge of her nose. "No, we're not going to pretend to take the shadowkill prisoner."

Qisami stared at a section of the wall farther toward the end. "What about the corner there?"

The viperstrikes were still bickering. Qisami nudged Marhi's waist with an elbow. The taller woman elbowed her back in the boob.

"Hey." Qisami pointed. "What about there? That section of the wall is partially collapsed. We can climb to that cave-in and then to the third level."

Marhi squinted as she followed the finger. "That section is ripe for archers from every angle."

Qisami shrugged. "Probably still stand a better chance than playing in that boiling hot pot of death over there."

"Die from a sniper, or a random arrow or ax. It's all the same," said Sali. "Lead on."

It took a bit longer than Qisami had anticipated to hike up that section of rubble. A Katuia pod had lost a collision with the wall, and large sections of its wreckage were strewn all over the field. The pod was lying about in large pieces. Some parts of it were smoking, but most were piles of twisted metal and shattered wood. The smoke stung her eyes and there was a constant low-key growl of battle off in the distance echoing all around the walls. Evening was creeping forward, draping their surroundings in long shadows and blotted terrain, offering Qisami the perfect playground.

She darted forward, shadowstepping from crevice to nook, shade to corner, leaving soft puffs of air in her wake. Her training pool mother had called her the best cockroach she had ever trained.

Qisami was halfway up the pile leading to the second-story cave-in when Marhi's prediction of a trap was sprung. The viperstrikes were still farther down the path when a temple guard took shots at them, sending a crossbolt streaking toward Wani. Sali snatched it out of the air. Qisami jumped to cover and scanned for the sniper. By the sound of the bolt, it was a few stories above, in the vicinity of the collapsed wall. She locked in on his location from his second shot.

"I got you now," she muttered, giddy. This type of cat-and-mouse killing was more stimulating than the mundane mass slaughter that occurred in pitched battles. Everything felt so impersonal, and everyone stank, which was rude. Qisami liked to smell fresh during fights.

She shadowstepped three times, each time moving up half a floor until she stepped out from the darkness behind the sniper, who was hidden at the edge of the collapsed wall with a long-range dragon crossbow. She drew one of her painted knives and stabbed him at the base of his neck. The poor bastard didn't even know what hit him as he slumped forward and over the side of the broken floor.

Qisami eyed the body's descent as it bounced off another ledge on its way down. She chuckled and realized that she wasn't alone. She looked to the side and noticed two other guards: one was taking a dump in a basin while the other sat on the ground next to him drinking soup. Both looked startled at her. Then a black knife sliced through the air. It struck the soup drinker in the mouth as he stood. She had aimed for his forehead. The other guard stood with his sword and buckler, pants still down, his bits dangling in the breeze.

"Oh, for Tiandi's sake," snapped Qisami. She put her hand on her waist. "Pull your pants up."

The guard looked down and nodded. He bent down and reached for his trousers. Qisami sank another knife between the eyes. The viperstrikes by now had ascended up the rubble mound. Qisami noticed another sniper nest farther up, and homed in on it. She shadowstepped twice more, slipping to a small ledge below the window. When a bow appeared, she reached up, found a wrist, and yanked. The poor sap pitched forward, screaming, down to the rocky crag of rubble below. Then, for good measure, Qisami dropped a knife on his face.

The third nest was high on the opposite end of the collapsed area. Qisami had to make a running leap out across a low chasm and hurl her black knife at the highest point of her arc. She missed the sniper anyway, ricocheting the blade off the broken wall. He noticed her approach and tried to swivel the dragon crossbow toward her. It was too late. Qisami sidestepped into a darkened area and came out behind the archer. One blade slipped around his neck and she sliced him open in a clean drag.

Her knees wobbled and she lowered to one knee, huffing slightly. That last jump was long and took a bit out of her. Sali appeared a few moments later, having scaled the rubble free from enemy fire. She walked up to Qisami and offered a hand. "That climb wasn't bad. There were barely any defenders."

"Says you," Qisami grumbled.

The four women hurried down the side corridor, moving away in the direction of battle. They were fortunate to quickly get behind the temple guards' lines and into the ground level of the temple. Qisami's eyes scanned the zigzags spiderwebbing all the way up. "That's a lot of stairs," she muttered.

"Where do we go now?" asked Marhi.

A loud crack filled the air. A large figure was suddenly tossed over the side railings from one of the levels several stories up. The body plummeted toward the earth and crashed, shattering several marble tiles. There was a small explosion of shrapnel as a dozen metal Hansoo arm rings exploded from the impact.

Qisami's eyes widened. Anyone who could toss one of these big war monks like that had to be immensely strong. The four women followed his trajectory back up to the broken railing on the fifth floor. Not another word had to be said as Qisami and the three viperstrikes ran up the path along the stairs and ladders off to the side.

Qisami had come up with a trick early on. Those at the temple were on the lookout for Katuia. They would assume any Zhuun face was a friendly one, so Qisami had the three viperstrikes pull up their hoods while she pulled hers back. The ploy worked. Most servants gave her one look and dismissed the group. The only one who gave them grief was the guard manning the stairwell to the third level. Qisami wondered why anyone would stand guard during the middle of a siege. She would either be fighting or high-hoofing it out of here, not standing guard.

That guard, however, ordered them to stop and had the three viperstrikes pull back their hoods. Her dagger hissed from its sheath the moment he reached for a weapon. It arced across the air and the poor egg lost his hand, cut off at the wrist. She then tossed him over the side of the railing to drop several stories to the ground level far below.

The rest of their journey was unimpeded. They stayed in the back channels, avoiding as many people as they could. The few they encountered were easily dispatched. The group had just passed the third floor and were climbing up a wall of vines to reach the next level when Qisami's forearm began to itch, as if the blood just beneath were boiling. She shuddered, and then her gaze moved to a far corner off to the side. She could just make out a lookout platform jutting over the side of the mountain. There was a small cluster of figures observing the battle.

There, standing in the center of the group, was her death mark, the one person in the entire world Qisami wanted to kill most. Top of the list! Her heart went double time. Her body became taut as her vision narrowed. Her sense of touch and smell heightened and the sickly sweet taste of blood filled her mouth.

"Maza Qisami, you're falling behind," said Wani, helping Marhi to her feet at the top of the wall.

Qisami couldn't look away. "There's something I have to do."

"What, like right now?" the viperstrike sputtered. "Could you have gone before we set out?"

"No, it's—listen, there's someone I need to kill really quick. You go on ahead. I'll be right back."

Sali, far ahead, hissed back, "What is the holdup? The khan and his Sacred Cohort are just ahead."

Qisami's arms burned. "I have to go. You can thank me later."

"But . . ." said Wani.

She launched herself off the vined wall and shadowstepped into the near corner, emerging on the opposite end, dangling between floors. She reached out and grabbed hold of the upper ledge and pulled herself over. She glanced back and noticed Marhi staring. There was disappointment in her eyes. She had vouched for Qisami to Salminde.

Qisami felt a little bad about it, but this was important! It was about Akiya and Akiana, the souls of those two little girls under her care back in Allanto. This was their chance for their souls to finally find peace. And it was Qisami who would deliver it. She broke into a sprint, darting through the darkness, avoiding the lit areas. The sconces and chandeliers in these open pavilions offered plenty of scattered shade to play with. As Qisami neared her mark, she studied the three individuals. The one on the left was a servant girl; the one on the right an elderly scholar. Neither would give her any trouble. It was the one in the middle who counted. Then she noticed the mute man standing off to the side. She would have to eliminate him first.

Qisami took three more large steps and launched herself at a full sprint at the nearby corner. There was a rush of whimsical bubbles, swirling euphorically around her as she stretched. She crossed to the other side, emerging from the covered ceiling above her death mark. Qisami's lips curled as she launched downward, her knees angled at the point and both arms reverse-gripping her big black dagger as she came down on the mute man. Not even their famous tough bodies could heal from a dagger in the skull. She yanked the dagger free, releasing a putrid goo like tar on the blade.

She was already moving, however, leaping forward and kicking the old man and then backhanding the servant girl out of the way. It was probably unnecessary, but she didn't want the distractions.

Finally, she landed in front of her mark and growled. "Hey, remember me?"

Duchess Sunri of Caobiu just stood there and frowned. She shook her head. "No, can't say I do."

CHAPTER SIXTY-FOUR

FREEDOM

S ali crept through the mostly deserted paths spiderwebbing along the cliff face of the Skyfall Temple. Most of the streets and walkways were deserted; only those fighting remaining outside. She crept along the shade of a servants' catwalk running below the spines of the roofs overhead and stopped to watch when a group of monks sped below them, sprinting down the stairs toward the sixth level, where a large group of Katuia had gathered. The two sides charged and clashed, another pitched battle exploding in the open square with a large statue of a cow at its center.

Why would these Zhuun worship cows? What strange people.

A wave of black and white slammed into a wave of yellow-clad monks. The battle lines momentarily washed one way, and then another. They stayed in place and came to a standstill for several tense moments until a group of Hansoo joined the fracas. The Katuia ranks shattered as the big beasts of men smashed through their spears.

Sali's blood boiled to join her people against their ancestral enemies. She wanted nothing more than to swoop down and fight alongside the many notable war artists within the horde ranks. But this was not why Sali was here. There was a larger monster to hunt here. Sali continued, using the maze of servant walkways near the ceilings to avoid the chaos below. There was no need to be quiet. There were so many waterfalls trickling around that she could barely hear herself think. She had never been good at skulking, anyway.

Several footsteps approached from behind, joined by soft, heated whispers and giggles. Marhi and Wani joined her a moment later. She had sent them to scout the divergent paths, and the two young viper-strikes were greatly enjoying this adventure.

Marhi reported first. "A bunch of their big meaty people built a blockade at the foot of the main stairs. They're holding the main way up. Bull's balls, we're cut off."

"What happened to the shadowkill?"

Wani gulped. "She said she had to go kill someone really quick and that she would be right back."

"And you just let her go?"

Wani looked bug-eyed. "How was I supposed to stop her?"

Sali turned to Marhi. "And you did nothing either?"

The older neophyte shrugged. "I thought she went off to take a piss."

"I always thought it was just Hampa who was dumb," Sali muttered, "but maybe they all are at that age."

The sound of the battle erupted to an ear-deafening ruckus. A mix of Hansoo, battlemonks, and Black Orchid nuns were fighting a much smaller number of Katuia, all Sacred Cohort by the looks of them. The tide in the melee changed as the black and white broke through the stalemate and surged forward. One of the Hansoo was slain while the other retreated with the rest of the monks. What had been the difference? Then she noticed the Katuia figure, long strands of hair flapping in the breeze beneath a silver helm. Chest armor shimmering pale like the full moon.

Sali's breath caught every time she saw the Moonlight Lord, as he was known in battle. There was a warm glory that bathed over her whenever she fought alongside the khan. She was aware he wielded a natural compulsion, but the knowledge was buried within a numbed mind. She didn't care. She just wanted to fight alongside him to glory and greatness. This was Sali's path to immortality. . . .

The Eternal Khan of Katuia was a large man, half a head taller than most Katuia warriors, but he was only one man. The Zhuun had a dozen of their large meaty monks, each as tall and wide as the khan. However, size didn't equate to strength. Visan destroyed the large Hansoo and monks alike, cutting through them with brutal efficiency. There was an aggressive gleefulness to Visan's movements as he smashed a Hansoo to the ground, throwing short, sharp punches and elbows in his Eight Limbed Art style.

It wasn't long before the Tiandi monks broke. Then it became a rout as the Katuia surged forward. Sali and her neophytes had to sprint along the upper level to keep up. The panic of people fleeing on the Tiandi side was infectious.

Sali noticed that most of those Zhuun were not war artists or militia, but civilians, part of the harmless herd that required protection from warriors. Yet Visan ordered his forces to relentlessly pursue them. Slaughtering sheep was not the raidlife way. It was not the Katuia way. It felt off, disturbing.

The khan caught hold of a dazed Hansoo who had fallen behind. He lifted him off the ground by the front of his robes and cracked his jaw with his elbow, twisting the war monk's neck at an unnatural angle. The khan tossed the body aside.

Sali had to look away. The constant fighting the past few weeks had been too much, even for someone as seasoned as she. Contrary to what outsiders of the Grass Sea believe, the Katuia were not a warring society. The terrible influence of the new khan had already dramatically shaped Katuia culture. Visan was a warmonger, and within a shockingly brief period of time, he had realigned the entire horde to his violent aggression. Within a few short weeks, Sali had witnessed more battle and death than she had seen in the last ten years combined.

It wasn't long before the remnants of this group ran out of places to flee. They came up against a dead-end curve of stairs leading to the next level. Hundreds of the Tiandi were trapped as the Katuia closed in. The handful of Hansoo still standing put themselves in between their devout and the Katuia.

"The Katuia should move on," she muttered. "There's no point in this slaughter."

Visan walked to the front of the Katuia line and sneered at the trapped Tiandi monks. "The Katuia do not take prisoners. Kill them all."

"What is that man doing?" she muttered. This wasn't right. This offended Sali to her core. Her honor as a warrior and as a Katuia required her to act. She broke into a sprint along the upper walkway until she was directly over the trapped Zhuun. Sali launched herself off the railing, somersaulting down to the ground between the Eternal Khan of Katuia and the defenseless monks.

She dropped to one knee, leaning forward aggressively, her head bowed. "The Katuia do not take prisoners. We let the innocent go. They are not part of the raidlife."

"Who cares about these weeds? They need to be pulled before they can spread." Visan looked at her curiously. "I would have thought your clan would be scurrying halfway back to the Grass Sea by now."

"My task isn't complete." She stood to face him, her eyes piercing and intense.

"You challenge me on the field?" he sneered. "And to defend these land-chained vermin?"

"I defend the honor of our people and our ways. The Katuia abandoned slaughter and enslavement centuries ago. You will try to drag us back to a darker time. Slaughtering these people is a disgraceful act, great khan."

"You speak to me of disgrace, Salminde the Viperstrike. You raised a rebellion against the horde, you killed many of the Katuia who followed you into battle, and you murdered a will of the khan!"

Sali screamed her contempt, letting loose thoughts she otherwise would not have dared utter aloud. "You committed slavery and genocide!"

"Our enemies deserve nothing less than extinction!" he roared.

"You are an excited boy playing with a new toy with a temperament undignified for a khan. You are making decrees your immature mind does not fully grasp. We cannot allow wholesale slaughter to pollute our people's identity. There is no returning from that. Let these people go, Visan. Complete your conquest with your honor intact."

"You dare speak of honor, traitor," he snarled. "Honor is written by the victor."

"I cannot allow you to steer the Katuia down this dark path."

Visan's face twisted in rage as he drew Ageless Sky, his legendary diamond-edged hooked spear with its wavy blade that was half as tall as she. He brought it down upon her, intent on cleaving her in two. There was no subtlety or finesse, just a killing blow. Sali was pleased by the surprised look on Visan's face when she sidestepped, as if he had expected her to just stand there and take it.

She lashed back, her tongue leaping from its holster. The whip form snapped, the sharpened tip of the spearhead gashing against the khan's silver armor, raking sparks across the front, until it found a gap just below the shoulder, splattering a small spray of blood on the grass. The khan looked more surprised than injured as he winced. Several of the wills of the khan grew enraged and surged forward.

The first to reach Sali tried to drag her to the ground. She twisted away, using his momentum against him as she threw him flying head over heels onto his back. She turned to face the second, connecting a looping ax kick that smashed the nose of the woman darting in. Sali was familiar with the Eight Limbed Art style, and these freshly minted new wills of the khan weren't good at it. Like Visan, they were young, most still in their teens since they were likely the khan's childhood friends, just as she had been Jiamin's. But to someone with Sali's experience, they were little more than wobbly-legged pups.

She manhandled the next two wills with ease, sweeping one's legs from under them. They were skilled for their age, their abilities no doubt bolstered by their connection to the khan, but in the end, they were still children to a master war artist like Sali. None of these whelps had had time to grow into their roles. Jiamin studied for years as khan before unleashing his might against the rest of the world.

Sali continued to flow against the stream of wills of the khan, fighting hand battles and kick exchanges, her arms whipping like a coiled snake striking while at the same time avoiding the quick sharp elbows and punches. These young warriors were powerful, if raw, and too predictable. Sali was breathing heavier, but it wasn't long until four of the khan's Sacred Cohort lay injured at her feet.

"Enough!" Visan raised Ageless Sky. "I will oversee this personally."

The khan's Sacred Cohort cleared away as the Eternal Khan of Katuia launched at Sali. She sent a jolt to stiffen the shaft of her tongue as she parried the heavy, swinging blade of his hooked spear. Visan was frighteningly quick and strong. His long two-handed hooked spear, which he wielded easily with one, released a thunderclap with each strike. Sali's arms rattled as she deflected blow after blow. The brutal impact from each still sapped her strength.

Sali had one decided advantage, however. The viperstrike's Serpent Fang was a natural counter to the dominating Eight Limbed Art style. And though Visan had strength and speed, Sali's experience and savvy, coupled with her style's advantages, made them evenly matched at first. She seized the opening when the khan, having hacked relentlessly at her as if trying to smack an annoying gnat, exposed an opening. Sali sent the bite of her tongue flying straight toward his exposed ribs. The spearhead thudded as if striking marble, but its tip was crimson when it fell. Visan staggered, clutching the wound.

Sali pulled her tongue back to her hands and relished the blow. They both knew she could hurt him now. It made him hesitate and second-guess his movements. He fought less arrogantly, less confidently.

Sali remained calm and resolute. "Are you sure you wish to continue, khan? You have a battle to finish. Why waste your time here with fodder who can't fight back?"

Visan, still hunched forward clutching his waist, straightened.

"That was a good hit, viperstrike. Let's see if you can do it again." The few remaining wills of the khan circled her, blocking her retreat.

Sali obliged, falling into her familiar Serpent Fang. To her surprise, Visan followed suit, abandoning the more upright Eight Limbed Art stance to a similarly relaxed guard. Then he attacked, somehow fighting with her sect style. Except his movements were older by several generations. Fork Snake Tastes the Air met Dead Baby's Rattle. What tactical advantage her Serpent Fang style afforded her was now nullified. Visan somehow matched her prowess wielding her own sect style. He was certainly rawer in his movements but his vast power still carried over.

"The Viperstrike sect has the honor of having had three former hosts serve as khan." Visan's eyes glistened. "It took a few exchanges to awaken those old memories."

He lashed out unexpectedly, the hooked spear looking to sever her head from her body. Sali had no choice but to block with the shaft of her tongue. The impact was as bone-jarring as the others. Sali felt the khan's jing ripple up her arm and into her body, sending her flying back. She managed to stay on her feet, barely, as she skidded to a standing pose. Then her legs gave way and she fell to a knee.

"You thought you could dethrone your god!" Visan sprinted at her and threw a flying knee, connecting to her entire left side and sending her spinning through the air. She crashed into a group of the Zhuun, bowling them over as she rolled to her feet.

Sali blinked, trying to clear her thoughts. She couldn't remember the last time she had been struck so hard. "I don't need to beat you. I just need to show the world that you can be beaten."

"You should know by now that one soul cannot possibly defeat the aggregate of hundreds!" He launched into the air and came down at her head just as she rolled away. The impact knocked several of the nearby Zhuun off their feet. Sali tried to jump up but a boot in her chest sent her down on her back. Sali caught the khan's foot as he crushed the sole down on her. Her arms shook from the strain.

A new figure flew down from an upper landing, bounding off the head of a marble statue, then streaked straight toward Visan, aiming a

dark sword with a hazy blue hue in its wake. Visan caught sight of the
flying Zhuun. He parried the attack with Ageless Sky at the last possible moment. A sharp clang rang across the air as the Zhuun war artist
was blown back as if picked up by a gale. Their clash put to rest any
thought that the Prophesied Hero of the Tiandi stood a chance against
the Eternal Khan of Katuia. The difference in strength in their opposing jing was stark. Wen Jian was fairly strong, more powerful than
most. Certainly not at Sali's level, but defeating him now would require some effort. Compared to the Eternal Khan of Katuia, however,
he was a mosquito jabbing at an elephant. This was the chosen one of
the Zhuun who was supposed to defeat their immortal god king? This
was a joke.

Visan swiped with Ageless Sky, smacking Jian out of the air like an
annoying insect.

The prophesied hero disappeared in the crowd and then was
launched back into the sky a moment later, throwing a somersault as
he brought his straight sword hacking down at the khan's shoulder.
Ageless Sky met the Swallow Dances, each blow sending a clear ring
into the air like a bell. Each contact of metal sent a spark illuminating
the surroundings.

The distraction allowed Sali to slip away from under the khan's
heel, scrambling back to her feet a few moments later. Both she and
the khan watched as the young Zhuun flew over the heads of several
wills of the khan, his foot rebounding off Horsaw's helm as he landed
just outside of Sali's spear.

She recognized the young man from back in Jiayi all those years
ago, when she suspected he had been the Prophesied Hero of the Tiandi. Sali tsked. Wen Jian was older now, certainly not a boy any longer. He was maturing into his destiny, unlike previously. It had nothing
to do with his armor or the dozen nuns desperately trying to protect
him. It was in his demeanor, his bearing, and the intensity on his face.
This young man had been seasoned.

For a brief glimmer, Sali entertained the possibility that these crazy
Zhuun were going to fulfill their prophecy today. It shouldn't make
any difference. Even with his obvious inexperience in this body and

mind, the sheer strength of the khan's jing should make this duel trivial. Visan should crush Jian like a little bitch beetle.

Jian drew his sword, a blue shimmering blade, and launched himself at the khan, flying through the air with his blade extended. The Prophesied Hero of the Tiandi certainly had a flair for drama. "I am Wen Jian, Prophesied Hero of the Tiandi, Champion of the Five Under Heaven, and destroyer of gods. You will not touch my friend."

Visan's mouth dropped. He turned to Sali. "Since when did you become friends with our people's sworn enemies?"

Sali was offended. "He's not talking about me. I tried to kill him once already. How insulting. How dare you!"

"Zofi, are you all right?" asked Jian.

One of the fallen Zhuun crawled back to her feet. "I'm all right."

"Good. Get the others to safety."

The girl began herding the Zhuun toward the stairs in the back.

When Visan made as if to go after them, Jian shook his head. "I'm the prize you want. Let them go."

"Very well." Visan hefted Ageless Sky over one shoulder. "You must be the one who beckoned me in my dreams. That must mean you welcome an end to our eternal struggle."

"You sound like a madman," said Jian, "but it doesn't matter. I'm going to save my people."

Visan bowed and fell into his Eight Limbed Art stance. "It is time then, little one. Honor is the way."

The Prophesied Hero of the Tiandi raised his guard, his straight sword reflecting blue light from the setting sun. "It is the only way."

One of Visan's wills of the khan rushed past Sali, trying to go to the aid of her khan. Sali backfisted the woman's face, knocking her unconscious before her body hit the ground.

She stared down the other wills of the khan. "This is destiny beckoning. Let them cook."

CHAPTER SIXTY-FIVE

PROPHECY'S END

Wen Jian felt good about his chances against the Eternal Khan of Katuia through the first six exchanges. The two clashed as Jian skirted through the air, jumping and riding the dozens of nimble currents surrounding the two. The Swallow Dances was a blur as he parried and countered the khan's long, shimmering weapon.

"It's not too late for you to turn around and walk away." Sometimes Jian couldn't help himself.

"It's too late for you." The khan studied him. "I am surprised the Zhuun champion is so diminutive."

"That makes two of us," Jian replied. "I bet I can fit through doors easier."

"Doors and holes in the ground like the rest of the vermin," said the khan.

Strange, Jian would have thought the Eternal Khan of Katuia more eloquent. Instead, the man taunted like a war arts school bully. It made him seem more human, beatable.

As their duel continued, the reputed savage Eternal Khan of Katuia, the lord of death and supposed bringer of doom, or whatever they called him, didn't look so tough. He was large, sure, but no larger than most of the Hansoo. He just had more hair. Sure, the khan looked terrifying, but it was mostly because of his black-and-white armor with those horns and spikes. Someone seemed to be trying to compensate for some inadequacy. The khan was quick and powerful, but nothing Jian hadn't faced against Taishi or any of the other masters dozens of times. Lastly, sure, the khan radiated so much jing Jian could feel his power, but as Taishi always said, the power wasn't as important as knowing how to wield it. In this case, the khan's war art was surprisingly ineloquent. His spear work was quick but in detectable patterns. Jian was able to avoid or parry most of the thrusts with ease. The khan appeared somewhat raw and disjointed, which was surprising for someone Taishi had once claimed was an artist of death.

Jian bounced around his prophesied enemy like a pestering gnat, always avoiding the khan's diamond-edged hooked spear while the tip of the Swallow Dances slashed and probed for gaps in the khan's guard and armor. He even managed to draw first blood—a slice right across the khan's chin—much to both their surprise. The small nick probably cut more beard than skin, but it was gratifying to know that he not only could hurt the supposed god king but also could hurt the man.

The windwhispering Three Starlings Blink the Sky countered what looked like a Katuia variation of Long Bird's Neck Pecks. The result was three spear thrusts that were off-angle and hurried, easily avoidable.

Jian's confidence continued to grow with every exchange. He discovered that he could match the khan blow for blow. He was beginning to believe that he could actually win. The best teachers and masters had trained him. He had survived the Celestial Palace, survived Jiayi and the Cloud Pillars. He had fought mute men in Allanto and had been further battle tested in Vauzan. Jian was ready to face his destiny and to finally put this damn prophecy to rest.

"I can do this!" Jian didn't mean to scream it aloud, but he roared the words, and backed his claim by drawing more of the khan's blood, this time slicing open his forearm. A powerful creature such as the Eternal Khan of Katuia could not be felled with one blow. It would require several great blows to wear this monster down.

Who knew the way to make Jian believe in himself was to put him up against the very thing he feared most? Now he knew that he could defeat the Eternal Khan of Katuia. He whooped in victory, and leaped toward a quicker passing current, his self-belief higher than it had ever been. Jian completed his sequence, drawing blood two more times.

Jian could actually fulfill the prophecy!

He might finally forge his destiny!

His name would be leg—

Five beefy fingers curled around Jian's ankle just as he was about to make his escape. They clamped down, holding him in place. The air current slipped away.

Jian looked down. "Oh, no—"

The khan's iron grip closed around Jian's leg, slammed him down on the ground like an abused doll. Luckily, it was over grass. Jian's body would have likely shattered on marble. He groaned as he bounced off the soft dirt, the wind suddenly knocked out of him. He felt his last meal crawling back up his throat. To his chagrin, the khan lifted him again and was about to slam him down, this time on the marble walkway, when he hesitated.

Jian turned around until he faced the khan. The man's face was a great deal bigger than Jian's head. What exactly did everyone expect him to do against such a monstrous man?

"All this effort for such a little, weak thing." The khan studied him. "I do not understand. There is nothing special about this one. How did he ever expect to defeat me?"

"I have no idea," admitted Jian. "The prophecy was pretty light on details."

"That's a shame for you," said the khan. "I still have to make an example of you, but please know, I also pity you."

"Is that supposed to make me feel better?"

The khan slammed him down on the ground.

Luckily, Jian had just enough wits about him to gather a few air currents to cushion the blow. His face came to a rest just a few fingers' breadth from the hard stone. He blinked, his head still jumbled. He was surprised he was alive. The khan roared and this time heaved Jian, sending him spinning, limbs flailing out of control through the air until he landed with a crash as he tumbled and skidded along the ground, barreling into a crowd of nuns. This time, he did throw up. He peed on himself a little as well, although he would never admit it.

Many nearby Tiandi nuns surrounded him, mothering him to his feet and, unsurprisingly, trying to give him advice.

"You have to fight harder, prophesied hero!" one said. "Hit him before he hits you!"

"Stick him with the pointy end," said another.

"I hear the khan's weakness is his fat toe, his left one! Crush it and he dies!"

Then their ideas became progressively worse.

"Stand strong," a nearby nun, back hunched, crowed in her weak, wiry voice. "We will fight by your side."

"Once a Black Orchid," one proclaimed.

"Always a Black Orchid," several elderly nuns around him cheered.

This was a bad idea.

"That's all right," Jian stammered, picking himself up.

"Your death will build a better future, Prophesied Hero of the Tiandi." The khan approached, his face bleeding and his expression dark. He looked scarier now.

Then, to Jian's dismay, the nuns meant what they said. A whole surge of them, young and old, healthy and hunched over, all charged the khan. "No, don't!" he screamed.

It was too late. The nuns converged on the khan. Some were armed with reaping swords, others with broomsticks. Many were wielding their Mosaic prayer parchments as well, as if that were going to do any good. The khan looked confused as the squawking nuns converged on him. He raised his big diamond-edged spear.

That monster was going to butcher these old women. The fighting was getting worse. Large groups of Tiandi devout had come out from inside the mountain, and the face of Skyfall had devolved into a terrible and chaotic melee. None of his friends were in sight. He had left them a few levels down to help these trapped Tiandi devout, but now he was alone with them, facing the most powerful war artist in the world. The first of the nuns, a former Black Orchid from the cut of her robe, attacked the khan. Their spears clashed, bursting sparks with every exchange. The Black Orchid was older and wily. For several moments she confused the khan, but then power and reach and speed won out. Jian watched, horrified, as the khan's silver spear sliced down, splintering her reaper sword. Then he thrust it forward deep into her chest. The nun stiffened and then fell when he yanked his blade from her body.

Jian had to do something! There was only one thing that could get the khan's attention. He picked up his fallen sword—relieved that Taishi wasn't around to see him drop it—and waved his arms at the Eternal Khan of Katuia.

"Hey, you, Khan!" He tried his most threatening roar. "Visan, you hairy dog!"

That caught the man's attention. Their eyes locked. "What is it, friend Jian?"

"It's getting too crowded around here. Catch me if you can." Jian stepped onto a strong current and lifted into the air.

The khan's face was trained on him. The man swatted several nuns aside as he took a few steps and then began loping forward in long strides. Jian surfed atop a particularly fast-moving current. The giant man was a lumbering beast. There was no way he could catch up.

And then the khan took three long leaps and bounded forward, arcing over Jian's head and landing at the middle of the staircase in front of him. Visan palmed the top of the nearby stone pedestal and separated the top stone globe from its base. He snarled at Jian and hurled it with blinding force.

The projectile reached Jian quicker than he expected. He just managed to lean to his left as parts of its jagged edges scraped his chest. Another rock followed. He was ready for it this time. The Swallow Dances sang out of its scabbard as its blue light sliced the stone in half. Yet another ruffled the hair on his head.

Jian was a fat flying chicken up here. There was little chance he could escape the khan's range, not with the strength he was throwing these pieces. That left him with no other option. Jian ducked another piece of stone and charged at the khan. The two crashed together in a clearing at the north side of the seventh level. At least there was no one else around to get hurt.

Jian did the only thing he could do: he closed the distance and attacked. Swooping Dragon Steals the Sheep met Soliloquy of Blades. The khan's looping slashes blurred the air. Jian found himself on his back heel more times than he was comfortable with. Windwhispering was tiring work and he had to keep flitting about to avoid getting skewered like a fish. He had to stay as close to the khan as possible, however, in order to seize any openings that presented themselves.

Like right there. Visan was careless holding his spear, allowing the butt end to drift away from his body. It was bad, lazy form, strange for a war arts master.

Jian shot in, past the spearhead and around the flexing shaft, the Swallow Dances aiming true at the khan's chest. Blades clashed as Jian was thwarted at the last possible moment. The two renewed their next exchange, and there it was again. The khan held the spear too high and far from his body. Another easy opening. He didn't seem to learn from his mistakes. Jian took advantage again, abruptly changing angles and diving like an eagle, talons out, bombing its prey.

The khan bounded upward, leaping in a ridiculous jumping uppercut. Yet somehow, the stupid thing connected. The khan's meaty hand punched into Jian's belly. He felt the back of his spine rattle, felt it splinter. He tasted blood, felt a strange pressure behind his eyes, and then his body went limp. His head pitched forward, followed by his body. Jian was only vaguely conscious as the world turned upside down. Strange, the air tasted like metal. Then he blinked and lost all control of his senses.

When he came to, his head hurt. He looked up and saw the khan stalking toward him. Jian tried to push himself up to a sitting position, but his head felt too heavy to hold himself up. He blinked another time and watched, numbly, a large silhouette of a tall and broad-shouldered man standing against the backdrop of a burning city. The sight of his approaching death stiffened Jian's spine. Groaning, he picked himself up and hobbled away. He needed to clear his head before he could attempt to take to the air. Taishi always chastised him for his reliance on currents when he windwhispered. Now he felt like a grounded goose. He got to his feet and began to limp away. Each step sent a jolt of pain shooting up his leg.

"Where do you think you're going, Prophesied Hero of the Tiandi?" Visan boomed. "This is as good of a place as any for you to make your final stand. Right here in your house of worship," he mused. "There's something poetic about that, don't you think? It reminds me of a poem I once wrote."

"I'd rather you just kill me quickly instead," Jian shot back.

Sharp anguish flashed across the khan's face. The man must really think highly of his poetry. "As you wish, Prophesied Hero of the Tiandi."

Jian, looking over his shoulder, saw the Eternal Khan of Katuia heft his spear like a javelin. He knew he was a dead man. The scorching pain in his ankles was subsiding, but he would be an even easier target on a current, especially hobbled. He tried to pick up his pace limping away.

Jian sensed the air splitting the moment the spear left the khan's hand. He already knew he wouldn't be quick enough to duck it. All he could do was brace for the impact. Perhaps avoid a vital organ, if possible. Maybe not shit his pants. That was probably the last dignity he could offer the Tiandi devout for his utter failure as their prophesied hero.

Something flashed nearby, and then a powerful force shoved him to the side. The khan's spear streaked between them, miraculously narrowly missing him. Then a sharp pull nearly dislocated his shoulder but kept him upright. Jian was startled to see a Katuia woman helping him. It was one of their warriors, although she was dressed differently in banded green armor. Now that he looked at her more closely . . .

Jian squinted. "I know you."

She nodded. "You do. Salminde the Viperstrike."

"You tried to kill me before."

"I did, yes, back in Jiayi."

His eyes widened. "Are you here to finish the job?"

She pointed at the khan. "No, that's his job."

"Wasn't he just trying to kill *you* earlier?"

"You're a more important target."

Jian was confused. "So are we on the same side now?"

"Definitely not." Sali stared down the khan. "But against him, perhaps this one time."

CHAPTER SIXTY-SIX

THE FINAL FIGHT

S ali couldn't believe this was happening. She closed her eyes. This was humiliating. It would have never occurred to her in ten centuries that she would ally with the Prophesied Hero of the Tiandi against the Eternal Khan of Katuia. Yet here she was, standing shoulder to shoulder with this land-chained Zhuun, the most hated individual in history, facing down the leader of her people. She was glad that her parents, teachers, ancestors, and everyone else in her life who had ever cared about or looked up to her weren't here to witness her blasphemy.

This was a new low, which was saying something because she had been hitting so many of those recently.

Sali's only solace was that she knew this was the right thing to do. Within a short time, the Eternal Khan of Katuia, at least this latest iteration of the khan, had razed a city, enslaved people, and committed genocide. He would lead the Katuia down a dark path in the name of glory, one from which there would be no turning back.

This was not the Katuia way, and it could not be their path forward.

Sali opened her eyes and studied her new ally. Not that it mattered. Wen Jian at least looked the part: muscles in the right places, held his sword correctly, and moved competently as a war artist. He looked perfectly adequate, but from what little she had observed so far, there was nothing special about him. He certainly did not look like he would be a problem for the Eternal Khan of Katuia. The only reason he held up well so far was because the khan had been battling since dawn, which included several hard exchanges with Sali. Both she and Jian had lost to Visan individually. Perhaps they would fare better working together.

"Are you ready, lad?" she asked.

"No," he replied. "Any idea how to beat him?"

She shrugged. "I don't know what you're good at, but I just stab him with the sharp end."

Jian scowled. "Why does everyone keep giving me such obvious advice?"

"Perhaps you should learn to start taking it then. Be wary. He adapts." Sali attacked first, drawing the hilt of her tongue from its holster. Her tongue cracked the air. Sali whirled it overhead and curved it at Visan, hoping to bend it around his defenses. The khan dodged it with ease, ducking and sidestepping as his diamond-edged hooked spear homed in on her. Then Sali wrapped her hand around the rope, wrapping it around her back and shoulders as she continued swinging and whipping her tongue. This was a game both had played many times before, while training in a previous lifetime. Sali continued to work, switching between the supple rope and the shaft, guiding and manipulating her tongue around her opponent.

Visan, back in his Eight Limbed Art stance, blocked her shots easily. He continued plodding toward her. She sent a jolt into her tongue, stiffening its shaft. Now spear met spear, and the two clashed in a duel of sharp teeth. Sali's spear was more supple, bending when necessary, while the khan's was rigid brute force, an extension of his jing. The two sparred, spearheads snapping and cutting. Sali gashed Visan's chest open while he slicked her lower leg up pretty fierce in that last exchange. It was debatable if she won this round.

"Your ancestors will not forgive this shame, Salminde," said the khan. "This treachery will stain your bloodline."

"You are a parasite," she hissed, "feeding upon our people for hundreds of generations."

"The Katuia only reached these heights because of me!" he retorted. "You stand upon the legacy that I built. So who is the parasite?"

"You have sacrificed and consumed so many of our young. It is monstrous."

He laughed. "You think they are the ones who made the greater sacrifice? If you only knew, young one. Your life is nothing more than a drop in the vast river of time."

Their chatter gave Wen Jian the opportunity to attack Visan from above, although it wasn't effective. The khan's lightning-quick reflexes repelled the Prophesied Hero of the Tiandi's attack, their guards clashing and knocking Jian. The two allies kept up their pressure, his blue sword writing glowing calligraphy in soft dusk light, while Sali's metallic tongue continued to bite at the khan. The constant pressure they put on the khan with their flurry of attacks proved effective, with several small blotches of red staining the khan's white armor.

But while they were able to whittle and weaken him small cut by small cut, all Visan needed was one good shot, which he seized a moment later.

Neither Sali nor Jian could maintain their intensity for long. Fatigue and exhaustion set in after the first dozen exchanges. The khan did not seem to tire. That was when Sali made a mistake. The weight of her thrust was too far forward, and she was a blink too late to pull back. Visan caught hold of her tongue and yanked. She was not quick enough to react and was pulled off her feet. Her stance had been too weak and her center of gravity too high. As she stumbled forward, Visan threw a hard elbow that connected to her chin, sending her mind into darkness as she fell forward.

Death certainly would come next.

When Sali opened her eyes, everything moved with disjointed slowness. There was buzzing in her ears. The world throbbed; she could feel the heavy bass in the depths of her guts. Everything around

her was swimming. She blinked. She had suffered enough brain rat-
tles to know when it was a concussion.

Visan approached, moving slowly, columns of smoke drifting up
into the background. His mouth moved, sound came out, but Sali
could not make out the meaning. The khan shook his head and
pointed the hooked spearhead at her chest.

Sali supposed she should feel honored. To die by the Eternal Khan
of Katuia's own hand, being killed by Ageless Sky. The weapon's name
was apt, its power an extension of its wielder's jing. In the hands of the
mighty, it was doubly so. The khan took one slow step toward her, and
then another, and stabbed.

There was a flash of blue and Wen Jian was there, sweeping the
khan's thrust aside to land harmlessly a few paces to Sali's left. Then
the prophesied hero countered. The blue wake from his sword colored
the air as he splintered the khan's armor. Then, just as he sneaked a
few more licks in, Visan snatched Jian out of the air, his fingers curled
around the prophesied hero's neck. Jian choked, pawing at the khan's
wrists.

Sali tried to stand, but the world swooned. She could hardly take a
step forward, and then she fell to one knee. Visan stared down at her,
his lips curled into a sneer. He turned back to Jian, whose face had
turned blue.

Then there was the sound of glass crashing, and falling from the
higher levels were two bodies shrouded in what appeared to be wisps
of darkness. They fell to the earth and happened to barrel into the
khan's back, causing him to stumble. Visan dropped Jian and fell forward onto his hands and knees.

Darkness evaporated from the newcomers' bodies like steam. It
took a moment for Sali's eyes to focus. She recognized the little shadowkill with her wild mane of hair. The other person Sali recognized as
well, only because she was the most famous woman in the world.

Qisami looked at Sali, and then at Sunri. Sunri looked back at her,
and then they both looked at the khan. Qisami raised her hand. "What
is going on here? And, oh my . . ." Her voice trailed off. "Who is that
handsome, hunky, hairy man?"

Qisami couldn't believe this was happening. Of all the places to find her future husband, she never thought he would be a Kati, let alone a giant of a man and a murderous psychopath. Well, the last bit was probably half likely considering her line of work. Upon closer examination, she found that his face was only all right—she didn't care for his nose—but his hair was like a stallion's mane. His eyes were two big bull's-eyes. His fit body seemed to have leaped straight out of a Burning Hearts romance book.

Qisami looked over at Sali and considered; maybe she just had a thing for Katuia people. "Hey," she called. "Are you all right there, business? Who's that hairy brisket over there? I'd like to dig my face in that shrub of chest hair."

Salminde stared at her, puzzled. "Are you referring to the Eternal Khan of Katuia?"

"Oh, *that's* the khan?" Qisami chortled. "He can ravage my heart any day."

Sunri stepped next to her, eyes trained forward. "That's the most dangerous man in the world, and you want to bed him?"

"I don't claim to make the best life choices!" she shot back.

"Why are you fighting, Duchess Sunri of Caobiu?" demanded Sali. "Aren't you both Zhuun?"

"Why are you fighting your own khan?" Sunri shot back. "Aren't you both Kati?"

"Watch your words, land-chained," Sali snarled.

"Who's that Kati speaking as if her words carry weight?" Sunri demanded. She pointed at Jian. "Is he dead?"

Sali shrugged. "I did my best, either way. Right now, we have a bigger problem to worry about."

The only problem that was bigger than the death of the Prophesied Hero of the Tiandi certainly had to be the Eternal Khan of Katuia, that handsome hunk of a man staring back at her from across the field. Qisami's face flushed. Those big puppy dog eyes.

"Duchess Sunri," said the khan. "I am honored by your presence."

"Oh." Qisami scowled. "He's looking at you."

"We need to kill him," said Sali, voice muffled.

"I don't have any quarrel with him right now," said Sunri. "If he wants to pillage his way through Xing and Lawkan, he can be my guest."

"I thought you said you were the empress," Jian groaned, sitting up, clutching his neck.

"That's just a technicality until I clean up everyone's mess."

The khan walked to the weapon he had dropped, a pretty giant spear with diamond etchings, and picked it up. Qisami was going to steal that after the battle was over, assuming she won and he was dead. The huge man pointed at each of them. "Everyone who needs killing has come to me in one place. How considerate." He paused. "It still is unknown, however, who amongst you called to me."

"Do you all stand with me against him?" asked Sali.

"Won't he just come back if we kill him?" asked Jian. "Because he died before."

"Yes, but it would be another decade or two before he does. This particular host seeks domination and chaos. Not all khans harbor such capacity for violence and aggression. Perhaps he will be wiser in his next life. His death will be the only way you can stop this current attack on Skyfall Temple."

Jian's face tightened. "That's all you needed to say." He stood and took the first unsteady step toward the khan. His next was more assured.

Sali put her hand on his shoulder. "*I* will take him from the front. You slide in from the right flank."

Qisami raised her hand. "Can I have the right flank? It's everyone's blind side." She waggled a finger at Jian. "He'll just waste the advantage."

"Hey," said Jian. "That's rude. I don't even know you."

Her hackles rose. "You don't remember? I tried to kill you!"

He shook his head and shrugged. "Doesn't jog any memories. A lot of people have tried to kill me. It must not have been that memorable."

"Why, you little cockroach." Qisami's eyes narrowed. She then caught the attention of Sunri moving next to her. "Hey, we have a truce until this is over, right?"

Sunri looked disgusted. "You tried to assassinate the Empress of the Enlightened States and now you want to talk truce?"

"No, I still want to kill you. I just want to wait until we kill him first, okay?"

"Fine, whatever. Let's just get on with this." Sunri sniffed. "I'm an empress. I don't have all day."

"How many times an hour do you tell yourself that?"

The khan watched them with contempt as they fanned out around him. "The four of you think you can stand against the Eternal Khan of Katuia? Haven't you failed enough today, hero?"

"I'm still standing," Jian retorted.

"You're just a boy in a god's body, Visan," said Sali. "Now you've brought ruin and death to thousands."

"I brought death to our enemies!" Visan screamed.

"Death is death," she replied. "It is the foundation of our way of life. You would know that if you had studied. The spirit shamans rushed you out, didn't they? Jiamin had studied a full five years before assuming the mantle."

Visan pointed at his temple. "His memories are in me right now. I know all I need to know. Think about this vast, fertile land, Salminde. All this, as far as our hawks can soar, could be under our dominion. No longer will our people have to eke out an existence in the Grass Sea. Our cities can roam free here, as the masters of these lands."

"Not if I have anything to say about that, great khan." Sunri's words dripped with rage and malice. "Apologies, but these lands are already taken."

"It appears the fate of the entire world rests upon this battle." He glanced farther down the mountain at the battle on the lower levels. "We should at least have an audience to witness this momentous event."

"They're mostly your people," said Qisami. "Hardly fair."

"Three women and a boy. Was there ever any doubt about the victor?"

"Hey!" Jian protested.

The hubris of an overconfident war artist was often their own worst enemy. Believing himself at an advantage, Visan thought he controlled the initiative, which often led to tiresome monologues.

They came at him all at once, each striking, kicking, or stabbing from a different angle, from above, from the shadows. The khan stood his ground against all four, not retreating. His spear clashed with Sali's tongue, their fencing ringing in sharp rhythm. He knocked Jian out of the air while the windwhisper dove down from above. That kid could use a little more seasoning.

Sunri attacked next, slipping out from the khan's shadow—a difficult and impressive shadowstepping maneuver—and tried to skewer the man between the legs. The khan somehow evaded her as her sharp thrusts met no resistance. Then he swept her leg with such force her foot flipped over her head. While she was still in the air, he bodychecked her with his shoulder, shooting her through the wall of a nearby building.

Qisami stepped into the shadow behind a statue of a rabbit standing on its hindquarters wearing a court official's hat. She took off for the khan, staying directly behind the large man. Whenever he turned one way, she veered toward the other, staying light on her feet.

The khan was preoccupied with Salminde, both Katuia wielding flexible spears that bent and whipped at each other. He was driving Sali back, only to be confronted by Jian and his shiny blue blade. The khan made quick work of the prophesied hero, however, knocking him aside with relative ease.

Then it was Qisami's turn, pouncing onto his back and driving a blade between his shoulders, drawing blood a finger digit deep. She snarled at the sight of blood and rammed the blade back down for another taste. Clinging to his shoulders like a rabid monkey, she tried to jam the dagger straight into the handsome khan's ear.

Beauty was such a terrible thing to waste.

The khan threw his shoulders side to side, trying to buck her off, causing her stab to miss its mark and graze the side of his head instead. One of those meaty hands reached over and grabbed hold of Qisami's robes. The large Katuia tossed her over his shoulder like a child with a ball. Qisami flailed through the air, her trajectory sending her off the side of the mountain. Being in broad, clear daylight meant there was nowhere for her to shadowstep. She was about to go over the edge when there was a soft pop nearby. Something barreled into Qisami, sending them both crashing into the balcony just shy of falling off the sheer cliff.

"You have time for one strike, not two, against this man," said Sunri, hauling Qisami to her feet.

"I hate that it's you who saved my life," Qisami replied.

"Worry about repaying your honor debt later." Sunri motioned to her left. "Execute the Bo Po Mo Fo Dancing Shadows. Now!" She took off sprinting to the right, disappearing into a shadow.

Qisami was impressed that the duchess remembered their training pool's signature tactic. She followed suit, streaking to the left and disappearing into a shadow behind a hedge. She popped up in a nearby goldwood tree, sprinting along its long, flat branches until she was almost directly over the fighting. She leaped at the khan just as Sunri emerged from the side.

The khan had enough time to react to one of them, as he swung his spear and knocked Sunri off her path. Qisami succeeded in landing a long cut along the khan's chest, breaking through armor and finding more blood. Qisami fell directly into the khan's shadow and, using the momentum from gravity to shoot out from the shaded corner of two walls directly facing the khan, aimed a killing blow.

Kill the head, and the body has no head, as the Goramh saying goes, or something like that. Qisami had never been a great student. In any case, the tips of her blades were aimed squarely at the khan's exposed throat. She had already cut him several times. Now she was going to end it. Much to her chagrin, right as she passed that familiar wall of bubbles, a hand wrapped around her throat, holding her in place.

The khan, still dashingly handsome, sneered. "There used to be a clan of your type of nightblossoms known as the Triangle Eye, night walkers who jumped through shadows. I personally ripped the lungs out of every one of their sect when I caught them spying on my court so many centuries ago. Their clan is forbidden from rising ever again."

"Seems like a terrible waste of knowledge. I guess a bunch of invisible assassins and spies wouldn't have been useful in your war against the Zhuun," she hissed back. The vise around her neck was tight. "Idiot."

A moment later, Sunri rejoined the attack, only to suffer a similar fate, as if the Eternal Khan of Katuia could somehow detect their shadowstepping. The khan struck Sunri so hard with a sharp elbow that the duchess went limp before she hit the ground. He then threw Qisami across the yard, sending her skidding against the hard stone. She groaned, her vision hazy.

Salminde hit next, the bite of her tongue snapping the air once, twice, before retracting. Then, just as she stiffened her tongue to its spear form, the khan dropped his spear and shot forward with blinding quickness to snatch the neck of her spear. Before she could react, he torqued the shaft one way, using the leverage of the flexible shaft to swing the viperstrike to the side and smash her with deafening force into the nearby wall, cracking the marble Mosaic of the Tiandi mural.

A sudden blast of wind followed by a loud boom caused the khan to stumble as the windwhisper descended on him. Qisami blinked, head still groggy. She was impressed that the boy could muster this much jing.

Curlew Pokes the Ponds met Sway Hands Carry the Wave, except the khan's large arms and hands made exceptionally large waves. Jian's blue blade continued to seek its mark, twirling from Hummingbird Darts Toward the Sun before transitioning to Drill, Big Baby, Drill.

The khan's turtle shell defense coupled with his long reach made any sustained attack difficult. Then, with a sudden roar, he burst forward, knocked the sword from Wen Jian's hands, and curled his fingers around the young man's neck. Arms extended, the khan lifted the Prophesied Hero of the Tiandi off his feet, dangling him like a helpless fish hanging off a hook.

His eyes bulged and his face went purple as his legs kicked and flailed helplessly. Qisami tried to get up, but failed.

"Enough!" the high-pitched voice of a child called. The war artists momentarily stopped their struggles and looked toward this strange source of authority, surprising coming from one so young.

There, walking out from a nearby tunnel entrance, was Ling Taishi. Standing next to her was a little girl in strange garb holding a fox.

The girl spoke again. "Enough, Warrior, enough of this fighting. It is time to lay down the blade."

Taishi couldn't believe everything that had happened so far only for them to lose so badly. It was obvious to her from the beginning that Jian and his ragtag group of allies were going to get crushed by the Eternal Khan of Katuia. Even raw, the enormous man was too quick, too powerful. He shook off their attacks with ease, his raw power able to overcome four master war artists. Well, three and Jian. The boy was certainly skilled, now with experience tempered by the fighting in Vauzan, but he was still a far cry from a true master.

That shadowkill was noteworthy because their paths had crossed so many times. You rarely survived an encounter with one of their kind once, let alone two or three times. That little one had tried to kill her in Sanba and then at Jiayi a few weeks later. It was the same one who was blamed for killing Duke Saan. That had been a surprise. At the time, Taishi had assumed the negotiations in Allanto were where the action was hottest, so of course they would attract the best diamond-tier operatives. But now, years later, Taishi's third encounter with this shadowkill meant this was not a coincidence.

The viperstrike, on the other hand, was another matter. Salminde was *the* viperstrike, if Taishi recalled. She had been a Katuia war artist of repute long before the Jiayi incident. It didn't surprise Taishi that the viperstrike would be here along with the khan. This was the deadliest Katuia attack ever launched at the Enlightened States. What surprised Taishi was that the viperstrike was fighting *against* the khan. This was the same woman who had tried to kill Jian back in Jiayi. Now she was fighting alongside him. Strange allies, indeed.

This wasn't even what shocked Taishi the most. She looked down at little Pei, the Oracle of the Tiandi, standing next to her stroking Floppy's fur. The girl had somehow called to her from all the way up Skyfall Mountain in the midst of battle. The compulsion was like nothing Taishi had ever felt. It was jarringly strong, a gravitational pull, but also didn't feel forced. Taishi had *wanted* to find Pei. She had *wanted* to bring her here. For whatever reason, Pei wanted to see this fight. Taishi had assumed it was because the oracle wanted to bear witness to this occasion, but she wasn't sure why.

Taishi just knew that she had to help the oracle at all costs, so here they were. She had spent a few moments watching the exchange. Jian had loosened up, but he was still too frantic in his movements. His unique spin of windwhispering was certainly interesting, but the boy was going to wear himself out working this hard in every fight. Assuming he survived this fight, which appeared unlikely. The viperstrike was holding the khan's attention. The others were hyenas at the lion's heels. She grimaced. Jian's shoulders were still so tight, he was going to get a cramp.

The group had stopped brawling and faced her. The diminutive oracle broke free from Taishi's clasped hand and stepped out of the tunnel into the clearing, much to Taishi's chagrin. Her worries grew as Pei moved to within a few feet of the khan. He could reach out and crush the life out of the little girl in a heartbeat. He certainly would the moment he discovered who she was. The oracle was just as central to the Tiandi religion as Jian.

Unless, of course, he already knew.

The Eternal Khan of Katuia stared at the girl, and then his expression morphed, his facade of strength revealing the pain and grief beneath. His face contorted in its own journey: anger to confusion to shock to disbelief to . . . Taishi couldn't read his last emotions.

He fell to his knees, weeping. What was happening here? How did the Oracle of the Tiandi wield such power over the Eternal Khan of Katuia?

Taishi wasn't the only one befuddled. The viperstrike woman looked equally shocked. Her mouth open, she held her spear loosely as if she couldn't believe what she was seeing. Then, as if snapping out of her stupor, she raised her spear and moved as if to seize the moment and stab the khan in the back.

Taishi seized what little string of jing she could muster and sent her voice across the battlefield to Salminde. "No, viperstrike, stay your spear."

Salminde looked her way, and then back at the khan and the child huddled together. She finally lowered her weapon. All eyes focused on the Oracle of the Tiandi, the progenitor of the Zhuun religion whose every word from her divine lips was considered sacrosanct, with the Eternal Khan of Katuia's head in her small hands, their foreheads touching.

What could all this mean?

The khan's low baritone voice broke. "I searched for you everywhere. For a century, I did," the khan swore. Each word brimmed with regret. "Then I stopped looking. I failed you."

"You failed no one, brave Warrior. You have fought far longer than anyone else. But now it is time to rest."

The Eternal Khan of Katuia deflated, as if all the tension seeped from his body. He bowed his head and wept. The Oracle of the Tiandi wrapped her arms around him and murmured into his ear.

The khan, after several moments, nodded with his head bowed as he rose to stand. He eyed Jian first, then the two shadowkills, Taishi, and finally, Sali. He spoke in his low but proud, rumbling voice. "I, the Eternal Khan of Katuia, leader of the Katuia horde, clan chief of Chaqra, surrender the Katuia horde to the Exiles Rebellion, for now and forever."

This time, the spear clattered from Salminde's hands. "Why?" was all she could muster.

The khan walked up to her. "On condition that I am brought back to the place of our birth for my final rest."

Salminde hesitated. "You wish to return to the Sun Under Lagoon?"

He nodded. "Deliver me, and you will have your peace, and we will have our rest."

Who was we?

Pei turned to the others. "You have all played your parts . . . adequately." Her eyes narrowed and she jabbed a finger at Jian. "Except you. *You* really messed things up."

He huffed. "I don't have to dance to your puppet strings—"

Floppy the fox leaped out of her hands and crept up to Jian, baring his teeth. The boy still didn't know when to keep his mouth shut.

The girl crossed her arms and stomped up to him. "Kill the old lady. That's all you had to do. Do you know how many hundreds of thousands of lives were lost, all because you wouldn't fulfill your stupid destiny—it was your only job!—to assume the mantle of the Master Windwhisper? Your one job! It was literally the thing you signed up for when you became Taishi's student."

Pei turned to face the shadowkill. "Maza Qisami, your father was a fool for offering his brightest seed to the Consortium, but for being so shortsighted, he saved your people by giving them you." She bowed.

Qisami looked uncomfortable. "Does that mean I *shouldn't* kill him? Because that was going to be my next stop."

The oracle took her comment in stride. "Whether he lives or dies matters not. You are fit to follow your heart. The scales of your deeds are balanced."

"Does that mean yes?"

"It means the fates don't give a shit." The mouth on this girl.

Qisami still looked confused when Pei turned to Sali. "Salminde the Viperstrike."

Salminde was still stunned and looked unsteady. She was probably still grappling with the fact that the khan had surrendered just as he was on the cusp of victory. She placed her fist over her forehead, chin, and then heart. "What does this mean?" she asked. "And what would be the fate of my clan, my family?"

Pei smiled. "Always my favorite player because you constantly think of your people. That makes your free will consistent and predictable. I worried the least about you through all this. Your star always pointed toward the righteous way."

"My former capital city was burned to the ground as well," Sali said. "Was that avoidable?"

"Your Nezra clan had to fall to ashes so you could rise, Salminde the Viperstrike. All your other paths led to quick and glorious, but utterly useless death."

Pei turned last to Taishi. "My old friend. You did your best."

Taishi sputtered. "That's all you have to say? I did my best? I got us here, didn't I?"

"It's precious and amusing you think that." Pei smirked. "The truth is you fell ass-backward here, but yes, we are *here*. But then there was a way to reach *here* without having to ransack two Zhuun cities and two Katuia capitals."

"I don't regret my choice!" Jian tried to pipe in.

The oracle stared daggers at him.

Taishi shrugged. "The boy has his own free will."

"That's the problem," Pei hissed. "You were supposed to prepare him for battle, not to make stupid, impulsive choices."

"I don't think sparing my life was stupid or impulsive."

"Please, I can read your thoughts, Ling Taishi."

"That's not fair." Taishi looked around. "What happens now? We won? What do we do with the khan?"

"There is one more task that must be done, Ling Taishi, one that I can only entrust to you."

Taishi snorted. "Didn't you say I did a lousy job, and now only I can be entrusted with this task?"

"Sadly, two things can be true at the same time. Now shut up and listen. This is important. I don't want you to screw it up again."

EPILOGUE

Koteuni landed beneath a windowsill and climbed in through the cracked opening, her long legs slinking through one at a time like a spider. She skulked lightly on her feet, slithering around walls and shadowstepping into the many dark corners of this modest estate.

It was one of those mid-priced estates that were a little too ostentatious for a commoner but would be laughed out of court for the nobility. The market for these were either the new-rich peasants or the impoverished lords. Koteuni had been getting into real estate at Manjing. She couldn't be shadowkilling forever, could she?

The rest of the cell slipped in after her. There was Zwei and Burandin, and the newest crew, Jahko and Bingwing. Koteuni, of course, was in charge of this copper-tier shadowkill cell. It was a modest step down from her peak being part of a diamond-tier cell, but at least she was the boss this time. They were just going through a rough patch. Things would pick up.

The room, a library with a burning fireplace at its center, was nicely furnished in velvet and silk. It was far too nice for an estate this modest. That pointed to a declining lord then, nobility whose wealth and power had weakened. That was typical, too.

Sitting at a desk next to the roaring fire was an ancient man, spindly and hunched, poring over several stacks of parchment. The sometimes-revered emeritus Senior Mnemonic of the Gyian Court, Maza Ziyak, was more bones than brains now. He flipped through the pages, noticing nothing as the cell crept up on him. He had to be deaf because they weren't that quiet. It was a little embarrassing, really. Yet the old man was muttering to himself and noticed nothing.

The five shadowkills fanned out and then closed in, finally getting his attention. The old man stuck his nose out of his book as they converged and raised a hand. "Now, what reason would anyone have to assassinate an old, retired mnemonic lord? His life isn't worth the liang."

"Apparently it is, because someone paid to have you strangled," said Zwei, their long hair flowing from under their hood.

"Humph," the old man considered. "If this is it, do you mind giving me a day and coming back tomorrow? I wish to settle my affairs and perhaps try to sleep with one of my mistresses one last time. I'll pay handsomely."

Koteuni perked up. They could use the extra margins. "How many liang is that worth to you?"

A loud, slow clap resounded; its deliberate cadence drew attention to itself until it held everyone's attention. The color in Koteuni's face drained when Qisami stepped out from the shadows.

Koteuni and Burandin leaped back and drew their weapons. Zwei tried to as well, but somehow bobbled and dropped their sword in the process.

Qisami shushed them. "Oh, stop. The old egg is right. What reason could anyone possibly have to hire shadowkills for this doddering man?" She turned to him. "Hi, ba."

Maza Ziyak blinked at her several times. "Have we met?"

Qisami looked as if she wanted to stab him right then and there. She looked at Koteuni. "You look awful. Hard times?"

Koteuni's butt cheeks clenched. "Hi, Kiki, I'm glad to see you're back on your feet. I knew you would be fine in the end. I always believed in—"

Qisami cut her off. "Stop talking or I'm going to stick a knife through your throat." She turned to the others. "By the way, I'm the client who hired you, so you can put your blades away before you get hurt *and* not get any death pay to your beneficiaries. The only reason you're all still alive is because I haven't killed you yet." She pointed at Jahko and Bingwing standing confused off to the side. "You two I don't know. Get out of here before I decide to kill you."

Koteuni put on a smile. "It's good to see you, Kiki. You look . . . okay."

"Five years in a penal colony can wreak havoc on one's complexion. It's hard to keep the skincare regimen when you're starving and freezing."

"Qisami? Is that you, my child?" Her father doddered to his feet and reached for her.

"We're past introductions. Catch up, ba."

Qisami's black knives appeared in her hands. "Now, you're all wondering why you're here. I had some unfinished business with all of you, and I thought it'd be easier if I got you in a room at the same time. It will save me the hassle of hunting each of you down."

"Qisami, your mother would be—"

"I said shut it, ba. Why are you always cutting me off? You never cut off any of my brothers, but you always cut me off. Is it because I have the biggest dick among all of you or because I'm a woman?"

Ziyak frowned. "No, of course not. It was because you never stopped talking. And have you heard her sing? There are rocks less tone-deaf than my little Qisami."

"Hey, Kiki," said Koteuni. "It looks like you and your ba have a lot to discuss. I'm glad you two can bond. Why don't I take my cell out of your way? We'll just need to settle on the kill fee." She stopped. "You know what, forget the kill fee. Let's call it square."

Qisami stabbed the nearby table with a hard downward thrust, splintering the wood. "Nobody move."

"That's mahogany!" Ziyak moaned.

Everyone else obliged.

Qisami paced around them. "Now that I have all of your attention, it's time I get what I'm owed." She yanked the dagger off the table and eyed both her father and Koteuni. "I . . ." She swallowed, as if tasting bile. "I would like to start with an apology first." She stopped and waited, and then spoke again. "An apology from you two, of course."

The *Hana Iceberg* approached the outer smoke curtain of the fabled Sun Under Lagoon. The arctic barge, a giant chunk of floating ice with three giant masts and four large paddlehouses attached to it, plowed through the icy blue waters of the True Freeze like a pregnant whale. Sali had made this journey several times since her visit to cure her soul rot and still basked in the frigid beauty of the icy landscape as well as stared at the hellish horror of the smoke ring surrounding the Sun Under Lagoon.

A string of curses broke the quiet awe among the small group standing at the forward platform. Sali looked over to see Ling Taishi, eyes wide and marked with terror, her face drained as white as the snow around them, gawking at the smoke ring. The Happan home of Hrusha was set on an island in the center of the mouth of an active underwater volcano. The perpetual wall of soot, smoke, and ash rose high and fanned out into the heavens.

It felt unnatural standing so close to the war artist grandmaster, a Zhuun, a formidable former enemy who now stood alongside her working toward a common cause. Sali looked down at the little girl standing next to Ling Taishi. They made for strange allies, especially considering recent events. What could it all mean? How were the Eternal Khan of Katuia and the Oracle of the Tiandi so familiar with each other? Taishi was curious as well and had tried unsuccessfully to pry this knowledge from the little oracle, just as Sali had with the khan. So far, neither would say.

Taishi caught Sali staring. "Are you sure this isn't a trap?"

"I am never sure. Having second thoughts, master?"

Taishi looked back at the girl standing at the tip of the barge's bow, studying the approaching black curtain. "Every damn day."

The young Oracle of the Tiandi had insisted on accompanying the Eternal Khan of Katuia back to Hrusha for his final rest. Ling Taishi, as well as practically the entire Tiandi religion, had been set against the girl coming. It had nearly sparked another war, this time with the high seats abbots getting aggressively protective of their little prophet. The oracle—her name was Pei—had put her foot down about traveling here to the True Freeze, so here they were with Taishi serving as the girl's chaperone.

A large man in a white polar bear suit walked up to the platform next to the viperstrike. "We're approaching the smoke ring now, landlady."

"Thank you, Captain Lehuangxi Thiraput Cungle."

When the call had gone out that the Eternal Khan of Katuia requested transport to Hrusha, dozens of arctic barges showed up at the pier requesting the privilege of ferrying the khan home. Among them was the *Hana Iceberg*. Sali was gladdened to see her old friend and had given his barge the honor of ferrying the khan to his final return to the Sun Under Lagoon.

A collection of chimes rang throughout the barge, and the *Hana Iceberg* picked up speed. Nearly half the barges that had decided to accompany the *Hana Iceberg* formed up around them, creating a large fleet of escorts. Other chimes joined in from several of the other nearby ships, forming a strange harmony. It was eerily beautiful and warm—almost joyous—out here in this otherwise stark, barren landscape.

The crowd at the bow of the *Hana Iceberg* braced as they entered the smoke ring. Sali put her arms around Wani and shielded the girl. This was her younger neophyte's first journey to the Sun Under Lagoon, and apparently her first time on a seabound craft. The lass's face had been green during most of the voyage, and she was terrified of the vast open water as well. This giant, hellish wall of smoke did nothing to calm her fears. The acrid stench of smoke and sulfur tickled Sali's nose with its sour tang, burning her eyes. Tendrils of smoke clung to her cloak, leaving a Salminde-shaped hole in her wake.

Taishi attempted to herd Pei into one of the nearby tents for shelter, but the girl would have none of it. She pushed her chaperone away and stepped forward to the edge of the bow, closing her eyes and spreading her arms wide as if trying to embrace the smoke ring, even as the smoke choked Taishi's frail body. She clung to the nearby railing and retched.

Sali fought back the urge to come to the grandmaster's aid. It was obvious that the last of the master war artist's days were near, and often during the end of life all one had was their pride. Sali would never insult the woman in such a way.

Pei had no such qualms. The girl hurried to Taishi and touched her arm. "The pain will pass soon." And it seemed like it did. The older woman stopped coughing and stood more erect.

"That sounds ominous, girl," Taishi muttered, wiping the spittle from her mouth.

A moment later, the *Hana Iceberg* emerged on the other side, and they were enveloped by bright shimmering blue light. Sali blinked the last of the irritant from her eyes and studied the island off in the distance. Hrusha, the island city and the birthplace of the Xoangiagu. Three streaks of colored lights shot up from the center of the island, exploding into a kaleidoscope of patterned flower lights. The Happan must be expecting them. Of course, considering the fleet at their back, they probably looked like an invasion.

"We will dock soon," said Sali. "I will inform our guest of honor."

"That will not be necessary." Visan stepped onto the platform at the bow of the barge. The khan was not dressed in his usual armor or in Chaqra robes, but in plain white pilgrimage garb. Every member of the crew bowed respectfully as he passed. The Happan crew nearby went a step further, placing both palms to their foreheads and squatting close to the ground.

Visan went to Pei. The two had often been together since his surrender, their heads touching, much to both Taishi's and Sali's chagrin.

They were an odd pair, certainly. Visan towered a half body above most other men, while Pei was diminutive even for her age. The wind-whisper often studied the two from a distance. Sali could just make out their conversation.

"This is a strange ending, no?" said the khan.

The oracle smiled. "What if I were to tell you that there is no final ending?"

"Is it at least a good one?"

"We are long past good and bad endings. It is *an* ending, which is all we can ask for at this time."

He grunted. "I'm glad it's with you and not the Scholar. He's insufferable."

"Yes, he was, but his thoughts were always in the right place."

Taishi eventually backed away to give them space and joined Sali at the other end of the platform as the *Hana Iceberg* pulled into the mouth of the harbor. Sali eyed the many lines of fursuited Happans crowding the walls and paths along the steep cliffs above the narrow water channel silently watching them pass. The *Hana Iceberg* pulled into the docks to thick crowds waiting at the water's edge with a pair of older, elaborately dressed men, one in puffin-feather fursuit and the other in rags wearing a leather apron.

Sali pointed at the two distinguished men leading the reception. "Rich Man Yuraki and Ritualist Conchitsha Abu Suriptika. Yuraki is Hrusha's leader, while Suriptika is their ritualist, or shaman."

"Charlatan," one of the Chaqra spirit shamans snorted. Some prejudices would never die.

"Watch your tongue, spirit shaman," Sali snapped. "The old ways are done."

The elderly spirit shaman looked offended at first but was properly cowed.

The *Hana Iceberg* came to a rumbling stop, shedding ice as its sides banged against the stone docks. The ramps were extended, and several of the crew disembarked to moor the barge.

The captain signaled to Salminde first. "My crew can't do their job until these crowds clear, so get this pageantry over with first. Let the procession begin, landlady."

She nodded. "You have my thanks, friend. Hrusha will cover the costs of this travel."

"Your honor and friendship is better than coin, Salminde the Viperstrike." That was considered the highest compliment among Tsunarcos. "Besides, think of the publicity once everyone in the True Freeze learns that it was the *Hana Iceberg* that carried the Eternal Khan of Katuia back to the Sun Under Lagoon."

Of course.

Visan, as the Eternal Khan of Katuia and leader of the horde, had the honor of stepping off the *Hana Iceberg* first. The chatter in the crowd quieted when he emerged. The harbor became hushed, with only the sloshing sound of the water lapping the shores and the barges bumping against the docks interrupting the stillness.

To a man, woman, and child, every Happan looked stone-faced, anxious, fearful even.

The khan looked uncomfortable as well. He took a deep breath, his large chest expanding and contracting. "My people." His voice carried across the city and then broke. "My people, I have returned to beg your forgiveness. Know that in my heart, my duty has always been to protect you. I am sorry."

The khan's return to Hrusha must be bittersweet. The Warrior had been their patron and defender, the last of the Xoangiagu, before defecting to Katuia and becoming their conqueror. The tale that the Happan crew told was that he had betrayed them. The story from the spirit shamans' Keeper of Legends who was on board with them was that the khan's capitulation was the Katuia horde's price for peace with the Happan. The story from the khan himself was that his sacrifice was necessary to save his people from extinction.

Everyone had a justification if they only believed hard enough.

The khan was at first met with silence; several of the Happan even turned their backs to him. Betrayal was a difficult thing to forgive. The khan accepted his frosty reception and continued down the ramp. Not all rejected him, however. Several of the Happan reached out, touching his arm as he passed. A surprised buzz passed through the audience when Ritualist Conchitsha Abu Suriptika stepped forward to meet the khan. There was tension in the air as the two faced each other. Then Suriptika reached out and embraced the Xoangiagu, sending a wave of relief and a few cheers through the crowds.

It was a somber moment, but also one filled with relief. All of them collectively, the Happan and the khan, had finally let a burden go.

Next came the delegation from Chaqra. The spirit shamans almost came to blows jockeying for a place in this delegation. A mountain of jeers and boos filled the valley as the city let them know how they felt about their former oppressors. The haughty spirit shamans seemed unnerved, not expecting this sort of reception. Sali pursed her lips. Most of these senior shamans of the council had never stepped foot off their capital city. They were unaware just how hated they were among many in the horde.

Following them was supposed to be the Oracle of the Tiandi, the most exalted and senior of the Zhuun delegation. However, the girl became shy walking up the ramp and fled into Taishi's arms. Rather than try to coax her out, Sali decided to go ahead and walk up next.

However, as soon as she appeared at the top of the ramp, a cheer rose from the crowds. She was taken aback. She had come to Hrusha half a dozen times since their alliance was formed, and it had always been quiet and unassuming. She could feel their admiration, love, and gratitude. Their thunderous roars seemed to shake the very mountains, agitating the clear waters and sending a large murmuration of starlings into flight.

"Salminde the Viperstrike!"

"Salminde the Liberator!"

"Salminde the Hero!"

Sali stood on the ramp, frozen, dismayed and touched by the reception. Tears welled in her eyes. Her mind wandered to her parents, Faalsa and Mileene, Alyna her mentor, and her neophyte Hampa, how each of them had been so instrumental in leading her to where she stood now. Hampa would have loved this. Sali did the only thing she could. She raised a fist in the air, placed it over her forehead, and then her heart, and fell to both knees.

"Humility is the greatest strength a leader can wield," Alyna, her mentor, had once taught her.

If possible, the cheers grew even louder, stronger, and more deafening.

The chants of "Nezra! Nezra! Nezra!" filled the mountain range.

After several moments, Sali picked herself up and walked off the ramp to the docks. She was mobbed by fursuits, touching and thanking her for their deliverance to freedom. The chants continued on for several more minutes before finally dying. Sali embraced Rich Man Yuraki and stood next to him as Taishi came next, holding shy Pei's hand.

The Oracle of the Tiandi peeked out from behind Taishi. She waved. The pair were initially met with confused stares. A murmur passed through the crowds. Then a loud, nearly panicked cry cut through the low chatter.

"No, it is not possible. It can't be!" Ritualist Conchitsha Abu Suriptika darted forward, running and stumbling on spindly feet, twice falling onto all fours before he made it, halfway hunched over, up the ramp to them. Taishi, looking alarmed, placed herself between Pei and this madman charging them.

The ritualist cried out. He sounded as if his heart had broken. The old man was on his knees, crying shoulder-wracking sobs as he clutched her feet. It was awkward and humbling. A mutter rose through the crowd, many uncomfortable as their spiritual leader cried and prostrated himself in front of a foreign Zhuun child.

Pei knelt down and cupped the ritualist's face. The two exchanged soft words in the presence of thousands. Suriptika, after a few moments, stood, his face wet. He beamed as he wept openly, fat wet tears rolling down his cheeks, wetting his wrinkles. He wiped his face with his dirty sleeves, stared toward the sky, and breathed deep before speaking with unsteady breath.

"My people, my friends, my family. I bring glorious news. It is her!

The missing orphan Xoangiagu, long thought lost to us centuries ago, has returned to the Happan of Hrusha! The pure Child has returned home!"

The cheers erupted the moment Kaiyu reached the top of the Three Hands to Heaven Tower. There were no gongs to ring so he waved a yellow-and-brown banner, the colors of Shulan. From there, the gathering crowds at the base grew even louder and more boisterous as the new Master of the Houtou descended, adroitly swinging and dropping several floors at a time, catching the handholds and clinging on to the many statues and eaves on his way to the ground. The residents of the city had turned out in force when they learned that one of their heroes of the Siege of Vauzan was completing his final test for his ascension. By the time he reached the ground, a large audience had gathered, cheering the Houtou name and singing the victorious songs of Shulan Duchy.

It was a small bright spot in an otherwise dark and turbulent time for the citizens of Vauzan. The ducal court had negotiated a good and kind conditional surrender to the Caobiu Duchy, but a surrender was still a surrender, and almost always bittersweet. The weight of being defeated people was still difficult to bear, not to mention having to begin the long and arduous process of rebuilding the city from the devastation caused by the siege.

The surviving lords of the Shulan Court were already jockeying for position to become the next Duke of Shulan. For a moment, the people feared that a ducal civil war would break out among the court, but the newly crowned Empress Sunri of the Enlightened States, may her greatness ever last, had put her foot down, decreeing that the only violence allowed in this succession would be champions' duels made public in arenas. It was a genius move by the empress, preventing further violence for the war-torn people while entertaining the masses.

Sunri had initially offered to attend this ceremony, but in the end reconsidered, claiming her new duties keeping the fractured empire together required her to stay at the Celestial Palace. That was for the best. There was little love for the empress here in Shulan. The people's wounds ran deep, and their scars would take years to heal, if ever. In the end, just about everyone had to acknowledge that the best and most qualified person won the Heart of the Tiandi Throne.

The cheers for Kaiyu reached their peak when he swung off the edge of an eave some three stories up, somersaulting like only the Houtou style could, snatching Summer Bow out of the air—thrown flipping through the air by Hachi as only a whipfinger could—before landing in the traditional Houtou guard stance.

Both Kaiyu and Hachi were immediately surrounded by gaggles of children as a fleet of floating paper lanterns were released into the air. The city was celebrating its heroes, but they were also marking the opening of the new Houtou & Whipfinger School of Heroic War Arts at the Holy Glow Plaza at the base of Peony Peak. The two friends had decided to open brotherhood schools in the same location, mainly due to their close relationship but also to save on rent. They had asked Jian if he had wanted to join in, but a school was not the windwhisper way.

Kaiyu's climb and his ascension to the Master of the Houtou was as good marketing as any. Zofi, standing off to the side, received deposits from many eager parents and practitioners vying for a limited spot on each school's roster, while Master Sohn stood by to keep the crowds in line.

Jian stood off to the side alongside Sonaya with a grin on his lips that wouldn't die. It had been a month since they had returned from Skyfall Temple, and everything had already changed. Peace had finally come to the Enlightened States. Order had returned as well. For the first time in years, the daily lives of the people here finally seemed to have stabilized.

The important next thing they had to do, however, was bury their friends.

The first was Xinde, who had died saving Taishi's life. His funeral was surprisingly large. He had many friends and admirers in the city, including the magistrates he served with, war artists from other schools, and hundreds of young women who admired the handsome man from afar. The procession was long, almost that of a venerated abbot, before they sent his body back to his family in Allanto. Sunri had deified him upon his death, making him a Defender of the Tiandi. His father had wept when he recovered his body. The son he had thrown out of his household for being too soft was now returning for burial, given the highest honor within the Enlightened States.

Fausan and Bhasani were moved to the drowned fists' family mausoleum in one of the burial mountains near Vauzan. The couple who quarreled endlessly in life but loved each other intensely would have the opportunity to continue doing so for the rest of their afterlife. Sonaya had grieved for her mother for weeks, and had only recently emerged from mourning, now wearing the mantle of the Mother of the Drowned Fist.

That left Sohn, somewhat ironically, the only survivor among that group. The eternal bright light master, now also a Defender of the Tiandi, had his opportunity to choose any of thousands of young men and women clamoring to be his heir. Yet surprisingly, he had turned everyone down, and appeared content to let fate take its course.

"I'm too old to teach anyone anymore," he had grumbled at the funeral. "Besides, who wants to spend the last of their days training a bunch of entitled snots? I'd much rather spend it enjoying the company of friends." He had looked mournfully at the funeral pyres and bowed his head, weeping. His meaning had been clear, and it was now too late.

The last two were Jian and Sonaya. Jian was surprised at how quickly he had been forgotten by the masses after his time as the Prophesied Hero of the Tiandi had concluded. Sure, people had come to touch his shoulders and speak to him, but they rarely spoke about the prophecy or his place in their religion. When they did stop him on the streets, they thanked him for defending their city and bringing hope to their people. It was as if the prophecy wasn't as important to them as what had actually mattered to them personally. Things like having a life to return to, a city to go back to, and friends to reunite with. It confused Jian at first, but then he became appreciative of them. They actually *saw* Wen Jian, not just the Prophesied Hero of the Tiandi.

Hachi walked past, leading a parade of new students toward the new school for a tour. Walking alongside him, leaning into the crook of his neck, was Neeshan. Wrapped around both their wrists were wedding bracelets. That jerk really did go off on his own and get married without telling his friends. Hachi apologized later on, saying that after Skyfall, he couldn't wait another day to marry Neeshan.

Jian looked at Sonaya chatting with Templeabbot Lee Mori. The apology was unnecessary. He understood why his friend felt that way.

Kaiyu passed by next, leading another procession. The new Houtou master wore a wide stupid grin that took up half his face. He noticed Jian and waved. Jian waved back, feeling every bit a proud big brother. The young man certainly deserved this day.

"See you at the grand opening party tonight?" Kaiyu hollered.

Jian tapped his chest over his heart once with his right fist and raised it. He wrinkled his nose, smelling the scent of lemon and strawberries. A chin touched his right shoulder. "Now that you're unemployed, Five Champ, maybe you can ask those boys for a job. You would think being the Prophesied Hero of the Tiandi would earn you a stipend from your own religion."

"Right?"

"You could always ask the empress. I'm sure she would gladly provide for you."

That would mean he would be under her thumb forever. Just because they had allied briefly didn't mean he liked the woman. Jian grunted. "No thanks."

They joined the flow of traffic making their way toward the Holy Glow Plaza, passing several large rose arrangements leaning against the walls to their left. These bouquets were the Zhuun way of congratulating new businesses.

Sonaya, holding his hand, stopped to smell a bunch of roses. "What are you going to do then?"

Jian considered. "I think I'm going to go back to the Cloud Pillars and fix up the Diyu Temple."

"Why would you want to go to that weird dump?"

Jian looked to the northeast. That's where his master was at this moment. "Taishi always loved the Cloud Pillars. I don't know how much time she has left, but I think she'd like to spend it there. I want to offer her the same sacrifice that she has given me. I'm going to go back and get it ready. You'll come with me, right?"

Sonaya snorted. "By the Tiandi, no. Why would I want to go there?"

"Because I'm there." Hurt stung him.

She leaned in and kissed his cheek. "And I love you no matter where you are, but I'm not going to live in the middle of Tiandi forsaken wilderness just for you. The drowned fist master does not hide in a hovel. I have to show my face to the lunar court." He had learned the other day that the drowned fist lineage was obscenely wealthy, as opposed to the windwhisper lineage, which was obscenely poor.

"I have to take care of Taishi first," he said. "I want to be there for her like she was for me."

"And I'll still be here while you're being a good son." Sonaya slapped his chest over his heart playfully. "Just not with you physically, because I love running water far too much. When is Taishi coming back anyway?"

Jian looked to the northeast. She would be somewhere there. "I don't know. Soon, I hope. I miss her."

"Well, it's time for my first costume change. I'll see you tonight for the celebration." Sonaya broke away and headed the other direction.

Jian watched blankly, and then he asked, "Hey, Sonaya, do you think the prophecy actually made a difference? Like, did anything I do as the Prophesied Hero of the Tiandi actually matter?"

She stopped and considered for a few moments. "Does it make a difference to you if it did, if the outcome's all the same?"

Jian pondered. "No, I suppose it doesn't."

"Then there's your answer." Sonaya looked back and blew him a kiss. "Change your robes, Five Champ. They're filthy, and you stink. Clean up for me. I'll see you tonight, love."

☯

Taishi's mind was a jumble as she walked alongside Pei up the road running up the side of the mountain. She still felt numb from the recent revelations. The Oracle of the Tiandi was a Xoangiagu, just like the Eternal Khan of Katuia. These two figures had cast a long shadow over both their people for so many centuries. All along, they had been the same creatures. She had heard the legends about Xoangiagu, the six spirits, as their legend goes. She had always brushed those off as shamanistic tales, stories told around their hearth, word of mouth from less civilized people tucked far away in the world.

What could it all mean?

Pei, still holding Taishi's hand, looked up. "Why does it matter that the Warrior and I came from the same place?"

Taishi couldn't answer that. "Our two people have been mortal enemies for centuries. So much bloodshed. So much death. Couldn't all this death and destruction have been somehow avoided? Why did both the Zhuun and Katuia have to suffer such dreadful fates?"

"How do you know this isn't one of the better outcomes?"

"It can't possibly be. There's been so much destruction. So many have perished. So many lives broken. How could this possibly be a good outcome?"

The oracle offered a small sad smile. "I have seen all the possibilities, Ling Taishi. There are many better endings, but far more terrible ones."

The two followed a procession of the Happan up the mountain, past dozens of ramshackle houses, most carved out of ice with colorful metal roofs. The Happan had sung the entire way, banging tin cups and beating sticks. There was dancing and swaying, sauntering, as they hiked up a street they called Orca Way.

Ritualist Conchitsha Abu Suriptika led the procession carrying a torn banner depicting each of the six Xoangiagu. The old man moved with a determined quickness that defied his age. Taishi's gaze focused on the third among the six, next to the giant Warrior, a smaller person: the pure Child.

For the hundredth time, she wondered what she had gotten herself into. More importantly, she hoped Jian was all right. The Prophesied

Hero of the Tiandi was not safe in Katuia lands, regardless of their circumstances and this new world post-destiny. Taishi would not take any chances with him until she was lying at rest in her family tomb. She tasted the acrid metallic bile in her throat and the creeping coughs crawling up her lungs. That only meant she had to stay vigilant for a little while longer. She couldn't wait until this business was concluded and she could return home to Jian. Maybe not to Vauzan, but perhaps to the Ngyn Ocean coast or perhaps the Sea of Flowers. She even missed that dump of hers back at the Cloud Pillars. Anyway, as long as she was reunited with her family, Taishi didn't care where they ended up.

Suriptika noticed her worried expression and slowed to walk alongside her. "Master Windwhisper, you honor us with your presence, but your duty has been fulfilled. The *Hana Iceberg* will return you back to your lands if you wish."

"Not yet." Taishi glanced down at Pei. "What happens to her now?"

"The two Xoangiagu will return to their natural homes down in the depths of the Sun Under Lagoon. Their return will finally end the eternal cycle tread upon this land reincarnating within human hosts. Our people will finally break the curse."

Taishi wasn't comfortable with the sound of that. "What happens to Pei?"

"The pure Child—"

"I don't give a shit about the spirits," Taishi snapped. "What bloody happens to the girl?"

The ritualist pursed his lips. "I regret to inform you, Master Windwhisper. There is nothing that can be done for the host."

"No! The Oracle of the Tiandi did not travel all this way so you can sacrifice her life!" Taishi stopped. Her instincts took over as she clutched a fistful of the ritualist's dirty, matted fursuit.

Several Happan nearby gasped. More than a few drew their sticks. Taishi felt the end of a stick jab her back. She didn't care. Walking the little girl to her death was not what she signed up for when she agreed to escort Pei here to Hrusha.

Salminde appeared an instant later. "I remind you, Master Windwhisper, that you are a guest among the Happan. Threatening violence upon their ritualist is, perhaps, not a wise decision."

Taishi rounded on her. "Did you know about this?"

"Know about what?"

"Did you know that your ritualist was going to kill an innocent little girl?"

The surprised look on the viperstrike's face was answer enough. She turned to the ritualist. "Is it true? You were able to cure me of the soul rot." Salminde sounded angry, almost accusatory. That meant a lot to Taishi. At least she wasn't the only one trying to protect the girl.

Suriptika shook his head. "The joining of a Xoangiagu to a host cannot be undone. The two are, in essence, one."

"I did not know. I am sorry, Ling Taishi." Salminde pursed her lips, bowing, resigned. "There is no greater and more noble sacrifice than the ones we make today for a brighter future tomorrow."

Taishi's heart shattered. Her knees wobbled, making it difficult to stand. The cold Hrusha air chilled her lungs. Her breathing became labored. She was helpless to do anything about this situation. She could resist and fight the Happan, but it was a meaningless gesture. She was too feeble to take on any of these Happan with sticks, let alone the many thousands here. Still, sometimes the helpless had to make a stand. Her right hand closed into a fist. "A better future cannot start with the sacrifice of an innocent child."

Taishi felt a light touch on her forearm. Calm surged up her shoulder. Her fist unclenched. Pei stared at her with bright moon-shaped eyes, one hand reassuring this weepy old woman and the other clutching her pet fox. The diminutive Oracle of the Tiandi smiled her strangely vapid, yet knowing smile. "Everything will turn out as best as it can. I am pleased with the outcome. It's not a sacrifice if more good comes from it."

"That's what you said when Jian spared my life and refused to take the final test."

Pei smiled. "Free will can be a cruel bitch sometimes."

"Language, child," Taishi admonished, not that it mattered. It was more out of habit than anything else, but the words carried their desired effect. Pei clamped her mouth shut and made a petulant face. She was still the little girl from all those years ago.

The procession reached a gated area Salminde referred to as Hightop Cluster. The large gates opened with great ceremony, with drums rattling and sticks banging. Hundreds of bodies, lining the streets, faces poking out the windows, people sitting on roofs, children sitting on shoulders, and young people squatting on walls and rafters watched as the procession entered the cluster.

The cheering grew louder as they passed through the gates, moving into a community square surrounded by several more stories of oddly shaped buildings half carved out of ice. Pei's grip on Taishi's hand tightened, and the oracle seemed to wither from this terrible and heavy attention.

"Stay close, child." Taishi pulled her in, as if attempting to shield her. Pei was trembling. She was nervous, worried. No, not just that. She was frightened.

Suriptika brought them to a run-down shop near the back of the cluster. Two boys wearing penguin fursuits were hard at work sewing bits of leather together. The ritualist exchanged a few quiet words with them and they scurried off.

"Since when did you get new apprentices?" asked Sali.

"Someone has to make them for this city." Suriptika became animated, shaking his fist. "And you know that Jawapa's crap is garbage." He spat.

Taishi nudged Sali. "Is he still talking about the Xoangiagu?"

"He's one of two cobblers in the city."

"You mean this is a shoe shop? Where's the temple?"

Salminde pointed at the shop. "Right through the shop."

They continued through the front door, passed several dirty workspaces, before exiting the building into an even dirtier trash heap. Why would the Happan place their sacred beliefs in such squalor? Taishi looked back at the way they came, puzzled, not certain that this wasn't some assassination hit. She was only mildly mollified when she saw the khan speaking at the back of the heap, standing at what appeared to be an entrance to an ancient temple.

The three joined the khan and ritualist. Taishi felt Pei tremble next to her. It felt like nerves, or fear. She had to remind herself that Pei was still a girl. And she knew what awaited at the end of this journey. How does anyone, let alone this girl, face death without fear? Taishi's stomach churned at the thought. It wasn't right.

"The ceremony is quick," explained the ritualist. "All each of you need to do is return to the pool from which you came, and let the physical body go."

"The host dies?" Taishi pressed. The words were such a heavy vise upon her heart.

"The body dies," admitted Suriptika. "The soul stays with the spirit."

Pei's grip on Taishi's hand tightened.

"Are you sure about this, girl?" Taishi must have asked this question five or six times by now.

The Oracle of the Tiandi, for the first time that Taishi could recall, nodded, looking anything but sure.

The small group entered the temple leading into what was an ancient and well-traveled cave system. They continued deeper into the mountain, past openings and chambers, constantly descending down carved stairs and winding tunnels. The freezing air stung when Taishi breathed in. It had a flavor like rust and sulfur.

They finally reached a cavern. As soon as they entered the round hole that served as an entrance, the air went from frigid to hot and wet, as if they had passed through a curtain of humidity. Inside the chambers was a barren room with a small ledge overlooking a large pool of a strange rainbow-hued viscous liquid, slurping and rolling in a seemingly bottomless cauldron.

The ritualist spoke in a loud and raspy voice, his words echoing around the cavern walls. "Six Xoangiagu rose from the depths of wondrous Hrusha, Oasis of the True Freeze: the beautiful Woman, the pure Child, the wise Scholar, the giant Bull, the sharp Owl, and the staunch Warrior. Now, after a thousand years, two return to their home, their final resting place. The Happan weep with joy for our beloved Xoangiagu." He turned to Visan and Pei. "Are you ready, staunch Warrior?"

The Eternal Khan of Katuia, Visan as his host was known, nodded. He dropped to a knee and spoke to Pei. "Thank you for bringing me home." Without another word, he stepped into the glowing colorful pool, and sank like quicksand into the depths of the pool until he was submerged.

Taishi watched, aghast, as the khan's body spasmed and went limp. Then a figure, the same shape, except translucent and colorful, separated from him. The figure, still the Warrior, but now in some strange gaseous state contained within a translucent membrane, looked out of the pool at the small group standing around the rim. He beckoned to Pei.

Ritualist Suriptika next turned to Pei. "Are you ready, pure Child?"

Pei raised her arms and offered Floppy. Taishi accepted the gift and embraced the child. "You will always be loved." Her voice was more intense, near frantic. "You don't have to do this."

"I know that I do not have to, but I also know that I must." Pei, the Oracle of the Tiandi, the pure Child, shook her head. "This has been the purpose of my existence ever since I was severed from the others during an ambush by the Chaqra spirit shamans and driven into Zhuun lands. I lay hidden among your people for centuries, eking out a small existence with no way to return to my beloved Sun Under Lagoon. One day I heard news about this new Khan of Katuia, and my heart despaired. That was when I embarked on this quest to see the many paths of the future through the maze of possibilities to find a way to reach this very singular outcome." Her voice broke. "All I've ever wanted was to save the last of my kind, Ling Taishi. I have you to thank for accomplishing this."

Taishi didn't fight the tears as they streamed down her withered cheeks and into the glowing pool. She pulled the girl in and squeezed with what little strength she possessed. It wasn't fair. Every child deserved a chance to live their life. Her thoughts drifted momentarily to Sanso, then Jian, and then back to Pei. A pained, motherly moan filled with a lifetime of heartache and loss escaped her lips as Pei stepped one foot into the glowing rainbow pool, and then the other. The girl blinked, her eyes wide as she walked along the pool's surface. Then a high-pitched squeal escaped her lips as she began to sink.

"It feels warm and it tickles." Pei giggled as the surface of the shimmering substance rose to her waist, and then her chest. She looked over at Taishi and waved. "You don't have to worry anymore. I'm going to be okay now, but I'll miss you, Taishi. The cold won't do Floppy any good. Promise you'll take him back to the Sea of Flowers? He loves the salt air there." Then the colorful liquid reached to her neck, and then she was gone, sinking below the surface of the pool.

Taishi's one good arm reached for empty air, and then she fell to her knees, not able to look away. Her heart shattered when Pei, now submerged, experienced panic, her body flailing in the thick viscous gunk, before suddenly relaxing. Then, a rainbow membrane, like the King's rays reflecting off oil on water, came into being wearing Pei's silhouette.

The pure Child submerged fully within the vast depth beneath the pool, darting agilely back and forth like a dolphin frolicking about. She didn't know how long—it must have been hours—but she stayed sitting on her knees watching the two spirits, the Warrior and Child, dancing around each other. Every once in a while, the Child, still shaped like Pei, would stop in the middle of her play and look up, directly at Taishi, as if reassured to see her still there.

More time passed. Taishi's knees and back ached, but still she couldn't bear to look away. Exhaustion finally set in, and with a mewling snarl, Taishi forced herself up to her feet. She tried to stand, stopping just short of straightening her back. Every bone in her spine popped and ground in protest. A long resigned breath loosed from her lips. Taishi looked down and met Pei's large luminous eyes staring back.

The Child looked alarmed and darted from deep within the depths back up toward the surface. She reached for Taishi, her palm touching the surface of the pool from the other side. Taishi hesitated, and reached down with her lone good hand, pressing down, her old frail and bony hand eclipsing the small child's smaller hand.

Taishi heard the words spoken inside her head. "Do you really have to go?"

A choke escaped Taishi's lips as she nodded. "I must. You're safe. You're home now."

A ripple passed over the pure Child. Taishi could sense her sadness through touch. She could feel the child's fear, her insecurities and doubts. Most of all, Taishi could feel Pei still in there, somewhere inside the essence of this strange being.

Finally, Pei spoke. "Will you come back and visit me sometime? It is so quiet here. I will be so lonely without my friends."

Taishi nodded between body-wracking sobs. "I will, dear child."

Salminde came to her side, her boots clicking on the cavern floor. "Captain Lehuangxi Thiraput Cungle has sent word that he intends to depart tonight and would be honored to return you back to the mainland."

Taishi acknowledged the viperstrike and turned to leave. Her job was complete. It was time to go home, back to Jian and Zofi, where she belonged. She looked back at the pool one last time and saw Pei staring back intently.

Taishi closed her eyes and made her choice. "My duty was to watch over the Oracle of the Tiandi. That task is not yet complete. She still needs me, perhaps more than ever. Send word to my son, Wen Jian. Tell him . . ." She drew in a deep breath and closed her eyes. "Tell him I'm sorry. She needs me."

The Story So Far

The Burning Hearts Romance Book Synopsis

(#42-#45)

BURNING HEARTS ROMANCE #42:
The Spark That Showers the Heavens with Rays of Love

Our heroine, Shao Hua, daughter of Shao Lai (BHR #35–41), grand-daughter of Shao Soo (BHR #26–34), was sent to the Celestial Palace at the age of thirteen to serve as a scullerymaiden. It was there, with her pale luminescent moonlight skin, delicate porcelain features, and dainty small feet, alongside her razor wit and pure heart, that she ensnared the love of Wen Jian, the young and dashing Prophesied Hero of the Tiandi. Shao Hua and Wen Jian fell deeply in forbidden love, for how could a lowly scullerymaiden with no family or political power serve as a match for the great and important and obviously very wealthy Savior of the Zhuun?

Yet their love was real and true. Under the shrine of the Celestial Family, Wen Jian pledged his devotion to Shao Hua for all eternity. He planned to return to her after he fulfilled the Prophecy of the Tiandi by slaying the evil demonic Eternal Khan of Katuia. Then they would settle down together and live a humble and holy life in obscurity under the Celestial Family back in her home village on the southern banks of the Yukian River.

The two were destined to live happily ever after, until the evil Ling Taishi kidnapped Wen Jian and whisked him away from the Celestial Palace one fateful night.

Shao Hua vowed to search the ends of the earth for her beloved, for she came from a long lineage of the war arts style Heart Plunger. She would make that evil witch Ling Taishi pay!

BURNING HEARTS ROMANCE #43:
Fanning the Flames of Hot Burning Desire Again and Again

After a year of fruitless searching and dead ends, our heroine Shao Hua bought a lead that took her to the lawless and brutal city of Jiayi, where she finally found her beloved, Wen Jian, the Prophesied Hero of the Tiandi. But he did not remember her. The evil witch Ling Taishi had wiped his memory! The poor, noble people's savior was now disguised as the street urchin Lu Hiro, a body servant at the lowly war arts school.

Determined to save him, Shao Hua searched for the magic potion to break the spell and cross paths with the terrible, evil, wretched Ling Taishi. The two powerful war artists waged an epic duel across the ugly city, their balletic dance of death soaring above the rooftops, there for all the people to see. To this day, there are still songs about Shao Hua's glistening, beautiful raven hair. The battle was terrible. In the end, Shao Hua was not strong enough to defeat the horrid witch Ling Taishi, falling to the villainous war artist's mighty windwhispering blow.

Our heroine could only watch, helpless, as Ling Taishi escaped with her beloved once more.

BURNING HEARTS ROMANCE #44:
Licking the Lips of the Fiery Fires of Passion

Shao Hua never gave up her search for her beloved, Wen Jian. Her search brought her to a remote settlement called Bahngtown in the savage and primitive lands of the Cloud Pillars. It was nearby where she finally located the evil and awful and repugnant Ling Taishi's cannibal lair. Knowing she could not defeat the master windwhisper on her own, Shao Hua recruited the noble war artists of the Lotus Lotus Sect. A mighty naval battle ensued in which Shao Hua and her noble comrades nearly defeated Ling Taishi and her henchmen. Just as victory was within Shao Hua's grasp, Ling Taishi sold Wen Jian to the mighty Duke Saan of Shulan to save her own neck.

Shao Hua was once again thwarted from saving her beloved.

BURNING HEARTS ROMANCE #45:
Explosion of Destiny upon the Many Wonderful Corpses of My Beloveds

Shao Hua chased after the Shulan army all the way to Allanto, the capital city of Gyian Duchy. There was danger at every corner, and the temptation of handsome lords filled the streets as well as her gaze, but Shao Hua was determined to rescue Wen Jian, carefully and skillfully navigating the deadly Gyian Court politics and streets.

The city burst into violence when the just and wise and noble Duchess Sunri of Caobiu rallied the poor and despondent people of Gyian Province to shake off their oppressors. The great Sunri waged a mighty battle against both Dukes Saan's and Yanso's forces, and in a mighty display of martial prowess, defeated both armies and seized the city!

The treacherous Ling Taishi had the audacity to ambush noble Sunri, the Duchess of Caobiu, and nearly slay her! Fortunately, Shao Hua arrived just in time to save the day. An even greater fight erupted as the two women fought for the last time with the love and soul of Wen Jian as the prize.

This time, Shao Hua was triumphant. She struck down Ling Taishi with a mighty blow and then broke the terrible spell that had been cast over her beloved Wen Jian's mind. He immediately awoke and recognized Shao Hua, his true love. The two joined Sunri's righteous army and defeated the two evil dukes of the Enlightened States.

Afterward, Shao Hua, our heroine, and Wen Jian retired to Vau-zan, where they lived happily ever after.

Until now. A new evil approaches. Read what happens next!

Coming soon to a teahouse near you:

BURNING HEARTS ROMANCE #46:
Swirling Deeply the Blistering Melt of True Love

Salminde the Viperstrike
Chaqra Spirit Shaman Book Storage Archive

First Taint: Salminde the Viperstrike returned home from the raidlife to find her city and clan, Nezra, razed and sunk under the Grass Sea. Her duty as the Will of the Khan was to return to the Whole, where she was to be received with honor alongside the other Wills of the Khan. Instead of fulfilling her duty, Salminde cowardly avoided death and responsibility and proclaimed herself a soulseeker.

Second Taint: Salminde the Viperstrike was ordered to ride south to the Blue Sea for her first pilgrimage as a soulseeker. Instead, she disobeyed the will of the spirit shamans and went to Jiayi, the home of the indentured Nezra clan. Regardless of her standing within the horde, the woman was blatantly disregarding and disrespecting the very spirit of Katuia!

Third Taint: Salminde made contact with the remnants of her clan in Jiayi, against the spirit shamans' explicit wisdom! She rallied her people and devised a way to escape the city with them. Several large fires were set throughout the city, and Salminde led her clan out under the chaos of the night.

Fourth Taint: Salminde the Viperstrike committed treason to the Katuia by freeing Nezra from their agreed-upon indentured servitude as required by the armistice. Her selfish, childish impulses to free her clan endangered the entire horde. Katuia was not yet ready to shake off the yoke of the Zhuun. We needed more time, and her brash behavior risked everything.

For these sins, as laid out by the wisdom of the Chaqra, Salminde was exiled from all Katuia.

Fifth Taint: Salminde the Viperstrike and her rogue Nezra had evaded the khan's justice for too long. The capital city Liqusa was dispatched to hunt the rogue clan down. For years, the cowardly Nezra clan escaped the spirit shamans' justice, fleeing north toward the fringe of the horde's realm.

Sixth Taint: In a shocking turn of events, Salminde the Viperstrike emerged in the holy city of Hrusha. There, in the True Freeze, she led an uprising of the native Happan population and threw out the spirit shamans there tending to the holy Grand Monastery of the Dawn Song. This treachery overwhelmed our peaceful shamans and evicted Katuia from the fabled Sun Under Lagoon.

Seventh Taint: Salminde the Viperstrike emerged from the events on Hrusha three cycles later, leading an entire capital city fleet. She has raised the flag of rebellion against Katuia, against her khan, and against her people. She must be stopped!

For these sins, as laid out by the wisdom of Chaqra, unless overwritten by a higher power, Salminde the Viperstrike of Nezra is sentenced to immediate death.

Consortium Logs: Maza Qisami Cell: Grunt Tsang

GRUNT'S JOURNAL: #511

Man, Sanba sucks! Tunnel life is the worst. Everything smells like fungus and fart. I always get the worst assignments. All I'm doing is staring at this dumb map store for the past two days. It's the worst. We're after some old lady that used to be some big deal. They're all fussing over this Ling Taishi woman. She supposedly was a scary monster within the lunar court in some primitive ancient times past. Like ten years ago or something. Pretty sure she's irrelevant now. Probably an easy bag once we find her. Damn, the cats here are fat.

GRUNT'S JOURNAL: #512

Who in the Tiandi is that mean witch bitch Ling Taishi? That woman is death incarnate! She beat the crap out of everyone. Every member of the cell is cut and busted up! Burandin is pooping blood. Do you know how much laundry and tailoring I have to do now? I think Qisami bit off more than she could chew, but she's so pigheaded she will never admit it. As far as I can tell, she still wants to keep at it. Right now, we just left Zhuun lands and are following the mapmaker's pretty map to some remote temple. This is the worst trip!

GRUNT'S JOURNAL: #513

That terrifying Taishi nearly killed everyone! The cell is getting annoyed with the recent events. Everyone is tired of getting beat up, but no one is willing to stand up to Qisami. Boss is getting obsessed and crazy over this. Anyway, we're now heading to Jiayi. We have a lead on the boy, this Prophesied Hero of the Tiandi. Funny thing, I didn't even know he was a real person. I had just assumed he was some stupid story the Tiandi religion peddled to trick the masses. Stories ba told us when we were kids to keep us in line. "Don't slouch or the Prophesied Hero of the Tiandi will drag you in front of the class by your ear! If you don't eat your cabbage, you will fail the Champion of the Five Under Heaven!" Stuff like that. And now I get to actually meet and kill him! It'll be great! Best of all, we'll be stupid rich once we collect the bounty. I can just retire and skip all this stupid shadowkill training.

GRUNT'S JOURNAL: #514

Every time we step up to Ling Taishi, she beats our asses. We're hunting for this prophecy boy in Jiayi. Boss has a new obsession now. This Kati woman, Salminde. She is all hot and bothered by her. But Boss always had weird taste.

It's Haaren's turn to cook tonight. He always adds too much salt and keeps trying to give me a shoulder rub. Anyway, we allied with the local underworld and this Kati. Going to tighten the noose around prophecy boy, and then it's hello, retirement!

GRUNT'S JOURNAL: #515

Why do all the quests have to lead down into the sewers? Sewers are the worst! Qisami and her new Kati girlfriend set up the trap for the prophecy boy, and lo and behold, we're fighting with that frightening viperstrike woman, and I think we're winning. Everyone's going grand. We're doing our shadowkill thing. The Kati's doing her Kati thing, and we're just about to win!

All of a sudden Qisami gets into a lovers' spat with her Kati and the two start killing each other! Right in the middle of our battle against that Ling Taishi witch! What in the Tiandi happened? Can't we focus on one thing at a time? In any case, prophecy boy escapes, and there went my early retirement plans. The cell's pissed. Oh, and Haaren died. That's a shame, but more shares for the rest of us!

Consortium Logs: Maza Qisami Cell: Grunt Cyyk

GRUNT'S JOURNAL: #001

Words are stupid.

GRUNT'S JOURNAL: #002

Writing a diary is stupid. I'm not doing it.

GRUNT'S JOURNAL: #015

It's either write in this thing or Burandin is going to switch me, so fine. He always did like to hit people for fun. We're in some backwater settlement doing backwater things. It sucks. Some wife wants to kill another wife in the deadly game of spousal politics. The cell barely gets by on these low-rent jobs. So much for Qisami being good at her stupid job.

Hmm, it actually feels good to get these thoughts out. They've been grating on my last nerve for a while now. Maybe I should try to write more.

GRUNT'S JOURNAL: #016

Burandin is the dumbest person to ever walk upright. It's insulting for someone of my family name, my station, to have to associate with this forehead-smashed-the-ground hairy cretin. My father is a high lord! Why did my ba give me away like this? Koteuni is encouraging me to kill him one day, and do you know what? I think I will! Anyway, I think we've been kidnapped. The last job tanked and now the entire cell is locked up in dog cages. Dog cages! Do they know who I am?

GRUNT'S JOURNAL: #016B

Zwei keeps asking me to train with the rest of the cell. I keep refusing. They are starting to think I dislike them, and it's true, I don't like anyone on this stupid team. But that's not why I refuse to train with them. I simply have never met a war artist who is so awful at war arting. I'm afraid if I spar with them, their laughably incompetent war arts taint is going to rub off on me. I come from a very distinguished war arts family! I'm not some commoner learning junk off the streets!

Anyway, Qisami made a big deal of having met Sunri—I met her dozens of times. My father is Quan Sah, after all. Right now, though, we're sitting on this rickety cart walking to Allanto. Walking! My humiliation knows no depths. I'm going to kill every one of these people one of these days.

GRUNT'S JOURNAL: #017

I really hope none of my old university mates recognize me. It'll be so humiliating. I'll never live it down, which means I'll probably have to kill them then. It is a grave injustice to embarrass nobility.

I really don't think the rest of the cell appreciates my contribution. I think it's safe to say after Qisami, I'm the most important person in the cell. I have the best blood. I'm a high lord's son! I'm also the best-looking by far.

We're undercover working in Uncle Yanso's estates. At least that's what I called him when I was a little lion. I am always jealous of Allanto estates, and Yanso's is by far the best. But no wonder Gyian armies stink. They spend all their liang on their palaces instead of their military. Ha, idiots!

GRUNT'S JOURNAL: #018

I'm sitting here watching the south exit toward the city. It's completely dead right now so here's my stupid entry.

Everyone is acting strangely. The negotiations between the three dukes have commenced. Yanso, Sunri, and Saan are going to forge an alliance. As the child of a high lord, I'm sure only I can grasp how staggering this alliance will be. This meeting will dictate the future of the Enlightened States. Everyone is excited and on edge.

I'm in the tunnels underneath the arena. Something just happened above. Sounds of yells and thundering footsteps. Is that the sound of battle overhead? What is going on? For some reason Koteuni just bloodscrawled me. She wants to get eyes on Qisami. That's strange. Why would we need to do that?

All right, new orders. Finally, some action. Koteuni is pulling me off my assignment and summoning me to the ground garage. I'll finish the entry later. If I'm late one more time, Qisami said she was going to toss me into prison and throw away the key.

ACKNOWLEDGMENTS

Well, 'tis done. After five years and seven hundred thousand words, the War Arts Saga trilogy has concluded. This has been a project filled with love, tears, doubt, and absolute joy. I am, at the same time, relieved and saddened to close this page of my life.

The War Arts Saga didn't begin back in 2019 when I first imagined Ling Taishi. It began a long time ago, before I even knew how to speak English. You see, my parents immigrated to the United States for university when I was five years old and brought my brother and me along to Lincoln, Nebraska. Back in the eighties, there weren't many people like us around those parts, so I had no idea what it meant to be Asian.

One day, I discovered wuxia movies from a television series called *Samurai Sunday*. They were a bunch of badly dubbed kung fu movies from the sixties, but to a kid searching for belonging, they were a mind-blowing revelation. My ancestors could fly and punch through walls! This began a lifelong love for martial arts and wuxia. I was a voracious reader as a kid and couldn't find any English books in this genre, so I vowed to write my own one day. Fast-forward four decades and fourteen books later, here we are.

Now, there's no way I could have pulled this off without an entire army at my back, so here goes:

To my mother and father, Yukie and Mike, I keep falling, yet you're always still there, giving me that soft landing and picking me back up.

To my brother, Stephen, I'm never going to admit to you how much I look up to you.

To my sister, Amy, nothing else is more important than family.

To Hunter and River, my boys, you are the greatest gifts I will ever bring to the world. I am so privileged to be your dad.

To my editor, Tricia, you've honed my storytelling skills and blade to a sharp point. My experience collaborating with you has been a joy. I am honored to have worked with one of the great editors of our time.

To my agent, Russ, I owe you more than words can convey. Thank you for being my shield, protecting and guiding me through this often-turbulent publishing journey.

To Sarah, thank you for cleaning up all my ugly bits.

To the team at Del Rey, the best in publishing: Keith Clayton, Scott Shannon, Alex Larned, Julie Leung, Ayesha Shibli, Ashleigh Heaton, Tori Henson, Sabrina Shen, Kay Popple, David Moench, Ada Maduka, Cassie Vu, Jo Anne Metsch, Paul Gilbert, Mark Maguire, and Abby Duval. Thank you all for being part of this army.

To Tran Nguyen, your talents are sublime. Your cover art brings all readers to the yard.

To all you readers, I wouldn't be here without you, and I hope we go on many more adventures together. Every word in these books is written with you in mind. I hope you all have enjoyed these adventures as much as I enjoyed writing them.

Finally, to Taishi, Jian, Salminde, Qisami, and the rest of the War Arts crew, I'm really going to miss all of you. I finally have that wuxia story I wanted to read as a kid. Thank you for making the lifelong dream of this lonely little kid from Nebraska come true.

ABOUT THE AUTHOR

WESLEY CHU is the #1 *New York Times* bestselling author of thirteen published novels, including *The Art of Prophecy, The Art of Destiny, Time Salvager, The Rise of Io,* and *The Walking Dead: Typhoon.* He won the Astounding Award for Best New Writer. His debut, *The Lives of Tao,* won the Young Adult Library Services Association's Alex Award. Chu is an accomplished martial artist and a former member of the Screen Actors Guild. He has acted in film and television, worked as a model and stuntman, and summited Kilimanjaro. He currently resides in Los Angeles with his two boys, Hunter and River.

wesleychu.com
X: @wes_chu
Instagram: @wesleychu1

ABOUT THE TYPE

This book was set in Electra, a typeface designed for
Linotype by W. A. Dwiggins, the renowned type designer
(1880–1956). Electra is a fluid typeface, avoiding the con-
trasts of thick and thin strokes that are prevalent in most
modern typefaces.